STEPHEN CRANE

Collected Works

CASTLE

Copyright ©1986 by Castle, a Division of Book Sales, Inc.
of Secaucus, N.J. 07094

ISBN 1-55521-114-3

Manufactured in the United States of America

The Castle trademark is registered in the U.S. Patent and
Trademark Office

85 86 87 88   0 9 8 7 6 5 4 3 2

Contents

THE
RED BADGE
OF
COURAGE

An Episode
of the
American Civil War

THE RED BADGE OF COURAGE

Chapter 1

The cold passed reluctantly from the earth, and the retiring fogs revealed an army stretched out on the hills, resting. As the landscape changed from brown to green, the army awakened, and began to tremble with eagerness at the noise of rumors. It cast its eyes upon the roads, which were growing from long troughs of liquid mud to proper thoroughfares. A river, amber-tinted in the shadow of its banks, purled at the army's feet; and at night, when the stream had become of a sorrowful blackness, one could see across it the red, eyelike gleam of hostile campfires set in the low brows of distant hills.

Once a certain tall soldier developed virtues and went resolutely to wash a shirt. He came flying back from a brook waving his garment bannerlike. He was swelled with a tale he had heard from a reliable friend, who had heard it from a truthful cavalryman, who had heard it from his trustworthy brother, one of the orderlies at division headquarters. He adopted the important air of a herald in red and gold.

"We're goin' t' move t' morrah—sure," he said pompously to a group in the company street. "We're goin' 'way up the river, cut across, an' come around in behint 'em."

To his attentive audience he drew a loud and elaborate plan of a very brilliant campaign. When he had finished, the blue-clothed men scattered into small arguing groups between the rows of squat brown huts. A negro teamster who had been dancing upon a cracker box with the hilarious encouragement of twoscore soldiers was deserted. He sat mournfully down. Smoke drifted lazily from a multitude of quaint chimneys.

"It's a lie! that's all it is—a thunderin' lie!" said another private loudly. His smooth face was flushed, and his hands were thrust sulkily into his trousers' pockets. He took the matter as an affront to him. "I don't believe the derned old army's ever going to move. We're set. I've got ready to move eight times in the last two weeks, and we ain't moved yet."

The tall soldier felt called upon to defend the truth of a rumor he himself had introduced. He and the loud one came near to fighting over it.

A corporal began to swear before the assemblage. He had just put a costly board floor in his house, he said. During the early spring he had refrained from adding extensively to the comfort of his environment because he had felt that the army might start on the march at any moment. Of late, however, he had been impressed that they were in a sort of eternal camp.

Many of the men engaged in a spirited debate. One outlined in a peculiarly lucid manner all the plans of the commanding general. He was opposed by men who advocated that there were other plans of campaign. They clamored at each other, numbers making futile bids for the popular attention. Meanwhile, the soldier who had fetched the rumor bustled about with much importance. He was continually assailed by questions.

"What's up, Jim?"

"Th' army's goin' t' move."

"Ah, what yeh talkin' about? How yeh know it is?"

"Well, yeh kin b'lieve me er not, jest as yeh like. I don't care a hang."

There was much food for thought in the manner in which he replied. He came near to convincing them by disdaining to produce proofs. They grew much excited over it.

There was a youthful private who listened with eager ears to the words of the tall soldier and to the varied comments of his comrades. After receiving a fill of discussions concerning marches and attacks, he went to his hut and crawled through an intricate hole that served it as a door. He wished to be alone with some new thoughts that had lately come to him.

He lay down on a wide bank that stretched across the end of the room. In the other end, cracker boxes were made to serve as furniture. They were grouped about the fireplace. A picture from an illustrated weekly was upon the log walls, and three rifles were paralleled on pegs. Equipments hung on handy projections, and some tin dishes lay upon a small pile of firewood. A folded tent was serving as a roof. The sunlight, without, beating upon it, made it glow a light yellow shade. A small window shot an oblique square of whiter light upon the cluttered floor. The smoke from the fire at times neglected the clay chimney and wreathed into the room, and this flimsy chimney of clay and sticks made endless threats to set ablaze the whole establishment.

The youth was in a little trance of astonishment. So they were at last going to fight. On the morrow, perhaps, there would be a battle, and he would be in it. For a time he was obliged to labor to make himself believe. He could not accept with assurance an omen that he was about to mingle in one of those great affairs of the earth.

He had, of course, dreamed of battles all his life—of vague and bloody conflicts that had thrilled him with their sweep and fire. In visions he had seen himself in many struggles. He had imagined peoples secure in the shadow of his eagle-eyed prowess. But awake he had regarded battles as crimson blotches on the pages of the past. He had put them as things of the bygone with his thought-images of heavy crowns and high castles. There was a portion of the world's history which he had regarded as the time of wars, but it, he thought, had been long gone over the horizon and had disappeared forever.

From his home his youthful eyes had looked upon the war in his own country with distrust. It must be some sort of a play affair. He had long despaired of witnessing a Greeklike struggle. Such would be no more, he had said. Men were better, or more timid. Secular and religious education had effaced the throat-grappling instinct, or else firm finance held in check the passions.

He had burned several times to enlist. Tales of great movements shook the land. They might not be distinctly Homeric, but there seemed to be much glory in them. He had read of marches, sieges, conflicts, and he had longed to see it all. His busy mind had drawn for him large pictures extravagant in color, lurid with breathless deeds.

But his mother had discouraged him. She had affected to look with some contempt upon the quality of his war ardor and patriotism. She could calmly seat herself and with no apparent difficulty give him many hundreds of reasons why he was of vastly more importance on the farm than on the field of battle. She had had certain ways of expression that told him that her statements on the subject came from a deep conviction. Moreover, on her side, was his belief that her ethical motive in the argument was impregnable.

At last, however, he had made firm rebellion against this yellow light thrown upon the color of his ambitions. The newspapers, the gossip of the village, his own picturings, had aroused him to an uncheckable degree. They were in truth fighting finely down there. Almost every day the newspapers printed accounts of a decisive victory.

One night, as he lay in bed, the winds had carried to him the clangoring of the church bell as some enthusiast jerked the rope frantically to tell the twisted news of a great battle. This voice of the people rejoicing in the night had made him shiver in a prolonged ecstasy of excitement. Later, he had gone down to his mother's room and had spoken thus: "Ma, I'm going to enlist."

"Henry, don't you be a fool," his mother had replied. She had then covered her face with the quilt. There was an end to the matter for that night.

Nevertheless, the next morning he had gone to a town that was near his mother's farm and had enlisted in a company that was forming there. When he had returned home his mother was milking the brindle cow. Four others stood waiting. "Ma, I've enlisted," he had said to her diffidently. There was a short silence. "The Lord's will be done, Henry," she had finally replied, and had then continued to milk the brindle cow.

When he had stood in the doorway with his soldier's clothes on his back, and with the light of excitement and expectancy in his eyes almost defeating the glow of regret for the home bonds, he had seen two tears leaving their trails on his mother's scarred cheeks.

Still, she had disappointed him by saying nothing whatever about returning with his shield or on it. He had privately primed himself for a beautiful scene. He had prepared certain sentences which he thought could be used with touching effect. But her words destroyed his plans. She had doggedly peeled potatoes and addressed him as follows: "You watch out, Henry, an' take good care of yerself in this here fighting business—you watch out, an' take good care of yerself. Don't go a-thinkin' you can lick the hull rebel army at the start, because yeh can't. Yer jest one little feller amongst a hull lot of others, and yeh've got to keep quiet an' do what they tell yeh. I know how you are, Henry.

"I've knet yeh eight pair of socks, Henry, and I've put in all yer best shirts, because I want my boy to be jest as warm and comf'able as anybody in the army. Whenever they get holes in 'em, I want yeh to send 'em right-away back to me, so's I kin dern 'em.

"An' allus be careful an' choose yer comp'ny. There's lots of bad men in the army, Henry. The army makes 'em wild, and they like nothing better than the job of leading off a young feller like you, as ain't never been away from home much and has allus had a mother, an' a-learning 'em to drink and swear. Keep clear of them folks, Henry. I don't want yeh to ever do anything, Henry, that yeh would be 'shamed to let me know about. Jest think as if I was a-watchin' yeh. If yeh keep that in yer mind allus, I guess yeh'll come out about right.

"Yeh must allus remember yer father, too, child, an' remember he never drunk a drop of licker in his life, and seldom swore a cross oath.

"I don't know what else to tell yeh, Henry, excepting that yeh must never do no shirking, child, on my account. If so be a time comes when yeh have to be kilt or do a mean thing, why, Henry, don't think of anything 'cept what's right, because there's many a woman has to bear up 'ginst sech things these times, and the Lord 'll take keer of us all.

"Don't forgit about the socks and the shirts, child; and I've put a cup of blackberry jam with yer bundle, because I know yeh like it above all things. Good-by, Henry. Watch out, and be a good boy."

He had, of course, been impatient under the ordeal of this speech. It had not been quite what he expected, and he had borne it with an air of irritation. He departed feeling vague relief.

Still, when he had looked back from the gate, he had seen his mother kneeling among the potato parings. Her brown face, upraised, was stained with tears, and her spare form was quivering. He bowed his head and went on, feeling suddenly ashamed of his purposes.

From his home he had gone to the seminary to bid adieu to many schoolmates. They had thronged about him with wonder and admiration. He had felt the gulf now between them and had swelled with calm pride. He and some of his fellows who had donned blue were quite overwhelmed with privileges for all of one afternoon, and it had been a very delicious thing. They had strutted.

A certain light-haired girl had made vivacious fun at his martial spirit, but there was another and darker girl whom he had gazed at steadfastly, and he thought she grew demure and sad at sight of his blue and brass. As he had walked down the path between the rows of oaks, he had turned his head and detected her at a window watching his departure. As he perceived her, she had immediately begun to stare up through the high tree branches at the sky. He had seen a good deal of flurry and haste in her movement as she changed her attitude. He often thought of it.

On the way to Washington his spirit had soared. The regiment was fed and caressed at station after station until the youth had believed that he must be a hero. There was a lavish expenditure of bread and cold meats, coffee, and pickles and cheese. As he basked in the smiles of the girls and was patted and complimented by the old men, he had felt growing within him the strength to do mighty deeds of arms.

After complicated journeyings with many pauses, there had come months of monotonous life in a camp. He had had the belief that real war was a series of death struggles with small time in between for sleep and meals; but since his regiment had come to the field the army had done little but sit still and try to keep warm.

He was brought then gradually back to his old ideas. Greeklike struggles would be no more. Men were better, or more timid. Secular and religious education had effaced the throat-grappling instinct, or else firm finance held in check the passions.

He had grown to regard himself merely as a part of a vast blue demonstration. His province was to look out, as far as he could, for his personal comfort. For recreation he could twiddle his thumbs and speculate on the thoughts which must agitate the minds of the generals. Also, he was drilled and drilled and reviewed, and drilled and drilled and reviewed.

The only foes he had seen were some pickets along the river bank. They were a sun-tanned, philosophical lot, who sometimes shot reflectively at the blue pickets. When reproached for this afterward, they usually expressed sorrow, and swore by their gods that the guns had exploded without their permission. The youth, on guard duty one night, conversed across the stream with one of them. He was a slightly ragged man, who spat skillfully between his shoes and possessed a great fund of bland and infantile assurance. The youth liked him personally.

"Yank," the other had informed him, "yer a right dum good feller." This sentiment, floating to him upon the still air, had made him temporarily regret war.

Various veterans had told him tales. Some talked of gray, bewhiskered hordes who were advancing with relentless curses and chewing tobacco with unspeakable valor; tremendous bodies of fierce soldiery who were sweeping along like the Huns. Others spoke of tattered and eternally hungry men who fired despondent powders. "They'll charge through hell's fire an' brimstone t' git a holt on a haversack, an' sech stomachs ain't a-lastin' long," he was told. From the stories, the youth imagined the red, live bones sticking out through slits in the faded uniforms.

Still, he could not put a whole faith in veterans' tales, for recruits were their prey. They talked much of smoke, fire, and blood, but he could not tell how much might be lies. They persistently yelled "Fresh fish!" at him, and were in no wise to be trusted.

However, he perceived now that it did not greatly matter what kind of soldiers he was going to fight, so long as they fought, which fact no one disputed. There was a more serious problem. He lay in his bunk pondering upon it. He tried to mathematically prove to himself that he would not run from a battle.

Previously he had never felt obliged to wrestle too seriously with this question. In his life he had taken certain things for granted, never challenging his belief in ultimate success, and bothering little about means and roads. But here he was confronted with a thing of moment. It had suddenly appeared to him that perhaps in a battle he might run. He was forced to admit that as far as war was concerned he knew nothing of himself.

A sufficient time before he would have allowed the problem to kick its heels at the outer portals of his mind, but now he felt compelled to give serious attention to it.

A little panic-fear grew in his mind. As his imagination went forward to a fight, he saw hideous possibilities. He contemplated the lurking menaces of the future, and failed in an effort to see himself standing stoutly in the midst of them. He recalled his visions of broken-bladed glory, but in the shadow of the impending tumult he suspected them to be impossible pictures.

He sprang from the bunk and began to pace nervously to and fro. "Good Lord, what's th' matter with me?" he said aloud.

He felt that in this crisis his laws of life were useless. Whatever he had learned of himself was here of no avail. He was an unknown quantity. He saw that he would again be obliged to experiment as he had in early youth. He must accumulate information of himself, and meanwhile he resolved to remain close upon his guard lest those qualities of which he knew nothing should everlastingly disgrace him. "Good Lord!" he repeated in dismay.

After a time the tall soldier slid dexterously through the hole. The loud private followed. They were wrangling.

"That's all right," said the tall soldier as he entered. He waved his hand expressively. "You can believe me or not, jest as you like. All you got to do is to sit down and wait as quiet as you can. Then pretty soon you'll find out I was right."

His comrade grunted stubbornly. For a moment he seemed to be searching for a formidable reply. Finally he said: 'Well, you don't know everything in the world, do you?"

"Didn't say I knew everything in the world," retorted the other sharply. He began to stow various articles snugly into his knapsack.

The youth, pausing in his nervous walk, looked down at the busy figure. "Going to be a battle, sure, is there, Jim?" he asked.

"Of course there is," replied the tall soldier. "Of course there is. You jest wait 'til to-morrow, and you'll see one of the biggest battles ever was. You jest wait."

"Thunder!" said the youth.

"Oh, you'll see fighting this time, my boy, what'll be regular out-and-out fighting," added the tall soldier, with the air of a man who is about to exhibit a battle for the benefit of his friends.

"Huh!" said the loud one from a corner.

"Well," remarked the youth, "like as not this story'll turn out jest like them others did."

"Not much it won't," replied the tall soldier, exasperated. "Not much it won't. Didn't the cavalry all start this morning?" He glared about him. No one denied his statement. "The cavalry started this morning," he continued. "They say there ain't hardly any cavalry left in camp. They're going to Richmond, or some place, while we fight all the Johnnies. It's some dodge like that. The regiment's got orders, too. A feller what seen 'em go to headquarters told me a little while ago. And they're raising blazes all over camp—anybody can see that."

"Shucks!" said the loud one.

The youth remained silent for a time. At last he spoke to the tall soldier. "Jim!"

"What?"

"How do you think the reg'ment 'll do?"

"Oh, they'll fight all right, I guess, after they once get into it," said the other with cold judgment. He made a fine use of the third person. "There's been heaps of fun poked at 'em because they're new, of course, and all that; but they'll fight all right, I guess."

"Think any of the boys 'll run?" persisted the youth.

"Oh, there may be a few of 'em run, but there's them kind in every regiment, 'specially when they first goes under fire," said the other in a tolerant way. "Of course it might happen that the hull kit-and-boodle might start and run, if some big fighting came first-off, and then again they might stay and fight like fun. But you can't bet on nothing. Of course they ain't never been under fire yet, and it ain't likely they'll lick the hull rebel army all-to-oncet the first time; but I think they'll fight better than some, if worse than others. That's the way I figger. They call the reg'ment 'Fresh fish' and everything; but the boys come of good stock, and most of 'em 'll fight like sin after they oncet git shootin'," he added, with a mighty emphasis on the last four words.

"Oh, you think you know——" began the loud soldier with scorn.

The other turned savagely upon him. They had a rapid altercation, in which they fastened upon each other various strange epithets.

The youth at last interrupted them. "Did you ever think you might run yourself, Jim?" he asked. On concluding the sentence he laughed as if he had meant to aim a joke. The loud soldier also giggled.

The tall private waved his hand. "Well," said he profoundly, "I've thought it might get too hot for Jim Conklin in some of them scrimmages, and if a whole lot of boys started and run, why, I s'pose I'd start and run. And if I once started to run, I'd run like the devil, and no mistake. But if everybody was a-standing and a-fighting, why, I'd stand and fight. Be jiminey, I would. I'll bet on it."

"Huh!" said the loud one.

The youth of this tale felt gratitude for these words of his comrade. He had feared that all of the untried men possessed a great and correct confidence. He now was in a measure reassured.

Chapter 2

The next morning the youth discovered that his tall comrade had been the fast-flying messenger of a mistake. There was much scoffing at the latter by those who had yesterday been firm adherents of his views, and there was even a little sneering by men who had never believed the rumor. The tall one fought with a man from Chatfield Corners and beat him severely.

The youth felt, however, that his problem was in no wise lifted from him. There was, on the contrary, an irritating prolongation. The tale had created in him a great concern for himself. Now, with the newborn question in his mind, he was compelled to sink back into his old place as part of a blue demonstration.

For days he made ceaseless calculations, but they were all wondrously unsatisfactory. He found that he could establish nothing. He finally concluded that the only way to prove himself was to go into the blaze, and then figuratively to watch his legs to discover their merits and faults. He reluctantly admitted that he could not sit still and with a mental slate and pencil derive an answer. To gain it, he must have blaze, blood, and danger, even as a chemist requires this, that, and the other. So he fretted for an opportunity.

Meanwhile he continually tried to measure himself by his comrades. The tall soldier, for one, gave him some assurance. This man's serene unconcern dealt him a measure of confidence, for he had known him since childhood, and from his intimate knowledge he did not see how he could be capable of anything that was beyond him, the youth. Still, he thought that his comrade might be mistaken about himself. Or, on the other hand, he might be a man heretofore doomed to peace and obscurity, but, in reality, made to shine in war.

The youth would have liked to have discovered another who suspected himself. A sympathetic comparison of mental notes would have been a joy to him.

He occasionally tried to fathom a comrade with seductive sentences. He looked about to find men in the proper mood. All attempts failed to bring forth any statement which looked in any way like a confession to those doubts which he privately acknowledged in himself. He was afraid to make an open declaration of his concern, because he dreaded to place some unscrupulous confidant upon the high plane of the unconfessed from which elevation he could be derided.

In regard to his companions his mind wavered between two opinions, according to his mood. Sometimes he inclined to believing them all heroes. In fact, he usually admitted in secret the superior development of the higher qualities in others. He could conceive of men going very insignificantly about the world bearing a load of courage unseen, and although he had known many of his comrades through boyhood, he began to fear that his judgment of them had been blind. Then, in other moments, he flouted these theories, and assured himself that his fellows were all privately wondering and quaking.

His emotions made him feel strange in the presence of men who talked excitedly of a prospective battle as of a drama they were about to witness, with nothing but eagerness and curiosity apparent in their faces. It was often that he suspected them to be liars.

He did not pass such thoughts without severe condemnation of himself. He dinned reproaches at times. He was convicted by himself of many shameful crimes against the gods of traditions.

In his great anxiety his heart was continually clamoring at what he considered the intolerable slowness of the generals. They seemed content to perch tranquilly on the river bank, and leave him bowed down by the weight of a great problem. He wanted it settled forthwith. He could not long bear such a load, he said. Sometimes his anger at the commanders reached an acute stage, and he grumbled about the camp like a veteran.

One morning, however, he found himself in the ranks of his prepared regiment. The men were whispering speculations and recounting the old rumors. In the gloom before the break of the day their uniforms glowed a deep purple hue. From across the river the red eyes were still peering. In the eastern sky there was a yellow patch like a rug laid for the feet of the coming sun; and against it, black and patternlike, loomed the gigantic figure of the colonel on a gigantic horse.

From off in the darkness came the trampling of feet. The youth could occasionally see dark shadows that moved like monsters. The regiment stood at rest for what seemed a long time. The youth grew impatient. It was unendurable the way these affairs were managed. He wondered how long they were to be kept waiting.

As he looked all about him and pondered upon the mystic gloom, he began to believe that at any moment the ominous distance might be aflare, and the rolling crashes of an engagement come to his ears. Staring once at the red eyes across the river, he conceived them to be growing larger, as the orbs of a row of dragons advancing. He turned toward the colonel and saw him lift his gigantic arm and calmly stroke his mustache.

At last he heard from along the road at the foot of the hill the clatter of a horse's galloping hoofs. It must be the coming of orders. He bent forward, scarce breathing. The exciting clickety-click, as it grew louder and louder, seemed to be beating upon his soul. Presently a horseman with jangling equipment drew rein before the colonel of the regiment. The two held a short, sharp-worded conversation. The men in the foremost ranks craned their necks.

As the horseman wheeled his animal and galloped away he turned to shout over his shoulder, "Don't forget that box of cigars!" The colonel mumbled in reply. The youth wondered what a box of cigars had to do with war.

A moment later the regiment went swinging off into the darkness. It was now like one of those moving monsters wending with many feet. The air was heavy, and cold with dew. A mass of wet grass, marched upon, rustled like silk.

There was an occasional flash and glimmer of steel from the backs of all these huge crawling reptiles. From the road came creakings and grumblings as some surly guns were dragged away.

The men stumbled along still muttering speculations. There was a subdued debate. Once a man fell down, and as he reached for his rifle a comrade, unseeing, trod upon his hand. He of the injured fingers swore bitterly and aloud. A low, tittering laugh went among his fellows.

Presently they passed into a roadway and marched forward with easy strides. A dark regiment moved before them, and from behind also came the tinkle of equipments on the bodies of marching men.

The rushing yellow of the developing day went on behind their backs. When the sunrays at last struck full and mellowingly upon the earth, the youth saw that the landscape was streaked with two long, thin, black columns which disappeared on the brow of a hill in front and rearward vanished in a wood. They were like two serpents crawling from the cavern of the night.

The river was not in view. The tall soldier burst into praises of what he thought to be his powers of perception.

Some of the tall one's companions cried with emphasis that they, too, had evolved the same thing, and they congratulated themselves upon it. But there were others who said that the tall one's plan was not the true one at all. They persisted with other theories. There was a vigorous discussion.

The youth took no part in them. As he walked along in careless line he was engaged with his own eternal debate. He could not hinder himself from dwelling upon it. He was despondent and sullen, and threw shifting glances about him. He looked ahead, often expecting to hear from the advance the rattle of firing.

But the long serpents crawled slowly from hill to hill without bluster of smoke. A dun-colored cloud of dust floated away to the right. The sky overhead was of a fairy blue.

The youth studied the faces of his companions, ever on the watch to detect kindred emotions. He suffered disappointment. Some ardor of the air which was causing the veteran commands to move with glee—almost with song—had infected the new regiment. The men began to speak of victory as of a thing they knew. Also, the tall soldier received his vindication. They were certainly going to come around in behind the enemy. They expressed commiseration for that part of the army which had been left upon the river bank, felicitating themselves upon being a part of a blasting host.

The youth, considering himself as separated from the others, was saddened by the blithe and merry speeches that went from rank to rank. The company wags all made their best endeavors. The regiment tramped to the tune of laughter.

The blatant soldier often convulsed whole files by his biting sarcasms aimed at the tall one.

And it was not long before all the men seemed to forget their mission. Whole brigades grinned in unison, and regiments laughed.

A rather fat soldier attempted to pilfer a horse from a dooryard. He planned to load his knapsack upon it. He was escaping with his prize when a young girl rushed from the house and grabbed the animal's mane. There followed a wrangle. The young girl, with pink cheeks and shining eyes, stood like a dauntless statue.

The observant regiment, standing at rest in the roadway, whooped at once, and entered whole-souled upon the side of the maiden. The men became so engrossed in this affair that they entirely ceased to remember their own large war. They jeered the piratical private, and called attention to various defects in his personal appearance; and they were wildly enthusiastic in support of the young girl.

To her, from some distance, came bold advice. "Hit him with a stick."

There were crows and catcalls showered upon him when he retreated without the horse. The regiment rejoiced at his downfall. Loud and vociferous congratulations were showered upon the maiden, who stood panting and regarding the troops with defiance.

At nightfall the column broke into regimental pieces, and the fragments went into the fields to camp. Tents sprang up like strange plants. Camp fires, like red, peculiar blossoms, dotted the night.

The youth kept from intercourse with his companions as much as circumstances would allow him. In the evening he wandered a few paces into the gloom. From this little distance the many fires, with the black forms of men passing to and fro before the crimson rays, made weird and satanic effects.

He lay down in the grass. The blades pressed tenderly against his cheek. The moon had been lighted and was hung in a treetop. The liquid stillness of the night enveloping him made him feel vast pity for himself. There was a caress in the soft winds; and the whole mood of the darkness, he thought, was one of sympathy for himself in his distress.

He wished, without reserve, that he was at home again making the endless rounds from the house to the barn, from the barn to the fields, from the fields to the barn, from the barn to the house. He remembered he had often cursed the brindle cow and her mates, and had sometimes flung milking stools. But, from his present point of view, there was a halo of happiness about each of their heads, and he would have sacrificed all the brass buttons on the continent to have been enabled to return to them. He told himself that he was not formed for a soldier. And he mused seriously upon the radical differences between himself and those men who were dodging implike around the fires.

As he mused thus he heard the rustle of grass, and, upon turning his head, discovered the loud soldier. He called out, "Oh! Wilson!"

The latter approached and looked down. "Why, hello, Henry; is it you? What you doing here?"

"Oh, thinking," said the youth.

The other sat down and carefully lighted his pipe. "You're getting blue, my boy. You're looking thundering peeked. What the dickens is wrong with you?"

"Oh, nothing," said the youth.

The loud soldier launched then into the subject of the anticipated fight. "Oh, we've got 'em now!" As he spoke his boyish face was wreathed in a gleeful smile, and his voice had an exultant ring. "We've got 'em now. At last, by the eternal thunders, we'll lick 'em good!"

"If the truth was known," he added, more soberly, "*they've* licked *us* about every clip up to now; but this time—this time—we'll lick 'em good!"

"I thought you was objecting to this march a little while ago," said the youth coldly.

"Oh, it wasn't that," explained the other. "I don't mind marching, if there's going to be fighting at the end of it. What I hate is this getting moved here and moved there, with no good coming of it, as far as I can see, excepting sore feet and damned short rations."

"Well, Jim Conklin says we'll get a plenty of fighting this time."

"He's right for once, I guess, though I can't see how it come. This time we're in for a big battle, and we've got the best end of it, certain sure. Gee rod! how we will thump 'em!"

He arose and began to pace to and fro excitedly. The thrill of his enthusiasm made him walk with an elastic step. He was sprightly, vigorous, fiery in his belief in success. He looked into the future with clear, proud eye, and he swore with the air of an old soldier.

The youth watched him for a moment in silence. When he finally spoke his voice was as bitter as dregs. "Oh, you're going to do great things, I s'pose!"

The loud soldier blew a thoughtful cloud of smoke from his pipe. "Oh, I don't know," he remarked with dignity; "I don't know. I s'pose I'll do as well as the rest. I'm going to try like thunder." He evidently complimented himself upon the modesty of this statement.

"How do you know you won't run when the time comes?" asked the youth.

"Run?" said the loud one; "run?—of course not!" He laughed.

"Well," continued the youth, "lots of good-a-'nough men have thought they was going to do great things before the fight, but when the time come they skedaddled."

"Oh, that's all true, I s'pose," replied the other; "but I'm not going to skedaddle. The man that bets on my running will lose his money, that's all." He nodded confidently.

"Oh, shucks!" said the youth. "You ain't the bravest man in the world, are you?"

"No, I ain't," exclaimed the loud soldier indignantly; "and I didn't say I was the bravest man in the world, neither. I said I was going to do my share of fighting—that's what I said. And I am, too. Who are you, anyhow? You talk as if you thought you was Napoleon Bonaparte." He glared at the youth for a moment, and then strode away.

The youth called in a savage voice after his comrade: "Well, you needn't git mad about it!" But the other continued on his way and made no reply.

He felt alone in space when his injured comrade had disappeared. His failure to discover any mite of resemblance in their view points made him more miserable than before. No one seemed to be wrestling with such a terrific personal problem. He was a mental outcast.

He went slowly to his tent and stretched himself on a blanket by the side of the snoring tall soldier. In the darkness he saw visions of a thousand-tongued fear that would babble at his back and cause him to flee, while others were going coolly about their country's business. He admitted that he would not be able to cope with this monster. He felt that every nerve in his body would be an ear to hear the voices, while other men would remain stolid and deaf.

And as he sweated with the pain of these thoughts, he could hear low, serene sentences. "I'll bid five." "Make it six." "Seven." "Seven goes."

He stared at the red, shivering reflection of a fire on the white wall of his tent until, exhausted and ill from the monotony of his suffering, he fell asleep.

Chapter 3

When another night came the columns, changed to purple streaks, filed across two pontoon bridges. A glaring fire wine-tinted the waters of the river. Its rays, shining upon the moving masses of troops, brought forth here and there sudden gleams of silver or gold. Upon the other shore a dark and mysterious range of hills was curved against the sky. The insect voices of the night sang solemnly.

After this crossing the youth assured himself that at any moment they might be suddenly and fearfully assaulted from the caves of the lowering woods. He kept his eyes watchfully upon the darkness.

But his regiment went unmolested to a camping place, and its soldiers slept the brave sleep of wearied men. In the morning they were routed out with early energy, and hustled along a narrow road that led deep into the forest.

It was during this rapid march that the regiment lost many of the marks of a new command.

The men had begun to count the miles upon their fingers, and they grew tired. "Sore feet an' damned short rations, that's all," said the loud soldier. There was perspiration and grumblings. After a time they began to shed their knapsacks. Some tossed them unconcernedly down; others hid them carefully, asserting their plans to return for them at some convenient time. Men extricated themselves from thick shirts. Presently few carried anything but their necessary clothing, blankets, haversacks, canteens, and arms and ammunition. "You can now eat and shoot," said the tall soldier to the youth. "That's all you want to do."

There was sudden change from the ponderous infantry of theory to the light and speedy infantry of practice. The regiment, relieved of a burden, received a new impetus. But there was much loss of valuable knapsacks, and, on the whole, very good shirts.

But the regiment was not yet veteranlike in appearance. Veteran regiments in the army were likely to be very small aggregations of men. Once, when the command had first come to the field, some perambulating veterans, noting the length of their column, had accosted them thus: "Hey, fellers, what brigade is that?" And when the men had replied that they formed a regiment and not a brigade, the other soldiers had laughed, and said, "O Gawd!"

Also, there was too great a similarity in the hats. The hats of a regiment should properly represent the history of headgear for a period of years. And, moreover, there were no letters of faded gold speaking from the colors. They were new and beautiful, and the color bearer habitually oiled the pole.

Presently the army again sat down to think. The odor of the peaceful pines was in the men's nostrils. The sound of monotonous axe blows rang through the forest, and the insects, nodding upon their perches, crooned like old women. The youth returned to his theory of a blue demonstration.

One gray dawn, however, he was kicked in the leg by the tall soldier, and then, before he was entirely awake, he found himself running down a wood road in the midst of men who were panting from the first effects of speed. His canteen banged rhythmically upon his thigh, and his haversack bobbed softly. His musket bounced a trifle from his shoulder at each stride and made his cap feel uncertain upon his head.

He could hear the men whisper jerky sentences: "Say—what's all this—about?" "What th' thunder—we—skedaddlin' this way fer?" "Billie—keep off m' feet. Yeh run—like a cow." And the loud soldier's shrill voice could be heard: "What th' devil they in sich a hurry for?"

The youth thought the damp fog of early morning moved from the rush of a great body of troops. From the distance came a sudden spatter of firing.

He was bewildered. As he ran with his comrades he strenuously tried to think, but all he knew was that if he fell down those coming behind would tread upon him. All his faculties seemed to be needed to guide him over and past obstructions. He felt carried along by a mob.

The sun spread disclosing rays, and, one by one, regiments burst into view like armed men just born of the earth. The youth perceived that the time had come. He was about to be measured. For a moment he felt in the face of his great trial like a babe, and the flesh over his heart seemed very thin. He seized time to look about him calculatingly.

But he instantly saw that it would be impossible for him to escape from the regiment. It inclosed him. And there were iron laws of tradition and law on four sides. He was in a moving box.

As he perceived this fact it occurred to him that he had never wished to come to the war. He had not enlisted of his free will. He had been dragged by the merciless government. And now they were taking him out to be slaughtered.

The regiment slid down a bank and wallowed across a little stream. The mournful current moved slowly on, and from the water, shaded black, some white bubble eyes looked at the men.

As they climbed the hill on the farther side artillery began to boom. Here the youth forgot many things as he felt a sudden impulse of curiosity. He scrambled up the bank with a speed that could not be exceeded by a bloodthirsty man.

He expected a battle scene.

There were some little fields girted and squeezed by a forest. Spread over the grass and in among the tree trunks, he could see knots and waving lines of skirmishers who were running hither and thither and firing at the landscape. A dark battle line lay upon a sunstruck clearing that gleamed orange color. A flag fluttered.

Other regiments floundered up the bank. The brigade was formed in line of battle, and after a pause started slowly through the woods in the rear of the receding skirmishers, who were continually melting into the scene to appear again farther on. They were always busy as bees, deeply absorbed in their little combats.

The youth tried to observe everything. He did not use care to avoid trees and branches, and his forgotten feet were constantly knocking against stones or getting entangled in briers. He was aware that these battalions with their commotions were woven red and startling into the gentle fabric of softened greens and browns. It looked to be a wrong place for a battle field.

The skirmishers in advance fascinated him. Their shots into thickets and at distant and prominent trees spoke to him of tragedies—hidden, mysterious, solemn.

Once the line encountered the body of a dead soldier. He lay upon his back staring at the sky. He was dressed in an awkward suit of yellowish brown. The youth could see that the soles of his shoes had been worn to the thinness of writing paper, and from a great rent in one the dead foot projected piteously. And it was as if fate had betrayed the soldier. In death it exposed to his enemies that poverty which in life he had perhaps concealed from his friends.

The ranks opened covertly to avoid the corpse. The invulnerable dead man forced a way for himself. The youth looked keenly at the ashen face. The wind raised the tawny beard. It moved as if a hand were stroking it. He vaguely desired to walk around and around the body and stare; the impulse of the living to try to read in dead eyes the answer to the Question.

During the march the ardor which the youth had acquired when out of view of the field rapidly faded to nothing. His curiosity was quite easily satisfied. If an intense scene had caught him with its wild swing as he came to the top of the bank he might have gone roaring on. This advance upon Nature was too calm. He had opportunity to reflect. He had time in which to wonder about himself and to attempt to probe his sensations.

Absurd ideas took hold upon him. He thought that he did not relish the landscape. It threatened him. A coldness swept over his back, and it is true that his trousers felt to him that they were not fit for his legs at all.

A house standing placidly in distant fields had to him an ominous look. The shadows of the woods were formidable. He was certain that in this vista there lurked fierce-eyed hosts. The swift thought came to him that the generals did not know what they were about. It was all a trap. Suddenly those close forests would bristle with rifle barrels. Ironlike brigades would appear in the rear. They were all going to be sacrificed. The generals were stupids. The enemy would presently swallow the whole command. He glared about him, expecting to see the stealthy approach of his death.

He thought that he must break from the ranks and harangue his comrades. They must not all be killed like pigs; and he was sure it would come to pass unless they were informed of these dangers. The generals were idiots to send them marching into a regular pen. There was but one pair of eyes in the corps. He would step forth and make a speech. Shrill and passionate words came to his lips.

The line, broken into moving fragments by the ground, went calmly on through fields and woods. The youth looked at the men nearest him, and saw, for the most part, expressions of deep interest, as if they were investigating something that had fascinated them. One or two stepped with overvaliant airs as if they were already plunged into war. Others walked as upon thin ice. The greater part of the untested men appeared quiet and absorbed. They were going to look at war, the red animal—war, the blood-swollen god. And they were deeply engrossed in this march.

As he looked the youth gripped his outcry at his throat. He saw that even if the men were tottering with fear they would laugh at his warning. They would jeer him, and, if practicable, pelt him with missiles. Admitting that he might be wrong, a frenzied declamation of the kind would turn him into a worm.

He assumed, then, the demeanor of one who knows that he is doomed alone to unwritten responsibilities. He lagged, with tragic glances at the sky.

He was surprised presently by the young lieutenant of his company, who began heartily to beat him with a sword, calling out in a loud and insolent voice: "Come, young man, get up into ranks there. No skulking'll do here." He mended his pace with suitable haste. And he hated the lieutenant, who had no appreciation of fine minds. He was a mere brute.

After a time the brigade was halted in the cathedral light of a forest. The busy skirmishers were still popping. Through the aisles of the wood could be seen the floating smoke from their rifles. Sometimes it went up in little balls, white and compact.

During this halt many men in the regiment began erecting tiny hills in front of them. They used stones, sticks, earth, and anything they thought might turn a bullet. Some built comparatively large ones, while others seemed content with little ones.

This procedure caused a discussion among the men. Some wished to fight like duelists, believing it to be correct to stand erect and be, from their feet to their foreheads, a mark. They said they scorned the devices of the cautious. But the others scoffed in reply, and pointed to the veterans on the flanks who were digging at the ground like terriers. In a short time there was quite a barricade along the regimental fronts. Directly, however, they were ordered to withdraw from that place.

This astounded the youth. He forgot his stewing over the advance movement. "Well, then, what did they march us out here for?" he demanded of the tall soldier. The latter with calm faith began a heavy explanation, although he had been compelled to leave a little protection of stones and dirt to which he had devoted much care and skill.

When the regiment was aligned in another position each man's regard for his safety caused another line of small intrenchments. They ate their noon meal behind a third one. They were moved from this one also. They were marched from place to place with apparent aimlessness.

The youth had been taught that a man became another thing in a battle. He saw his salvation in such a change. Hence this waiting was an ordeal to him. He was in a fever of impatience. He considered that there was denoted a lack of purpose on the part of the generals. He began to complain to the tall soldier. "I can't stand this much longer," he cried, "I don't see what good it does to make us wear out our legs for nothin'." He wished to return to camp, knowing that this affair was a blue demonstration; or else to go into a battle and discover that he had been a fool in his doubts, and was, in truth, a man of traditional courage. The strain of present circumstances he felt to be intolerable.

The philosophical tall soldier measured a sandwich of cracker and pork and swallowed it in a nonchalant manner. "Oh, I suppose we must go reconnoitering around the country jest to keep 'em from getting too close, or to develop 'em, or something."

"Huh!" said the loud soldier.

"Well," cried the youth, still fidgeting, "I'd rather do anything 'most than go tramping 'round the country all day doing no good to nobody and jest tiring ourselves out."

"So would I," said the loud soldier. "It ain't right. I tell you if anybody with any sense was a-runnin' this army it——"

"Oh, shut up!" roared the tall private. "You little fool. You little damn' cuss. You ain't had that there coat and them pants on for six months, and yet you talk as if——"

"Well, I wanta do some fighting anyway," interrupted the other. "I didn't come here to walk. I could 'ave walked to home—'round an' 'round the barn, if I jest wanted to walk."

The tall one, red-faced, swallowed another sandwich as if taking poison in despair.

But gradually, as he chewed, his face became again quiet and contented. He could not rage in fierce argument in the presence of such sandwiches. During his meals he always wore an air of blissful contemplation of the food he had swallowed. His spirit seemed then to be communing with the viands.

He accepted new environment and circumstance with great coolness, eating from his haversack at every opportunity. On the march he went along with the stride of a hunter, objecting to neither gait nor distance. And he had not raised his voice when he had been ordered away from three little protective piles of earth and stone, each of which had been an engineering feat worthy of being made sacred to the name of his grandmother.

In the afternoon the regiment went out over the same ground it had taken in the morning. The landscape then ceased to threaten the youth. He had been close to it and become familiar with it.

When, however, they began to pass into a new region, his old fears of stupidity and incompetence reassailed him, but this time he doggedly let them babble. He was occupied with his problem, and in his desperation he concluded that the stupidity did not greatly matter.

Once he thought he had concluded that it would be better to get killed directly and end his troubles. Regarding death thus out of the corner of his eye, he conceived it to be nothing but rest, and he was filled with a momentary astonishment that he should have made an extraordinary commotion over the mere matter of getting killed. He would die; he would go to some place where he would be understood. It was useless to expect appreciation of his profound and fine senses from such men as the lieutenant. He must look to the grave for comprehension.

The skirmish fire increased to a long clattering sound. With it was mingled far-away cheering. A battery spoke.

Directly the youth would see the skirmishers running. They were pursued by the sound of musketry fire. After a time the hot, dangerous flashes of the rifles were visible. Smoke clouds went slowly and insolently across the fields like observant phantoms. The din became crescendo, like the roar of an oncoming train.

A brigade ahead of them and on the right went into action with a rending roar. It was as if it had exploded. And thereafter it lay stretched in the distance behind a long gray wall, that one was obliged to look twice at to make sure that it was smoke.

The youth, forgetting his neat plan of getting killed, gazed spell bound. His eyes grew wide and busy with the action of the scene. His mouth was a little ways open.

Of a sudden he felt a heavy and sad hand laid upon his shoulder. Awakening from his trance of observation he turned and beheld the loud soldier.

"It's my first and last battle, old boy," said the latter, with intense gloom. He was quite pale and his girlish lip was trembling.

"Eh?" murmured the youth in great astonishment.

"It's my first and last battle, old boy," continued the loud soldier. "Something tells me——"

"What?"

"I'm a gone coon this first time and—and I w-want you to take these here things—to—my—folks." He ended in a quavering sob of pity for himself. He handed the youth a little packet done up in a yellow envelope.

"Why, what the devil——" began the youth again.

But the other gave him a glance as from the depths of a tomb, and raised his limp hand in a prophetic manner and turned away.

Chapter 4

The brigade was halted in the fringe of a grove. The men crouched among the trees and pointed their restless guns out at the fields. They tried to look beyond the smoke.

Out of this haze they could see running men. Some shouted information and gestured as they hurried.

The men of the new regiment watched and listened eagerly, while their tongues ran on in gossip of the battle. They mouthed rumors that had flown like birds out of the unknown.

"They say Perry has been driven in with big loss."

"Yes, Carrott went t' th' hospital. He said he was sick. That smart lieutenant is commanding 'G' Company. Th' boys say they won't be under Carrott no more if they all have t' desert. They allus knew he was a——"

"Hannises' batt'ry is took."

"It ain't either. I saw Hannises' batt'ry off on th' left not more'n fifteen minutes ago."

"Well——"

"Th' general, he ses he is goin' t' take th' hull cammand of th' 304th when we go inteh action, an' then he ses we'll do sech fightin' as never another one reg'ment done."

"They say we're catchin' it over on th' left. They say th' enemy driv' our line inteh a devil of a swamp an' took Hannises' batt'ry."

"No sech thing. Hannises' batt'ry was 'long here 'bout a minute ago."

"That young Hasbrouck, he makes a good off'cer. He ain't afraid 'a nothin'."

"I met one of th' 148th Maine boys an' he ses his brigade fit th' hull rebel army fer four hours over on th' turnpike road an' killed about five thousand of 'em. He ses one more sech fight as that an' th' war'll be over."

"Bill wasn't scared either. No, sir! It wasn't that. Bill ain't a-gittin' scared easy. He was jest mad, that's what he was. When that feller trod on his hand, he up an' sed that he was willin' t' give his hand t' his country, but he be dumbed if he was goin' t' have every dumb bushwhacker in th' kentry walkin' 'round on it. Se he went t' th' hospital disregardless of th' fight. Three fingers was crunched. Th' dern doctor wanted t' amputate 'm, an' Bill, he raised a heluva row, I hear. He's a funny feller."

The din in front swelled to a tremendous chorus. The youth and his fellows were frozen to silence. They could see a flag that tossed in the smoke angrily. Near it were the blurred and agitated forms of troops. There came a turbulent stream of men across the fields. A battery changing position at a frantic gallop scattered the stragglers right and left.

A shell screaming like a storm banshee went over the huddled heads of the reserves. It landed in the grove, and exploding redly flung the brown earth. There was a little shower of pine needles.

Bullets began to whistle among the branches and nip at the trees. Twigs and leaves came sailing down. It was as if a thousand axes, wee and invisible, were being wielded. Many of the men were constantly dodging and ducking their heads.

The lieutenant of the youth's company was shot in the hand. He began to swear so wondrously that a nervous laugh went along the regimental line. The officer's profanity sounded conventional. It relieved the tightened senses of the new men. It was as if he had hit his fingers with a tack hammer at home.

He held the wounded member carefully away from his side so that the blood would not drip upon his trousers.

The captain of the company, tucking his sword under his arm, produced a handkerchief and began to bind with it the lieutenant's wound. And they disputed as to how the binding should be done.

The battle flag in the distance jerked about madly. It seemed to be struggling to free itself from an agony. The billowing smoke was filled with horizontal flashes.

Men running swiftly emerged from it. They grew in numbers until it was seen that the whole command was fleeing. The flag suddenly sank down as if dying. Its motion as it fell was a gesture of despair.

Wild yells came from behind the walls of smoke. A sketch in gray and red dissolved into a moblike body of men who galloped like wild horses.

The veteran regiments on the right and left of the 304th immediately began to jeer. With the passionate song of the bullets and the banshee shrieks of shells were mingled loud catcalls and bits of facetious advice concerning places of safety.

But the new regiment was breathless with horror. "Gawd! Saunders's got crushed!" whispered the man at the youth's elbow. They shrank back and crouched as if compelled to await a flood.

The youth shot a swift glance along the blue ranks of the regiment. The profiles were motionless, carven; and afterward he remembered that the color sergeant was standing with his legs apart, as if he expected to be pushed to the ground.

The following throng went whirling around the flank. Here and there were officers carried along on the stream like exasperated chips. They were striking about them with their swords and with their left fists, punching every head they could reach. They cursed like highwaymen.

A mounted officer displayed the furious anger of a spoiled child. He raged with his head, his arms, and his legs.

Another, the commander of the brigade, was galloping about bawling. His hat was gone and his clothes were awry. He resembled a man who has come from bed to go to a fire. The hoofs of his horse often threatened the heads of the running men, but they scampered with singular fortune. In this rush they were apparently all deaf and blind. They heeded not the largest and longest of the oaths that were thrown at them from all directions.

Frequently over this tumult could be heard the grim jokes of the critical veterans; but the retreating men apparently were not even conscious of the presence of an audience.

The battle reflection that shone for an instant in the faces on the mad current made the youth feel that forceful hands from heaven would not have been able to have held him in place if he could have got intelligent control of his legs.

There was an appalling imprint upon these faces. The struggle in the smoke had pictured an exaggeration of itself on the bleached cheeks and in the eyes wild with one desire.

The sight of this stampede exerted a floodlike force that seemed able to drag sticks and stones and men from the ground. They of the reserves had to hold on. They grew pale and firm, and red and quaking.

The youth achieved one little thought in the midst of this chaos. The composite monster which had caused the other troops to flee had not then appeared. He resolved to get a view of it, and then, he thought he might very likely run better than the best of them.

Chapter 5

There were moments of waiting. The youth thought of the village street at home before the arrival of the circus parade on a day in the spring. He remembered how he had stood, a small, thrillful boy, prepared to follow the dingy lady upon the white horse, or the band in its faded chariot. He saw the yellow road, the lines of expectant people, and the sober houses. He particularly remembered an old fellow who used to sit upon a cracker box in front of the store and feign to despise such exhibitions. A thousand details of color and form surged in his mind. The old fellow upon the cracker box appeared in middle prominence.

Some one cried, "Here they come!"

There was rustling and muttering among the men. They displayed a feverish desire to have every possible cartridge ready to their hands. The boxes were pulled around into various positions, and adjusted with great care. It was as if seven hundred new bonnets were being tried on.

The tall soldier, having prepared his rifle, produced a red handkerchief of some kind. He was engaged in knitting it about his throat with exquisite attention to its position, when the cry was repeated up and down the line in a muffled roar of sound.

"Here they come! Here they come!" Gun locks clicked.

Across the smoke-infested fields came a brown swarm of running men who were giving shrill yells. They came on, stooping and swinging their rifles at all angles. A flag, titled forward, sped near the front.

As he caught sight of them the youth was momentarily startled by a thought that perhaps his gun was not loaded. He stood trying to rally his faltering intellect so that he might recollect the moment when he had loaded, but he could not.

A hatless general pulled his dripping horse to a stand near the colonel of the 304th. He shook his fist in the other's face. "You've got to hold 'em back!" he shouted, savagely; "you've got to hold 'em back!"

In his agitation the colonel began to stammer. "A-all r-right, General, all right, by Gawd! We-we'll do our—we-we'll d-d-do— do our best, General." The general made a passionate gesture and galloped away. The colonel, perchance to relieve his feelings, began to scold like a wet parrot. The youth, turning swiftly to make sure that the rear was unmolested, saw the commander regarding his men in a highly resentful manner, as if he regretted above everything his association with them.

The man at the youth's elbow was mumbling, as if to himself: "Oh, we're in for it now! oh, we're in for it now!"

The captain of the company had been pacing excitedly to and fro in the rear. He coaxed in schoolmistress fashion, as to a congregation of boys with primers. His talk was an endless repetition. "Reserve your fire, boys—don't shoot till I tell you—save your fire—wait till they get close up—don't be damned fools——"

Perspiration streamed down the youth's face, which was soiled like that of a weeping urchin. He frequently, with a nervous movement, wiped his eyes with his coat sleeve. His mouth was still a little way open.

He got the one glance at the foe-swarming field in front of him, and instantly ceased to debate the question of his piece being loaded. Before he was ready to begin—before he had announced to himself that he was about to fight— he threw the obedient, well-balanced rifle into position and fired a first wild shot. Directly he was working at his weapon like an automatic affair.

He suddenly lost concern for himself, and forgot to look at a menacing fate. He became not a man but a member. He felt that something of which he was a part—a regiment, an army, a cause, or a country—was in a crisis. He was welded into a common personality which was dominated by a single desire. For some moments he could not flee no more than a little finger can commit a revolution from a hand.

If he had thought the regiment was about to be annihilated perhaps he could have amputated himself from it. But its noise gave him assurance. The regiment was like a firework that, once ignited, proceeds superior to circum- stances until its blazing vitality fades. It wheezed and banged with a mighty power. He pictured the ground before it as strewn with the discomfited.

There was a consciousness always of the presence of his comrades about him. He felt the subtle battle brotherhood more potent even than the cause for which they were fighting. It was a mysterious fraternity born of the smoke and danger of death.

He was at a task. He was like a carpenter who has made many boxes, making still another box, only there was furious haste in his movements. He, in his thought, was careering off in other places, even as the carpenter who as he works whistles and thinks of his friend or his enemy, his home or a saloon. And these jolted dreams were never perfect to him afterward, but remained a mass of blurred shapes.

Presently he began to feel the effects of the war atmosphere—a blistering sweat, a sensation that his eyeballs were about to crack like hot stones. A burning roar filled his ears.

Following this came a red rage. He developed the acute exasperation of a pestered animal, a well-meaning cow worried by dogs. He had a mad feeling against his rifle, which could only be used against one life at a time. He wished to rush forward and strangle with his fingers. He craved a power that would enable him to make a world-sweeping gesture and brush all back. His impotency appeared to him, and made his rage into that of a driven beast.

Buried in the smoke of many rifles his anger was directed not so much against the men whom he knew were rushing toward him as against the swirling battle phantoms which were choking him, stuffing their smoke robes down his parched throat. He fought frantically for respite for his senses, for air, as a babe being smothered attacks the deadly blankets.

There was a blare of heated rage mingled with a certain expression of intentness on all faces. Many of the men were making low-toned noises with their mouths, and these subdued cheers, snarls, imprecations, prayers, made a wild, barbaric song that went as an undercurrent of sound, strange and chantlike with the resounding chords of the war march. The man at the youth's elbow was babbling. In it there was something soft and tender like the monologue of a babe. The tall soldier was swearing in a loud voice. From his lips came a black procession of curious oaths. Of a sudden another broke out in a querulous way like a man who has mislaid his hat. "Well, why don't they support us? Why don't they send supports? Do they think——"

The youth in his battle sleep heard this as one who dozes hears.

There was a singular absence of heroic poses. The men bending and surging in their haste and rage were in every impossible attitude. The steel ramrods clanked and clanged with incessant din as the men pounded them furiously into the hot rifle barrels. The flaps of the cartridge boxes were all unfastened, and bobbed idiotically with each movement. The rifles, once loaded, were jerked to the shoulder and fired without apparent aim into the smoke or at one of the blurred and shifting forms which upon the field before the regiment had been growing larger and larger like puppets under a magician's hand.

The officers, at their intervals, rearward, neglected to stand in picturesque attitudes. They were bobbing to and fro roaring directions and encouragements. The dimensions of their howls were extraordinary. They expended their lungs with prodigal wills. And often they nearly stood upon their heads in their anxiety to observe the enemy on the other side of the tumbling smoke.

The lieutenant of the youth's company had encountered a soldier who had fled screaming at the first volley of his comrades. Behind the lines these two were acting a little isolated scene. The man was blubbering and staring with sheeplike eyes at the lieutenant, who had seized him by the collar and was pommeling him. He drove him back into the ranks with many blows. The soldier went mechanically, dully, with his animal-like eyes upon the officer. Perhaps there was to him a divinity expressed in the voice of the other—stern, hard, with no reflection of fear in it. He tried to reload his gun, but his shaking hands prevented. The lieutenant was obliged to assist him.

The men dropped here and there like bundles. The captain of the youth's company had been killed in an early part of the action. His body lay stretched out in the position of a tired man resting, but upon his face there was an astonished and sorrowful look, as if he thought some friend had done him an ill turn. The babbling man was grazed by a shot that made the blood stream widely down his face. He clapped both hands to his head. "Oh!" he said, and ran. Another grunted suddenly as if he had been struck by a club in the stomach. He sat down and gazed ruefully. In his eyes there was mute, indefinite reproach. Farther up the line a man, standing behind a tree, had had his knee joint splintered by a ball. Immediately he had dropped his rifle and gripped the tree with both arms. And there he remained, clinging desperately and crying for assistance that he might withdraw his hold upon the tree.

At last an exultant yell went along the quivering line. The firing dwindled from an uproar to a last vindictive popping. As the smoke slowly eddied away, the youth saw that the charge had been repulsed. The enemy were scattered into reluctant groups. He saw a man climb to the top of the fence, straddle the rail, and fire a parting shot. The waves had receded, leaving bits of dark *débris* upon the ground.

Some in the regiment began to whoop frenziedly. Many were silent. Apparently they were trying to contemplate themselves.

After the fever had left his veins, the youth thought that at last he was going to suffocate. He became aware of the foul atmosphere in which he had been struggling. He was grimy and dripping like a laborer in a foundry. He grasped his canteen and took a long swallow of the warmed water.

A sentence with variations went up and down the line. "Well, we've helt 'em back. We've helt 'em back; derned if we haven't." The men said it blissfully, leering at each other with dirty smiles.

The youth turned to look behind him and off to the right and off to the left. He experienced the joy of a man who at last finds leisure in which to look about him.

Under foot there were a few ghastly forms motionless. They lay twisted in fantastic contortions. Arms were bent and heads were turned in incredible ways. It seemed that the dead men must have fallen from some great height to get into such positions. They looked to be dumped out upon the ground from the sky.

From a position in the rear of the grove a battery was throwing shells over it. The flash of the guns startled the youth at first. He thought they were aimed directly at him. Through the trees he watched the black figures of the gunners as they worked swiftly and intently. Their labor seemed a complicated thing. He wondered how they could remember its formula in the midst of confusion.

The guns squatted in a row like savage chiefs. They argued with abrupt violence. It was a grim pow-wow. Their busy servants ran hither and thither.

A small procession of wounded men were going drearily toward the rear. It was a flow of blood from the torn body of the brigade.

To the right and to the left were the dark lines of other troops. Far in front he thought he could see lighter masses protruding in points from the forest. They were suggestive of unnumbered thousands.

Once he saw a tiny battery go dashing along the line of the horizon. The tiny riders were beating the tiny horses.

From a sloping hill came the sound of cheerings and clashes. Smoke welled slowly through the leaves.

Batteries were speaking with thunderous oratorical effort. Here and there were flags, the red in the stripes dominating. They splashed bits of warm color upon the dark lines of troops.

The youth felt the old thrill at the sight of the emblem. They were like beautiful birds strangely undaunted in a storm.

As he listened to the din from the hillside, to a deep pulsating thunder that came from afar to the left, and to the lesser clamors which came from many directions, it occurred to him that they were fighting, too, over there, and over there, and over there. Heretofore he had supposed that all the battle was directly under his nose.

As he gazed around him the youth felt a flash of astonishment at the blue, pure sky and the sun gleamings on the trees and fields. It was surprising that Nature had gone tranquilly on with her golden process in the midst of so much devilment.

Chapter 6

The youth awakened slowly. He came gradually back to a position from which he could regard himself. For moments he had been scrutinizing his person in a dazed way as if he had never before seen himself. Then he picked up his cap from the ground. He wriggled in his jacket to make a more comfortable fit, and kneeling relaced his shoe. He thoughtfully mopped his reeking features.

So it was all over at last! The supreme trial had been passed. The red, formidable difficulties of war had been vanquished.

He went into an ecstasy of self-satisfaction. He had the most delightful sensations of his life. Standing as if apart from himself, he viewed that last scene. He perceived that the man who had fought thus was magnificent.

He felt that he was a fine fellow. He saw himself even with those ideals which he had considered as far beyond him. He smiled in deep gratification.

Upon his fellows he beamed tenderness and good will. "Gee! ain't it hot, hey?" he said affably to a man who was polishing his streaming face with his coat sleeves.

"You bet!" said the other, grinning sociably. "I never seen sech dumb hotness." He sprawled out luxuriously on the ground. "Gee, yes! An' I hope we don't have no more fightin' till a week from Monday."

There were some handshakings and deep speeches with men whose features were familiar, but with whom the youth now felt the bonds of tied hearts. He helped a cursing comrade to bind up a wound of the shin.

But, of a sudden, cries of amazement broke out along the ranks of the new regiment. "Here they come ag'in! Here they come ag'in!" The man who had sprawled upon the ground started up and said, "Gosh!"

The youth turned quick eyes upon the field. He discerned forms begin to swell in masses out of a distant wood. He again saw the tilted flag speeding forward.

The shells, which had ceased to trouble the regiment for a time, came swirling again, and exploded in the grass or among the leaves of the trees. They looked to be strange war flowers bursting into fierce bloom.

The men groaned. The luster faded from their eyes. Their smudged countenances now expressed a profound dejection. They moved their stiffened bodies slowly, and watched in sullen mood the frantic approach of the enemy. The slaves toiling in the temple of this god began to feel rebellion at his harsh tasks.

They fretted and complained each to each. "Oh, say, this is too much of a good thing! Why can't somebody send us supports?"

"We ain't never goin' to stand this second banging. I didn't come here to fight the hull damn' rebel army."

There was one who raised a doleful cry. "I wish Bill Smithers had trod on my hand, insteader me treddin' on his'n." The sore joints of the regiment creaked as it painfully floundered into position to repulse.

The youth stared. Surely, he thought, this impossible thing was not about to happen. He waited as if he expected the enemy to suddenly stop, apologize, and retire bowing. It was all a mistake.

But the firing began somewhere on the regimental line and ripped along in both directions. The level sheets of flame developed great clouds of smoke that tumbled and tossed in the mild wind near the ground for a moment, and then rolled through the ranks as through a gate. The clouds were tinged an earthlike yellow in the sunrays and in the shadow were a sorry blue. The flag was sometimes eaten and lost in this mass of vapor, but more often it projected, sun-touched, resplendent.

Into the youth's eyes there came a look that one can see in the orbs of a jaded horse. His neck was quivering with nervous weakness and the muscles of his arms felt numb and bloodless. His hands, too, seemed large and awkward as if he was wearing invisible mittens. And there was a great uncertainty about his knee joints.

The words that comrades had uttered previous to the firing began to recur to him. "Oh, say, this is too much of a good thing! What do they take us for— why don't they send supports? I didn't come here to fight the hull damned rebel army."

He began to exaggerate the endurance, the skill, and the valor of those who were coming. Himself reeling from exhaustion, he was astonished beyond measure at such persistency. They must be machines of steel. It was very gloomy struggling against such affairs, wound up perhaps to fight until sundown.

He slowly lifted his rifle and catching a glimpse of the thickspread field he blazed at a cantering cluster. He stopped then and began to peer as best he could through the smoke. He caught changing views of the ground covered with men who were all running like pursued imps, and yelling.

To the youth it was an onslaught of redoubtable dragons. He became like the man who lost his legs at the approach of the red and green monster. He waited in a sort of a horrified, listening attitude. He seemed to shut his eyes and wait to be gobbled.

A man near him who up to this time had been working feverishly at his rifle suddenly stopped and ran with howls. A lad whose face had borne an expression of exalted courage, the majesty of he who dares give his life, was, at an instant, smitten abject. He blanched like one who has come to the edge of a cliff at midnight and is suddenly made aware. There was a revelation. He, too, threw down his gun and fled. There was no shame in his face. He ran like a rabbit.

Others began to scamper away through the smoke. The youth turned his head, shaken from his trance by this movement as if the regiment was leaving him behind. He saw the few fleeing forms.

He yelled then with fright and swung about. For a moment, in the great clamor, he was like a proverbial chicken. He lost the direction of safety. Destruction threatened him from all points.

Directly he began to speed toward the rear in great leaps. His rifle and cap were gone. His unbuttoned coat bulged in the wind. The flap of his cartridge box bobbed wildly, and his canteen, by its slender cord, swung out behind. On his face was all the horror of those things which he imagined.

The lieutenant sprang forward bawling. The youth saw his features wrathfully red, and saw him make a dab with his sword. His one thought of the incident was that the lieutenant was a peculiar creature to feel interested in such matters upon this occasion.

He ran like a blind man. Two or three times he fell down. Once he knocked his shoulder so heavily against a tree that he went headlong.

Since he had turned his back upon the fight his fears had been wondrously magnified. Death about to thrust him between the shoulder blades was far more dreadful than death about to smite him between the eyes. When he thought of it later, he conceived the impression that it is better to view the appalling than to be merely within hearing. The noises of the battle were like stones; he believed himself liable to be crushed.

As he ran on he mingled with others. He dimly saw men on his right and on his left, and he heard footsteps behind him. He thought that all the regiment was fleeing, pursued by these ominous crashes.

In his flight the sound of these following footsteps gave him his one meager relief. He felt vaguely that death must make a first choice of the men who were nearest; the initial morsels for the dragons would be then those who were following him. So he displayed the zeal of an insane sprinter in his purpose to keep them in the rear. There was a race.

As he, leading, went across a little field, he found himself in a region of shells. They hurtled over his head with long wild screams. As he listened he imagined them to have rows of cruel teeth that grinned at him. Once one lit before him and the livid lightning of the explosion effectually barred the way in his chosen direction. He groveled on the ground and then springing up went careering off through some bushes.

He experienced a thrill of amazement when he came within view of a battery in action. The men there seemed to be in conventional moods, altogether unaware of the impending annihilation. The battery was disputing with a distant antagonist and the gunners were wrapped in admiration of their shooting. They were continually bending in coaxing postures over the guns. They seemed to be patting them on the back and encouraging them with words. The guns, stolid and undaunted, spoke with dogged valor.

The precise gunners were coolly enthusiastic. They lifted their eyes every chance to the smoke-wreathed hillock from whence the hostile battery addressed them. The youth pitied them as he ran. Methodical idiots! Machine-like fools! The refined joy of planting shells in the midst of the other battery's formation would appear a little thing when the infantry came swooping out of the woods.

The face of a youthful rider, who was jerking his frantic horse with an abandon of temper he might display in a placid barnyard, was impressed deeply upon his mind. He knew that he looked upon a man who would presently be dead.

Too, he felt a pity for the guns, standing, six good comrades, in a bold row.

He saw a brigade going to the relief of its pestered fellows. He scrambled upon a wee hill and watched it sweeping finely, keeping formation in difficult places. The blue of the line was crusted with steel color, and the brilliant flags projected. Officers were shouting.

This sight also filled him with wonder. The brigade was hurrying briskly to be gulped into the infernal mouths of the war god. What manner of men were they, anyhow? Ah, it was some wondrous breed! Or else they didn't comprehend—the fools.

A furious order caused commotion in the artillery. An officer on a bounding horse made maniacal motions with his arms. The teams went swinging up from the rear, the guns were whirled about, and the battery scampered away. The cannon with their noses poked slantingly at the ground grunted and grumbled like stout men, brave but with objections to hurry.

The youth went on, moderating his pace since he had left the place of noises.

Later he came upon a general of division seated upon a horse that pricked its ears in an interested way at the battle. There was a great gleaming of yellow and patent leather about the saddle and bridle. The quiet man astride looked mouse-colored upon such a splendid charger.

A jingling staff was galloping hither and thither. Sometimes the general was surrounded by horsemen and at other times he was quite alone. He looked to be much harassed. He had the appearance of a business man whose market is swinging up and down.

The youth went slinking around this spot. He went as near as he dared trying to overhear words. Perhaps the general, unable to comprehend chaos, might call upon him for information. And he could tell him. He knew all concerning it. Of a surety the force was in a fix, and any fool could see that if they did not retreat while they had opportunity—why——

He felt that he would like to thrash the general, or at least approach and tell him in plain words exactly what he thought him to be. It was criminal to stay calmly in one spot and make no effort to stay destruction. He loitered in a fever of eagerness for the division commander to apply to him.

As he warily moved about, he heard the general call out irritably: "Tompkins, go over an' see Taylor, an' tell him not t' be in such an all-fired hurry; tell him t' halt his brigade in th' edge of th' woods; tell him t' detach a reg'ment—say I think th' center 'll break if we don't help it out some; tell him t' hurry up."

A slim youth on a fine chestnut horse caught these swift words from the mouth of his superior. He made his horse bound into a gallop almost from a walk in his haste to go upon his mission. There was a cloud of dust.

A moment later the youth saw the general bounce excitedly in his saddle.

"Yes, by heavens, they have!" The officer leaned forward. His face was aflame with excitement. "Yes, by heavens, they've held 'im! They've held 'im!"

He began to blithely roar at his staff: "We'll wallop 'im now. We'll wallop 'im now. We've got 'em sure." He turned suddenly upon an aid: "Here—you—Jones—quick—ride after Tompkins—see Taylor—tell him t' go in—everlastingly—like blazes—anything."

As another officer sped his horse after the first messenger, the general beamed upon the earth like a sun. In his eyes was a desire to chant a pæan. He kept repeating, "They've held 'em, by heavens!"

His excitement made his horse plunge, and he merrily kicked and swore at it. He held a little carnival of joy on horseback.

Chapter 7

The youth cringed as if discovered in a crime. By heavens, they had won after all! The imbecile line had remained and become victors. He could hear cheering.

He lifted himself upon his toes and looked in the direction of the fight. A yellow fog lay wallowing on the treetops. From beneath it came the clatter of musketry. Hoarse cries told of an advance.

He turned away amazed and angry. He felt that he had been wronged.

He had fled, he told himself, because annihilation approached. He had done a good part in saving himself, who was a little piece of the army. He had considered the time, he said, to be one in which it was the duty of every little piece to rescue itself if possible. Later the officers could fit the little pieces together again, and make a battle front. If none of the little pieces were wise enough to save themselves from the flurry of death at such a time, why, then, where would be the army? It was all plain that he had proceeded according to very correct and commendable rules. His actions had been sagacious things. They had been full of strategy. They were the work of a master's legs.

Thoughts of his comrades came to him. The brittle blue line had withstood the blows and won. He grew bitter over it. It seemed that the blind ignorance and stupidity of those little pieces had betrayed him. He had been overturned and crushed by their lack of sense in holding the position, when intelligent deliberation would have convinced them that it was impossible. He, the enlightened man who looks afar in the dark, had fled because of his superior perceptions and knowledge. He felt a great anger against his comrades. He knew it could be proved that they had been fools.

He wondered what they would remark when later he appeared in camp. His mind heard howls of derision. Their density would not enable them to understand his sharper point of view.

He began to pity himself acutely. He was ill used. He was trodden beneath the feet of an iron injustice. He had proceeded with wisdom and from the most righteous motives under heaven's blue only to be frustrated by hateful circum-stances.

A dull, animal-like rebellion against his fellows, war in the abstract, and fate grew within him. He shambled along with bowed head, his brain in a tumult of

36

agony and despair. When he looked loweringly up, quivering at each sound, his eyes had the expression of those of a criminal who thinks his guilt and his punishment great, and knows that he can find no words.

He went from the fields into a thick wood, as if resolved to bury himself. He wished to get out of hearing of the crackling shots which were to him like voices.

The ground was cluttered with vines and bushes, and the trees grew close and spread out like bouquets. He was obliged to force his way with much noise. The creepers, catching against his legs, cried out harshly as their sprays were torn from the barks of trees. The swishing saplings tried to make known his presence to the world. He could not conciliate the forest. As he made his way, it was always calling out protestations. When he separated embraces of trees and vines the disturbed foliages waved their arms and turned their face leaves toward him. He dreaded lest these noisy motions and cries should bring men to look at him. So he went far, seeking dark and intricate places.

After a time the sound of musketry grew faint and the cannon boomed in the distance. The sun, suddenly apparent, blazed among the trees. The insects were making rhythmical noises. They seemed to be grinding their teeth in unison. A woodpecker stuck his impudent head around the side of a tree. A bird flew on lighthearted wing.

Off was the rumble of death. It seemed now that Nature had no ears.

This landscape gave him assurance. A fair field holding life. It was the religion of peace. It would die if its timid eyes were compelled to see blood. He conceived Nature to be a woman with a deep aversion to tragedy.

He threw a pine cone at a jovial squirrel, and he ran with chattering fear. High in a treetop he stopped, and, poking his head cautiously from behind a branch, looked down with an air of trepidation.

The youth felt triumphant at this exhibition. There was the law, he said. Nature had given him a sign. The squirrel, immediately upon recognizing danger, had taken to his legs without ado. He did not stand stolidly baring his furry belly to the missile, and die with an upward glance at the sympathetic heavens. On the contrary, he had fled as fast as his legs could carry him; and he was but an ordinary squirrel, too—doubtless no philosopher of his race. The youth wended, feeling that Nature was of his mind. She re-enforced his argument with proofs that lived where the sun shone.

Once he found himself almost into a swamp. He was obliged to walk upon bog tufts and watch his feet to keep from the oily mire. Pausing at one time to look about him he saw, out at some black water, a small animal pounce in and emerge directly with a gleaming fish.

The youth went again into the deep thickets. The brushed branches made a noise that drowned the sounds of cannon. He walked on, going from obscurity into promises of a greater obscurity.

At length he reached a place where the high, arching boughs made a chapel. He softly pushed the green doors aside and entered. Pine needles were a gentle brown carpet. There was a religious half light.

Near the threshold he stopped, horror-stricken at the sight of a thing.

He was being looked at by a dead man who was seated with his back against a columnlike tree. The corpse was dressed in a uniform that once had been blue, but was now faded to a melancholy shade of green. The eyes, staring at the youth, had changed to the dull hue to be seen on the side of a dead fish.

The mouth was open. Its red had changed to an appalling yellow. Over the gray skin of the face ran little ants. One was trundling some sort of a bundle along the upper lip.

The youth gave a shriek as he confronted the thing. He was for moments turned to stone before it. He remained staring into the liquid-looking eyes. The dead man and the living man exchanged a long look. Then the youth cautiously put one hand behind him and brought it against a tree. Leaning upon this he retreated, step by step, with his face still toward the thing. He feared that if he turned his back the body might spring up and stealthily pursue him.

The branches, pushing against him, threatened to throw him over upon it. His unguided feet, too, caught aggravatingly in brambles; and with it all he received a subtle suggestion to touch the corpse. As he thought of his hand upon it he shuddered profoundly.

At last he burst the bonds which had fastened him to the spot and fled, unheeding the underbrush. He was pursued by a sight of the black ants swarming greedily upon the gray face and venturing horribly near to the eyes.

After a time he paused, and, breathless and panting, listened. He imagined some strange voice would come from the dead throat and squawk after him in horrible menaces.

The trees about the portal of the chapel moved soughingly in a soft wind. A sad silence was upon the little guarding edifice.

Chapter 8

The trees began softly to sing a hymn of twilight. The sun sank until slanted bronze rays struck the forest. There was a lull in the noises of insects as if they had bowed their beaks and were making a devotional pause. There was silence save for the chanted chorus of the trees.

Then, upon this stillness, there suddenly broke a tremendous clangor of sounds. A crimson roar came from the distance.

The youth stopped. He was transfixed by this terrific medley of all noises. It was as if worlds were being rended. There was the ripping sound of musketry and the breaking crash of the artillery.

His mind flew in all directions. He conceived the two armies to be at each other panther fashion. He listened for a time. Then he began to run in the direction of the battle. He saw that it was an ironical thing for him to be running thus toward that which he had been at such pains to avoid. But he said, in substance, to himself that if the earth and the moon were about to clash, many persons would doubtless plan to get upon the roofs to witness the collision.

As he ran, he became aware that the forest had stopped its music, as if at last becoming capable of hearing the foreign sounds. The trees hushed and stood motionless. Everything seemed to be listening to the crackle and clatter and ear-shaking thunder. The chorus pealed over the still earth.

It suddenly occurred to the youth that the fight in which he had been was, after all, but perfunctory popping. In the hearing of this present din he was doubtful if he had seen real battle scenes. This uproar explained a celestial battle; it was tumbling hordes a-struggle in the air.

Reflecting, he saw a sort of a humor in the point of view of himself and his fellows during the late encounter. They had taken themselves and the enemy very seriously and had imagined that they were deciding the war. Individuals must have supposed that they were cutting the letters of their names deep into everlasting tablets of brass, or enshrining their reputations forever in the hearts of their countrymen, while, as to fact, the affair would appear in printed reports under a meek and immaterial title. But he saw that it was good, else, he said, in battle every one would surely run save forlorn hopes and their ilk.

He went rapidly on. He wished to come to the edge of the forest that he might peer out.

As he hastened, there passed through his mind pictures of stupendous conflicts. His accumulated thought upon such subjects was used to form scenes. The noise was as the voice of an eloquent being, describing.

Sometimes the brambles formed chains and tried to hold him back. Trees, confronting him, stretched out their arms and forbade him to pass. After its previous hostility this new resistance of the forest filled him with a fine bitterness. It seemed that Nature could not be quite ready to kill him.

But he obstinately took roundabout ways, and presently he was where he could see long gray walls of vapor where lay battle lines. The voices of cannon shook him. The musketry sounded in long irregular surges that played havoc with his ears. He stood regardant for a moment. His eyes had an awestruck expression. He gawked in the direction of the fight.

Presently he proceeded again on his forward way. The battle was like the grinding of an immense and terrible machine to him. Its complexities and powers, its grim processes, fascinated him. He must go close and see it produce corpses.

He came to a fence and clambered over it. On the far side, the ground was littered with clothes and guns. A newspaper, folded up, lay in the dirt. A dead soldier was stretched with his face hidden in his arm. Farther off there was a group of four or five corpses keeping mournful company. A hot sun had blazed upon the spot.

In this place the youth felt that he was an invader. This forgotten part of the battle ground was owned by the dead men, and he hurried, in the vague apprehension that one of the swollen forms would rise and tell him to begone.

He came finally to a road from which he could see in the distance dark and agitated bodies of troops, smoke-fringed. In the lane was a blood-stained crowd streaming to the rear. The wounded men were cursing, groaning, and wailing. In the air, always, was a mighty swell of sound that it seemed could sway the earth. With the courageous words of the artillery and the spiteful sentences of the musketry mingled red cheers. And from this region of noises came the steady current of the maimed.

One of the wounded men had a shoeful of blood. He hopped like a schoolboy in a game. He was laughing hysterically.

One was swearing that he had been shot in the arm through the commanding general's mismanagement of the army. One was marching with an air imitative of some sublime drum major. Upon his features was an unholy mixture of merriment and agony. As he marched he sang a bit of doggerel in a high and quavering voice:

> "Sing a song a' vic'try,
>   A pocketful 'a bullets,
>   Five an' twenty dead men
>   Baked in a—pie."

Parts of the procession limped and staggered to this tune.

Another had the gray seal of death already upon his face. His lips were curled in hard lines and his teeth were clinched. His hands were bloody from where he had pressed them upon his wound. He seemed to be awaiting the moment when he should pitch headlong. He stalked like the specter of a soldier, his eyes burning with the power of a stare into the unknown.

There were some who proceeded sullenly, full of anger at their wounds, and ready to turn upon anything as an obscure cause.

An officer was carried along by two privates. He was peevish. "Don't joggle so, Johnson, yeh fool," he cried. "Think m' leg is made of iron? If yeh can't carry me decent, put me down an' let some one else do it."

He bellowed at the tottering crowd who blocked the quick march of his bearers. "Say, make way there, can't yeh? Make way, dickens take it all."

They sulkily parted and went to the roadsides. As he was carried past they made pert remarks to him. When he raged in reply and threatened them, they told him to be damned.

The shoulder of one of the tramping bearers knocked heavily against the spectral soldier who was staring into the unknown.

The youth joined this crowd and marched along with it. The torn bodies expressed the awful machinery in which the men had been entangled.

Orderlies and couriers occasionally broke through the throng in the roadway, scattering wounded men right and left, galloping on followed by howls. The melancholy march was continually disturbed by the messengers, and sometimes by bustling batteries that came swinging and thumping down upon them, the officers shouting orders to clear the way.

There was a tattered man, fouled with dust, blood and powder stain from hair to shoes, who trudged quietly at the youth's side. He was listening with eagerness and much humility to the lurid descriptions of a bearded sergeant. His lean features wore an expression of awe and admiration. He was like a listener in a country store to wondrous tales told among the sugar barrels. He eyed the story-teller with unspeakable wonder. His mouth was agape in yokel fashion.

The sergeant, taking note of this, gave pause to his elaborate history while he administered a sardonic comment. "Be keerful, honey, you 'll be a-ketchin' flies," he said.

The tattered man shrank back abashed.

After a time he began to sidle near to the youth, and in a different way try to make him a friend. His voice was gentle as a girl's voice and his eyes were pleading. The youth saw with surprise that the soldier had two wounds, one in the head, bound with a blood-soaked rag, and the other in the arm, making that member dangle like a broken bough.

After they had walked together for some time the tattered man mustered sufficient courage to speak. "Was pretty good fight, wa'n't it?" he timidly said. The youth, deep in thought, glanced up at the bloody and grim figure with its lamblike eyes. "What?"

"Was pretty good fight, wa'n't it?"

"Yes," said the youth shortly. He quickened his pace.

But the other hobbled industriously after him. There was an air of apology in his manner, but he evidently thought that he needed only to talk for a time, and the youth would perceive that he was a good fellow.

"Was pretty good fight, wa'n't it?" he began in a small voice, and then he achieved the fortitude to continue. "Dern me if I ever see fellers fight so. Laws, how they did fight! I knowed th' boys 'd like when they onct got square at it. Th' boys ain't had no fair chanct up t' now, but this time they showed what they was. I knowed it 'd turn out this way. Yeh can't lick them boys. No, sir! They're fighters, they be."

He breathed a deep breath of humble admiration. He had looked at the youth for encouragement several times. He received none, but gradually he seemed to get absorbed in his subject.

"I was talkin' 'cross pickets with a boy from Georgie, onct, an' that boy, he ses, 'Your fellers 'll all run like hell when they onct hearn a gun,' he ses. 'Mebbe they will,' I ses, 'but I don't b'lieve none of it,' I ses; 'an' b'jiminey,' I ses back t' 'um, 'mebbe your fellers 'll all run like hell when they onct hearn a gun,' I ses. He larfed. Well, they didn't run t' day, did they, hey? No, sir! They fit, an' fit, an' fit."

His homely face was suffused with a light of love for the army which was to him all things beautiful and powerful.

After a time he turned to the youth. "Where yeh hit, ol' boy?" he asked in a brotherly tone.

The youth felt instant panic at this question, although at first its full import was not borne in upon him.

"What?" he asked.

"Where yeh hit?" repeated the tattered man.

"Why," began the youth, "I—I—that is—why—I——"

He turned away suddenly and slid through the crowd. His brow was heavily flushed, and his fingers were picking nervously at one of his buttons. He bent his head and fastened his eyes studiously upon the button as if it were a little problem.

The tattered man looked after him in astonishment.

Chapter 9

The youth fell back in the procession until the tattered soldier was not in sight. Then he started to walk on with the others.

But he was amid wounds. The mob of men was bleeding. Because of the tattered soldier's question he now felt that his shame could be viewed. He was continually casting sidelong glances to see if the men were contemplating the letters of guilt he felt burned into his brow.

At times he regarded the wounded soldiers in an envious way. He conceived persons with torn bodies to be peculiarly happy. He wished that he, too, had a wound, a red badge of courage.

The spectral soldier was at his side like a stalking reproach. The man's eyes were still fixed in a stare into the unknown. His gray, appalling face had attracted attention in the crowd, and men, slowing to his dreary pace, were walking with him. They were discussing his plight, questioning him and giving him advice. In a dogged way he repelled them, signing to them to go on and leave him alone. The shadows of his face were deepening and his tight lips seemed holding in check the moan of great despair. There could be seen a certain stiffness in the movements of his body, as if he were taking infinite care not to arouse the passion of his wounds. As he went on, he seemed always looking for a place, like one who goes to choose a grave.

Something in the gesture of the man as he waved the bloody and pitying soldiers away made the youth start as if bitten. He yelled in horror. Tottering forward he laid a quivering hand upon the man's arm. As the latter slowly turned his waxlike features toward him, the youth screamed:

"Gawd! Jim Conklin!"

The tall soldier made a little commonplace smile. "Hello, Henry," he said.

The youth swayed on his legs and glared strangely. He stuttered and stammered. "Oh, Jim—oh, Jim—oh, Jim——"

The tall soldier held out his gory hand. There was a curious red and black combination of new blood and old blood upon it. "Where yeh been, Henry?" he asked. He continued in a monotonous voice, "I thought mebbe yeh got keeled over. There's been thunder t' pay t'-day. I was worryin' about it a good deal."

The youth still lamented, "Oh, Jim—oh, Jim—oh, Jim——"

"Yeh know," said the tall soldier, "I was out there." He made a careful gesture. "An', Lord, what a circus! An', b'jiminey, I got shot—I got shot. Yes, b'jiminey, I got shot." He reiterated this fact in a bewildered way, as if he did not know how it came about.

The youth put forth anxious arms to assist him, but the tall soldier went firmly on as if propelled. Since the youth's arrival as a guardian for his friend, the other wounded men had ceased to display much interest. They occupied themselves again in dragging their own tragedies toward the rear.

Suddenly, as the two friends marched on, the tall soldier seemed to be overcome by a terror. His faced turned to a semblance of gray paste. He clutched the youth's arm and looked all about him, as if dreading to be overheard. Then he began to speak in a shaking whisper:

"I tell yeh what I'm 'fraid of, Henry—I'll tell yeh what I'm 'fraid of. I'm 'fraid I'll fall down—an' then yeh know—them damned artillery wagons—they like as not 'll run over me. That's what I'm 'fraid of——"

The youth cried out to him hysterically: "I'll take care of yeh, Jim! I'll take care of yeh! I swear t' Gawd I will!"

"Sure—will yeh, Henry?" the tall soldier beseeched.

"Yes—yes—I tell yeh—I'll take care of yeh, Jim!" protested the youth. He could not speak accurately because of the gulpings in his throat.

But the tall soldier continued to beg in a lowly way. He now hung babelike to the youth's arm. His eyes rolled in the wildness of his terror. "I was allus a good friend t' yeh, wa'n't I, Henry? I've allus been a pretty good feller, ain't I? An' it ain't much t' ask, is it? Jest t' pull me along outer th' road? I'd do it fer you, wouldn't I, Henry?"

He paused in piteous anxiety to await his friend's reply.

The youth had reached an anguish where the sobs scorched him. He strove to express his loyalty, but he could only make fantastic gestures.

However, the tall soldier seemed suddenly to forget all those fears. He became again the grim, stalking specter of a soldier. He went stonily forward. The youth wished his friend to lean upon him, but the other always shook his head and strangely protested. "No—no—no—leave me be—leave me be——"

His look was fixed again upon the unknown. He moved with mysterious purpose, and all of the youth's offers he brushed aside. "No—no—leave me be— leave me be——"

The youth had to follow.

Presently the latter heard a voice talking softly near his shoulders. Turning he saw that it belonged to the tattered soldier. "Ye 'd better take 'im outa th' road, partner. There's a batt'ry comin' helitywhoop down th' road an' he'll git runned over. He's a goner anyhow in about five minutes—yeh kin see that. Ye'd better take 'im outa th' road. Where th' blazes does he git his stren'th from?"

"Lord knows!" cried the youth. He was shaking his hands helplessly.

He ran forward presently and grasped the tall soldier by the arm. "Jim! Jim!" he coaxed, "come with me."

The tall soldier weakly tried to wrench himself free. "Huh," he said vacantly. He stared at the youth for a moment. At last he spoke as if dimly comprehending. "Oh! Inteh th' fields? Oh!"

He started blindly through the grass.

The youth turned once to look at the lashing riders and jouncing guns of the battery. He was startled from this view by a shrill outcry from the tattered man.

"Gawd! He's running'!"

Turning his head swiftly, the youth saw his friend running in a staggering and stumbling way toward a little clump of bushes. His heart seemed to wrench itself almost free from his body at this sight. He made a noise of pain. He and the tattered man began a pursuit. There was a singular race.

When he overtook the tall soldier he began to plead with all the words he could find. "Jim—Jim—what are you doing—what makes you do this way—you 'll hurt yerself."

The same purpose was in the tall soldier's face. He protested in a dulled way, keeping his eyes fastened on the mystic place of his intentions.

"No—no—don't tech me—leave me be—leave me be——"

The youth, aghast and filled with wonder at the tall soldier, began quaveringly to question him.

"Where yeh goin', Jim? What you thinking about? Where you going? Tell me, won't you, Jim?"

The tall soldier faced about as upon relentless pursuers. In his eyes there was a great appeal. "Leave me be, can't yeh? Leave me be fer a minnit."

The youth recoiled. "Why, Jim," he said, in a dazed way, "what's the matter with you?"

The tall soldier turned and, lurching dangerously, went on. The youth and the tattered soldier followed, sneaking as if whipped, feeling unable to face the stricken man if he should again confront them. They began to have thoughts of a solemn ceremony. There was something rite-like in these movements of the doomed soldier. And there was a resemblance in him to a devotee of a mad religion, blood-sucking, muscle-wrenching, bone-crushing. They were awed and afraid. They hung back lest he have at command a dreadful weapon.

At last, they saw him stop and stand motionless. Hastening up, they perceived that his face wore an expression telling that he had at last found the place for which he had struggled. His spare figure was erect; his bloody hands were quietly at his side. He was waiting with patience for something that he had come to meet. He was at the rendezvous. They paused and stood, expectant.

There was a silence.

Finally, the chest of the doomed soldier began to heave with a strained motion. It increased in violence until it was as if an animal was within and was kicking and tumbling furiously to be free.

This spectacle of gradual strangulation made the youth writhe, and once as his friend rolled his eyes, he saw something in them that made him sink wailing to the ground. He raised his voice in a last supreme call.

"Jim—Jim—Jim——"

The tall soldier opened his lips and spoke. He made a gesture. "Leave me be—don't tech me—leave me be——"

There was another silence while he waited.

Suddenly, his form stiffened and straightened. Then it was shaken by a prolonged ague. He stared into space. To the two watchers there was a curious and profound dignity in the firm lines of his awful face.

He was invaded by a creeping strangeness that slowly enveloped him. For a moment the tremor of his legs caused him to dance a sort of hideous hornpipe. His arms beat wildly about his head in expression of implike enthusiasm.

His tall figure stretched itself to its full height. There was a slight rending sound. Then it began to swing forward, slow and straight, in the manner of a falling tree. A swift muscular contortion made the left shoulder strike the ground first.

The body seemed to bounce a little way from the earth. "God!" said the tattered soldier.

The youth had watched, spellbound, this ceremony at the place of meeting. His face had been twisted into an expression of every agony he had imagined for his friend.

He now sprang to his feet and, going closer, gazed upon the pastelike face. The mouth was open and the teeth showed in a laugh.

As the flap of the blue jacket fell away from the body, he could see that the side looked as if it had been chewed by wolves.

The youth turned, with sudden, livid rage, toward the battlefield. He shook his fist. He seemed about to deliver a philippic.

"Hell——"

The red sun was pasted in the sky like a wafer.

Chapter 10

The tattered man stood musing.

"Well, he was reg'lar jim-dandy fer nerve, wa'n't he," said he finally in a litle awestruck voice. "A reg'lar jim-dandy." He thoughtfully poked one of the docile hands with his foot. "I wonner where he got 'is stren'th from? I never seen a man do like that before. It was a funny thing. Well, he was a reg'lar jim-dandy."

The youth desired to screech out his grief. He was stabbed, but his tongue lay dead in the tomb of his mouth. He threw himself again upon the ground and began to brood.

The tattered man stood musing.

"Look-a-here, pardner," he said, after a time. He regarded the corpse as he spoke. "He's up an' gone, ain't 'e, an' we might as well begin t' look out fer ol' number one. This here thing is all over. He's up an' gone, ain't 'e? An' he's all right here. Nobody won't bother 'im. An' I must say I ain't enjoying any great health m'self these days."

The youth, awakened by the tattered soldier's tone, looked quickly up. He saw that he was swinging uncertainly on his legs and that his face had turned to a shade of blue.

"Good Lord!" he cried, "you ain't goin' t'—not you, too."

The tattered man waved his hand. "Nary die," he said. "All I want is some pea soup an' a good bed. Some pea soup," he repeated dreamfully.

The youth arose from the ground. "I wonder where he came from. I left him over there." He pointed. "And now I find 'im here. And he was coming from over there, too." he indicated a new direction. They both turned toward the body as if to ask of it a question.

"Well," at length spoke the tattered man, "there ain't no use in our stayin' here an' tryin' t' ask him anything."

The youth nodded an assent wearily. They both turned to gaze for a moment at the corpse.

The youth murmured something.

"Well, he was a jim-dandy, wa'n't 'e?" said the tattered man as if in response.

They turned their backs upon it and started away. For a time they stole softly, treading with their toes. It remained laughing there in the grass.

"I'm commencin' t' feel pretty bad," said the tattered man, suddenly breaking one of his little silences. "I'm commencin' t' feel pretty damn' bad."

The youth groaned. "O Lord!" He wondered if he was to be the tortured witness of another grim encounter.

But his companion waved his hand reassuringly. "Oh, I'm not goin' t' die yit! There too much dependin' on me fer me t' die yit. No, sir! Nary die! I *can't!* Ye'd oughta see th' swad a' chil'ren I've got, an' all like that."

The youth glancing at his companion could see by the shadow of a smile that he was making some kind of fun.

As they plodded on the tattered soldier continued to talk. "Besides, if I died, I wouldn't die th' way that feller did. That was th' funniest thing. I'd jest flop down, I would. I never seen a feller die th' way that feller did.

"Yeh know Tom Jamison, he lives next door t' me up home. He's a nice feller, he is, an' we was allus good friends. Smart, too. Smart as a steel trap. Well, when we was a-fightin' this afternoon, all-of-a-sudden he begin t' rip up an' cuss an' beller at me. 'Yer shot, yeh blamed infernal!'—he swear horrible— he ses t' me. I put up m' hand t' m' head an' when I looked at m' fingers, I seen, sure 'nough, I was shot. I give a holler an' begin t' run, but b'fore I could git away another one hit me in th' arm an' whirl' me clean 'round. I got skeared when they was all a-shootin' b'hind me an' I run t' beat all, but I cotch it pretty bad. I've an idee I'd a' been fightin' yit, if t'was n't fer Tom Jamison."

Then he made a calm announcement: "There's two of 'em—little ones—but they're beginnin' t' have fun with me now. I don't b'lieve I kin walk much furder."

They went slowly on in silence. "Yeh look pretty peek-ed yerself," said the tattered man at last. "I bet yeh've got a worser one than yeh think. Ye'd better take keer of yer hurt. It don't do t' let sech things go. It might be inside mostly, an' them plays thunder. Where is it located?" But he continued his harangue without waiting for a reply. "I see 'a feller git hit plum in th' head when my reg'ment was a-standin' at ease onct. An' everybody yelled out to 'im: Hurt, John? Are yeh hurt much? 'No,' ses he. He looked kinder surprised, an' he went on tellin' 'em how he felt. He sed he didn't feel nothin'. But, by dad, th' first thing that feller knowed he was dead. Yes, he was dead—stone dead. So, yeh wanta watch out. Yeh might have some queer kind 'a hurt yerself. Yeh can't never tell. Where is your'n located?"

The youth had been wriggling since the introduction of this topic. He now gave a cry of exasperation and made a furious motion with his hand. "Oh, don't bother me!" he said. He was enraged against the tattered man, and could have strangled him. His companions seemed ever to play intolerable parts. They were ever upraising the ghost of shame on the stick of their curiosity. He turned toward the tattered man as one at bay. "Now, don't bother me," he repeated with desperate menace.

"Well, Lord knows I don't wanta bother anybody," said the other. There was a little accent of despair in his voice as he replied, "Lord knows I've gota 'nough m' own t' tend to."

The youth, who had been holding a bitter debate with himself and casting glances of hatred and contempt at the tattered man, here spoke in a hard voice. "Good-by," he said.

The tattered man looked at him in gaping amazement. "Why—why, pardner, where yeh goin'?" he asked unsteadily. The youth looking at him, could see that he, too, like that other one, was beginning to act dumb and animal-like. His thoughts seemed to be floundering about in his head. "Now—now—look—a—here, you Tom Jamison—now—I won't have this—this here won't do. Where—where yeh goin'?"

The youth pointed vaguely, "Over there," he replied.

"Well, now look—a—here—now," said the tattered man, rambling on in idiot fashion. His head was hanging forward and his words were slurred. "This thing won't do, now, Tom Jamison. It won't do. I know yeh, yeh pig-headed devil. Yeh wanta go trompin' off with a bad hurt. It ain't right—now—Tom Jamison—it ain't. Yeh wanta leave me take keer of yeh, Tom Jamison. It ain't—right—it ain't—fer yeh t' go—trompin' off—with a bad hurt—it ain't—ain't—ain't right—it ain't."

In reply the youth climbed a fence and started away. He could hear the tattered man bleating plaintively.

Once he faced about angrily. "What?"

"Look—a—here, now, Tom Jamison—now—it ain't——"

The youth went on. Turning at a distance he saw the tattered man wandering about helplessly in the field.

He now thought that he wished he was dead. He believed that he envied those men whose bodies lay strewn over the grass of the fields and on the fallen leaves of the forest.

The simple questions of the tattered man had been knife thrusts to him. They asserted a society that probes pitilessly at secrets until all is apparent. His late companion's chance persistency made him feel that he could not keep his crime concealed in his bosom. It was sure to be brought plain by one of those arrows which cloud the air and are constantly pricking, discovering, proclaiming those things which are willed to be forever hidden. He admitted that he could not defend himself against this agency. It was not within the power of vigilance.

Chapter 11

He became aware that the furnace roar of the battle was growing louder. Great brown clouds had floated to the still heights of air before him. The noise, too, was approaching. The woods filtered men and the fields became dotted.

As he rounded a hillock, he perceived that the roadway was now a crying mass of wagons, teams, and men. From the heaving tangle issued exhortations, commands, imprecations. Fear was sweeping it all along. The cracking whips bit and horses plunged and tugged. The white-topped wagons strained and stumbled in their exertions like fat sheep.

The youth felt comforted in a measure by this sight. They were all retreating. Perhaps, then, he was not so bad after all. He seated himself and watched the terror-stricken wagons. They fled like soft, ungainly animals. All the roarers and lashers served to help him to magnify the dangers and horrors of the engagement that he might try to prove to himself that the thing with which men could charge him was in truth a symmetrical act. There was an amount of pleasure to him in watching the wild march of this vindication.

Presently the calm head of a forward-going column of infantry appeared in the road. It came swiftly on. Avoiding the obstructions gave it the sinuous movement of a serpent. The men at the head butted mules with their musket stocks. They prodded teamsters indifferent to all howls. The men forced their way through parts of the dense mass by strength. The blunt head of the column pushed. The raving teamsters swore many strange oaths.

The commands to make way had the ring of a great importance in them. The men were going forward to the heart of the din. They were to confront the eager rush of the enemy. They felt the pride of their onward movement when the remainder of the army seemed trying to dribble down this road. They tumbled teams about with a fine feeling that it was no matter so long as their column got to the front in time. This importance made their faces grave and stern. And the backs of the officers were very rigid.

As the youth looked at them the black weight of his woe returned to him. He felt that he was regarding a procession of chosen beings. The separation was as great to him as if they had marched with weapons of flame and banners of sunlight. He could never be like them. He could have wept in his longings.

He searched about in his mind for an adequate malediction for the indefinite cause, the thing upon which men turn the words of final blame. It—whatever it was—was responsible for him, he said. There lay the fault.

The haste of the column to reach the battle seemed to the forlorn young man to be something much finer than stout fighting. Heroes, he thought, could find excuses in that long seething lane. They could retire with perfect self-respect and make excuses to the stars.

He wondered what those men had eaten that they could be in such haste to force their way to grim chances of death. As he watched his envy grew until he thought that he wished to change lives with one of them. He would have liked to have used a tremendous force, he said, throw off himself and become a better. Swift pictures of himself, apart, yet in himself, came to him—a blue desperate figure leading lurid charges with one knee forward and a broken blade high—a blue, determined figure standing before a crimson and steel asssault, getting calmly killed on a high place before the eyes of all. He thought of the magnificent pathos of his dead body.

These thoughts uplifted him. He felt the quiver of war desire. In his ears, he heard the ring of victory. He knew the frenzy of a rapid successful charge. The music of the trampling feet, the sharp voices, the clanking arms of the column near him made him soar on the red wings of war. For a few moments he was sublime.

He thought that he was about to start for the front. Indeed, he saw a picture of himself, dust-stained, haggard, panting, flying to the front at the proper moment to seize and throttle the dark, leering witch of calamity.

Then the difficulties of the thing began to drag at him. He hesitated, balancing awkwardly on one foot.

He had no rifle; he could not fight with his hands, said he resentfully to his plan. Well, rifles could be had for the picking. They were extraordinarily profuse.

Also, he continued, it would be a miracle if he found his regiment. Well, he could fight with any regiment.

He started forward slowly. He stepped as if he expected to tread upon some explosive thing. Doubts and he were struggling.

He would truly be a worm if any of his comrades should see him returning thus, the marks of his flight upon him. There was a reply that the intent fighters did not care for what happened rearward saving that no hostile bayonets appeared there. In the battle-blur his face would, in a way be hidden, like the face of a cowled man.

But then he said that his tireless fate would bring forth, when the strife lulled for a moment, a man to ask of him an explanation. In imagination he felt the scrutiny of his companions as he painfully labored through some lies.

Eventually, his courage expended itself upon these objections. The debates drained him of his fire.

He was not cast down by this defeat of his plan, for, upon studying the affair carefully, he could not but admit that the objections were very formidable.

Furthermore, various ailments had begun to cry out. In their presence he could not persist in flying high with the wings of war; they rendered it almost impossible for him to see himself in a heroic light. He tumbled headlong.

He discovered that he had a scorching thirst. His face was so dry and grimy that he thought he could feel his skin crackle. Each bone of his body had an ache in it, and seemingly threatened to break with each movement. His feet were like two sores. Also, his body was calling for food. It was more powerful than a direct hunger. There was a dull, weight like feeling in his stomach, and, when he tried to walk, his head swayed and he tottered. He could not see with distinctness. Small patches of green mist floated before his vision.

While he had been tossed by many emotions, he had not been aware of ailments. Now they beset him and made clamor. As he was at last compelled to pay attention to them, his capacity for self-hate was multiplied. In despair, he declared that he was not like those others. He now conceded it to be impossible that he should ever become a hero. He was a craven loon. Those pictures of glory were piteous things. He groaned from his heart and went staggering off.

A certain mothlike quality within him kept him in the vicinity of the battle. He had a great desire to see, and to get news. He wished to know who was winning.

He told himself that, despite his unprecedented suffering, he had never lost his greed for a victory, yet, he said, in a half-apologetic manner to his conscience, he could not but know that a defeat for the army this time might mean many favorable things for him. The blows of the enemy would splinter regiments into fragments. Thus, many men of courage, he considered, would be obliged to desert the colors and scurry like chickens. He would appear as one of them. They would be sullen brothers in distress, and he could then easily believe he had not run any farther or faster than they. And if he himself could believe in his virtuous perfection, he conceived that there would be small trouble in convincing all others.

He said, as if in excuse for this hope, that previously the army had encountered great defeats and in a few months had shaken off all blood and tradition of them, emerging as bright and valiant as a new one; thrusting out of sight the memory of disaster, and appearing with the valor and confidence of unconquered legions. The shrilling voices of the people at home would pipe dismally for a time, but various generals were usually compelled to listen to these ditties. He of course felt no compunctions for proposing a general as a sacrifice. He could not tell who the chosen for the barbs might be, so he could center no direct sympathy upon him. The people were afar and he did not conceive public opinion to be accurate at long range. It was quite probable they would hit the wrong man who, after he had recovered from his amazement would perhaps spend the rest of his days in writing replies to the songs of his alleged failure. It would be very unfortunate, no doubt, but in this case a general was of no consequence to the youth.

In a defeat there would be a roundabout vindication of himself. He thought it would prove, in a manner, that he had fled early because of his superior powers of perception. A serious prophet upon predicting a flood should be the first man to climb a tree. This would demonstrate that he was indeed a seer.

A moral vindication was regarded by the youth as a very important thing. Without salve, he could not, he thought, wear the sore badge of his dishonor through life. With his heart continually assuring him that he was despicable, he could not exist without making it, through his actions, apparent to all men.

If the army had gone gloriously on he would be lost. If the din meant that now his army's flags were tilted forward he was a condemned wretch. He would be compelled to doom himself to isolation. If the men were advancing, their indifferent feet were trampling upon his chances for a successful life.

As these thoughts went rapidly through his mind, he turned upon them and tried to thrust them away. He denounced himself as a villain. He said that he was the most unutterably selfish man in existence. His mind pictured the soldiers who would place their defiant bodies before the spear of the yelling battle fiend, and as he saw their dripping corpses on an imagined field, he said that he was their murderer.

Again he thought that he wished he was dead. He believed that he envied a corpse. Thinking of the slain, he achieved a great contempt for some of them, as if they were guilty for thus becoming lifeless. They might have been killed by lucky chances, he said, before they had had opportunities to flee or before they had been really tested. Yet they would receive laurels from tradition. He cried out bitterly that their crowns were stolen and their robes of glorious memories were shams. However, he still said that it was a great pity he was not as they.

A defeat of the army had suggested itself to him as a means of escape from the consequences of his fall. He considered, now, however, that it was useless to think of such a possibility. His education had been that success for that mighty blue machine was certain; that it would make victories as a contrivance turns out buttons. He presently discarded all his speculations in the other direction. He returned to the creed of soldiers.

When he perceived again that it was not possible for the army to be defeated, he tried to bethink him of a fine tale which he could take back to his regiment, and with it turn the expected shafts of derision.

But, as he mortally feared these shafts, it became impossible for him to invent a tale he felt he could trust. He experimented with many schemes, but threw them aside one by one as flimsy. He was quick to see vulnerable places in them all.

Furthermore, he was much afraid that some arrow of scorn might lay him mentally low before he could raise his protecting tale.

He imagined the whole regiment saying: "Where's Henry Fleming? He run, didn't 'e? Oh, my!" He recalled various persons who would be quite sure to leave him no peace about it. They would doubtless question him with sneers, and laugh at his stammering hesitation. In the next engagement they would try to keep watch of him to discover when he would run.

Wherever he went in camp, he would encounter insolent and lingeringly cruel stares. As he imagined himself passing near a crowd of comrades, he could hear some one say, "There he goes!"

Then, as if the heads were moved by one muscle, all the faces were turned toward him with wide, derisive grins. He seemed to hear some one make a humorous remark in a low tone. At it the others all crowed and cackled. He was a slang phrase.

Chapter 12

The column that had butted stoutly at the obstacles in the roadway was barely out of the youth's sight before he saw dark waves of men come sweeping out of the woods and down through the fields. He knew at once that the steel fibers had been washed from their hearts. They were bursting from their coats and their equipments as from entanglements. They charged down upon him like terrified buffaloes.

Behind them blue smoke curled and clouded above the treetops, and through the thickets he could sometimes see a distant pink glare. The voices of the cannon were clamoring in interminable chorus.

The youth was horrorstricken. He stared in agony and amazement. He forgot that he was engaged in combating the universe. He threw aside his mental pamphlets on the philosophy of the retreated and rules for the guidance of the damned.

The fight was lost. The dragons were coming with invincible strides. The army, helpless in the matted thickets and blinded by the overhanging night, was going to be swallowed. War, the red animal, war, the blood-swollen god, would have bloated fill.

Within him something bade to cry out. He had the impulse to make a rallying speech, to sing a battle hymn, but he could only get his tongue to call into the air: "Why—why—what—what 's th' matter?"

Soon he was in the midst of them. They were leaping and scampering all about him. Their blanched faces shone in the dusk. They seemed, for the most part, to be very burly men. The youth turned from one to another of them as they galloped along. His incoherent questions were lost. They were heedless of his appeals. They did not seem to see him.

They sometimes gabbled insanely. One huge man was asking of the sky: "Say, where de plank road? Where de plank road!" It was as if he had lost a child. He wept in his pain and dismay.

Presently, men were running hither and thither in all ways. The artillery booming, forward, rearward, and on the flanks made jumble of ideas of direction. Landmarks had vanished into the gathered gloom. The youth began to imagine that he had got into the center of the tremendous quarrel, and he could perceive no way out of it. From the mouths of the fleeing men came a thousand wild questions, but no one made answers.

The youth, after rushing about and throwing interrogations at the heedless bands of retreating infantry, finally clutched a man by the arm. They swung around face to face.

"Why—why——" stammered the youth struggling with his balking tongue.

The man screamed: "Let go me! Let go me!" His face was livid and his eyes were rolling uncontrolled. He was heaving and panting. He still grasped his rifle, perhaps having forgotten to release his hold upon it. He tugged frantically, and the youth being compelled to lean forward was dragged several paces.

"Let go me! Let go me!"

"Why—why——" stuttered the youth.

"Well, then!" bawled the man in a lurid rage. He adroitly and fiercely swung his rifle. It crushed upon the youth's head. The man ran on.

The youth's fingers had turned to paste upon the other's arm. The energy was smitten from his muscles. He saw the flaming wings of lightning flash before his vision. There was a deafening rumble of thunder within his head.

Suddenly his legs seemed to die. He sank writhing to the ground. He tried to arise. In his efforts against the numbing pain he was like a man wrestling with a creature of the air.

There was a sinister struggle.

Sometimes he would achieve a position half erect, battle with the air for a moment, and then fall again, grabbing at the grass. His face was of a clammy pallor. Deep groans were wrenched from him.

At last, with a twisting movement, he got upon his hands and knees, and from thence, like a babe trying to walk, to his feet. Pressing his hands to his temples he went lurching over the grass.

He fought an intense battle with his body. His dulled senses wished him to swoon and he opposed them stubbornly, his mind portraying unknown dangers and mutilations if he should fall upon the field. He went tall soldier fashion. He imagined secluded spots where he could fall and be unmolested. To search for one he strove against the tide of his pain.

Once he put his hand to the top of his head and timidly touched the wound. The scratching pain of the contact made him draw a long breath through his clinched teeth. His fingers were dabbled with blood. He regarded them with a fixed stare.

Around him he could hear the grumble of jolted cannon as the scurrying horses were lashed toward the front. Once, a young officer on a besplashed charger nearly ran him down. He turned and watched the mass of guns, men, and horses sweeping in a wide curve toward a gap in a fence. The officer was making excited motions with a gauntleted hand. The guns followed the teams with an air of unwillingness, of being dragged by the heels.

Some officers of the scattered infantry were cursing and railing like fishwives. Their scolding voices could be heard above the din. Into the unspeakable jumble in the roadway rode a squadron of cavalry. The faded yellow of their facings shone bravely. There was a mighty altercation.

The artillery were assembling as if for a conference.

The blue haze of evening was upon the field. The lines of forest were long purple shadows. One cloud lay along the western sky partly smothering the red.

As the youth left the scene behind him, he heard the guns suddenly roar out. He imagined them shaking in black rage. They belched and howled like brass devils guarding a gate. The soft air was filled with the tremendous remonstrance. With it came the shattering peal of opposing infantry. Turning to look behind him, he could see sheets of orange light illumine the shadowy distance. There were subtle and sudden lightnings in the far air. At times he thought he could see heaving masses of men.

He hurried on in the dusk. The day had faded until he could barely distinguish place for his feet. The purple darkness was filled with men who lectured and jabbered. Sometimes he could see them gesticulating against the blue and somber sky. There seemed to be a great ruck of men and munitions spread about in the forest and in the fields.

The little narrow roadway now lay lifeless. There were overturned wagons like sun-dried bowlders. The bed of the former torrent was choked with the bodies of horses and splintered parts of war machines.

It had come to pass that his wound pained him but little. He was afraid to move rapidly, however, for a dread of disturbing it. He held his head very still and took many precautions against stumbling. He was filled with anxiety, and his face was pinched and drawn in anticipation of the pain of any sudden mistake of his feet in the gloom.

His thoughts, as he walked, fixed intently upon his hurt. There was a cool, liquid feeling about it and he imagined blood moving slowly down under his hair. His head seemed swollen to a size that made him think his neck to be inadequate.

The new silence of his wound made much worriment. The little blistering voices of pain that had called out from his scalp were, he thought, definite in their expression of danger. By them he believed that he could measure his plight. But when they remained ominously silent he became frightened and imagined terrible fingers that clutched into his brain.

Amid it he began to reflect upon various incidents and conditions of the past. He bethought him of certain meals his mother had cooked at home, in which those dishes of which he was particularly fond had occupied prominent positions. He saw the spread table. The pine walls of the kitchen were glowing in the warm light from the stove. Too, he remembered how he and his companions used to go from the schoolhouse to the bank of a shaded pool. He saw his clothes in disorderly array upon the grass of the bank. He felt the swash of the fragrant water upon his body. The leaves of the overhanging maple rustled with melody in the wind of youthful summer.

He was overcome presently by a dragging weariness. His head hung forward and his shoulders were stooped as if he were bearing a great bundle. His feet shuffled along the ground.

He held continuous arguments as to whether he should lie down and sleep at some near spot, or force himself on until he reached a certain haven. He often tried to dismiss the question, but his body persisted in rebellion and his senses nagged at him like pampered babies.

At last he heard a cheery voice near his shoulder: "Yeh seem t' be in a pretty bad way, boy?"

The youth did not look up, but he assented with thick tongue. "Uh!"

The owner of the cheery voice took him firmly by the arm. "Well," he said, with a round laugh, 'I'm goin' your way. Th' hull gang is goin' your way. An' I guess I kin give yeh a lift." They began to walk like a drunken man and his friend.

As they went along, the man questioned the youth and assisted him with the replies like one manipulating the mind of a child. Sometimes he interjected anecdotes. "What reg'ment do yeh b'long teh? Eh? What's that? Th' 304th N' York? Why, what corps is that in? Oh, it is? Why, I thought they wasn't engaged t'-day—they're way over in th' center. Oh, they was, eh? Well, pretty near everybody got their share a' fightin' t'-day. By dad, I give myself up fer dead any number 'a times. There was shootin' here an' shootin' there, an' hollerin' here an hollerin' there, in th' damn' darkness, until I couldn't tell t' save m' soul which side I was on. Sometimes I thought I was sure 'nough from Ohier, an' other times I could 'a swore I was from th' bitter end of Florida. It was th' most mixed up dern thing I ever see. An' these here hull woods is a reg'lar mess. It'll be a miracle if we find our reg'ments t'-night. Pretty soon, though, we'll meet a-plenty of guards an' provost-guards, an' one thing an' another. Ho! there they go with an off'cer, I guess. Look at his hand a-draggin'. He's got all th' war he wants, I bet. He won't be talkin' so big about his reputation an' all when they go t' sawin' off his leg. Poor feller! My brother 's got whiskers jest like that. How did yeh git 'way over here, anyhow? You reg'ment is a long way from here, ain't it? Well, I guess we can find it. Yeh know there was a boy killed in my comp'ny t'-day that I thought th' world an' all of. Jack was a nice feller. By ginger, it hurt like thunder t' see ol' Jack jest git knocked flat. We was a-standin' purty peaceable fer a spell, 'though there was men runnin' ev'ry way all 'round us, an' while we was a-standin' like that, 'long come a big fat feller. He began t' peck at Jack's elbow, an' he ses: 'Say, where's th' road t' th' river?' An' Jack, he never paid no attention, an' th' feller kept on a-peckin' at his elbow an' sayin': 'Say, where's th' road t' th' river?' Jack was a-lookin' ahead all th' time tryin' t' see th' Johnnies comin' through th' woods, an' he never paid no attention t' this big fat feller fer a long time, but at last he turned 'round an' he ses: 'Ah, go t' hell an' find th' road t' th' river!' An' jest then a shot slapped him bang on th' side th' head. He was a sergeant, too. Them was his last words. Thunder, I wish we was sure 'a findin' our reg'ments t'-night. It's goin' t' be long huntin'. But I guess we kin do it."

In the search which followed, the man of the cheery voice seemed to the youth to possess a wand of a magic kind. He threaded the mazes of the tangled forest with a strange fortune. In encounters with guards and patrols he displayed the keenness of a detective and the valor of a gamin. Obstacles fell before him and became of assistance. The youth, with his chin still on his breast, stood woodenly by while his companion beat ways and means out of sullen things.

The forest seemed a vast hive of men buzzing about in frantic circles, but the cheery man conducted the youth without mistakes, until at last he began to chuckle with glee and self-satisfaction.

"Ah, there yeh are! See that fire?"

The youth nodded stupidly.

"Well, there's where your reg'ment is. An' now, good-by, ol' boy, good luck t' yeh."

A warm and strong hand clasped the youth's languid fingers for an instant, and then he heard a cheerful and audacious whistling as the man strode away. As he who had so befriended him was thus passing out of his life, it suddenly occurred to the youth that he had not once seen his face.

Chapter 13

The youth went slowly toward the fire indicated by his departed friend. As he reeled, he bethought him of the welcome his comrades would give him. He had a conviction that he would soon feel in his sore heart the barbed missiles of ridicule. He had no strength to invent a tale; he would be a soft target.

He made vague plans to go off into the deeper darkness and hide, but they were all destroyed by the voices of exhaustion and pain from his body. His ailments, clamoring, forced him to seek the place of food and rest, at whatever cost.

He swung unsteadily toward the fire. He could see the forms of men throwing black shadows in the red light, and as he went nearer it became known to him in some way that the ground was strewn with sleeping men.

Of a sudden he confronted a black and monstrous figure. A rifle barrel caught some glinting beams. "Halt! halt!" He was dismayed for a moment, but he presently thought that he recognized the nervous voice. As he stood tottering before the rifle barrel, he called out: "Why, hello, Wilson, you—you here?"

The rifle was lowered to a position of caution and the loud soldier came slowly forward. He peered into the youth's face. "That you, Henry?"

"Yes, it's—it's me."

"Well, well, ol' boy," said the other, "by ginger, I'm glad t' see yeh! I give yeh up fer a goner. I thought yeh was dead sure enough." There was husky emotion in his voice.

The youth found that now he could barely stand upon his feet. There was a sudden sinking of his forces. He thought he must hasten to produce his tale to protect him from the missiles already at the lips of his redoubtable comrades. So, staggering before the loud soldier, he began: "Yes, yes. I've—I've had an awful time. I've been all over. Way over on th' right. Ter'ble fightin' over there. I had an awful time. I got separated from the reg'ment. Over on th' right, I got shot. In th' head. I never see sech fightin'. Awful time. I don't see how I could a' got separated from th' reg'ment. I got shot, too."

His friend had stepped forward quickly.

"What? Got shot? Why didn't yeh say so first? Poor ol' boy, we must—hol' on a minnit; what am I doin'. I'll call Simpson."

Another figure at that moment loomed in the gloom. They could see that it was the corporal. "Who yeh talkin' to, Wilson?" he demanded. His voice was anger-toned. "Who yeh talkin' to? Yeh th' derndest sentinel—why—hello, Henry, you here? Why, I thought you was dead four hours ago! Great Jerusalem, they keep turnin' up every ten minutes or so! We thought we'd lost forty-two men by straight count, but if they keep on a-coming' this way, we'll git th' comp'ny all back by mornin' yit. Where was yeh?"

"Over on th' right. I got separated"—began the youth with considerable glibness.

But his friend had interrupted hastily. "Yes, an' he got shot in th' head an' he's in a fix, an' we must see t' him right away." He rested his rifle in the hollow of his left arm and his right around the youth's shoulder.

"Gee, it must hurt like thunder!" he said.

The youth leaned heavily upon his friend. "Yes, it hurts—hurts a good deal," he replied. There was a faltering in his voice.

"Oh," said the corporal. He linked his arm in the youth's and drew him forward. "Come on, Henry. I'll take keer 'a yeh."

As they went on together the loud private called out after them: "Put 'im t' sleep in my blanket, Simpson. An'—hol' on a minnit—here's my canteen. It's full 'a coffee. Look at his head by th' fire an' see how it looks. Maybe it's a pretty bad un. When I git relieved in a couple 'a minnits, I'll be over an' see t' him."

The youth's senses were so deadened that his friend's voice sounded from afar and he could scarcely feel the pressure of the corporal's arm. He submitted passively to the latter's directing strength. His head was in the old manner hanging forward upon his breast. His knees wobbled.

The corporal led him into the glare of the fire. "Now, Henry," he said, "let's have look at yer ol' head."

The youth sat down obediently and the corporal, laying aside his rifle, began to fumble in the bushy hair of his comrade. He was obliged to turn the other's head so that the full flush of the fire light would beam upon it. He puckered his mouth with a critical air. He drew back his lips and whistled through his teeth when his fingers came in contact with the splashed blood and the rare wound.

"Ah, here we are!" he said. He awkwardly made further investigations. "Jest as I thought," he added, presently. "Yeh've been grazed by a ball. It's raised a queer lump jest as if some feller had lammed yeh on th' head with a club. It stopped a-bleedin' long time ago. Th' most about it is that in th' mornin' yeh'll feel that a number ten hat wouldn't fit yeh. An' your head'll be all het up an' feel as dry as burnt pork. An' yeh may git a lot 'a other sicknesses, too, by mornin'. Yeh can't never tell. Still, I don't much think so. It's jest a damn' good belt on th' head, an' nothin' more. Now, you jest sit here an' don't move, while I go rout out th' relief. Then I'll send Wilson t' take keer 'a yeh."

The corporal went away. The youth remained on the ground like a parcel. He stared with a vacant look into the fire.

After a time he aroused, for some part, and the things about him began to take form. He saw that the ground in the deep shadows was cluttered with men, sprawling in every conceivable posture. Glancing narrowly into the more distant darkness, he caught occasional glimpses of visages that loomed pallid and ghostly, lit with a phosphorescent glow. These faces expressed in their lines the deep stupor of the tired soldiers. They made them appear like men drunk with wine. This bit of forest might have appeared to an ethereal wanderer as a scene of the result of some frightful debauch.

On the other side of the fire the youth observed an officer asleep, seated bolt upright, with his back against a tree. There was something perilous in his position. Badgered by dreams, perhaps, he swayed with little bounces and starts, like an old, toddy-stricken grandfather in a chimney corner. Dust and stains were upon his face. His lower jaw hung down as if lacking strength to assume its normal position. He was the picture of an exhausted soldier after a feast of war.

He had evidently gone to sleep with his sword in his arms. These two had slumbered in an embrace, but the weapon had been allowed in time to fall unheeded to the ground. The brass-mounted hilt lay in contact with some parts of the fire.

Within the gleam of rose and orange light from the burning sticks were other soldiers, snoring and heaving, or lying deathlike in slumber. A few pairs of legs were stuck forth, rigid and straight. The shoes displayed the mud or dust of marches and bits of rounded trousers, protruding from the blankets, showed rents and tears from hurried pitchings through the dense brambles.

The fire crackled musically. From it swelled light smoke. Overhead the foliage moved softly. The leaves, with their faces turned toward the blaze, were colored shifting hues of silver, often edged with red. Far off to the right, through a window in the forest could be seen a handful of stars lying, like glittering pebbles, on the black level of the night.

Occasionally, in this low-arched hall, a soldier would arouse and turn his body to a new position, the experience of his sleep having taught him of uneven and objectionable places upon the ground under him. Or, perhaps, he would lift himself to a sitting posture, blink at the fire for an unintelligent moment, throw a swift glance at his prostrate companion, and then cuddle down again with a grunt of sleepy content.

The youth sat in a forlorn heap until his friend the loud young soldier came, swinging two canteens by their light strings. "Well, now, Henry, ol' boy," said the latter, "we'll have yeh fixed up in jest about a minnit."

He had the bustling ways of an amateur nurse. He fussed around the fire and stirred the sticks to brilliant exertions. He made his patient drink largely from the canteen that contained the coffee. It was to the youth a delicious draught. He tilted his head afar back and held the canteen long to his lips. The cool mixture went caressingly down his blistered throat. Having finished, he sighed with comfortable delight.

The loud soldier watched his comrade with an air of satisfaction. He later produced an extensive handkerchief from his pocket. He folded it into a manner of bandage and soused water from the other canteen upon the middle of it. This crude arrangement he bound over the youth's head, trying the ends in a queer knot at the back of the neck.

"There," he said, moving off and surveying his deed, "yeh look like th' devil, but I bet yeh feel better."

The youth contemplated his friend with grateful eyes. Upon his aching and swelling head the cold cloth was like a tender woman's hand.

"Yeh don't holler ner say nothin'," remarked his friend approvingly. "I know I'm a blacksmith at takin' keer 'a sick folks, an' yeh never squeaked. Yer a good un, Henry. Most 'a men would a' been in th' hospital long ago. A shot in th' head ain't foolin' business."

The youth made no reply, but began to fumble with the buttons of his jacket.

"Well, come, now," continued his friend, "come on. I must put yeh t' bed an' see that yeh git a good night's rest."

The other got carefully erect, and the loud young soldier led him among the sleeping forms lying in groups and rows. Presently he stooped and picked up his blankets. He spread the rubber one upon the ground and placed the woolen one about the youth's shoulders.

"There now," he said, "lie down an' git some sleep."

The youth, with his manner of doglike obedience, got carefully down like a crone stooping. He stretched out with a murmur of relief and comfort. The ground felt like the softest couch.

But of a sudden he ejaculated: "Hol' on a minnit! Where you goin' t' sleep?"

His friend waved his hand impatiently. "Right down there by yeh."

"Well, but hol' on a minnit," continued the youth. "What yeh goin' t' sleep in? I've got your——"

The loud young soldier snarled: "Shet up an' go on t' sleep. Don't be makin' a damn' fool 'a yerself," he said severely.

After the reproof the youth said no more. An exquisite drowsiness had spread through him. The warm comfort of the blanket enveloped him and made a gentle languor. His head fell forward on his crooked arm and his weighted lids went softly down over his eyes. Hearing a splatter of musketry from the distance, hs wondered indifferently if those men sometimes slept. He gave a long sigh, snuggled down into his blanket, and in a moment was like his comrades.

Chapter 14

When the youth awoke it seemed to him that he had been asleep for a thousand years, and he felt sure that he opened his eyes upon an unexpected world. Gray mists were slowly shifting before the first efforts of the sun rays. An impending splendor could be seen in the eastern sky. An icy dew had chilled his face, and immediately upon arousing he curled farther down into his blanket. He stared for a while at the leaves overhead, moving in a heraldic wind of the day.

The distance was splintering and blaring with the noise of fighting. There was in the sound an expression of a deadly persistency, as if it had not begun and was not to cease.

About him were the rows and groups of men that he had dimly seen the previous night. They were getting a last draught of sleep before the awakening. The gaunt, careworn features and dusty figures were made plain by this quaint light at the dawning, but it dressed the skin of the men in corpselike hues and made the tangled limbs appear pulseless and dead. The youth started up with a little cry when his eyes first swept over this motionless mass of men, thick-spread upon the ground, pallid, and in strange postures. His disordered mind interpreted the hall of the forest as a charnel place. He believed for an instant that he was in the house of the dead, and he did not dare to move lest these corpses start up, squalling and squawking. In a second, however, he achieved his proper mind. He swore a complicated oath at himself. He saw that this somber picture was not a fact of the present, but a mere prophecy.

He heard then the noise of a fire crackling briskly in the cold air, and, turning his head, he saw his friend pottering busily about a small blaze. A few other figures moved in the fog, and he heard the hard cracking of axe blows.

Suddenly there was a hollow rumble of drums. A distant bugle sang faintly. Similar sounds, varying in strength, came from near and far over the forest. The bugles called to each other like brazen gamecocks. The near thunder of the regimental drums rolled.

The body of men in the woods rustled. There was a general uplifting of heads. A murmuring of voices broke upon the air. In it there was much bass of grumbling oaths. Strange gods were addressed in condemnation of the early hours necessary to correct war. An officer's peremptory tenor rang out and quickened the stiffened movement of the men. The tangled limbs unraveled. The corpse-hued faces were hidden behind fists that twisted slowly in the eye sockets.

The youth sat up and gave vent to an enormous yawn. "Thunder!" he remarked petulantly. He rubbed his eyes, and then putting up his hand felt carefully of the bandage over his wound. His friend, perceiving him to be awake, came from the fire. "Well, Henry, ol' man, how do yeh feel this mornin'?" he demanded.

The youth yawned again. Then he puckered his mouth to a little pucker. His head, in truth, felt precisely like a melon, and there was an unpleasant sensation at his stomach.

"Oh, Lord, I feel pretty bad," he said.

"Thunder!" exclaimed the other. "I hoped ye'd feel all right this mornin'." Let's see th' bandage—I guess it's slipped." He began to tinker at the wound in rather a clumsy way until the youth exploded.

"Gosh-dern it!" he said in sharp irritation; "you're the hangdest man I ever saw! You wear muffs on your hands. Why in good thunderation can't you be more easy? I'd rather you'd stand off an' throw guns at it. Now, go slow, an' don't act as if you was nailing down carpet."

He glared with insolent command at his friend, but the latter answered soothingly. "Well, well, come now, an' git some grub," he said. "Then, maybe, yeh'll feel better."

At the fireside the loud young soldier watched over his comrade's wants with tenderness and care. He was very busy marshaling the little black vagabonds of tin cups and pouring into them the streaming, iron colored mixture from a small and sooty tin pail. He had some fresh meat, which he roasted hurriedly upon a stick. He sat down then and contemplated the youth's appetite with glee.

The youth took note of a remarkable change in his comrade since those days of camp life upon the river bank. He seemed no more to be continually regarding the proportions of his personal prowess. He was not furious at small words that pricked his conceits. He was no more a loud young soldier. There was about him now a fine reliance. He showed a quiet belief in his purposes and his abilities. And this inward confidence enabled him to be indifferent to little words of other men aimed at him.

The youth reflected. He had been used to regarding his comrade as a blatant child with an audacity grown from his inexperience, thoughtless, headstrong, jealous, and filled with a tinsel courage. A swaggering babe accustomed to strut in his own dooryard. The youth wondered where had been born these new eyes; when his comrade had made the great discovery that there were many men who would refuse to be subjected by him. Apparently, the other had now climbed a peak of wisdom from which he could perceive himself as a very wee thing. And the youth saw that ever after it would be easier to live in his friend's neighborhood.

His comrade balanced his ebony coffee-cup on his knee. "Well, Henry," he said, "what d'yeh think th' chances are? D'yeh think we'll wallop 'em?"

The youth considered for a moment. "Day-b'fore-yesterday," he finally replied, with boldness, "you would 'a' bet you'd lick the hull kit-an'-boodle all by yourself."

His friend looked a trifle amazed. "Would I?" he asked. He pondered. "Well, perhaps I would," he decided at last. He stared humbly at the fire.

The youth was quite disconcerted at this surprising reception of his remarks. "Oh, no, you wouldn't either," he said, hastily trying to retrace.

But the other made a deprecating gesture. "Oh, yeh needn't mind, Henry," he said. "I believe I was a pretty big fool in those days." He spoke as after a lapse of years.

There was a little pause.

"All th' officers say we've got th' rebs in a pretty tight box," said the friend, clearing his throat in a commonplace way. "They all seem t' think we've got 'em jest where we want 'em."

"I don't know about that," the youth replied. "What I seen over on th' right makes me think it was th' other way about. From where I was, it looked as if we was gettin' a good poundin' yestirday."

"D'yeh think so?" inquired the friend. "I thought we handled 'em pretty rough yestirday."

"Not a bit," said the youth. "Why, lord, man, you didn't see nothing of the fight. Why!" Then a sudden thought came to him. "Oh! Jim Conklin's dead."

His friend started. "What? Is he? Jim Conklin?"

The youth spoke slowly. "Yes. He's dead. Shot in th' side."

"Yeh don't say so. Jim Conklin. . . . poor cuss!"

All about them were other small fires surrounded by men with their little black utensils. From one of these near came sudden sharp voices in a row. It appeared that two light-footed soldiers had been teasing a huge, bearded man, causing him to spill coffee upon his blue knees. The man had gone into a rage and had sworn comprehensively. Stung by his language, his tormentors had immediately bristled at him with a great show of resenting unjust oaths. Possibly there was going to be a fight.

The friend arose and went over to them, making pacific motions with his arms. "Oh, here, now, boys, what's th' use?" he said. "We'll be at th' rebs in less'n an hour. What's th' good fightin' 'mong ourselves?"

One of the light-footed soldiers turned upon him red-faced and violent. "Yeh needn't come around here with yer preachin'. I s'pose yeh don't approve 'a fightin' since Charley Morgan licked yeh; but I don't see what business this here is 'a yours or anybody else."

"Well, it ain't," said the friend mildly. "Still I hate t' see——"

There was a tangled argument.

"Well, he——," said the two, indicating their opponent with accusative forefingers.

The huge soldier was quite purple with rage. He pointed at the two soldiers with his great hand, extending clawlike. "Well, they——"

But during this argumentative time the desire to deal blows seemed to pass, although they said much to each other. Finally the friend returned to his old seat. In a short while the three antagonists could be seen together in an amiable bunch.

"Jimmie Rogers ses I'll have t' fight him after th' battle t'-day," announced the friend as he again seated himself. "He ses he don't allow no interferin' in his business. I hate t' see th' boys fightin' 'mong themselves."

The youth laughed. "Yer changed a good bit. Yeh ain't at all like yeh was. I remember when you an' that Irish feller——" He stopped and laughed again.

"No, I didn't use t' be that way," said his friend thoughtfully. "That's true 'nough."

"Well, I didn't mean——" began the youth.

The friend made another deprecatory gesture. "Oh, yeh needn't mind, Henry."

There was another little pause.

"Th' reg'ment lost over half th' men yestirday," remarked the friend eventually. "I thought a course they was all dead, but, laws, they kep' a-comin' back last night until it seems, after all, we didn't lose but a few. They'd been scattered all over, wanderin' around in th' woods, fightin' with other reg'ments, an' everything. Jest like you done."

"So?" said the youth.

Chapter 15

The regiment was standing at order arms at the side of a lane, waiting for the command to march, when suddenly the youth remembered the little packet enwrapped in a faded yellow envelope which the loud young soldier with lugubrious words had intrusted to him. It made him start. He uttered an exclamation and turned toward his comrade.

"Wilson!"

"What?"

His friend, at his side in the ranks, was thoughtfully staring down the road. From some cause his expression was at that moment very meek. The youth, regarding him with sidelong glances, felt impelled to change his purpose. "Oh, nothing," he said.

His friend turned his head in some surprise, "Why, what was yeh goin' t' say?"

"Oh, nothing," repeated the youth.

He resolved not to deal the little blow. It was sufficient that the fact made him glad. It was not necessary to knock his friend on the head with the misguided packet.

He had been possessed of much fear of his friend, for he saw how easily questionings could make holes in his feelings. Lately, he had assured himself that the altered comrade would not tantalize him with a persistent curiosity, but he felt certain that during the first period of leisure his friend would ask him to relate his adventures of the previous day.

He now rejoiced in the possession of a small weapon with which he could prostrate his comrade at the first signs of a cross-examination. He was master. It would now be he who could laugh and shoot the shafts of derision.

The friend had, in a weak hour, spoken with sobs of his own death. He had delivered a melancholy oration previous to his funeral, and had doubtless in the packet of letters, presented various keepsakes to relatives. But he had not died, and thus he had delivered himself into the hands of the youth.

The latter felt immensely superior to his friend, but he inclined to condescension. He adopted toward him an air of patronizing good humor.

His self-pride was now entirely restored. In the shade of its flourishing growth he stood with braced and self-confident legs, and since nothing could now be discovered he did not shrink from an encounter with the eyes of judges, and allowed no thoughts of his own to keep him from an attitude of manfulness. He had performed his mistakes in the dark, so he was still a man.

Indeed, when he remembered his fortunes of yesterday, and looked at them from a distance he began to see something fine there. He had license to be pompous and veteranlike.

His panting agonies of the past he put out of his sight.

In the present, he declared to himself that it was only the doomed and the damned who roared with sincerity at circumstance. Few but they ever did it. A man with a full stomach and the respect of his fellows had no business to scold about anything that he might think to be wrong in the ways of the universe, or even with the ways of society. Let the unfortunates rail; the others may play marbles.

He did not give a great deal of thought to these battles that lay directly before him. It was not essential that he should plan his ways in regard to them. He had been taught that many obligations of a life were easily avoided. The lessons of yesterday had been that retribution was a laggard and blind. With these facts before him he did not deem it necessary that he should become feverish over the possibilities of the ensuing twenty-four hours. He could leave much to chance. Besides, a faith in himself had secretly blossomed. There was a little flower of confidence growing within him. He was now a man of experience. He had been out among the dragons, he said, and he assured himself that they were not so hideous as he had imagined them. Also, they were inaccurate; they did not sting with precision. A stout heart often defied, and defying, escaped.

And, furthermore, how could they kill him who was the chosen of gods and doomed to greatness?

He remembered how some of the men had run from the battle. As he recalled their terror-struck faces he felt a scorn for them. They had surely been more fleet and more wild than was absolutely necessary. They were weak mortals. As for himself, he had fled with discretion and dignity.

He was aroused from this reverie by his friend, who, having hitched about nervously and blinked at the trees for a time, suddenly coughed in an introductory way, and spoke.

"Fleming!"

"What?"

The friend put his hand up to his mouth and coughed again. He fidgeted in his jacket.

"Well," he gulped, at last, "I guess yeh might as well give me back them letters." Dark, prickling blood had flushed into his cheeks and brow.

"All right, Wilson," said the youth. He loosened two buttons of his coat, thrust in his hand, and brought forth the packet. As he extended it to his friend the latter's face was turned from him.

He had been slow in the act of producing the packet because during it he had been trying to invent a remarkable comment upon the affair. He could conjure nothing of sufficient point. He was compelled to allow his friend to escape unmolested with his packet. And for this he took unto himself considerable credit. It was a generous thing.

His friend at his side seemed suffering great shame. As he contemplated him, the youth felt his heart grow more strong and stout. He had never been compelled to blush in such manner for his acts; he was an individual of extraordinary virtues.

He reflected, with condescending pity: "Too bad! Too bad! The poor devil, it makes him feel tough!"

After this incident, and as he reviewed the battle pictures he had seen, he felt quite competent to return home and make the hearts of the people glow with stories of war. He could see himself in a room of warm tints telling tales to listeners. He could exhibit laurels. They were insignificant; still, in a district where laurels were infrequent, they might shine.

He saw his gaping audience picturing him as the central figure in blazing scenes. And he imagined the consternation and the ejaculations of his mother and the young lady at the seminary as they drank his recitals. Their vague feminine formula for beloved ones doing brave deeds on the field of battle without risk of life would be destroyed.

Chapter 16

A sputtering of musketry was always to be heard. Later, the cannon had entered the dispute. In the fog-filled air their voices made a thudding sound. The reverberations were continued. This part of the world led a strange, battlefield existence.

The youth's regiment was marched to relieve a command that had lain long in some damp trenches. The men took positions behind a curving line of rifle pits that had been turned up, like a large furrow, along the line of woods. Before them was a level stretch, peopled with short, deformed stumps. From the woods beyond came the dull popping of the skirmishers and pickets, firing in the fog. From the right came the noise of a terrific fracas.

The men cuddled behind the small embankment and sat in easy attitudes awaiting their turn. Many had their backs to the firing. The youth's friend lay down, buried his face in his arms, and almost instantly, it seemed, he was in a deep sleep.

The youth leaned his breast against the brown dirt and peered over at the woods and up and down the line. Curtains of trees interfered with his ways of vision. He could see the low line of trenches but for a short distance. A few idle flags were perched on the dirt hills. Behind them were rows of dark bodies with a few heads sticking curiously over the top.

Always the noise of skirmishers came from the woods on the front and left, and the din on the right had grown to frightful proportions. The guns were roaring without an instant's pause for breath. It seemed that the cannon had come from all parts and were engaged in a stupendous wrangle. It became impossible to make a sentence heard.

The youth wished to launch a joke—a quotation from newspapers. He desired to say, "All quiet on the Rappahannock," but the guns refused to permit even a comment upon their uproar. He never successfully concluded the sentence. But at last the guns stopped, and among the men in the rifle pits rumors again flew, like birds, but they were now for the most part black creatures who flapped their wings drearily near to the ground and refused to rise on any wings of hope. The men's faces grew doleful from the interpreting of omens. Tales of hesitation and uncertainty on the part of those high in place and responsibility came to their ears. Stories of disaster were borne into their minds

70

with many proofs. This din of musketry on the right, growing like a released genie of sound, expressed and emphasized the army's plight.

The men were disheartened and began to mutter. They made gestures expressive of the sentence: "Ah, what more can we do?" And it could always be seen that they were bewildered by the alleged news and could not fully comprehend a defeat.

Before the gray mists had been totally obliterated by the sun rays, the ,regiment was marching in a spread column that was retiring carefully through the woods. The disordered, hurrying lines of the enemy could sometimes be seen down through the groves and little fields. They were yelling, shrill and exultant.

At this sight the youth forgot many personal matters and became greatly enraged. He exploded in loud sentences. "B'jiminey, we're generaled by a lot 'a lunkheads."

"More than one feller has said that t'-day," observed a man.

His friend, recently aroused, was still very drowsy. He looked behind him until his mind took in the meaning of the movement. Then he sighed. "Oh, well, I s'pose we got licked," he remarked sadly.

The youth had a thought that it would not be handsome for him to freely condemn other men. He made an attempt to restrain himself, but the words upon his tongue were too bitter. He presently began a long and intricate denunciation of the commander of the forces.

"Mebbe, it wa'n't all his fault—not all together. He did th' best he knowed. It's our luck t' git licked often," said his friend in a weary tone. He was trudging along with stooped shoulders and shifting eyes like a man who has been caned and kicked.

"Well, don't we fight like the devil? Don't we do all that men can?" demanded the youth loudly.

He was secretly dumfounded at this sentiment when it came from his lips. For a moment his face lost its valor and he looked guiltily about him. But no one questioned his right to deal in such words, and presently he recovered his air of courage. He went on to repeat a statement he had heard going from group to group at the camp that morning. "The brigadier said he never saw a new reg'ment fight the way we fought yesterday, didn't he? And we didn't do better than many another reg'ment, did we? Well, then, you can't say it's th' army's fault, can you?"

In his reply, the friend's voice was stern. "'A course not," he said. "No man dare say we don't fight like th' devil. No man will ever dare say it. Th' boys fight like hell-roosters. But still—still, we don't have no luck."

"Well, then, if we fight like the devil an' don't ever whip, it must be the general's fault," said the youth grandly and decisively. "And I don't see any sense in fighting and fighting and fighting, yet always losing through some derned old lunkhead of a general."

A sarcastic man who was tramping at the youth's side, then spoke lazily. "Mebbe yeh think yeh fit th' hull battle yesterday, Fleming," he remarked.

The speech pierced the youth. Inwardly he was reduced to an abject pulp by these chance words. His legs quaked privately. He cast a frightened glance at the sarcastic man.

"Why, no," he hastened to say in a conciliating voice, "I don't think I fought the whole battle yesterday.''

But the other seemed innocent of any deeper meaning. Apparently, he had no information. It was merely his habit. ''Oh!'' he replied in the same tone of calm derision.

The youth, nevertheless, felt a threat. His mind shrank from going near to the danger, and thereafter he was silent. The significance of the sarcastic man's words took from him all loud moods that would make him appear prominent. He became suddenly a modest person.

There was low-toned talk among the troops. The officers were impatient and snappy, their countenances clouded with the tales of misfortune. The troops, sifting through the forest, were sullen. In the youth's company once a man's laugh rang out. A dozen soldiers turned their faces quickly toward him and frowned with vague displeasure.

The noise of firing dogged their footsteps. Sometimes, it seemed to be driven a little way, but it always returned again with increased insolence. The men muttered and cursed, throwing black looks in its direction.

In a clear space the troops were at last halted. Regiments and brigades, broken and detached through their encounters with thickets, grew together again and lines were faced toward the pursuing bark of the enemy's infantry.

This noise, following like the yellings of eager, metallic hounds, increased to a loud and joyous burst, and then, as the sun went serenely up the sky, throwing illuminating rays into the gloomy thickets, it broke forth into prolonged pealings. The woods began to crackle as if afire.

''Whoop-a-dadee,'' said a man, ''here we are! Everybody fightin'. Blood an' destruction.''

''I was willin' t' bet they'd attack as soon as th' sun got fairly up,'' savagely asserted the lieutenant who commanded the youth's company. He jerked without mercy at his little mustache. He strode to and fro with dark dignity in the rear of his men, who were lying down behind whatever protection they had collected.

A battery had trundled into position in the rear and was thoughtfully shelling the distance. The regiment, unmolested as yet, awaited the moment when the gray shadows of the woods before them should be slashed by the lines of flame. There was much growling and swearing.

''Good Gawd,'' the youth grumbled, ''we're always being chased around like rats! It makes me sick. Nobody seems to know where we go or why we go. We just get fired around from pillar to post and get licked here and get licked there, and nobody knows what it's done for. It makes a man feel like a damn' kitten in a bag. Now, I'd like to know what the eternal thunders we was marched into these woods for anyhow, unless it was to give the rebs a regular pot shot at us. We came in here and got our legs all tangled up in these cussed briers, and then we begin to fight and the rebs had an easy time of it. Don't tell me it's just luck! I know better. It's this derned old——''

The friend seemed jaded, but he interrupted his comrade with a voice of calm confidence. ''It'll turn out all right in th' end,'' he said.

''Oh, the devil it will! You always talk like a dog-hanged parson. Don't tell me! I know——''

At this time there was an interposition by the savage-minded lieutenant, who was obliged to vent some of his inward dissatisfaction upon his men. ''You boys shut right up! There no need 'a your wastin' your breath in long-winded arguments about this an' that an' th' other. You've been jawin' like a lot 'a old hens. All you've got t' do is to fight, an' you'll get plenty 'a that t' do in about ten minutes. Less talkin' an' more fightin' is what's best for you boys. I never saw sech gabbling jackasses.''

He paused, ready to pounce upon any man who might have the temerity to reply. No words being said, he resumed his dignified pacing.

''There's too much chin music an' too little fightin' in this war, anyhow,'' he said to them, turning his head for a final remark.

The day had grown more white, until the sun shed his full radiance upon the thronged forest. A sort of a gust of battle came sweeping toward that part of the line where lay the youth's regiment. The front shifted a trifle to meet it squarely. There was a wait. In this part of the field there passed slowly the intense moments that precede the tempest.

A single rifle flashed in a thicket before the regiment. In an instant it was joined by many others. There was a mighty song of clashes and crashes that went sweeping through the woods. The guns in the rear, aroused and enraged by shells that had been thrown burr-like at them, suddenly involved themselves in a hideous altercation with another band of guns. The battle roar settled to a rolling thunder, which was a single, long explosion.

In the regiment there was a peculiar kind of hesitation denoted in the attitudes of the men. They were worn, exhausted, having slept but little and labored much. They rolled their eyes toward the advancing battle as they stood awaiting the shock. Some shrank and flinched. They stood as men tied to stakes.

Chapter 17

This advance of the enemy had seemed to the youth like a ruthless hunting. He began to fume with rage and exasperation. He beat his foot upon the ground, and scowled with hate at the swirling smoke that was approaching like a phantom flood. There was a maddening quality in this seeming resolution of the foe to give him no rest, to give him no time to sit down and think. Yesterday he had fought and had fled rapidly. There had been many adventures. For to-day he felt that he had earned opportunities for contemplative repose. He could have enjoyed portraying to uninitiated listeners various scenes at which he had been a witness or ably discussing the processes of war with other proved men. Too it was important that he should have time for physical recuperation. He was sore and stiff from his experiences. He had received his fill of all exertions, and he wished to rest.

But those other men seemed never to grow weary; they were fighting with their old speed. He had a wild hate for the relentless foe. Yesterday, when he had imagined the universe to be against him, he had hated it, little gods and big gods; to-day he hated the army of the foe with the same great hatred. He was not going to be badgered of his life, like a kitten chased by boys, he said. It was not well to drive men into final corners; at those moments they could all develop teeth and claws.

He leaned and spoke into his friend's ear. He menaced the woods with a gesture. "If they keep on chasing us, by Gawd, they'd better watch out. Can't stand *too* much."

The friend twisted his head and made a calm reply. "If they keep on a-chasin' us they'll drive us all inteh th' river."

The youth cried out savagely at this statement. He crouched behind a little tree with his eyes burning hatefully and his teeth set in a cur-like snarl. The awkward bandage was still about his head, and upon it, over his wound, there was a spot of dry blood. His hair was wondrously tousled, and some straggling, moving locks hung over the cloth of the bandage down toward his forehead. His jacket and shirt were open at the throat, and exposed his young bronzed neck. There could be seen spasmodic gulpings at his throat.

His fingers twined nervously about his rifle. He wished that it was an engine of annihilating power. He felt that he and his companions were being taunted and derided from sincere convictions that they were poor and puny. His knowledge of his inability to take vengeance for it made his rage into a dark and stormy specter, that possessed him and made him dream of abominable cruelties. The tormentors were flies sucking insolently at his blood, and he thought that he would have given his life for a revenge of seeing their faces in pitiful plights.

The winds of battle had swept all about the regiment, until the one rifle, instantly followed by others, flashed in its front. A moment later the regiment roared forth its sudden and valiant retort. A dense wall of smoke settled slowly down. It was furiously slit and slashed by the knifelike fire from the rifles.

To the youth the fighters resembled animals tossed for a death struggle into a dark pit. There was a sensation that he and his fellows, at bay, were pushing back, always pushing fierce onslaughts of creatures who were slippery. Their beams of crimson seemed to get no purchase upon the bodies of their foes; the latter seemed to evade them with ease, and come through, between, around, and about with unopposed skill.

When, in a dream, it occurred to the youth that his rifle was an impotent stick, he lost sense of everything but his hate, his desire to smash into pulp the glittering smile of victory which he could feel upon the faces of his enemies.

The blue smoke-swallowed line curled and writhed like a snake stepped upon. It swung its ends to and fro in an agony of fear and rage.

The youth was not conscious that he was erect upon his feet. He did not know the direction of the ground. Indeed, once he even lost the habit of balance and fell heavily. He was up again immediately. One thought went through the chaos of his brain at the time. He wondered if he had fallen because he had been shot. But the suspicion flew away at once. He did not think more of it.

He had taken up a first position behind the little tree, with a direct determination to hold it against the world. He had not deemed it possible that his army could that day succeed, and from this he felt the ability to fight harder. But the throng had surged in all ways, until he lost directions and locations, save that he knew where lay the enemy.

The flames bit him, and the hot smoke broiled his skin. His rifle barrel grew so hot that ordinarily he could not have borne it upon his palms; but he kept on stuffing cartridges into it, and pounding them with his clanking, bending ramrod. If he aimed at some changing form through the smoke, he pulled his trigger with a fierce grunt, as if he were dealing a blow of the fist with all his strength.

When the enemy seemed falling back before him and his fellows, he went instantly forward, like a dog who, seeing his foes lagging, turns and insists upon being pursued. And when he was compelled to retire again, he did it slowly, sullenly, taking steps of wrathful despair.

Once he, in his intent hate, was almost alone, and was firing, when all those near him had ceased. He was so engrossed in his occupation that he was not aware of a lull.

He was recalled by a hoarse laugh and a sentence that came to his ears in a voice of contempt and amazement. "Yeh infernal fool, don't yeh know enough t' quit when there ain't anything t' shoot at? Good Gawd!"

He turned then and, pausing with his rifle thrown half into position, looked at the blue line of his comrades. During this moment of leisure they seemed all to be engaged in staring with astonishment at him. They had become spectators. Turning to the front again he saw, under the lifted smoke, a deserted ground.

He looked bewildered for a moment. Then there appeared upon the glazed vacancy of his eyes a diamond point of intelligence. "Oh," he said, comprehending.

He returned to his comrades and threw himself upon the ground. He sprawled like a man who had been thrashed. His flesh seemed strangely on fire, and the sounds of the battle continued in his ears. He groped blindly for his canteen.

The lieutenant was crowing. He seemed drunk with fighting. He called out to the youth: "By heavens, if I had ten thousand wild cats like you I could tear th' stomach outa this war in less'n a week!" He puffed out his chest with large dignity as he said it.

Some of the men muttered and looked at the youth in awe-struck ways. It was plain that as he had gone on loading and firing and cursing without the proper intermission, they had found time to regard him. And they now looked upon him as a war devil.

The friend came staggering to him. There was some fright and dismay in his voice. "Are yeh all right, Fleming? Do yeh feel all right? There ain't nothin' th' matter with yeh, Henry, is there?"

"No," said the youth with difficulty. His throat seemed full of knobs and burs.

These incidents made the youth ponder. It was revealed to him that he had been a barbarian, a beast. He had fought like a pagan who defends his religion. Regarding it, he saw that it was fine, wild, and, in some ways, easy. He had been a tremendous figure, no doubt. By this struggle he had overcome obstacles which he had admitted to be mountains. They had fallen like paper peaks, and he was now what he called a hero. And he had not been aware of the process. He had slept and, awakening, found himself a knight.

He lay and basked in the occasional stares of his comrades. Their faces were varied in degrees of blackness from the burned powder. Some were utterly smudged. They were reeking with perspiration, and their breaths came hard and wheezing. And from these soiled expanses they peered at him.

"Hot work! Hot work!" cried the lieutenant deliriously. He walked up and down, restless and eager. Sometimes his voice could be heard in a wild, incomprehensible laugh.

When he had a particularly profound thought upon the science of war he always unconsciously addressed himself to the youth.

There was some grim rejoicing by the men. "By thunder, I bet this army'll never see another new reg'ment like us!"

"You bet!"

"A dog, a woman, an' a walnut tree,
Th' more yeh beat 'em, th' better they be!

That's like us."

"Lost a piler men, they did. If an' ol' woman swep' up th' woods she'd git a dustpanful."

"Yes, an' if she'll come around ag'in in 'bout an' hour she'll git a pile more."

The forest still bore its burden of clamor. From off under the trees came the rolling clatter of the musketry. Each distant thicket seemed a strange porcupine with quills of flame. A cloud of dark smoke, as from smoldering ruins, went up toward the sun now bright and gay in the blue, enameled sky.

Chapter 18

The ragged line had respite for some minutes, but during its pause the struggle in the forest became magnified until the trees seemed to quiver from the firing and the ground to shake from the rushing of the men. The voices of the cannon were mingled in a long and interminable row. It seemed difficult to live in such an atmosphere. The chests of the men strained for a bit of freshness, and their throats craved water.

There was one shot through the body, who raised a cry of bitter lamentation when came this lull. Perhaps he had been calling out during the fighting also, but at that time no one had heard him. But now the men turned at the woeful complaints of him upon the ground.

"Who is it? Who is it?"

"It's Jimmie Rogers. Jimmie Rogers."

When their eyes first encountered him there was a sudden halt, as if they feared to go near. He was thrashing about in the grass, twisting his shuddering body into many strange postures. He was screaming loudly. This instant's hesitation seemed to fill him with a tremendous, fantastic contempt, and he damned them in shrieked sentences.

The youth's friend had a geographical illusion concerning a stream, and he obtained permission to go for some water. Immediately canteens were showered upon him. "Fill mine, will yeh?" "Bring me some, too." "And me, too." He departed, ladened. The youth went with his friend, feeling a desire to throw his heated body onto the stream and, soaking there, drink quarts.

They made a hurried search for the supposed stream, but did not find it. "No water here," said the youth. They turned without delay and began to retrace their steps.

From their position as they again faced toward the place of the fighting, they could of course comprehend a greater amount of the battle than when their visions had been blurred by the hurling smoke of the line. They could see dark stretches winding along the land, and on one cleared space there was a row of guns making gray clouds, which were filled with large flashes of orange-colored flame. Over some foliage they could see the roof of a house. One window, glowing a deep murder red, shone squarely through the leaves. From the edifice a tall leaning tower of smoke went far into the sky.

Looking over their own troops, they saw mixed masses slowly getting into regular form. The sunlight made twinkling points of the bright steel. To the rear there was a glimpse of a distant roadway as it curved over a slope. It was crowded with retreating infantry. From all the interwoven forest arose the smoke and bluster of the battle. The air was always occupied by a blaring.

Near where they stood shells were flip-flapping and hooting. Occasional bullets buzzed in the air and spanged into tree trunks. Wounded men and other stragglers were slinking through the woods.

Looking down an aisle of the grove, the youth and his companion saw a jangling general and his staff almost ride upon a wounded man, who was crawling on his hands and knees. The general reined strongly at his charger's opened and foamy mouth and guided it with dexterous horsemanship past the man. The latter scrambled in wild and torturing haste. His strength evidently failed him as he reached a place of safety. One of his arms suddenly weakened, and he fell, sliding over upon his back. He lay stretched out, breathing gently.

A moment later the small, creaking cavalcade was directly in front of the two soldiers. Another officer, riding with the skillful abandon of a cowboy, galloped his horse to a position directly before the general. The two unnoticed foot soldiers made a little show of going on, but they lingered near in the desire to overhear the conversation. Perhaps, they thought, some great inner historical things would be said.

The general, whom the boys knew as the commander of their division, looked at the other officer and spoke coolly, as if he were criticising his clothes. "Th' enemy's formin' over there for another charge," he said. "It'll be directed against Whiterside, an' I fear they'll break through there unless we work like thunder t' stop them."

The other swore at his restive horse, and then cleared his throat. He made a gesture toward his cap. "It'll be hell t' pay stoppin' them," he said shortly.

"I presume so," remarked the general. Then he began to talk rapidly and in a lower tone. He frequently illustrated his words with a pointing finger. The two infantrymen could hear nothing until finally he asked: "What troops can you spare?"

The officer who rode like a cowboy reflected for an instant. "Well," he said, "I had to order in th' 12th to help th' 76th, an' I haven't really got any. But there's th' 304th. They fight like a lot 'a mule drivers. I can spare them best of any."

The youth and his friend exchanged glances of astonishment.

The general spoke sharply. "Get 'em ready, then. I'll watch developments from here, an' send you word when t' start them. It'll happen in five minutes."

As the other officer tossed his fingers toward his cap and wheeling his horse, started away, the general called out to him in a sober voice: "I don't believe many of your mule drivers will get back."

The other shouted something in reply. He smiled.

With scared faces, the youth and his companion hurried back to the line.

These happenings had occupied an incredibly short time, yet the youth felt that in them he had been made aged. New eyes were given to him. And the most startling thing was to learn suddenly that he was very insignificant. The officer spoke of the regiment as if he referred to a broom. Some part of the woods needed sweeping, perhaps, and he merely indicated a broom in a tone properly indifferent to its fate. It was war, no doubt, but it appeared strange.

As the two boys approached the line, the lieutenant perceived them and swelled with wrath. "Fleming—Wilson—how long does it take yeh to git water, anyhow—where yeh been to."

But his oration ceased as he saw their eyes, which were large with great tales. "We're goin' t' charge—we're goin' t' charge!" cried the youth's friend, hastening with his news.

"Charge?" said the lieutenant. "Charge? Well, b'Gawd! Now, this is real fightin'." Over his soiled countenance there went a boastful smile. "Charge? Well, b'Gawd!"

A little group of soldiers surrounded the two youths. "Are we, sure 'nough? Well, I'll be derned! Charge? What fer? What at? Wilson, you're lyin'."

"I hope to die," said the youth, pitching his tones to the key of angry remonstrance. "Sure as shooting, I tell you."

And his friend spoke in re-enforcement. "Not by a blame sight, he ain't lyin'. We heard 'em talkin'."

They caught sight of two mounted figures a short distance from them. One was the colonel of the regiment and the other was the officer who had received orders from the commander of the division. They were gesticulating at each other. The soldier, pointing at them, interpreted the scene.

One man had a final objection: "How could yeh hear 'em talkin'?" But the men, for a large part, nodded, admitting that previously the two friends had spoken truth.

They settled back into reposeful attitudes with airs of having accepted the matter. And they mused upon it, with a hundred varieties of expression. It was an engrossing thing to think about. Many tightened their belts carefully and hitched at their trousers.

A moment later the officers began to bustle among the men, pushing them into a more compact mass and into a better alignment. They chased those that straggled and fumed at a few men who seemed to show by their attitudes that they had decided to remain at that spot. They were like critical shepherds struggling with sheep.

Presently, the regiment seemed to draw itself up and heave a deep breath. None of the men's faces were mirrors of large thoughts. The soldiers were bended and stooped like sprinters before a signal. Many pairs of glinting eyes peered from the grimy faces toward the curtains of the deeper woods. They seemed to be engaged in deep calculations of time and distance.

They were surrounded by the noises of the monstrous altercation between the two armies. The world was fully interested in other matters. Apparently, the regiment had its small affair to itself.

The youth, turning, shot a quick, inquiring glance at his friend. The latter returned to him the same manner of look. They were the only ones who possessed an inner knowledge. "Mule drivers—hell t' pay—don't believe many will get back." It was an ironical secret. Still, they saw no hesitation in each other's faces, and they nodded a mute and unprotesting assent when a shaggy man near them said in a meek voice: "We'll git swallowed."

Chapter 19

The youth stared at the land in front of him. Its foliages now seemed to veil powers and horrors. He was unaware of the machinery of orders that started the charge, although from the corners of his eyes he saw an officer, who looked like a boy a-horseback, come galloping, waving his hat. Suddenly he felt a straining and heaving among the men. The line fell slowly forward like a toppling wall, and, with a convulsive gasp that was intended for a cheer, the regiment began its journey. The youth was pushed and jostled for a moment before he understood the movement at all, but directly he lunged ahead and began to run.

He fixed his eye upon a distant and prominent clump of trees where he had concluded the enemy were to be met, and he ran toward it as toward a goal. He had believed throughout that it was a mere question of getting over an unpleasant matter as quickly as possible, and he ran desperately, as if pursued for a murder. His face was drawn hard and tight with the stress of his endeavor. His eyes were fixed in a lurid glare. And with his soiled and disordered dress, his red and inflamed features surmounted by the dingy rag with its spot of blood, his wildly swinging rifle and banging accouterments, he looked to be an insane soldier.

As the regiment swung from its position out into a cleared space the woods and thickets before it awakened. Yellow flames leaped toward it from many directions. The forest made a tremendous objection.

The line lurched straight for a moment. Then the right wing swung forward; it in turn was surpassed by the left. Afterward the center careered to the front until the regiment was a wedge-shaped mass, but an instant later the opposition of the bushes, trees, and uneven places on the ground split the command and scattered it into detached clusters.

The youth, light-footed, was unconsciously in advance. His eyes still kept note of the clump of trees. From all places near it the clannish yell of the enemy could be heard. The little flames of rifles leaped from it. The song of the bullets was in the air and shells snarled among the treetops. One tumbled directly into the middle of a hurrying group and exploded in crimson fury. There was an instant's spectacle of a man, almost over it, throwing up his hands to shield his eyes.

Other men, punched by bullets, fell in grotesque agonies. The regiment left a coherent trail of bodies.

They had passed into a clearer atmosphere. There was an effect like a revelation in the new appearance of the landscape. Some men working madly at a battery were plain to them, and the opposing infantry's lines were defined by the gray walls and fringes of smoke.

It seemed to the youth that he saw everything. Each blade of the green grass was bold and clear. He thought that he was aware of every change in the thin, transparent vapor that floated idly in sheets. The brown or gray trunks of the trees showed each roughness of their surfaces. And the men of the regiment, with their starting eyes and sweating faces, running madly, or falling, as if thrown headlong, to queer, heaped-up corpses—all were comprehended. His mind took a mechanical but firm impression, so that afterward everything was pictured and explained to him, save why he himself was there.

But there was a frenzy made from this furious rush. The men, pitching forward insanely, had burst into cheerings, moblike and barbaric, but tuned in strange keys that can arouse the dullard and the stoic. It made a mad enthusiasm that, it seemed, would be incapable of checking itself before granite and brass. There was the delirium that encounters despair and death, and is heedless and blind to the odds. It is a temporary but sublime absence of selfishness. And because it was of this order was the reason, perhaps, why the youth wondered, afterward, what reasons he could have had for being there.

Presently the straining pace ate up the energies of the men. As if by agreement, the leaders began to slacken their speed. The volleys directed against them had had a seeming windlike effect. The regiment snorted and blew. Among some stolid trees it began to falter and hesitate. The men, staring intently, began to wait for some of the distant walls of smoke to move and disclose to them the scene. Since much of their strength and their breath had vanished, they returned to caution. They were become men again.

The youth had a vague belief that he had run miles, and he thought, in a way, that he was now in some new and unknown land.

The moment the regiment ceased its advance the protesting splutter of musketry became a steadied roar. Long and accurate fringes of smoke spread out. From the top of a small hill came level belchings of yellow flame that caused an inhuman whistling in the air.

The men, halted, had opportunity to see some of their comrades dropping with moans and shrieks. A few lay under foot, still or wailing. And now for an instant the men stood, their rifles slack in their hands, and watched the regiment dwindle. They appeared dazed and stupid. This spectacle seemed to paralyze them, overcome them with a fatal fascination. They stared woodenly at the sights, and, lowering their eyes, looked from face to face. It was a strange pause, and a strange silence.

Then, above the sounds of the outside commotion, arose the roar of the lieutenant. He strode suddenly forth, his infantile features blank with rage.

"Come on, yeh fools!" he bellowed. "Come on! Yeh can't stay here. Yeh must come on." He said more, but much of it could not be understood.

He started rapidly forward, with his head turned toward the men. "Come on," he was shouting. The men stared with blank and yokel-like eyes at him. He was obliged to halt and retrace his steps. He stood then with his back to the enemy and delivered gigantic curses into the faces of the men. His body vibrated from the weight and force of his imprecations. And he could string oaths with the facility of a maiden who strings beads.

The friend of the youth aroused. Lurching suddenly forward and dropping to his knees, he fired an angry shot at the persistent woods. This action awakened the men. They huddled no more like sheep. They seemed suddenly to bethink them of their weapons, and at once commenced firing. Belabored by their officers, they began to move forward. The regiment, involved like a cart involved in mud and muddle, started unevenly with many jolts and jerks. The men stopped now every few paces to fire and load, and in this manner moved slowly on from trees to trees.

The flaming opposition in their front grew with their advance until it seemed that all forward ways were barred by the thin leaping tongues, and off to the right an ominous demonstration could sometimes be dimly discerned. The smoke lately generated was in confusing clouds that made it difficult for the regiment to proceed with intelligence. As he passed through each curling mass the youth wondered what would confront him on the farther side.

The command went painfully forward until an open space interposed between them and the lurid lines. Here, crouching and cowering behind some trees, the men clung with desperation, as if threatened by a wave. They looked wild-eyed, and as if amazed at this furious disturbance they had stirred. In the storm there was an ironical expression of their importance. The faces of the men, too, showed a lack of a certain feeling of responsibility for being there. It was as if they had been driven. It was the dominant animal failing to remember in the supreme moments the forceful causes of various superficial qualities. The whole affair seemed incomprehensible to many of them.

As they halted thus the lieutenant again began to bellow profanely. Regardless of the vindictive threats of the bullets, he went about coaxing, berating, and bedamning. His lips, that were habitually in a soft and childlike curve, were now writhed into unholy contortions. He swore by all possible deities.

Once he grabbed the youth by the arm. "Come on, yeh lunkhead!" he roared. "Come on! We'll all git killed if we stay here. We've on'y got t' go across that lot. An' then"—the remainder of his idea disappeared in a blue haze of curses.

The youth stretched forth his arm. "Cross there?" His mouth was puckered in doubt and awe.

"Certainly. Jest 'cross th' lot! We can't stay here," screamed the lieutenant. He poked his face close to the youth and waved his bandaged hand. "Come on!" Presently he grappled with him as if for a wrestling bout. It was as if he planned to drag the youth by the ear on to the assault.

The private felt a sudden unspeakable indignation against his officer. He wrenched fiercely and shook him off.

"Come on yerself, then," he yelled. There was a bitter challenge in his voice.

They galloped together down the regimental front. The friend scrambled after them. In front of the colors the three men began to bawl: "Come on! come on!" They danced and gyrated like tortured savages.

The flag, obedient to these appeals, bended its glittering form and swept toward them. The men wavered in indecision for a moment, and then with a long, wailful cry the dilapidated regiment surged forward and began its new journey.

Over the field went the scurrying mass. It was a handful of men splattered into the faces of the enemy. Toward it instantly sprang the yellow tongues. A vast quantity of blue smoke hung before them. A mighty banging made ears valueless.

The youth ran like a madman to reach the woods before a bullet could discover him. He ducked his head low, like a football player. In his haste his eyes almost closed, and the scene was a wild blur. Pulsating saliva stood at the corners of his mouth.

Within him, as he hurled himself forward, was born a love, a despairing fondness for this flag which was near him. It was a creation of beauty and invulnerability. It was a goddess, radiant, that bended its form with an imperious gesture to him. It was a woman, red and white, hating and loving, that called him with the voice of his hopes. Because no harm could come to it he endowed it with power. He kept near, as if it could be a saver of lives, and an imploring cry went from his mind.

In the mad scramble he was aware that the color sergeant flinched suddenly, as if struck by a bludgeon. He faltered, and then became motionless, save for his quivering knees.

He made a spring and a clutch at the pole. At the same instant his friend grabbed it from the other side. They jerked at it, stout and furious, but the color sergeant was dead, and the corpse would not relinquish its trust. For a moment there was a grim encounter. The dead man, swinging with bended back, seemed to be obstinately tugging, in ludicrous and awful ways, for the possession of the flag.

It was past in an instant of time. They wrenched the flag furiously from the dead man, and, as they turned again, the corpse swayed forward with bowed head. One arm swung high, and the curved hand fell with heavy protest on the friend's unheeding shoulder.

Chapter 20

When the two youths turned with the flag they saw that much of the regiment had crumbled away, and the dejected remnant was coming slowly back. The men, having hurled themselves in projectile fashion, had presently expended their forces. They slowly retreated, with their faces still toward the spluttering woods, and their hot rifles still replying to the din. Several officers were giving orders, their voices keyed to screams.

"Where in hell yeh goin'?" the lieutenant was asking in a sarcastic howl. And a red-bearded officer, whose voice of triple brass could plainly be heard, was commanding: "Shoot into 'em! Shoot into 'em, Gawd damn their souls!" There was a *melée* of screeches, in which the men were ordered to do conflicting and impossible things.

The youth and his friend had a small scuffle over the flag. "Give it t' me!" "No, let me keep it!" Each felt satisfied with the other's possession of it, but each felt bound to declare, by an offer to carry the emblem, his willingness to further risk himself. The youth roughly pushed his friend away.

The regiment fell back to the stolid trees. There it halted for a moment to blaze at some dark forms that had begun to steal upon its track. Presently it resumed its march again, curving among the tree trunks. By the time the depleted regiment had again reached the first open space they were receiving a fast and merciless fire. There seemed to be mobs all about them.

The greater part of the men, discouraged, their spirits worn by the turmoil, acted as if stunned. They accepted the pelting of the bullets with bowed and weary heads. It was of no purpose to strive against walls. It was of no use to batter themselves against granite. And from this consciousness that they had attempted to conquer an unconquerable thing there seemed to arise a feeling that they had been betrayed. They glowered with bent brows, but dangerously, upon some of the officers, more particularly upon the red-bearded one with the voice of triple brass.

However, the rear of the regiment was fringed with men, who continued to shoot irritably at the advancing foes. They seemed resolved to make every trouble. The youthful lieutenant was perhaps the last man in the disordered mass. His forgotten back was toward the enemy. He had been shot in the arm. It hung straight and rigid. Occasionally he would cease to remember it, and be about to emphasize an oath with a sweeping gesture. The multiplied pain caused him to swear with incredible power.

The youth went along with slipping, uncertain feet. He kept watchful eyes rearward. A scowl of mortification and rage was upon his face. He had thought of a fine revenge upon the officer who had referred to him and his fellows as mule drivers. But he saw that it could not come to pass. His dreams had collapsed when the mule drivers, dwindling rapidly, had wavered and hesitated on the little clearing, and then had recoiled. And now the retreat of the mule drivers was a march of shame to him.

A dagger-pointed gaze from without his blackened face was held toward the enemy, but his greater hatred was riveted upon the man, who, not knowing him, had called him a mule driver.

When he knew that he and his comrades had failed to do anything in successful ways that might bring the little pangs of a kind of remorse upon the officer, the youth allowed the rage of the baffled to possess him. This cold officer upon a monument, who dropped epithets unconcernedly down, would be finer as a dead man, he thought. So grievous did he think it that he could never possess the secret right to taunt truly in answer.

He had pictured red letters of curious revenge. "We *are* mule drivers, are we?" And now he was compelled to throw them away.

He presently wrapped his heart in the cloak of his pride and kept the flag erect. He harangued his fellows, pushing against their chests with his free hand. To those he knew well he made frantic appeals, beseeching them by name. Between him and the lieutenant, scolding and near to losing his mind with rage, there was felt a subtle fellowship and equality. They supported each other in all manner of hoarse, howling protests.

But the regiment was a machine run down. The two men babbled at a forceless thing. The soldiers who had heart to go slowly were continually shaken in their resolves by a knowledge that comrades were slipping with speed back to the lines. It was difficult to think of reputation when others were thinking of skins. Wounded men were left crying on this black journey.

The smoke fringes and flames blustered always. The youth, peering once through a sudden rift in a cloud, saw a brown mass of troops, interwoven and magnified until they appeared to be thousands. A fierce-hued flag flashed before his vision.

Immediately, as if the uplifting of the smoke had been prearranged, the discovered troops burst into a rasping yell, and a hundred flames jetted toward the retreating band. A rolling gray cloud again interposed as the regiment doggedly replied. The youth had to depend again upon his misused ears, which were trembling and buzzing from the *mêlée* of musketry and yells.

The way seemed eternal. In the clouded haze men became panicstricken with the thought that the regiment had lost its path, and was proceeding in a perilous direction. Once the men who headed the wild procession turned and came pushing back against their comrades, screaming that they were being fired upon from points which they had considered to be toward their own lines. At this cry a hysterical fear and dismay beset the troops. A soldier, who heretofore had been ambitious to make the regiment into a wise little band that would proceed calmly amid the huge-appearing difficulties, suddenly sank down and buried his face in his arms with an air of bowing to a doom. From another a shrill lamentation rang out filled with profane illusions to a general. Men ran hither and thither, seeking with their eyes roads of escape. With serene regularity, as if controlled by a schedule, bullets buffed into men.

The youth walked stolidly into the midst of the mob, and with his flag in his hands took a stand as if he expected an attempt to push him to the ground. He unconsciously assumed the attitude of color bearer in the fight of the preceding day. He passed over his brow a hand that trembled. His breath did not come freely. He was choking during this small wait for the crisis.

His friend came to him. "Well, Henry, I guess this is good-by—John."

"Oh, shut up, you damned fool!" replied the youth, and he would not look at the other.

The officers labored like politicians to beat the mass into a proper circle to face the menaces. The ground was uneven and torn. The men curled into depressions and fitted themselves snugly behind whatever would frustrate a bullet.

The youth noted with vague surprise that the lieutenant was standing mutely with his legs far apart and his sword held in the manner of a cane. The youth wondered what had happened to his vocal organs that he no more cursed.

There was something curious in this little intent pause of the lieutenant. He was like a babe which, having wept its fill, raises its eyes and fixes them upon a distant toy. He was engrossed in this contemplation, and the soft under lip quivered from self-whispered words.

Some lazy and ignorant smoke curled slowly. The men, hiding from the bullets, waited anxiously for it to lift and disclose the plight of the regiment.

The silent ranks were suddenly thrilled by the eager voice of the youthful lieutenant bawling out: "Here they come! Right onto us, b'Gawd!" His further words were lost in a roar of wicked thunder from the men's rifles.

The youth's eyes had instantly turned in the direction indicated by the awakened and agitated lieutenant, and he had seen the haze of treachery disclosing a body of soldiers of the enemy. They were so near that he could see their features. There was a recognition as he looked at the types of faces. Also he perceived with dim amazement that their uniforms were rather gay in effect, being light gray, accented with a brilliant-hued facing. Moreoever, the clothes seemed new.

These troops had apparently been going foward with caution, their rifles held in readiness, when the youthful lieutenant had discovered them and their movement had been interrupted by the volley from the blue regiment. From the moment's glimpse, it was derived that they had been unaware of the proximity of their dark-suited foes or had mistaken the direction. Almost instantly they were shut utterly from the youth's sight by the smoke from the energetic rifles of his companions. He strained his vision to learn the accomplishment of the volley, but the smoke hung before him.

The two bodies of troops exchanged blows in the manner of a pair of boxers. The fast angry firings went back and forth. The men in blue were intent with the despair of their circumstances and they seized upon the revenge to be had at close range. Their thunder swelled loud and valiant. Their curving front bristled with flashes and the place resounded with the clangor of their ramrods. The youth ducked and dodged for a time and achieved a few unsatisfactory views of the enemy. There appeared to be many of them and they were replying swiftly. They seemed moving toward the blue regiment, step by step. He seated himself gloomily on the ground with his flag between his knees.

As he noted the vicious, wolflike temper of his comrades he had a sweet thought that if the enemy was about to swallow the regimental broom as a large prisoner, it could at least have the consolation of going down with bristles forward.

But the blows of the antagonist began to grow more weak. Fewer bullets ripped the air, and finally, when the men slackened to learn of the fight, they could see only dark, floating smoke. The regiment lay still and gazed. Presently some chance whim came to the pestering blur, and it began to coil heavily away. The men saw a ground vacant of fighters. It would have been an empty stage if it were not for a few corpses that lay thrown and twisted into fantastic shapes upon the sward.

At sight of this tableau, many of the men in blue sprang from behind their covers and made an ungainly dance of joy. Their eyes burned and a hoarse cheer of elation broke from their dry lips.

It had begun to seem to them that events were trying to prove that they were impotent. These little battles had evidently endeavored to demonstrate that the men could not fight well. When on the verge of submission to these opinions, the small duel had showed them that the proportions were not impossible, and by it they had revenged themselves upon their misgivings and upon the foe.

The impetus of enthusiasm was theirs again. They gazed about them with looks of uplifted pride, feeling new trust in the grim, always confident weapons in their hands. And they were men.

Chapter 21

Presently they knew that no firing threatened them. All ways seemed once more opened to them. The dusty blue lines of their friends were disclosed a short distance away. In the distance there were many colossal noises, but in all this part of the field there was a sudden stillness.

They perceived that they were free. The depleted band drew a long breath of relief and gathered itself into a bunch to complete its trip.

In this last length of journey the men began to show strange emotions. They hurried with nervous fear. Some who had been dark and unfaltering in the grimmest moments now could not conceal an anxiety that made them frantic. It was perhaps that they dreaded to be killed in insignificant ways after the times for proper military deaths had passed. Or, perhaps, they thought it would be too ironical to get killed at the portals of safety. With backward looks of perturbation, they hastened.

As they approached their own lines there was some sarcasm exhibited on the part of a gaunt and bronzed regiment that lay resting in the shade of trees. Questions were wafted to them.

"Where th' hell yeh been?"

"What yeh comin' back fer?"

"Why didn't yeh stay there?"

"Was it warm out there, sonny?"

"Goin' home now, boys?"

One shouted in taunting mimicry: "Oh, mother, come quick an' look at th' sojers!"

There was no reply from the bruised and battered regiment, save that one man made broadcast challenges to fist fights and the red-bearded officer walked rather near and glared in great swashbuckler style at a tall captain in the other regiment. But the lieutenant suppressed the man who wished to fist fight, and the tall captain, flushing at the little fanfare of the red-bearded one, was obliged to look intently at some trees.

The youth's tender flesh was deeply stung by these remarks. From under his creased brows he glowered with hate at the mockers. He meditated upon a few revenges. Still, many in the regiment hung their heads in criminal fashion, so that it came to pass that the men trudged with sudden heaviness, as if they bore upon their bended shoulders the coffin of their honor. And the youthful lieutenant, recollecting himself, began to mutter softly in black curses.

They turned when they arrived at their old position to regard the ground over which they had charged.

The youth in this contemplation was smitten with a large astonishment. He discovered that the distances, as compared with the brilliant measurings of his mind, were trivial and ridiculous. The stolid trees, where much had taken place, seemed incredibly near. The time, too, now that he reflected, he saw to have been short. He wondered at the number of emotions and events that had been crowded into such little spaces. Elfin thoughts must have exaggerated and enlarged everything, he said.

It seemed, then, that there was bitter justice in the speeches of the gaunt and bronzed veterans. He veiled a glance of disdain at his fellows who strewed the ground, choking with dust, red from perspiration, misty-eyed, disheveled.

They were gulping at their canteens, fierce to wring every mite of water from them, and they polished at their swollen and watery features with coat sleeves and bunches of grass.

However, to the youth there was a considerable joy in musing upon his performances during the charge. He had had very little time previously in which to appreciate himself, so that there was now much satisfaction in quietly thinking of his actions. He recalled bits of color that in the flurry had stamped themselves unawares upon his engaged senses.

As the regiment lay heaving from its hot exertions the officer who had named them as mule drivers came galloping along the line. He had lost his cap. His tousled hair streamed wildly, and his face was dark with vexation and wrath. His temper was displayed with more clearness by the way in which he managed his horse. He jerked and wrenched savagely at his bridle, stopping the hard-breathing animal with a furious pull near the colonel of the regiment. He immediately exploded in reproaches which came unbidden to the ears of the men. They were suddenly alert, being always curious about black words between officers.

"Oh, thunder, MacChesnay, what an awful bull you made of this thing!" began the officer. He attempted low tones, but his indignation caused certain of the men to learn the sense of his words. "What an awful mess you made! Good Lord, man, you stopped about a hundred feet this side of a very pretty success! If your men had gone a hundred feet farther you would have made a great charge, but as it is—what a lot of mud diggers you've got anyway!"

The men, listening with bated breath, now turned their curious eyes upon the colonel. They had a ragamuffin interest in this affair.

The colonel was seen to straighten his form and put one hand forth in oratorical fashion. He wore an injured air; it was as if a deacon had been accused of stealing. The men were wiggling in an ecstasy of excitement.

But of a sudden the colonel's manner changed from that of a deacon to that of a Frenchman. He shrugged his shoulders. "Oh, well, general, we went as far as we could," he said calmly.

"As far as you could? Did you, b'Gawd?" snorted the other. "Well, that wasn't very far, was it?" he added, with a glance of cold contempt into the other's eyes. "Not very far, I think. You were intended to make a diversion in favor of Whiterside. How well you succeeded your own ears can now tell you."

He wheeled his horse and rode stiffly away.

The colonel, bidden to hear the jarring noises of an engagement in the woods to the left, broke out in vague damnations.

The lieutenant, who had listened with an air of impotent rage to the interview, spoke suddenly in firm and undaunted tones. "I don't care what a man is—whether he is a general or what—if he says th' boys didn't put up a good fight out there he's a damned fool."

"Lieutenant," began the colonel, severely, "this is my own affair, and I'll trouble you——"

The lieutenant made an obedient gesture. "All right, colonel, all right," he said. He sat down with an air of being content with himself.

The news that the regiment had been reproached went along the line. For a time the men were bewildered by it. "Good thunder!" they ejaculated, staring at the vanishing form of the general. They conceived it to be a huge mistake.

Presently, however, they began to believe that in truth their efforts had been called light. The youth could see this conviction weigh upon the entire regiment until the men were like cuffed and cursed animals, but withal rebellious.

The friend, with a grievance in his eye, went to the youth. "I wonder what he does want," he said. "He must think we went out there an' played marbles! I never see sech a man!"

The youth developed a tranquil philosophy for these moments of irritation. "Oh, well," he rejoined, "he probably didn't see nothing of it at all and got mad as blazes, and concluded we were a lot of sheep, just because we didn't do what he wanted done. It's a pity old Grandpa Henderson got killed yestirday—he'd have known that we did our best and fought good. It's just our awful luck, that's what."

"I should say so," replied the friend. He seemed to be deeply wounded at an injustice. "I should say we did have awful luck! There's no fun in fightin' fer people when everything yeh do—no matter what—ain't done right. I have a notion t' stay behind next time an' let 'em take their ol' charge an' go t' th' devil with it."

The youth spoke soothingly to his comrade. "Well, we both did good. I'd like to see the fool what'd say we both didn't do as good as we could!"

"Of course we did," declared the friend stoutly. "An' I'd break th' feller's neck if he was as big as a church. But we're all right, anyhow, for I heard one feller say that we two fit th' best in th' reg'ment, an' they had a great argument 'bout it. Another feller, 'a course, he had t' up an' say it was a lie—he seen all what was goin' on an' he never seen us from th' beginnin' t' th' end. An' a lot more struck in an' ses it wasn't a lie—we did fight like thunder, an' they give us quite a send-off. But this is what I can't stand—these everlastin' ol' soldiers, titterin' an' laughin,' an' then that general, he's crazy."

The youth exclaimed with sudden exasperation: "He's a lunkhead! He makes me mad. I wish he'd come along next time. We'd show 'im what——"

He ceased because several men had come hurrying up. Their faces expressed a bringing of great news.

"O Flem, yeh jest oughta heard!" cried one, eagerly.

"Heard what?" said the youth.

"Yeh jest oughta heard!" repeated the other, and he arranged himself to tell his tidings. The others made an excited circle. "Well, sir, th' colonel met your lieutenant right by us—it was damnedest thing I ever heard—an' he ses: 'Ahem! ahem! he ses. 'Mr. Hasbrouck!' he ses, 'by th' way, who was that lad what carried th' flag?' he ses. There, Flemin', what d' yeh think 'a that? 'Who was th' lad what carried th' flag?' he ses, an' th' lieutenant, he speaks up right away: 'That's Flemin', an' he's a jimhickey,' he ses, right away. What? I say he did. 'A jimhickey,' he ses—those 'r his words. He did, too. I say he did. If you kin tell this story better than I kin, go ahead an' tell it. Well, then, keep yer mouth shet. Th' lieutenant, he ses: 'He's a jimhickey,' an' th' colonel, he ses: 'Ahem! ahem! he is, indeed, a very good man t' have, ahem! He kep' th' flag 'way t' th' front. I saw 'im. He's a good un,' ses th' colonel. 'You bet,' ses th' lieutenant, 'he an' a feller named Wilson was at th' head 'a th' charge, an' howlin' like Indians all th' time,' he ses. 'Head 'a th' charge all th' time,' he ses. 'A feller named Wilson,' he ses. There, Wilson, m'boy, put that in a letter an' send it hum t' yer mother, hay? 'A feller named Wilson,' he ses. An' th' colonel, he ses: 'Were they, indeed? Ahem! ahem! My sakes!' he ses. 'At th' head 'a th' reg'ment?' he ses. 'They were,' es th' lieutenant. 'My sakes!' ses th' colonel. He ses: 'Well, well, well,' he ses, 'those two babies?' 'They were,' ses th' lieutenant. 'Well, well,' ses th' colonel, 'they deserve t' be major generals,' he ses. 'They deserve t' be major-generals.'

The youth and his friend had said: "Huh!" "Yer lyin', Thompson." "Oh, go t' blazes!" "He never sed it." "Oh what a lie!" "Huh!" But despite these youthful scoffings and embarrassments, they knew that their faces were deeply flushing from thrills of pleasure. They exchanged a secret glance of joy and congratulation.

They speedily forgot many things. The past held no pictures of error and disappointment. They were very happy, and their hearts swelled with grateful affection for the colonel and the youthful lieutenant.

Chapter 22

When the woods again began to pour forth the dark-hued masses of the enemy the youth felt serene self-confidence. He smiled briefly when he saw men dodge and duck at the long screechings of shells that were thrown in giant handfuls over them. He stood, erect and tranquil, watching the attack begin against a part of the line that made a blue curve along the side of an adjacent hill. His vision being unmolested by smoke from the rifles of his companions, he had opportunities to see parts of the hard fight. It was a relief to perceive at last from whence came some of these noises which had been roared into his ears.

Off a short way he saw two regiments fighting a little separate battle with two other regiments. It was in a cleared space, wearing a set-apart look. They were blazing as if upon a wager, giving and taking tremendous blows. The firings were incredibly fierce and rapid. These intent regiments apparently were oblivious of all larger purposes of war, and were slugging each other as if at a matched game.

In another direction he saw a magnificent brigade going with the evident intention of driving the enemy from a wood. They passed in out of sight and presently there was a most awe-inspiring racket in the wood. The noise was unspeakable. Having stirred this prodigious uproar, and, apparently, finding it too prodigious, the brigade, after a little time, came marching airily out again with its fine formation in nowise disturbed. There were no traces of speed in its movements. The brigade was jaunty and seemed to point a proud thumb at the yelling wood.

On a slope to the left there was a long row of guns, gruff and maddened, denouncing the enemy, who, down through the woods, were forming for another attack in the pitiless monotony of conflicts. The round red discharges from the guns made a crimson flare and a high, thick smoke. Occasional glimpses could be caught of groups of the toiling artillerymen. In the rear of this row of guns stood a house, calm and white, amid bursting shells. A congregation of horses, tied to a long railing, were tugging frenziedly at their bridles. Men were running hither and thither.

The detached battle between the four regiments lasted for some time. There chanced to be no interference, and they settled their dispute by themselves.

They struck savagely and powerfully at each other for a period of minutes, and then the lighter-hued regiments faltered and drew back, leaving the dark-blue lines shouting. The youth could see the two flags shaking with laughter amid the smoke remnants.

Presently there was a stillness, pregnant with meaning. The blue lines shifted and changed a trifle and stared expectantly at the silent woods and fields before them. The hush was solemn and churchlike, save for a distant battery that, evidently unable to remain quiet, sent a faint rolling thunder over the ground. It irritated, like the noises of unimpressed boys. The men imagined that it would prevent their perched ears from hearing the first words of the new battle.

Of a sudden the guns on the slope roared out a message of warning. A spluttering sound had begun in the woods. It swelled with amazing speed to a profound clamor that involved the earth in noises. The splitting crashes swept along the lines until an interminable roar was developed. To those in the midst of it it became a din fitted to the universe. It was the whirring and thumping of gigantic machinery, complications among the smaller stars. The youth's ears were filled up. They were incapable of hearing more.

On an incline over which a road wound he saw wild and desperate rushes of men perpetually backward and forward in riotous surges. These parts of the opposing armies were two long waves that pitched upon each other madly at dictated points. To and fro they swelled. Sometimes, one side by its yells and cheers would proclaim decisive blows, but a moment later the other side would be all yells and cheers. Once the youth saw a spray of light forms go in houndlike leaps toward the waving blue lines. There was much howling, and presently it went away with a vast mouthful of prisoners. Again, he saw a blue wave dash with such thunderous force against a gray obstruction that it seemed to clear the earth of it and leave nothing but trampled sod. And always in their swift and deadly rushes to and fro the men screamed and yelled like maniacs.

Particular pieces of fence or secure positions behind collections of trees were wrangled over, as gold thrones or pearl bedsteads. There were desperate lunges at these chosen spots seemingly every instant, and most of them were bandied like light toys between the contending forces. The youth could not tell from the battle flags flying like crimson foam in many directions which color of cloth was winning.

His emaciated regiment bustled forth with undiminished fierceness when its time came. When assaulted again by bullets, the men burst out in a barbaric cry of rage and pain. They bent their heads in aims of intent hatred behind the projected hammers of their guns. Their ramrods clanged loud with fury as their eager arms pounded the cartridges into the rifle barrels. The front of the regiment was a smoke-wall penetrated by the flashing points of yellow and red.

Wallowing in the fight, they were in an astonishingly short time resmudged. They surpassed in stain and dirt all their previous appearances. Moving to and fro with strained exertion, jabbering the while, they were, with their swaying bodies, black faces, and glowing eyes, like strange and ugly friends jigging heavily in the smoke.

The lieutenant, returning from a tour after a bandage, produced from a hidden receptacle of his mind new and portentous oaths suited to the emergency. Strings of expletives he swung lashlike over the backs of his men, and it was evident that his previous efforts had in nowise impaired his resources.

The youth, still the bearer of the colors, did not feel his idleness. He was deeply absorbed as a spectator. The crash and swing of the great drama made him lean forward, intent-eyed, his face working in small contortions. Sometimes he prattled, words coming unconsciously from him in grotesque exclamations. He did not know that he breathed; that the flag hung silently over him, so absorbed was he.

A formidable line of the enemy came within dangerous range. They could be seen plainly—tall, gaunt men with excited faces running with long strides toward a wandering fence.

At sight of this danger the men suddenly ceased their cursing monotone. There was an instant of strained silence before they threw up their rifles and fired a plumping volley at the foes. There had been no order given; the men, upon recognizing the menace, had immediately let drive their flock of bullets without waiting for word of command.

But the enemy were quick to gain the protection of the wandering line of fence. They slid down behind it with remarkable celerity, and from this position they began briskly to slice up the blue men.

These latter braced their energies for a great struggle. Often, white clinched teeth shone from the dusky faces. Many heads surged to and fro, floating upon a pale sea of smoke. Those behind the fence frequently shouted and yelped in taunts and gibelike cries, but the regiment maintained a stressed silence. Perhaps, at this new assault the men recalled the fact that they had been named mud diggers, and it made their situation thrice bitter. They were breathlessly intent upon keeping the ground and thrusting away the rejoicing body of the enemy. They fought swiftly and with a despairing savageness denoted in their expressions.

The youth had resolved not to budge whatever should happen. Some arrows of scorn that had buried themselves in his heart had generated strange and unspeakable hatred. It was clear to him that his final and absolute revenge was to be achieved by his dead body lying, torn and gluttering, upon the field. This was to be a poignant retaliation upon the officer who had said "mule drivers," and later "mud diggers," for in all the wild graspings of his mind for a unit responsible for his sufferings and commotions he always seized upon the man who had dubbed him wrongly. And it was his idea, vaguely formulated, that his corpse would be for those eyes a great and salt reproach.

The regiment bled extravagantly. Grunting bundles of blue began to drop. The orderly sergeant of the youth's company was shot through the cheeks. Its supports being injured, his jaw hung afar down, disclosing in the wide cavern of his mouth a pulsing mass of blood and teeth. And with it all he made attempts to cry out. In his endeavor there was a dreadful earnestness, as if he conceived that one great shriek would make him well.

The youth saw him presently go rearward. His strength seemed in nowise impaired. He ran swiftly, casting wild glances for succor.

Others fell down about the feet of their companions. Some of the wounded crawled out and away, but many lay still, their bodies twisted into impossible shapes.

The youth looked once for his friend. He saw a vehement young man, powder-smeared and frowzled, whom he knew to be him. The lieutenant, also, was unscathed in his position at the rear. He had continued to curse, but it was now with the air of a man who was using his last box of oaths.

For the fire of the regiment had begun to wane and drip. The robust voice, that had come strangely from the thin ranks, was growing rapidly weak.

Chapter 23

The colonel came running along back of the line. There were other officers following him. "We must charge'm!" they shouted. "We must charge'm!" they cried with resentful voices, as if anticipating a rebellion against this plan by the men.

The youth, upon hearing the shouts, began to study the distance between him and the enemy. He made vague calculations. He saw that to be firm soldiers they must go forward. It would be death to stay in the present place, and with all the circumstances to go backward would exalt too many others. Their hope was to push the galling foes away from the fence.

He expected that his companions, weary and stiffened, would have to be driven to this assault, but as he turned toward them he perceived with a certain surprise that they were giving quick and unqualified expressions of assent. There was an ominous, clanging overture to the charge when the shafts of the bayonets rattled upon the rifle barrels. At the yelled words of command the soldiers sprang forward in eager leaps. There was new and unexpected force in the movement of the regiment. A knowledge of its faded and jaded condition made the charge appear like a paroxysm, a display of the strength that comes before a final feebleness. The men scampered in insane fever of haste, racing as if to achieve a sudden success before an exhilarating fluid should leave them. It was a blind and despairing rush by the collection of men in dusty and tattered blue, over a green sward and under a sapphire sky, toward a fence, dimly outlined in smoke, from behind which spluttered the fierce rifles of enemies.

The youth kept the bright colors to the front. He was waving his free arm in furious circles, the while shrieking mad calls and appeals, urging on those that did not need to be urged, for it seemed that the mob of blue men hurling themselves on the dangerous group of rifles were again grown suddenly wild with an enthusiasm of unselfishness. From the many firings starting toward them, it looked as if they would merely succeed in making a great sprinkling of corpses on the grass between their former position and the fence. But they were in a state of frenzy, perhaps because of forgotten vanities, and it made an exhibition of sublime recklessness. There was no obvious questioning, nor figurings, nor diagrams. There was, apparently, no considered loopholes. It appeared that the swift wings of their desires would have shattered against the iron gates of the impossible.

He himself felt the daring spirit of a savage religion-mad. He was capable of profound sacrifices, a tremendous death. He had no time for dissections, but he knew that he thought of the bullets only as things that could prevent him from reaching the place of his endeavor. There were subtle flashings of joy within him that thus should be his mind.

He strained all his strength. His eyesight was shaken and dazzled by the tension of thought and muscle. He did not see anything excepting the mist of smoke gashed by the little knives of fire, but he knew that in it lay the aged fence of a vanished farmer protecting the snuggled bodies of the gray men.

As he ran a thought of the shock of contact gleamed in his mind. He expected a great concussion when the two bodies of troops crashed together. This became a part of his wild battle madness. He could feel the onward swing of the regiment about him and he conceived of a thunderous, crushing blow that would prostrate the resistance and spread consternation and amazement for miles. The flying regiment was going to have a catapultian effect. This dream made him run faster among his comrades, who were giving vent to hoarse and frantic cheers.

But presently he could see that many of the men in gray did not intend to abide the blow. The smoke, rolling, disclosed men who ran, their faces still turned. These grew to a crowd, who retired stubbornly. Individuals wheeled frequently to send a bullet at the blue wave.

But at one part of the line there was a grim and obdurate group that made no movement. They were settled firmly down behind posts and rails. A flag, ruffled and fierce, waved over them and their rifles dinned fiercely.

The blue whirl of men got very near, until it seemed that in truth there would be a close and frightful scuffle. There was an expressed disdain in the opposition of the little group, that changed the meaning of the cheers of the men in blue. They became yells of wrath, directed, personal. The cries of the two parties were now in sound an interchange of scathing insults.

They in blue showed their teeth; their eyes shone all white. They launched themselves as at the throats of those who stood resisting. The space between dwindled to an insignificant distance.

The youth had centered the gaze of his soul upon that other flag. Its possession would be high pride. It would express bloody minglings, near blows. He had a gigantic hatred for those who made great difficulties and complications. They caused it to be as a craved treasure of mythology, hung amid tasks and contrivances of danger.

He plunged like a mad horse at it. He was resolved it should not escape if wild blows and darings of blows could seize it. His own emblem, quivering and aflare, was winging toward the other. It seemed there would shortly be an encounter of strange beaks and claws, as of eagles.

The swirling body of blue men came to a sudden halt at close and disastrous range and roared a swift volley. The group in gray was split and broken by this fire, but its riddled body still fought. The men in blue yelled again and rushed in upon it.

The youth, in his leapings, saw, as through a mist, a picture of four or five men stretched upon the ground or writhing upon their knees with bowed heads as if they had been stricken by bolts from the sky. Tottering among them was the rival color bearer, whom the youth saw had been bitten vitally by the bullets of the last formidable volley. He perceived this man fighting a last struggle, the struggle of one whose legs are grasped by demons. It was a ghastly battle. Over his face was the bleach of death, but set upon it was the dark and hard lines of desperate purpose. With this terrible grin of resolution he hugged his precious flag to him and was stumbling and staggering in his design to go the way that led to safety for it.

But his wounds always made it seem that his feet were retarded, held, and he fought a grim fight, as with invisible ghouls fastened greedily upon his limbs. Those in advance of the scampering blue men, howling cheers, leaped at the fence. The despair of the lost was in his eyes as he glanced back at them.

The youth's friend went over the obstruction in a tumbling heap and sprang at the flag as a panther at prey. He pulled at it and, wrenching it free, swung up its red brilliancy with a mad cry of exultation even as the color bearer, gasping, lurched over in a final throe and, stiffening convulsively, turned his dead face to the ground. There was much blood upon the grass blades.

At the place of success there began more wild clamorings of cheers. The men gesticulated and bellowed in an ecstasy. When they spoke it was as if they considered their listener to be a mile away. What hats and caps were left to them they often slung high in the air.

At one part of the line four men had been swooped upon, and they now sat as prisoners. Some blue men were about them in an eager and curious circle. The soldiers had trapped strange birds, and there was an examination. A flurry of fast questions was in the air.

One of the prisoners was nursing a superficial wound in the foot. He cuddled it, baby-wise, but he looked up from it often to curse with an astonishing utter abandon straight at the noses of his captors. He consigned them to red regions; he called upon the pestilential wrath of strange gods. And with it all he was singularly free from recognition of the finer points of the conduct of prisoners of war. It was as if a clumsy clod had trod upon his toe and he conceived it to be his privilege, his duty, to use deep, resentful oaths.

Another, who was a boy in years, took his plight with great calmness and apparent good nature. He conversed with the men in blue, studying their faces with his bright and keen eyes. They spoke of battles and conditions. There was an acute interest in all their faces during this exchange of view points. It seemed a great satisfaction to hear voices from where all had been darkness and speculation.

The third captive sat with a morose countenance. He preserved a stoical and cold attitude. To all advances he made one reply without variation, "Ah, go t' hell!"

The last of the four was always silent and, for the most part, kept his face turned in unmolested directions. From the views the youth received he seemed to be in a state of absolute dejection. Shame was upon him, and with it profound regret that he was, perhaps, no more to be counted in the ranks of his fellows. The youth could detect no expression that would allow him to believe that the other was giving a thought to his narrowed future, the pictured dungeons, perhaps, and starvations and brutalities, liable to the imagination. All to be seen was shame for captivity and regret for the right to antagonize.

After the men had celebrated sufficiently they settled down behind the old rail fence, on the opposite side to the one from which their foes had been driven. A few shot perfunctorily at distant marks.

There was some long grass. The youth nestled in it and rested, making a convenient rail support the flag. His friend, jubilant, and glorified, holding his treasure with vanity, came to him there. They sat side by side and congratulated each other.

Chapter 24

The roarings that had stretched in a long line of sound across the face of the forest began to grow intermittent and weaker. The stentorian speeches of the artillery continued in some distant encounter, but the crashes of the musketry had almost ceased. The youth and his friend of a sudden looked up, feeling a deadened form of distress at the waning of these noises, which had become a part of life. They could see changes going on among the troops. There were marchings this way and that way. A battery wheeled leisurely. On the crest of a small hill was the thick gleam of many departing muskets.

The youth arose. "Well, what now, I wonder?" he said. By his tone he seemed to be preparing to resent some new monstrosity in the way of dins and smashes. He shaded his eyes with his grimy hand and gazed over the field.

His friend also arose and stared. "I bet we're goin' t' git along out of this an' back over th' river," said he.

"Well, I swan!" said the youth.

They waited, watching. Within a little while the regiment received orders to retrace its way. The men got up grunting from the grass, regretting the soft repose. They jerked their stiffened legs, and stretched their arms over their heads. One man swore as he rubbed his eyes. They all groaned "O Lord!" They had as many objections to this change as they would have had to a proposal for a new battle.

They trampled slowly back over the field across which they had run in a mad scamper.

The regiment marched until it had joined its fellows. The reformed brigade, in column, aimed through a wood at the road. Directly they were in a mass of dust-covered troops, and were trudging along in a way parallel to the enemy's lines as these had been defined by the previous turmoil.

They passed within view of a stolid white house, and saw in front of it groups of their comrades lying in wait behind a neat breastwork. A row of guns were booming at a distant enemy. Shells thrown in reply were raising clouds of dust and splinters. Horsemen dashed along the line of intrenchments.

At this point of its march the division curved away from the field and went

101

winding off in the direction of the river. When the significance of this movement had impressed itself upon the youth he turned his head and looked over his shoulder toward the trampled and *débris*-strewed ground. He breathed a breath of new satisfaction. He finally nudged his friend. "Well, it's all over," he said to him.

His friend gazed backward. 'B'Gawd, it is," he assented. They mused.

For a time the youth was obliged to reflect in a puzzled and uncertain way. His mind was undergoing a subtle change. It took moments for it to cast off its battleful ways and resume its accustomed course of thought. Gradually his brain emerged from the clogged clouds, and at last he was enabled to more closely comprehend himself and circumstance.

He understood then that the existence of shot and counter-shot was in the past. He had dwelt in a land of strange, squalling upheavals and had come forth. He had been where there was red of blood and black of passion, and he was escaped. His first thoughts were given to rejoicings at this fact.

Later he began to study his deeds, his failures, and his achievements. Thus, fresh from scenes where many of his usual machines of reflection had been idle, from where he had proceeded sheeplike, he struggled to marshal all his acts.

At last they marched before him clearly. From this present view point he was enabled to look upon them in spectator fashion and to criticise them with some correctness, for his new condition had already defeated certain sympathies.

Regarding his procession of memory he felt gleeful and unregretting, for in it his public deeds were paraded in great and shining prominence. Those performances which had been witnessed by his fellows marched now in wide purple and gold, having various deflections. They went gayly with music. It was pleasure to watch these things. He spent delightful minutes viewing the gilded images of memory.

He saw that he was good. He recalled with a thrill of joy the respectful comments of his fellows upon his conduct.

Nevertheless, the ghost of his flight from the first engagement appeared to him and danced. There were small shoutings in his brain about these matters. For a moment he blushed, and the light of his soul flickered with shame.

A specter of reproach came to him. There loomed the dogging memory of the tattered soldier—he who, gored by bullets and faint for blood, had fretted concerning an imagined wound in another; he who had loaned his last of strength and intellect for the tall soldier; he who, blind with weariness and pain, had been deserted in the field.

For an instant a wretched chill of sweat was upon him at the thought that he might be detected in the thing. As he stood persistently before his vision, he gave vent to a cry of sharp irritation and agony.

His friend turned. "What's the matter, Henry?" he demanded. The youth's reply was an outburst of crimson oaths.

As he marched along the little branch-hung roadway among his prattling companions this vision of cruelty brooded over him. It clung near him always and darkened his view of these deeds in purple and gold. Whichever way his thoughts turned they were followed by the somber phantom of the desertion in the fields. He looked stealthily at his companions, feeling sure that they must discern in his face evidences of this pursuit. But they were plodding in ragged array, discussing with quick tongues the accomplishments of the late battle.

"Oh, if a man should come up an' ask me, I'd say we got a dum good lickin'."

"Lickin'—in yer eye! We ain't licked, sonny. We're goin' down here aways, swing aroun', an' come in behint 'em."

"Oh, hush, with your comin' in behint 'em. I've seen all 'a that I wanta. Don't tell me about comin' in behint——"

"Bill Smithers, he ses he'd rather been in ten hundred battles than been in that heluva hospital. He ses they got shootin' in th' night-time, an' shells dropped plum among 'em in th' hospital. He ses sech hollerin' he never see."

"Hasbrouck? He's th' best off'cer in this here reg'ment. He's a whale."

"Didn't I tell yeh we'd come aroun' in behint 'em? Didn't I tell yeh so? We——"

"Oh, shet yeh mouth!"

For a time this pursuing recollection of the tattered man took all elation from the youth's veins. He saw his vivid error, and he was afraid that it would stand before him all his life. He took no share in the chatter of his comrades, nor did he look at them or know them, save when he felt sudden suspicion that they were seeing his thoughts and scrutinizing each detail of the scene with the tattered soldier.

Yet gradually he mustered force to put the sin at a distance. And at last his eyes seemed to open to some new ways. He found that he could look back upon the brass and bombast of his earlier gospels and see them truly. He was gleeful when he discovered that he now despised them.

With this conviction came a store of assurance. He felt a quiet manhood, nonassertive but of sturdy and strong blood. He kew that he would no more quail before his guides wherever they should point. He had been to touch the great death, and found that, after all, it was but the great death. He was a man.

So it came to pass that as he trudged from the place of blood and wrath his soul changed. He came from hot plowshares to prospects of clover tranquilly, and it was as if hot plowshares were not. Scars faded as flowers.

It rained. The procession of weary soldiers became a bedraggled train, despondent and muttering, marching with churning effort in a trough of liquid brown mud under a low, wretched sky. Yet the youth smiled, for he saw that the world was a world for him, though many discovered it to be made of oaths and walking sticks. He had rid himself of the red sickness of battle. The sultry nightmare was in the past. He had been an animal blistered and sweating in the heat and pain of war. He turned now with a lover's thirst to images of tranquil skies, fresh meadows, cool brooks—an existence of soft and eternal peace.

Over the river a golden ray of sun came through the hosts of leaden rain clouds.

THE
LITTLE REGIMENT

and other episodes
of the American Civil War

CONTENTS

THE LITTLE REGIMENT

The fog made the clothes of the men of the column in the roadway seem of a luminous quality. It imparted to the heavy infantry overcoats a new colour, a kind of blue which was so pale that a regiment might have been merely a long, low shadow in the mist. However, a muttering, one part grumble, three parts joke, hovered in the air above the thick ranks, and blended in an undertoned roar, which was the voice of the column.

The town on the southern shore of the little river loomed spectrally, a faint etching upon the gray cloud-masses which were shifting with oily languor. A long row of guns upon the northern bank had been pitiless in their hatred, but a little battered belfry could be dimly seen still pointing with invincible resolution toward the heavens.

The enclouded air vibrated with noises made by hidden colossal things. The infantry tramplings, the heavy rumbling of the artillery, made the earth speak of gigantic preparation. Guns on distant heights thundered from time to time with sudden, nervous roar, as if unable to endure in silence a knowledge of hostile troops massing, other guns going to position. These sounds, near and remote, defined an immense battleground, described the tremendous width of the stage of the prospective drama. The voices of the guns, slightly casual, unexcited in their challenges and warnings, could not destroy the unutterable eloquence of the word in the air, a meaning of impending struggle which made the breath halt at the lips.

The column in the roadway was ankle-deep in mud. The men swore piously at the rain which drizzled upon them, compelling them to stand always very erect in fear of the drops that would sweep in under their coat-collars. The fog was as cold as wet cloths. The men stuffed their hands deep in their pockets, and huddled their muskets in their arms. The machinery of orders had rooted these soldiers deeply into the mud precisely as almighty nature roots mullein stalks.

They listened and speculated when a tumult of fighting came from the dim town across the river. When the noise lulled for a time they resumed their descriptions of the mud and graphically exaggerated the number of hours they had been kept waiting. The general commanding their division rode along the ranks, and they cheered admiringly, affectionately, crying out to him gleeful prophecies of the coming battle. Each man scanned him with a peculiarly keen personal interest, and afterward spoke of him with unquestioning devotion and

109

confidence, narrating anecdotes which were mainly untrue.

When the jokers lifted the shrill voices which invariably belonged to them, flinging witticisms at their comrades, a loud laugh would sweep from rank to rank, and soldiers who had not heard would lean forward and demand repetition. When were borne past them some wounded men with gray and blood-smeared faces, and eyes that rolled in that helpless beseeching for assistance from the sky which comes with supreme pain, the soldiers in the mud watched intently, and from time to time asked of the bearers an account of the affair. Frequently they bragged of their corps, their division, their brigade, their regiment. Anon they referred to the mud and the cold drizzle. Upon this threshold of a wild scene of death they, in short, defied the proportion of events with that splendour of heedlessness which belongs only to veterans.

"Like a lot of wooden soldiers," swore Billie Dempster, moving his feet in the thick mass, and casting a vindictive glance indefinitely; "standing in the mud for a hundred years."

"Oh, shut up!" murmured his brother Dan. The manner of his words implied that this fraternal voice near him was an indescribable bore.

"Why should I shut up?" demanded Billie.

"Because you're a fool," cried Dan, taking no time to debate it; "the biggest fool in the regiment."

There was but one man between them, and he was habituated. These insults from brother to brother had swept across his chest, flown past his face, many times during two long campaigns. Upon this occasion he simply grinned first at one, then at the other.

The way of these brothers was not an unknown topic in regimental gossip. They had enlisted simultaneously, with each sneering loudly at the other for doing it. They left their little town, and went forward with the flag, exchanging protestations of undying suspicion. In the camp life they so openly despised each other that, when entertaining quarrels were lacking, their companions often contrived situations calculated to bring forth display of this fraternal dislike.

Both were large-limbed, strong young men, and often fought with friends in camp unless one was near to interfere with the other. This latter happened rather frequently, because Dan, preposterously willing for any manner of combat, had a very great horror of seeing Billie in a fight; and Billie, almost odiously ready himself, simply refused to see Dan stripped to his shirt and with his fists aloft. This sat queerly upon them, and made them the objects of plots.

When Dan jumped through a ring of eager soldiers and dragged forth his raving brother by the arm, a thing often predicted would almost come to pass. When Billie performed the same office for Dan, the prediction would again miss fulfilment by an inch. But indeed they never fought together, although they were perpetually upon the verge.

They expressed longing for such conflict. As a matter of truth, they had at one time made full arrangement for it, but even with the encouragement and interest of half of the regiment they somehow failed to achieve collision.

If Dan became a victim of police duty, no jeering was so destructive to the feelings as Billie's comment. If Billie got a call to appear at the headquarters, none would so genially prophesy his complete undoing as Dan. Small misfortunes to one were, in truth, invariably greeted with hilarity by the other, who seemed to see in them great re-enforcement of his opinion.

As soldiers, they expressed each for each a scorn intense and blasting. After a certain battle, Billie was promoted to corporal. When Dan was told of it, he seemed smitten dumb with astonishment and patriotic indignation. He stared in silence, while the dark blood rushed to Billie's forehead, and he shifted his weight from foot to foot. Dan at last found his tongue, and said: "Well, I'm durned!" If he had heard that an army mule had been appointed to the post of corps commander, his tone could not have had more derision in it. Afterward, he adopted a fervid insubordination, an almost religious reluctance to obey the new corporal's orders, which came near to developing the desired strife.

It is here finally to be recorded also that Dan, most ferociously profane in speech, very rarely swore in the presence of his brother; and that Billie, whose oaths came from his lips with the grace of falling pebbles, was seldom known to express himself in this manner when near his brother Dan.

At last the afternoon contained a suggestion of evening. Metallic cries rang suddenly from end to end of the column. They inspired at once a quick, business-like adjustment. The long thing stirred in the mud. The men had hushed, and were looking across the river. A moment later the shadowy mass of pale blue figures was moving steadily toward the stream. There could be heard from the town a clash of swift fighting and cheering. The noise of the shooting coming through the heavy air had its sharpness taken from it, and sounded in thuds.

There was a halt upon the bank above the pontoons. When the column went winding down the incline, and streamed out upon the bridge, the fog had faded to a great degree, and in the clearer dusk the guns on a distant ridge were enabled to perceive the crossing. The long whirling outcries of the shells came into the air above the men. An occasional solid shot struck the surface of the river, and dashed into view a sudden vertical jet. The distance was subtly illuminated by the lightning from the deep-booming guns. One by one the batteries on the northern shore aroused, the innumerable guns bellowing in angry oration at the distant ridge. The rolling thunder crashed and reverberated as a wild surf sounds on a still night, and to this music the column marched across the pontoons.

The waters of the grim river curled away in a smile from the ends of the great boats and slid swiftly beneath the planking. The dark, riddled walls of the town upreared before the troops, and from a region hidden by these hammered and tumbled houses came incessantly the yells and firings of a prolonged and close skirmish.

When Dan had called his brother a fool, his voice had been so decisive, so brightly assured, that many men had laughed, considering it to be great humour under the circumstances. The incident happened to rankle deep in Billie. It was not any strange thing that his brother had called him a fool. In fact, he often called him a fool with exactly the same amount of cheerful and prompt conviction, and before large audiences, too. Billie wondered in his own mind why he took such profound offence in this case; but, at any rate, as he slid down the bank and on to the bridge with his regiment, he was searching his knowledge for something that would pierce Dan's blithesome spirit. But he could contrive nothing at this time, and his impotency made the glance which he was once able to give his brother still more malignant.

The guns far and near were roaring a fearful and grand introduction for this column which was marching upon the stage of death. Billie felt it, but only in a numb way. His heart was cased in that curious dissonant metal which covers a man's emotions at such times. The terrible voices from the hills told him that in this wide conflict his life was an insignificant fact, and that his death would be an insignificant fact. They portended the whirlwind to which he would be as necessary as a butterfly's waved wing. The solemnity, the sadness of it came near enough to make him wonder why he was neither solemn nor sad. When his mind vaguely adjusted events according to their importance to him, it appeared that the uppermost thing was the fact that upon the eve of battle, and before many comrades, his brother had called him a fool.

Dan was in a particularly happy mood. "Hurray! Look at 'em shoot," he said, when the long witches' croon of the shells came into the air. It enraged Billie when he felt the little thorn in him, and saw at the same time that his brother had completely forgotten it.

The column went from the bridge into more mud. At this southern end there was a chaos of hoarse directions and commands. Darkness was coming upon the earth, and regiments were being hurried up the slippery bank. As Billie floundered in the black mud, amid the swearing, sliding crowd, he suddenly resolved that, in the absence of other means of hurting Dan, he would avoid looking at him, refrain from speaking to him, pay absolutely no heed to his existence; and this done skilfully would, he imagined, soon reduce his brother to a poignant sensitiveness.

At the top of the bank the column again halted and rearranged itself, as a man after a climb rearranges his clothing. Presently the great steel-backed brigade, an infinitely graceful thing in the rhythm and ease of its veteran movement, swung up a little narrow, slanting street.

Evening had come so swiftly that the fighting on the remote borders of the town was indicated by thin flashes of flame. Some building was on fire, and its reflection upon the clouds was an oval of delicate pink.

* * *

All demeanour of rural serenity had been wrenched violently from the little town by the guns and by the waves of men which had surged through it. The hand of war laid upon this village had in an instant changed it to a thing of remnants. It resembled the place of a monstrous shaking of the earth itself. The windows, now mere unsightly holes, made the tumbled and blackened dwellings seem skeletons. Doors lay splintered to fragments. Chimneys had flung their bricks everywhere. The artillery fire had not neglected the rows of gentle shade-trees which had lined the streets. Branches and heavy trunks cluttered the mud in driftwood tangles, while a few shattered forms had contrived to remain dejectedly, mournfully upright. They expressed an innocence, a helplessness, which perforce created a pity for their happening into this cauldron of battle. Furthermore, there was under foot a vast collection of odd things reminiscent of the charge, the fight, the retreat. There were boxes and barrels filled with earth, behind which riflemen had lain snugly, and in these little trenches were the dead in blue with the dead in gray, the poses eloquent of the struggles for possession of the town until the history of the whole conflict was written plainly in the streets.

And yet the spirit of this little city, its quaint individuality, poised in the air above the ruins, defying the guns, the sweeping volleys; holding in contempt those avaricious blazes which had attacked many dwellings. The hard earthen sidewalks proclaimed the games that had been played there during long lazy days, in the careful shadows of the trees. "General Merchandise," in faint letters upon a long board, had to be read with a slanted glance, for the sign dangled by one end; but the porch of the old store was a palpable legend of wide-hatted men, smoking.

This subtle essence, this soul of the life that had been, brushed like invisible wings the thoughts of the men in the swift columns that came up from the river.

In the darkness a loud and endless humming arose from the great blue crowds bivouacked in the streets. From time to time a sharp spatter of firing from far picket lines entered this bass chorus. The smell from the smouldering ruins floated on the cold night breeze.

Dan, seated ruefully upon the doorstep of a shot-pierced house, was proclaiming the campaign badly managed. Orders had been issued forbidding camp-fires.

Suddenly he ceased his oration, and scanning the group of his comrades, said: "Where's Billie? Do you know?"

"Gone on picket."

"Get out! Has he?" said Dan. "No business to go on picket. Why don't some of them other corporals take their turn?"

A bearded private was smoking his pipe of confiscated tobacco, seated comfortably upon a horse-hair trunk which he had dragged from the house. He observed: "*Was* his turn."

"No such thing," cried Dan. He and the man on the horse-hair trunk held discussion in which Dan stoutly maintained that if his brother had been sent on picket it was an injustice. He ceased his argument when another soldier, upon whose arms could faintly be seen the two stripes of a corporal, entered the circle. "Humph," said Dan, "where you been?"

The corporal made no answer. Presently Dan said: "Billie, where you been?"

His brother did not seem to hear these inquiries. He glanced at the house which towered above them, and remarked casually to the man on the horse-hair trunk: "Funny, ain't it? After the pelting this town got, you'd think there wouldn't be one brick left on another."

"Oh," said Dan, glowering at his brother's back. "Getting mighty smart, ain't you?"

The absence of camp-fires allowed the evening to make apparent its quality of faint silver light in which the blue clothes of the throng became black, and the faces became white expanses, void of expression. There was considerable excitement a short distance from the group around the doorstep. A soldier had chanced upon a hoop-skirt, and arrayed in it he was performing a dance amid the applause of his companions. Billie and a greater part of the men immediately poured over there to witness the exhibition.

"What's the matter with Billie?" demanded Dan of the man upon the horse-hair trunk.

"How do I know?" rejoined the other in mild resentment. He arose and walked away. When he returned he said briefly, in a weather-wise tone, that it would rain during the night.

Dan took a seat upon one end of the horse-hair trunk. He was facing the crowd around the dancer, which in its hilarity swung this way and that way. At times he imagined that he could recognise his brother's face.

He and the man on the other end of the trunk thoughtfully talked of the army's position. To their minds, infantry and artillery were in a most precarious jumble in the streets of the town; but they did not grow nervous over it, for they were used to having the army appear in a precarious jumble to their minds. They had learned to accept such puzzling situations as a consequence of their position in the ranks, and were now usually in possession of a simple but perfectly immovable faith that somebody understood the jumble. Even if they had been convinced that the army was a headless monster, they would merely have nodded with the veteran's singular cynicism. It was none of their business as soldiers. Their duty was to grab sleep and food when occasion permitted, and cheerfully fight wherever their feet were planted until more orders came. This was a task sufficiently absorbing.

They spoke of other corps, and this talk being confidential, their voices dropped to tones of awe. "The Ninth"—"The First"—"The Fifth"—"The Sixth"—"The Third"—the simple numerals rang with eloquence, each having a meaning which was to float through many years as no intangible arithmetical mist, but as pregnant with individuality as the names of cities.

Of their own corps they spoke with a deep veneration, an idolatry, a supreme confidence which apparently would not blanch to see it match against everything.

It was as if their respect for other corps was due partly to a wonder that organizations not blessed with their own famous numeral could take such an interest in war. They could prove that their division was the best in the corps, and that their brigade was the best in the division. And their regiment—it was plain that no fortune of life was equal to the chance which caused a man to be born, so to speak, into this command, the keystone of the defending arch.

At times Dan covered with insults the character of a vague, unnamed general to whose petulance and busy-body spirit he ascribed the order which made hot coffee impossible.

Dan said that victory was certain in the coming battle. The other man seemed rather dubious. He remarked upon the fortified line of hills, which had impressed him even from the other side of the river. "Shucks," said Dan. "Why, we—" He pictured a splendid overflowing of these hills by the sea of men in blue. During the period of this conversation Dan's glance searched the merry throng about the dancer. Above the babble of voices in the street a far-away thunder could sometimes be heard—evidently from the very edge of the horizon—the boom-boom of restless guns.

* * *

Ultimately the night deepened to the tone of black velvet. The outlines of the fireless camp were like the faint drawings upon ancient tapestry. The glint of a rifle, the shine of a button, might have been of threads of silver and gold sewn upon the fabric of the night. There was little presented to the vision, but to a sense more subtle there was discernible in the atmosphere something like a pulse; a mystic beating which would have told a stranger of the presence of a giant thing—the slumbering mass of regiments and batteries.

With fires forbidden, the floor of a dry old kitchen was thought to be a good exchange for the cold earth of December, even if a shell had exploded in it and knocked it so out of shape that when a man lay curled in his blanket his last waking thought was likely to be of the wall that bellied out above him as if strongly anxious to topple upon the score of soldiers.

Billie looked at the bricks ever about to descend in a shower upon his face, listened to the industrious pickets plying their rifles on the border of the town, imagined some measure of the din of the coming battle, thought of Dan and Dan's chagrin, and rolling over in his blanket went to sleep with satisfaction.

At an unknown hour he was aroused by the creaking of boards. Lifting himself upon his elbow, he saw a sergeant prowling among the sleeping forms. The sergeant carried a candle in an old brass candle-stick. He would have resembled some old farmer on an unusual midnight tour if it were not for the significance of his gleaming buttons and striped sleeves.

Billie blinked stupidly at the light until his mind returned from the journeys of slumber. The sergeant stooped among the unconscious soldiers, holding the candle close, and peering into each face.

"Hello, Haines," said Billie. "Relief?"

"Hello, Billie," said the sergeant. "Special duty."

"Dan got to go?"

'Jameson, Hunter, McCormack, D. Dempster. Yes. Where is he?"

"Over there by the winder," said Billie, gesturing. "What is it for, Haines?"

"You don't think I know, do you?" demanded the sergeant. He began to pipe sharply but cheerily at men upon the floor. "Come, Mac, get up here. Here's a special for you. Wake up, Jameson. Come along, Dannie, me boy."

Each man at once took this call to duty as a personal affront. They pulled themselves out of their blankets, rubbed their eyes, and swore at whoever was responsible. "Them's orders," cried the sergeant. "Come! Get out of here." An undetailed head with dishevelled hair thrust out from a blanket, and a sleepy voice said: "Shut up, Haines, and go home."

When the detail clanked out of the kitchen, all but one of the remaining men seemed to be again asleep. Billie, leaning on his elbow, was gazing into darkness. When the footsteps died to silence, he curled himself into his blanket.

At the first cool lavender lights of day-break he aroused again, and scanned his recumbent companions. Seeing a wakeful one he asked: "Is Dan back yet?"

The man said: "Hain't seen 'im."

Billie put both hands behind his head, and scowled into the air. "Can't see the use of these cussed details in the night-time," he muttered in his most unreasonable tones. "Darn nuisances. Why can't they—" He grumbled at length and graphically.

When Dan entered with the squad, however, Billie was convincingly asleep.

* * *

The regiment trotted in double time along the street, and the colonel seemed to quarrel over the right of way with many artillery officers. Batteries were waiting in the mud, and the men of them, exasperated by the bustle of this ambitious infantry, shook their fists from saddle and caisson, exchanging all manner of taunts and jests. The slanted guns continued to look reflectively at the ground.

On the outskirts of the crumbled town a fringe of blue figures were firing into the fog. The regiment swung out into skirmish lines, and the fringe of blue figures departed, turning their backs and going joyfully around the flank.

The bullets began a low moan off toward a ridge which loomed faintly in the heavy mist. When the swift crescendo had reached its climax, the missiles zipped just overhead, as if piercing an invisible curtain. A battery on the hill was crashing with such tumult that it was as if the guns had quarrelled and had fallen pell-mell and snarling upon each other. The shells howled on their journey toward the town. From short range distance there came a spatter of musketry, sweeping along an invisible line and making faint sheets of orange light.

Some in the new skirmish lines were beginning to fire at various shadows discerned in the vapour, forms of men suddenly revealed by some humour of the laggard masses of clouds. The crackle of musketry began to dominate the purring of the hostile bullets. Dan, in the front rank, held his rifle poised, and looked into the fog keenly, coldly, with the air of a sportsman. His nerves were so steady that it was as if they had been drawn from his body, leaving him merely a muscular machine; but his numb heart was somehow beating to the pealing march of the fight.

The waving skirmish line went backward and forward, ran this way and that way. Men got lost in the fog, and men were found again. Once they got too close to the formidable ridge, and the thing burst out as if repulsing a general attack. Once another blue regiment was apprehended on the very edge of firing into them. Once a friendly battery began an elaborate and scientific process of extermination. Always as busy as brokers, the men slid here and there over the plain, fighting their foes, escaping from their friends, leaving a history of many movements in the wet yellow turf, cursing the atmosphere, blazing away every time they could identify the enemy.

In one mystic changing of the fog, as if the fingers of spirits were drawing aside these draperies, a small group of the gray skirmishers, silent, statuesque, were suddenly disclosed to Dan and those about him. So vivid and near were they that there was something uncanny in the revelation.

There might have been a second of mutual staring. Then each rifle in each group was at the shoulder. As Dan's glance flashed along the barrel of his weapon, the figure of a man suddenly loomed as if the musket had been a telescope. The short black beard, the slouch hat, the pose of the man as he sighted to shoot, made a quick picture in Dan's mind. The same moment, it would seem, he pulled his own trigger, and the man, smitten, lurched forward, while his exploding rifle made a slanting crimson streak in the air, and the slouch hat fell before the body. The billows of the fog, governed by singular impulses, rolled between.

"You got that feller sure enough," said a comrade to Dan. Dan looked at him absent-mindedly.

* * *

When the next morning calmly displayed another fog, the men of the regiment exchanged eloquent comments; but they did not abuse it at length, because the streets of the town now contained enough galloping aides to make three troops of cavalry, and they knew that they had come to the verge of the great fight.

Dan conversed with the man who had once possessed a horse-hair trunk; but they did not mention the line of hills which had furnished them in more careless moments with an agreeable topic. They avoided it now as condemned men do the subject of death, and yet the thought of it stayed in their eyes as they looked at each other and talked gravely of other things.

The expectant regiment heaved a long sigh of relief when the sharp call: "Fall in," repeated indefinitely, arose in the streets. It was inevitable that a bloody battle was to be fought, and they wanted to get it off their minds. They were, however, doomed again to spend a long period planted firmly in the mud. They craned their necks, and wondered where some of the other regiments were going.

At last the mists rolled carelessly away. Nature made at this time all provisions to enable foes to see each other, and immediately the roar of guns resounded from every hill. The endless cracking of the skirmishers swelled to rolling crashes of musketry. Shells screamed with panther-like noises at the houses. Dan looked at the man of the horse-hair trunk, and the man said: "Well, here she comes!"

The tenor voices of younger officers and the deep and hoarse voices of the older ones rang in the streets. These cries pricked like spurs. The masses of men vibrated from the suddenness with which they were plunged into the situation of troops about to fight. That the orders were long-expected did not concern the emotion.

Simultaneous movement was imparted to all these thick bodies of men and horses that lay in the town. Regiment after regiment swung rapidly into the streets that faced the sinister ridge.

This exodus was theatrical. The little sober-hued village had been like the cloak which disguises the king of drama. It was now put aside, and an army, splendid thing of steel and blue, stood forth in the sunlight.

Even the soldiers in the heavy columns drew deep breaths at the sight, more majestic than they had dreamed. The heights of the enemy's position were crowded with men who resembled people come to witness some mighty pageant. But as the column moved steadily to their positions, the guns, matter-of-fact warriors, doubled their number, and shells burst with red thrilling tumult on the crowded plain. One came into the ranks of the regiment, and after the smoke and the wrath of it had faded, leaving motionless figures, everyone stormed according to the limits of his vocabulary, for veterans detest being killed when they are not busy.

The regiment sometimes looked sideways at its brigade companions composed of men who had never been in battle; but no frozen blood could withstand the heat of the splendour of this army before the eyes on the plain, these lines so long that the flanks were little streaks, this mass of men of one intention. The recruits carried themselves heedlessly. At the rear was an idle battery, and three artillery men in a foolish row on a caisson nudged each other and grinned at the recruits. "You'll catch it pretty soon," they called out. They were impersonally gleeful, as if they themselves were not also likely to catch it pretty soon. But with this picture of an army in their hearts, the new men perhaps felt the devotion which the drops may feel for the wave; they were of its power and glory; they smiled jauntily at the foolish row of gunners, and told them to go to blazes.

The column trotted across some little bridges, and spread quickly into lines of battle. Before them was a bit of plain, and back of the plain was the ridge. There was no time left for considerations. The men were staring at the plain, mightily wondering how it would feel to be out there, when a brigade in advance yelled and charged. The hill was all gray smoke and fire-points.

That fierce elation in the terrors of war, catching a man's heart and making it burn with such ardour that he becomes capable of dying, flashed in the faces of the men like coloured lights, and made them resemble leashed animals, eager, ferocious, daunting at nothing. The line was really in its first leap before the wild, hoarse crying of the orders.

The greed for close quarters which is the emotion of a bayonet charge, came then into the minds of the men and developed until it was a madness. The field, with its faded grass of a Southern winter, seemed to this fury miles in width.

High, slow-moving masses of smoke, with an odour of burning cotton, engulfed the line until the men might have been swimmers. Before them the ridge, the shore of this gray sea, was outlined, crossed, and recrossed by sheets of flame. The howl of the battle arose to the noise of innumerable wind demons.

The line, galloping, scrambling, plunging like a herd of wounded horses, went over a field that was sown with corpses, the records of other charges.

Directly in front of the black-faced, whooping Dan, carousing in this onward sweep like a new kind of fiend, a wounded man appeared, raising his shattered body, and staring at this rush of men down upon him. It seemed to occur to him that he was to be trampled; he made a desperate, piteous effort to escape; then finally huddled in a waiting heap. Dan and the soldier near him widened the interval between them without looking down, without appearing to heed the wounded man. This little clump of blue seemed to reel past them as boulders reel past a train.

Bursting through a smoke-wave, the scampering, unformed bunches came upon the wreck of the brigade that had preceded them, a floundering mass stopped afar from the hill by the swirling volleys.

It was as if a necromancer had suddenly shown them a picture of the fate which awaited them; but the line with muscular spasm hurled itself over this wreckage and onward, until men were stumbling amid the relics of other assaults, the point where the fire from the ridge consumed.

The men, panting, perspiring, with crazed faces, tried to push against it; but it was as if they had come to a wall. The wave halted, shuddered in an agony from the quick struggle of its two desires, then toppled, and broke into a fragmentary thing which has no name.

Veterans could now at last be distinguished from recruits. The new regiments were instantly gone, lost, scattered, as if they never had been. But the sweeping failure of the charge, the battle, could not make the veterans forget their business. With a last throe, the band of maniacs drew itself up and blazed a volley at the hill, insignificant to those iron intrenchments, but nevertheless expressing that singular final despair which enables men coolly to defy the walls of a city of death.

After this episode the men renamed their command. They called it the Little Regiment.

* * *

"I seen Dan shoot a feller yesterday. Yes sir. I'm sure it was him that done it. And maybe he thinks about that feller now, and wonders if *he* tumbled down just about the same way. Them things come up in a man's mind."

Bivouac fires upon the sidewalks, in the streets, in the yards, threw high their wavering reflections, which examined, like slim, red fingers, the dingy, scarred walls and the piles of tumbled brick. The droning of voices again arose from great blue crowds.

The odour of frying bacon, the fragrance from countless little coffee-pails floated among the ruins. The rifles, stacked in the shadows, emitted flashes of steely light. Wherever a flag lay horizontally from one stack to another was the bed of an eagle which had led men into the mystic smoke.

The men about a particular fire were engaged in holding in check their jovial spirits. They moved whispering around the blaze, although they looked at it with a certain fine contentment, like labourers after a day's hard work.

There was one who sat apart. They did not address him save in tones suddenly changed. They did not regard him directly, but always in little sidelong glances.

At last a soldier from a distant fire came into this circle of light. He studied for a time the man who sat apart. Then he hesitatingly stepped closer, and said: "Got any news, Dan?"

"No," said Dan.

The new-comer shifted his feet. He looked at the fire, at the sky, at the other men, at Dan. His face expressed a curious despair; his tongue was plainly in rebellion. Finally, however, he contrived to say: "Well, there's some chance yet, Dan. Lots of the wounded are still lying out there, you know. There's some chance yet."

"Yes," said Dan.

The soldier shifted his feet again, and looked miserably into the air. After another struggle he said: "Well, there's some chance yet, Dan." He moved hastily away.

One of the men of the squad, perhaps encouraged by this example, now approached the still figure. "No news yet, hey?" he said, after coughing behind his hand.

"No," said Dan.

"Well," said the man, "I've been thinking of how he was fretting about you the night you went on special duty. You recollect? Well, sir, I was surprised. He couldn't say enough about it. I swan, I don't believe he slep' a wink after you left, but just lay awake cussing special duty and worrying. I was surprised. But there he lay cussing. He——"

Dan made a curious sound, as if a stone had wedged in his throat. He said: "Shut up, will you?"

Afterward the men would not allow this moody contemplation of the fire to be interrupted.

"Oh, let him alone, can't you?"

"Come away from there, Casey!"

"Say, can't you leave him be?"

They moved with reverence about the immovable figure, with its countenance of mask-like invulnerability.

* * *

After the red round eye of the sun had stared long at the little plain and its burden, darkness, a sable mercy, came heavily upon it, and the wan hands of the dead were no longer seen in strange frozen gestures.

The heights in front of the plain shone with tiny camp-fires, and from the town in the rear, small shimmerings ascended from the blazes of the bivouac. The plain was a black expanse upon which, from time to time, dots of light, lanterns, floated slowly here and there. These fields were long steeped in grim mystery.

Suddenly, upon one dark spot, there was a resurrection. A strange thing had been groaning there, prostrate. Then it suddenly dragged itself to a sitting posture, and became a man.

The man stared stupidly for a moment at the lights on the hill, then turned and contemplated the faint colouring over the town. For some moments he remained thus, staring with dull eyes, his face unemotional, wooden.

Finally he looked around him at the corpses dimly to be seen. No change flashed into his face upon viewing these men. They seemed to suggest merely that his information concerning himself was not too complete. He ran his fingers over his arms and chest, bearing always the air of an idiot upon a bench at an almshouse door.

Finding no wound in his arms nor in his chest, he raised his hand to his head, and the fingers came away with some dark liquid upon them. Holding these fingers close to his eyes, he scanned them in the same stupid fashion, while his body gently swayed.

The soldier rolled his eyes again toward the town. When he arose, his clothing peeled from the frozen ground like wet paper. Hearing the sound of it, he seemed to see reason for deliberation. He paused and looked at the ground, then at his trousers, then at the ground.

Finally he went slowly off toward the faint reflection, holding his hands palm outward before him, and walking in the manner of a blind man.

* * *

The immovable Dan again sat unaddressed in the midst of comrades, who did not joke aloud. The dampness of the usual morning fog seemed to make the little camp-fires furious.

Suddenly a cry arose in the streets, a shout of amazement and delight. The men making breakfast at the fire looked up quickly. They broke forth in clamorous exclamation: "Well! Of all things! Dan! Dan! Look who's coming! Oh, Dan!"

Dan the silent raised his eyes and saw a man, with a bandage of the size of a helmet about his head, receiving a furious demonstration from the company. He was shaking hands, and explaining, and haranguing to a high degree.

Dan started. His face of bronze flushed to his temples. He seemed about to leap from the ground, but then suddenly he sank back, and resumed his impassive gazing.

The men were in a flurry. They looked from one to the other. "Dan! Look! See who's coming!" some cried again. "Dan! Look!"

He scowled at last, and moved his shoulders sullenly. "Well, don't I know it?"

But they could not be convinced that his eyes were in service. "Dan! Why can't you look? See who's coming!"

He made a gesture then of irritation and rage. "Curse it! Don't I know it?"

The man with a bandage of the size of a helmet moved forward, always shaking hands and explaining. At times his glance wandered to Dan, who sat with his eyes riveted.

After a series of shiftings, it occurred naturally that the man with the bandage was very near to the man who saw the flames. He paused, and there was a little silence. Finally he said: "Hello, Dan."

"Hello, Billie."

THREE MIRACULOUS SOLDIERS

The girl was in the front room on the second floor, peering through the blinds. It was the "best room." There was a very new rag carpet on the floor. The edges of it had been dyed with alternate stripes of red and green. Upon the wooden mantel there were two little puffy figures in clay—a shepherd and a shepherdess probably. A triangle of pink and white wool hung carefully over the edge of this shelf. Upon the bureau there was nothing at all save a spread newspaper, with edges folded to make it into a mat. The quilts and sheets had been removed from the bed and were stacked upon a chair. The pillows and the great feather mattress were muffled and tumbled until they resembled great dumplings. The picture of a man terribly leaden in complexion hung in an oval frame on one white wall and steadily confronted the bureau.

From between the slats of the blinds she had a view of the road as it wended across the meadow to the woods, and again where it reappeared crossing the hill, half a mile away. It lay yellow and warm in the summer sunshine. From the long grasses of the meadow came the rhythmic click of the insects. Occasional frogs in the hidden brook made a peculiar chug-chug sound, as if somebody throttled them. The leaves of the wood swung in gentle winds. Through the dark-green branches of the pines that grew in the front yard could be seen the mountains, far to the southeast, and inexpressibly blue.

Mary's eyes were fastened upon the little streak of road that appeared on the distant hill. Her face was flushed with excitement, and the hand which stretched in a strained pose on the sill trembled because of the nervous shaking of the wrist. The pines whisked their green needles with a soft, hissing sound against the house.

At last the girl turned from the window and went to the head of the stairs. "Well, I just know they're coming, anyhow," she cried argumentatively to the depths.

A voice from below called to her angrily: "They ain't. We've never seen one yet. They never come into this neighbourhood. You just come down here and 'tend to your work insteader watching for soldiers."

"Well, ma, I just know they're coming."

A voice retorted with the shrillness and mechanical violence of occasional housewives. The girl swished her skirts defiantly and returned to the window.

Upon the yellow streak of road that lay across the hillside there now was a handful of black dots—horsemen. A cloud of dust floated away. The girl flew to the head of the stairs and whirled down into the kitchen.

"They're coming! They're coming!"

It was as if she had cried "Fire!" Her mother had been peeling potatoes while seated comfortably at the table. She sprang to her feet. "No—it can't be—how you know it's them—where?" The stubby knife fell from her hand, and two or three curls of potato skin dropped from her apron to the floor.

The girl turned and dashed upstairs. Her mother followed, gasping for breath, and yet contriving to fill the air with questions, reproach, and remonstrance. The girl was already at the window, eagerly pointing. "There! There! See 'em! See 'em!"

Rushing to the window, the mother scanned for an instant the road on the hill. She crouched back with a groan. "It's them, sure as the world! It's them!" She waved her hands in despairing gestures.

The black dots vanished into the wood. The girl at the window was quivering and her eyes were shining like water when the sun flashes. "Hush! They're in the woods! They'll be here directly." She bent down and intently watched the green archway whence the road emerged. "Hush! I hear 'em coming," she swiftly whispered to her mother, for the elder woman had dropped dolefully upon the mattress and was sobbing. And indeed the girl could hear the quick, dull trample of horses. She stepped aside with sudden apprehension, but she bent her head forward in order to still scan the road.

"Here they are!"

There was something very theatrical in the sudden appearance of these men to the eyes of the girl. It was as if a scene had been shifted. The forest suddenly disclosed them—a dozen brown-faced troopers in blue—galloping.

"Oh, look!" breathed the girl. Her mouth was puckered into an expression of strange fascination as if she had expected to see the troopers change into demons and gloat at her. She was at last looking upon those curious beings who rode down from the North—those men of legend and colossal tale—they who were possessed of such marvellous hallucinations.

The little troop rode in silence. At its head was a youthful fellow with some dim yellow stripes upon his arm. In his right hand he held his carbine, slanting upward, with the stock resting upon his knee. He was absorbed in a scrutiny of the country before him.

At the heels of the sergeant the rest of the squad rode in thin column, with creak of leather and tinkle of steel and tin. The girl scanned the faces of the horsemen, seeming astonished vaguely to find them of the type she knew.

The lad at the head of the troop comprehended the house and its environments in two glances. He did not check the long, swinging stride of his horse. The troopers glanced for a moment like casual tourists, and then returned to their study of the region in front. The heavy thudding of the hoofs became a small noise. The dust, hanging in sheets, slowly sank.

The sobs of the woman on the bed took form in words which, while strong in their note of calamity, yet expressed a querulous mental reaching for some near thing to blame. "And it'll be lucky fer us if we ain't both butchered in our sleep—plundering and running off horses—old Santo's gone—you see if he ain't—plundering——"

"But, ma," said the girl, perplexed and terrified in the same moment, "they've gone."

"Oh, but they'll come back!" cried the mother, without pausing her wail. "They'll come back—trust them for that—running off horses. O John, John! why did you, why did you?" She suddenly lifted herself and sat rigid, staring at her daughter. "Mary," she said in tragic whisper, "the kitchen door isn't locked!" Already she was bended forward to listen, her mouth agape, her eyes fixed upon her daughter.

"Mother," faltered the girl.

Her mother again whispered, "The kitchen door isn't locked."

Motionless and mute they stared into each other's eyes.

At last the girl quavered, "We better—we better go and lock it." The mother nodded. Hanging arm in arm they stole across the floor toward the head of the stairs. A board of the floor creaked. They halted and exchanged a look of dumb agony.

At last they reached the head of the stairs. From the kitchen came the bass humming of the kettle and frequent sputterings and cracklings from the fire. These sounds were sinister. The mother and the girl stood incapable of movement. "There's somebody down there!" whispered the elder woman.

Finally, the girl made a gesture of resolution. She twisted her arm from her mother's hands and went two steps downward. She addressed the kitchen: "Who's there?" Her tone was intended to be dauntless. It rang so dramatically in the silence that a sudden new panic seized them as if the suspected presence in the kitchen had cried out to them. But the girl ventured again: "Is there anybody there?" No reply was made save by the kettle and the fire.

With a stealthy tread the girl continued her journey. As she neared the last step the fire cracked explosively and the girl screamed. But the mystic presence had not swept around the corner to grab her, so she dropped to a seat on the step and laughed. "It was—was only the—the fire," she said, stammering hysterically.

Then she arose with sudden fortitude and cried: "Why, there isn't anybody there! I know there isn't." She marched down into the kitchen. In her face was dread, as if she half expected to confront something, but the room was empty. She cried joyously: "There's nobody here! Come on down, ma." She ran to the kitchen door and locked it.

The mother came down to the kitchen. "Oh, dear, what a fright I've had! It's given me the sick headache. I know it has."

"Oh, ma," said the girl.

"I know it has—I know it. Oh, if your father was only here! He'd settle those Yankees mighty quick—he'd settle 'em! Two poor helpless women——"

"Why, ma, what makes you act so? The Yankees haven't——"

"Oh, they'll be back—they'll be back. Two poor helpless women! Your father and your uncle Asa and Bill off galavanting around and fighting when they ought to be protecting their home! That's the kind of men they are. Didn't I say to your father just before he left——"

"Ma," said the girl, coming suddenly from the window, "the barn door is open. I wonder if they took old Santo?"

"Oh, of course they have—of course—— Mary, I don't see what we are going to do—I don't see what we are going to do."

The girl said, "Ma, I'm going to see if they took old Santo."

"Mary," cried the mother, "don't you dare!"

"But think of poor old Sant, ma."

"Never you mind old Santo. We're lucky to be safe ourselves, I tell you. Never mind old Santo. Don't you dare to go out there, Mary—Mary!"

The girl had unlocked the door and stepped out upon the porch. The mother cried in despair, "Mary!"

"Why, there isn't anybody out here," the girl called in response. She stood for a moment with a curious smile upon her face as of gleeful satisfaction at her daring.

The breeze was waving the boughs of the apple trees. A rooster with an air importantly courteous was conducting three hens upon a foraging tour. On the hillside at the rear of the gray old barn the red leaves of a creeper flamed amid the summer foliage. High in the sky clouds rolled toward the north. The girl swung impulsively from the little stoop and ran toward the barn.

The great door was open, and the carved peg which usually performed the office of a catch lay on the ground. The girl could not see into the barn because of the heavy shadows. She paused in a listening attitude and heard a horse munching placidly. She gave a cry of delight and sprang across the threshold. Then she suddenly shrank back and gasped. She had confronted three men in gray seated upon the floor with their legs stretched out and their backs against Santo's manger. Their dust-covered countenances were expanded in grins.

* * *

As Mary sprang backward and screamed, one of the calm men in gray, still grinning, announced, "I knowed you'd holler." Sitting there comfortably the three surveyed her with amusement.

Mary caught her breath, throwing her hand up to her throat. "Oh!" she said, "you—you frightened me!"

"We're sorry, lady, but couldn't help it no way," cheerfully responded another. "I knowed you'd holler when I seen you coming yere, but I raikoned we couldn't help it no way. We hain't a-troubling this yere barn, I don't guess. We been doing some mighty tall sleeping yere. We done woke when them Yanks loped past."

"Where did you come from? Did—did you escape from the—the Yankees?" The girl still stammered and trembled. The three soldiers laughed. "No, m'm. No, m'm. They never cotch us. We was in a muss down the road yere about two mile. And Bill yere they gin it to him in the arm, kehplunk. And they pasted me thar, too. Curious. And Sim yere, he didn't get nothing, but they chased us all quite a little piece, and we done lose track of our boys."

"Was it—was it those who passed here just now? Did they chase you?"

The men in gray laughed again. "What—them? No, indeedee! There was a mighty big swarm of Yanks and a mighty big swarm of our boys, too. What—that little passel? No, m'm."

She became calm enough to scan them more attentively. They were much begrimed and very dusty. Their gray clothes were tattered. Splashed mud had dried upon them in reddish spots. It appeared, too, that the men had not shaved in many days. In the hats there was a singular diversity. One soldier wore the little blue cap of the Northern infantry, with corps emblem and regimental number; one wore a great slouch hat with a wide hole in the crown; and the other wore no hat at all. The left sleeve of one man and the right sleeve of another had been slit and the arms were neatly bandaged with clean cloth. "These hain't no more than two little cuts," explained one. "We stopped up yere to Mis' Leavitts—she said her name was—and she bind them for us. Bill yere, he had the thirst come on him. And the fever too. We——"

"Did you ever see my father in the army?" asked Mary. "John Hinckson—his name is."

The three soldiers grinned again, but they replied kindly: "No, m'm. No, m'm, we hain't never. What is he—in the cavalry?"

"No," said the girl. "He and my uncle Asa and my cousin—his name is Bill Parker—they are all with Longstreet—they call him."

"Oh," said the soldiers. "Longstreet? Oh, they're a good smart ways from yere. 'Way off up nawtheast. There hain't nothing but cavalry down yere. They're in the infantry, probably."

"We haven't heard anything from them for days and days," said Mary.

"Oh, they're all right in the infantry," said one man, to be consoling. "The infantry don't do much fighting. They go bellering out in a big swarm and only a few of 'em get hurt. But if they was in the cavalry—the cavalry——"

Mary interrupted him without intention. "Are you hungry?" she asked.

The soldiers looked at each other, struck by some sudden and singular shame. They hung their heads. "No, m'm," replied one at last.

Santo, in his stall, was tranquilly chewing and chewing. Sometimes he looked benevolently over at them. He was an old horse and there was something about his eyes and his forelock which created the impression that he wore spectacles. Mary went and patted his nose. "Well, if you are hungry, I can get you something," she told the men. "Or you might come to the house."

"We wouldn't dast go to the house," said one. "That passel of Yanks was only a scouting crowd, most like. Just an advance. More coming, likely."

"Well, I can bring you something," cried the girl eagerly. "Won't you let me bring you something?"

"Well," said a soldier with embarrassment, "we hain't had much. If you could bring us a little snack-like—just a snack—we'd——"

Without waiting for him to cease, the girl turned toward the door. But before she had reached it she stopped abruptly. "Listen!" she whispered. Her form was bent forward, her head turned and lowered, her hand extended toward the men in a command for silence.

They could faintly hear the thudding of many hoofs, the clank of arms, and frequent calling voices.

"By cracky, it's the Yanks!" The soldiers scrambled to their feet and came toward the door. "I knowed that first crowd was only an advance."

The girl and the three men peered from the shadows of the barn. The view of the road was intersected by tree trunks and a little henhouse. However, they could see many horsemen streaming down the road. The horsemen were in blue. "Oh, hide—hide—hide!" cried the girl, with a sob in her voice.

"Wait a minute," whispered a gray soldier excitedly. "Maybe they're going along by. No, by thunder, they hain't! They're halting. Scoot, boys!"

They made a noiseless dash into the dark end of the barn. The girl, standing by the door, heard them break forth an instant later in clamorous whispers.

"Where'll we hide? Where'll we hide? There hain't a place to hide!" The girl turned and glanced wildly about the barn. It seemed true. The stock of hay had grown low under Santo's endless munching, and from occasional levyings by passing troopers in gray. The poles of the mow were barely covered, save in one corner where there was a little bunch.

The girl espied the great feed box. She ran to it and lifted the lid. "Here! here!" she called. "Get in here."

They had been tearing noiselessly around the rear part of the barn. At her low call they came and plunged at the box. They did not all get in at the same moment without a good deal of a tangle. The wounded men gasped and muttered, but they at last were flopped down on the layer of feed which covered the bottom. Swiftly and softly the girl lowered the lid and then turned like a flash toward the door.

No one appeared there, so she went close to survey the situation. The troopers had dismounted and stood in silence by their horses. A gray-bearded man, whose red cheeks and nose shone vividly above the whiskers, was strolling about with two or three others. They wore double-breasted coats, and faded yellow sashes were wound under their black leather sword belts. The gray-bearded soldier was apparently giving orders, pointing here and there.

Mary tiptoed to the feed box. "They've all got off their horses," she said to it. A finger projected from a knothole near the top and said to her very plainly, "Come closer." She obeyed, and then a muffled voice could be heard: "Scoot for the house, lady, and if we don't see you again, why, much obliged for what you done."

"Good-bye," she said to the feed box.

She made two attempts to walk dauntlessly from the barn, but each time she faltered and failed just before she reached the point where she could have been seen by the blue-coated troopers. At last, however, she made a sort of a rush forward and went out into the bright sunshine.

The group of men in double-breasted coats wheeled in her direction at the instant. The gray-bearded officer forgot to lower his arm which had been stretched forth in giving an order.

She felt that her feet were touching the ground in a most unnatural manner. Her bearing, she believed, was suddenly grown awkward and ungainly. Upon her face she thought that this sentence was plainly written: "There are three men hidden in the feed box."

The gray-bearded soldier came toward her. She stopped; she seemed about to run away. But the soldier doffed his little blue cap and looked amiable. "You live here, I presume?" he said.

"Yes," she answered.

"Well, we are obliged to camp here for the night, and as we've got two wounded men with us I don't suppose you's mind if we put them in the barn."

"In—in the barn?"

He became aware that she was agitated. He smiled assuringly. "You needn't be frightened. We won't hurt anything around here. You'll all be safe enough."

The girl balanced on one foot and swung the other to and fro in the grass. She was looking down at it. "But—but I don't think ma would like it if—if you took the barn."

The old officer laughed. "Wouldn't she?" said he. "That's so. Maybe she wouldn't." He reflected for a time and then decided cheerfully: "Well, we will have to go ask her, anyhow. Where is she? In the house?"

"Yes," replied the girl, "she's in the house. She—she'll be scared to death when she sees you!"

"Well, you go and ask her then," said the soldier, always wearing a benign smile. "You go ask her and then come and tell me."

When the girl pushed open the door and entered the kitchen, she found it empty. "Ma!" she called softly. There was no answer. The kettle still was humming its low song. The knife and the curl of potato skin lay on the floor.

She went to her mother's room and entered timidly. The new, lonely aspect of the house shook her nerves. Upon the bed was a confusion of coverings. "Ma!" called the girl, quaking in fear that her mother was not there to reply. But there was a sudden turmoil of the quilts, and her mother's head was thrust forth. "Mary!" she cried, in what seemed to be a supreme astonishment, "I thought—I thought——"

"Oh, ma" blurted the girl, "there's over a thousand Yankees in the yard, and I've hidden three of our men in the feed box!"

The elder woman, however, upon the appearance of her daughter had begun to thrash hysterically about on the bed and wail.

"Ma," the girl exclaimed, "and now they want to use the barn—and our men in the feed box! What shall I do, ma? What shall I do?"

Her mother did not seem to hear, so absorbed was she in her grievous flounderings and tears. "Ma!" appealed the girl. "Ma!"

For a moment Mary stood silently debating, her lips apart, her eyes fixed. Then she went to the kitchen window and peeked.

The old officer and the others were staring up the road. She went to another window in order to get a proper view of the road, and saw that they were gazing at a small body of horsemen approaching at a trot and raising much dust. Presently she recognised them as the squad that had passed the house earlier, for the young man with the dim yellow chevron still rode at their head. An unarmed horseman in gray was receiving their close attention.

As they came very near to the house she darted to the first window again. The gray-bearded officer was smiling a fine broad smile of satisfaction. "So you got him?" he called out. The young sergeant sprang from his horse and his brown hand moved in a salute. The girl could not hear his reply. She saw the unarmed horseman in gray stroking a very black mustache and looking about him coolly and with an interested air. He appeared so indifferent that she did not understand he was a prisoner until she heard the graybeard call out: "Well, put him in the barn. He'll be safe there, I guess." A party of troopers moved with the prisoner toward the barn.

The girl made a sudden gesture of horror, remembering the three men in the feed box.

* * *

The busy troopers in blue scurried about the long lines of stamping horses. Men crooked their backs and perspired in order to rub with cloths or bunches of grass these slim equine legs, upon whose splendid machinery they depended so greatly. The lips of the horses were still wet and frothy from the steel bars which had wrenched at their mouths all day. Over their backs and about their noses sped the talk of the men.

"Moind where yer plug is steppin', Finerty! Keep 'im aff me!"

"An ould elephant! He shtrides like a schoolhouse."

"Bill's little mar—she was plum beat when she come in with Crawford's crowd."

"Crawford's the hardest-ridin' cavalryman in the army. An he don't use up a horse, neither—much. They stay fresh when the others are most a-droppin'."

"Finerty, will yeh moind that cow a yours?"

Amid a bustle of gossip and banter, the horses retained their air of solemn rumination, twisting their lower jaws from side to side and sometimes rubbing noses dreamfully.

Over in front of the barn three troopers sat talking comfortably. Their carbines were leaned against the wall. At their side and outlined in the black of the open door stood a sentry, his weapon resting in the hollow of his arm. Four horses, saddled and accoutred, were conferring with their heads close together. The four bridle reins were flung over a post.

Upon the calm green of the land, typical in every way of peace, the hues of war brought thither by the troops shone strangely. Mary, gazing curiously, did not feel that she was contemplating a familiar scene. It was no longer the home acres. The new blue, steel, and faded yellow thoroughly dominated the old green and brown. She could hear the voices of the men, and it seemed from their tone that they had camped there for years. Everything with them was usual. They had taken possession of the landscape in such a way that even the old marks appeared strange and formidable to the girl.

Mary had intended to go and tell the commander in blue that her mother did not wish his men to use the barn at all, but she paused when she heard him speak to the sergeant. She thought she perceived then that it mattered little to him what her mother wished, and that an objection by her or by anybody would be futile. She saw the soldiers conduct the prisoner in gray into the barn, and for a long time she watched the three chatting guards and the pondering sentry. Upon her mind in desolate weight was the recollection of the three men in the feed box.

It seemed to her that in a case of this description it was her duty to be a heroine. In all the stories she had read when at boarding school in Pennsylvania, the girl characters, confronted with such difficulties, invariably did hair breadth things. True, they were usually bent upon rescuing and recovering their lovers, and neither the calm man in gray nor any of the three in the feed box was lover of hers, but then a real heroine would not pause over this minor question. Plainly a heroine would take measures to rescue the four men. If she did not at least make the attempt, she would be false to those carefully constructed ideals which were the accumulation of years of dreaming.

But the situation puzzled her. There was the barn with only one door, and with four armed troopers in front of this door, one of them with his back to the rest of the world, engaged, no doubt, in a steadfast contemplation of the calm man and, incidentally, of the feed box. She knew, too, that even if she should open the kitchen door, three heads and perhaps four would turn casually in her direction. Their ears were real ears.

Heroines, she knew, conducted these matters with infinite precision and despatch. They severed the hero's bonds, cried a dramatic sentence, and stood between him and his enemies until he had run far enough away. She saw well, however, that even should she achieve all things up to the point where she might take glorious stand between the escaping and the pursuers, those grim troopers in blue would not pause. They would run around her, make a circuit. One by one she saw the gorgeous contrivances and expedients of fiction fall before the plain, homely difficulties of this situation. They were of no service. Sadly, ruefully, she thought of the calm man and of the contents of the feed box.

The sum of her invention was that she could sally forth to the commander of the blue cavalry, and confessing to him that there were three of her friends and his enemies secreted in the feed box, pray him to let them depart unmolested. But she was beginning to believe the old graybeard to be a bear. It was hardly probable that he would give this plan his support. It was more probable that he and some of his men would at once descend upon the feed box and confiscate her three friends. The difficulty with her idea was that she could not learn its value without trying it, and then in case of failure it would be too late for remedies and other plans. She reflected that war made men very unreasonable.

All that she could do was to stand at the window and mournfully regard the barn. She admitted this to herself with a sense of deep humiliation. She was not, then, made of that fine stuff, that mental satin, which enabled some other beings to be of such mighty service to the distressed. She was defeated by a barn with one door, by four men with eight eyes and eight ears—trivialities that would not impede the real heroine.

The vivid white light of broad day began slowly to fade. Tones of gray came upon the fields, and the shadows were of lead. In this more sombre atmosphere the fires built by the troops down in the far end of the orchard grew more brilliant, becoming spots of crimson colour in the dark grove.

The girl heard a fretting voice from her mother's room. "Mary!" She hastily obeyed the call. She perceived that she had quite forgotten her mother's existence in this time of excitement.

The elder woman still lay upon the bed. Her face was flushed and perspiration stood amid new wrinkles upon her forehead. Weaving wild glances from side to side, she began to whimper. "Oh, I'm just sick—I'm just sick! Have those men gone yet? Have they gone?"

The girl smoothed a pillow carefully for her mother's head. 'No, ma. They're here yet. But they haven't hurt anything—it doesn't seem. Will I get you something to eat?"

Her mother gestured her away with the impatience of the ill. "No—no—just don't bother me. My head is splitting, and you know very well that nothing can be done for me when I get one of these spells. It's trouble—that's what makes them. When are those men going? Look here, don't you go 'way. You stick close to the house now."

"I'll stay right here," said the girl. She sat in the gloom and listened to her mother's incessant moaning. When she attempted to move, her mother cried out at her. When she desired to ask if she might try to alleviate the pain, she was interrupted shortly. Somehow her sitting in passive silence within hearing of this illness seemed to contribute to her mother's relief. She assumed a posture of submission. Sometimes her mother projected questions concerning the local condition, and although she laboured to be graphic and at the same time soothing, unalarming, her form of reply was always displeasing to the sick woman, and brought forth ejaculations of angry impatience.

Eventually the woman slept in the manner of one worn from terrible labour. The girl went slowly and softly to the kitchen. When she looked from the window, she saw the four soldiers still at the barn door. In the west, the sky was yellow. Some tree trunks intersecting it appeared black as streaks of ink. Soldiers hovered in blue clouds about the bright spendour of the fires in the orchard. There were glimmers of steel.

The girl sat in the new gloom of the kitchen and watched. The soldiers lit a lantern and hung it in the barn. Its rays made the form of the sentry seem gigantic. Horses whinnied from the orchard. There was a low hum of human voices. Sometimes small detachments of troopers rode past the front of the house. The girl heard the abrupt calls of sentries. She fetched some food and ate it from her hand, standing by the window. She was so afraid that something would occur that she barely left her post for an instant.

A picture of the interior of the barn hung vividly in her mind. She recalled the knotholes in the boards at the rear, but she admitted that the prisoners could not escape through them. She remembered some inadequacies of the roof, but these also counted for nothing. When confronting the problem, she felt her ambitions, her ideals tumbling headlong like cottages of straw.

Once she felt that she had decided to reconnoitre at any rate. It was night; the lantern at the barn and the camp fires made everything without their circle into masses of heavy mystic blackness. She took two steps toward the door. But there she paused. Innumerable possibilities of danger had assailed her mind. She returned to the window and stood wavering. At last, she went swiftly to the door, opened it, and slid noiselessly into the darkness.

For a moment she regarded the shadows. Down in the orchard the camp fires of the troops appeared precisely like a great painting, all in reds upon a black cloth. The voices of the troopers still hummed. The girl started slowly off in the opposite direction. Her eyes were fixed in a stare; she studied the darkness in front for a moment, before she ventured upon a forward step. Unconsciously, her throat was arranged for a sudden shrill scream. High in the tree branches she could hear the voice of the wind, a melody of the night, low and sad, the plaint of an endless, incommunicable sorrow. Her own distress, the plight of the men in gray—these near matters as well as all she had known or imagined of grief—everything was expressed in this soft mourning of the wind in the trees. At first she felt like weeping. This sound told her of human impotency and doom. Then later the trees and the wind breathed strength to her, sang of sacrifice, of dauntless effort, of hard carven faces that did not blanch when Duty came at midnight or at noon.

She turned often to scan the shadowy figures that moved from time to time in the light at the barn door. Once she trod upon a stick, and it flopped, crackling in the intolerable manner of all sticks. At this noise, however, the guards at the barn made no sign. Finally, she was where she could see the knotholes in the rear of the structure gleaming like pieces of metal from the effect of the light within. Scarcely breathing in her excitement she glided close and applied an eye to a knothole. She had barely achieved one glance at the interior before she sprang back shuddering.

For the unconscious and cheerful sentry at the door was swearing away in flaming sentences, heaping one gorgeous oath upon another, making a conflagration of his description of his troop horse.

"Why," he was declaring to the calm prisoner in gray, "you ain't got a horse in your hull——army that can run forty rod with that there little mar'!"

As in the outer darkness Mary cautiously returned to the knothole, the three guards in front suddenly called in low tones: "S-s-s-h!" "Quit, Pete; here comes the lieutenant." The sentry had apparently been about to resume his declamation, but at these warnings he suddenly posed in a soldierly manner.

A tall and lean officer with a smooth face entered the barn. The sentry saluted primly. The officer flashed a comprehensive glance about him. "Everything all right?"

"All right, sir."

This officer had eyes like the points of stilettos. The lines from his nose to the corners of his mouth were deep and gave him a slightly disagreeable aspect, but somewhere in his face there was a quality of singular thoughtfulness, as of the absorbed student dealing in generalities, which was utterly in opposition to the rapacious keenness of the eyes which saw everything.

Suddenly he lifted a long finger and pointed. "What's that?"

"That? That's a feed box, I suppose."

"What's in it?"

"I don't know. I——"

"You ought to know," said the officer sharply. He walked over to the feed box and flung up the lid. With a sweeping gesture, he reached down and scooped a handful of feed. "You ought to know what's in everything when you have prisoners in your care," he added, scowling.

During the time of this incident, the girl had nearly swooned. Her hands searched weakly over the boards for something to which to cling. With the pallor of the dying she had watched the downward sweep of the officer's arm, which after all had only brought forth a handful of feed. The result was a stupefaction of her mind. She was astonished out of her senses at this spectacle of three large men metamorphosed into a handful of feed.

* * *

It is perhaps a singular thing that this absence of the three men from the feed box at the time of the sharp lieutenant's investigation should terrify the girl more than it should joy her. That for which she had prayed had come to pass. Apparently the escape of these men in the face of every improbability had been granted her, but her dominating emotion was fright. The feed box was a mystic and terrible machine, like some dark magician's trap. She felt it almost possible that she should see the three weird men floating spectrally away through the air. She glanced with swift apprehension behind her, and when the dazzle from the lantern's light had left her eyes, saw only the dim hillside stretched in solemn silence.

The interior of the barn possessed for her another fascination because it was now uncanny. It contained that extraordinary feed box. When she peeped again at the knothole, the calm, gray prisoner was seated upon the feed box, thumping it with his dangling, careless heels as if it were in nowise his conception of a remarkable feed-box. The sentry also stood facing it. His carbine he held in the hollow of his arm. His legs were spread apart, and he mused. From without came the low mumble of the three other troopers. The sharp lieutenant had vanished.

The trembling yellow light of the lantern caused the figures of the men to cast monstrous wavering shadows. There were spaces of gloom which shrouded ordinary things in impressive garb. The roof presented an inscrutable blackness, save where small rifts in the shingles glowed phosphorescently. Frequently old Santo put down a thunderous hoof. The heels of the prisoner made a sound like the booming of a wild kind of drum. When the men moved their heads, their eyes shone with ghoulish whiteness, and their complexions were always waxen and unreal. And there was that profoundly strange feed box, imperturbable with its burden of fantastic mystery.

Suddenly from down near her feet the girl heard a crunching sound, a sort of a nibbling, as if some silent and very discreet terrier was at work upon the turf. She faltered back; here was no doubt another grotesque detail of this most unnatural episode. She did not run, because physically she was in the power of these events. Her feet chained her to the ground in submission to this march of terror after terror. As she stared at the spot from which this sound seemed to come, there floated through her mind a vague, sweet vision—a vision of her safe little room, in which at this hour she usually was sleeping.

The scratching continued faintly and with frequent pauses, as if the terrier was then listening. When the girl first removed her eyes from the knothole the scene appeared of one velvet blackness; then gradually objects loomed with a dim lustre. She could see now where the tops of the trees joined the sky and the form of the barn was before her dyed in heavy purple. She was ever about to shriek, but no sound came from her constricted throat. She gazed at the ground with the expression of countenance of one who watches the sinister-moving grass where a serpent approaches.

Dimly she saw a piece of sod wrenched free and drawn under the great foundation beam of the barn. Once she imagined that she saw human hands, not outlined at all, but sufficient in colour, form, or movement to make subtle suggestion.

Then suddenly a thought that illuminated the entire situation flashed in her mind like a light. The three men, late of the feed box, were beneath the floor of the barn and were now scraping their way under this beam. She did not consider for a moment how they could come there. They were marvellous creatures. The supernatural was to be expected of them. She no longer trembled, for she was possessed upon this instant of the most unchangeable species of conviction. The evidence before her amounted to no evidence at all, but nevertheless her opinion grew in an instant from an irresponsible acorn to a rooted and immovable tree. It was if she was on a jury.

She stooped down hastily and scanned the ground. There she indeed saw a pair of hands hauling at the dirt where the sod had been displaced. Softly, in a whisper like a breath, she said, "Hey!"

The dim hands were drawn hastily under the barn. The girl reflected for a moment. Then she stooped and whispered: 'Hey! It's me!''

After a time there was a resumption of the digging. The ghostly hands began once more their cautious mining. She waited. In hollow reverberations from the interior of the barn came the frequent sounds of old Santo's lazy movements. The sentry conversed with the prisoner.

At last the girl saw a head thrust slowly from under the beam. She perceived the face of one of the miraculous soldiers from the feed box. A pair of eyes glintered and wavered, then finally settled upon her, a pale statue of a girl. The eyes became lit with a kind of humorous greeting. An arm gestured at her.

Stooping, she breathed, "All right." The man drew himself silently back under the beam. A moment later the pair of hands resumed their cautious task. Ultimately the head and arms of the man were thrust strangely from the earth. He was lying on his back. The girl thought of the dirt in his hair. Wriggling slowly and pushing at the beam above him he forced his way out of the curious little passage. He twisted his body and raised himself upon his hands. He grinned at the girl and drew his feet carefully from under the beam. When he at last stood erect beside her, he at once began mechanically to brush the dirt from his clothes with his hands. In the barn the sentry and his prisoner were evidently engaged in an argument.

The girl and the first miraculous soldier signalled warily. It seemed that they feared that their arms would make noises in passing through the air. Their lips moved, conveying dim meanings.

In this sign language the girl described the situation in the barn. With guarded motions, she told him of the importance of absolute stillness. He nodded, and then in the same manner he told her of his two companions under the barn floor. He informed her again of their wounded state, and wagged his head to express his despair. He contorted his face to tell how sore were their arms; and jabbed the air mournfully, to express their remote geographical position.

This signalling was interrupted by the sound of a body being dragged or dragging itself with slow, swishing sound under the barn. The sound was too loud for safety. They rushed to the hole and began to semaphore until a shaggy head appeared with rolling eyes and quick grin.

With frantic downward motions of their arms they suppressed this grin and with it the swishing noise. In dramatic pantomime they informed this head of the terrible consequences of so much noise. The head nodded, and painfully but with extreme care the second man pushed and pulled himself from the hole.

In a faint whisper the first man said, "Where's Sim?"

The second man made low reply. "He's right here." He motioned reassuringly toward the hole.

When the third head appeared, a soft smile of glee came upon each face, and the mute group exchanged expressive glances.

When they all stood together, free from this tragic barn, they breathed a long sigh that was contemporaneous with another smile and another exchange of glances.

One of the men tiptoed to a knothole and peered into the barn. The sentry was at that moment speaking. "Yes, we know 'em all. There isn't a house in this region that we don't know who is in it most of the time. We collar 'em once in a while—like we did you. Now, that house out yonder, we——"

The man suddenly left the knothole and returned to the others. Upon his face, dimly discerned, there was an indication that he had made an astonishing discovery. The others questioned him with their eyes, but he simply waved an arm to express his inability to speak at that spot. He led them back toward the hill, prowling carefully. At a safe distance from the barn he halted and as they grouped eagerly about him, he exploded in an intense undertone: "Why, that— that's Cap'n Sawyer they got in yonder."

"Cap'n Sawyer!" incredulously whispered the other men.

But the girl had something to ask. "How did you get out of that feed box?" He smiled. "Well, when you put us, in there, we was just in a minute when we allowed it wasn't a mighty safe place, and we allowed we'd get out. And we did. We skedaddled 'round and 'round until it 'peared like we was going to get cotched, and then we flung ourselves down in the cow stalls where it's low-like—just dirt floor—and then we just naturally went a-whooping under the barn floor when the Yanks come. And we didn't know Cap'n Sawyer by his voice nohow. We heard 'im discoursing, and we allowed it was a mighty pert man, but we didn't know that it was him. No, m'm."

These three men, so recently from a situation of peril, seemed suddenly to have dropped all thought of it. They stood with sad faces looking at the barn. They seemed to be making no plans at all to reach a place of more complete safety. They were halted and stupefied by some unknown calamity.

"How do you raikon they cotch him, Sim?" one whispered mournfully.

"I don't know," replied another, in the same tone.

Another with a low snarl expressed in two words his opinion of the methods of Fate: "Oh, hell!"

The three men started then as if simultaneously stung and gazed at the young girl who stood silently near them. The man who had sworn began to make agitated apology: "Pardon, miss! 'Pon my soul I clean forgot you was by. 'Deed, and I wouldn't swear like that if I had knowed. 'Deed, I wouldn't."

The girl did not seem to hear him. She was staring at the barn. Suddenly she turned and whispered, "Who is he?"

"He's Cap'n Sawyer, m'm," they told her sorrowfully. "He's our own cap'n. He's been in command of us yere since a long time. He's got folks about yere. Raikon they cotch him while he was a-visiting."

She was still for a time and then, awed, she said "Will they—will they hang him?"

"No, m'm. Oh, no, m'm. Don't raikon no such thing. No, m'm."

The group became absorbed in a contemplation of the barn. For a time no one moved nor spoke. At last the girl was aroused by slight sounds, and turning, she perceived that the three men who had so recently escaped from the barn were now advancing toward it.

* * *

The girl, waiting in the darkness, expected to hear the sudden crash and uproar of a fight as soon as the three creeping men should reach the barn. She reflected in an agony upon the swift disaster that would befall any enterprise so desperate. She had an impulse to beg them to come away. The grass rustled in silken movements as she sped toward the barn.

When she arrived, however, she gazed about her bewildered. The men were gone. She searched with her eyes, trying to detect some moving thing, but she could see nothing.

Left alone again, she began to be afraid of the night. The great stretches of darkness could hide crawling dangers. From sheer desire to see a human, she was obliged to peep again at the knothole. The sentry had apparently wearied of talking. Instead, he was reflecting. The prisoner still sat on the feed box, moodily staring at the floor. The girl felt in one way that she was looking at a ghastly group in wax. She started when the old horse put down an echoing hoof. She wished the men would speak; their silence re-enforced the strange aspect. They might have been two dead men.

The girl felt impelled to look at the corner of the interior where were the cow stalls. There was no light there save the appearance of peculiar gray haze which marked the track of the dimming rays of the lantern. All else was sombre shadow. At last she saw something move there. It might have been as small as a rat, or it might have been a part of something as large as a man. At any rate, it proclaimed that something in that spot was alive. At one time she saw it plainly and at other times it vanished, because her fixture of gaze caused her occasionally to greatly tangle and blur those peculiar shadows and faint lights. At last, however, she perceived a human head. It was monstrously dishevelled and wild. It moved slowly forward until its glance could fall upon the prisoner and then upon the sentry. The wandering rays caused the eyes to glitter like silver. The girl's heart pounded so that she put her hand over it.

The sentry and the prisoner remained immovably waxen, and over in the gloom the head thrust from the floor watched them with its silver eyes.

Finally, the prisoner slipped from the feed box, and, raising his arms, yawned at great length. "Oh, well," he remarked, "you boys will get a good licking if you fool around here much longer. That's some satisfaction, anyhow, even if you did bag me. You'll get a good walloping." He reflected for a moment, and decided: "I'm sort of willing to be captured if you fellows only get a d——d good licking for being so smart."

The sentry looked up and smiled a superior smile. "Licking, hey? Nixey!" He winked exasperatingly at the prisoner. "You fellows are not fast enough, my boy. Why didn't you lick us at ——? and at ——? and at ——?" He named some of the great battles.

To this the captive officer blurted in angry astonishment, "Why, we did!"

The sentry winked again in profound irony. "Yes—I know you did. Of course. You whipped us, didn't you? Fine kind of whipping that was! Why, we——"

He suddenly ceased, smitten mute by a sound that broke the stillness of the night. It was the sharp crack of a distant shot that made wild echoes among the hills. It was instantly followed by the hoarse cry of a human voice, a far-away yell of warning, singing of surprise, peril, fear of death. A moment later there was a distant, fierce spattering of shots. The sentry and the prisoner stood facing each other, their lips apart, listening.

The orchard at that instant awoke to sudden tumult. There were the thud and scramble and scamper of feet, the mellow, swift clash of arms, men's voices in question, oath, command, hurried and unhurried, resolute and frantic. A horse sped along the road at a raging gallop. A loud voice shouted, "What is it,

Ferguson?'' Another voice yelled something incoherent. There was a sharp, discordant chorus of command. An uproarious volley suddenly rang from the orchard. The prisoner in gray moved from his intent, listening attitude. Instantly the eyes of the sentry blazed, and he said with a new and terrible sternness, "Stand where you are!"

The prisoner trembled in his excitement. Expressions of delight and triumph bubbled to his lips. "A surprise, by Gawd! Now—now, you'll see!"

The sentry stolidly swung his carbine to his shoulder. He sighted carefully along the barrel until it pointed at the prisoner's head, about at his nose. "Well, I've got you, anyhow. Remember that! Don't move!"

The prisoner could not keep his arms from nervously gesturing. "I won't; but——"

"And shut your mouth!"

The three comrades of the sentry flung themselves into view. "Pete—devil of a row!—can you——"

"I've got him," said the sentry calmly and without moving. It was as if the barrel of the carbine rested on piers of stone, The three comrades turned and plunged into the darkness.

In the orchard it seemed as if two gigantic animals were engaged in a mad, floundering encounter, snarling, howling in a whirling chaos of noise and motion. In the barn the prisoner and his guard faced each other in silence.

As for the girl at the knothole, the sky had fallen at the beginning of this clamour. She would not have been astonished to see the stars swinging from their abodes, and the vegetation, the barn, all blow away. It was the end of everything, the grand universal murder. When two of the three miraculous soldiers who formed the original feed-box corps emerged in detail from the hole under the beam and slid away into the darkness, she did no more than glance at them.

Suddenly she recollected the head with silver eyes. She started forward and again applied her eyes to the knot hole. Even with the din resounding from the orchard, from up the road and down the road, from the heavens and from the deep earth, the central fascination was this mystic head. There, to her, was the dark god of the tragedy.

The prisoner in gray at this moment burst into a laugh that was no more than a hysterical gurgle. "Well, you can't hold that gun out forever! Pretty soon you'll have to lower it."

The sentry's voice sounded slightly muffled, for his cheek was pressed against the weapon. "I won't be tired for some time yet."

The girl saw the head slowly rise, the eyes fixed upon the sentry's face. A tall, black figure slunk across the cow stalls and vanished back of old Santo's quarters. She knew what was to come to pass. She knew this grim thing was upon a terrible mission, and that it would reappear again at the head of the little passage between Santo's stall and the wall, almost at the sentry's elbow; and yet when she saw a faint indication as of a form crouching there, a scream from an utterly new alarm almost escaped her.

The sentry's arms, after all, were not of granite. He moved restively. At last he spoke in his even, unchanging tone: "Well, I guess you'll have to climb into that feed box. Step back and lift the lid."

"Why, you don't mean——"

"Step back!"

The girl felt a cry of warning arising to her lips as she gazed at this sentry. She noted every detail of his facial expression. She saw, moreover, his mass of brown hair bunching disgracefully about his ears, his clear eyes lit now with a hard, cold light, his forehead puckered in a mighty scowl, the ring upon the third finger of the left hand. "Oh, they won't kill him! Surely they won't kill him!" The noise of the fight in the orchard was the loud music, the thunder and lightning, the rioting of the tempest which people love during the critical scene of a tragedy.

When the prisoner moved back in reluctant obedience, he faced for an instant the entrance of the little passage, and what he saw there must have been written swiftly, graphically in his eyes. And the sentry read it and knew then that he was upon the threshold of his death. In a fraction of time, certain information went from the grim thing in the passage to the prisoner, and from the prisoner to the sentry. But at that instant the black formidable figure arose, towered, and made its leap. A new shadow flashed across the floor when the blow was struck.

As for the girl at the knot hole, when she returned to sense she found herself standing with clinched hands and screaming with her might.

As if her reason had again departed from her, she ran around the barn, in at the door, and flung herself sobbing beside the body of the soldier in blue.

The uproar of the fight became at last coherent, inasmuch as one party was giving shouts of supreme exultation. The firing no longer sounded in crashes; it was now expressed in spiteful crackles, the last words of the combat, spoken with feminine vindictiveness.

Presently there was a thud of flying feet. A grimly panting, red-faced mob of troopers in blue plunged into the barn, became instantly frozen to attitudes of amazement and rage, and then roared in one great chorus, "He's gone!"

The girl who knelt beside the body upon the floor turned toward them her lamenting eyes and cried: "He's not dead, is he? He can't be dead?"

They thronged forward. The sharp lieutenant who had been so particular about the feed box knelt by the side of the girl and laid his head against the chest of the prostrate soldier. "Why, no," he said, rising and looking at the man. "He's all right. Some of you boys throw some water on him."

"Are you sure?" demanded the girl, feverishly.

"Of course! He'll be better after awhile."

"Oh!" said she softly, and then looked down at the sentry. She started to arise, and the lieutenant reached down and hoisted rather awkwardly at her arm.

"Don't you worry about him. He's all right."

She turned her face with its curving lips and shining eyes once more toward the unconscious soldier upon the floor. The troopers made a lane to the door, the lieutenant bowed, the girl vanished.

"Queer," said a young officer. "Girl very clearly worst kind of rebel, and yet she falls to weeping and wailing like mad over one of her enemies. Be around in the morning with all sorts of doctoring—you see if she ain't. Queer."

The sharp lieutenant shrugged his shoulders. After reflection he shrugged his shoulders again. He said: "War changes many things; but it doesn't change everything, thank God!"

A MYSTERY OF HEROISM

The dark uniforms of the men were so coated with dust from the incessant wrestling of the two armies that the regiment almost seemed a part of the clay bank which shielded them from the shells. On the top of the hill a battery was arguing in tremendous roars with some other guns, and to the eye of the infantry, the artillerymen, the guns, the caissons, the horses, were distinctly outlined upon the blue sky. When a piece was fired, a red streak as round as a log flashed low in the heavens, like a monstrous bolt of lightning. The men of the battery wore white duck trousers, which somehow emphasized their legs; and when they ran and crowded in little groups at the bidding of the shouting officers, it was more impressive than usual to the infantry.

Fred Collins, of A Company, was saying: "Thunder! I wisht I had a drink. Ain't there any water round here?" Then somebody yelled, "There goes th' bugler!"

As the eyes of half the regiment swept in one machinelike movement there was an instant's picture of a horse in a great convulsive leap of a death wound and a rider leaning back with a crooked arm and spread fingers before his face. On the ground was the crimson terror of an exploding shell, with fibres of flame that seemed like lances. A glittering bugle swung clear of the rider's back as fell headlong the horse and the man. In the air was an odour as from a conflagration.

Sometimes they of the infantry looked down at a fair little meadow which spread at their feet. Its long, green grass was rippling gently in a breeze. Beyond it was the gray form of a house half torn to pieces by shells and by the busy axes of soldiers who had pursued firewood. The line of an old fence was now dimly marked by long weeds and by an occasional post. A shell had blown the well-house to fragments. Little lines of gray smoke ribboning upward from some embers indicated the place where had stood the barn.

From beyond the curtain of green woods there came the sound of some stupendous scuffle, as if two animals of the size of islands were fighting. At a distance there were occasional appearances of swift-moving men, horses, batteries, flags, and, with the crashing of infantry volleys were heard, often, wild and frenzied cheers. In the midst of it all Smith and Ferguson, two privates of A Company, were engaged in a heated discussion, which involved the greatest questions of the national existence.

The battery on the hill presently engaged in a frightful duel. The white legs of the gunners scampered this way and that way, and the officers redoubled their shouts. The guns, with their demeanours of stolidity and courage, were typical of something infinitely self-possessed in this clamour of death that swirled around the hill.

One of a "swing" team was suddenly smitten quivering to the ground, and his maddened brethren dragged his torn body in their struggle to escape from this turmoil and danger. A young soldier astride one of the leaders swore and fumed in his saddle, and furiously jerked at the bridle. An officer screamed out an order so violently that his voice broke and ended the sentence in a falsetto shriek.

The leading company of the infantry regiment was somewhat exposed, and the colonel ordered it moved more fully under the shelter of the hill. There was the clank of steel against steel.

A lieutenant of the battery rode down and passed them, holding his right arm carefully in his left hand. And it was as if this arm was not at all a part of him, but belonged to another man. His sober and reflective charger went slowly. The officer's face was grimy and perspiring, and his uniform was tousled as if he had been in direct grapple with an enemy. He smiled grimly when the men stared at him. He turned his horse toward the meadow.

Collins, of A Company, said: "I wisht I had a drink. I bet there's water in that there ol' well yonder!"

"Yes; but how you goin' to git it?"

For the little meadow which intervened was now suffering a terrible onslaught of shells. Its green and beautiful calm had vanished utterly. Brown earth was being flung in monstrous handfuls. And there was a massacre of the young blades of grass. They were being torn, burned, obliterated. Some curious fortune of the battle had made this gentle little meadow the object of the red hate of the shells, and each one as it exploded seemed like an imprecation in the face of a maiden.

The wounded officer who was riding across this expanse said to himself, "Why, they couldn't shoot any harder if the whole army was massed here!"

A shell struck the gray ruins of the house, and as, after the roar, the shattered wall fell in fragments, there was a noise which resembled the flapping of shutters during a wild gale of winter. Indeed, the infantry paused in the shelter of the bank appeared as men standing upon a shore contemplating a madness of the sea. The angel of calamity had under its glance the battery upon the hill. Fewer white-legged men laboured about the guns. A shell had smitten one of the pieces, and after the flare, the smoke, the dust, the wrath of this blow were gone, it was possible to see white legs stretched horizontally upon the ground. And at that interval to the rear, where it is the business of battery horses to stand with their noses to the fight awaiting the command to drag their guns out of the destruction or into it or wheresoever these incomprehensible humans demanded with whip and spur—in this line of passive and dumb spectators, whose fluttering hearts yet would not let them forget the iron laws of man's control of them—in this rank of brute-soldiers there had been relentless and hideous carnage. From the ruck of bleeding and prostrate horses, the men of the infantry could see one animal raising its stricken body with its fore legs, and turning its nose with mystic and profound eloquence toward the sky.

Some comrades joked Collins about his thirst. "Well, if yeh want a drink so bad, why don't yeh go git it!"

"Well, I will in a minnet, if yeh don't shut up!"

A lieutenant of artillery floundered his horse straight down the hill with as great concern as if it were level ground. As he galloped past the colonel of the infantry, he threw up his hand in swift salute. "We've got to get out of that," he roared angrily. He was a black-bearded officer, and his eyes, which resembled beads, sparkled like those of an insane man. His jumping horse sped along the column of infantry.

The fat major, standing carelessly with his sword held horizontally behind him and with his legs far apart, looked after the receding horseman and laughed. "He wants to get back with orders pretty quick, or there'll be no batt'ry left," he observed.

The wise young captain of the second company hazarded to the lieutenant colonel that the enemy's infantry would probably soon attack the hill, and the lieutenant colonel snubbed him.

A private in one of the rear companies looked out over the meadow, and then turned to a companion and said, "Look there, Jim!" It was the wounded officer from the battery, who some time before had started to ride across the meadow, supporting his right arm carefully with his left hand. This man had encountered a shell apparently at a time when no one perceived him, and he could now be seen lying face downward with a stirruped foot stretched across the body of his dead horse. A leg of the charger extended slantingly upward precisely as stiff as a stake. Around this motionless pair the shells still howled.

There was a quarrel in A Company. Collins was shaking his fist in the faces of some laughing comrades. "Dern yeh! I ain't afraid t' go. If yeh say much, I will go!"

"Of course, yeh will! You'll run through that there medder, won't yeh?"

Collins said, in a terrible voice, "You see now!" At this ominous threat his comrades broke into renewed jeers.

Collins gave them a dark scowl and went to find his captain. The latter was conversing with the colonel of the regiment.

"Captain," said Collins, saluting and standing at attention—in those days all trousers bagged at the knees—"captain, I want t' get permission to go git some water from that there well over yonder!"

The colonel and the captain swung about simultaneously and stared across the meadow. The captain laughed. "You must be pretty thirsty, Collins?"

"Yes, sir, I am."

"Well—ah," said the captain. After a moment, he asked, "Can't you wait?"

"No, sir."

The colonel was watching Collins's face. "Look here, my lad," he said, in a pious sort of a voice—"look here, my lad"—Collins was not a lad—"don't you think that's taking pretty big risks for a little drink of water?"

"I dunno," said Collins uncomfortably. Some of the resentment toward his companions, which perhaps had forced him into this affair, was beginning to fade. "I dunno wether 'tis."

The colonel and the captain contemplated him for a time.

"Well," said the captain finally.

"Well," said the colonel, "if you want to go, why, go."

Collins saluted. "Much obliged t' yeh."

As he moved away the colonel called after him. "Take some of the other boys' canteens with you an' hurry back now."

"Yes, sir, I will."

The colonel and the captain looked at each other then, for it had suddenly occurred that they could not for the life of them tell whether Collins wanted to go or whether he did not.

They turned to regard Collins, and as they perceived him surrounded by gesticulating comrades, the colonel said: "Well, by thunder! I guess he's going."

Collins appeared as a man dreaming. In the midst of the questions, the advice, the warnings, all the excited talk of his company mates, he maintained a curious silence.

They were very busy in preparing him for his ordeal. When they inspected him carefully it was somewhat like the examination that grooms give a horse before a race; and they were amazed, staggered by the whole affair. Their astonishment found vent in strange repetitions.

"Are yeh sure a-goin'?" they demanded again and again.

"Certainly I am," cried Collins, at last furiously.

He strode sullenly away from them. He was swinging five or six canteens by their cords. It seemed that his cap would not remain firmly on his head, and often he reached and pulled it down over his brow.

There was a general movement in the compact column. The long animal-like thing moved slightly. Its four hundred eyes were turned upon the figure of Collins.

"Well, sir, if that ain't th' derndest thing! I never thought Fred Collins had the blood in him for that kind of business."

"What's he goin' to do, anyhow?"

"He's goin' to that well there after water."

"We ain't dyin' of thirst, are we? That's foolishness."

"Well, somebody put him up to it, an' he's doin' it.

"Say, he must be a desperate cuss."

When Collins faced the meadow and walked away from the regiment, he was vaguely conscious that a chasm, the deep valley of all prides, was suddenly between him and his comrades. It was provisional, but the provision was that he return as a victor. He had blindly been led by quaint emotions, and laid himself under an obligation to walk squarely up to the face of death.

But he was not sure that he wished to make a retraction, even if he could do so without shame. As a matter of truth, he was sure of very little. He was mainly surprised.

It seemed to him supernaturally strange that he had allowed his mind to manœuvre his body into such a situation. He understood that it might be called dramatically great.

However, he had no full appreciation of anything, excepting that he was actually conscious of being dazed. He could feel his dulled mind groping after the form and colour of this incident. He wondered why he did not feel some keen agony of fear cutting his sense like a knife. He wondered at this, because human expression had said loudly for centuries that men should feel afraid of certain things, and that all men who did not feel this fear were phenomena— heroes.

He was, then, a hero. He suffered that disappointment which we would all have if we discovered that we were ourselves capable of those deeds which we most admire in history and legend. This, then, was a hero. After all, heroes were not much.

No, it could not be true. He was not a hero. Heroes had no shames in their lives, and, as for him, he remembered borrowing fifteen dollars from a friend and promising to pay it back the next day, and then avoiding that friend for ten months. When at home his mother had aroused him for the early labour of his life on the farm, it had often been his fashion to be irritable, childish, diabolical; and his mother had died since he had come to the war.

He saw that, in this matter of the well, the canteens, the shells, he was an intruder in the land of fine deeds.

He was now about thirty paces from his comrades. The regiment had just turned its many faces toward him.

From the forest of terrific noises there suddenly emerged a little uneven line of men. They fired fiercely and rapidly at distant foliage on which appeared little puffs of white smoke. The spatter of skirmish firing was added to the thunder of the guns on the hill. The little line of men ran forward. A colour sergeant fell flat with his flag as if he had slipped on ice. There was hoarse cheering from this distant field.

Collins suddenly felt that two demon fingers were pressed into his ears. He could see nothing but flying arrows, flaming red. He lurched from the shock of this explosion, but he made a mad rush for the house, which he viewed as a man submerged to the neck in a boiling surf might view the shore. In the air, little pieces of shell howled and the earthquake explosions drove him insane with the menace of their roar. As he ran the canteens knocked together with a rhythmical tinkling.

As he neared the house, each detail of the scene became vivid to him. He was aware of some bricks of the vanished chimney lying on the sod. There was a door which hung by one hinge.

Rifle bullets called forth by the insistent skirmishers came from the far-off bank of foliage. They mingled with the shells and the pieces of shells until the air was torn in all directions by hootings, yells, howls. The sky was full of fiends who directed all their wild rage at his head.

When he came to the well, he flung himself face downward and peered into its darkness. There were furtive silver glintings some feet from the surface. He grabbed one of the canteens and, unfastening its cap, swung it down by the cord. The water flowed slowly in with an indolent gurgle.

And now as he lay with his face turned away he was suddenly smitten with the terror. It came upon his heart like the grasp of claws. All the power faded from his muscles. For an instant he was no more than a dead man.

The canteen filled with a maddening slowness, in the manner of all bottles. Presently he recovered his strength and addressed a screaming oath to it. He leaned over until it seemed as if he intended to try to push water into it with his hands. His eyes as he gazed down into the well shone like two pieces of metal and in their expression was a great appeal and a great curse. The stupid water derided him.

There was the blaring thunder of a shell. Crimson light shone through the swift-boiling smoke and made a pink reflection on part of the wall of the well. Collins jerked out his arm and canteen with the same motion that a man would use in withdrawing his head from a furnace.

He scrambled erect and glared and hesitated. On the ground near him lay the old well bucket, with a length of rusty chain. He lowered it swiftly into the well. The bucket struck the water and then, turning lazily over, sank. When, with hand reaching tremblingly over hand, he hauled it out, it knocked often against the walls of the well and spilled some of its contents.

In running with a filled bucket, a man can adopt but one kind of gait. So through this terrible field over which screamed practical angels of death Collins ran in the manner of a farmer chased out of a dairy by a bull.

His face went staring white with anticipation—anticipation of a blow that would whirl him around and down. He would fall as he had seen other men fall, the life knocked out of them so suddenly that their knees were no more quick to touch the ground than their heads. He saw the long blue line of the regiment, but his comrades were standing looking at him from the edge of an impossible star. He was aware of some deep wheel ruts and hoofprints in the sod beneath his feet.

The artillery officer who had fallen in this meadow had been making groans in the teeth of the tempest of sound. These futile cries, wrenched from him by his agony, were heard only by shells, bullets. When wild-eyed Collins came running, this officer raised himself. His face contorted and blanched from pain, he was about to utter some great beseeching cry. But suddenly his face straightened and he called: "Say, young man, give me a drink of water, will you?"

Collins had no room amid his emotions for surprise. He was mad from the threats of destruction.

"I can't!" he screamed, and in his reply was a full description of his quaking apprehension. His cap was gone and his hair was riotous. His clothes made it appear that he had been dragged over the ground by the heels. He ran on.

The officer's head sank down and one elbow crooked. His foot in its brass-bound stirrup still stretched over the body of his horse and the other leg was under the steed.

But Collins turned. He came dashing back. His face had now turned gray and in his eyes was all terror. "Here it is! here it is!"

The officer was as a man gone in drink. His arm bent like a twig. His head drooped as if his neck were of willow. He was sinking to the ground, to lie face downward.

Collins grabbed him by the shoulder. "Here it is. Here's your drink. Turn over. Turn over, man, for God's sake!"

With Collins hauling at his shoulder, the officer twisted his body and fell with his face turned toward that region where lived the unspeakable noises of the swirling missiles. There was the faintest shadow of a smile on his lips as he looked at Collins. He gave a sigh, a little primitive breath like that from a child.

Collins tried to hold the bucket steadily, but his shaking hands caused the water to splash all over the face of the dying man. Then he jerked it away and ran on.

The regiment gave him a welcoming roar. The grimed faces were wrinkled in laughter.

His captain waved the bucket away. "Give it to the men!"

The two genial, skylarking young lieutenants were the first to gain possession of it. They played over it in their fashion.

When one tried to drink the other teasingly knocked his elbow. "Don't, Billie! You'll make me spill it," said the one. The other laughed.

Suddenly there was an oath, the thud of wood on the ground, and a swift murmur of astonishment among the ranks. The two lieutenants glared at each other. The bucket lay on the ground empty.

AN INDIANA CAMPAIGN

When the able-bodied citizens of the village formed a company and marched away to the war, Major Tom Boldin assumed in a manner the burden of the village cares. Everybody ran to him when they felt obliged to discuss their affairs. The sorrows of the town were dragged before him. His little bench at the sunny side of Migglesville tavern became a sort of an open court where people came to speak resentfully of their grievances. He accepted his position and struggled manfully under the load. It behooved him, as a man who had seen the sky red over the quaint, low cities of Mexico, and the compact Northern bayonets gleaming on the narrow roads.

One warm summer day the major sat asleep on his little bench. There was a lull in the tempest of discussion which usually enveloped him. His cane, by use of which he could make the most tremendous and impressive gestures, reposed beside him. His hat lay upon the bench, and his old bald head had swung far forward until his nose actually touched the first button of his waistcoat.

The sparrows wrangled desperately in the road, defying perspiration. Once a team went jangling and creaking past, raising a yellow blur of dust before the soft tones of the field and sky. In the long grass of the meadow across the road the insects chirped and clacked eternally.

Suddenly a frouzy-headed boy appeared in the roadway, his bare feet pattering rapidly. He was extremely excited. He gave a shrill whoop as he discovered the sleeping major and rushed toward him. He created a terrific panic among some chickens who had been scratching intently near the major's feet. They clamoured in an insanity of fear, and rushed hither and thither seeking a way of escape, whereas in reality all ways lay plainly open to them.

This tumult caused the major to arouse with a sudden little jump of amazement and apprehension. He rubbed his eyes and gazed about him. Meanwhile, some clever chicken had discovered a passage to safety and led the flock into the garden, where they squawked in sustained alarm.

Panting from his run and choked with terror, the little boy stood before the major, struggling with a tale that was ever upon the tip of his tongue.

"Major—now—major——"

The old man, roused from a delicious slumber, glared impatiently at the little boy. "Come, come! What's th' matter with yeh?" he demanded. "What's th' matter? Don't stand there shaking! Speak up!"

"Lots is th' matter!" the little boy shouted valiantly, with a courage born of

146

the importance of his tale, "My ma's chickens 'uz all stole, an'—now—he's over in th' woods!"

"Who is? Who is over in the woods? Go ahead!"

"Now—th' rebel is!"

"What?" roared the major.

"Th' rebel!" cried the little boy, with the last of his breath.

The major pounced from his bench in tempestuous excitement. He seized the little boy by the collar and gave him a great jerk. "Where? Are yeh sure? Who saw 'im? How long ago? Where is he now? Did you see 'im?"

The little boy, frightened at the major's fury, began to sob. After a moment he managed to stammer: "He—now—he's in the woods. I saw 'im. He looks uglier'n anythin'."

The major released his hold upon the boy, and, pausing for a time, indulged in a glorious dream. Then he said: "By thunder! we'll ketch th' cuss. You wait here," he told the boy, "an' don't say a word t' anybody. Do yeh hear?"

The boy, still weeping, nodded, and the major hurriedly entered the inn. He took down from its pegs an awkward, smoothbore rifle and carefully examined the enormous percussion cap that was fitted over the nipple. Mistrusting the cap, he removed it and replaced it with a new one. He scrutinized the gun keenly, as if he could judge in this manner of the condition of the load. All his movements were deliberate and deadly.

When he arrived upon the porch of the tavern he beheld the yard filled with people. Peter Witheby, sooty-faced and grinning, was in the van. He looked at the major. "Well?" he said.

"Well?" returned the major, bridling.

"Well, what's 'che got?" said old Peter.

"'Got?' Got a rebel over in th' woods!" roared the major.

At this sentence the women and boys, who had gathered eagerly about him, gave vent to startled cries. The women had come from adjacent houses, but the little boys represented the entire village. They had miraculously heard the first whisper of rumour, and they performed wonders in getting to the spot. They clustered around the important figure of the major and gazed in silent awe. The women, however, burst forth. At the word "rebel," which represented to them all terrible things, they deluged the major with questions which were obviously unanswerable.

He shook them off with violent impatience. Meanwhile Peter Witheby was trying to force exasperating interrogations through the tumult to the major's ears. "What? No! Yes! How d' I know?" the maddened veteran snarled as he struggled with his friends. "No! Yes! What? How in thunder d' I know?" Upon the steps of the tavern the landlady sat, weeping forlornly.

At last the major burst through the crowd, and went to the roadway. There, as they all streamed after him, he turned and faced them. "Now, look a' here, I don't know any more about this than you do," he told them forcibly. "All that I know is that there's a rebel over in Smith's woods, an' all I know is that I'm agoin' after 'im."

"But hol' on a minnet," said old Peter. "How do yeh know he's a rebel?"

"I know he is!" cried the major. "Don't yeh think I know what a rebel is?"

Then, with a gesture of disdain at the babbling crowd, he marched determinedly away, his rifle held in the hollow of his arm. At this heroic moment a new clamour arose, half admiration, half dismay. Old Peter hobbled after the major, continually repeating, "Hol' on a minnet."

The little boy who had given the alarm was the centre of a throng of lads who gazed with envy and awe, discovering in him a new quality. He held forth to them eloquently. The women stared after the figure of the major and old Peter, his pursuer. Jerozel Bronson, a half-witted lad who comprehended nothing save an occasional genial word, leaned against the fence and grinned like a skull. The major and the pursuer passed out of view around the turn in the road where the great maples lazily shook the dust that lay on their leaves.

For a moment the little group of women listened intently as if they expected to hear a sudden shot and cries from the distance. They looked at each other, their lips a little ways apart. The trees sighed softly in the heat of the summer sun. The insects in the meadow continued their monotonous humming, and, somewhere, a hen had been stricken with fear and was crackling loudly.

Finally, Mrs Goodwin said, "Well, I'm goin' up to th' turn a' th' road, anyhow." Mrs. Willets and Mrs. Joe Petersen, her particular friends, cried out at this temerity, but she said, "Well, I'm goin', anyhow."

She called Bronson. "Come on, Jerozel, You're a man, an' if he should chase us, why, you mus' pitch inteh 'im. Hey?"

Bronson always obeyed everybody. He grinned an assent, and went with her down the road.

A little boy attempted to follow them, but a shrill scream from his mother made him halt.

The remaining women stood motionless, their eyes fixed upon Mrs. Goodwin and Jerozel. Then at last one gave a laugh of triumph at her conquest of caution and fear, and cried, "Well, I'm goin' too!"

Another instantly said, "So am I." There began a general movement. Some of the little boys had already ventured a hundred feet away from the main body, and at this unanimous advance they spread out ahead in little groups. Some recounted terrible stories of rebel ferocity. Their eyes were large with excitement. The whole thing with its possible dangers had for them a delicious element. Johnnie Peterson, who could whip any boy present, explained what he would do in case the enemy should happen to pounce out at him.

The familiar scene suddenly assumed a new aspect. The field of corn which met the road upon the left was no longer a mere field of corn. It was a darkly mystic place whose recesses could contain all manner of dangers. The long green leaves, waving in the breeze, rustled from the passing of men. In the song of the insects there were now omens, threats.

There was a warning in the enamel blue of the sky, in the stretch of yellow road, in the very atmosphere. Above the tops of the corn loomed the distant foliage of Smith's woods, curtaining the silent action of a tragedy whose horrors they imagined.

The women and the little boys came to a halt, overwhelmed by the impressiveness of the landscape. They waited silently.

Mrs. Goodwin suddenly said, "I'm goin' back." The others, who all wished to return, cried at once disdainfully:

"Well, go back, if yeh want to!"

A cricket at the roadside exploded suddenly in his shrill song, and a woman who had been standing near shrieked in startled terror. An electric movement went through the group of women. They jumped and gave vent to sudden screams. With the fears still upon their agitated faces, they turned to berate the one who had shrieked. "My! what a goose you are, Sallie! Why, it took my breath away. Goodness sakes, don't holler like that again!"

* * *

"Hol' on a minnet!" Peter Witheby was crying to the major, as the latter, full of the importance and dignity of his position as protector of Migglesville, paced forward swiftly. The veteran already felt upon his brow a wreath formed of the flowers of gratitude, and as he strode he was absorbed in planning a calm and self-contained manner of wearing it. "Hol' on a minnet!" piped old Peter in the rear.

At last the major, aroused from his dream of triumph, turned about wrathfully. "Well, what?"

"Now, look a' here," said Peter. "What 'che goin' t' do?"

The major, with a gesture of supreme exasperation, wheeled again and went on. When he arrived at the cornfield he halted and waited for Peter. He had suddenly felt that indefinable menace in the landscape.

"Well?" demanded Peter, panting.

The major's eyes wavered a trifle. "Well," he repeated—"well, I'm goin' in there an' bring out that there rebel."

They both paused and studied the gently swaying masses of corn, and behind them the looming woods, sinister with possible secrets.

"Well," said old Peter.

The major moved uneasily and put his hand to his brow. Peter waited in obvious expectation.

The major crossed through the grass at the roadside and climbed the fence. He put both legs over the topmost rail and then sat perched there, facing the woods. Once he turned his head and asked, "What?"

"I hain't said anythin'," answered Peter.

The major clambered down from the fence and went slowly into the corn, his gun held in readiness. Peter stood in the road.

Presently the major returned and said, in a cautious whisper, "If yeh hear anythin', you come a-runnin', will yeh?"

"Well, I hain't got no gun nor nuthin'," said Peter, in the same low tone; "what good 'ud I do?"

"Well, yeh might come along with me an' watch," said the major. "Four eyes is better'n two."

"If I had a gun——" began Peter.

"Oh, yeh don't need no gun," interrupted the major, waving his hand. "All I'm afraid of is that I won't find 'im. My eyes ain't so good as they was."

"Well——"

"Come along," whispered the major. "Yeh hain't afraid, are yeh?"

"No, but——"

"Well, come along, then. What's th' matter with yeh?"

Peter climbed the fence. He paused on the top rail and took a prolonged stare at the inscrutable woods. When he joined the major in the cornfield he said, with a touch of anger:

"Well, you got the gun. Remember that. If he comes for me, I hain't got a blame thing!"

"Shucks!" answered the major. "He ain't agoin' t' come for yeh."

The two then began a wary journey through the corn. One by one the long aisles between the rows appeared. As they glanced along each of them it seemed as if some gruesome thing had just previously vacated it. Old Peter halted once and whispered: "Say, look a' here; supposin'—supposin'——"

"Supposin' what?" demanded the major.

"Supposin'——" said Peter. "Well, remember you got th' gun, an' I hain't got anythin'."

"Thunder!" said the major.

When they got to where the stalks were very short because of the shade cast by the trees of the wood, they halted again. The leaves were gently swishing in the breeze. Before them stretched the mystic green wall of the forest, and there seemed to be in it eyes which followed each of their movements.

Peter at last said, "I don't believe there's anybody in there."

"Yes, there is, too," said the major. "I'll bet anythin' he's in there."

"How d' yeh know?" asked Peter. "I'll bet he ain't within a mile o' here."

The major suddenly ejaculated, "Listen!"

They bent forward, scarce breathing, their mouths agape, their eyes glinting. Finally, the major turned his head. "Did yeh hear that?" he said hoarsely.

"No," said Peter, in a low voice. "What was it?"

The major listened for a moment. Then he turned again. "I thought I heered somebody holler!" he explained cautiously.

They both bent forward and listened once more. Peter in the intentness of his attitude lost his balance and was obliged to lift his foot hastily and with noise. "S-s-sh!" hissed the major.

After a minute Peter spoke quite loudly, "Oh, shucks! I don't believe yeh heered anythin'."

The major made a frantic downward gesture with his hand. "Shet up, will yeh!" he said, in an angry undertone.

Peter became silent for a moment, but presently he said again, 'Oh, yeh didn't hear anythin'."

The major turned to glare at his companion in despair and wrath.

"What's th' matter with yeh? Can't yeh shet up?"

"Oh, this here ain't no use. If you're goin' in after 'im, why don't yeh go in after 'im?"

"Well, gimme time, can't yeh?" said the major, in a growl. And, as if to add more to this reproach, he climbed the fence that compassed the woods, looking resentfully back at his companion.

"Well," said Peter, when the major paused.

The major stepped down upon the thick carpet of brown leaves that stretched under the trees. He turned then to whisper, "You wait here, will yeh?" His face was red with determination.

"Well, hol' on a minnet!" said Peter. "You—I—we'd better——"

"No," said the major. "You wait here."

He went stealthily into the thickets. Peter watched him until he grew to be a vague, slow-moving shadow. From time to time he could hear the leaves crackle and twigs snap under the major's awkward tread. Peter, intent, breathless, waited for the peal of sudden tragedy. Finally, the woods grew silent in a solemn and impressive hush that caused Peter to feel the thumping of his heart. He began to look about him to make sure that nothing should spring upon him from the sombre shadows. He scrutinized this cool gloom before him, and at times he thought he could perceive the moving of swift silent shapes. He concluded that he had better go back and try to muster some assistance to the major.

As Peter came through the corn, the women in the road caught sight of the glittering figure and screamed. Many of them began to run. The little boys, with all their valour, scurried away in clouds. Mrs. Joe Peterson, however, cast a glance over her shoulders as she, with her skirts gathered up, was running as best she could. She instantly stopped and, in tones of deepest scorn, called out to the others, "Why, it's on'y Pete Witheby!" They came faltering back then, those who had been naturally swiftest in the race avoiding the eyes of those whose limbs had enabled them to flee a short distance.

Peter came rapidly, appreciating the glances of vivid interest in the eyes of the women. To their lightning-like questions, which hit all sides of the episode, he opposed a new tranquillity gained from his sudden ascent in importance. He made no answer to their clamour. When he had reached the top of the fence, he called out commandingly: "Here you, Johnnie, you and George, run an' git my gun! It's hangin' on th' pegs over th' bench in th' shop."

At this terrible sentence, a shuddering cry broke from the women. The boys named sped down the road, accompanied by a retinue of envious companions.

Peter swung his legs over the rail and faced the woods again. He twisted his head once to say: "Keep still, can't yeh? Quit scufflin' aroun'!" They could see by his manner that this was a supreme moment. The group became motionless and still. Later, Peter turned to say, "S-s-sh!" to a restless boy, and the air with which he said it smote them all with awe.

The little boys who had gone after the gun came pattering along hurriedly, the weapon borne in the midst of them. Each was anxious to share in the honour. The one who had been delegated to bring it was bullying and directing his comrades.

Peter said, "S-s-sh!" He took the gun and poised it in readiness to sweep the cornfield. He scowled at the boys and whispered angrily: "Why didn't yeh bring th' powder horn an' th' thing with th' bullets in?" I told yeh t' bring 'em. I'll send somebody else next time."

"Yeh didn't tell us!" cried the two boys shrilly.

"S-s-sh! Quit yeh noise," said Peter, with a violent gesture.

However, this reproof enabled other boys to recover that peace of mind which they had lost when seeing their friends loaded with honours.

The women had cautiously approached the fence and, from time to time, whispered feverish questions; but Peter repulsed them savagely, with an air of being infinitely bothered by their interference in his intent watch. They were forced to listen again in silence to the weird and prophetic chanting of the insects and the mystic silken rustling of the corn.

At last the thud of hurrying feet in the soft soil of the field came to their ears. A dark form sped toward them. A wave of a mighty fear swept over the group, and the screams of the women came hoarsely from their choked throats. Peter swung madly from his perch, and turned to use the fence as a rampart.

But it was the major. His face was inflamed and his eyes were glaring. He clutched his rifle by the middle and swung it wildly. He was bounding at a great speed for his fat, short body.

"It's all right! it's all right!" he began to yell, some distance away. "It's all right! It's on'y ol' Milt' Jacoby!"

When he arrived at the top of the fence, he paused and mopped his brow.

"What?" they thundered, in an agony of sudden unreasoning disappointment.

Mrs. Joe Petersen, who was a distant connection of Milton Jacoby, thought to forestall any damage to her social position by saying at once disdainfully, "Drunk, I s'pose!"

"Yep," said the major, still on the fence, and mopped his brow. "Drunk as a fool. Thunder! I was surprised. I—I—thought it was a rebel, sure."

The thoughts of all these women wavered for a time. They were at a loss for precise expression of their emotion. At last, however, they hurled this superior sentence at the major:

"Well, yeh might have known."

A GRAY SLEEVE

"It looks as if it might rain this afternoon," remarked the lieutenant of artillery.

"So it does," the infantry captain assented. He glanced casually at the sky. When his eyes had lowered to the green-shadowed landscape before him, he said fretfully: "I wish those fellows out yonder would quit pelting at us. They've been at it since noon."

At the edge of a grove of maples, across wide fields, there occasionally appeared little puffs of smoke of a dull hue in this gloom of sky which expressed an impending rain. The long wave of blue and steel in the field moved uneasily at the eternal barking of the far-away sharpshooters, and the men, leaning upon their rifles, stared at the grove of maples. Once a private turned to borrow some tobacco from a comrade in the rear rank, but, with his hand still stretched out, he continued to twist his head and glance at the distant trees. He was afraid the enemy would shoot him at a time when he was not looking.

Suddenly the artillery officer said, "See what's coming!"

Along the rear of the brigade of infantry a column of cavalry was sweeping at a hard gallop. A lieutenant, riding some yards to the right of the column, bawled furiously at the four troopers just at the rear of the colours. They had lost distance and made a little gap, but at the shouts of the lieutenant they urged their horses forward. The bugler, careering along behind the captain of the troop, fought and tugged like a wrestler to keep his frantic animal from bolting far ahead of the column.

On the springy turf the innumerable hoofs thundered in a swift storm of sound. In the brown faces of the troopers their eyes were set like bits of flashing steel.

The long line of the infantry regiments standing at ease underwent a sudden movement at the rush of the passing squadron. The foot soldiers turned their heads to gaze at the torrent of horses and men.

The yellow folds of the flag fluttered back in silken, shuddering waves as if it were a reluctant thing. Occasionally a giant spring of a charger would rear the firm and sturdy figure of a soldier suddenly head and shoulders above his comrades. Over the noise of the scudding hoofs could be heard the creaking of leather trappings, the jingle and clank of steel, and the tense, low-toned commands or appeals of the men to their horses. And the horses were mad with the headlong sweep of this movement. Powerful under jaws bent back and straightened so that the bits were clamped as rigidly as vices upon the teeth, and glistening necks arched in desperate resistance to the hands at the bridles. Swinging their heads in rage at the granite laws of their lives, which compelled even their angers and their ardours to chosen directions and chosen faces, their flight was as a flight of harnessed demons.

The captain's bay kept its pace at the head of the squadron with the lithe bounds of a thoroughbred, and this horse was proud as a chief at the roaring trample of his fellows behind him. The captain's glance was calmly upon the grove of maples whence the sharpshooters of the enemy had been picking at the blue line. He seemed to be reflecting. He stolidly rose and fell with the plunges of his horse in all the indifference of a deacon's figure seated plumply in church. And it occurred to many of the watching infantry to wonder why this officer could remain imperturbable and reflective when his squadron was thundering and swarming behind him like the rushing of a flood.

The column swung in a sabre-curve toward a break in a fence, and dashed into a roadway. Once a little plank bridge was encountered, and the sound of the hoofs upon it was like the long roll of many drums. An old captain in the infantry turned to his first lieutenant and made a remark which was a compound of bitter disparagement of cavalry in general and soldiery admiration of this particular troop.

Suddenly the bugle sounded, and the column halted with a jolting upheaval amid sharp, brief cries. A moment later the men had tumbled from their horses, and, carbines in hand, were running in a swarm toward the grove of maples. In the road one of every four of the troopers was standing with braced legs, and pulling and hauling at the bridles of four frenzied horses.

The captain was running awkwardly in his boots. He held his sabre low so that the point often threatened to catch in the turf. His yellow hair ruffled out from under his faded cap. "Go in hard now!" he roared, in a voice of hoarse fury. His face was violently red.

The troopers threw themselves upon the grove like wolves upon a great animal. Along the whole front of woods there was the dry, crackling of musketry, with bitter, swift flashes and smoke that writhed like stung phantoms. The troopers yelled shrilly and spanged bullets low into the foliage.

For a moment, when near the woods, the line almost halted. The men struggled and fought for a time like swimmers encountering a powerful current. Then with a supreme effort they went on again. They dashed madly at the grove, whose foliage from the high light of the field was as inscrutable as a wall.

Then suddenly each detail of the calm trees became apparent, and with a few more frantic leaps the men were in the cool gloom of the woods. There was a heavy odour as from burned paper. Wisps of gray smoke wound upward. The men halted and, grimy, perspiring, and puffing, they searched the recesses of the woods with eager, fierce glances. Figures could be seen flitting afar off. A dozen carbines rattled at them in an angry volley.

During this pause the captain strode along the line, his face lit with a broad smile of contentment. "When he sends this crowd to do anything, I guess he'll find we do it pretty sharp," he said to the grinning lieutenant.

"Say, they didn't stand that rush a minute, did they?" said the subaltern. Both officers were profoundly dusty in their uniforms, and their faces were soiled like those of two urchins.

Out in the grass behind them were three tumbled and silent forms.

Presently the line moved forward again. The men went from tree to tree like hunters stalking game. Some at the left of the line fired occasionally, and those at the right gazed curiously in that direction. The men still breathed heavily from their scramble across the field.

Of a sudden a trooper halted and said: "Hello! there's a house!" Every one paused. The men turned to look at their leader.

The captain stretched his neck and swung his head from side to side. "By George, it is a house!" he said.

Through the wealth of leaves there vaguely loomed the form of a large, white house. These troopers, brown-faced from many days of campaigning, each feature of them telling of their placid confidence and courage, were stopped abruptly by the appearance of this house. There was some subtle suggestion— some tale of an unknown thing—which watched them from they knew not what part of it.

A rail fence girded a wide lawn of tangled grass. Seven pines stood along a driveway which led from two distant posts of a vanished gate. The blue-clothed troopers moved forward until they stood at the fence peering over it.

The captain put one hand on the top rail and seemed to be about to climb the fence, when suddenly he hesitated, and said in a low voice, "Watson, what do you think of it?"

The lieutenant stared at the house. "Derned if I know!" he replied.

The captain pondered. It happened that the whole company had turned a gaze of profound awe and doubt upon this edifice which confronted them. The men were very silent.

At last the captain swore and said: "We are certainly a pack of fools. Derned old deserted house halting a company of Union cavalry, and making us gape like babies!"

"Yes, but there's something—something——" insisted the subaltern in a half stammer.

"Well, if there's 'something—something' in there, I'll get it out," said the captain."Send Sharpe clean around to the other side with about twelve men, so we will sure bag your 'something—something,' and I'll take a few of the boys and find out what's in the d——d old thing!"

He chose the nearest eight men for his "storming party," as the lieutenant called it. After he had waited some minutes for the others to get into position, he said "Come ahead" to his eight men, and climbed the fence.

The brighter light of the tangled lawn made him suddenly feel tremendously apparent, and he wondered if there could be some mystic thing in the house which was regarding this approach. His men trudged silently at his back. They stared at the windows and lost themselves in deep speculations as to the probability of there being, perhaps, eyes behind the blinds—malignant eyes, piercing eyes.

Suddenly a corporal in the party gave vent to a startled exclamation, and half threw his carbine into position. The captain turned quickly, and the corporal said: "I saw an arm move the blinds. An arm with a gray sleeve!"

"Don't be a fool, Jones, now!" said the captain sharply.

"I swear t'——" began the corporal, but the captain silenced him.

When they arrived at the front of the house, the troopers paused, while the captain went softly up the front steps. He stood before the large front door and studied it. Some crickets chirped in the long grass, and the nearest pine could be heard in its endless sighs. One of the privates moved uneasily, and his foot crunched the gravel. Suddenly the captain swore angrily and kicked the door with a loud crash. It flew open.

* * *

The bright lights of the day flashed into the old house when the captain angrily kicked open the door. He was aware of a wide hallway carpeted with matting and extending deep into the dwelling. There was also an old walnut hatrack and a little marble-topped table with a vase and two books upon it. Farther back was a great, venerable fireplace containing dreary ashes.

But directly in front of the captain was a young girl. The flying open of the door had obviously been an utter astonishment to her, and she remained transfixed there in the middle of the floor, staring at the captain with wide eyes.

She was like a child caught at the time of a raid upon the cake. She wavered to and fro upon her feet, and held her hands behind her. There were two little points of terror in her eyes, as she gazed up at the young captain in dusty blue, with his reddish, bronze complexion, his yellow hair, his bright sabre held threateningly.

These two remained motionless and silent, simply staring at each other for some moments.

The captain felt his rage fade out of him and leave his mind limp. He had been violently angry, because this house had made him feel hesitant, wary. He did not like to be wary. He liked to feel confident, sure. So he had kicked the door open, and had been prepared to march in like a soldier of wrath.

But now he began, for one thing, to wonder if his uniform was so dusty and old in appearance. Moreover, he had a feeling that his face was covered with a compound of dust, grime, and perspiration. He took a step forward and said, "I didn't mean to frighten you." But his voice was coarse from his battle-howling. It seemed to him to have hempen fibres in it.

The girl's breath came in little, quick gasps, and she looked at him as she would have looked at a serpent.

"I didn't mean to frighten you," he said again.

The girl, still with her hands behind her, began to back away.

"Is there any one else in the house?" he went on, while slowly following her. "I don't wish to disturb you, but we had a fight with some rebel skirmishers in the woods, and I thought maybe some of them might have come in here. In fact, I was pretty sure of it. Are there any of them here?"

The girl looked at him and said, "No!" He wondered why extreme agitation made the eyes of some women so limpid and bright.

"Who is here besides yourself?"

By this time his pursuit had driven her to the end of the hall, and she remained there with her back to the wall and her hands still behind her. When she answered this question, she did not look at him but down at the floor. She cleared her voice and then said, "There is no one here."

"No one?"

She lifted her eyes to him in that appeal that the human being must make even to falling trees, crashing bowlders, the sea in a storm, and said, "No, no, there is no one here." He could plainly see her tremble.

Of a sudden he bethought him that she continually kept her hands behind her. As he recalled her air when first discovered, he remembered she appeared precisely as a child detected at one of the crimes of childhood. Moreover, she had always backed away from him. He thought now that she was concealing something which was an evidence of the presence of the enemy in the house.

"What are you holding behind you?" he said suddenly.

She gave a little quick moan, as if some grim hand had throttled her.

"What are you holding behind you?"

"Oh, nothing—please. I am not holding anything behind me; indeed I'm not."

"Very well. Hold your hands out in front of you, then."

"Oh, indeed, I'm not holding anything behind me. Indeed, I'm not."

"Well," he began. Then he paused, and remained for a moment dubious. Finally, he laughed. "Well, I shall have my men search the house, anyhow. I'm sorry to trouble you, but I feel sure that there is some one here whom we want." He turned to the corporal, who with the other men was gaping quietly in at the door, and said, "Jones, go through the house."

As for himself, he remained planted in front of the girl, for she evidently did not dare to move and allow him to see what she held so carefully behind her back. So she was his prisoner.

The men rummaged around on the ground floor of the house. Sometimes the captain called to them, "Try that closet," "Is there any cellar?" But they found no one, and at last they went trooping toward the stairs which led to the second floor.

But at this movement on the part of the men the girl uttered a cry—a cry of such fright and appeal that the men paused. "Oh, don't go up there! Please don't go up there!—ple—ease! There is no one there! Indeed—indeed there is not! Oh, ple—ease!"

"Go on, Jones," sad the captain calmly.

The obedient corporal made a preliminary step, and the girl bounded toward the stairs with another cry.

As she passed him, the captain caught sight of that which she had concealed behind her back, and which she had forgotten in this supreme moment. It was a pistol.

She ran to the first step, and standing there, faced the men, one hand extended with perpendicular palm, and the other holding the pistol at her side. "Oh, please, don't go up there! Nobody is there—indeed, there is not! P-l-e-a-s-e!" Then suddenly she sank swiftly down upon the step, and, huddling forlornly, began to weep in the agony and with the convulsive tremors of an infant. The pistol fell from her fingers and rattled down to the floor.

The astonished troopers looked at their astonished captain. There was a short silence.

Finally, the captain stooped and picked up the pistol. It was a heavy weapon of the army pattern. He ascertained that it was empty.

He leaned toward the shaking girl, and said gently, "Will you tell me what you were going to do with this pistol?"

He had to repeat the question a number of times, but at last a muffled voice said, "Nothing."

"Nothing!" He insisted quietly upon a further answer. At the tender tones of the captain's voice, the phlegmatic corporal turned and winked gravely at the man next to him.

"Won't you tell me?"

The girl shook her head.

"Please tell me!"

The silent privates were moving their feet uneasily and wondering how long they were to wait.

The captain said, "Please won't you tell me?"

Then the girl's voice began in stricken tones half coherent, and amid violent sobbing: "It was grandpa's. He—he—he said he was going to shoot anybody who came in here—— he didn't care if there were thousands of 'em. And—and I know he would, and I was afraid they'd kill him. And so—and—so I stole away his pistol—and I was going to hide it when you—you—you kicked open the door."

The men straightened up and looked at each other. The girl began to weep again.

The captain mopped his brow. He peered down at the girl. He mopped his brow again. Suddenly he said, "Ah, don't cry like that."

He moved restlessly and looked down at his boots. He mopped his brow again.

Then he gripped the corporal by the arm and dragged him some yards back from the others. "Jones," he said, in an intensely earnest voice, "will you tell me what in the devil I am going to do?"

The corporal's countenance became illuminated with satisfaction at being thus requested to advise his superior officer. He adopted an air of great thought, and finally said: "Well, of course, the feller with the gray sleeve must be upstairs, and we must get past the girl and up there somehow. Suppose I take her by the arm and lead her——"

"What!" interrupted the captain from between his clinched teeth. As he turned away from the corporal, he said fiercely over his shoulder, "You touch that girl and I'll split your skull!"

* * *

The corporal looked after his captain with an expression of mingled amazement, grief, and philosophy. He seemed to be saying to himself that there unfortunately were times, after all, when one could not rely upon the most reliable of men. When he returned to the group he found the captain bending over the girl and saying, "Why is it that you don't want us to search upstairs?"

The girl's head was buried in her crossed arms. Locks of her hair had escaped from their fastenings and these fell upon her shoulder.

"Won't you tell me?"

The corporal here winked again at the man next to him.

"Because," the girl moaned—"because—there isn't anybody up there."

The captain at last said timidly, "Well, I'm afraid—I'm afraid we'll have to——"

The girl sprang to her feet again, and implored him with her hands. She looked deep into his eyes with her glance, which was at this time like that of the fawn when it says to the hunter, "Have mercy upon me!"

These two stood regarding each other. The captain's foot was on the bottom step, but he seemed to be shrinking. He wore an air of being deeply wretched and ashamed. There was a silence.

Suddenly the corporal said in a quick, low tone, "Look out, captain!"

All turned their eyes swiftly toward the head of the stairs. There had appeared there a youth in a gray uniform. He stood looking coolly down at them. No word was said by the troopers. The girl gave vent to a little wail of desolation, "O Harry!"

He began slowly to descend the stairs. His right arm was in a white sling, and there were some fresh blood stains upon the cloth. His face was rigid and deathly pale, but his eyes flashed like lights. The girl was again moaning in an utterly dreary fashion, as the youth came slowly down toward the silent men in blue.

Six steps from the bottom of the flight he halted and said, "I reckon it's me you're looking for."

The troopers had crowded forward a trifle and, posed in lithe, nervous attitudes, were watching him like cats. The captain remained unmoved. At the youth's question he merely nodded his head and said, "Yes."

The young man in gray looked down at the girl, and then, in the same even tone which now, however, seemed to vibrate with suppressed fury, he said, "And is that any reason why you should insult my sister?"

At this sentence, the girl intervened, desperately, between the young man in gray and the officer in blue. "Oh, don't, Harry, don't! He was good to me! He was good to me, Harry—indeed he was!"

The youth came on in his quiet, erect fashion until the girl could have touched either of the men with her hand, for the captain still remained with his foot upon the first step. She continually repeated: "O Harry! O Harry!"

The youth in gray manœuvred to glare into the captain's face, first over one shoulder of the girl and then over the other. In a voice that rang like metal, he said: "You are armed and unwounded, while I have no weapons and am wounded; but——"

The captain had stepped back and sheathed his sabre. The eyes of these two men were gleaming fire, but otherwise the captain's countenance was imperturbable. He said: "You are mistaken. You have no reason to——"

"You lie!"

All save the captain and the youth in gray started in an electric movement. These two words crackled in the air like shattered glass. There was a breathless silence.

The captain cleared his throat. His look at the youth contained a quality of singular and terrible ferocity, but he said in his stolid tone, "I don't suppose you mean what you say now."

Upon his arm he had felt the pressure of some unconscious little fingers. The girl was leaning against the wall as if she no longer knew how to keep her balance, but those fingers—he held his arm very still. She murmured: "Oh Harry, don't! He was good to me—indeed he was!"

The corporal had come forward until he in a measure confronted the youth in gray, for he saw those fingers upon the captain's arm, and he knew that sometimes very strong men were not able to move hand nor foot under such conditions.

The youth had suddenly seemed to become weak. He breathed heavily and clung to the rail. He was glaring at the captain, and apparently summoning all his will power to combat his weakness. The corporal addressed him with profound straightforwardness, "Don't you be a derned fool!" The youth turned toward him so fiercely that the corporal threw up a knee and an elbow like a boy who expects to be cuffed.

The girl pleaded with the captain. "You won't hurt him, will you? He don't know what he's saying. He's wounded, you know. Please don't mind him!"

"I won't touch him," said the captain, with rather extraordinary earnestness; "don't you worry about him at all. I won't touch him!"

Then he looked at her, and the girl suddenly withdrew her fingers from his arm.

The corporal contemplated the top of the stairs, and remarked without surprise, "There's another of 'em coming!"

An old man was clambering down the stairs with much speed. He waved a cane wildly. "Get out of my house, you thieves! Get out! I won't have you cross my threshold! Get out!" He mumbled and wagged his head in an old man's fury. It was plainly his intention to assault them.

And so it occurred that a young girl became engaged in protecting a stalwart captain, fully armed, and with eight grim troopers at his back, from the attack of an old man with a walking-stick!

A blush passed over the temples and brow of the captain, and he looked particularly savage and weary. Despite the girl's efforts, he suddenly faced the old man.

"Look here," he said distinctly, "we came in because we had been fighting in the woods yonder, and we concluded that some of the enemy were in this house, especially when we saw a gray sleeve at the window. But this young man is wounded, and I have nothing to say to him. I will even take it for granted that there are no others like him upstairs. We will go away, leaving your d——d old house just as we found it! And we are no more thieves and rascals than you are!"

The old man simply roared: "I haven't got a cow nor a pig nor a chicken on the place! Your soldiers have stolen everything they could carry away. They have torn down half my fences for firewood. This afternoon some of your accursed bullets even broke my window panes!"

The girl had been faltering: "Grandpa! O grandpa!"

The captain looked at the girl. She returned his glance from the shadow of the old man's shoulder. After studying her face a moment, he said, "Well, we will go now." He strode toward the door and his men clanked docilely after him.

At this time there was the sound of harsh cries and rushing footsteps from without. The door flew open, and a whirlwind composed of blue-coated troopers came in with a swoop. It was headed by the lieutenant. "Oh, here you are!" he cried, catching his breath. "We thought—— Oh, look at the girl!"

The captain said intensely, "Shut up, you fool!"

The men settled to a halt with a clash and a bang. There could be heard the dulled sound of many hoofs outside of the house.

"Did you order up the horses?" inquired the captain.

"Yes. We thought——"

"Well, then, let's get out of here," interrupted the captain morosely.

The men began to filter out into the open air. The youth in gray had been hanging dismally to the railing of the stairway. He now was climbing slowly up to the second floor. The old man was addressing himself directly to the serene corporal.

"Not a chicken on the place!" he cried.

"Well I didn't take your chickens, did I?"

"No, maybe you didn't, but——"

The captain crossed the hall and stood before the girl in rather a culprit's fashion. "You are not angry at me, are you?" he asked timidly.

"No," she said. She hesitated a moment, and then suddenly held out her hand. "You were good to me—and I'm—much obliged."

The captain took her hand, and then he blushed, for he found himself unable to formulate a sentence that applied in any way to the situation.

She did not seem to heed that hand for a time.

He loosened his grasp presently, for he was ashamed to hold it so long without saying anything clever. At last, with an air of charging an intrenched brigade, he contrived to say, 'I would rather do anything than frighten or trouble you."

His brow was warmly perspiring. He had a sense of being hideous in his dusty uniform and with his grimy face.

She said, "Oh, I'm so glad it was you instead of somebody who might have—might have hurt brother Harry and grandpa!"

He told her, "I wouldn't have hurt 'em for anything!"

There was a little silence.

"Well, good-bye!" he said at last.

"Good-bye!"

He walked toward the door past the old man, who was scolding at the vanishing figure of the corporal. The captain looked back. She had remained there watching him.

At the bugle's order, the troopers standing beside their horses swung briskly into the saddle. The lieutenant said to the first sergeant:

"Williams, did they ever meet before?"

"Hanged if I know!"

"Well, say——"

The captain saw a curtain move at one of the windows. He cantered from his position at the head of the column and steered his horse between two flower beds.

"Well, good-bye!"

The squadron trampled slowly past.

"Good-bye!"

They shook hands.

He evidently had something enormously important to say to her, but it seems that he could not manage it. He struggled heroically. The bay charger, with his great mystically solemn eyes, looked around the corner of his shoulder at the girl.

The captain studied a pine tree. The girl inspected the grass beneath the window. The captain said hoarsely, "I don't suppose—I don't suppose—I'll ever see you again!"

She looked at him affrightedly and shrank back from the window. He seemed to have woefully expected a reception of this kind for his question. He gave her instantly a glance of appeal.

She said, "Why, no, I don't suppose we will."

"Never?"

"Why, no, 'tain't possible. You—you are a—Yankee!"

"Oh, I know it, but——" Eventually he continued, "Well, some day, you know, when there's no more fighting, we might——" He observed that she had again withdrawn suddenly into the shadow, so he said, "Well, good-bye!"

When he held her fingers she bowed her head, and he saw a pink blush steal over the curves of her cheek and neck.

"Am I never going to see you again?"

She made no reply.

"Never?" he repeated

After a long time, he bent over to hear a faint reply: "Sometimes—when there are no troops in the neighbourhood—grandpa don't mind if I—walk over as far as that old oak tree yonder—in the afternoons."

It appeared that the captain's grip was very strong, for she uttered an exclamation and looked at her fingers as if she expected to find them mere fragments. He rode away.

The bay horse leaped a flower bed. They were almost to the drive, when the girl uttered a panic-stricken cry.

The captain wheeled his horse violently and upon his return journey went straight through a flower bed.

The girl had clasped her hands. She beseeched him wildly with her eyes. "Oh, please, don't believe it! I never walk to the old oak tree. Indeed, I don't! I never—never—never walk there."

The bridle drooped on the bay charger's neck. The captain's figure seemed limp. With an expression of profound dejection and gloom he stared off at where the leaden sky met the dark green line of the woods. The long-impending rain began to fall with a mournful patter, drop and drop. There was a silence.

At last a low voice said, "Well—I might—sometimes I might—perhaps—but only once in a great while—I might walk to the old tree—in the afternoons."

THE VETERAN

Out of the low window could be seen three hickory trees placed irregularly in a meadow that was resplendent in springtime green. Farther away, the old, dismal belfry of the village church loomed over the pines. A horse meditating in the shade of one of the hickories lazily swished his tail. The warm sunshine made an oblong of vivid yellow on the floor of the grocery.

"Could you see the whites of their eyes?" said the man who was seated on a soap box.

"Nothing of the kind," replied old Henry warmly. "Just a lot of flitting figures, and I let go at where they 'peared to be the thickest. Bang!"

"Mr. Fleming," said the grocer—his deferential voice expressed somehow the old man's exact social weight—"Mr. Fleming, you never was frightened much in them battles, was you?"

The veteran looked down and grinned. Observing his manner, the entire group tittered. "Well, I guess I was," he answered finally. "Pretty well scared, sometimes. Why, in my first battle I thought the sky was falling down. I thought the world was coming to an end. You bet I was scared."

Every one laughed. Perhaps it seemed strange and rather wonderful to them that a man should admit the thing, and in the tone of their laughter there was probably more admiration than if old Fleming had declared that he had always been a lion. Moreover, they knew that he had ranked as an orderly sergeant, and so their opinion of his heroism was fixed. None, to be sure, knew how an orderly sergeant ranked, but then it was understood to be somewhere just shy of a major general's stars. So, when old Henry admitted that he had been frightened, there was a laugh.

"The trouble was," said the old man, "I thought they were all shooting at me. Yes, sir, I thought every man in the other army was aiming at me in particular, and only me. And it seemed so darned unreasonable, you know, I wanted to explain to 'em what an almighty good fellow I was, because I thought then they might quit all trying to hit me. But I couldn't explain, and they kept on being unreasonable—blim!—blam!—bang! So I run!"

Two little triangles of wrinkles appeared at the corners of his eyes. Evidently he appreciated some comedy in this recital. Down near his feet, however, little Jim, his grandson, was visibly horror-stricken. His hands were clasped nervously, and his eyes were wide with astonishment at this terrible scandal, his most magnificent grandfather telling such a thing.

163

"That was at Chancellorsville. Of course, afterward I got kind of used to it. A man does. Lots of men, though, seem to feel all right from the start. I did, as soon as I 'got on to it,' as they say now; but at first I was pretty well flustered. Now, there was young Jim Conklin, old Si Conklin's son—that used to keep the tannery—you none of you recollect him—well, he went into it from the start just as if he was born to it. But with me it was different. I had to get used to it."

When little Jim walked with his grandfather he was in the habit of skipping along on the stone pavement in front of the three stores and the hotel of the town and betting that he could avoid the cracks. But upon this day he walked soberly, with his hand gripping two of his grandfather's fingers. Sometimes he kicked abstractedly at dandelions that curved over the walk. Any one could see that he was much troubled.

"There's Sickles's colt over in the medder, Jimmie," said the old man. "Don't you wish you owned one like him?"

"Um," said the boy, with a strange lack of interest. He continued his reflections. Then finally he ventured, "Grandpa—now—was that true what you was telling those men?"

"What?" asked the grandfather. "What was I telling them?"

"Oh, about your running."

"Why, yes, that was true enough, Jimmie. It was my first fight, and there was an awful lot of noise, you know."

Jimmie seemed dazed that this idol, of its own will, should so totter. His stout boyish idealism was injured.

Presently the grandfather said: "Sickles's colt is going for a drink. Don't you wish you owned Sickles's colt, Jimmie?"

The boy merely answered, "He ain't as nice as our'n." He lapsed then into another moody silence.

* * *

One of the hired men, a Swede, desired to drive to the county seat for purposes of his own. The old man loaned a horse and an unwashed buggy. It appeared later that one of the purposes of the Swede was to get drunk.

After quelling some boisterous frolic of the farm hands and boys in the garret, the old man had that night gone peacefully to sleep, when he was aroused by clamouring at the kitchen door. He grabbed his trousers, and they waved out behind as he dashed forward. He could hear the voice of the Swede, screaming and blubbering. He pushed the wooden button, and, as the door flew open, the Swede, a maniac, stumbled inward, chattering, weeping, still screaming: "De barn fire! Fire! Fire! De barn fire! Fire! Fire! Fire!"

There was a swift and indescribable change in the old man. His face ceased instantly to be a face; it became a mask, a gray thing, with horror written about the mouth and eyes. He hoarsely shouted at the foot of the little rickety stairs, and immediately, it seemed, there came down an avalanche of men. No one knew that during this time the old lady had been standing in her night clothes at the bedroom door, yelling: "What's th' matter? What's th' matter? What's th' matter?"

When they dashed toward the barn it presented to their eyes its usual appearance, solemn, rather mystic in the black night. The Swede's lantern was overturned at a point some yards in front of the barn doors. It contained a wild little conflagration of its own, and even in their excitement some of those who ran felt a gentle secondary vibration of the thrifty part of their minds at the sight of this overturned lantern. Under ordinary circumstances it would have been a calamity.

But the cattle in the barn were trampling, trampling, trampling, and above this noise could be heard a humming like the song of innumerable bees. The old man hurled aside the great doors, and a yellow flame leaped out at one corner and sped and wavered frantically up the old gray wall. It was glad, terrible, this single flame, like the wild banner of deadly and triumphant foes.

The motley crowd from the garret had come with all the pails of the farm. They flung themselves upon the well. It was a leisurely old machine, long dwelling in indolence. It was in the habit of giving out water with a sort of reluctance. The men stormed at it, cursed it; but it continued to allow the buckets to be filled only after the wheezy windlass had howled many protests at the mad-handed men.

With his opened knife in his hand old Fleming himself had gone headlong into the barn, where the stifling smoke swirled with the air currents, and where could be heard in its fulness the terrible chorus of the flames, laden with tones of hate and death, a hymn of wonderful ferocity.

He flung a blanket over an old mare's head, cut the halter close to the manger, led the mare to the door, and fairly kicked her out to safety. He returned with the same blanket, and rescued one of the work horses. He took five horses out, and then came out himself, with his clothes bravely on fire. He had no whiskers, and very little hair on his head. They soused five pailfuls of water on him. His eldest son made a clean miss with the sixth pailful, because the old man had turned and was running down the decline and around to the basement of the barn, where were the stanchions of the cows. Some one noticed at the time that he ran very lamely, as if one of the frenzied horses had smashed his hip.

The cows, with their heads held in the heavy stanchions, had thrown themselves, strangled themselves, tangled themselves: done everything which the ingenuity of their exuberant fear could suggest to them.

Here, as at the well, the same thing happened to every man save one. Their hands went mad. They became incapable of everything save the power to rush into dangerous situations.

The old man released the cow nearest the door, and she, blind drunk with terror, crashed into the Swede. The Swede had been running to and fro babbling. He carried an empty milk pail, to which he clung with an unconscious, fierce enthusiasm. He shrieked like one lost as he went under the cow's hoofs, and the milk pail, rolling across the floor, made a flash of silver in the gloom.

Old Fleming took a fork, beat off the cow, and dragged the paralyzed Swede to the open air. When they had rescued all the cows save one, which had so fastened herself that she could not be moved an inch, they returned to the front of the barn and stood sadly, breathing like men who had reached the final point of human effort.

Many people had come running. Some one had even gone to the church, and now, from the distance, rang the tocsin note of the old bell. There was a long flare of crimson on the sky, which made remote people speculate as to the whereabouts of the fire.

The long flames sang their drumming chorus in voices of the heaviest bass. The wind whirled clouds of smoke and cinders into the faces of the spectators. The form of the old barn was outlined in black amid these masses of orange-hued flames.

And then came this Swede again, crying as one who is the weapon of the sinister fates. "De colts! De colts! You have forgot de colts!"

Old Fleming staggered. It was true; they had forgotten the two colts in the box stalls at the back of the barn. "Boys," he said, "I must try to get 'em out." They clamoured about him then, afraid for him, afraid of what they should see. Then they talked wildly each to each. "Why, it's sure death!" "He would never get out!" "Why, it's suicide for a man to go in there!" Old Fleming stared absentmindedly at the open doors. "The poor little things!" he said. He rushed into the barn.

When the roof fell in, a great funnel of smoke swarmed toward the sky, as if the old man's mighty spirit, released from its body—a little bottle—had swelled like the genie of fable. The smoke was tinted rose-hue from the flames, and perhaps the unutterable midnights of the universe will have no power to daunt the colour of this soul.

THE
OPEN BOAT
and other tales of adventure

CONTENTS

THE OPEN BOAT

N one of them knew the color of the sky. Their eyes glanced level, and were fastened upon the waves that swept toward them. These waves were of the hue of slate, save for the tops, which were of foaming white, and all of the men knew the colors of the sea. The horizon narrowed and widened, and dipped and rose, and at all times its edge was jagged with waves that seemed thrust up in points like rocks.

Many a man ought to have a bath-tub larger than the boat which here rode upon the sea. These waves were most wrongfully and barbarously abrupt and tall, and each froth-top was a problem in small-boat navigation.

The cook squatted in the bottom, and looked with both eyes at the six inches of gunwale which separated him from the ocean. His sleeves were rolled over his fat forearms, and the two flaps of his unbuttoned vest dangled as he bent to bail out the boat. Often he said, "Gawd! that was a narrow clip." As he remarked it he invariably gazed eastward over the broken sea.

The oiler, steering with one of the two oars in the boat, sometimes raised himself suddenly to keep clear of water that swirled in over the stern. It was a thin little oar, and it seemed often ready to snap.

The correspondent, pulling at the other oar, watched the waves and wondered why he was there.

The injured captain, lying in the bow, was at this time buried in that profound dejection and indifference which comes, temporarily at least, to even the bravest and most enduring when, willy-nilly, the firm fails, the army loses, the ship goes down. The mind of the master of a vessel is rooted deep in the timbers of her, though he command for a day or a decade; and this captain had on him the stern impression of a scene in the grays of dawn of seven turned faces, and later a stump of a topmast with a white ball on it, that slashed to and fro at the waves, went low and lower, and down. Thereafter there was something strange in his voice. Although steady, it was deep with mourning, and of a quality beyond oration or tears.

"Keep 'er a little more south, Billie," said he.

"A little more south, sir," said the oiler in the stern.

A seat in this boat was not unlike a seat upon a bucking broncho, and, by the same token, a broncho is not much smaller. The craft pranced and reared

171

and plunged like an animal. As each wave came, and she rose for it, she seemed like a horse making at a fence outrageously high. The manner of her scramble over these walls of water is a mystic thing, and, moreover, at the top of them were ordinarily these problems in white water, the foam racing down from the summit of each wave, requiring a new leap, and a leap from the air. Then, after scornfully bumping a crest, she would slide and race and splash down a long incline, and arrive bobbing and nodding in front of the next menace.

A singular disadvantage of the sea lies in the fact that, after successfully surmounting one wave, you discover that there is another behind it, just as important and just as nervously anxious to do something effective in the way of swamping boats. In a ten-foot dinghy one can get an idea of the resources of the sea in the line of waves that is not probable to the average experience, which is never at sea in a dinghy. As each slaty wall of water approached, it shut all else from the view of the men in the boat, and it was not difficult to imagine that this particular wave was the final outburst of the ocean, the last effort of the grim water. There was a terrible grace in the move of the waves, and they came in silence, save for the snarling of the crests.

In the wan light the faces of the men must have been gray. Their eyes must have glinted in strange ways as they gazed steadily astern. Viewed from a balcony, the whole thing would, doubtless, have been weirdly picturesque. But the men in the boat had no time to see it, and if they had had leisure, there were other things to occupy their minds. The sun swung steadily up the sky, and they knew it was broad day because the color of the sea changed from slate to emerald-green streaked with amber lights, and the foam was like tumbling snow. The process of the breaking day was unknown to them. They were aware only of this effect upon the color of the waves that rolled toward them.

In disjointed sentences the cook and the correspondent argued as to the difference between a life-saving station and a house of refuge. The cook had said: "There's a house of refuge just north of the Mosquito Inlet Light, and as soon as they see us they'll come off in their boat and pick us up."

"As soon as who see us?" said the correspondent.

"The crew," said the cook.

"Houses of refuge don't have crews," said the correspondent. "As I understand them, they are only places where clothes and grub are stored for the benefit of shipwrecked people. They don't carry crews."

"Oh, yes, they do," said the cook.

"No, they don't," said the correspondent.

"Well, we're not there yet, anyhow," said the oiler in the stern.

"Well," said the cook, "perhaps it's not a house of refuge that I'm thinking of as being near Mosquito Inlet Light; perhaps it's a life-saving station."

"We're not there yet," said the oiler in the stern.

* * *

As the boat bounced from the top of each wave the wind tore through the hair of the hatless men, and as the craft plopped her stern down again the spray slashed past them. The crest of each of these waves was a hill, from the top of which the men surveyed for a moment a broad, tumultuous expanse, shining and wind-riven. It was probably splendid, it was probably glorious, this play of the free sea, wild with lights of emerald and white and amber.

"Bully good thing it's an on-shore wind," said the cook. "If not, where would we be? Would n't have a show."

"That's right," said the correspondent.

The busy oiler nodded his assent.

Then the captain, in the bow, chuckled in a way that expressed humor, contempt, tragedy, all in one. "Do you think we've got much of a show now, boys?" said he.

Whereupon the three were silent, save for a trifle of hemming and hawing. To express any particular optimism at this time they felt to be childish and stupid, but they all doubtless possessed this sense of the situation in their minds. A young man thinks doggedly at such times. On the other hand, the ethics of their condition was decidedly against any open suggestion of hopelessness. So they were silent.

"Oh, well," said the captain, soothing his children, "we'll get ashore all right."

But there was that in his tone which made them think; so the oiler quoth, "Yes! if this wind holds."

The cook was bailing. "Yes! if we don't catch hell in the surf."

Canton-flannel gulls flew near and far. Sometimes they sat down on the sea, near patches of brown seaweed that rolled over the waves with a movement like carpets on a line in a gale. The birds sat comfortably in groups, and they were envied by some in the dinghy, for the wrath of the sea was no more to them than it was to a covey of prairie-chickens a thousand miles inland. Often they came very close and stared at the men with black, bead-like eyes. At these times they were uncanny and sinister in their unblinking scrutiny, and the men hooted angrily at them, telling them to be gone. One came, and evidently decided to alight on the top of the captain's head. The bird flew parallel to the boat, and did not circle, but made short sidelong jumps in the air in chicken fashion. His black eyes were wistfully fixed upon the captain's head. "Ugly brute," said the oiler to the bird. "You look as if you were made with a jack-knife." The cook and the correspondent swore darkly at the creature. The captain naturally wished to knock it away with the end of the heavy painter, but he did not dare do it, because anything resembling an emphatic gesture would have capsized this freighted boat; and so, with his open hand, the captain gently and carefully waved the gull away. After it had been discouraged from the pursuit the captain breathed easier on account of his hair, and others breathed easier because the bird struck their minds at this time as being somehow gruesome and ominous.

In the meantime the oiler and the correspondent rowed; and also they rowed. They sat together in the same seat, and each rowed an oar. Then the oiler took both oars; then the correspondent took both oars; then the oiler; then the correspondent. They rowed and they rowed. The very ticklish part of the business was when the time came for the reclining one in the stern to take his turn at the oars. By the very last star of truth, it is easier to steal eggs from under a hen than it was to change seats in the dinghy. First the man in the stern slid his hand along the thwart and moved with care, as if he were of Sèvres. Then the man in the rowing-seat slid his hand along the other thwart. It was all done with the most extraordinary care. As the two sidled past each other, the whole party kept watchful eyes on the coming wave, and the captain cried: "Look out, now! Steady, there!"

The brown mats of seaweed that appeared from time to time were like islands, bits of earth. They were traveling, apparently, neither one way nor the other. They were, to all intents, stationary. They informed the men in the boat that it was making progress slowly toward the land.

The captain, rearing cautiously in the bow after the dinghy soared on a great swell, said that he had seen the lighthouse at Mosquito Inlet. Presently the cook remarked that he had seen it. The correspondent was at the oars then, and for some reason he too wished to look at the lighthouse; but his back was toward the far shore, and the waves were important, and for some time he could not seize an opportunity to turn his head. But at last there came a wave more gentle than the others, and when at the crest of it he swiftly scoured the western horizon.

"See it?" said the captain.

"No," said the correspondent, slowly; "I didn't see anything."

"Look again," said the captain. He pointed. "It's exactly in that direction."

At the top of another wave the correspondent did as he was bid, and this time his eyes chanced on a small, still thing on the edge of the swaying horizon. It was precisely like the point of a pin. It took an anxious eye to find a lighthouse so tiny.

"Think we'll make it, Captain?"

"If this wind holds and the boat don't swamp, we can't do much else," said the captain.

The little boat, lifted by each towering sea and splashed viciously by the crests, made progress that in the absence of seaweed was not apparent to those in her. She seemed just a wee thing wallowing miraculously, top up, at the mercy of five oceans. Occasionally a great spread of water, like white flames, swarmed into her.

"Bail her, cook," said the captain, serenely.

"All right, Captain," said the cheerful cook.

* * *

It would be difficult to describe the subtle brotherhood of men that was here established on the seas. No one said that it was so. No one mentioned it. But it dwelt in the boat, and each man felt it warm him. They were a captain, an oiler, a cook, and a correspondent, and they were friends—friends in a more curiously iron-bound degree than may be common. The hurt captain, lying against the water-jar in the bow, spoke always in a low voice and calmly; but he could never command a more ready and swiftly obedient crew than the motley three of the dinghy. It was more than a mere recognition of what was best for the common safety. There was surely in it a quality that was personal and heartfelt. And after this devotion to the commander of the boat, there was this comradeship, that the correspondent, for instance, who had been taught to be cynical of men, knew even at the time was the best experience of his life. But no one said that it was so. No one mentioned it.

"I wish we had a sail," remarked the captain. "We might try my overcoat on the end of an oar, and give you two boys a chance to rest." So the cook and the correspondent held the mast and spread wide the overcoat; the oiler steered; and the little boat made good way with her new rig. Sometimes the oiler had to scull sharply to keep a sea from breaking into the boat, but otherwise sailing was a success.

Meanwhile the lighthouse had been growing slowly larger. It had now almost assumed color, and appeared like a little gray shadow on the sky. The man at the oars could not be prevented from turning his head rather often to try for a glimpse of this little gray shadow.

At last, from the top of each wave, the men in the tossing boat could see land. Even as the lighthouse was an upright shadow on the sky, this land seemed but a long black shadow on the sea. It certainly was thinner than paper. "We must be about opposite New Smyrna," said the cook, who had coasted this shore often in schooners. "Captain, by the way, I believe they abandoned that life-saving station there about a year ago."

"Did they?" said the captain.

The wind slowly died away. The cook and the correspondent were not now obliged to slave in order to hold high the oar; but the waves continued their old impetuous swooping at the dinghy, and the little craft, no longer under way, struggled woundily over them. The oiler or the correspondent took the oars again.

Shipwrecks are *apropos* of nothing. If men could only train for them and have them occur when the men had reached pink condition, there would be less drowning at sea. Of the four in the dinghy none had slept any time worth mentioning for two days and two nights previous to embarking in the dinghy, and in the excitement of clambering about the deck of a foundering ship they had also forgotten to eat heartily.

For these reasons, and for others, neither the oiler nor the correspondent was fond of rowing at this time. The correspondent wondered ingenuously how in the name of all that was sane could there be people who thought it amusing to row a boat. It was not an amusement; it was a diabolical punishment, and even a genius of mental aberrations could never conclude that it was anything but a horror to the muscles and a crime against the back. He mentioned to the boat in general how the amusement of rowing struck him, and the weary-faced oiler smiled in full sympathy. Previously to the foundering, by the way, the oiler had worked double watch in the engine-room of the ship.

"Take her easy now, boys," said the captain. "Don't spend yourselves. If we have to run a surf you'll need all your strength, because we'll sure have to swim for it. Take your time."

Slowly the land arose from the sea. From a black line it became a line of black and a line of white—trees and sand. Finally the captain said that he could make out a house on the shore. "That's the house of refuge, sure," said the cook. "They'll see us before long, and come out after us."

The distant lighthouse reared high. "The keeper ought to be able to make us out now, if he's looking through a glass," said the captain. "He'll notify the life-saving people."

"None of those other boats could have got ashore to give word of the wreck," said the oiler, in a low voice, "else the life-boat would be out hunting us."

Slowly and beautifully the land loomed out of the sea. The wind came again. It had veered from the northeast to the southeast. Finally a new sound struck the ears of the men in the boat. It was the low thunder of the surf on the shore. "We'll never be able to make the lighthouse now," said the captain. "Swing her head a little more north, Billie."

"A little more north, sir," said the oiler.

Whereupon the little boat turned her nose once more down the wind, and all but the oarsman watched the shore grow. Under the influence of this expansion doubt and direful apprehension were leaving the minds of the men. The management of the boat was still most absorbing, but it could not prevent a quiet cheerfulness. In an hour, perhaps, they would be ashore.

Their backbones had become thoroughly used to balancing in the boat, and they now rode this wild colt of a dinghy like circus men. The correspondent thought that he had been drenched to the skin, but happening to feel in the top pocket of his coat, he found therein eight cigars. Four of them were soaked with sea-water; four were perfectly scatheless. After a search, somebody produced three dry matches; and thereupon the four waifs rode in their little boat and, with an assurance of an impending rescue shining in their eyes, puffed at the big cigars, and judged well and ill of all men. Everybody took a drink of water.

* * *

"Cook," remarked the captain, "there don't seem to be any signs of life about your house of refuge."

"No," replied the cook. "Funny they don't see us!"

A broad stretch of lowly coast lay before the eyes of the men. It was of low dunes topped with dark vegetation. The roar of the surf was plain, and sometimes they could see the white lip of a wave as it spun up the beach. A tiny house was blocked out black upon the sky. Southward, the slim lighthouse lifted its little gray length.

Tide, wind, and waves were swinging the dinghy northward. "Funny they don't see us," said the men.

The surf's roar was here dulled, but its tone was nevertheless thunderous and mighty. As the boat swam over the great rollers the men sat listening to this roar. "We'll swamp sure," said everybody.

It is fair to say here that there was not a life-saving station within twenty miles in either direction; but the men did not know this fact, and in consequence they made dark and opprobrious remarks concerning the eyesight of the nation's life-savers. Four scowling men sat in the dinghy, and surpassed records in the invention of epithets.

"Funny they don't see us."

The light-heartedness of a former time had completely faded. To their sharpened minds it was easy to conjure pictures of all kinds of incompetency and blindness and, indeed, cowardice. There was the shore of the populous land,

and it was bitter and bitter to them that from it came no sign.

"Well," said the captain, ultimately, "I suppose we'll have to make a try for ourselves. If we stay out here too long, we'll none of us have strength left to swim after the boat swamps."

And so the oiler, who was at the oars, turned the boat straight for the shore. There was a sudden tightening of muscles. There was some thinking.

"If we don't all get ashore," said the captain,—"if we don't all get ashore, I suppose you fellows know where to send news of my finish?"

They then briefly exchanged some addresses and admonitions. As for the reflections of the men, there was a great deal of rage in them. Perchance they might be formulated thus: "If I am going to be drowned—if I am going to be drowned—if I am going to be drowned, why, in the name of the seven mad gods who rule the sea, was I allowed to come thus far and contemplate sand and trees? Was I brought here merely to have my nose dragged away as I was about to nibble the sacred cheese of life? It is preposterous! If this old ninny-woman, Fate, cannot do better than this, she should be deprived of the management of men's fortunes. She is an old hen who knows not her intention. If she has decided to drown me, why did she not do it in the beginning, and save me all this trouble? The whole affair is absurd.... But no; she cannot mean to drown me. She dare not drown me. She cannot drown me. Not after all this work!" Afterward the man might have had an impulse to shake his fist at the clouds. "Just you drown me, now, and then hear what I call you!"

The billows that came at this time were more formidable. They seemed always just about to break and roll over the little boat in a turmoil of foam. There was a preparatory and long growl in the speech of them. No mind unused to the sea would have concluded that the dinghy could ascend these sheer heights in time. The shore was still afar. The oiler was a wily surfman. "Boys," he said swiftly, "she won't live three minutes more, and we're too far out to swim. Shall I take her to sea again, Captain?"

"Yes; go ahead!" said the captain.

This oiler, by a series of quick miracles and fast and steady oarsmanship, turned the boat in the middle of the surf and took her safely to sea again.

There was a considerable silence as the boat bumped over the furrowed sea to deeper water. Then somebody in gloom spoke: "Well, anyhow, they must have seen us from the shore by now."

The gulls went in slanting flight up the wind toward the gray, desolate east. A squall, marked by dingy clouds, and clouds brick-red, like smoke from a burning building, appeared from the southeast.

"What do you think of those life-saving people? Ain't they peaches?"

"Funny they haven't seen us."

"Maybe they think we're out here for sport! Maybe they think we're fishin'. Maybe they think we're damned fools."

It was a long afternoon. A changed tide tried to force them southward, but wind and wave said northward. Far ahead, where coast-line, sea, and sky formed their mighty angle, there were little dots which seemed to indicate a city on the shore.

"St. Augustine?"

The captain shook his head. "Too near Mosquito Inlet."

And the oiler rowed, and then the correspondent rowed; then the oiler rowed. It was a weary business. The human back can become the seat of more aches and pains than are registered in books for the composite anatomy of a regiment. It is a limited area, but it can become the theater of innumerable muscular conflicts, tangles, wrenches, knots, and other comforts.

"Did you ever like to row, Billie?" asked the correspondent.

"No," said the oiler; "hang it!"

When one exchanged the rowing-seat for a place in the bottom of the boat, he suffered a bodily depression that caused him to be careless of everything save an obligation to wiggle one finger. There was cold sea-water swashing to and fro in the boat, and he lay in it. His head, pillowed on a thwart, was within an inch of the swirl of a wave-crest, and sometimes a particularly obstreperous sea came inboard and drenched him once more. But these matters did not annoy him. It is almost certain that if the boat had capsized he would have tumbled comfortably out upon the ocean as if he felt sure that it was a great, soft mattress.

"Look! There's a man on the shore!"

"Where?"

"There! See 'im? See 'im?"

"Yes, sure ! He's walking along."

"Now he's stopped. Look! He's facing us!"

"He's waving at us!"

"So he is! By thunder!"

"Ah, now we're all right! Now we're all right! There'll be a boat out here for us in half an hour."

"He's going on. He's running. He's going up to that house there."

The remote beach seemed lower than the sea, and it required a searching glance to discern the little black figure. The captain saw a floating stick, and they rowed to it. A bath towel was by some weird chance in the boat, and tying this on the stick, the captain waved it. The oarsman did not dare turn his head, so he was obliged to ask questions.

"What's he doing now?"

"He's standing still again. He's looking, I think. ... There he goes again— toward the house. ... Now he's stopped again."

"Is he waving at us?"

"No, not now; he was, though."

"Look! There comes another man!"

"He's running."

"Look at him go, would you!"

"Why, he's on a bicycle. Now he's met the other man. They're both waving at us. Look!"

"There comes something up the beach."

"What the devil is that thing?"

"Why, it looks like a boat."

"Why, certainly, it's a boat."

"No; it's on wheels."

"Yes, so it is. Well, that must be the life-boat. They drag them along shore on a wagon."

"That's the life-boat, sure."

"No, by——,it's—it's an omnibus."

"I tell you it's a life-boat."

"It is not! It's an omnibus. I can see it plain. See? One of these big hotel omnibuses."

"By thunder, you're right. It's an omnibus, sure as fate. What do you suppose they are doing with an omnibus? Maybe they are going around collecting the life-crew, hey?"

"That's it, likely. Look! There's a fellow waving a little black flag. He's standing on the steps of the omnibus. There come those other two fellows. Now they're all talking together. Look at the fellow with the flag. Maybe he ain't waving it!"

"That ain't a flag, is it? That's his coat. Why, certainly, that's his coat."

"So it is; it's his coat. He's taken it off and is waving it around his head. But would you look at him swing it!"

"Oh, say, there isn't any life-saving station there. That's just a winter-resort hotel omnibus that has brought over some of the boarders to see us drown."

"What's that idiot with the coat mean? What's he signaling, anyhow?"

"It looks as if he were trying to tell us to go north. There must be a life-saving station up there."

"No; he thinks we're fishing. Just giving us a merry hand. See? Ah, there, Willie!"

"Well, I wish I could make something out of those signals. What do you suppose he means?"

"He don't mean anything; he's just playing."

"Well, if he'd just signal us to try the surf again, or to go to sea and wait, or go north, or go south, or go to hell, there would be some reason in it. But look at him! He just stands there and keeps his coat revolving like a wheel. The ass!"

"There come more people."

"Now there's quite a mob. Look! Isn't that a boat?"

"Where? Oh, I see where you mean. No, that's no boat."

"That fellow is still waving his coat."

"He must think we like to see him do that. Why don't he quit it? It don't mean anything."

"I don't know. I think he is trying to make us go north. It must be that there's a life-saving station there somewhere."

"Say, he ain't tired yet. Look at 'im wave!"

"Wonder how long he can keep that up. He's been revolving his coat ever since he caught sight of us. He's an idiot. Why aren't they getting men to bring a boat out? A fishing-boat—one of those big yawls—could come out here all right. Why don't he do something?"

"Oh, it's all right now."

"They'll have a boat out here for us in less than no time, now that they've seen us."

A faint yellow tone came into the sky over the low land. The shadows on the sea slowly deepened. The wind bore coldness with it, and the men began to shiver.

"Holy smoke!" said one, allowing his voice to express his impious mood, "if we keep on monkeying out here! If we've got to flounder out here all night!"

"Oh, we'll never have to stay here all night! Don't you worry. They've seen us now, and it won't be long before they'll come chasing out after us."

The shore grew dusky. The man waving a coat blended gradually into this gloom, and it swallowed in the same manner the omnibus and the group of people. The spray, when it dashed uproariously over the side, made the voyagers shrink and swear like men who were being branded.

"I'd like to catch the chump who waved the coat. I feel like soaking him one, just for luck."

"Why? What did he do?"

"Oh, nothing, but then he seemed so damned cheerful."

In the meantime the oiler rowed, and then the correspondent rowed, and then the oiler rowed. Gray-faced and bowed forward, they mechanically, turn by turn, plied the leaden oars. The form of the lighthouse had vanished from the southern horizon, but finally a pale star appeared, just lifting from the sea. The streaked saffron in the west passed before the all-merging darkness, and the sea to the east was black. The land had vanished, and was expressed only by the low and drear thunder of the surf.

"If I am going to be drowned—if I am going to be drowned—if I am going to be drowned, why, in the name of the seven mad gods who rule the sea, was I allowed to come thus far and contemplate sand and trees? Was I brought here merely to have my nose dragged away as I was about to nibble the sacred cheese of life?"

The patient captain, drooped over the water-jar, was sometimes obliged to speak to the oarsman.

"Keep her head up! Keep her head up!"

"Keep her head up, sir." The voices were weary and low.

This was surely a quiet evening. All save the oarsman lay heavily and listlessly in the boat's bottom. As for him, his eyes were just capable of noting the tall black waves that swept forward in a most sinister silence, save for an occasional subdued growl of a crest.

The cook's head was on a thwart, and he looked without interest at the water under his nose. He was deep in other scenes. Finally he spoke. "Billie," he murmured dreamfully, "what kind of pie do you like best?"

* * *

"Pie!" said the oiler and the correspondent, agitatedly. "Don't talk about those things, blast you!"

"Well," said the cook, "I was just thinking about ham sandwiches, and—"

A night on the sea in an open boat is a long night. As darkness settled finally, the shine of the light, lifting from the sea in the south, changed to full gold. On the northern horizon a new light appeared, a small bluish gleam on the edge of the waters. These two lights were the furniture of the world. Otherwise there was nothing but waves.

Two men huddled in the stern, and distances were so magnificent in the dinghy that the rower was enabled to keep his feet partly warm by thrusting them under his companions. Their legs indeed extended far under the rowing-seat until they touched the feet of the captain forward. Sometimes, despite the efforts of the tired oarsman, a wave came piling into the boat, an icy wave of the night, and the chilling water soaked them anew. They would twist their bodies for a moment and groan, and sleep the dead sleep once more, while the water in the boat gurgled about them as the craft rocked.

The plan of the oiler and the correspondent was for one to row until he lost the ability, and then arouse the other from his sea-water couch in the bottom of the boat.

The oiler plied the oars until his head drooped forward and the overpowering sleep blinded him; and he rowed yet afterward. Then he touched a man in the bottom of the boat, and called his name. "Will you spell me for a little while?" he said meekly.

"Sure, Billie," said the correspondent, awaking and dragging himself to a sitting position. They exchanged places carefully, and the oiler, cuddling down in the sea-water at the cook's side, seemed to go to sleep instantly.

The particular violence of the sea had ceased. The waves came without snarling. The obligation of the man at the oars was to keep the boat headed so that the tilt of the rollers would not capsize her, and to preserve her from filling when the crests rushed past. The black waves were silent and hard to be seen in the darkness. Often one was almost upon the boat before the oarsman was aware.

In a low voice the correspondent addressed the captain. He was not sure that the captain was awake, although this iron man seemed to be always awake. "Captain, shall I keep her making for that light north, sir?"

The same steady voice answered him. "Yes. Keep it about two points off the port bow."

The cook had tied a life-belt around himself in order to get even the warmth which this clumsy cork contrivance could donate, and he seemed almost stovelike when a rower, whose teeth invariably chattered wildly as soon as he ceased his labor, dropped down to sleep.

The correspondent, as he rowed, looked down at the two men sleeping under foot. The cook's arm was around the oiler's shoulders, and, with their fragmentary clothing and haggard faces, they were the babes of the sea—a grotesque rendering of the old babes in the wood.

Later he must have grown stupid at his work, for suddenly there was a growling of water, and a crest came with a roar and a swash into the boat, and it was a wonder that it did not set the cook afloat in his life-belt. The cook continued to sleep, but the oiler sat up, blinking his eyes and shaking with the new cold.

"Oh, I'm awful sorry, Billie," said the correspondent, contritely.

"That's all right, old boy," said the oiler, and lay down again and was asleep.

Presently it seemed that even the captain dozed, and the correspondent thought that he was the one man afloat on all the oceans. The wind had a voice as it came over the waves, and it was sadder than the end.

There was a long, loud swishing astern of the boat, and a gleaming trail of phosphorescence, like blue flame, was furrowed on the black waters. It might have been made by a monstrous knife.

Then there came a stillness, while the correspondent breathed with the open mouth and looked at the sea.

Suddenly there was another swish and another long flash of bluish light, and this time it was alongside the boat, and might almost have been reached with an oar. The correspondent saw an enormous fin speed like a shadow through the water, hurling the crystalline spray and leaving the long glowing trail.

The correspondent looked over his shoulder at the captain. His face was hidden, and he seemed to be asleep. He looked at the babes of the sea. They certainly were asleep. So, being bereft of sympathy, he leaned a little way to one side and swore softly into the sea.

But the thing did not then leave the vicinity of the boat. Ahead or astern, on one side or the other, at intervals long or short, fled the long sparkling streak, and there was to be heard the whiroo of the dark fin. The speed and power of the thing was greatly to be admired. It cut the water like a gigantic and keen projectile.

The presence of this biding thing did not affect the man with the same horror that it would if he had been a picnicker. He simply looked at the sea dully and swore in an undertone.

Nevertheless, it is true that he did not wish to be alone with the thing. He wished one of his companions to awake by chance and keep him company with it. But the captain hung motionless over the water-jar, and the oiler and the cook in the bottom of the boat were plunged in slumber.

* * *

"If I am going to be drowned—if I am going to be drowned—if I am going to be drowned, why, in the name of the seven mad gods who rule the sea, was I allowed to come thus far and contemplate sand and trees?"

During this dismal night, it may be remarked that a man would conclude that it was really the intention of the seven mad gods to drown him, despite the abominable injustice of it. For it was certainly an abominable injustice to drown a man who had worked so hard, so hard. The man felt it would be a crime most unnatural. Other people had drowned at sea since galleys swarmed with painted sails, but still—

When it occurs to a man that nature does not regard him as important, and that she feels she would not maim the universe by disposing of him, he at first wishes to throw bricks at the temple, and he hates deeply the fact that there are no bricks and no temples. Any visible expression of nature would surely be pelleted with his jeers.

Then, if there be no tangible thing to hoot, he feels, perhaps, the desire to confront a personification and indulge in pleas, bowed to one knee, and with hands supplicant, saying, "Yes, but I love myself."

A high cold star on a winter's night is the word he feels that she says to him. Thereafter he knows the pathos of his situation.

The men in the dinghy had not discussed these matters, but each had, no doubt, reflected upon them in silence and according to his mind. There was seldom any expression upon their faces save the general one of complete weariness. Speech was devoted to the business of the boat.

To chime the notes of his emotion, a verse mysteriously entered the correspondent's head. He had even forgotten that he had forgotten this verse, but it suddenly was in his mind.

> A soldier of the Legion lay dying in Algiers;
> There was lack of woman's nursing, there was dearth of woman's tears;
> But a comrade stood beside him, and he took that comrade's hand,
> And he said, "I never more shall see my own, my native land."

In his childhood the correspondent had been made acquainted with the fact that a soldier of the Legion lay dying in Algiers, but he had never regarded it as important. Myriads of his school-fellows had informed him of the soldier's plight, but the dinning had naturally ended by making him perfectly indifferent. He had never considered it his affair that a soldier of the Legion lay dying in Algiers, nor had it appeared to him as a matter for sorrow. It was less to him than breaking of a pencil's point.

Now, however, it quaintly came to him as a human, living thing. It was no longer merely a picture of a few throes in the breast of a poet, meanwhile drinking tea and warming his feet at the grate; it was an actuality—stern, mournful, and fine.

The correspondent plainly saw the soldier. He lay on the sand with his feet out straight and still. While his pale left hand was upon his chest in an attempt to thwart the going of his life, the blood came between his fingers. In the far Algerian distance, a city of low square forms was set against a sky that was faint with the last sunset hues. The correspondent, plying the oars and dreaming of the slow and slower movements of the lips of the soldier, was moved by a profound and perfectly impersonal comprehension. He was sorry for the soldier of the Legion who lay dying in Algiers.

The thing which had followed the boat and waited had evidently grown bored at the delay. There was no longer to be heard the slash of the cutwater, and there was no longer the flame of the long trail. The light in the north still glimmered, but it was apparently no nearer to the boat. Sometimes the boom of the surf rang in the correspondent's ears, and he turned the craft seaward then and rowed harder. Southward, some one had evidently built a watch-fire on the beach. It was too low and too far to be seen, but it made a shimmering, roseate reflection upon the bluff back of it, and this could be discerned from the boat. The wind came stronger, and sometimes a wave suddenly raged out like a mountain-cat, and there was to be seen the sheen and sparkle of a broken crest.

The captain, in the bow, moved on his water-jar and sat erect. "Pretty long night," he observed to the correspondent. He looked at the shore. "Those life-saving people take their time."

"Did you see that shark playing around?"

"Yes, I saw him. He was a big fellow, all right."

"Wish I had known you were awake."

Later the correspondent spoke into the bottom of the boat.

"Billie!" There was a slow and gradual disentanglement. "Billie, will you spell me?"

"Sure," said the oiler.

As soon as the correspondent touched the cold, comfortable sea-water in the bottom of the boat and had huddled close to the cook's life-belt he was deep in sleep, despite the fact that his teeth played all the popular airs. This sleep was so good to him that it was but a moment before he heard a voice call his name in a tone that demonstrated the last stages of exhaustion. "Will you spell me?"

"Sure, Billie."

The light in the north had mysteriously vanished, but the correspondent took his course from the wide-awake captain.

Later in the night they took the boat farther out to sea, and the captain directed the cook to take one oar at the stern and keep the boat facing the seas. He was to call out if he should hear the thunder of the surf. This plan enabled the oiler and the correspondent to get respite together. "We'll give those boys a chance to get into shape again," said the captain. They curled down and, after a few preliminary chatterings and trembles, slept once more the dead sleep. Neither knew they had bequeathed to the cook the company of another shark, or perhaps the same shark.

As the boat caroused on the waves, spray occasionally bumped over the side and gave them a fresh soaking, but this had no power to break their repose. The ominous slash of the wind and the water affected them as it would have affected mummies.

"Boys," said the cook, with the notes of every reluctance in his voice, "she's drifted in pretty close. I guess one of you had better take her to sea again." The correspondent, aroused, heard the crash of the toppled crests.

As he was rowing, the captain gave him some whisky and water, and this steadied the chills out of him. "If I ever get ashore and anybody shows me even a photograph of an oar—"

At last there was a short conversation.

"Billie! . . . Billie, will you spell me?"

"Sure," said the oiler.

* * *

When the correspondent again opened his eyes, the sea and the sky were each of the gray hue of the dawning. Later, carmine and gold was painted upon the waters. The morning appeared finally, in its splendor, with a sky of pure blue, and the sunlight flamed on the tips of the waves.

On the distant dunes were set many little black cottages, and a tall white windmill reared above them. No man, nor dog, nor bicycle appeared on the beach. The cottages might have formed a deserted village.

The voyagers scanned the shore. A conference was held in the boat. "Well," said the captain, "if no help is coming, we might better try a run through the surf right away. If we stay out here much longer we will be too weak to do anything for ourselves at all." The others silently acquiesced in this reasoning. The boat was headed for the beach. The correspondent wondered if none ever ascended the tall wind-tower, and if then they never looked seaward. This tower was a giant, standing with its back to the plight of the ants. It represented in a degree, to the correspondent, the serenity of nature amid the struggles of the individual—nature in the wind, and nature in the vision of men. She did not seem cruel to him then, nor beneficent, nor treacherous, nor wise. But she was indifferent, flatly indifferent. It is, perhaps, plausible that a man in this situation, impressed with the unconcern of the universe, should see the innumerable flaws of his life and have them taste wickedly in his mind and wish for another chance. A distinction between right and wrong seems absurdly clear to him, then, in this new ignorance of the grave-edge, and he understands that if he were given another opportunity he would mend his conduct and his words, and be better and brighter during an introduction or at a tea.

"Now, boys," said the captain, "she is going to swamp sure. All we can do is to work her in as far as possible, and then when she swamps, pile out and scramble for the beach. Keep cool now, and don't jump until she swamps sure."

The oiler took the oars. Over his shoulders he scanned the surf. "Captain," he said, "I think I'd better bring her about, and keep her head-on to the seas, and back her in."

"All right, Billie," said the captain. "Back her in." The oiler swung the boat then, and, seated in the stern, the cook and the correspondent were obliged to look over their shoulders to contemplate the lonely and indifferent shore.

The monstrous inshore rollers heaved the boat high until the men were again enabled to see the white sheets of water scudding up the slanted beach. "We won't get in very close," said the captain. Each time a man could wrest his attention from the rollers, he turned his glance toward the shore, and in the expression of the eyes during this contemplation there was a singular quality. The correspondent, observing the others, knew that they were not afraid, but the full meaning of their glances was shrouded.

As for himself, he was too tired to grapple fundamentally with the fact. He tried to coerce his mind into thinking of it, but the mind was dominated at this time by the muscles, and the muscles said they did not care. It merely occurred to him that if he should drown it would be a shame.

There were no hurried words, no pallor, no plain agitation. The men simply looked at the shore. "Now, remember to get well clear of the boat when you jump," said the captain.

Seaward the crest of a roller suddenly fell with a thunderous crash, and the long white comber came roaring down upon the boat.

"Steady now," said the captain. The men were silent. They turned their eyes from the shore to the comber and waited. The boat slid up the incline, leaped at the furious top, bounced over it, and swung down the long back of the wave. Some water had been shipped, and the cook bailed it out.

But the next crest crashed also. The tumbling, boiling flood of white water caught the boat and whirled it almost perpendicular. Water swarmed in from all sides. The correspondent had his hands on the gunwale at this time, and when the water entered at that place he swiftly withdrew his fingers, as if he objected to wetting them.

The little boat, drunken with this weight of water, reeled and snuggled deeper into the sea.

"Bail her out, cook! Bail her out!" said the captain.

"All right, Captain," said the cook.

"Now, boys, the next one will do for us sure," said the oiler. "Mind to jump clear of the boat."

The third wave moved forward, huge, furious, implacable. It fairly swallowed the dinghy, and almost simultaneously the men tumbled into the sea. A piece of life-belt had lain in the bottom of the boat, and as the correspondent went overboard he held this to his chest with his left hand.

The January water was icy, and he reflected immediately that it was colder than he had expected to find it off the coast of Florida. This appeared to his dazed mind as a fact important enough to be noted at the time. The coldness of the water was sad; it was tragic. This fact was somehow mixed and confused with his opinion of his own situation so that it seemed almost a proper reason for tears. The water was cold.

When he came to the surface he was conscious of little but the noisy water. Afterward he saw his companions in the sea. The oiler was ahead in the race. He was swimming strongly and rapidly. Off to the correspondent's left, the cook's great white and corked back bulged out of the water; and in the rear the captain was hanging with his one good hand to the keel of the overturned dinghy.

There is a certain immovable quality to a shore, and the correspondent wondered at it amid the confusion of the sea.

It seemed also very attractive; but the correspondent knew that it was a long journey, and he paddled leisurely. The piece of life-preserver lay under him, and sometimes he whirled down the incline of a wave as if he were on a hand-sled.

But finally he arrived at a place in the sea where travel was beset with difficulty. He did not pause swimming to inquire what manner of current had caught him, but there his progress ceased. The shore was set before him like a bit of scenery on a stage, and he looked at it, and understood with his eyes each detail of it.

As the cook passed, much farther to the left, the captain was calling to him, "Turn over on your back, cook! Turn over on your back and use the oar."

"All right, sir." The cook turned on his back, and, paddling with an oar, went ahead as if he were a canoe.

Presently the boat also passed to the left of the correspondent, with the captain clinging with one hand to the keel. He would have appeared like a man raising himself to look over a board fence if it were not for the extraordinary gymnastics of the boat. The correspondent marveled that the captain could still hold to it.

They passed on nearer to shore,—the oiler, the cook, the captain,—and following them went the water-jar, bouncing gaily over the seas.

The correspondent remained in the grip of this strange new enemy, a current. The shore, with its white slope of sand and its green bluff, topped with little silent cottages, was spread like a picture before him. It was very near to him then, but he was impressed as one who, in a gallery, looks at a scene from Brittany or Algiers.

He thought: "I am going to drown? Can it be possible? Can it be possible? Can it be possible?" Perhaps an individual must consider his own death to be the final phenomenon of nature.

But later a wave perhaps whirled him out of this small deadly current, for he found suddenly that he could again make progress toward the shore. Later still he was aware that the captain, clinging with one hand to the keel of the dinghy, had his face turned away from the shore and toward him, and was calling his name. "Come to the boat! Come to the boat!"

In his struggle to reach the captain and the boat, he reflected that when one gets properly wearied drowning must really be a comfortable arrangement—a cessation of hostilities accompanied by a large degree of relief; and he was glad of it, for the main thing in his mind for some moments had been horror of the temporary agony; he did not wish to be hurt.

Presently he saw a man running along the shore. He was undressing with most remarkable speed. Coat, trousers, shirt, everything flew magically off him.

"Come to the boat!" called the captain.

"All right, Captain." As the correspondent paddled, he saw the captain let himself down to bottom and leave the boat. Then the correspondent performed his one little marvel of the voyage. A large wave caught him and flung him with ease and supreme speed completely over the boat and far beyond it. It struck him even then as an event in gymnastics and a true miracle of the sea. An overturned boat in the surf is not a plaything to a swimming man.

The correspondent arrived in water that reached only to his waist, but his condition did not enable him to stand for more than a moment. Each wave knocked him into a heap, and the undertow pulled at him.

Then he saw the man who had been running and undressing, and undressing and running, come bounding into the water. He dragged ashore the cook, and then waded toward the captain; but the captain waved him away and sent him to the correspondent. He was naked—naked as a tree in winter; but a halo was about his head, and he shone like a saint. He gave a strong pull, and a long drag, and a bully heave at the correspondent's hand. The correspondent, schooled in the minor formulæ, said, "Thanks, old man." But suddenly the man cried, "What's that?" He pointed a swift finger. The correspondent said, "Go."

In the shallows, face downward, lay the oiler. His forehead touched sand that was periodically, between each wave, clear of the sea.

The correspondent did not know all that transpired afterward. When he achieved safe ground he fell, striking the sand with each particular part of his body. It was as if he had dropped from a roof, but the thud was grateful to him.

It seems that instantly the beach was populated with men with blankets, clothes, and flasks, and women with coffee-pots and all the remedies sacred to their minds. The welcome of the land to the men from the sea was warm and generous; but a still and dripping shape was carried slowly up the beach, and the land's welcome for it could only be the different and sinister hospitality of the grave.

When it came night, the white waves paced to and fro in the moonlight, and the wind brought the sound of the great sea's voice to the men on shore, and they felt that they could then be interpreters.

A MAN AND SOME OTHERS

Dark mesquit spread from horizon to horizon. There was no house or horseman from which a mind could evolve a city or a crowd. The world was declared to be a desert and unpeopled. Sometimes, however, on days when no heat-mist arose, a blue shape, dim, of the substance of a specter's veil, appeared in the southwest, and a pondering sheep-herder might remember that there were mountains.

In the silence of these plains the sudden and childish banging of a tin pan could have made an iron-nerved man leap into the air. The sky was ever flawless; the manœuvering of clouds was an unknown pageant; but at times a sheep-herder could see, miles away, the long, white streamers of dust rising from the feet of another's flock, and the interest became intense.

Bill was arduously cooking his dinner, bending over the fire and toiling like a blacksmith. A movement, a flash of strange color, perhaps, off in the bushes, caused him suddenly to turn his head. Presently he arose, and, shading his eyes with his hand, stood motionless and gazing. He perceived at last a Mexican sheep-herder winding through the brush toward his camp.

"Hello!" shouted Bill.

The Mexican made no answer, but came steadily forward until he was within some twenty yards. There he paused, and, folding his arms, drew himself up in the manner affected by the villain in the play. His serape muffled the lower part of his face, and his great sombrero shaded his brow. Being unexpected and also silent, he had something of the quality of an apparition; moreover, it was clearly his intention to be mystic and sinister.

The American's pipe, sticking carelessly in the corner of his mouth, was twisted until the wrong side was uppermost, and he held his frying-pan poised in the air. He surveyed with evident surprise this apparition in the mesquit. "Hello, José!" he said; "what's the matter?"

The Mexican spoke with the solemnity of funeral tollings: "Beel, you mus' geet off range. We want you geet off range. We no like. Un'erstan'? We no like."

"What you talking about?" said Bill. "No like what?"

"We no like you here. Un'erstan'? Too mooch. You mus' geet out. We no like. Un'erstan'?"

"Understand? No; I don't know what the blazes you're gittin' at." Bill's eyes wavered in bewilderment, and his jaw fell. "I must git out? I must git off the range? What you givin' us?"

The Mexican unfolded his serape with his small yellow hand. Upon his face was then to be seen a smile that was gently, almost caressingly, murderous. "Beel," he said, "git out!"

Bill's arm dropped until the frying-pan was at his knee. Finally he turned again toward the fire. "Go on, you dog-gone little yaller rat!" he said over his shoulder. "You fellers can't chase me off this range. I got as much right here as anybody."

"Beel," answered the other in a vibrant tone, thrusting his head forward and moving one foot, "you geet out or we keel you."

"Who will?" said Bill.

"I—and the others." The Mexican tapped his breast gracefully.

Bill reflected for a time, and then he said: "You ain't got no manner of license to warn me off'n this range, and I won't move a rod. Understand? I've got rights, and I suppose if I don't see 'em through, no one is likely to give me a good hand and help me lick you fellers, since I'm the only white man in half a day's ride. Now, look: if you fellers try to rush this camp, I'm goin' to plug about fifty per cent. of the gentlemen present, sure. I'm goin' in for trouble, an' I'll git a lot of you. 'Nuther thing: if I was a fine valuable caballero like you, I'd stay in the rear till the shootin' was done, because I'm goin' to make a particular p'int of shootin' you through the chest." He grinned affably, and made a gesture of dismissal.

As for the Mexican, he waved his hands in a consummate expression of indifference. "Oh, all right," he said. Then, in a tone of deep menace and glee, he added: "We will keel you eef you no geet. They have decide."

"They have, have they?" said Bill. "Well, you tell them to go to the devil!"

* * *

Bill had been a mine-owner in Wyoming, a great man, an aristocrat, one who possessed unlimited credit in the saloons down the gulch. He had the social weight that could interrupt a lynching or advise a bad man of the particular merits of a remote geographical point. However, the fates exploded the toy balloon with which they had amused Bill, and on the evening of the same day he was a professional gambler with ill fortune dealing him unspeakable irritation in the shape of three big cards whenever another fellow stood pat. It is well here to inform the world that Bill considered his calamities of life all dwarfs in comparison with the excitement of one particular evening, when three kings came to him with criminal regularity against a man who always filled a straight. Later he became a cow-boy, more weirdly abandoned than if he had never been an aristocrat. By this time all that remained of his former splendor was his pride, or his vanity, which was one thing which need not have remained. He killed the foreman of the ranch over an inconsequent matter as to which of them was a liar, and the midnight train carried him eastward. He became a brakeman on the Union Pacific, and really gained high honors in the hobo war that for many years has devastated the beautiful railroads of our country. A creature of ill fortune himself, he practised all the ordinary cruelties upon these other creatures of ill fortune. He was of so fierce a mien that tramps usually surrendered at once whatever coin or tobacco they had in their possession; and if afterward he kicked them from the train, it was only because this was a recognized treachery of the war upon the hoboes. In a famous battle fought in Nebraska in 1879, he would have achieved a lasting distinction if it had not been for a deserter from the United States army. He was at the head of a heroic and sweeping charge, which really broke the power of the hoboes in that county for three months; he had already worsted four tramps with his own coupling-stick, when a stone thrown by the ex-third baseman of F Troop's nine laid him flat on the prairie, and later enforced a stay in the hospital in Omaha. After his recovery he engaged with other railroads, and shuffled cars in countless yards. An order to strike came upon him in Michigan, and afterward the vengeance of the railroad pursued him until he assumed a name. This mask is like the darkness in which the burglar chooses to move. It destroys many of the healthy fears. It is a small thing, but it eats that which we call our conscience. The conductor of No. 419 stood in the caboose within two feet of Bill's nose, and called him a liar. Bill requested him to use a milder term. He had not bored the foreman of Tin Can Ranch with any such request, but had killed him with expedition. The conductor seemed to insist, and so Bill let the matter drop.

He became the bouncer of a saloon on the Bowery in New York. Here most of his fights were as successful as had been his brushes with the hoboes in the West. He gained the complete admiration of the four clean bartenders who stood behind the great and glittering bar. He was an honored man. He nearly killed Bad Hennessy, who, as a matter of fact, had more reputation than ability, and his fame moved up the Bowery and down the Bowery.

But let a man adopt fighting as his business, and the thought grows constantly within him that it is his business to fight. These phrases became mixed in Bill's mind precisely as they are here mixed; and let a man get this idea in his mind, and defeat begins to move toward him over the unknown ways of circumstances. One summer night three sailors from the U.S.S. *Seattle* sat in the saloon drinking and attending to other people's affairs in an amiable fashion. Bill was a proud man since he had thrashed so many citizens, and it suddenly occurred to him that the loud talk of the sailors was very offensive. So he swaggered upon their attention, and warned them that the saloon was the flowery abode of peace and gentle silence. They glanced at him in surprise, and without a moment's pause consigned him to a worse place than any stoker of them knew. Whereupon he flung one of them through the side door before the others could prevent it. On the sidewalk there was a short struggle, with many hoarse epithets in the air, and then Bill slid into the saloon again. A frown of false rage was upon his brow, and he strutted like a savage king. He took a long yellow night-stick from behind the lunch-counter, and started importantly toward the main doors to see that the incensed seamen did not again enter.

The ways of sailormen are without speech, and, together in the street, the three sailors exchanged no word, but they moved at once. Landsmen would have required three years of discussion to gain such unanimity. In silence, and immediately, they seized a long piece of scantling that lay handily. With one forward to guide the battering-ram, and with two behind him to furnish the power, they made a beautiful curve, and came down like the Assyrians on the front door of that saloon.

Strange and still strange are the laws of fate. Bill, with his kingly frown and his long night-stick, appeared at precisely that moment in the doorway. He stood like a statue of victory; his pride was at its zenith; and in the same second this atrocious piece of scantling punched him in the bulwarks of his stomach, and he vanished like a mist. Opinions differed as to where the end of the scantling landed him, but it was ultimately clear that it landed him in southwestern Texas, where he became a sheep-herder.

The sailors charged three times upon the plate-glass front of the saloon, and when they had finished, it looked as if it had been the victim of a rural fire company's success in saving it from the flames. As the proprietor of the place surveyed the ruins, he remarked that Bill was a very zealous guardian of property. As the ambulance surgeon surveyed Bill, he remarked that the wound was really an excavation.

* * *

As his Mexican friend tripped blithely away, Bill turned with a thoughtful face to his frying-pan and his fire. After dinner he drew his revolver from its scarred old holster, and examined every part of it. It was the revolver that had dealt death to the foreman, and it had also been in free fights in which it had dealt death to several or none. Bill loved it because its allegiance was more than that of man, horse, or dog. It questioned neither social nor moral position; it obeyed alike the saint and the assassin. It was the claw of the eagle, the tooth of the lion, the poison of the snake; and when he swept it from its holster, this minion smote where he listed, even to the battering of a far penny. Wherefore it was his dearest possession, and was not to be exchanged in southwestern Texas for a handful of rubies, nor even the shame and homage of the conductor of No. 419.

During the afternoon he moved through his monotony of work and leisure with the same air of deep meditation. The smoke of his supper-time fire was curling across the shadowy sea of mesquit when the instinct of the plainsman warned him that the stillness, the desolation, was again invaded. He saw a motionless horseman in black outline against the pallid sky. The silhouette displayed serape and sombrero, and even the Mexican spurs as large as pies. When this black figure began to move toward the camp, Bill's hand dropped to his revolver.

The horseman approached until Bill was enabled to see pronounced American features, and a skin too red to grow on a Mexican face. Bill released his grip on his revolver.

"Hello!" called the horseman.

"Hello!" answered Bill.

The horseman cantered forward. "Good evening," he said, as he again drew rein.

"Good evenin'," answered Bill, without committing himself by too much courtesy.

For a moment the two men scanned each other in a way that is not ill-mannered on the plains, where one is in danger of meeting horse-thieves or tourists.

Bill saw a type which did not belong in the mesquit. The young fellow had invested in some Mexican trappings of an expensive kind. Bill's eyes searched the outfit for some sign of craft, but there was none. Even with his local regalia, it was clear that the young man was of a far, black Northern city. He had discarded the enormous stirrups of his Mexican saddle; he used the small English stirrup, and his feet were thrust forward until the steel tightly gripped his ankles. As Bill's eyes traveled over the stranger, they lighted suddenly upon the stirrups and the thrust feet, and immediately he smiled in a friendly way. No dark purpose could dwell in the innocent heart of a man who rode thus on the plains.

As for the stranger, he saw a tattered individual with a tangle of hair and beard, and with a complexion turned brick-color from the sun and whisky. He saw a pair of eyes that at first looked at him as the wolf looks at the wolf, and then became childlike, almost timid, in their glance. Here was evidently a man who had often stormed the iron walls of the city of success, and who now sometimes valued himself as the rabbit values his prowess.

The stranger smiled genially, and sprang from his horse. "Well, sir, I suppose you will let me camp here with you to-night?"

"Eh?" said Bill.

"I suppose you will let me camp here with you to-night?"

Bill for a time seemed too astonished for words. "Well," he answered, scowling in inhospitable annoyance, "well, I don't believe this here is a good place to camp to-night, mister."

The stranger turned quickly from his saddle-girth.

"What?" he said in surprise. "You don't want me here? You don't want me to camp here?"

Bill's feet scuffled awkwardly, and he looked steadily at a cactus-plant. "Well, you see, mister," he said, "I'd like your company well enough, but—you see, some of these here greasers are goin' to chase me off the range to-night; and while I might like a man's company all right, I couldn't let him in for no such game when he ain't got nothin' to do with the trouble."

"Going to chase you off the range?" cried the stranger.

"Well, they said they were goin' to do it," said Bill.

"And—great heavens!—will they kill you, do you think?"

"Don't know. Can't tell till afterward. You see, they take some feller that's alone like me, and then they rush his camp when he ain't quite ready for 'em, and ginerally plug 'im with a sawed-off shot-gun load before he has a chance to git at 'em. They lay around and wait for their chance, and it comes soon enough. Of course a feller alone like me has got to let up watching some time. Maybe they ketch 'im asleep. Maybe the feller gits tired waiting, and goes out in broad day, and kills two or three just to make the whole crowd pile on him and settle the thing. I heard of a case like that once. It's awful hard on a man's mind—to git a gang after him."

"And so they're going to rush your camp to-night?" cried the stranger. "How do you know? Who told you?"

"Feller come and told me."

"And what are you going to do? Fight?"

"Don't see nothin' else to do," answered Bill, gloomily, still staring at the cactus-plant.

There was a silence. Finally the stranger burst out in an amazed cry. "Well, I never heard of such a thing in my life! How many of them are there?"

"Eight," answered Bill. "And now look-a-here; you ain't got no manner of business foolin' around here just now, and you might better lope off before dark. I don't ask no help in this here row. I know your happening along here just now don't give me no call on you, and you'd better hit the trail."

"Well, why in the name of wonder don't you go get the sheriff?" cried the stranger.

"Oh, h——!" said Bill.

* * *

Long, smouldering clouds spread in the western sky, and to the east sliver mists lay on the purple gloom of the wilderness.

Finally, when the great moon climbed the heavens and cast its ghastly radiance upon the bushes, it made a new and more brilliant crimson of the camp-fire, where the flames capered merrily through its mesquit branches, filling the silence with the fire chorus, an ancient melody which surely bears a message of the inconsequence of individual tragedy—a messsage that is in the boom of the sea, the sliver of the wind through the grass-blades, the silken clash of hemlock boughs.

No figures moved in the rosy space of the camp, and the search of the moon-beams failed to disclose a living thing in the bushes. There was no owl-faced clock to chant the weariness of the long silence that brooded upon the plain.

The dew gave the darkness under the mesquit a velvet quality that made air seem nearer to water, and no eye could have seen through it the black things that moved like monster lizards toward the camp. The branches, the leaves, that are fain to cry out when death approaches in the wilds, were frustrated by these mystic bodies gliding with the finesse of the escaping serpent. They crept forward to the last point where assuredly no frantic attempt of the fire could discover them, and there they paused to locate the prey. A romance relates the tale of the black cell hidden deep in the earth, where, upon entering, one sees only the little eyes of snakes fixing him in menaces. If a man could have approached a certain spot in the bushes, he would not have found it romantically necessary to have his hair rise. There would have been a sufficient expression of horror in the feeling of the death-hand at the nape of his neck and in his rubber knee-joints.

Two of these bodies finally moved toward each other until for each there grew out of the darkness a face placidly smiling with tender dreams of assassination. "The fool is asleep by the fire, God be praised!" The lips of the other widened in a grin of affectionate appreciation of the fool and his plight. There was some signaling in the gloom, and then began a series of subtle rustlings, interjected often with pauses, during which no sound arose but the sound of faint breathing.

A bush stood like a rock in the stream of firelight, sending its long shadow backward. With painful caution the little company traveled along this shadow, and finally arrived at the rear of the bush. Through its branches they surveyed for a moment of comfortable satisfaction a form in a gray blanket extended on the ground near the fire. The smile of joyful anticipation fled quickly, to give place to a quiet air of business. Two men lifted shot-guns with much of the barrels gone, and sighting these weapons through the branches, pulled trigger together.

The noise of the explosions roared over the lonely mesquit as if these guns wished to inform the entire world; and as the gray smoke fled, the dodging company back of the bush saw the blanketed form twitching. Whereupon they burst out in chorus in a laugh, and arose as merry as a lot of banqueters. They gleefully gestured congratulations, and strode bravely into the light of the fire.

Then suddenly a new laugh rang from some unknown spot in the darkness. It was a fearsome laugh of ridicule, hatred, ferocity. It might have been demoniac. It smote them motionless in their gleeful prowl, as the stern voice from the sky smites the legendary malefactor. They might have been a weird group in wax, the light of the dying fire on their yellow faces, and shining athwart their eyes turned toward the darkness whence might come the unknown and the terrible.

The thing in the gray blanket no longer twitched; but if the knives in their hands had been thrust toward it, each knife was now drawn back, and its owner's elbow was thrown upward, as if he expected death from the clouds.

This laugh had so chained their reason that for a moment they had no wit to flee. They were prisoners to their terror. Then suddenly the belated decision arrived, and with bubbling cries they turned to run; but at that instant there was a long flash of red in the darkness, and with the report one of the men shouted a bitter shout, spun once, and tumbled headlong. The thick bushes failed to impede the rout of the others.

The silence returned to the wilderness. The tired flames faintly illumined the blanketed thing and the flung corpse of the marauder, and sang the fire chorus, the ancient melody which bears the message of the inconsequence of human tragedy.

* * *

"Now you are worse off than ever," said the young man, dry-voiced and awed.

"No, I ain't," said Bill rebelliously. "I'm one ahead."

After reflection, the stranger remarked, "Well, there's seven more."

They were cautiously and slowly approaching the camp. The sun was flaring its first warming rays over the gray wilderness. Upreared twigs, prominent branches, shone with golden light, while the shadows under the mesquit were heavily blue.

Suddenly the stranger uttered a frightened cry. He had arrived at a point whence he had, through openings in the thicket, a clear view of a dead face.

"Gosh!" said Bill, who at the next instant had seen the thing; "I thought at first it was that there José. That would have been queer, after what I told 'im yesterday."

They continued their way, the stranger wincing in his walk, and Bill exhibiting considerable curiosity.

The yellow beams of the new sun were touching the grim hues of the dead

Mexican's face, and creating there an inhuman effect, which made his countenance more like a mask of dulled brass. One hand, grown curiously thinner, had been flung out regardlessly to a cactus-bush.

Bill walked forward and stood looking respectfully at the body. "I know that feller; his name is Miguel. He—"

The stranger's nerves might have been in that condition when there is no backbone to the body, only a long groove. "Good heavens!" he exclaimed, much agitated; "don't speak that way!"

"What way?" said Bill. "I only said his name was Miguel."

After a pause the stranger said:

"Oh, I know; but—" He waved his hand. "Lower your voice, or something. I don't know. This part of the business rattles me, don't you see?"

"Oh, all right," replied Bill, bowing to the other's mysterious mood. But in a moment he burst out violently and loud in the most extraordinary profanity, the oaths winging from him as the sparks go from the funnel.

He had been examining the contents of the bundled gray blanket, and he had brought forth, among other things, his frying-pan. It was now only a rim with a handle; the Mexican volley had centered upon it. A Mexican shot-gun of the abbreviated description is ordinarily loaded with flat-irons, stove-lids, lead pipe, old horseshoes, sections of chain, window weights, railroad sleepers and spikes, dumb-bells, and any other junk which may be at hand. When one of these loads encounters a man vitally, it is likely to make an impression upon him, and a cooking-utensil may be supposed to subside before such an assault of curiosities.

Bill held high his desecrated frying-pan, turning it this way and that way. He swore until he happened to note the absence of the stranger. A moment later he saw him leading his horse from the bushes. In silence and sullenly the young man went about saddling the animal. Bill said, "Well, goin' to pull out?"

The stranger's hands fumbled uncertainly at the throat-latch. Once he exclaimed irritably, blaming the buckle for the trembling of his fingers. Once he turned to look at the dead face with the light of the morning sun upon it. At last he cried, "Oh, I know the whole thing was all square enough—couldn't be squarer—but—somehow or other, that man there takes the heart out of me." He turned his troubled face for another look. "He seems to be all the time calling me a—he makes me feel like a murderer."

"But," said Bill, puzzling, "you didn't shoot him, mister; I shot him."

"I know; but I feel that way, somehow. I can't get rid of it."

Bill considered for a time; then he said diffidently, "Mister, you're a' eddycated man, ain't you?"

"What?"

"You're what they call a'—a' eddycated man, ain't you?"

The young man, perplexed, evidently had a question upon his lips, when there was a roar of guns, bright flashes, and in the air such hooting and whistling as would come from a swift flock of steam-boilers. The stranger's horse gave a mighty, convulsive spring, snorting wildly in its sudden anguish, fell upon its knees, scrambled afoot again, and was away in the uncanny death-run known to men who have seen the finish of brave horses.

"This comes from discussin' things," cried Bill, angrily.

He had thrown himself flat on the ground facing the thicket whence had come the firing. He could see the smoke winding over the bush-tops. He lifted his revolver, and the weapon came slowly up from the ground and poised like the glittering crest of a snake. Somewhere on his face there was a kind of smile, cynical, wicked, deadly, of a ferocity which at the same time had brought a deep flush to his face, and had caused two upright lines to glow in his eyes.

"Hello, José!" he called, amiable for satire's sake. "Got your old blunder-busses loaded up again yet?"

The stillness had returned to the plain. The sun's brilliant rays swept over the sea of mesquit, painting the far mists of the west with faint rosy light, and high in the air some great bird fled toward the south.

"You come out here," called Bill, again addressing the landscape, "and I'll give you some shootin' lessons. That ain't the way to shoot." Receiving no reply, he began to invent epithets and yell them at the thicket. He was something of a master of insult, and, moreover, he dived into his memory to bring forth imprecations tarnished with age, unused since fluent Bowery days. The occupation amused him, and sometimes he laughed so that it was uncomfortable for his chest to be against the ground.

Finally the stranger, prostrate near him, said wearily, "Oh, they've gone."

"Don't you believe it," replied Bill, sobering swiftly. "They're there yet— every man of 'em."

"How do you know?"

"Because I do. They won't shake us so soon. Don't put your head up, or they'll get you, sure."

Bill's eyes, meanwhile, had not wavered from their scrutiny of the thicket in front. "They're there, all right; don't you forget it. Now you listen." So he called out: "José! Ojo, José! Speak up, *hombre!* I want have talk. Speak up, you yaller cuss, you!"

Whereupon a mocking voice from off in the bushes said, "Señor?"

"There," said Billy to his ally; "didn't I tell you? The whole batch." Again he lifted his voice. "José—look—ain't you gittin' kinder tired? You better go home, you fellers, and git some rest."

The answer was a sudden furious chatter of Spanish, eloquent with hatred, calling down upon Bill all the calamities which life holds. It was as if some one had suddenly enraged a cageful of wildcats. The spirits of all the revenges which they had imagined were loosened at this time, and filled the air.

"They're in a holler," said Bill, chuckling, "or there'd be shootin'."

Presently he began to grow angry. His hidden enemies called him nine kinds of coward, a man who could fight only in the dark, a baby who would run from the shadows of such noble Mexican gentlemen, a dog that sneaked. They described the affair of the previous night, and informed him of the base advantage he had taken of their friend. In fact, they in all sincerity endowed him with every quality which he no less earnestly believed them to possess. One could have seen the phrases bite him as he lay there on the ground fingering his revolver.

* * *

It is sometimes taught that men do the furious and desperate thing from an emotion that is as even and placid as the thoughts of a village clergyman on

Sunday afternoon. Usually, however, it is to be believed that a panther is at the time born in the heart, and that the subject does not resemble a man picking mulberries.

"B' G——!" said Bill, speaking as from a throat filled with dust, "I'll go after 'em in a minute."

"Don't you budge an inch!" cried the stranger, sternly. "Don't you budge!"

"Well," said Bill, glaring at the bushes—"well."

"Put your head down!" suddenly screamed the stranger, in white alarm. As the guns roared, Bill uttered a loud grunt, and for a moment leaned panting on his elbow, while his arm shook like a twig. Then he upreared like a great and bloody spirit of vengeance, his face lighted with the blaze of his last passion. The Mexicans came swiftly and in silence.

The lightning action of the next few moments was of the fabric of dreams to the stranger. The muscular struggle may not be real to the drowning man. His mind may be fixed on the far, straight shadows back of the stars, and the terror of them. And so the fight, and his part in it, had to the stranger only the quality of a picture half drawn. The rush of feet, the spatter of shots, the cries, the swollen faces seen like masks on the smoke, resembled a happening of the night.

And yet afterward certain lines, forms, lived out so strongly from the incoherence that they were always in his memory.

He killed a man, and the thought went swiftly by him, like the feather on the gale, that it was easy to kill a man.

Moreover, he suddenly felt for Bill, this grimy sheep-herder, some deep form of idolatry. Bill was dying, and the dignity of last defeat, the superiority of him who stands in his grave, was in the pose of the lost sheep-herder.

The stranger sat on the ground idly mopping the sweat and powder-stain from his brow. He wore the gentle idiot smile of an aged beggar as he watched three Mexicans limping and staggering in the distance. He noted at this time that one who still possessed a serape had from it none of the grandeur of the cloaked Spaniard, but that against the sky the silhouette resembled a cornucopia of childhood's Christmas.

They turned to look at him, and he lifted his weary arm to menace them with his revolver. They stood for a moment banded together, and hooted curses at him.

Finally he arose, and, walking some paces, stooped to loosen Bill's gray hands from a throat. Swaying as if slightly drunk, he stood looking down into the still face.

Struck suddenly with a thought, he went about with dulled eyes on the ground, until he plucked his gaudy blanket from where it lay, dirty from trampling feet. He dusted it carefully, and then returned and laid it over Bill's form. There he again stood motionless, his mouth just agape and the same stupid glance in his eyes, when all at once he made a gesture of fright and looked wildly about him.

He had almost reached the thicket when he stopped, smitten with alarm. A body contorted, with one arm stiff in the air, lay in his path. Slowly and warily he moved around it, and in a moment the bushes, nodding and whispering, their leaf-faces turned toward the scene behind him, swung and swung again into stillness and the peace of the wilderness.

ONE DASH—HORSES

Richardson pulled up his horse and looked back over the trail, where the crimson serape of his servant flamed amid the dusk of the mesquit. The hills in the west were carved into peaks, and were painted the most profound blue. Above them, the sky was of that marvelous tone of green—like still, sun-shot water—which people denounce in pictures.

José was muffled deep in his blanket, and his great toppling sombrero was drawn low over his brow. He shadowed his master along the dimming trail in the fashion of an assassin. A cold wind of the impending night swept over the wilderness of mesquit.

"Man," said Richardson, in lame Mexican, as the servant drew near, "I want eat! I want sleep! Understand no? Quickly! Understand?"

"Si, señor," said José, nodding. He stretched one arm out of his blanket, and pointed a yellow finger into the gloom. "Over there, small village! Si, señor."

They rode forward again. Once the American's horse shied and breathed quiveringly at something which he saw or imagined in the darkness, and the rider drew a steady, patient rein, and leaned over to speak tenderly, as if he were addressing a frightened woman. The sky had faded to white over the mountains, and the plain was a vast, pointless ocean of black.

Suddenly some low houses appeared squatting amid the bushes. The horsemen rode into a hollow until the houses rose against the somber, sundown sky, and then up a small hillock, causing these habitations to sink like boats in the sea of shadow.

A beam of red firelight fell across the trail. Richardson sat sleepily on his horse while the servant quarreled with somebody—a mere voice in the gloom—over the price of bed and board. The houses about him were for the most part like tombs in their whiteness and silence, but there were scudding black figures that seemed interested in his arrival.

José came at last to the horses' heads, and the American slid stiffly from his seat. He muttered a greeting as with his spurred feet he clicked into the adobe house that confronted him. The brown, stolid face of a woman shone in the light of the fire. He seated himself on the earthen floor, and blinked drowsily at the blaze. He was aware that the woman was clinking earthenware, and hieing here

198

and everywhere in the manœuvres of the housewife. From a dark corner of the room there came the sound of two or three snores twining together.

The woman handed him a bowl of tortillas. She was a submissive creature, timid and large-eyed. She gazed at his enormous silver spurs, his large and impressive revolver, with the interest and admiration of the highly privileged cat of the adage. When he ate, she seemed transfixed off there in the gloom, her white teeth shining.

José entered, staggering under two Mexican saddles large enough for building-sites. Richardson decided to smoke a cigarette, and then changed his mind. It would be much finer to go to sleep. His blanket hung over his left shoulder, furled into a long pipe of cloth, according to a Mexican fashion. By doffing his sombrero, unfastening his spurs and his revolver-belt, he made himself ready for the slow, blissful twist into the blanket. Like a cautious man, he lay close to the wall, and all his property was very near his hand.

The mesquit brush burned long. José threw two gigantic wings of shadow as he flapped his blanket about him—first across his chest under his arms, and then around his neck and across his chest again, this time over his arms, with the end tossed on his right shoulder. A Mexican thus snugly enveloped can nevertheless free his fighting arm in a beautifully brisk way, merely shrugging his shoulder as he grabs for the weapon at his belt. They always wear their serapes in this manner.

The firelight smothered the rays which, streaming from a moon as large as a drum-head, were struggling at the open door. Richardson heard from the plain the fine, rhythmical trample of the hoofs of hurried horses. He went to sleep wondering who rode so fast and so late. And in the deep silence the pale rays of the moon must have prevailed against the red spears of the fire until the room was slowly flooded to its middle with a rectangle of silver light.

Richardson was awakened by the sound of a guitar. It was badly played—in this land of Mexico, from which the romance of the instrument ascends to us like a perfume. The guitar was groaning and whining like a badgered soul. A noise of scuffling feet accompanied the music. Sometimes laughter arose, and often the voices of men saying bitter things to each other; but always the guitar cried on, the treble sounding as if some one were beating iron, and the bass humming like bees.

"D——it! they' re having a dance," muttered Richardson, fretfully. He heard two men quarreling in short, sharp words like pistol-shots; they were calling each other worse names than common people know in other countries.

He wondered why the noise was so loud. Raising his head from his saddle-pillow, he saw, with the help of the valiant moonbeams, a blanket hanging flat against the wall at the farther end of the room. Being of the opinion that it concealed a door, and remembering that Mexican drink made men very drunk, he pulled his revolver closer to him and prepared for sudden disaster.

Richardson was dreaming of his far and beloved North.

"Well, I would kill him, then!"

"No, you must not!"

"Yes, I will kill him! Listen! I will ask this American beast for his beautiful pistol and spurs and money and saddle, and if he will not give them—you will see!"

"But these Americans—they are a strange people. Look out, señor."

Then twenty voices took part in the discussion. They rose in quivering shrillness, as from men badly drunk.

Richardson felt the skin draw tight around his mouth, and his knee-joints turned to bread. He slowly came to a sitting posture, glaring at the motionless blanket at the far end of the room. This stiff and mechanical movement, accomplished entirely by the muscles of the wrist, must have looked like the rising of a corpse in the wan moonlight, which gave everything a hue of the grave.

My friend, take my advice, and never be executed by a hangman who does n't talk the English language. It, or anything that resembles it, is the most difficult of deaths. The tumultuous emotions of Richardson's terror destroyed that slow and careful process of thought by means of which he understood Mexican. Then he used his instinctive comprehension of the first and universal language, which is tone. Still, it is disheartening not to be able to understand the detail of threats against the blood of your body.

Suddenly the clamor of voices ceased. There was a silence—a silence of decision. The blanket was flung aside, and the red light of a torch flared into the room. It was held high by a fat, round-faced Mexican, whose little snake-like mustache was as black as his eyes, and whose eyes were black as jet. He was insane with the wild rage of a man whose liquor is dully burning at his brain. Five or six of his fellows crowded after him. The guitar, which had been thrummed doggedly during the time of the high words, now suddenly stopped.

They contemplated each other. Richardson sat very straight and still, his right hand lost in the folds of his blanket. The Mexicans jostled in the light of the torch, their eyes blinking and glittering.

The fat one posed in the manner of a grandee. Presently his hand dropped to his belt, and from his lips there spun an epithet—a hideous word which often foreshadows knife-blows, a word peculiarly of Mexico, where people have to dig deep to find an insult that has not lost its savor.

The American did not move. He was staring at the fat Mexican with a strange fixedness of gaze, not fearful, not dauntless, not anything that could be interpreted; he simply stared.

The fat Mexican must have been disconcerted, for he continued to pose as a grandee, with more and more sublimity, until it would have been easy for him to have fallen over backward. His companions were swaying in a very drunken manner. They still blinked their beady eyes at Richardson. Ah, well, sirs, here was a mystery. At the approach of their menacing company, why did not this American cry out and turn pale, or run, or pray them mercy? The animal merely sat still, and stared, and waited for them to begin. Well, evidently he was a great fighter; or perhaps he was an idiot. Indeed, this was an embarrassing situation, for who was going forward to discover whether he was a great fighter or an idiot?

To Richardson, whose nerves were tingling and twitching like live wires, and whose heart jolted inside him, this pause was a long horror; and for these men who could so frighten him there began to swell in him a fierce hatred—a hatred that made him long to be capable of fighting all of them, a hatred that made him capable of fighting all of them. A 44-caliber revolver can make a hole large enough for little boys to shoot marbles through, and there was a certain fat Mexican with a mustache like a snake, who came extremely near to have eaten his last tomale merely because he frightened a man too much.

José had slept the first part of the night in his fashion, his body hunched into a heap, his legs crooked, his head touching his knees. Shadows had obscured him from the sight of the invaders. At this point he arose, and began to prowl quakingly over toward Richardson, as if he meant to hide behind him.

Of a sudden the fat Mexican gave a howl of glee. José had come within the torch's circle of light. With roars of singular ferocity the whole group of Mexicans pounced on the American's servant.

He shrank shuddering away from them, beseeching by every device of word and gesture. They pushed him this way and that. They beat him with their fists. They stung him with their curses. As he groveled on his knees, the fat Mexican took him by the throat and said: "I' m going to kill!" And continually they turned their eyes to see if they were to succeed in causing the initial demonstration by the American.

Richardson looked on impassively. Under the blanket, however, his fingers were clinched as rigidly as iron upon the handle of his revolver.

Here suddenly two brilliant clashing chords from the guitar were heard, and a woman's voice, full of laughter and confidence, cried from without: "Hello! hello! Where are you?"

The lurching company of Mexicans instantly paused and looked at the ground. One said, as he stood with his legs wide apart in order to balance himself: "It is the girls! They have come!" He screamed in answer to the question of the woman: "Here!" And without waiting he started on a pilgrimage toward the blanket-covered door. One could now hear a number of female voices giggling and chattering.

Two other Mexicans said: "Yes; it is the girls! Yes!" They also started quietly away. Even the fat Mexican's ferocity seemed to be affected. He looked uncertainly at the still immovable American. Two of his friends grasped him gaily. "Come, the girls are here! Come!" He cast another glower at Richardson. "But this—" he began. Laughing, his comrades hustled him toward the door. On its threshold, and holding back the blanket with one hand, he turned his yellow face with a last challenging glare toward the American. José, bewailing his state in little sobs of utter despair and woe, crept to Richardson and huddled near his knee. Then the cries of the Mexicans meeting the girls were heard, and the guitar burst out in joyous humming.

The moon clouded, and but a faint square of light fell through the open main door of the house. The coals of the fire were silent save for occasional sputters. Richardson did not change his position. He remained staring at the blanket which hid the strategic door in the far end. At his knees José was arguing, in a low, aggrieved tone, with the saints. Without the Mexicans laughed and danced, and—it would appear from the sound—drank more.

In the stillness and night Richardson sat wondering if some serpent-like Mexican was sliding toward him in the darkness, and if the first thing he knew of it would be the deadly sting of the knife. "Sssh," he whispered to José. He drew his revolver from under the blanket and held it on his leg.

The blanket over the door fascinated him. It was a vague form, black and unmoving. Through the opening it shielded was to come, probably, menace, death. Sometimes he thought he saw it move.

As grim white sheets, the black and silver of coffins, all the panoply of death, affect us because of that which they hide, so this blanket, dangling before a hole in an adobe wall, was to Richardson a horrible emblem, and a horrible thing in itself. In his present mood Richardson could not have been brought to touch it with his finger.

The celebrating Mexicans occasionally howled in song. The guitarist played with speed and enthusiasm.

Richardson longed to run. But in this threatening gloom, his terror convinced him that a move on his part would be a signal for the pounce of death. José, crouching abjectly, occasionally mumbled. Slowly and ponderous as stars the minutes went.

Suddenly Richardson thrilled and started. His breath, for a moment, left him. In sleep his nerveless fingers had allowed his revolver to fall and clang upon the hard floor. He grabbed it up hastily, and his glance swept apprehensively over the room.

A chill blue light of dawn was in the place. Every outline was slowly growing; detail was following detail. The dread blanket did not move. The riotous company had gone or become silent.

Richardson felt in his blood the effect of this cold dawn. The candor of breaking day brought his nerve. He touched José. "Come," he said. His servant lifted his lined, yellow face and comprehended. Richardson buckled on his spurs and strode up; José obediently lifted the two great saddles. Richardson held two bridles and a blanket on his left arm; in his right hand he held his revolver. They sneaked toward the door.

The man who said that spurs jingled was insane. Spurs have a mellow clash—clash—clash. Walking in spurs—notably Mexican spurs—you remind yourself vaguely of a telegraphic lineman. Richardson was inexpressibly shocked when he came to walk. He sounded to himself like a pair of cymbals. He would have known of this if he had reflected; but then he was escaping, not reflecting. He made a gesture of despair, and from under the two saddles, José tried to make one of hopeless horror. Richardson stooped, and with shaking fingers unfastened the spurs. Taking them in his left hand, he picked up his revolver and they slunk on toward the door.

On the threshold Richardson looked back. In a corner he saw, watching him with large eyes, the Indian man and woman who had been his hosts. Throughout the night they had made no sign, and now they neither spoke nor moved. Yet Richardson thought he detected meek satisfaction at his departure.

The street was still and deserted. In the eastern sky there was a lemon-colored patch.

José had picketed the horses at the side of the house. As the two men came around the corner, Richardson's animal set up a whinny of welcome. The little horse had evidently heard them coming. He stood facing them, his ears cocked forward, his eyes bright with welcome.

Richardson made a frantic gesture, but the horse, in his happiness at the appearance of his friends, whinnied with enthusiasm.

The American felt at this time that he could have strangled his well-beloved steed. Upon the threshold of safety he was being betrayed by his horse, his friend. He felt the same hate for the horse that he would have felt for a dragon. And yet, as he glanced wildly about him, he could see nothing stirring in the street, nor at the doors of the tomb-like houses.

José had his own saddle-girth and both bridles buckled in a moment. He curled the picket ropes with a few sweeps of his arm. The fingers of Richardson, however, were shaking so that he could hardly buckle the girth. His hands were in invisible mittens. He was wondering, calculating, hoping about his horse. He knew the little animal's willingness and courage under all circumstances up to this time, but then—here it was different. Who could tell if some wretched instance of equine perversity was not about to develop. Maybe the little fellow would not feel like smoking over the plain at express-speed this morning, and so he would rebel and kick and be wicked. Maybe he would be without feeling of interest, and run listlessly. All men who have had to hurry in the saddle know what it is to be on a horse who does not understand the dramatic situation. Riding a lame sheep is bliss to it. Richardson, fumbling furiously at the girth, thought of these things.

Presently he had it fastened. He swung into the saddle, and as he did so his horse made a mad jump forward. The spurs of José scratched and tore the flanks of his great black animal, and side by side the two horses raced down the village street. The American heard his horse breathe a quivering sigh of excitement.

Those four feet skimmed. They were as light as fairy puff-balls. The houses of the village glided past in a moment, and the great, clear, silent plain appeared like a pale-blue sea of mist and wet bushes. Above the mountains the colors of the sunlight were like the first tones, the opening chords of the mighty hymn of the morning.

The American looked down at his horse. He felt in his heart the first thrill of confidence. The little animal, unurged and quite tranquil, moving his ears this way and that way with an air of interest in the scenery, was nevertheless bounding into the eye of the breaking day with the speed of a frightened antelope. Richardson, looking down, saw the long, fine reach of fore limb as steady as steel machinery. As the ground reeled past, the long, dried grasses hissed, and cactus-plants were dull blurs. A wind whirled the horse's mane over his rider's bridle hand.

José's profile was lined against the pale sky. It was as that of a man who swims alone in an ocean. His eyes glinted like metal fastened on some unknown point ahead of him, some mystic place of safety. Occasionally his mouth puckered in a little unheard cry; and his legs, bent back, worked spasmodically as his spurred heels sliced the flanks of his charger.

Richardson consulted the gloom in the west for signs of a hard-riding, yelling cavalcade. He knew that whereas his friends the enemy had not attacked him when he had sat still and with apparent calmness confronted them, they would certainly take furiously after him now that he had run from them—now that he had confessed to them that he was the weaker. Their valor would grow like weeds in the spring, and upon discovering his escape they would ride forth dauntless warriors.

Sometimes he was sure he saw them. Sometimes he was sure he heard them. Continually looking backward over his shoulder, he studied the purple expanses where the night was marching away. José rolled and shuddered in his saddle, persistently disturbing the stride of the black horse, fretting and worrying him until the white foam flew, and the great shoulders shone like satin from the sweat.

At last Richardson drew his horse carefully down to a walk. José wished to rush insanely on, but the American spoke to him sternly. As the two paced forward side by side, Richardson's little horse thrust over his soft nose and inquired into the black's condition.

Riding with José was like riding with a corpse. His face resembled a cast in lead. Sometimes he swung forward and almost pitched from his seat. Richardson was too frightened himself to do anything but hate this man for his fear. Finally he issued a mandate which nearly caused José's eyes to slide out of his head and fall to the ground like two silver coins.

"Ride behind me—about fifty paces."

"Señor—" stuttered the servant.

"Go!" cried the American, furiously. He glared at the other and laid his hand on his revolver. José looked at his master wildly. He made a piteous gesture. Then slowly he fell back, watching the hard face of the American for a sign of mercy.

Richardson had resolved in his rage that at any rate he was going to use the eyes and ears of extreme fear to detect the approach of danger; and so he established his servant as a sort of an outpost.

As they proceeded he was obliged to watch sharply to see that the servant did not slink forward and join him. When José made beseeching circles in the air with his arm he replied by menacingly gripping his revolver.

José had a revolver, too; nevertheless it was very clear in his mind that the revolver was distinctly an American weapon. He had been educated in the Rio Grande country.

Richardson lost the trail once. He was recalled to it by the loud sobs of his servant.

Then at last José came clattering forward, gesticulating and wailing. The little horse sprang to the shoulder of the black. They were off.

Richardson, again looking backward, could see a slanting flare of dust on the whitening plain. He thought that he could detect small moving figures in it.

José's moans and cries amounted to a university course in theology. They broke continually from his quivering lips. His spurs were as motors. They forced the black horse over the plain in great headlong leaps.

But under Richardson there was a little insignificant rat-colored beast, who was running apparently with almost as much effort as it requires for a bronze statue to stand still. As a matter of truth, the ground seemed merely something to be touched from time to time with hoofs that were as light as blown leaves. Occasionally Richardson lay back and pulled stoutly at his bridle to keep from abandoning his servant.

José harried at his horse's mouth, flopped around in the saddle, and made his two heels beat like flails. The black ran like a horse in despair.

Crimson serapes in the distance resemble drops of blood on the great cloth of plain.

Richardson began to dream of all possible chances. Although quite a humane man, he did not once think of his servant. José being a Mexican, it was natural that he should be killed in Mexico; but for himself, a New-Yorker—

He remembered all the tales of such races for life, and he thought them badly written.

The great black horse was growing indifferent. The jabs of José's spurs no longer caused him to bound forward in wild leaps of pain. José had at last succeeded in teaching him that spurring was to be expected, speed or no speed, and now he took the pain of it dully and stolidly, as an animal who finds that doing his best gains him no respite.

José was turned into a raving maniac. He bellowed and screamed, working his arms and his heels like one in a fit. He resembled a man on a sinking ship, who appeals to the ship. Richardson, too, cried madly to the black horse.

The spirit of the horse responded to these calls, and, quivering and breathing heavily, he made a great effort, a sort of a final rush, not for himself apparently, but because he understood that his life's sacrifice, perhaps, had been invoked by these two men who cried to him in the universal tongue. Richardson had no sense of appreciation at this time—he was too frightened—but often now he remembers a certain black horse.

From the rear could be heard a yelling, and once a shot was fired—in the air evidently. Richardson moaned as he looked back. He kept his hand on his revolver. He tried to imagine the brief tumult of his capture—the flurry of dust from the hoofs of horses pulled suddenly to their haunches, the shrill biting curses of the men, the ring of the shots, his own last contortion. He wondered, too, if he could not somehow manage to pelt that fat Mexican, just to cure his abominable egotism.

It was José, the terror-stricken, who at last discovered safety. Suddenly he gave a howl of delight, and astonished his horse into a new burst of speed. They were on a little ridge at the time, and the American at the top of it saw his servant gallop down the slope and into the arms, so to speak, of a small column of horsemen in gray and silver clothes. In the dim light of the early morning they were as vague as shadows, but Richardson knew them at once for a detachment of rurales, that crack cavalry corps of the Mexican army which polices the plain so zealously, being of themselves the law and the arm of it—a fierce and swift-moving body that knows little of prevention, but much of vengeance. They drew up suddenly, and the rows of great silver-trimmed sombreros bobbed in surprise.

Richardson saw José throw himself from his horse and begin to jabber at the leader of the party. When he arrived he found that his servant had already outlined the entire situation, and was then engaged in describing him, Richardson, as an American señor of vast wealth, who was the friend of almost every governmental potentate within two hundred miles. This seemed to profoundly impress the officer. He bowed gravely to Richardson and smiled significantly at his men, who unslung their carbines.

The little ridge hid the pursuers from view, but the rapid thud of their horses' feet could be heard. Occasionally they yelled and called to each other.

Then at last they swept over the brow of the hill, a wild mob of almost fifty drunken horsemen. When they discerned the pale-uniformed rurales they were sailing down the slope at top-speed.

If toboggans half-way down a hill should suddenly make up their minds to turn around and go back, there would be an effect somewhat like that now produced by the drunken horsemen. Richardson saw the rurales serenely swing their carbines forward, and, peculiar-minded person that he was, felt his heart leap into his throat at the prospective volley. But the officer rode forward alone.

It appeared that the man who owned the best horse in this astonished company was the fat Mexican with the snaky mustache, and, in consequence, this gentleman was quite a distance in the van. He tried to pull up, wheel his horse, and scuttle back over the hill as some of his companions had done, but the officer called to him in a voice harsh with rage.

"——!" howled the officer. "This señor is my friend, the friend of my friends. Do you dare pursue him, ——? ——! ——! ——! ——!" These lines represent terrible names, all different, used by the officer.

The fat Mexican simply groveled on his horse's neck. His face was green; it could be seen that he expected death.

The officer stormed with magnificent intensity: "——! ——! ——!"

Finally he sprang from his saddle, and, running to the fat Mexican's side, yelled: "Go!" and kicked the horse in the belly with all his might. The animal gave a mighty leap into the air, and the fat Mexican, with one wretched glance at the contemplative rurales, aimed his steed for the top of the ridge. Richardson again gulped in expectation of a volley, for, it is said, this is one of the favorite methods of the rurales for disposing of objectionable people. The fat, green Mexican also evidently thought that he was to be killed while on the run, from the miserable look he cast at the troops. Nevertheless, he was allowed to vanish in a cloud of yellow dust at the ridge-top.

José was exultant, defiant, and, oh! bristling with courage. The black horse was drooping sadly, his nose to the ground. Richardson's little animal, with his ears bent forward, was staring at the horses of the rurales as if in an intense study. Richardson longed for speech, but he could only bend forward and pat the shining, silken shoulders. The little horse turned his head and looked back gravely.

FLANAGAN

And his Short Filibustering Adventure

"I have got twenty men at me back who will fight to the death," said the warrior to the old filibuster.

"And they can be blowed, for all me," replied the old filibuster. "Common as sparrows—cheap as cigarettes. Show me twenty men with steel clamps on their mouths, with holes in their heads where memory ought to be, and I want 'em. But twenty brave men merely? I'd rather have twenty brave onions."

Thereupon the warrior removed sadly, feeling that no salaams were paid to valor in these days of mechanical excellence.

Valor, in truth, is no bad thing to have when filibustering; but many medals are to be won by the man who knows not the meaning of powwow, before or afterward. Twenty brave men with tongues hung lightly may make trouble rise from the ground like smoke from grass because of their subsequent fiery pride, whereas twenty cow-eyed villains who accept unrighteous and far-compelling kicks as they do the rain of heaven may halo the ultimate history of an expedition with gold, and plentifully bedeck their names, winning forty years of gratitude from patriots, simply by remaining silent. As for the cause, it may be only that they have no friends or other credulous furniture.

If it were not for the curse of the swinging tongue, it is surely to be said that the filibustering industry, flourishing now in the United States, would be pie. Under correct conditions it is merely a matter of dealing with some little detectives whose skill at search is rated by those who pay them at a value of twelve or twenty dollars each week. It is nearly axiomatic that normally a twelve-dollar-per-week detective cannot defeat a one-hundred-thousand-dollar filibustering excursion. Against the criminal the detective represents the commonwealth; but in this other case he represents his desire to show cause why his salary should be paid. He represents himself merely, and he counts no more than a grocer's clerk.

But the pride of the successful filibuster often smites him and his cause like an ax, and men who have not confided in their mothers go prone with him. It can make the dome of the Capitol tremble, and incite the senators to overturning benches. It can increase the salaries of detectives who could not detect the location of a pain in the chest. It is a wonderful thing, this pride.

Filibustering was once such a simple game. It was managed blandly by gentle captains and smooth and undisturbed gentlemen who at other times dealt in the law, soap, medicine, and bananas. It was a great pity that the little cote of doves in Washington was obliged to rustle officially, and naval men were kept from their berths at night, and sundry custom-house people got wiggings, all because the returned adventurer powwowed in his pride. A yellow-and-red banner would have been long since smothered in a shame of defeat if a contract to filibuster had been let to some admirable organization like one of our trusts.

And yet the game is not obsolete; it is still played by the wise and the silent—men whose names are not display-typed and blathered from one end of the country to the other.

There is in mind now a man who knew one side of a fence from the other side when he looked sharply. They were hunting for captains then to command the first vessels of what has since become a famous little fleet. One was recommended to this man, and he said: "Send him down to my office, and I'll look him over." He was an attorney, and he liked to lean back in his chair, twirl a paper-knife, and let the other fellow talk.

The seafaring man came, and stood, and appeared confounded. The attorney asked the terrible first question of the filibuster to the applicant; he said: "Why do you want to go?"

The captain reflected, changed his attitude three times, and decided ultimately that he didn't know. He seemed greatly ashamed. The attorney, looking at him, saw that he had eyes that resembled a lambkin's eyes.

"Glory?" said the attorney, at last.

"No-o," said the captain.

"Pay?"

"No-o; not that so much."

"Think they'll give you a land grant when they win out?"

"No; never thought."

"No glory. No immense pay. No land grant. What are you going for, then?"

"Well, I don't know," said the captain, with his glance on the floor, and shifting his position again. "I don't know. I guess it's just for fun, mostly." The attorney asked him out to have a drink.

When he stood on the bridge of his outgoing steamer the attorney saw him again. His shore meekness and uncertainty were gone. He was clear-eyed and strong, aroused like a mastiff at night. He took his cigar out of his mouth, and yelled some sudden language at the deck.

This steamer had about her a quality of unholy medieval disrepair which is usually accounted the principal prerogative of the United States revenue marine. There is many a seaworthy ice-house if she was a good ship. She swashed through the seas as genially as an old wooden clock, burying her head under waves that came only like children at play, and on board it cost a ducking to go from anywhere to anywhere.

The captain had commanded vessels that shore people thought were liners, but when a man gets the ant of desire-to-see-what-it-'s-like stirring in his heart, he will wallow out to sea in a pail. The thing surpasses a man's love for his sweetheart. The great tank-steamer *Thunder Voice* had long been Flanagan's sweetheart, but he was far happier off Hatteras, watching this wretched little portmanteau boom down the slant of a wave.

The crew scraped acquaintance, one with another, gradually. Each man came ultimately to ask his neighbor what particular turn of ill fortune or inherited deviltry caused him to try this voyage. When one frank, bold man saw another frank, bold man aboard, he smiled, and they became friends. There was not a mind on board the ship that was not fastened to the dangers of the coast of Cuba, and taking wonder at this prospect and delight in it. Still, in jovial moments they termed each other accursed idiots.

At first there was some trouble in the engine-room, where there were many steel animals, for the most part painted red and in other places very shiny, bewildering, complex, incomprehensible to any one who don't care, usually thumping, thumping, thumping, with the monotony of a snore.

It seems that this engine was as whimsical as a gas-meter. The chief engineer was a fine old fellow with a gray mustache; but the engine told him that it didn't intend to budge until it felt better. He came to the bridge and said: "The blamed old thing has laid down on us, sir."

"Who was on duty?" roared the captain.

"The second, sir."

"Why didn't he call you?"

"Don't know, sir." Later the stokers had occasion to thank the stars that they were not second engineers.

The *Foundling* was soundly thrashed by the waves for loitering, while the captain and the engineers fought the obstinate machinery. During this wait on the sea the first gloom came to the faces of the company. The ocean is wide, and a ship is a small place for the feet, and an ill ship is worriment. Even when she was again under way the gloom was still upon the crew. From time to time men went to the engine-room doors and, looking down, wanted to ask questions of the chief engineer, who slowly prowled to and fro and watched with careful eye his red-painted mysteries. No man wished to have a companion know that he was anxious, and so questions were caught at the lips. Perhaps none commented save the first mate, who remarked to the captain, "Wonder what the bally old thing will do, sir, when we're chased by a Spanish cruiser?"

The captain merely grinned. Later he looked over the side and said to himself with scorn: "Sixteen knots! sixteen knots!—sixteen hinges on the inner gates of Hades! Sixteen knots! Seven is her gait, and nine if you crack her up to it."

There may never be a captain whose crew can't sniff his misgivings. They scent it as a herd scents the menace far through the trees and over the ridges. A captain that does not know that he is on a foundering ship sometimes can take his men to tea and buttered toast twelve minutes before the disaster; but let him fret for a moment in the loneliness of his cabin, and in no time it affects the liver of a distant and sensitive seaman. Even as Flanagan reflected on the *Foundling*, viewing her as a filibuster, word arrived that a winter of discontent had come to the stoke-room.

The captain knew that it requires sky to give a man courage. He sent for a stoker, and talked to him on the bridge. The man, standing under the sky, instantly and shamefacedly denied all knowledge of the business. Nevertheless, a jaw had presently to be broken by a fist because the *Foundling* could only steam nine knots and because the stoke-room has no sky, no wind, no bright horizon.

When the *Foundling* was somewhere off Savannah a blow came from the northeast, and the steamer, headed southeast, rolled like a boiling potato. The first mate was a fine officer, and so a wave crashed him into the deck-house and broke his arm. The cook was a good cook, and so the heave of the ship flung him heels over head with a pot of boiling water and caused him to lose interest in everything save his legs. "By the piper!" said Flanagan to himself, "this filibustering is no trick with cards."

Later there was more trouble in the stoke-room. All the stokers participated save the one with a broken jaw, who had become discouraged. The captain had an excellent chest development. When he went aft roaring, it was plain that a man could beat carpets with a voice like that one.

* * *

One night the *Foundling* was off the southern coast of Florida and running at half-speed toward the shore. The captain was on the bridge. "Four flashes at intervals of one minute," he said to himself, gazing steadfastly toward the beach. Suddenly a yellow eye opened in the black face of the night, and looked at the *Foundling,* and closed again. The captain studied his watch and the shore. Three times more the eye opened, and looked at the *Foundling,* and closed again. The captain called to the vague figures on the deck below him. "Answer it." The flash of a light from the bow of the steamer displayed for a moment in golden color the crests of the inriding waves.

The *Foundling* lay to, and waited. The long swells rolled her gracefully, and her two stub masts, reaching into the darkness, swung with the solemnity of batons timing a dirge. When the ship had left Boston she had been as incrusted with ice as a Dakota stagedriver's beard; but now the gentle wind of Florida softly swayed the lock on the forehead of the coatless Flanagan, and he lit a new cigar without troubling to make a shield of his hands.

Finally a dark boat came plashing over the waves. As it came very near, the captain leaned forward, and perceived that the men in her rowed like seamstresses, and at the same time a voice hailed him in bad English. "It's a dead sure connection," said he to himself.

At sea, to load two hundred thousand rounds of rifle ammunition, seven hundred and fifty rifles, two rapid-fire field-guns with a hundred shells, forty bundles of machetes, and a hundred pounds of dynamite, from yawls, and by men who are not born stevedores, and in a heavy ground-swell, and with the search-light of a United States cruiser sometimes flashing like lightning in the sky to the southward, is no business for a Sunday-school class. When at last the *Foundling* was steaming for the open, over the gray sea, at dawn, there was not a man of the forty come aboard from the Florida shore, nor of the fifteen sailed from Boston, who was not glad, standing with his hair matted to his forehead with sweat, smiling at the broad wake of the *Foundling* and the dim streak on the horizon which was Florida.

But there is a point of the compass in these waters which men call the northeast. When the strong winds come from that direction they kick up a turmoil that is not good for a *Foundling* stuffed with coal and war stores. In the gale which came this ship was no more than a drunken soldier.

The Cuban leader, standing on the bridge with the captain, was presently informed that of his men thirty-nine out of a possible thirty-nine were seasick. And in truth they were seasick. There are degrees in this complaint, but that matter was waived between them. They were all sick to the limits. They strewed the deck in every posture of human anguish; and when the *Foundling* ducked and water came sluicing down from the bows, they let it sluice. They were satisfied if they could keep their heads clear of the wash; and if they could not keep their heads clear of the wash they didn't care. Presently the *Foundling* swung her course to the southeast, and the waves pounded her broadside. The patriots were all ordered below decks, and there they howled and measured their misery one against another. All day the *Foundling* plopped and foundered over a blazing bright meadow of an ocean whereon the white foam was like flowers.

The captain on the bridge mused and studied the bare horizon. He said a strong word to himself, and the word was more in amazement than in indignation or sorrow. "Thirty-nine seasick passengers, the mate with a broken arm, a stoker with a broken jaw, the cook with a pair of scalded legs, and an engine likely to be taken with all these diseases, if not more! If I get back to a home port with a spoke of the wheel gripped in my hands, it'll be fair luck."

There is a kind of corn whisky bred in Florida which the natives declare is potent in the proportion of seven fights to a drink. Some of the Cuban volunteers had had the forethought to bring a small quantity of this whisky aboard with them; and being now in the fire-room and seasick, and feeling that they would not care to drink liquor for two or three years to come, they gracefully tendered their portions to the stokers. The stokers accepted these gifts without avidity, but with a certain earnestness of manner.

As they were stokers and toiling, the whirl of emotion was delayed, but it arrived ultimately and with emphasis. One stoker called another stoker a weird name; and the latter, righteously inflamed at it, smote his mate with an iron shovel, and the man fell headlong over a heap of coal, which crashed gently, while piece after piece rattled down upon the deck.

A third stoker was providentially enraged at the scene, and assailed the second stoker. They fought for some moments, while the seasick Cubans sprawled on the deck watched with languid, rolling glances the ferocity of this scuffle. One was so indifferent to the strategic importance of the space he occupied that he was kicked in the shins.

When the second engineer came to separate the combatants, he was sincere in his efforts, and he came near to disabling them for life.

The captain said, "I'll go down there and—"

But the leader of the Cubans restrained him. "No, no," he cried; "you must not. We must treat them like children, very gently, all the time, you see, or else when we get back to a United States port they will—what you call—spring?— yes, spring the whole business. We must—jolly them. You see?"

"You mean," said the captain, thoughtfully, "they are likely to get mad and give the expedition dead away when we reach port again, unless we blarney them now?"

"Yes, yes," cried the Cuban leader; "unless we are so very gentle with them they will make many troubles afterward for us in the newspapers, and then in court."

"Well, but I won't have my crew—" began the captain.

"But you must," interrupted the Cuban. "You must. It is the only thing. You are like the captain of a pirate ship. You see? Only you can't throw them overboard like him. You see?"

"Hum," said the captain, "this here filibustering business has got a lot to it when you come to look it over."

He called the fighting stokers to the bridge, and the three came, meek and considerably battered. He was lecturing them soundly, but sensibly, when he suddenly tripped a sentence and cried: "Here! Where's that other fellow? How does it come he wasn't in the fight?

The row of stokers cried at once eagerly: "He's hurt, sir. He's got a broken jaw, sir."

"So he has, so he has," murmured the captain, much embarrassed.

And because of all these affairs the *Foundling* steamed toward Cuba with its crew in a sling, if one may be allowed to speak in that way.

* * *

At night the *Foundling* approached the coast like a thief. Her lights were muffled so that from the deck the sea shone with its own radiance, like the faint shimmer of some kinds of silk. The men on deck spoke in whispers, and even down in the fire-room the hidden stokers, working before the blood-red furnace doors, used no words, and walked tiptoe. The stars were out in the blue velvet sky, and their light, with the soft shine of the sea, caused the coast to appear black as the side of a coffin. The surf boomed in low thunder on the distant beach.

The *Foundling's* engines ceased their thumping for a time. She glided quietly forward until a bell chimed faintly in the engine-room. Then she paused, with a flourish of phosphorescent waters.

"Give the signal," said the captain. Three times a flash of light went from the bow. There was a moment of waiting. Then an eye like the one on the coast of Florida opened and closed, opened and closed, opened and closed. The Cubans, grouped in a great shadow on deck, burst into a low chatter of delight. A hiss from their leader silenced them.

"Well?" said the captain.

"All right," said the leader.

At the giving of the word it was not apparent that any one on board of the *Foundling* had ever been seasick. The boats were lowered swiftly—too swiftly. Boxes of cartridges were dragged from the hold and passed over the side with a rapidity that made men in the boats exclaim against it. They were being bombarded. When a boat headed for shore, its rowers pulled like madmen. The captain paced slowly to and fro on the bridge. In the engine-room the engineers stood at their station, and in the stoke-hole the firemen fidgeted silently around the furnace doors.

On the bridge Flanagan reflected. "Oh, I don't know," he observed; "this filibustering business isn't so bad. Pretty soon I'll be off to sea again, with nothing to do but some big lying when I get into port."

In one of the boats returning from shore came twelve Cuban officers, the greater number of them convalescing from wounds, while two or three of them had been ordered to America on commissions from the insurgents. The captain welcomed them, and assured them of a speedy and safe voyage.

Presently he went again to the bridge and scanned the horizon. The sea was lonely, like the spaces amid the suns. The captain grinned, and softly smote his chest. "It's dead easy," said he. It was near the end of the cargo, and the men were breathing like spent horses, although their elation grew with each moment, when suddenly a voice spoke from the sky. It was not a loud voice, but the quality of it brought every man on deck to full stop and motionless as if they had all been changed to wax. "Captain," said the man at the masthead, "there's a light to the west'ard, sir. Think it's a steamer, sir."

There was a still moment until the captain called, "Well, keep your eye on it now." Speaking to the deck, he said, "Go ahead with your unloading."

The second engineer went to the galley to borrow a tin cup. "Hear the news, second?" asked the cook. "Steamer coming up from the west'ard."

"Gee!" said the second engineer. In the engine-room he said to the chief: "Steamer coming up to the west'ard, sir."

The chief engineer began to test various little machines with which his domain was decorated. Finally he addressed the stoke-room: "Boys, I want you to look sharp now. There's a steamer coming up to the west'ard."

"All right, sir," said the stoke-room.

From time to time the captain hailed the masthead. "How is she now?"

"Seems to be coming down on us pretty fast, sir."

The Cuban leader came anxiously to the captain. "Do you think we can save all the cargo? It is rather delicate business. No?"

"Go ahead," said Flanagan. "Fire away. I'll wait for you."

There continued the hurried shuffling of feet on deck and the low cries of the men unloading the cargo. In the engine-room the chief and his assistant were staring at the gong. In the stoke-room the firemen breathed through their teeth. A shovel slipped from where it leaned against the side, and banged on the floor. The stokers started, and looked around quickly.

Climbing to the rail and holding on to a stay, the captain gazed westward. A light had raised out of the deep. After watching this light for a time, he called to the Cuban leader, "Well, as soon as you're ready now, we might as well be skipping out."

Finally the Cuban leader told him: "Well, this is the last load. As soon as the boats come back you can be off."

"Sha'n't wait for the boats," said the captain. "That fellow is too close." As the last boat went shoreward the *Foundling* turned, and like a black shadow stole seaward to cross the bows of the oncoming steamer. "Waited about ten minutes too long," said the captain to himself.

Suddenly the light in the west vanished. "Hum," said Flanagan; "he's up to some meanness."

Everyone outside of the engine-rooms was set on watch. The *Foundling*, going at full speed into the northeast, slashed a wonderful trail of blue silver on the dark bosom of the sea.

A man on deck cried out hurriedly, "There she is, sir!" Many eyes searched the western gloom, and one after another the glances of the men found a tiny black shadow on the deep, with a line of white beneath it.

"He couldn't be heading better if he had a line to us," said Flanagan.

There was a thin flash of red in the darkness. It was long and keen, like a crimson rapier. A short, sharp report sounded, and then a shot whined swiftly in the air and blipped into the sea. The captain had been about to take a bite of plug tobacco at the beginning of this incident, and his arm was raised. He remained like a frozen figure while the shot whined, and then, as it blipped in the sea, his hand went to his mouth, and he bit the plug. He looked wide-eyed at the shadow with its line of white.

The senior Cuban officer came hurriedly to the bridge. "It is no good to surrender," he cried; "they would only shoot or hang all of us."

There was another thin red flash and a report. A loud whirring noise passed over the ship.

"I'm not going to surrender," said the captain, hanging with both hands to the rail. He appeared like a man whose traditions of peace are clinched in his heart. He was as astonished as if his hat had turned into a dog. Presently he wheeled quickly, and said: "What kind of a gun is that?"

"It is a one-pounder," cried the Cuban officer. "The boat is one of those little gunboats made from a yacht. You see?"

"Well, if it's only a yawl, he'll sink us in five more minutes," said Flanagan. For a moment he looked helplessly off at the horizon. His under jaw hung low. But a moment later something touched him like a stiletto-point of inspiration. He leaped to the pilot-house, and roared at the man at the wheel. The *Foundling* sheered suddenly to starboard, made a clumsy turn, and Flanagan was bellowing through the tube to the engine-room before anybody discovered that the old basket was heading straight for the Spanish gunboat. The ship lunged forward like a draft-horse on the gallop.

This strange manœuver by the *Foundling* first dealt consternation on board. Men instinctively crouched on the instant, and then swore their supreme oath, which was unheard by their own ears.

Later the manœuver of the *Foundling* dealt consternation on board of the gunboat. She had been going victoriously forward, dim-eyed from the fury of her pursuit. Then this tall, threatening shape had suddenly loomed over her like a giant apparition.

The people on board the *Foundling* heard panic shouts, hoarse orders. The little gunboat was paralyzed with astonishment.

Suddenly Flanagan yelled with rage, and sprang for the wheel. The helmsman had turned his eyes away. As the captain whirled the wheel far to starboard, he heard a crunch, as the *Foundling*, lifted on a wave, smashed her shoulder against the gunboat, and he saw, shooting past, a little launch sort of a thing with men on her than ran this way and that way. The Cuban officers, joined by the cook and a seaman, emptied their revolvers into the surprised terror of the seas.

There was naturally no pursuit. Under comfortable speed the *Foundling* stood to the northward.

The captain went to his berth chuckling. "There, now," he said. "There, now!"

* * *

When Flanagan came again on deck, the first mate, his arm in a sling, walked the bridge. Flanagan was smiling a wide smile. The bridge of the *Foundling* was dipping afar and then afar. With each lunge of the little steamer the water seethed and boomed alongside, and the spray dashed high and swiftly.

"Well," said Flanagan, inflating himself, "we've had a great deal of a time, and we've come through it all right, and thank Heaven it is all over."

The sky in the northeast was of a dull brick-red in tone, shaded here and there by black masses that billowed out in some fashion from the flat heavens.

"Look there," said the mate.

"Hum," said the captain. "Looks like a blow, don't it?"

Later the surface of the water rippled and flickered in the preliminary wind. The sea had become the color of lead. The swashing sound of the waves on the sides of the *Foundling* was now provided with some manner of ominous significance. The men's shouts were hoarse.

A squall struck the *Foundling* on her starboard quarter, and she leaned under the force of it as if she were never to return to the even keel. "I'll be glad when we get in," said the mate. "I'm going to quit then. I've got enough."

The steamer crawled on into the northwest. The white water sweeping out from her deadened the chug-chug-chug of the tired old engines.

Once, when the boat careened, she laid her shoulder flat on the sea and rested in that manner. The mate, looking down the bridge, which slanted more than a coal-chute, whistled softly to himself. Slowly, heavily, the *Foundling* arose to meet another sea.

At night waves thundered mightily on the bows of the steamer, and water, lighted with the beautiful phosphorescent glamour, went boiling and howling along the deck.

By good fortune the chief engineer crawled safely, but utterly drenched, to the galley for coffee. "Well, how goes it, chief?" said the cook, standing with his fat arms folded, in order to prove that he could balance himself under any condition.

The engineer shook his head slowly. "This old biscuit-box will never see port again. Why, she'll fall to pieces."

Finally, at night, the captain said, "Launch the boats." The Cubans hovered about him. "Is the ship going to sink?" The captain addressed them politely: "Gentlemen, we are in trouble; but all I ask of you is that you do just what I tell you, and no harm will come to anybody."

The mate directed the lowering of the first boat, and the men performed this task with all decency, like people at the side of a grave.

A young oiler came to the captain. "The chief sends word, sir, that the water is almost up to the fires."

"Keep at it as long as you can."

"Keep at it as long as we can, sir."

Flanagan took the senior Cuban officer to the rail, and, as the steamer sheered high on a great sea, showed him a yellow dot on the horizon. It was smaller than a needle when its point is toward you.

"There," said the captain. The wind-driven spray was lashing his face. "That's Jupiter Light on the Florida coast. Put your men in the boat we've just launched, and the mate will take you to that light."

Afterward Flanagan turned to the chief engineer. "We can never beach her," said the old man. "The stokers have got to quit in a minute." Tears were in his eyes.

The *Foundling* was a wounded thing. She lay on the water with gasping engines, and each wave resembled her death-blow.

Now the way of a good ship on the sea is finer than sword-play; but this is when she is alive. If a time comes that the ship dies, then her way is the way of a floating old glove, and she has that much vim, spirit, buoyancy. At this time many men on the *Foundling* suddenly came to know that they were clinging to a corpse.

The captain went to the stoke-room, and what he saw as he swung down the companion suddenly turned him hesitant and dumb. He had served the sea for many years, but this fire-room said something to him which he had not heard in his other voyages. Water was swirling to and fro with the roll of the ship, fuming greasily around half-strangled machinery that still attempted to perform its duty. Steam arose from the water, and through its clouds shone the red glare of the dying fires. As for the stokers, death might have been with silence in this room. One lay in his berth, his hands under his head, staring moodily at the wall. One sat near the foot of the companion, his face hidden in his arms. One leaned against the side, and gazed at the snarling water as it rose, and its made eddies among the machinery. In the unholy red light and gray mist of this stifling, dim inferno they were strange figures with their silence and their immobility. The wretched *Foundling* groaned deeply as she lifted, and groaned deeply as she sank into the trough, while hurried waves then thundered over her with the noise of land-slides.

But Flanagan took control of himself suddenly, and then he stirred the fire-room. The stillness had been so unearthly that he was not altogether inapprehensive of strange and grim deeds when he charged into them; but precisely as they had submitted to the sea, so they submitted to Flanagan. For a moment they rolled their eyes like hurt cows, but they obeyed the voice. The situation simply required a voice.

When the captain returned to the deck the hue of this fire-room was in his mind, and then he understood doom and its weight and complexion.

When finally the *Foundling* sank, she shifted and settled as calmly as an animal curls down in the bush-grass. Away over the waves three bobbing boats paused to witness this quiet death. It was a slow manœuver, altogether without the pageantry of uproar; but it flashed pallor into the faces of all men who saw it, and they groaned when they said, "There she goes!" Suddenly the captain whirled and knocked his head on the gunwale. He sobbed for a time, and then he sobbed and swore also.

There was a dance at the Imperial Inn. During the evening some irresponsible young men came from the beach, bringing the statement that several boat-loads of people had been perceived off shore. It was a charming dance, and none cared to take time to believe this tale. The fountain in the courtyard plashed softly, and couple after couple paraded through the aisles of palms, where lamps with red shades threw a rose light upon the gleaming leaves. High on some balcony a mocking-bird called into the evening. The band played its waltzes slumberously, and its music to the people among the palms came faintly and like the melodies in dreams.

Sometimes a woman said, "Oh, it is not really true, is it, that there was a wreck out at sea?"

A man usually said, "No; of course not."

At last, however, a youth came violently from the beach. He was triumphant in manner. "They're out there," he cried—"a whole boat-load!" He received eager attention, and he told all that he supposed. His news destroyed the dance. After a time the band was playing delightfully to space. The guests had donned wraps and hurried to the beach. One little girl cried, "Oh, mama, may I go too?" Being refused permission, she pouted.

As they came from the shelter of the great hotel, the wind was blowing swiftly from the sea, and at intervals a breaker shone livid. The women shuddered, and their bending companions seized opportunity to draw the cloaks closer. The sand of the beach was wet, and dainty slippers made imprints in it clear and deep.

"Oh dear," said a girl; "supposin' they were out there drowning while we were dancing!"

"Oh, nonsense!" said her younger brother; "that don't happen."

"Well, it might, you know, Roger. How can you tell?"

A man who was not her brother gazed at her then with profound admiration. Later she complained of the damp sand, and drawing back her skirts, looked ruefully at her little feet.

A mother's son was venturing too near to the water in his interest and excitement. Occasionally she cautioned and reproached him from the background.

Save for the white glare of the breakers, the sea was a great wind-crossed void. From the throng of charming women floated the perfume of many flowers. Later there floated to them a body with a calm face of an Irish type. The expedition of the *Foundling* will never be historic.

THE BRIDE
COMES TO YELLOW SKY

The great Pullman was whirling onward with such dignity of motion that a glance from the window seemed simply to prove that the plains of Texas were pouring eastward. Vast flats of green grass, dull-hued spaces of mesquit and cactus, little groups of frame houses, woods of light and tender trees, all were sweeping into the east, sweeping over the horizon, a precipice.

A newly married pair had boarded this coach at San Antonio. The man's face was reddened from many days in the wind and sun, and a direct result of his new black clothes was that his brick-colored hands were constantly performing in a most conscious fashion. From time to time he looked down respectfully at his attire. He sat with a hand on each knee, like a man waiting in a barber's shop. The glances he devoted to other passengers were furtive and shy.

The bride was not pretty, nor was she very young. She wore a dress of blue cashmere, with small reservations of velvet here and there, and with steel buttons abounding. She continually twisted her head to regard her puff sleeves, very stiff, straight, and high. They embarrassed her. It was quite apparent that she had cooked, and that she expected to cook, dutifully. The blushes caused by the careless scrutiny of some passengers as she had entered the car were strange to see upon this plain, under-class countenance, which was drawn in placid, almost emotionless lines.

They were evidently very happy. "Ever been in a parlor-car before?" he asked, smiling with delight.

"No," she answered; "I never was. It's fine, ain't it?"

"Great! And then after a while we'll go forward to the diner, and get a big lay-out. Finest meal in the world. Charge a dollar."

"Oh, do they?" cried the bride. "Charge a dollar? Why, that's too much—for us—ain't it, Jack?"

"Not this trip, anyhow," he answered bravely. "We're going to go the whole thing."

Later he explained to her about the trains. "You see, it's a thousand miles from one end of Texas to the other; and this train runs right across it, and never stops but four times." He had the pride of an owner. He pointed out to her the dazzling fittings of the coach; and in truth her eyes opened wider as she contemplated the sea-green figured velvet, the shining brass, silver, and glass, the wood that gleamed as darkly brilliant as the surface of a pool of oil. At one end a bronze figure sturdily held a support for a separated chamber, and at convenient places on the ceiling were frescos in olive and silver.

To the minds of the pair, their surroundings reflected the glory of their marriage that morning in San Antonio; this was the environment of their new estate; and the man's face in particular beamed with an elation that made him appear ridiculous to the negro porter. This individual at times surveyed them from afar with an amused and superior grin. On other occasions he bullied them with skill in ways that did not make it exactly plain to them that they were being bullied. He subtly used all the manners of the most unconquerable kind of snobbery. He oppressed them; but of this oppression they had small knowledge, and they speedily forgot that infrequently a number of travelers covered them with stares of derisive enjoyment. Historically there was supposed to be something infinitely humorous in their situation.

"We are due in Yellow Sky at 3:42," he said, looking tenderly into her eyes.

"Oh, are we?" she said, as if she had not been aware of it. To evince surprise at her husbands's statement was part of her wifely amiability. She took from a pocket a little silver watch; and as she held it before her, and stared at it with a frown of attention, the new husband's face shone.

"I bought it in San Anton' from a friend of mine," he told her gleefully.

"It's seventeen minutes past twelve," she said, looking up at him with a kind of shy and clumsy coquetry. A passenger, noting this play, grew excessively sardonic, and winked at himself in one of the numerous mirrors.

At last they went to the dining-car. Two rows of negro waiters, in glowing white suits, surveyed their entrance with the interest, and also the equanimity, of men who had been forewarned. The pair fell to the lot of a waiter who happened to feel pleasure in steering them through their meal. He viewed them with the manner of a fatherly pilot, his countenance radiant with benevolence. The patronage, entwined with the ordinary deference, was not plain to them. And yet, as they returned to their coach, they showed in their faces a sense of escape.

To the left, miles down a long purple slope, was a little ribbon of mist where moved the keening Rio Grande. The train was approaching it at an angle, and the apex was Yellow Sky. Presently it was apparent that, as the distance from Yellow Sky grew shorter, the husband became commensurately restless. His brick-red hands were more insistent in their prominence. Occasionally he was even rather absent-minded and far-away when the bride leaned forward and addressed him.

As a matter of truth, Jack Potter was beginning to find the shadow of a deed weigh upon him like a leaden slab. He, the town marshal of Yellow Sky, a man known, liked, and feared in his corner, a prominent person, had gone to San Antonio to meet a girl he believed he loved, and there, after the usual prayers, had actually induced her to marry him, without consulting Yellow Sky for any part of the transaction. He was now bringing his bride before an innocent and unsuspecting community.

Of course people in Yellow Sky married as it pleased them, in accordance with a general custom; but such was Potter's thought of his duty to his friends, or of their idea of his duty, or of an unspoken form which does not control men in these matters, that he felt he was heinous. He had committed an extra-ordinary crime. Face to face with this girl in San Antonio, and spurred by his sharp impulse, he had gone headlong over all the social hedges. At San Antonio he was like a man hidden in the dark. A knife to sever any friendly duty, any form, was easy to his hand in that remote city. But the hour of Yellow Sky—the hour of daylight—was approaching.

He knew full well that his marriage was an important thing to his town. It could only be exceeded by the burning of the new hotel. His friends could not forgive him. Frequently he had reflected on the advisability of telling them by telegraph, but a new cowardice had been upon him. He feared to do it. And now the train was hurrying him toward a scene of amazement, glee, and reproach. He glanced out of the window at the line of haze swinging slowly in toward the train.

Yellow Sky had a kind of brass band, which played painfully, to the delight of the populace. He laughed without heart as he thought of it. If the citizens could dream of his prospective arrival with his bride, they would parade the band at the station and escort them, amid cheers and laughing congratulations, to his adobe home.

He resolved that he would use all the devices of speed and plains-craft in making the journey from the station to his house. Once within that safe citadel, he could issue some sort of a vocal bulletin, and then not go among the citizens until they had time to wear off a little of their enthusiasm.

The bride looked anxiously at him. "What's worrying you, Jack?"

He laughed again. "I'm not worrying, girl; I'm only thinking of Yellow Sky."

She flushed in comprehension.

A sense of mutual guilt invaded their minds and developed a finer tenderness. They looked at each other with eyes softly aglow. But Potter often laughed the same nervous laugh; the flush upon the bride's face seemed quite permanent.

The traitor to the feelings of Yellow Sky narrowly watched the speeding landscape. "We're nearly there," he said.

Presently the porter came and announced the proximity of Potter's home. He held a brush in his hand, and, with all his airy superiority gone, he brushed Potter's new clothes as the latter slowly turned this way and that way. Potter fumbled out a coin and gave it to the porter, as he had seen others do. It was a heavy and muscle-bound business, as that of a man shoeing his first horse.

The porter took their bag, and as the train began to slow they moved forward to the hooded platform of the car. Presently the two engines and their long string of coaches rushed into the station of Yellow Sky.

"They have to take water here," said Potter, from a constricted throat and in mournful cadence, as one announcing death. Before the train stopped his eye had swept the length of the platform, and he was glad and astonished to see there was none upon it but the station-agent, who, with a slightly hurried and anxious air, was walking toward the water-tanks. When the train had halted, the porter alighted first, and placed in position a little temporary step.

"Come on, girl," said Potter, hoarsely. As he helped her down they each laughed on a false note. He took the bag from the negro, and bade his wife cling to his arm. As they slunk rapidly away, his hang-dog glance perceived that they were unloading the two trunks, and also that the station-agent, far ahead near the baggage-car, had turned and was running toward him, making gestures. He laughed, and groaned as he laughed, when he noted the first effect of his marital bliss upon Yellow Sky. He gripped his wife's arm firmly to his side, and they fled. Behind them the porter stood, chuckling fatuously.

* * *

The California express on the Southern Railway was due at Yellow Sky in twenty-one minutes. There were six men at the bar of the Weary Gentleman Saloon. One was a drummer, who talked a great deal and rapidly; three were Texans, who did not care to talk at that time; and two were Mexican sheep-herders, who did not talk as a general practice in the Weary Gentleman Saloon. The barkeeper's dog lay on the board walk that crossed in front of the door. His head was on his paws, and he glanced drowsily here and there with the constant vigilance of a dog that is kicked on occasion. Across the sandy street were some vivid green grass-plots, so wonderful in appearance, amid the sands that burned near them in a blazing sun, that they caused a doubt in the mind. They exactly resembled the grass mats used to represent lawns on the stage. At the cooler end of the railway station, a man without a coat sat in a tilted chair and smoked his pipe. The fresh-cut bank of the Rio Grande circled near the town, and there could be seen beyond it a great plum-colored plain of mesquit.

Save for the busy drummer and his companions in the saloon, Yellow Sky was dozing. The new-comer leaned gracefully upon the bar, and recited many tales with the confidence of a bard who has come upon a new field.

"—and at the moment that the old man fell down-stairs with the bureau in his arms, the old woman was coming up with two scuttles of coal, and of course—"

The drummer's tale was interrupted by a young man who suddenly appeared in the open door. He cried: "Scratchy Wilson's drunk, and has turned loose with both hands." The two Mexicans at once set down their glasses and faded out of the rear entrance of the saloon.

The drummer, innocent and jocular, answered: "All right, old man. S'pose he has? Come in and have a drink, anyhow."

But the information had made such an obvious cleft in every skull in the room that the drummer was obliged to see its importance. All had become instantly solemn. "Say," said he, mystified, "what is this?" His three companions made the introductory gesture of eloquent speech; but the young man at the door forestalled them.

"It means, my friend," he answered, as he came into the saloon, "that for the next two hours this town won't be a health resort."

The barkeeper went to the door, and locked and barred it; reaching out of the window, he pulled in heavy wooden shutters, and barred them. Immediately a solemn, chapel-like gloom was upon the place. The drummer was looking from one to another.

"But say," he cried, "what is this, anyhow? You don't mean there is going to be a gun-fight?"

"Don't know whether there'll be a fight or not," answered one man, grimly;

"but there'll be some shootin'—some good shootin'."

The young man who had warned them waved his hand. "Oh, there'll be a fight fast enough, if any one wants it. Anybody can get a fight out there in the street. There's a fight just waiting."

The drummer seemed to be swayed between the interest of a foreigner and a perception of personal danger.

"What did you say his name was?" he asked.

"Scratchy Wilson," they answered in chorus.

"And will he kill anybody? What are you going to do? Does this happen often? Does he rampage around like this once a week or so? Can he break in that door?"

"No; he can't break down that door," replied the barkeeper. "He's tried it three times. But when he comes you'd better lay down on the floor, stranger. He's dead sure to shoot at it, and a bullet may come through."

Thereafter the drummer kept a strict eye upon the door. The time had not yet been called for him to hug the floor, but, as a minor precaution, he sidled near to the wall. "Will he kill anybody?" he said again.

The men laughed low and scornfully at the question.

"He's out to shoot, and he's out for trouble. Don't see any good in experimentin' with him."

"But what do you do in a case like this? What do you do?"

A man responded: "Why, he and Jack Potter—"

"But," in chorus the other men interrupted, "Jack Potter's in San Anton'."

"Well, who is he? What's he got to do with it?"

"Oh, he's the town marshal. He goes out and fights Scratchy when he gets on one of these tears."

"Wow!" said the drummer, mopping his brow. "Nice job he's got."

The voices had toned away to mere whisperings. The drummer wished to ask further questions, which were born of an increasing anxiety and bewilderment; but when he attempted them, the men merely looked at him in irritation and motioned him to remain silent. A tense waiting hush was upon them. In the deep shadows of the room their eyes shone as they listened for sounds from the street. One man made three gestures at the barkeeper; and the latter, moving like a ghost, handed him a glass and a bottle. The man poured a full glass of whisky, and set down the bottle noiselessly. He gulped the whisky in a swallow, and turned again toward the door in immovable silence. The drummer saw that the barkeeper, without a sound, had taken a Winchester from beneath the bar. Later he saw this individual beckoning to him, so he tiptoed across the room.

"You better come with me back of the bar."

"No, thanks," said the drummer, perspiring; "I'd rather be where I can make a break for the back door."

Whereupon the man of bottles made a kindly but peremptory gesture. The drummer obeyed it, and, finding himself seated on a box with his head below the level of the bar, balm was laid upon his soul at sight of various zinc and copper fittings that bore a resemblance to armorplate. The barkeeper took a seat comfortably upon an adjacent box.

"You see," he whispered, "this here Scratchy Wilson is a wonder with a gun—a perfect wonder; and when he goes on the war-trail, we hunt our holes—naturally. He's about the last one of the old gang that used to hang out along the river here. He's a terror when he's drunk. When he's sober he's all right—kind of simple—wouldn't hurt a fly—nicest fellow in town. But when he's drunk—whoo!"

There were periods of stillness. "I wish Jack Potter was back from San Anton'," said the barkeeper. "He shot Wilson up once,—in the leg,—and he would sail in and pull out the kinks in this thing."

Presently they heard from a distance the sound of a shot, followed by three wild yowls. It instantly removed a bond from the men in the darkened saloon. There was a shuffling of feet. They looked at each other. "Here he comes," they said.

* * *

A man in a maroon-colored flannel shirt, which had been purchased for purposes of decoration, and made principally by some Jewish women on the East Side of New York, rounded a corner and walked into the middle of the main street of Yellow Sky. In either hand the man held a long, heavy, blue-black revolver. Often he yelled, and these cries rang through a semblance of a deserted village, shrilly flying over the roofs in a volume that seemed to have no relation to the ordinary vocal strength of a man. It was as if the surrounding stillness formed the arch of a tomb over him. These cries of ferocious challenge rang against walls of silence. And his boots had red tops with gilded imprints, of the kind beloved in winter by little sledding boys on the hillsides of New England.

The man's face flamed in a rage begot of whisky. His eyes, rolling, and yet keen for ambush, hunted the still doorways and windows. He walked with the creeping movement of the midnight cat. As it occurred to him, he roared menacing information. The long revolvers in his hands were as easy as straws; they were moved with an electric swiftness. The little fingers of each hand played sometimes in a musician's way. Plain from the low collar of the shirt, the cords of his neck straightened and sank, straightened and sank, as passion moved him. The only sounds were his terrible invitations. The calm adobes preserved their demeanor at the passing of this small thing in the middle of the street.

There was no offer of fight—no offer of fight. The man called to the sky. There were no attractions. He bellowed and fumed and swayed his revolvers here and everywhere.

The dog of the barkeeper of the Weary Gentleman Saloon had not appreciated the advance of events. He yet lay dozing in front of his master's door. At sight of the dog, the man paused and raised his revolver humorously. At sight of the man, the dog sprang up and walked diagonally away, with a sullen head, and growling. The man yelled, and the dog broke into a gallop. As it was about to enter an alley, there was a loud noise, a whistling, and something spat the ground directly before it. The dog screamed, and, wheeling in terror, galloped headlong in a new direction. Again there was a noise, a whistling, and sand was kicked viciously before it. Fear-stricken, the dog turned and flurried like an animal in a pen. The man stood laughing, his weapons at his hips.

Ultimately the man was attracted by the closed door of the Weary Gentleman Saloon. He went to it, and, hammering with a revolver, demanded drink.

The door remaining imperturbable, he picked a bit of paper from the walk, and nailed it to the framework with a knife. He then turned his back contemptuously upon this popular resort, and, walking to the opposite side of the street, and spinning there on his heel quickly and lithely, fired at the bit of paper. He missed it by a half-inch. He swore at himself, and went away. Later he comfortably fusilladed the windows of his most intimate friend. The man was playing with this town; it was a toy for him.

But still there was no offer of fight. The name of Jack Potter, his ancient antagonist, entered his mind, and he concluded that it would be a glad thing if he should go to Potter's house, and by bombardment induce him to come out and fight. He moved in the direction of his desire, chanting Apache scalp-music.

When he arrived at it, Potter's house presented the same still front as had the other adobes. Taking up a strategic position, the man howled a challenge. But this house regarded him as might a great stone god. It gave no sign. After a decent wait, the man howled further challenges, mingling with them wonderful epithets.

Presently there came the spectacle of a man churning himself into deepest rage over the immobility of a house. He fumed at it as the winter wind attacks a prairie cabin in the North. To the distance there should have gone the sound of a tumult like the fighting of two hundred Mexicans. As necessity bade him, he paused for breath or to reload his revolvers.

* * *

Potter and his bride walked sheepishly and with speed. Sometimes they laughed together shamefacedly and low.

"Next corner, dear," he said finally.

They put forth the efforts of a pair walking bowed against a strong wind. Potter was about to raise a finger to point the first appearance of the new home when, as they circled the corner, they came face to face with a man in a maroon-colored shirt, who was feverishly pushing cartridges into a large revolver. Upon the instant the man dropped his revolver to the ground, and, like lightning, whipped another from its holster. The second weapon was aimed at the bridegroom's chest.

There was a silence. Potter's mouth seemed to be merely a grave for his tongue. He exhibited an instinct to at once loosen his arm from the woman's grip, and he dropped the bag to the sand. As for the bride, her face had gone as yellow as old cloth. She was a slave to hideous rites, gazing at the apparitional snake.

The two men faced each other at a distance of three paces. He of the revolver smiled with a new and quiet ferocity.

"Tried to sneak up on me," he said. "Tried to sneak up on me!" His eyes grew more baleful. As Potter made a slight movement, the man thrust his revolver venomously forward. "No; don't you do it, Jack Potter. Don't you move a finger toward a gun just yet. Don't you move an eyelash. The time has come for me to settle with you, and I'm goin' to do it my own way, and loaf along with no interferin'. So if you don't want a gun bent on you, just mind what I tell you."

Potter looked at his enemy. "I ain't got a gun on me, Scratchy," he said. "Honest, I ain't." He was stiffening and steadying, but yet somewhere at the back of his mind a vision of the Pullman floated: the sea-green figured velvet, the shining brass, silver, and glass, the wood that gleamed as darkly brilliant as the surface of a pool of oil—all the glory of the marriage, the environment of the new estate. "You know I fight when it comes to fighting, Scratchy Wilson; but I ain't got a gun on me. You'll have to do all the shootin' yourself."

His enemy's face went livid. He stepped forward, and lashed his weapon to and fro before Potter's chest. "Don't you tell me you ain't got no gun on you, you whelp. Don't tell me no lie like that. There ain't a man in Texas ever seen you without no gun. Don't take me for no kid." His eyes blazed with light, and his throat worked like a pump.

"I ain't takin' you for no kid," answered Potter. His heels had not moved an inch backward. "I'm takin' you for a —— fool. I tell you I ain't got a gun, and I ain't. If you're goin' to shoot me up, you better begin now; you'll never get a chance like this again."

So much enforced reasoning had told on Wilson's rage; he was calmer. "If you ain't got a gun, why ain't you got a gun?" he sneered. "Been to Sunday-school?"

"I ain't got a gun because I've just come from San Anton' with my wife. I'm married," said Potter. "And if I'd thought there was going to be any galoots like you prowling around when I brought my wife home, I'd had a gun, and don't you forget it."

"Married!" said Scratchy, not at all comprehending.

"Yes, married. I'm married," said Potter, distinctly.

"Married?" said Scratchy. Seemingly for the first time, he saw the drooping, drowning woman at the other man's side. "No!" he said. He was like a creature allowed a glimpse of another world. He moved a pace backward, and his arm, with the revolver, dropped to his side. "Is this the lady?" he asked.

"Yes; this is the lady," answered Potter.

There was another period of silence.

"Well," said Wilson at last, slowly, "I s'pose it's all off now."

"It's all off if you say so, Scratchy. You know I didn't make the trouble." Potter lifted his valise.

"Well, I 'low it's off, Jack," said Wilson. He was looking at the ground. "Married!" He was not a student of chivalry; it was merely that in the presence of this foreign condition he was a simple child of the earlier plains. He picked up his starboard revolver, and, placing both weapons in their holsters, he went away. His feet made funnel-shaped tracks in the heavy sand.

THE WISE MEN

A Detail of American Life in Mexico

T hey were youths of subtle mind. They were very wicked, according to report, and yet they managed to have it reflect credit upon them. They often had the well informed and the great talkers of the American colony engaged in reciting their misdeeds, and facts relating to their sins were usually told with a flourish of awe and fine admiration.

One was from San Francisco, and one was from New York; but they resembled each other in appearance. This is an idiosyncrasy of geography.

They were never apart in the City of Mexico, at any rate, excepting, perhaps, when one had retired to his hotel for a respite; and then the other was usually camped down at the office, sending up servants with clamorous messages: "Oh, get up, and come on down."

They were two lads,—they were called the Kids,—and far from their mothers. Occasionally some wise man pitied them, but he usually was alone in his wisdom; the other folk frankly were transfixed at the splendor of the audacity and endurance of these Kids.

"When do those two boys ever sleep?" murmured a man, as he viewed them entering a café about eight o'clock one morning. Their smooth, infantile faces looked bright and fresh enough, at any rate. "Jim told me he saw them still at it about four-thirty this morning."

"Sleep?" ejaculated a companion, in a glowing voice. "They never sleep! They go to bed once in every two weeks." His boast of it seemed almost a personal pride.

"They'll end with a crash, though, if they keep it up at this pace," said a gloomy voice from behind a newspaper.

The "Café Colorado" has a front of white and gold, in which are set larger plate-glass windows than are commonly to be found in Mexico. Two little wings of willow, flip-flapping incessantly, serve as doors. Under them small stray dogs go furtively into the café, and are shied into the street again by the waiters. On the sidewalk there is always a decorative effect in loungers, ranging from the newly arrived and superior tourist to the old veteran of the silver-mines, bronzed by violent suns. They contemplate, with various shades of interest, the show of the street—the red, purple, dusty white, glaring forth against the walls in the furious sunshine.

One afternoon the Kids strolled into the Café Colorado. A half-dozen of the men, who sat smoking and reading with a sort of Parisian effect at the little tables which lined two sides of the room, looked up, and bowed, smiling; and although this coming of the Kids was anything but an unusual event, at least a dozen men wheeled in their seats to stare after them. Three waiters polished tables, and moved chairs noisily, and appeared to be eager. Distinctly these Kids were of importance.

Behind the distant bar the tall form of old "Pop" himself awaited them, smiling with broad geniality. "Well, my boys, how are you?" he cried in a voice of profound solicitude. He allowed five or six of his customers to languish in the care of Mexican bartenders, while he himself gave his eloquent attention to the Kids, lending all the dignity of a great event to their arrival. "How are the boys to-day, eh?"

"You're a smooth old guy," said one, eying him. "Are you giving us this welcome so we won't notice it when you push your worst whisky at us?"

Pop turned in appeal from one Kid to the other Kid. "There, now! Hear that, will you?" He assumed an oratorical pose. "Why, my boys, you always get the best—the very best—that this house has got."

"Yes; we do!" The Kids laughed. "Well, bring it out, anyhow; and if it's the same you sold us last night, we'll grab your cash-register and run."

Pop whirled a bottle along the bar, and then gazed at it with a rapt expression. "Fine as silk," he murmured. "Now just taste that, and if it isn't the finest whisky you ever put in your face, why, I'm a liar, that's all."

The Kids surveyed him with scorn, and poured out their allowances. Then they stood for a time, insulting Pop about his whisky. "Usually it tastes exactly like new parlor furniture," said the San Francisco Kid. "Well, here goes; and you want to look out for your cash-register."

"Your health, gentlemen," said Pop, with a grand air; and as he wiped his bristling gray mustache he wagged his head with reference to the cash-register question. "I could catch you before you got very far."

"Why, are you a runner?" said one, derisively.

"You just bank on me, my boy," said Pop, with deep emphasis. "I'm a flier."

The Kids set down their glasses suddenly, and looked at him. "You must be," they said. Pop was tall and graceful, and magnificent in manner, but he did not display those qualities of form which mean speed in the animal. His hair was gray; his face was round and fat from much living. The buttons of his glittering white vest formed a fine curve, so that if the concave surface of a piece of barrel-hoop had been laid against Pop, it would have touched each button. "You must be," observed the Kids again.

"Well, you can laugh all you like, but—no jolly, now, boys—I tell you I'm a winner. Why, I bet you I can skin anything in this town on a square go. When I kept my place in Eagle Pass, there wasn't anybody who could touch me. One of these sure things came down from San Anton'. Oh, he was a runner, he was—one of these people with wings. Well, I skinned 'im. What? Certainly I did. Never touched me."

The Kids had been regarding him in grave silence; but at this moment they grinned, and said, quite in chorus: "Oh, you old liar!"

Pop's voice took on a whining tone of earnestness: "Boys, I'm telling it to you straight. I'm a flier."

One of the Kids had had a dreamy cloud in his eye, and he cried out suddenly: "Say, what a joke to play this on Freddie!"

The other jumped ecstatically. "Oh, wouldn't it be, though? Say, he wouldn't do a thing but howl! He'd go crazy!"

They looked at Pop as if they longed to be certain that he was, after all, a runner. "Say, now, Pop,—on the level," said one of them, wistfully,—"can you run?"

"Boys," swore Pop, "I'm a peach! On the dead level, I'm a peach."

"By golly, I believe the old Indian can run," said one to the other, as if they were alone in conference.

"That's what I can," cried Pop.

The Kids said: "Well, so long, old man." They went to a table, and sat down. They ordered a salad. They were always ordering salads. This was because one Kid had a wild passion for salads, and the other did not care much. So at any hour of the day or night they might be seen ordering a salad. When this one came, they went into a sort of executive session. It was a very long consultation. Some of the men noted it; they said there was deviltry afoot. Occasionally the Kids laughed in supreme enjoyment of something unknown. The low rumble of wheels came from the street. Often could be heard the parrot-like cries of distant venders. The sunlight streamed through the green curtains and made some little amber-colored flitterings on the marble floor. High up among the severe decorations of the ceiling,—reminiscent of the days when the great building was a palace,—a small white butterfly was wending through the cool air-spaces. The long billiard-hall stretched back to a vague gloom. The balls were always clicking, and one could see endless elbows crooking. Beggars slunk through the wicker doors, and were ejected by the nearest waiter.

At last the Kids called Pop to them. "Sit down, Pop! Have a drink!" They scanned him carefully. "Say, now, Pop, on your solemn oath, can you run?"

"Boys," said Pop, piously, and raising his hand, "I can run like a rabbit."

"On your oath?"

"On my oath."

"Can you beat Freddie?"

Pop appeared to look at the matter from all sides. "Well, boys, I'll tell you: no man is cock-sure of anything in this world, and I don't want to say that I can best any man; but I've seen Freddie run, and I'm ready to swear I can beat 'im. In a hundred yards I'd just about skin 'im neat—you understand—just about neat. Freddie is a good average runner, but I—you understand—I'm just—a little—bit—better."

The Kids had been listening with the utmost attention. Pop spoke the latter part slowly and meaningly. They thought that he intended them to see his great confidence.

One said: "Pop, if you throw us in this thing, we'll come here and drink for two weeks without paying. We'll back you, and work a josh on Freddie! But oh—if you throw us!"

To this menace Pop cried: "Boys, I'll make the run of my life! On my oath!"

The salad having vanished, the Kids arose. "All right, now," they warned him. "If you play us for duffers, we'll get square. Don't you forget it!"

"Boys, I'll give you a race for your money. Bank on that. I may lose—

understand, I may lose—no man can help meeting a better man, but I think I can skin 'im, and I'll give you a run for your money, you bet."

"All right, then. But look here," they told him. "You keep your face closed. Nobody but us gets in on this. Understand?"

"Not a soul," Pop declared.

They left him, gesturing a last warning from the wicker doors.

In the street they saw Benson, his cane gripped in the middle, strolling among the white-clothed, jabbering natives on the shady side. They semaphored to him eagerly, their faces ashine with a plot. He came across cautiously, like a man who ventures into dangerous company.

"We're going to get up a race—Pop and Fred. Pop swears he can skin 'im. This is a tip; keep it dark, now. Say, won't Freddie be hot?"

Benson looked as if he had been compelled to endure these exhibitions of insanity for a century. "Oh, you fellows are off. Pop can't beat Freddie. He's an old bat. Why, it's impossible. Pop can't beat Freddie."

"Can't he? Want to bet he can't?" said the Kids. "There, now; let's see— you're talking so large."

"Well, you—"

"Oh, bet! Bet, or else close your trap. That's the way!"

"How do you know you can pull off the race? Seen Freddie?"

"No; but—"

"Well, see him, then. Can't bet now, with no race arranged. I'll bet with you all right, all right. I'll give you fellows a tip, though—you're a pair of asses. Pop can't run any faster than a brick school-house."

The Kids scowled at him, and defiantly said: "Can't he?"

They left him, and went to the "Casa Verde." Freddie, beautiful in his white jacket, was holding one of his innumerable conversations across the bar. He smiled when he saw them. "Where you boys been?" he demanded in a paternal tone. Almost all the proprietors of American cafés in the city used to adopt a paternal tone when they spoke to the Kids.

"Oh, been round," they replied.

"Have a drink," said the proprietor of the Casa Verde, forgetting his other social obligations.

During the course of this ceremony one of the Kids remarked: "Freddie, Pop says he can beat you running."

"Does he?" observed Freddie, without excitement. He was used to various snares of the Kids.

"That's what. He says he can leave you at the wire, and not see you again."

"Well, he lies," replied Freddie, placidly.

"And I'll bet you a bottle of wine that he can do it, too."

"Rats!" said Freddie.

"Oh, that's all right," pursued a Kid. "You can throw bluffs all you like; but he can lose you in a hundred-yard dash, you bet."

Freddie drank his whisky, and then settled his elbows on the bar. "Say, now, what do you boys keep coming in here with some pipe-story all the time for? You can't josh me. Do you think you can scare me about Pop? Why, I know I can beat 'im. He's an old man. He can't run with me; certainly not. Why, you fellows are just jollying me."

"Are we, though?" said the Kids.

"You daresn't bet the bottle of wine."

"Oh, of course I can bet you a bottle of wine," said Freddie, disdainfully. "Nobody cares about a bottle of wine, but—"

"Well, make it five, then," advised one of the Kids.

Freddie hunched his shoulders. "Why, certainly I will. Make it ten if you like, but—"

"We do," they said.

"Ten, is it? All right; that goes." A look of weariness came over Freddie's face. "But you boys are foolish. I tell you, Pop is an old man. How can you expect him to run? Of course I'm no great runner, but, then, I'm young and healthy, and—and a pretty smooth runner, too. Pop is old and fat, and, then, he does n't do a thing but tank all day. It's a cinch."

The Kids looked at him, and laughed rapturously. They waved their fingers at him. "Ah, there!" they cried. They meant that they had made a victim of him.

But Freddie continued to expostulate: "I tell you, he couldn't win—an old man like him. You're crazy! Of course I know that you don't care about ten bottles of wine, but then—to make such bets as that! You're twisted."

"Are we, though?" cried the Kids, in mockery. They had precipitated Freddie into a long and thoughtful treatise on every possible chance of the thing as he saw it. They disputed with him from time to time, and jeered at him. He labored on through his argument. Their childish faces were bright with glee.

In the midst of it Wilburson entered. Wilburson worked—not too much, though. He had hold of the Mexican end of a great importing-house of New York, and, as he was a junior partner, he worked—but not too much, though. "What's the howl?" he said.

The Kids giggled. "We've got Freddie rattled."

"Why," said Freddie, turning to him, "these two Indians are trying to tell me that Pop can beat me running."

"Like the devil?" said Wilburson, incredulously.

"Well, can't he?" demanded a Kid.

"Why, certainly not," said Wilburson, dismissing every possibility of it with a gesture. "That old bat? Certainly not! I'll bet fifty dollars that Freddie—"

"Take you," said a Kid.

"What?" said Wilburson. "That Freddie won't beat Pop?"

The Kid that had spoken now nodded his head.

"That Freddie won't beat Pop?" repeated Wilburson.

"Yes; is it a go?"

"Why, certainly," retorted Wilburson. "Fifty? All right."

"Bet you five bottles on the side," ventured the other Kid.

"Why, certainly," exploded Wilburson, wrathfully. "You fellows must take me for something easy. I'll take all those kind of bets that I can get. Cer-tain-ly."

They settled the details. The course was to be paced off on the asphalt of one of the adjacent side-streets; and then, at about eleven o'clock in the evening, the match would be run. Usually in Mexico the streets of a city grow lonely and dark but a little time after nine o'clock. There are occasional lurking figures, perhaps, but no crowds, lights, noise. The course would doubtless be undisturbed. As for the policemen in the vicinity, they—well, they were conditionally amiable.

The Kids went to see Pop. They told him of the arrangements; and then in deep tones they said: "Oh, Pop, if you throw us!"

Pop appeared to be a trifle shaken by the weight of responsibility thrust upon him, but he spoke out bravely: "Boys, I'll pinch that race. Now you watch me. I'll pinch it!"

The Kids went then on some business of their own, for they were not seen again until evening. When they returned to the neighborhood of the Café Colorado, the usual evening stream of carriages was whirling along the *calle*. The wheels hummed on the asphalt, and the coachmen towered in their great sombreros. On the sidewalk a gazing crowd sauntered, the better classes self-satisfied and proud in their derby hats and cutaway coats, the lower classes muffling their dark faces in their blankets, slipping along in leather sandals. An electric light sputtered and fumed over the throng. The afternoon shower had left the pave wet and glittering; the air was still laden with the odor of rain on flowers, grass, leaves.

In the Café Colorado a cosmopolitan crowd ate, drank, played billiards, gossiped, or read in the glaring yellow light. When the Kids entered, a large circle of men that had been gesticulating near the bar greeted them with a roar:

"Here they are now!"

"Oh, you pair of peaches!"

"Say, got any more money to bet with?"

The Kids smiled complacently. Old Colonel Hammigan, grinning, pushed his way to them. "Say, boys, we'll all have a drink on you now, because you won't have any money after eleven o'clock. You'll be going down the back stairs in your stocking-feet."

Although the Kids remained unnaturally serene and quiet, argument in the Café Colorado became tumultuous. Here and there a man who did not intend to bet ventured meekly that perchance Pop might win; and the others swarmed upon him in a whirlwind of angry denial and ridicule.

Pop, enthroned behind the bar, looked over at this storm with a shadow of anxiety upon his face; this wide-spread flouting affected him; but the Kids looked blissfully satisfied with the tumult they had stirred.

Blanco, honest man, ever worrying for his friends, came to them. "Say, you fellows, you aren't betting too much? This thing looks kind of shaky, don't it?"

The faces of the Kids grew sober, and after consideration one said: "No, I guess we've got a good thing, Blanco. Pop is going to surprise them, I think."

"Well, don't—"

"All right, old boy. We'll watch out."

From time to time the Kids had much business with certain orange, red, blue, purple, and green bills. They were making little memoranda on the backs of visiting-cards. Pop watched them closely, the shadow still upon his face. Once he called to them; and when they came, he leaned over the bar, and said intensely: "Say, boys, remember, now—I might lose this race. Nobody can ever say for sure, and if I do—why—"

"Oh, that's all right, Pop," said the Kids, reassuringly. "Don't mind it. Do your durndest, and let it go at that."

When they had left him, however, they went to a corner to consult. "Say, this is getting interesting. Are you in deep?" asked one, anxiously, of his friend.

"Yes; pretty deep," said the other, stolidly. "Are you?"

"Deep as the devil," replied the other, in the same tone.

They looked at each other stonily, and went back to the crowd. Benson had just entered the café. He approached them with a gloating smile of victory. "Well, where's all that money you were going to bet?"

"Right here," said the Kids, thrusting into their vest pockets.

At eleven o'clock a curious thing was learned. When Pop and Freddie, the Kids, and all, came to the little side-street, it was thick with people. It seems that the news of this great race had spread like the wind among the Americans, and they had come to witness the event. In the darkness the crowd moved, gesticulating and mumbling in argument.

The principals, the Kids, and those with them surveyed this scene with some dismay. "Say, here's a go." Even then a policeman might be seen approaching, the light from his little lantern flickering on his white cap, gloves, brass buttons, and on the butt of the old-fashioned Colt's revolver which hung at his belt. He addressed Freddie in swift Mexican. Freddie listened, nodding from time to time. Finally Freddie turned to the others to translate: "He says he'll get into trouble if he allows this race when all this crowd is here."

There was a murmur of discontent. The policeman looked at them with an expression of anxiety on his broad brown face.

"Oh, come on. We'll go hold it on some other fellow's beat," said one of the Kids.

The group moved slowly away, debating.

Suddenly the other Kid cried: "I know! The Paseo!"

"By jiminy!" said Freddie, "just the thing. We'll get a cab, and go out to the Paseo. S-s-sh! Keep it quiet. We don't want all this mob."

Later they tumbled in a cab—Pop, Freddie, the Kids, old Colonel Hammigan, and Benson. They whispered to the men who had wagered: "The Paseo." The cab whirled away up the black street. There were occasional grunts and groans—cries of: "Oh, get off me feet!" and of: "Quit! You're killing me!" Six people do not have fun in one cab. The principals spoke to each other with the respect and friendliness which comes to good men at such times.

Once a Kid put his head out of the window and looked backward. He pulled it in again, and cried: "Great Scott! Look at that, would you!"

The others struggled to do as they were bid, and afterward shouted: "Holy smoke!" "Well, I'll be blowed!" "Thunder and turf!"

Galloping after them came innumerable other cabs, their lights twinkling, streaming in a great procession through the night. "The street is full of them," ejaculated the old colonel.

The Paseo de la Reforma is the famous drive of the City of Mexico, leading to the castle of Chapultepec, which last ought to be well known in the United States.

It is a broad, fine avenue of macadam, with a much greater quality of dignity than anything of the kind we possess in our own land. It seems of the Old World, where to the beauty of the thing itself is added the solemnity of tradition and history, the knowledge that feet in buskins trod the same stones, that cavalcades of steel thundered there before the coming of carriages.

When the Americans tumbled out of their cabs, the giant bronzes of Aztec and Spaniard loomed dimly above them like towers. The four rows of poplar-trees rustled weirdly off there in the darkness. Pop took out his watch, and struck a match. "Well, hurry up this thing. It's almost midnight."

The other cabs came swarming, the drivers lashing their horses; for these Americans, who did all manner of strange things, nevertheless always paid well for it. There was a mighty hubbub then in the darkness. Five or six men began to pace off the distance and quarrel. Others knotted their handkerchiefs together to make a tape. Men were swearing over bets, fussing and fuming about the odds. Benson came to the Kids, swaggering. "You're a pair of asses." The cabs waited in a solid block down the avenue. Above the crowd, the tall statues hid their visages in the night.

At last a voice floated through the darkness: "Are you ready, there?" Everybody yelled excitedly. The men at the tape pulled it out straight. "Hold it higher, Jim, you fool!" A silence fell then upon the throng. Men bended down, trying to pierce the darkness with their eyes. From out at the starting-point came muffled voices. The crowd swayed and jostled.

The racers did not come. The crowd began to fret, its nerves burning. "Oh, hurry up!" shrilled some one.

The voice called again: "Ready, there?"

Everybody replied: "Yes; all ready! Hurry up!"

There was more muffled discussion at the starting-point. In the crowd a man began to make a proposition: "I'll bet twenty—" But the throng interrupted with a howl: "Here they come!" The thickly packed body of men swung as if the ground had moved. The men at the tape shouldered madly at their fellows, bawling: "Keep back! Keep back!"

From the profound gloom came the noise of feet pattering furiously. Vague forms flashed into view for an instant. A hoarse roar broke from the crowd. Men bended and swayed and fought. The Kids, back near the tape, exchanged another stolid look. A white form shone forth. It grew like a specter. Always could be heard the wild patter. A barbaric scream broke from the crowd: "By Gawd, it's Pop! Pop! Pop's ahead!"

The old man spun toward the tape like a madman, his chin thrown back, his gray hair flying. His legs moved like maniac machinery. And as he shot forward a howl as from forty cages of wild animals went toward the imperturbable chieftains in bronze. The crowd flung themselves forward. "Oh, you old Indian! You savage! You cuss, you! Durn my buttons, did you ever see such running?"

"Ain't he a peach? Well!"

"Say, this beats anything!"

"Where's the Kids? H-e-y, Kids!"

"Look at 'im, would you? Did you ever think?"

These cries flew in the air, blended in a vast shout of astonishment and laughter.

For an instant the whole great tragedy was in view. Freddie, desperate, his teeth shining, his face contorted, whirling along in deadly effort, was twenty feet behind the tall form of old Pop, who, dressed only in his—only in his underclothes—gained with each stride. One grand, insane moment, and then Pop had hurled himself against the tape—victor!

Freddie, falling into the arms of some men, struggled with his breath, and at last managed to stammer: "Say—can't—can't that old—old man run!"

Pop, puffing and heaving, could only gasp: "Where's my shoes? Who's got my shoes?"

Later Freddie scrambled, panting, through the crowd, and held out his hand. "Good man, Pop!" And then he looked up and down the tall, stout form. "Smoke! Who would think you could run like that?"

The Kids were surrounded by a crowd, laughing tempestuously.

"How did you know he could run?"

"Why didn't you give me a line on him?"

"Say,—great snakes!—you fellows had a nerve to bet on Pop."

"Why, I was cock-sure he couldn't win."

"Oh, you fellows must have seen him run before!"

"Who would ever think it!"

Benson came by, filling the midnight air with curses. They turned to jeer him. "What's the matter, Benson?"

"Somebody pinched my handkerchief. I tied it up in that string. Damn it!"

The Kids laughed blithely. "Why, hollo, Benson!" they said.

There was a great rush for cabs. Shouting, laughing, wondering, the crowd hustled into their conveyances, and the drivers flogged their horses toward the city again.

"Won't Freddie be crazy! Say, he'll be guyed about this for years."

"But who would ever think that old tank could run so?"

One cab had to wait while Pop and Freddie resumed various parts of their clothing.

As they drove home, Freddie said: "Well, Pop, you beat me!"

Pop said: "That's all right, old man."

The Kids, grinning, said: "How much did you lose, Benson?"

Benson said defiantly: "Oh, not so much. How much did you win?"

"Oh, not so much!"

Old Colonel Hammigan, squeezed down in a corner, had apparently been reviewing the event in his mind, for he suddenly remarked: "Well, I'm damned!"

They were late in reaching the Café Colorado; but when they did, the bottles were on the bar as thick as pickets on a fence.

DEATH AND THE CHILD

The peasants who were streaming down the mountain trail had, in their sharp terror, evidently lost their ability to count. The cattle and the huge round bundles seemed to suffice to the minds of the crowd if there were now two in each case where there had been three. This brown stream poured on with a constant wastage of goods and beasts. A goat fell behind to scout the dried grass, and its owner, howling, flogging his donkeys, passed far ahead. A colt, suddenly frightened, made a stumbling charge up the hillside. The expenditure was always profligate, and always unnamed, unnoted. It was as if fear was a river, and this horde had simply been caught in the torrent, man tumbling over beast, beast over man, as helpless in it as the logs that fall and shoulder grindingly through the gorges of a lumber country. It was a freshet that might sear the face of the tall, quiet mountain; it might draw a livid line across the land, this downpour of fear with a thousand homes adrift in the current— men, women, babes, animals. From it there arose a constant babble of tongues, shrill, broken, and sometimes choking, as from men drowning. Many made gestures, painting their agonies on the air with fingers that twirled swiftly.

The blue bay, with its pointed ships, and the white town lay below them, distant, flat, serene. There was upon this vista a peace that a bird knows when, high in air, it surveys the world, a great, calm thing rolling noiselessly toward the end of the mystery. Here on the height one felt the existence of the universe scornfully defining the pain in ten thousand minds. The sky was an arch of stolid sapphire. Even to the mountains, raising their mighty shapes from the valley, this headlong rush of the fugitives was too minute. The sea, the sky, and the hills combined in their grandeur to term this misery inconsequent. Then, too, it sometimes happened that a face seen as it passed on the flood reflected curiously the spirit of them all, and still more. One saw then a woman of the opinion of the vaults above the clouds. When a child cried, it cried always because of some adjacent misfortune—some discomfort of a pack-saddle or rudeness of an encircling arm. In the dismal melody of this flight there were often sounding chords of apathy. Into these preoccupied countenances one felt that needles could be thrust without purchasing a scream. The trail wound here and there, as the sheep had willed in the making of it.

Although this throng seemed to prove that the whole of humanity was fleeing in one direction,—with every tie severed that binds us to the soil,—a young man was walking rapidly up the mountain, hastening to a side of the path from time to time to avoid some particularly wide rush of people and cattle. He looked at everything in agitation and pity. Frequently he called admonitions to maniacal fugitives, and at other times he exchanged strange stares with the imperturbable ones. They seemed to him to wear merely the expressions of so many boulders rolling down the hill. He exhibited wonder and awe with his pitying glances.

Turning once toward the rear, he saw a man in the uniform of a lieutenant of infantry marching the same way. He waited then, subconsciously elate at a prospect of being able to make into words the emotion which heretofore had been expressed only in the flash of eyes and sensitive movements of his flexible mouth. He spoke to the officer in rapid French, waving his arms wildly, and often pointing with a dramatic finger. "Ah, this is too cruel, too cruel, too cruel! is it not? I did not think it would be as bad as this. I did not think—God's mercy!—I did not think at all. And yet, I am a Greek; or, at least, my father was a Greek. I did not come here to fight; I am really a correspondent; you see? I was to write for an Italian paper. I have been educated in Italy; I have spent nearly all my life in Italy—at the schools and universities. I knew nothing of war! I was a student—a student. I came here merely because my father was a Greek, and for his sake I thought of Greece. I loved Greece; but I did not dream—"

He paused, breathing heavily. His eyes glistened from that soft overflow which comes on occasion to the glance of a young woman. Eager, passionate, profoundly moved, his first words while facing the procession of fugitives had been an active definition of his own dimension, his personal relation to men, geography, life. Throughout he had preserved the fiery dignity of a tragedian.

The officer's manner at once deferred to this outburst. "Yes," he said, polite, but mournful; "these poor people—these poor people! I do not know what is to become of these poor people."

The young man declaimed again: "I had no dream—I had no dream that it would be like this! This is too cruel—too cruel! Now I want to be a soldier. Now I want to fight. Now I want to do battle for the land of my father." He made a sweeping gesture into the northwest.

The officer was also a young man, but he was bronzed and steady. Above his high military collar of crimson cloth with one silver star upon it appeared a profile stern, quiet, and confident, respecting fate, fearing only opinion. His clothes were covered with dust; the only bright spot was the flame of the crimson collar. At the violent cries of his companion he smiled as if to himself, meanwhile keeping his eyes fixed in a glance ahead.

From a land toward which their faces were bent came a continuous boom of artillery fire. It was sounding in regular measures, like the beating of a colossal clock—a clock that was counting the seconds in the lives of the stars, and men had time to die between the ticks. Solemn, oracular, inexorable, the great seconds tolled over the hills as if God fronted this dial rimmed by the horizon. The soldier and the correspondent found themselves silent. The latter in particular was sunk in a great mournfulness, as if he had resolved willy-nilly to swing to the bottom of the abyss where dwelt secrets of this kind, and had learned beforehand that all to be met there was cruelty and hopelessness. A strap of his bright new leather leggings came unfastened, and he bowed over it slowly, impressively, as one bending over the grave of a child.

Then, suddenly, the reverberations mingled until one could not separate one explosion from another, and into the hubbub came the drawling sound of a leisurely musketry fire. Instantly, for some reason of cadence, the noise was irritating, silly, infantile. This uproar was childish. It forced the nerves to object, to protest against this racket, which was as idle as the din of a lad with a drum.

The lieutenant lifted his finger and pointed. He spoke in vexed tones, as if he held the other man personally responsible for the noise. "Well, there!" he said. "If you wish for war, you now have an opportunity magnificent."

The correspondent raised himself upon his toes. He tapped his chest with gloomy pride. "Yes! There is war! There is the war I wish to enter. I fling myself in. I am a Greek—a Greek, you understand. I wish to fight for my country. You know the way. Lead me! I offer myself." Struck with a sudden thought, he brought a case from his pocket, and, extracting a card, handed it to the officer with a bow. "My name is Peza," he said simply.

A strange smile passed over the soldier's face. There was pity and pride— the vanity of experience—and contempt in it. "Very well," he said, returning the bow. "If my company is in the middle of the fight, I shall be glad for the honor of your companionship. If my company is not in the middle of the fight, I will make other arrangements for you."

Peza bowed once more, very stiffly, and correctly spoke his thanks. On the edge of what he took to be a great venture toward death, he discovered that he was annoyed at something in the lieutenant's tone. Things immediately assumed new and extraordinary proportions. The battle, the great carnival of woe, was sunk at once to an equation with a vexation by a stranger. He wanted to ask the lieutenant what was his meaning. He bowed again majestically. The lieutenant bowed. They flung a shadow of manners, of capering tinsel ceremony across a land that groaned, and it satisfied something within themselves completely.

In the meantime the river of fleeing villagers was changed to simply a last dropping of belated creatures, who fled past stammering and flinging their hands high. The two men had come to the top of the great hill. Before them was a green plain as level as an inland sea. It swept northward, and merged finally into a length of silvery mist. Upon the near part of this plain, and upon two gray, treeless mountains at the sides of it, were little black lines from which floated slanting sheets of smoke. It was not a battle, to the nerves; one could survey it with equanimity, as if it were a tea-table. But upon Peza's mind it struck a loud, clanging blow. It was war. Edified, aghast, triumphant, he paused suddenly, his lips apart. He remembered the pageants of carnage that had marched through the dreams of his childhood. Love he knew; that he had confronted alone, isolated, wondering, an individual, an atom taking the hand of a titanic principle. Like the faintest breeze on his forehead, he felt here the vibration from the hearts of forty thousand men.

The lieutenant's nostrils were moving. "I must go at once," he said. "I must go at once."

"I will go with you, wherever you go," shouted Peza, loudly.

A primitive track wound down the side of the mountain, and in their rush they bounded from here to there, choosing risks which in the ordinary caution of man would surely have seemed of remarkable danger. The ardor of the correspondent surpassed the full energy of the soldier. Several times he turned and shouted: "Come on! Come on!"

At the foot of the path they came to a wide road which extended toward the battle in a yellow and straight line. Some men were trudging wearily to the rear. They were without rifles; their clumsy uniforms were dirty and all awry. They turned eyes dully aglow with fever upon the pair striding toward the battle. Others were bandaged with the triangular kerchief, upon which one could still see, through blood-stains, the little explanatory pictures illustrating the ways to bind various wounds—"Fig. I," "Fig. 2," "Fig. 7." Mingled with the pacing soldiers were peasants, indifferent, capable of smiling, gibbering about the battle, which was to them an ulterior drama. A man was leading a string of three donkeys to the rear, and at intervals he was accosted by wounded or fevered soldiers, from whom he defended his animals with apelike cries and mad gesticulations. After much chattering they usually subsided gloomily, and allowed him to go with his sleek little beasts unburdened. Finally he encountered a soldier who walked slowly, with the assistance of a staff. His head was bound with a wide bandage, grimy from blood and mud. He made application to the peasant, and immediately they were involved in a hideous Levantine discussion. The peasant whined and clamored, sometimes spitting like a kitten. The wounded soldier jawed on thunderously, his great hands stretched in clawlike graspings over the peasant's head. Once he raised his staff and made threat with it. Then suddenly the row was at an end. The other sick men saw their comrade mount the leading donkey, and at once begin to drum with his heels. None attempted to gain the backs of the remaining animals. They gazed after him dully. Finally they saw the caravan outlined for a moment against the sky. The soldier was still waving his arms passionately, having it out with the peasant.

Peza was alive with despair for these men, who looked at him with such doleful, quiet eyes. "Ah, my God!" he cried to the lieutenant, "these poor souls!—these poor souls!"

The officer faced about angrily. "If you are coming with me, there is no time for this." Peza obeyed instantly and with a sudden meekness. In the moment some portion of egotism left him, and he modestly wondered if the universe took cognizance of him to an important degree. This theater for slaughter, built by the inscrutable needs of the earth, was an enormous affair, and he reflected that the accidental destruction of an individual, Peza by name, would perhaps be nothing at all.

With the lieutenant, he was soon walking along behind a series of little crescent-shaped trenches, in which were soldiers tranquilly interested, gossiping with the hum of a tea-party. Although these men were not at this time under fire, he concluded that they were fabulously brave, else they would not be so comfortable, so at home, in their sticky brown trenches. They were certain to be heavily attacked before the day was old. The universities had not taught him to understand this attitude. At the passing of the young man in very nice tweed, with his new leggings, his new white helmet, his new field-glass-case, his new revolver-holster, the soiled soldiers turned with the same curiosity which a being in strange garb meets at the corners of streets. He might as well have been promenading a populous avenue. The soldiers volubly discussed his identity.

To Peza there was something awful in the absolute familiarity of each tone, expression, gesture. These men, menaced with battle, displayed the curiosity of the café. Then, on the verge of his great encounter toward death, he found himself extremely embarrassed, composing his face with difficulty, wondering what to do with his hands, like a gawk at a levee.

He felt ridiculous, and also he felt awed, aghast at these men who could turn their faces from the ominous front and debate his clothes, his business. There was an element which was newborn into his theory of war.

He was not averse to the brisk pace at which the lieutenant moved along the line. The roar of fighting was always in Peza's ears. It came from some short hills ahead and to the left. The road curved suddenly and entered a wood. The trees stretched their luxuriant and graceful branches over grassy slopes. A breeze made all this verdure gently rustle and speak in long silken sighs. Absorbed in listening to the hurricane racket from the front, he still remembered that these trees were growing, the grass-blades were extending, according to their process. He inhaled a deep breath of moisture and fragrance from the grove, a wet odor which expressed the opulent fecundity of unmoved nature, marching on with her million plans for multiple life, multiple death.

Farther on, they came to a place where the Turkish shells were landing. There was a long, hurtling sound in the air, and then one had sight of a shell. To Peza it was of the conical missiles which friendly officers had displayed to him on board war-ships. Curiously enough, too, this first shell smacked of the foundry—of men with smudged faces, of the blare of furnace fires. It brought machinery immediately into his mind. He thought that if he was killed there at that time, it would be as romantic to the old standards as death by a bit of falling iron in a factory.

* * *

A child was playing on a mountain, and disregarding a battle that was waging on the plain. Behind him was the little cobbled hut of his fled parents. It was now occupied by a pearl-colored cow, that stared out from the darkness, thoughtful and tender-eyed. The child ran to and fro, fumbling with sticks, and making great machinations with pebbles. By a striking exercise of artistic license, the sticks were ponies, cows, and dogs, and the pebbles were sheep. He was managing large agricultural and herding affairs. He was too intent on them to pay much heed to the fight four miles away, which at that distance resembled in sound the beating of surf upon rocks. However, there were occasions when some louder outbreak of that thunder stirred him from his serious occupation, and he turned then a questioning eye upon the battle, a small stick poised in his hand, interrupted in the act of sending his dog after his sheep. His tranquillity in regard to the death on the plain was as invincible as that of the mountain on which he stood.

It was evident that fear had swept the parents away from their home in a manner that could make them forget this child, the first-born. Nevertheless, the hut was cleaned bare. The cow had committed no impropriety in billeting herself at the domicile of her masters. This smoke-colored and odorous interior contained nothing as large as a hummingbird. Terror had operated on these runaway people in its sinister fashion—elevating details to enormous heights, causing a man to remember a button while he forgot a coat, overpowering every one with recollections of a broken coffee-cup, deluging them with fears for the safety of an old pipe, and causing them to forget their first-born. Meanwhile the child played soberly with his trinkets.

He was solitary. Engrossed in his own pursuits, it was seldom that he lifted his head to inquire of the world why it made so much noise. The stick in his hand was much larger to him than was an army-corps of the distance. It was too childish for the mind of the child. He was dealing with sticks.

The battle-lines writhed at times in the agony of a sea-creature on the sands. These tentacles flung and waved in a supreme excitement of pain, and the struggles of the great outlined body brought it near and nearer to the child. Once he looked at the plain, and saw some men running wildly across a field. He had seen people chasing obdurate beasts in such fashion, and it struck him immediately that it was a manly thing, which he would incorporate in his game. Consequently he raced furiously at his stone sheep, flourishing a cudgel, crying the shepherd calls. He paused frequently to get a cue of manner from the soldiers fighting on the plain. He reproduced, to a degree, any movements which he accounted rational to his theory of sheep-herding, the business of men, the traditional and exalted living of his father.

* * *

It was as if Peza was a corpse walking on the bottom of the sea, and finding there fields of grain, groves, weeds, the faces of men, voices. War, a strange employment of the race, presented to him a scene crowded with familiar objects which wore the livery of their commonness placidly, undauntedly. He was smitten with keen astonishment; a spread of green grass, lit with the flames of poppies, was too old for the company of this new ogre. If he had been devoting the full lens of his mind to this phase, he would have known that he was amazed that the trees, the flowers, the grass, all tender and peaceful nature, had not taken to heels at once upon the outbreak of battle. He venerated the immovable poppies.

The road seemed to lead into the apex of an angle formed by the two defensive lines of the Greeks. There was a struggle of wounded men, and of gunless and jaded men. These latter did not seem to be frightened. They remained very cool, walking with unhurried steps, and busy in gossip. Peza tried to define them. Perhaps during the fight they had reached the limit of their mental storage, their capacity for excitement, for tragedy, and had then simply come away. Peza remembered his visit to a certain place of pictures, where he had found himself amid heavenly skies and diabolic midnights,—the sunshine beating red upon desert sands, nude bodies flung to the shore in the green moon-glow, ghastly and starving men clawing at a wall in darkness, a girl at her bath, with screened rays falling upon her pearly shoulders, a dance, a funeral, a review, an execution—all the strength of argus-eyed art; and he had whirled and whirled amid this universe, with cries of woe and joy, sin and beauty, piercing his ears until he had been obliged to simply come away. He remembered that as he had emerged he had lit a cigarette with unction, and advanced promptly to a café. A great hollow quiet seemed to be upon the earth.

This was a different case, but in his thoughts he conceded the same causes to many of these gunless wanderers. They, too, may have dreamed at lightning speed, until the capacity for it was overwhelmed. As he watched them, he again saw himself walking toward the café, puffing upon his cigarette. As if to reinforce his theory, a soldier stopped him with an eager but polite inquiry for a match. He watched the man light his little roll of tobacco and paper and begin to smoke ravenously.

Peza no longer was torn with sorrow at the sight of wounded men. Evidently he found that pity had a numerical limit, and when this was passed the emotion became another thing. Now, as he viewed them, he merely felt himself very lucky, and beseeched the continuance of his superior fortune. At the passing of these slouched and stained figures he now heard a reiteration of warning. A part of himself was appealing through the medium of these grim shapes. It was plucking at his sleeve and pointing, telling him to beware of these soldiers only as he would have cared for the harms of broken dolls. His whole vision was focused upon his own chance.

The lieutenant suddenly halted. "Look," he said; "I find that my duty is in another direction; I must go another way. But if you wish to fight, you have only to go forward, and any officer of the fighting line will give you opportunity." He raised his cap ceremoniously. Peza raised his new white helmet. The stranger to battles uttered thanks to his chaperon, the one who had presented him. They bowed punctiliously, staring at each other with civil eyes.

The lieutenant moved quietly away through a field. In an instant it flashed upon Peza's mind that this desertion was perfidious. He had been subjected to a criminal discourtesy. The officer had fetched him into the middle of the thing, and then left him to wander helplessly toward death. At one time he was upon the point of shouting at the officer.

In the vale there was an effect as if one was then beneath the battle. It was going on above, somewhere. Alone, unguided, Peza felt like a man groping in a cellar. He reflected, too, that one should always see the beginning of a fight. It was too difficult to thus approach it when the affair was in full swing. The trees hid all the movements of troops from him, and he thought he might be walking out to the very spot which chance had provided for the reception of a fool. He asked eager questions of passing soldiers. Some paid no heed to him; others shook their heads mournfully. They knew nothing, save that war was hard work. If they talked at all, it was in testimony of having fought well, savagely. They did not know if the army was going to advance, hold its ground, or retreat. They were weary.

A long, pointed shell flashed through the air, and struck near the base of a tree with a fierce upheaval, compounded of earth and flames. Looking back, Peza could see the shattered tree quivering from head to foot. Its whole being underwent a convulsive tremor which was an exhibition of pain and, furthermore, deep amazement. As he advanced through the vale, the shells continued to hiss and hurtle in long, low flights, and the bullets purred in the air. The missiles were flying into the breast of an astounded nature. The landscape, bewildered, agonized, was suffering a rain of infamous shots, and Peza imagined a million eyes gazing at him with the gaze of startled antelopes.

There was a resolute crashing of musketry from the tall hill on the left, and from directly in front there was a mingled din of artillery- and musketry-firing. Peza felt that his pride was playing a great trick in forcing him forward in this manner under conditions of strangeness, isolation, and ignorance; but he recalled the manner of the lieutenant, the smile on the hilltop among the flying peasants. Peza blushed, and pulled the peak of his helmet down on his forehead. He strode on firmly. Nevertheless, he hated the lieutenant, and he resolved that on some future occasion he would take much trouble to arrange a stinging social revenge upon that grinning jackanapes. It did not occur to him, until later, that he was now going to battle mainly because at a previous time a certain man had smiled.

* * *

The road moved around the base of a little hill, and on this hill a battery of mountain guns was leisurely shelling something unseen. In the lee of the height, the mules, contented under their heavy saddles, were quietly browsing the long grass. Peza ascended the hill by a slanting path. He felt his heart beat swiftly. Once at the top of the hill, he would be obliged to look this phenomenon in the face. He hurried with a mysterious idea of preventing by this strategy the battle from making his appearance a signal for some tremendous renewal. This vague thought seemed logical at the time. Certainly this living thing had knowledge of his coming. He endowed it with the intelligence of a barbaric deity. And so he hurried. He wished to surprise war, this terrible emperor, when it was only growling on its throne. The ferocious and horrible sovereign was not to be allowed to make the arrival a pretext for some fit of smoky rage and blood. In this half-lull, Peza had distinctly the sense of stealing upon the battle unawares.

The soldiers watching the mules did not seem to be impressed by anything august. Two of them sat side by side and talked comfortably; another lay flat upon his back, staring dreamily at the sky; another cursed a mule for certain refractions. Despite their uniforms, their bandoleers and rifles, they were dwelling in the peace of hostlers. However, the long shells were whooping from time to time over the brow of the hill, and swirling in almost straight lines toward the vale of trees, flowers, and grass. Peza, hearing and seeing the shells, and seeing the pensive guardians of the mules, felt reassured. They were accepting the conditons of war as easily as an old sailor accepts the chair behind the counter of a tobacco-shop. Or it was merely that the farm-boy had gone to sea, and he had adjusted himself to the circumstances immediately, and with only the usual first misadventures in conduct. Peza was proud and ashamed that he was not of them—these stupid peasants, who, throughout the world, hold potentates on their thrones, make statesmen illustrious, provide generals with lasting victories, all with ignorance, indifference, or half-witted hatred, moving the world with the strength of their arms, and getting their heads knocked together, in the name of God, the king, or the stock exchange—immortal, dreaming, hopeless asses, who surrender their reason to the care of a shining puppet, and persuade some toy to carry their lives in his purse. Peza mentally abased himself before them, and wished to stir them with furious kicks.

As his eyes ranged above the rim of the plateau, he saw a group of artillery officers talking busily. They turned at once, and regarded his ascent. A moment later a row of infantry soldiers, in a trench beyond the little guns, all faced him. Peza bowed to the officers. He understood at the time that he had made a good and cool bow, and he wondered at it; for his breath was coming in gasps—he was stifling from sheer excitement. He felt like a tipsy man trying to conceal his muscular uncertainty from the people in the street. But the officers did not display any knowledge. They bowed. Behind them Peza saw the plain, glittering green, with three lines of black marked upon it heavily. The front of the first of these lines was frothy with smoke. To the left of this hill was a craggy mountain, from which came a continual dull rattle of musketry. Its summit was ringed with the white smoke. The black lines on the plain slowly moved. The shells that came from there passed overhead, with the sound of great birds frantically flapping their wings. Peza thought of the first sight of the sea during a storm. He seemed to feel against his face the wind that races over the tops of cold and tumultuous billows.

He heard a voice afar off: "Sir, what would you?" He turned, and saw the dapper captain of the battery standing beside him. Only a moment had elapsed.

"Pardon me, sir," said Peza, bowing again.

The officer was evidently reserving his bows. He scanned the new-comer attentively. "Are you a correspondent?" he asked.

Peza produced a card. "Yes; I came as a correspondent," he replied. "But now, sir, I have other thoughts. I wish to help. You see? I wish to help."

"What do you mean?" said the captain. "Are you a Greek? Do you wish to fight?"

"Yes; I am a Greek; I wish to fight." Peza's voice surprised him by coming from his lips in even and deliberate tones. He thought with gratification that he was behaving rather well. Another shell, traveling from some unknown point on the plain, whirled close and furiously in the air, pursuing an apparently horizontal course, as if it were never going to touch the earth. The dark shape swished across the sky.

"Ah," cried the captain, now smiling, "I am not sure that we will be able to accommodate you with a fierce affair here just at this time, but—" He walked gaily to and fro behind the guns with Peza, pointing out to him the lines of the Greeks, and describing his opinion of the general plan of defense. He wore the air of an amiable host. Other officers questioned Peza in regard to the politics of the war. The king, the ministry, Germany, England, Russia—all these huge words were continually upon their tongues. "And the people in Athens, were they—?" Amid this vivacious babble, Peza, seated upon an ammunition-box, kept his glance high, watching the appearance of shell after shell. These officers were like men who had been lost for days in the forest. They were thirsty for any scrap of news. Nevertheless, one of them would occasionally dispute their informant courteously. What would Servia have to say to that? No, no; France and Russia could never allow it. Peza was elated. The shells killed no one. War was not so bad! He was simply having coffee in the smoking-room of some embassy where reverberate the names of nations.

A rumor had passed along the motley line of privates in the trench. The new arrival with the clean white helmet was a famous English cavalry officer, come to assist the army with his counsel. They stared at the figure of him, surrounded by officers. Peza, gaining sense of the glances and whispers, felt that his coming was an event.

Later, he resolved that he could, with temerity, do something finer. He contemplated the mountain where the Greek infantry was engaged, and announced leisurely to the captain of the battery that he thought presently of going in that direction and getting into the fight. He reaffirmed the sentiments of a patriot. The captain seemed surprised. "Oh, there will be fighting here at this knoll in a few minutes," he said orientally. "That will be sufficient. You had better stay with us. Besides, I have been ordered to resume fire." The officers all tried to dissuade him from departing. It was really not worth the trouble. The battery would begin again directly; then it would be amusing for him.

Peza felt that he was wandering, with his protestations of high patriotism, through a desert of sensible men. These officers gave no heed to his exalted declarations. They seemed too jaded. They were fighting the men who were fighting them. Palaver of the particular kind had subsided before their intense preoccupation in war as a craft. Moreover, many men had talked in that manner, and only talked.

Peza believed at first that they were treating him delicately; they were considerate of his inexperience. War had turned out to be such a gentle business that Peza concluded that he could scorn this idea. He bade them an heroic farewell, despite their objections.

However, when he reflected upon their ways afterward, he saw dimly that they were actuated principally by some universal childish desire for a spectator of their fine things. They were going into action, and they wished to be seen at war, precise and fearless.

* * *

Climbing slowly to the high infantry position, Peza was amazed to meet a soldier whose jaw had been half shot away, and who was being helped down the steep track by two tearful comrades. The man's breast was drenched with blood, and from a cloth which he held to the wound drops were splashing wildly upon the stones of the path. He gazed at Peza for a moment. It was a mystic gaze, which Peza withstood with difficulty. He was exchanging looks with a specter; all aspect of the man was somehow gone from this victim. As Peza went on, one of the unwounded soldiers loudly shouted to him to return and assist in this tragic march. But even Peza's fingers revolted. He was afraid of the specter; he would not have dared to touch it. He was surely craven in the movement of refusal he made to them. He scrambled hastily on up the path. He was running away!

At the top of the hill he came immediately upon a part of the line that was in action. Another battery of mountain guns was here, firing at the streaks of black on the plain. There were trenches filled with men lining parts of the crest, and near the base were other trenches, all crashing away mightily. The plain stretched as far as the eye could see, and from where silver mist ended this emerald ocean of grass, a great ridge of snow-topped mountains poised against a fleckless blue sky. Two knolls, green and yellow with grain, sat on the prairie, confronting the dark hills of the Greek position. Between them were the lines of the enemy. A row of trees, a village, a stretch of road, showed faintly on this great canvas, this tremendous picture; but men, the Turkish battalions, were emphasized startlingly upon it. The ranks of troops between the knolls and the Greek position were as black as ink. The first line, of course, was muffled in smoke; but at the rear of it, battalions crawled up, and to and fro, plainer than beetles on a plate. Peza had never understood that masses of men were so declarative, so unmistakable, as if nature makes every arrangement to give information of the coming and the presence of destruction, the end, oblivion. The firing was full, complete, a roar of cataracts, and this pealing of concerted volleys was adjusted to the grandeur of the far-off range of snowy mountains. Peza, breathless, pale, felt that he had been set upon a pillar, and was surveying mankind, the world. In the meantime dust had got in his eye. He took his handkerchief and mechanically administered to it.

An officer with a double stripe of purple on his trousers paced in the rear of the battery of howitzers. He waved a little cane. Sometimes he paused in his promenade to study the field through his glasses. "A fine scene, sir," he cried airily, upon the approach of Peza. It was like a blow in the chest to the wide-eyed volunteer. It revealed to him a point of view.

"Yes, sir; it is a fine scene," he answered.

They spoke in French. "I am happy to be able to entertain monsieur with a little fine practice," continued the officer. "I am firing upon that mass of troops you see there, a little to the right. They are probably forming for another attack."

Peza smiled. Here again appeared manners—manners erect by the side of death.

The right-flank gun of the battery thundered; there was a belch of fire and smoke; the shell, flung swiftly and afar, was known only to the ear in which rang a broadening, hooting wake of sound. The howitzer had thrown itself backward convulsively, and lay with its wheels moving in the air as a squad of men rushed toward it; and later, it seemed as if each little gun had made the supreme effort of its being in each particular shot. They roared with voices far too loud, and the thunderous effort caused a gun to bound as in a dying convulsion. And then occasionally one was hurled with wheels in air. These shuddering howitzers presented an appearance of so many cowards, always longing to bolt to the rear, but being implacably held up to their business by this throng of soldiers, who ran in squads to drag them up again to their obligation. The guns were herded and cajoled and bullied interminably. One by one, in relentless program, they were dragged forward to contribute a profound vibration of steel and wood, a flash and a roar, to the important happiness of men.

The adjacent infantry celebrated a good shot with smiles and an outburst of gleeful talk.

"Look, sir," cried an officer once to Peza. Thin smoke was drifting lazily before Peza, and, dodging impatiently, he brought his eyes to bear upon that part of the plain indicated by the officer's finger. The enemy's infantry was advancing to attack. From the black lines had come forth an inky mass, which was shaped much like a human tongue. It advanced slowly, casually, without apparent spirit, but with an insolent confidence that was like a proclamation of the inevitable.

The impetuous part was all played by the defensive side.

Officers called; men plucked each other by the sleeve. There were shouts—motion. All eyes were turned upon the inky mass, which was flowing toward the base of the hills, heavily, languorously, as oily and thick as one of the streams that ooze through a swamp.

Peza was chattering a question at every one. In the way, pushed aside, or in the way again, he continued to repeat it: "Can they take the position? Can they take the position? Can they take the position?" He was apparently addressing an assemblage of deaf men. Every eye was busy watching every hand. The soldiers did not even seem to see the interesting stranger in the white helmet, who was crying out so feverishly.

Finally, however, the hurried captain of the battery espied him, and heeded his question. "No, sir! No, sir! It is impossible!" he shouted angrily. His manner seemed to denote that if he had had sufficient time he would have completely insulted Peza. The latter swallowed the crumb of news without regard to the coating of scorn, and, waving his hand in adieu, he began to run along the crest of the hill toward the part of the Greek line against which the attack was directed.

* * *

Peza, as he ran along the crest of the mountain, believed that his action was receiving the wrathful attention of the hosts of the foe. To him, then, it was incredible foolhardiness thus to call to himself the stares of thousands of hateful eyes. He was like a lad induced by playmates to commit some indiscretion in a cathedral. He was abashed; perhaps he even blushed as he ran. It seemed to him that the whole solemn ceremony of war had paused during this commission. So he scrambled wildly over the rocks in his haste to end the embarrassing ordeal. When he came among the crowning rifle-pits, filled with eager soldiers, he wanted to yell with joy. None noticed him, save a young officer of infantry, who said: "Sir, what do you want?" It was obvious that people had devoted some attention to their own affairs.

Peza asserted, in Greek, that he wished above everything to battle for the fatherland. The officer nodded. With a smile he pointed to some dead men, covered with blankets, from which were thrust upturned dusty shoes.

"Yes; I know, I know," cried Peza. He thought the officer was poetically alluding to the danger.

"No," said the officer, at once. "I mean cartridges—a bandoleer. Take a bandoleer from one of them."

Peza went cautiously toward a body. He moved a hand toward a corner of a blanket. There he hesitated, stuck, as if his arm had turned to plaster. Hearing a rustle behind him, he spun quickly. Three soldiers of the close rank in the trench were regarding him. The officer came again, and tapped him on the shoulder. "Have you any tobacco?" Peza looked at him in bewilderment. His hand was still extended toward the blanket which covered the dead soldier.

"Yes," he said; "I have some tobacco." He gave the officer his pouch. As if in compensation, the other directed a soldier to strip the bandoleer from the corpse. Peza, having crossed the long cartridge-belt on his breast, felt that the dead man had flung his two arms around him.

A soldier, with a polite nod and smile, gave Peza a rifle—a relic of another dead man. Thus he felt, besides the clutch of a corpse about his neck, that the rifle was as unhumanly horrible as a snake that lives in a tomb. He heard at his ear something that was in effect like the voices of those two dead men, their low voices speaking to him of bloody death, mutilation. The bandoleer gripped him tighter; he wished to raise his hands to his throat, like a man who is choking. The rifle was clumsy; upon his palms he felt the movement of the sluggish currents of a serpent's life; it was crawling and frightful.

All about him were these peasants, with their interested countenances, gibbering of the fight. From time to time a soldier cried out in semi-humorous lamentations descriptive of his thirst. One bearded man sat munching a great bit of hard bread. Fat, greasy, squat, he was like an idol made of tallow. Peza felt dimly that there was a distinction between this man and a young student who could write sonnets and play the piano quite well. This old blockhead was coolly gnawing at the bread, while he—Peza—was being throttled by a dead man's arms.

He looked behind him, and saw that a head, by some chance, had been uncovered from its blanket. Two liquid-like eyes were staring into his face. The head was turned a little sideways, as if to get better opportunity for the scrutiny. Peza could feel himself blanch. He was being drawn and drawn by these dead men, slowly, firmly down, as to some mystic chamber under the earth, where they could walk, dreadful figures, swollen and blood-marked. He was bidden; they had commanded him; he was going, going, going.

When the man in the new white helmet bolted for the rear, many of the soldiers in the trench thought that he had been struck. But those who had been nearest to him knew better. Otherwise they would have heard the silken, sliding, tender noise of the bullet, and the thud of its impact. They bawled after him curses, and also outbursts of self-congratulation and vanity. Despite the prominence of the cowardly part, they were enabled to see in this exhibition a fine comment upon their own fortitude. The other soldiers thought that Peza had been wounded somewhere in the neck, because, as he ran, he was tearing madly at the bandoleer—the dead man's arms. The soldier with the bread paused in his eating, and cynically remarked upon the speed of the runaway.

An officer's voice was suddenly heard calling out the calculation of the distance to the enemy, the readjustment of the sights. There was a stirring rattle along the line. The men turned their eyes to the front. Other trenches, beneath them, to the right, were already heavily in action. The smoke was lifting toward the blue sky. The soldier with the bread placed it carefully on a bit of paper beside him as he turned to kneel in the trench.

* * *

In the late afternoon the child ceased his play on the mountain with his flocks and his dogs. Part of the battle had whirled very near to the base of his hill, and the noise was great. Sometimes he could see fantastic, smoky shapes, which resembled the curious figures in foam which one sees on the slant of a rough sea. The plain, indeed, was etched in white circles and whirligigs, like the slope of a colossal wave. The child took seat on a stone, and contemplated the fight. He was beginning to be astonished. He had never before seen cattle herded with such uproar. Lines of flame flashed out here and there. It was mystery.

Finally, without any preliminary indication, he began to weep. If the men struggling on the plain had had time, and greater vision, they could have seen this strange, tiny figure seated on a boulder, surveying them while the tears streamed. It was as simple as some powerful symbol.

As the magic clear light of day amid the mountains dimmed the distances, and the plain shone as a pallid blue cloth marked by the red threads of the firing, the child arose and moved off to the unwelcoming door of his home. He called softly for his mother, and complained of his hunger in the familiar formulæ. The pearl-colored cow, grinding her jaws thoughtfully, stared at him with her large eyes. The peaceful gloom of evening was slowly draping the hills.

The child heard a rattle of loose stones on the hillside, and, facing the sound, saw, a moment later, a man drag himself up to the crest of the hill and fall panting. Forgetting his mother and his hunger, filled with calm interest, the child walked forward, and stood over the heaving form. His eyes, too, were now large and inscrutably wise and sad, like those of the animal in the house.

After a silence, he spoke inquiringly: "Are you a man?"

Peza rolled over quickly, and gazed up into the fearless and cherubic countenance. He did not attempt to reply. He breathed as if life was about to leave his body. He was covered with dust; his face had been cut in some way, and his cheek was ribboned with blood. All the spick of his former appearance had vanished in a general dishevelment, in which he resembled a creature that had been flung to and fro, up and down, by cliffs and prairies during an earthquake. He rolled his eye glassily at the child.

They remained thus until the child repeated his words: "Are you a man?"

Peza gasped in the manner of a fish. Palsied, windless, and abject, he confronted the primitive courage, the sovereign child, the brother of the mountains, the sky, and the sea, and he knew that the definition of his misery could be written on a wee grass-blade.

THE FIVE WHITE MICE

reddie was mixing a cocktail. His hand with the long spoon was whirling swiftly, and the ice in the glass hummed and rattled like a cheap watch. Over by the window, a gambler, a millionaire, a railway conductor, and the agent of a vast American syndicate were playing seven-up. Freddie surveyed them with the ironical glance of a man who is mixing a cocktail.

From time to time a swarthy Mexican waiter came with his tray from the rooms at the rear, and called his orders across the bar. The sounds of the indolent stir of the city awakening from its siesta floated over the screens which barred the sun and the inquisitive eye. From the far-away kitchen could be heard the roar of the old French chef, driving, herding, and abusing his Mexican helpers.

A string of men came suddenly in from the street. They stormed up to the bar. There were impatient shouts. "Come now, Freddie, don't stand there like a portrait of yourself. Wiggle!" Drinks of many kinds and colors—amber, green, mahogany, strong and mild—began to swarm upon the bar, with all the attendants of lemon, sugar, mint, and ice. Freddie, with Mexican support, worked like a sailor in the provision of them, sometimes talking with that scorn for drink and admiration for those who drink which is the attribute of a good barkeeper.

At last a man was afflicted with a stroke of dice-shaking. A herculean discussion was waging, and he was deeply engaged in it, but at the same time he lazily flirted the dice. Occasionally he made great combinations. "Look at that, would you?" he cried proudly. The others paid little heed. Then violently the craving took them. It went along the line like an epidemic, and involved them all. In a moment they had arranged a carnival of dice-shaking, with money penalties and liquid prizes. They clamorously made it a point of honor with Freddie that he too should play, and take his chance of sometimes providing this large group with free refreshment. With bent heads, like foot-ball players, they surged over the tinkling dice, jostling, cheering, and bitterly arguing. One of the quiet company playing seven-up at the corner table said profanely that the row reminded him of a bowling contest at a picnic.

After the regular shower, many carriages rolled over the smooth *calle*, and sent a musical thunder through the Casa Verde. The shop-windows became aglow with light, and the walks were crowded with youths, callow and ogling, dressed vainly according to supposititious fashions. The policemen had muffled themselves in their gnome-like cloaks and placed their lanterns as obstacles for the carriages in the middle of the street. The City of Mexico gave forth the deep, mellow organ-tones of its evening resurrection.

But still the group at the bar of the Casa Verde were shaking dice. They had passed beyond shaking for drinks for the crowd, for Mexican dollars, for dinner, for the wine at dinner. They had even gone to the trouble of separating the cigars and cigarettes from the dinner's bill, and causing a distinct man to be responsible for them. Finally the were aghast. Nothing remained within sight of their minds which even remotely suggested further gambling. There was a pause for deep consideration.

"Well!"

"Well!"

A man called out in the exuberance of creation: "I know! Let's stake for a box to-night at the circus! A box at the circus!" The group was profoundly edified. "That's it! That's it! Come on, now! Box at the circus!" A dominating voice cried: "Three dashes—high man out!" An American, tall, and with a face of copper red from the rays that flash among the Sierra Madres and burn on the cactus deserts, took the little leathern cup, and spun the dice out upon the polished wood. A fascinated assemblage hung upon the bar-rail. Three kings turned their pink faces upward. The tall man flourished the cup, burlesquing, and flung the two other dice. From them he ultimately extracted one more pink king. "There," he said. "Now, let's see! Four kings!" He began to swagger in a sort of provisional way.

The next man took the cup, and blew softly on the top of it. Poising it in his hand, he then surveyed the company with a stony eye, and paused. They knew perfectly well that he was applying the magic of deliberation and ostentatious indifference, but they could not wait in tranquillity during the performance of all these rites. They began to call out impatiently: "Come, now! Hurry up!" At last the man, with a gesture that was singularly impressive, threw the dice. The others set up a howl of joy. "Not a pair!" There was another solemn pause. The men moved restlessly. "Come, now! Go ahead!" In the end, the man, induced and abused, achieved something that was nothing in the presence of four kings. The tall man climbed on the foot-rail, and leaned hazardously forward. "Four kings! My four kings are good to go out," he bellowed into the middle of the mob; and, although in a moment he did pass into the radiant region of exemption, he continued to bawl advice and scorn.

The mirrors and oiled woods of the Casa Verde were now dancing with blue flashes from a great buzzing electric lamp. A host of quiet members of the Anglo-Saxon colony had come in for their pre-dinner cocktails. An amiable person was exhibiting to some tourists this popular American saloon. It was a very sober and respectable time of day. Freddie reproved courageously the dice-shaking brawlers, and, in return, he received the choicest advice in a tumult of seven combined vocabularies. He laughed. He had been compelled to retire from the game, but he was keeping an interested, if furtive, eye upon it.

Down at the end of the line there was a youth at whom everybody railed for his flaming ill luck. At each disaster, Freddie swore from behind the bar, in a sort of affectionate contempt. "Why, this Kid has had no luck for two days. Did you ever see such throwin'?"

The contest narrowed eventually to the New York Kid and an individual who swung about placidly on legs that moved in nefarious circles. He had a grin that resembled a bit of carving. He was obliged to lean down and blink rapidly to ascertain the facts of his venture, but fate presented him with five queens. His smile did not change, but he puffed gently, like a man who has been running.

The others having emerged scatheless from this part of the conflict, waxed hilarious with the Kid. They smote him on either shoulder. "We've got you stuck for it, Kid! You can't beat that game! Five queens!"

Up to this time the Kid had displayed only the temper of the gambler; but the cheerful hoots of the players, supplemented now by a ring of guying non-combatants, caused him to feel profoundly that it would be fine to beat the five queens. He addressed a gambler's slogan to the interior of the cup:

> Oh, five white mice of chance,
> Shirts of wool and corduroy pants,
> Gold and wine, women and sin,
> All for you if you let me come in—
> Into the house of chance.

Flashing the dice sardonically out upon the bar, he displayed three aces. From two dice in the next throw he achieved one more ace. For his last throw he rattled the single dice for a long time. He already had four aces; if he accomplished another one, the five queens were vanquished, and the box at the circus came from the drunken man's pocket. All of the Kid's movements were slow and elaborate. For his last throw he planted the cup bottom up on the bar, with the one dice hidden under it. Then he turned and faced the crowd with the air of a conjuror or a cheat. "Oh, maybe it's an ace," he said in boastful calm—"maybe it's an ace." Instantly he was presiding over a little drama in which every man was absorbed. The Kid leaned with his back against the bar-rail and with his elbows upon it. "Maybe it's an ace," he repeated.

A jeering voice in the background said: "Yes; maybe it is, Kid."

The Kid's eyes searched for a moment among the men. "I'll bet fifty dollars it is an ace," he said.

Another voice asked: "American money?"

"Yes," answered the Kid.

"Oh!" There was a general laugh at this discomfiture. However, no one came forward at the Kid's challenge, and presently he turned to the cup. "Now I'll show you." With the manner of a mayor unveiling a statue, he lifted the cup. There was revealed naught but a ten-spot. In the roar which arose could be heard each man ridiculing the cowardice of his neighbor, and above all the din rang the voice of Freddie berating every one.

"Why, there isn't one liver to every five men in the outfit. That was the greatest cold bluff I ever saw worked. He wouldn't know how to cheat with dice if he wanted to. Don't know the first thing about it. I could hardly keep from laughin' when I seen him drillin' you around. Why, I tell you I had that fifty dollars right in my pocket, if I wanted to be a chump. You're an easy lot!"

Nevertheless, the group who had won in the circus-box game did not relinquish their triumph. They burst like a storm about the head of the Kid,

swinging at him with their fists. "'Five white mice!'" they quoted, choking,—
"'five white mice!'"

"Oh, they are not so bad," said the Kid.

Afterward it often occurred that a man would suddenly jeer a finger at the
Kid, and derisively say: "'Five white mice!'"

On the route from the dinner to the circus, others of the party often asked
the Kid if he had really intended to make his appeal to mice. They suggested
other animals—rabbits, dogs, hedgehogs, snakes, opossums. To this banter the
Kid replied with a serious expression of his belief in the fidelity and wisdom of
the five white mice. He presented a most eloquent case, decorated with fine
language and insults, in which he proved that, if one was going to believe in
anything at all, one might as well choose the five white mice. His companions,
however, at once and unanimously pointed out to him that his recent exploit did
not place him in the light of a convincing advocate.

The Kid discerned two figures in the street. They were making imperious
signs at him. He waited for them to approach, for he recognized one as the other
Kid—the 'Frisco Kid: there were two Kids. With the 'Frisco Kid was Benson.
They arrived almost breathless. "Where you been?" cried the 'Frisco Kid. It was
an arrangement that, upon meeting, the one that could first ask this question
was entitled to use a tone of limitless injury. "What you been doing? Where you
going? Come on with us! Benson and I have got a little scheme."

The New York Kid pulled his arm from the grapple of the other. "I can't.
I've got to take these sutlers to the circus. They stuck me for it, shaking dice at
Freddie's. I can't, I tell you."

The two did not at first attend to his remarks. "Come on; we've got a little
scheme."

"I can't. They've stuck me. I've got to take 'm to the circus."

At this time it did not suit the men with the scheme to recognize these
objections as important. "Oh, take 'm some other time." "Well, can't you take
'm some other time?" "Let 'm go." "Damn the circus." "Get cold feet!" "What
did you get stuck for?" "Get cold feet!"

But despite their fighting, the New York Kid broke away from them. "I
can't, I tell you. They stuck me."

As he left them, they yelled with rage. "Well, meet us, now, do you hear?—
in the Casa Verde, as soon as the circus quits! Hear?" They threw maledictions
after him.

In the City of Mexico a man goes to the circus without descending in any
way to infant amusements, because the Circo Teatro Orrin is one of the best in
the world, and too easily surpasses anything of the kind in the United States,
where it is merely a matter of a number of rings, if possible, and a great
professional agreement to lie to the public. Moreover, the American clown who
in the Mexican arena prances and gabbles is the clown to whom writers refer as
the delight of their childhood and lament that he is dead. At this circus the Kid
was not debased by the sight of mournful prisoner elephants and caged animals,
forlorn and sickly. He sat in his box until late, and laughed, and swore, when
past laughing, at the comic, foolish, wise clown.

When he returned to the Casa Verde, there was no display of the 'Frisco Kid
and Benson. Freddie was leaning upon the bar, listening to four men terribly
discuss a question that was not plain. There was a card game in the corner, of

course. Sounds of revelry pealed from the rear rooms.

When the Kid asked Freddie if he had seen his friend and Benson, Freddie looked bored. "Oh, yes; they were in here just a minute ago; but I don't know where they went. They've got their skates on. Where've they been? Came in here rolling across the floor like two little gilt gods. They wobbled around for a time, and then 'Frisco wanted me to send six bottles of wine around to Benson's rooms; but I didn't have anybody to send this time of night, and so they got mad and went out. Where did they get their loads?"

In the first deep gloom of the street the Kid paused a moment, debating. But presently he heard quavering voices: "Oh, Kid! Kid! Come 'ere!" Peering, he recognized two vague figures against the opposite wall. He crossed the street, and they said: "Hellokid."

"Say, where did you get it?" he demanded sternly. "You Indians better go home. What did you want to get scragged for?" His face was luminous with virtue.

As they swung to and fro they made angry denials: "We ain' load'. We ain' load'. Big chump! Comonangetadrink."

The sober youth turned then to his friend. "Hadn't you better go home, Kid? Come on; it's late. You'd better break away."

The 'Frisco Kid wagged his head decisively. "Got take Benson home first. He'll be wallowing round in a minute. Don't mind me; I'm all right."

"Ce'r'ly he's all right," said Benson, arousing from deep thought. "He's all right. But better take 'm home, though. That's ri-right. He's load'. But he's all right. No need go home any more 'n you. But better take 'm home. He's load'." He looked at his companion with compassion. "Kid, you're load'."

The sober Kid spoke abruptly to his friend from San Francisco. "Kid, pull yourself together, now. Don't fool. We've got to brace this ass of a Benson all the way home. Get hold of his other arm."

The 'Frisco Kid immediately obeyed his comrade, without a word or a glower. He seized Benson, and came to attention like a soldier. Later, indeed, he meekly ventured: "Can't we take cab?" But when the New York Kid snapped out that there were no convenient cabs, he subsided to an impassive silence. He seemed to be reflecting upon his state without astonishment, dismay, or any particular emotion. He submitted himself woodenly to the direction of his friend.

Benson had protested when they had grasped his arms. "Washa doing?" he said in a new and guttural voice. "Washa doing? I ain' load'. Comonangetadrink. I—"

"Oh, come along, you idiot," said the New York Kid. The 'Frisco Kid merely presented the mien of a stoic to the appeal of Benson, and in silence dragged away at one of his arms. Benson's feet came from that particular spot on the pavement with the reluctance of roots, and also with the ultimate suddenness of roots. The three of them lurched out into the street in the abandon of tumbling chimneys. Benson was meanwhile noisily challenging the others to produce any reasons for his being taken home. His toes clashed into the curb when they reached the other side of the *calle*, and for a moment the Kids hauled him along, with the points of his shoes scraping musically on the pavement. He balked formidably as they were about to pass the Casa Verde. "No, no! Leshavanoth-drink! Anothdrink! Onemore!"

But the 'Frisco Kid obeyed the voice of his partner in a manner that was blind, but absolute, and they scummed Benson on past the door. Locked together, the three swung into a dark street. The sober Kid's flank was continually careering ahead of the other wing. He harshly admonished the 'Frisco child, and the latter promptly improved in the same manner of unthinking, complete obedience. Benson began to recite the tale of a love-affair—a tale that didn't even have a middle. Occasionally the New York Kid swore. They toppled on their way like three comedians playing at it on the stage.

At midnight a little Mexican street burrowing among the walls of the city is as dark as a whale's throat at deep sea. Upon this occasion heavy clouds hung over the capital, and the sky was a pall. The projecting balconies could make no shadows.

"Shay," said Benson, breaking away from his escort suddenly, "what want gome for? I ain' load'. You got reg'lar spool-fact'ry in your head—you N' York Kid, there. Thish oth' Kid, he's mos' proper—mos' proper shober. He's drunk, but—but he's shober."

"Ah, shut up, Benson," said the New York Kid. "Come along, now. We can't stay here all night." Benson refused to be corralled, but spread his legs and twirled like a dervish, meanwhile under the evident impression that he was conducting himself most handsomely. It was not long before he gained the opinion that he was laughing at the others. "Eight purple dogsh-dogs! Eight purple dogs! Thas what Kid'll see in the morn'. Look ou' for 'em. They—"

As Benson, describing the canine phenomena, swung wildly across the sidewalk, it chanced that three other pedestrians were passing in shadowy rank. Benson's shoulder jostled one of them.

A Mexican wheeled upon the instant. His hand flashed to his hip. There was a moment of silence, during which Benson's voice was not heard raised in apology. Then an indescribable comment, one burning word, came from between the Mexican's teeth.

Benson, rolling about in a semi-detached manner, stared vacantly at the Mexican, who thrust his lean yellow face forward, while his fingers played nervously at his hip. The New York Kid could not follow Spanish well, but he understood when the Mexican breathed softly: "Does the señor want fight?"

Benson simply gazed in gentle surprise. The woman next to him at dinner had said something inventive—his tailor had presented his bill—something had occurred which was mildly out of the ordinary, and his surcharged brain refused to cope with it. He displayed only the agitation of a smoker temporarily without a light.

The New York Kid had almost instantly grasped Benson's arm, and was about to jerk him away when the other Kid, who up to this time had been an automaton, suddenly projected himself forward, thrust the rubber Benson aside, and said: "Yes."

There was no sound nor light in the world. The wall at the left happened to be of the common prison-like construction—no door, no window, no opening at all. Humanity was inclosed and asleep. Into the mouth of the sober Kid came a wretched, bitter taste, as if it had filled with blood. He was transfixed, as if he was already seeing the lightning ripples on the knife-blade.

But the Mexican's hand did not move at that time. His face went still further forward, and he whispered: "So?" The sober Kid saw this face as if he and it were alone in space—a yellow mask, smiling in eager cruelty, in satisfaction, and, above all, it was lit with sinister decision. As for the features, they were reminiscent of an unplaced, a forgotton type, which really resembled with precision those of a man who had shaved him three times in Boston in-1888. But the expression burned his mind as sealing-wax burns the palm, and, fascinated, stupefied, he actually watched the progress of the man's thought toward the point where a knife would be wrenched from its sheath. The emotion, a sort of mechanical fury, a breeze made by electric fans, a rage made by vanity, smote the dark countenance in wave after wave.

Then the New York Kid took a sudden step forward. His hand was also at his hip. He was gripping there a revolver of robust size. He recalled that upon its black handle was stamped a hunting scene in which a sportsman in fine leggings and a peaked cap was taking aim at a stag less than one eighth of an inch away.

His pace forward caused instant movement of the Mexicans. One immediately took two steps to face him squarely. There was a general adjustment, pair and pair. The opponent of the New York Kid was a tall man and quite stout. His sombrero was drawn low over his eyes; his serape was flung on his left shoulder; his back was bent in the supposed manner of a Spanish grandee. This concave gentleman cut a fine and terrible figure. The lad, moved by the spirits of his modest and perpendicular ancestors, had time to feel his blood roar at sight of the pose.

He was aware that the third Mexican was over on the left, fronting Benson; and he was aware that Benson was leaning against the wall, sleepily and peacefully eyeing the convention. So it happened that these six men stood, side fronting side, five of them with their right hands at their hips, and with their bodies lifted nervously, while the central pair exchanged a crescendo of provocations. The meaning of their words rose and rose. They were traveling in a straight line toward collision.

The New York Kid contemplated his Spanish grandee. He drew his revolver upward until the hammer was surely free of the holster. He waited, immovable and watchful, while the garrulous 'Frisco Kid expended two and a half lexicons on the middle Mexican.

The Eastern lad suddenly decided that he was going to be killed. His mind leaped forward and studied the aftermath. The story would be a marvel of brevity when first it reached the far New York home, written in a careful hand on a bit of cheap paper, topped and footed and backed by the printed fortifications of the cable company. But they are often as stones flung into mirrors, these bits of paper upon which are laconically written all the most terrible chronicles of the times. He witnessed the uprising of his mother and sister, and the invincible calm of his hard-mouthed old father, who would probably shut himself in his library and smoke alone. Then his father would come, and they would bring him here, and say: "This is the place." Then, very likely, each would remove his hat. They would stand quietly with their hats in their hands for a decent minute. He pitied his old financing father, unyielding and millioned, a man who commonly spoke twenty-two words a year to his beloved son. The Kid understood it at this time. If his fate was not impregnable, he might have turned out to be a man and have been liked by his father.

The other Kid would mourn his death. He would be preternaturally correct for some weeks, and recite the tale without swearing. But it would not bore him. For the sake of his dead comrade he would be glad to be preternaturally correct and to recite the tale without swearing.

These views were perfectly stereopticon, flashing in and away from his thought with an inconceivable rapidity, until, after all, they were simply one quick, dismal impression. And now, here is the unreal real: Into this Kid's nostrils, at the expectant moment of slaughter, had come the scent of new-mown hay, a fragrance from a field of prostrate grass, a fragrance which contained the sunshine, the bees, the peace of meadows, and the wonder of a distant crooning stream. It had no right to be supreme, but it was supreme, and he breathed it as he waited for pain and a sight of the unknown.

But in the same instant, it may be, his thought flew to the 'Frisco Kid, and it came upon him like a flicker of lightning that the 'Frisco Kid was not going to be there to perform, for instance, the extraordinary office of respectable mourner. The other Kid's head was muddled, his hand was unsteady, his agility was gone. This other Kid was facing the determined and most ferocious gentleman of the enemy. The New York Kid became convinced that his friend was lost. There was going to be a screaming murder. He was so certain of it that he wanted to shield his eyes from sight of the leaping arm and the knife. It was sickening—utterly sickening. The New York Kid might have been taking his first sea-voyage. A combination of honorable manhood and inability prevented him from running away.

He suddenly knew that it was possible to draw his own revolver, and by a swift manœuvre face down all three Mexicans. If he was quick enough he would probably be victor. If any hitch occurred in the draw he would undoubtedly be dead with his friends. It was a new game. He had never been obliged to face a situation of this kind in the Beacon Club in New York. In this test the lungs of the Kid still continued to perform their duty:

> Oh, five white mice of chance,
> Shirts of wool and corduroy pants,
> Gold and wine, women and sin,
> All for you if you let me come in—
> Into the house of chance.

He thought of the weight and size of his revolver, and dismay pierced him. He feared that in his hands it would be as unwieldy as a sewing-machine for this quick work. He imagined, too, that some singular providence might cause him to lose his grip as he raised his weapon; or it might get fatally entangled in the tails of his coat. Some of the eels of despair lay wet and cold against his back.

But at the supreme moment the revolver came forth as if it were greased, and it arose like a feather. This somnolent machine, after months of repose, was finally looking at the breasts of men.

Perhaps in this one series of movements the Kid had unconsciously used nervous force sufficient to raise a bale of hay. Before he comprehended it, he was standing behind his revolver, glaring over the barrel at the Mexicans, menacing first one and then another. His finger was tremoring on the trigger. The revolver gleamed in the darkness with a fine silver light.

The fulsome grandee sprang backward with a low cry. The man who had been facing the 'Frisco Kid took a quick step away. The beautiful array of Mexicans was suddenly disorganized.

The cry and the backward steps revealed something of great importance to the New York Kid. He had never dreamed that he did not have a complete monopoly of all possible trepidations. The cry of the grandee was that of a man who suddenly sees a poisonous snake. Thus the Kid was able to understand swiftly that they were all human beings. They were unanimous in not wishing for too bloody a combat. There was a sudden expression of the equality. He had vaguely believed that they were not going to evince much consideration for his dramatic development as an active factor. They even might be exasperated into an onslaught by it. Instead, they had respected his movement with a respect as great even as an ejaculation of fear and backward steps. Upon the instant he pounced forward, and began to swear, unreeling great English oaths as thick as ropes, and lashing the faces of the Mexicans with them. He was bursting with rage because these men had not previously confided to him that they were vulnerable. The whole thing had been an absurd imposition. He had been seduced into respectful alarm by the concave attitude of the grandee. And, after all, there had been an equality of emotion—an equality! He was furious. He wanted to take the serape of the grandee and swaddle him in it.

The Mexicans slunk back, their eyes burning wistfully. The Kid took aim first at one and then at another. After they had achieved a certain distance, they paused and drew up in a rank. They then resumed some of their old splendor of manner. A voice hailed him in a tone of cynical bravado, as if it had come from between high lips of smiling mockery: "Well, señor, it is finished?"

The Kid scowled into the darkness, his revolver drooping at his side. After a moment he answered: "I am willing." He found it strange that he should be able to speak after this silence of years.

"Good night, señor."

"Good night."

When he turned to look at the 'Frisco Kid, he found him in his original position, his hand upon his hip. He was blinking in perplexity at the point where the Mexicans had vanished.

"Well," said the sober Kid, crossly, "are you ready to go home now?"

The 'Frisco Kid said: "Where they gone?" His voice was undisturbed, but inquisitive.

Benson suddenly propelled himself from his dreamful position against the wall. "'Frisco Kid's all right. He's drunk 's fool, and he's all right. But you New York Kid, you're shober." He passed into a state of profound investigation. "Kid shober 'cause didn't go with us. Didn't go with us 'cause went to damn circus. Went to damn circus 'cause lose shakin' dice. Lose shakin' dice 'cause—what make lose shakin' dice, Kid?"

The New York Kid eyed the senile youth. "I don't know. The five white mice, maybe."

Benson puzzled so over this reply that he had to be held erect by his friends. Finally the 'Frisco Kid said: "Let's go home."

Nothing had happened.

ACTIVE
SERVICE

ACTIVE SERVICE

Chapter 1

Marjory walked pensively along the hall. In the cool shadows made by the palms on the window ledge, her face wore the expression of thoughtful melancholy expected on the faces of the devotees who pace in cloistered gloom. She halted before a door at the end of the hall and laid her hand on the knob. She stood hesitating; her head bowed. It was evident that this mission was to require great fortitude.

At last she opened the door. "Father," she began at once. There was disclosed an elderly, narrow-faced man seated at a large table and surrounded by manuscripts and books. The sunlight flowing through curtains of Turkey red fell sanguinely upon the bust of dead-eyed Pericles on the mantle. A little clock was ticking, hidden somewhere among the countless leaves of writing, the maps and broad heavy tomes that swarmed upon the table.

Her father looked up quickly with an ogreish scowl, "Go away!" he cried in a rage. "Go away. Go away. Get out!" He seemed on the point of arising to eject the visitor. It was plain to her that he had been interrupted in the writing of one of his sentences, ponderous, solemn and endless, in which wandered multitudes of homeless and friendless prepositions, adjectives looking for a parent, and quarrelling nouns, sentences which no longer symbolised the language-form of thought but which had about them a quaint aroma from the dens of long-dead scholars. "Get out," snarled the professor.

"Father," faltered the girl. Either because his formulated thought was now completely knocked out of his mind by his own emphasis in defending it, or because he detected something of portent in her expression, his manner suddenly changed, and with a petulant glance at his writing he laid down his pen and sank back in his chair to listen. "Well, what is it, my child?"

The girl took a chair near the window and gazed out upon the snow-stricken campus, where at the moment a group of students returning from a class room were festively hurling snow-balls. "I've got something important to tell you, father," said she, "but I don't quite know how to say it."

"Something important?" repeated the professor. He was not habitually interested in the affairs of his family, but this proclamation that something important could be connected with them, filled his mind with a capricious interest. "Well, what is it, Marjory?"

She replied calmly: "Rufus Coleman wants to marry me."

261

"What?" demanded the professor loudly. "Rufus Coleman. What do you mean?"

The girl glanced furtively at him. She did not seem to be able to frame a suitable sentence.

As for the professor, he had, like all men both thoughtless and thoughtful, told himself that one day his daughter would come to him with a tale of this kind. He had never forgotten that the little girl was to be a woman, and he had never forgotten that this tall, lithe creature, the present Marjory, was a woman. He had been entranced and confident or entranced and apprehensive according to the time. A man focussed upon astronomy, the pig market or social progression, may nevertheless have a secondary mind which hovers like a spirit over his dahlia tubers and dreams upon the mystery of their slow and tender revelations. The professor's secondary mind had dwelt always with his daughter and watched with a faith and delight the changing to a woman of a certain fat and mumbling babe. However, he now saw this machine, this self-sustaining, self-operative love, which had run with the ease of a clock, suddenly crumble to ashes and leave the mind of a great scholar staring at a calamity. "Rufus Coleman," he repeated, stunned. Here was his daughter, very obviously desirous of marrying Rufus Coleman. "Marjory," he cried in amazement and fear, "what possesses you? Marry Rufus Coleman?"

The girl seemed to feel a strong sense of relief at his prompt recognition of a fact. Being freed from the necessity of making a flat declaration, she simply hung her head and blushed impressively. A hush fell upon them. The professor stared long at his daughter. The shadow of unhappiness deepened upon his face. "Marjory, Marjory," he murmured at last. He had tramped heroically upon his panic and devoted his strength to bringing thought into some kind of attitude toward this terrible fact. "I am—I am surprised," he began. Fixing her then with a stern eye, he asked: "Why do you wish to marry this man? You, with your opportunities of meeting persons of intelligence. And you want to marry—" His voice grew tragic. "You want to marry the Sunday editor of the *New York Eclipse*."

"It is not so very terrible, is it?" said Marjory sullenly.

"Wait a moment; don't talk," cried the professor. He arose and walked nervously to and fro, his hands flying in the air. He was very red behind the ears as when in the class-room some student offended him. "A gambler, a sporter of fine clothes, an expert on champagne, a polite loafer, a witness knave who edits the Sunday edition of a great outrage upon our sensibilities. You want to marry him, this man? Marjory, you are insane. This fraud who asserts that his work is intelligent, this fool comes here to my house and—"

He became aware that his daughter was regarding him coldly. "I thought we had best have all this part of it over at once," she remarked.

He confronted her in a new kind of surprise. The little keen-eyed professor was at this time imperial, on the verge of a majestic outburst. "Be still," he said. "Don't be clever with your father. Don't be a dodger. Or, if you are, don't speak of it to me. I suppose this fine young man expects to see me personally?"

"He was coming to-morrow," replied Marjory. She began to weep. "He was coming to-morrow."

"Um," said the professor. He continued his pacing while Marjory wept with her head bowed to the arm of the chair. His brow made the three dark vertical crevices well known to his students. Sometimes he glowered murderously at the photographs of ancient temples which adorned the walls. "My poor child," he said once, as he paused near her, "to think I never knew you were a fool. I have been deluding myself. It has been my fault as much as it has been yours. I will not readily forgive myself."

The girl raised her face and looked at him. Finally, resolved to disregard the dishevelment wrought by tears, she presented a desperate front with her wet eyes and flushed cheeks. Her hair was disarrayed. "I don't see why you can call me a fool," she said. The pause before this sentence had been so portentous of a wild and rebellious speech that the professor almost laughed now. But still the father for the first time knew that he was being undauntedly faced by his child in his own library, in the presence of 372 pages of the book that was to be his masterpiece. At the back of his mind he felt a great awe as if his own youthful spirit had come from the past and challenged him with a glance. For a moment he was almost a defeated man. He dropped into a chair. "Does your mother know of this?" he asked mournfully.

"Yes," replied the girl. "She knows. She has been trying to make me give up Rufus."

"Rufus," cried the professor rejuvenated by anger.

"Well, his name is Rufus," said the girl.

"But please don't call him so before me," said the father with icy dignity. "I do not recognise him as being named Rufus. That is a contention of yours which does not arouse my interest. I know him very well as a gambler and a drunkard, and if incidentally, he is named Rufus, I fail to see any importance to it."

"He is not a gambler and he is not a drunkard," she said.

"Um. He drinks heavily—that is well known. He gambles. He plays cards for money—more than he possesses—at least he did when he was in college."

"You said you liked him when he was in college."

"So I did. So I did," answered the professor sharply. "I often find myself liking that kind of a boy in college. Don't I know them—those lads with their beer and their poker games in the dead of the night with a towel hung over the keyhole. Their habits are often vicious enough, but something remains in them through it all and they may go away and do great things. This happens. We know it. It happens with confusing insistence. It destroys theories. There—there isn't much to say about it. And sometimes we like this kind of a boy better than we do the—the others. For my part I know of many a pure, pious and fine-minded student that I have positively loathed from a personal point-of-view. But," he added, "this Rufus Coleman, his life in college and his life since, go to prove how often we get off the track. There is no gauge of collegiate conduct whatever, until we can get evidence of the man's work in the world. Your precious scoundrel's evidence is now all in and he is a failure, or worse."

"You are not habitually so fierce in judging people," said the girl.

"I would be if they all wanted to marry my daughter," rejoined the professor. "Rather than let that man make love to you—or even be within a short railway journey of you, I'll cart you off to Europe this winter and keep you there until you forget. If you persist in this silly fancy, I shall at once become medieval."

Marjory had evidently recovered much of her composure. "Yes, father, new climates are always supposed to cure one," she remarked with a kind of lightness.

"It isn't so much the old expedient," said the professor musingly, "as it is that I would be afraid to leave you here with no protection against that drinking gambler and gambling drunkard."

"Father, I have to ask you not to use such terms in speaking of the man that I shall marry."

There was a silence. To all intents the professor remained unmoved. He smote the tips of his fingers thoughtfully together. "Ye-es," he observed. "That sounds reasonable from your standpoint." His eyes studied her face in a long and steady glance. He arose and went into the hall. When he returned he wore his hat and great coat. He took a book and some papers from the table and went away.

Marjory walked slowly through the halls and up to her room. From a window she could see her father making his way across the campus labouriously against the wind and whirling snow. She watched it, this little black figure, bent forward, patient, steadfast. It was an inferior fact that her father was one of the famous scholars of the generation. To her, he was now a little old man facing the wintry winds. Recollecting herself and Rufus Coleman she began to weep again, wailing amid the ruins of her tumbled hopes. Her skies had turned to paper and her trees were mere bits of green sponge. But amid all this woe appeared the little black image of her father making its way against the storm.

Chapter 2

In a high-walled corridor of one of the college buildings, a crowd of students
waited amid jostlings and a loud buzz of talk. Suddenly a huge pair of doors
flew open and a wedge of young men inserted itself boisterously and deeply
into the throng. There was a great scuffle attended by a general banging of
books upon heads. The two lower classes engaged in herculean play while
members of the two higher classes, standing aloof, devoted themselves strictly
to the encouragement of whichever party for a moment lost ground or heart.
This was in order to prolong the conflict.

The combat, waged in the desperation of proudest youth, waxed hot and
hotter. The wedge had been instantly smitten into a kind of block of men. It had
crumpled into an irregular square and on three sides it was now assailed with
remarkable ferocity.

It was a matter of wall meet wall in terrific rushes, during which lads could
feel their very hearts leaving them in the compress of friends and foes. They on
the outskirts upheld the honour of their classes by squeezing into paper
thickness the lungs of those of their fellows who formed the centre of the mêlée.

In some way it resembled a panic at a theatre.

The first lance-like attack of the Sophomores had been formidable, but the
Freshmen outnumbering their enemies and smarting from continual Sophomoric
oppression, had swarmed to the front like drilled collegians and given the
arrogant foe the first serious check of the year. Therefore the tall Gothic
windows which lined one side of the corridor looked down upon as incomprehensible and enjoyable a tumult as could mark the steps of advanced education.
The Seniors and Juniors cheered themselves ill. Long freed from the joy of such
meetings, their only means for this kind of recreation was to involve the lower
classes, and they had never seen the victims fall to with such vigour and
courage. Bits of printed leaves, torn note-books, dismantled collars and cravats,
all floated to the floor beneath the feet of the warring hordes. There were no
blows; it was a battle of pressure. It was a deadly pushing where the leaders on
either side often suffered the most cruel and sickening agony caught thus
between phalanxes of shoulders with friend as well as foe contributing to the
pain.

Charge after charge of Freshmen beat upon the now compact and organised

265

Sophomores. Then, finally, the rock began to give slow way. A roar came from the Freshmen and they hurled themselves in a frenzy upon their betters.

To be under the gaze of the Juniors and Seniors is to be in sight of all men, and so the Sophomores at this important moment laboured with the desperation of the half-doomed to stem the terrible Freshmen.

In the kind of game, it was the time when bad tempers came strongly to the front, and in many Sophomores' minds a thought arose of the incomparable insolence of the Freshmen. A blow was struck; an infuriated Sophomore had swung an arm high and smote a Freshman.

Although it had seemed that no greater noise could be made by the given numbers, the din that succeeded this manifestation surpassed everything. The Juniors and Seniors immediately set up an angry howl. These veteran classes projected themselves into the middle of the fight, buffeting everybody with small thought as to merit. This method of bringing peace was as militant as a landslide, but they had much trouble before they could separate the central clump of antagonists into its parts. A score of Freshmen had cried out: "It was Coke. Coke punched him. Coke." A dozen of them were tempestuously endeavouring to register their protest against fisticuffs by means of an introduction of more fisticuffs.

The upper classmen were swift, harsh and hard. "Come, now, Freshies, quit it. Get back, get back, d'y' hear?" With a wrench of muscles they forced themselves in front of Coke, who was being blindly defended by his classmates from intensely earnest attacks by outraged Freshmen.

These meetings between the lower classes at the door of a recitation room were accounted quite comfortable and idle affairs, and a blow delivered openly and in hatred fractured a sharply defined rule of conduct. The corridor was in a hubbub. Many Seniors and Juniors, bursting from old and iron discipline, wildly clamoured that some Freshman should be given the privilege of a single encounter with Coke. The Freshmen themselves were frantic. They besieged the tight and dauntless circle of men that encompassed Coke. None dared confront the Seniors openly, but by headlong rushes at auspicious moments they tried to come to quarters with the rings of dark-browed Sophomores. It was no longer a festival, a game; it was a riot. Coke, wide-eyed, pallid with fury, a ribbon of blood on his chin, swayed in the middle of the mob of his classmates, comrades who waived the ethics of the blow under the circumstances of being obliged as a corps to stand against the scorn of the whole college, as well as against the tremendous assaults of the Freshmen. Shamed by their own man, but knowing full well the right time and the wrong time for a palaver of regret and disavowal, this battalion struggled in the desperation of despair. Once they were upon the verge of making unholy campaign against the interfering Seniors. This fiery impertinence was the measure of their state.

It was a critical moment in the play of the college. Four or five defeats from the Sophomores during the fall had taught the Freshmen much. They had learned the comparative measurements, and they knew now that their prowess was ripe to enable them to amply revenge what was, according to their standards, an execrable deed by a man who had not the virtue to play the rough game, but was obliged to resort to uncommon methods. In short, the Freshmen were almost out of control, and the Sophomores debased but defiant, were quite out of control. The Senior and Junior classes which, in American colleges dictate in these affrays, found their dignity toppling, and in consequence there was a sudden oncome of the entire force of upper classmen, football players naturally in advance. All distinctions were dissolved at once in a general fracas. The stiff and still Gothic windows surveyed a scene of dire carnage.

Suddenly a voice rang brazenly through the tumult. It was not loud, but it was different. "Gentlemen! Gentlemen!" Instantly there was a remarkable number of haltings, abrupt replacements, quick changes. Prof. Wainwright stood at the door of his recitation room, looking into the eyes of each member of the mob of three hundred. "Ssh!" said the mob. "Ssh! Quit! Stop! It's the Embassador! Stop!" He had once been minister to Austro-Hungary, and forever now to the students of the college his name was Embassador. He stepped into the corridor, and they cleared for him a little respectful zone of floor. He looked about him coldly. "It seems quite a general dishevelment. The Sophomores display an energy in the halls which I do not detect in the class room." A feeble murmur of appreciation arose from the outskirts of the throng. While he had been speaking several remote groups of battling men had been violently signaled and suppressed by other students. The professor gazed into terraces of faces that were still inflamed. "I needn't say that I am surprised," he remarked in the accepted rhetoric of his kind. He added musingly: "There seems to be a great deal of torn linen. Who is the young gentleman with blood on his chin?"

The throng moved restlessly. A manful silence, such as might be in the tombs of stern and honourable knights, fell upon the shadowed corridor. The subdued rustling had fainted to nothing. Then out of the crowd Coke, pale and desperate, delivered himself.

"Oh, Mr. Coke," said the professor, "I would be glad if you would tell the gentlemen they may retire to their dormitories." He waited while the students passed out to the campus.

The professor returned to his room for some books, and then began his own march across the snowy campus. The wind twisted his coat-tails fantastically, and he was obliged to keep one hand firmly on the top of his hat. When he arrived home he met his wife in the hall. "Look here, Mary," he cried. She followed him into the library. "Look here," he said. "What is this all about? Marjory tells me she wants to marry Rufus Coleman."

Mrs. Wainwright was a fat woman who was said to pride herself upon being very wise and if necessary, sly. In addition she laughed continually in an inexplicably personal way, which apparently made everybody who heard her feel offended. Mrs. Wainwright laughed.

"Well," said the professor, bristling, "what do you mean by that?"

"Oh, Harris," she replied. "Oh, Harris."

The professor straightened in his chair. "I do not see any illumination in those remarks, Mary. I understand from Marjory's manner that she is bent upon marrying Rufus Coleman. She said you knew of it."

"Why, of course I knew. It was as plain——"

"Plain!" scoffed the professor. "Plain!"

"Why, of course," she cried. "I knew it all along."

There was nothing in her tone which proved that she admired the event itself. She was evidently carried away by the triumph of her penetration. "I knew it all along," she added, nodding.

The professor looked at her affectionately. "You knew it all along, then,

Mary?'' Why didn't you tell me, dear?''

"Because you ought to have known it," she answered blatantly.

The professor was glaring. Finally he spoke in tones of grim reproach. "Mary, whenever you happen to know anything, dear, it seems only a matter of partial recompense that you should tell me."

The wife had been taught in a terrible school that she should never invent any inexpensive retorts concerning bookworms and so she yawed at once. "Really, Harris. Really, I didn't suppose the affair was serious. You could have knocked me down with a feather. Of course he has been here very often, but then Marjory gets a great deal of attention. A great deal of attention."

The professor had been thinking. "Rather than let my girl marry that scalawag, I'll take you and her to Greece this winter with the class. Separation. It is a sure cure that has the sanction of antiquity."

"Well," said Mrs. Wainwright, "you know best, Harris. You know best." It was a common remark with her, and it probably meant either approbation or disapprobation if it did not mean simple discretion.

Chapter 3

There had been a babe with no arms born in one of the western counties of Massachusetts. In place of upper limbs the child had growing from its chest a pair of fin-like hands, mere bits of skin-covered bone. Furthermore, it had only one eye. This phenomenon lived four days, but the news of the birth had travelled up this country road and through that village until it reached the ears of the editor of the *Michaelstown Tribune*. He was also a correspondent of the *New York Eclipse*. On the third day he appeared at the home of the parents accompanied by a photographer. While the latter arranged his instrument, the correspondent talked to the father and mother, two cow-eyed and yellow-faced people who seemed to suffer a primitive fright of the strangers. Afterwards as the correspondent and the photographer were climbing into their buggy, the mother crept furtively down to the gate and asked, in a foreigner's dialect, if they would send her a copy of the photograph. The correspondent carelessly indulgent, promised it. As the buggy swung away, the father came from behind an apple tree and the two semi-humans watched it with its burden of glorious strangers until it rumbled across the bridge and disappeared. The correspondent was elate; he told the photographer that the *Eclipse* would probably pay fifty dollars for the article and the photograph.

The office of the *New York Eclipse* was at the top of the immense building on Broadway. It was a sheer mountain to the heights of which the interminable thunder of the streets arose faintly. The Hudson was a broad path of silver in the distance. Its edge was marked by the tracery of sailing ships' rigging and by the huge and many-coloured stacks of ocean liners. At the foot of the cliff lay City Hall Park. It seemed no larger than a quilt. The grey walks patterned the snow-covering into triangles and ovals and upon them many tiny people scurried here and there, without sound, like a fish at the bottom of a pool. It was only the vehicles that sent high, unmistakable, the deep bass of their movement. And yet after listening one seemed to hear a singular murmurous note, a pulsation, as if the crowd made noise by its mere living, a mellow hum of the eternal strife. Then suddenly out of the deeps might ring a human voice, a newsboy shout perhaps, the cry of a faraway jackal at night.

From the level of the ordinary roofs, combined in many plateaus, dotted with short iron chimneys from which curled wisps of steam, arose other

269

mountains like the *Eclipse* Building. They were great peaks, ornate, glittering with paint or polish. Northward they subsided to sun-crowned ranges.

From some of the windows of the *Eclipse* office dropped the walls of a terrible chasm in the darkness of which could be seen vague struggling figures. Looking down into this appalling crevice one discovered only the tops of hats and knees which in spasmodic jerks seemed to touch the rims of the hats. The scene represented some weird fight or dance or carouse. It was not an exhibition of men hurrying along a narrow street.

It was good to turn one's eyes from that place to the vista of the city's splendid reaches, with spire and spar shining in the clear atmosphere and the marvel of the Jersey shore, pearl-misted or brilliant with detail. From this height the sweep of a snow-storm was defined and majestic. Even a slight summer shower, with swords of lurid yellow sunlight piercing its edges as if warriors were contesting every foot of its advance, was from the *Eclipse* office something so inspiring that the chance pilgrim felt a sense of exultation as if from this peak he was surveying the worldwide war of the elements and life. The staff of the *Eclipse* usually worked without coats and amid the smoke from pipes.

To one of the editorial chambers came a photograph and an article from Michaelstown, Massachusetts. A boy placed the packet and many others upon the desk of a young man who was standing before a window and thoughtfully drumming upon the pane. He turned at the thudding of the packets upon his desk. "Blast you," he remarked amiably. "Oh, I guess it won't hurt you to work," answered the boy, grinning with a comrade's insolence. Baker, an assistant editor for the Sunday paper, took seat at his desk and began the task of examining the packets. His face could not display any particular interest because he had been at the same work for nearly a fortnight.

The first long envelope he opened was from a woman. There was a neat little manuscript accompanied by a letter which explained that the writer was a widow who was trying to make her living by her pen and who, further, hoped that the generosity of the editor of the *Eclipse* would lead him to give her article the opportunity which she was sure it deserved. She hoped that the editor would pay her as well as possible for it, as she needed the money greatly. She added that her brother was a reporter on the *Little Rock Sentinel* and he had declared that her literary style was excellent.

Baker really did not read this note. His vast experience of a fortnight had enabled him to detect its kind in two glances. He unfolded the manuscript, looked at it woodenly and then tossed it with the letter to the top of his desk, where it lay with the other corpses. None could think of widows in Arkansas, ambitious from the praise of the reporter on the *Little Rock Sentinel*, waiting for a crown of literary glory and money. In the next envelope a man using the note-paper of a Boston journal begged to know if the accompanying article would be acceptable; if not it was to be kindly returned in the enclosed stamped envelope. It was a humourous essay on trolley cars. Adventuring through the odd scraps that were come to the great mill, Baker paused occasionally to relight his pipe.

As he went through envelope after envelope, the desks about him gradually were occupied by young men who entered from the hall with their faces still red from the cold of the streets. For the most part they bore the unmistakable stamp of the American college. They had that confident poise which is easily brought from the athletic field. Moreover, their clothes were quite in the way of being of the newest fashion. There was an air of precision about their cravats and linen. But on the other hand there might be with them some indifferent westerner who was obliged to resort to irregular means and harangue startled shop-keepers in order to provide himself with collars of a strange kind. He was usually very quick and brave of eye and noted for his inability to perceive a distinction between his own habit and the habit of others, his western character preserving itself inviolate amid a confusion of manners.

The men, coming one and one, or two and two, flung badinage to all corners of the room. Afterward, as they wheeled from time to time in their chairs, they bitterly insulted each other with the utmost good-nature, taking unerring aim at faults and riddling personalities with the quaint and cynical humour of a newspaper office. Throughout this banter, it was strange to note how infrequently the men smiled, particularly when directly engaged in an encounter.

A wide door opened into another apartment where were many little slanted tables, each under an electric globe with a green shade. Here a curly-headed scoundrel with a corncob pipe was hurling paper balls the size of apples at the head of an industrious man who, under these difficulties, was trying to draw a picture of an awful wreck with ghastly-faced sailors frozen in the rigging. Near this pair a lady was challenging a German artist who resembled Napoleon III. with having been publicly drunk at a music hall on the previous night. Next to the great gloomy corridor of this sixteenth floor was a little office presided over by an austere boy, and here waited in enforced patience a little dismal band of people who wanted to see the Sunday editor.

Baker took a manuscript and after glancing about the room, walked over to a man at another desk, "Here is something that I think might do," he said. The man at the desk read the first two pages. "But where is the photograph?" he asked then. "There should be a photograph with this thing."

"Oh, I forgot," said Baker. He brought from his desk a photograph of the babe that had been born lacking arms and one eye. Baker's superior braced a knee against his desk and settled back to a judicial attitude. He took the photograph and looked at it impassively. "Yes," he said, after a time, "that's a pretty good thing. You better show that to Coleman when he comes in."

In the little office where the dismal band waited, there had been a sharp hopeful stir when Rufus Coleman, the Sunday editor, passed rapidly from door to door and vanished within the holy precincts. It had evidently been in the minds of some to accost him then, but his eyes did not turn once in their direction. It was as if he had not seen them. Many experiences had taught him that the proper manner of passing through this office was at a blind gallop.

The dismal band turned then upon the austere office boy. Some demanded with terrible dignity that he should take in their cards at once. Others sought to ingratiate themselves by smiles of tender friendliness. He for his part employed what we would have called his knowledge of men and women upon the group, and in consequence blundered and bungled vividly, freezing with a glance an annoyed and importunate Arctic explorer who was come to talk of illustrations for an article that had been lavishly paid for in advance. The hero might have thought he was again in the northern seas. At the next moment the boy was treating almost courteously a German from the east side who wanted the *Eclipse* to print a grand full page advertising description of his invention, a gun which

was supposed to have a range of forty miles and to be able to penetrate anything
with equanimity and joy. The gun, as a matter of fact, had once been induced to
go off when it had hurled itself passionately upon its back, incidentally breaking
its inventor's leg. The projectile had wandered some four hundred yards
seaward, where it dug a hole in the water which was really a menace to
navigation. Since then there had been nothing tangible save the inventor, in
splints and out of splints, as the fortunes of science decreed. In short, this office
boy mixed his business in the perfect manner of an underdone lad dealing with
matters too large for him, and throughout he displayed the pride and assurance
of a god.

As Coleman crossed the large office his face still wore the stern expression
which he invariably used to carry him unmolested through the ranks of the
dismal band. As he was removing his London overcoat he addressed the
imperturbable back of one of his staff, who had a desk against the opposite wall.
"Has Hasskins sent in that drawing of the mine accident yet?" The man did not
lift his head from his work, but he answered at once: "No; not yet." Coleman
was laying his hat on a chair. "Well, why hasn't he?" he demanded. He glanced
toward the door of the room in which the curly-headed scoundrel with the
corncob pipe was still hurling paper balls at the man who was trying to invent
the postures of dead mariners frozen in the rigging. The office boy came timidly
from his post and informed Coleman of the waiting people. "All right," said the
editor. He dropped into his chair and began to finger his letters, which had been
neatly opened and placed in a little stack by a boy. Baker came in with the
photograph of the miserable babe.

It was publicly believed that the Sunday staff of the *Eclipse* must have a kind
of æsthetic delight in pictures of this kind, but Coleman's face betrayed no
emotion as he looked at this specimen. He lit a fresh cigar, tilted his chair and
surveyed it with a cold and stony stare. "Yes, that's all right," he said slowly.
There seemed to be no affectionate relation between him and this picture.
Evidently he was weighing its value as a morsel to be flung to a ravenous public,
whose wolf-life appetite could only satisfy itself upon mental entrails, abomina-
tions. As for himself, he seemed to be remote, exterior. It was a matter of the
Eclipse business.

Suddenly Coleman became executive. "Better give it to Schooner and tell
him to make a half-page—or, no, send him in here and I'll tell him my idea.
How's the article? Any good? Well, give it to Smith to rewrite."

An artist came from the other room and presented for inspection his
drawing of the seamen dead in the rigging of the wreck, a company of grizzly
and horrible figures, bony-fingered, shrunken and with awful eyes. "Hum," said
Coleman, after a prolonged study, "that's all right. That's good, Jimmie. But
you'd better work'em up around the eyes a little more." The office boy was
deploying in the distance, waiting for the correct moment to present some cards
and names.

The artist was cheerfully taking away his corpses when Coleman hailed
him. "Oh, Jim, let me see that thing again, will you? Now, how about this spar?
This don't look right to me."

"It looks right to me," replied the artist, sulkily.

"But, see. It's going to take up half a page. Can't you change it somehow?"

"How am I going to change it?" said the other, glowering at Coleman.

"That's the way it ought to be. How am I going to change it? That's the way it ought to be."

"No, it isn't at all," said Coleman. "You've got a spar sticking out of the main body of the drawing in a way that will spoil the look of the whole page."

The artist was a man of remarkable popular reputation and he was very stubborn and conceited of it, constantly making himself unbearable with covert threats that if he was not delicately placated at all points, he would freight his genius over to the office of the great opposition journal.

"That's the way it ought to be," he repeated, in a tone at once sullen and superior. "The spar is all right. I can't rig spars on ships just to suit you."

"And I can't give up the whole paper to your accursed spars, either," said Coleman, with animation. "Don't you see you use about a third of a page with this spar sticking off into space? Now, you were always so clever, Jimmie, in adapting yourself to the page. Can't you shorten it, or cut it off, or something? Or, break it—that's the thing. Make it a broken spar dangling down. See?"

"Yes, I s'pose I could do that," said the artist, mollified by a thought of the ease with which he could make the change, and mollified, too, by the brazen tribute to a part of his cleverness.

"Well, do it, then," said the Sunday editor, turning abruptly away. The artist, with head high, walked majestically back to the other room. Whereat the curly-headed one immediately resumed the rain of paper balls upon him. The office boy came timidly to Coleman and suggested the presence of the people in the outer office. "Let them wait until I read my mail," said Coleman. He shuffled the pack of letters indifferently through his hands. Suddenly he came upon a little grey envelope. He opened it at once and scanned its contents with the speed of his craft. Afterward he laid it down before him on the desk and surveyed it with a cool and musing smile. "So?" he remarked. "That's the case, is it?"

He presently swung around in his chair, and for a time held the entire attention of the men at the various desks. He outlined to them again their various parts in the composition of the next great Sunday edition. In a few brisk sentences he set a complex machine in proper motion. His men no longer thrilled with admiration at the precision with which he grasped each obligation of the campaign toward a successful edition. They had grown to accept it as they accepted his hat or his London clothes. At this time his face was lit with something of the self-contained enthusiasm of a general. Immediately afterward he arose and reached for his coat and hat.

The office boy, coming circuitously forward, presented him with some cards and also with a scrap of paper upon which was scrawled a long and semi-coherent word. "What are these?" grumbled Coleman.

"They are waiting outside," answered the boy, with trepidation. It was part of the law that the lion of the ante-room should cringe like a cold monkey, more or less, as soon as he was out of his private jungle. "Oh, Tallerman," cried the Sunday editor, "here's this Arctic man come to arrange about his illustration. I wish you'd go and talk it over with him." By chance he picked up the scrap of paper with its cryptic word. "Oh," he said, scowling at the office boy. "Pity you can't remember that fellow. If you can't remember faces any better than that you should be a detective. Get out now and tell him to go to the devil." The wilted slave turned at once, but Coleman hailed him. "Hold on. Come to think of it, I will see this idiot. Send him in," he commanded, grimly.

Coleman lapsed into a dream over the sheet of grey note paper. Presently, a middle-aged man, a palpable German, came hesitatingly into the room and bunted among the desks as unmanageably as a tempest-tossed scow. Finally he was impatiently towed in the right direction. He came and stood at Coleman's elbow and waited nervously for the engrossed man to raise his eyes. It was plain that this interview meant important things to him. Somehow on his common-place countenance was to be found the expression of a dreamer, a fashioner of great and absurd projects, a fine, tender fool. He cast hopeful and reverent glances at the man who was deeply contemplative of the grey note. He evidently believed himself on the threshold of a triumph of some kind, and he awaited his fruition with a joy that was only made sharper by the usual human suspicion of coming events.

Coleman glanced up at last and saw his visitor. "Oh, it's you, is it?" he remarked icily, bending upon the German the stare of a tyrant. "So you've come again, have you?" He wheeled in his chair until he could fully display a contemptuous, merciless smile. "Now, Mr. What's-your-name, you've called here to see me about twenty times already and at last I am going to say something definite about your invention." His listener's face, which had worn for a moment a look of fright and bewilderment, gladdened swiftly to a gratitude that seemed the edge of an outburst of tears. "Yes," continued Coleman, "I am going to say something definite. I am going to say that it is the most imbecile bit of nonsense that has come within the range of my large newspaper experience. It is simply the aberration of a rather remarkable lunatic. It is no good; it is not worth the price of a cheese sandwich. I understand that its one feat has been to break your leg; if it ever goes off again, persuade it to break your neck. And now I want you to take this nursery rhyme of yours and get out. And don't ever come here again. Do you understand? You understand, do you?" He arose and bowed in courteous dismissal.

The German was regarding him with the surprise and horror of a youth shot mortally. He could not find his tongue for a moment. Ultimately he gasped: "But, Mister Editor"—Coleman interrupted him tigerishly. "You heard what I said? Get out." The man bowed his head and went slowly toward the door.

Coleman placed the little grey note in his breast pocket. He took his hat and top coat, and evading the dismal band by a shameless manœuvre, passed through the halls to the entrance to the elevator shaft. He heard a movement behind him and saw that the German was also waiting for the elevator.

Standing in the gloom of the corridor, Coleman felt the mournful owlish eyes of the German resting upon him. He took a case from his pocket and elaborately lit a cigarette. Suddenly there was a flash of light and a cage of bronze, gilt and steel dropped, magically from above. Coleman yelled: "Down!" A door flew open. Coleman, followed by the German, stepped upon the elevator. "Well, Johnnie," he said cheerfully to the lad who operated this machine, "is business good?" "Yes, sir, pretty good," answered the boy, grinning. The little cage sank swiftly; floor after floor seemed to be rising with marvellous speed; the whole building was winging straight into the sky. There were soaring lights, figures and the opalescent glow of ground glass doors marked with black inscriptions. Other lifts were springing heavenward. All the lofty corridors rang with cries. "Up!" "Down!" "Down!" "Up!" The boy's hand grasped a lever and his machine obeyed his lightest movement with sometimes an unbalancing swiftness.

Coleman discoursed briskly to the youthful attendant. Once he turned and regarded with a quick stare of insolent annoyance the despairing countenance of the German whose eyes had never left him. When the elevator arrived at the ground floor, Coleman departed with the outraged air of a man who for a time had been compelled to occupy a cell in company with a harmless spectre.

He walked quickly away. Opposite a corner of the City Hall he was impelled to look behind him. Through the hordes of people with cable cars marching like panoplied elephants, he was able to distinguish the German, motionless and gazing after him. Coleman laughed. "That's a comic old boy," he said, to himself.

In the grill-room of a Broadway hotel he was obliged to wait some minutes for the fulfillment of his orders and he spent the time in reading and studying the little grey note. When his luncheon was served he ate with an expression of morose dignity.

Chapter 4

Marjory paused again at her father's door. After hesitating in the original way she entered the library. Her father almost represented an emblematic figure, seated upon a column of books. "Well," he cried. Then, seeing it was Marjory, he changed his tone. "Ah, under the circumstances, my dear, I admit your privilege of interrupting me at any hour of the day. You have important business with me." His manner was satanically indulgent.

The girl fingered a book. She turned the leaves in absolute semblance of a person reading. "Rufus Coleman called."

'Indeed," said the professor.

"And I've come to you, father, before seeing him."

The professor was silent for a time. "Well, Marjory," he said at last, "what do you want me to say?" He spoke very deliberately. "I am sure this is a singular situation. Here appears the man I formally forbid you to marry. I am sure I do not know what I am to say."

"I wish to see him," said the girl.

"You wish to see him?" enquired the professor. "You wish to see him? Marjory, I may as well tell you now that with all the books and plays I've read, I really don't know how the obdurate father should conduct himself. He is always pictured as an exceedingly dense gentleman with white whiskers, who does all the unintelligent things in the plot. You and I are going to play no drama, are we, Marjory? I admit that I have white whiskers, and I am an obdurate father. I am, as you well may say, a very obdurate father. You are not to marry Rufus Coleman. You understand the rest of the matter. He is here; you want to see him. What will you say to him when you see him?"

"I will say that you refuse to let me marry him, father and—" She hesitated a moment before she lifted her eyes fully and formidably to her father's face. "And that I shall marry him anyhow."

The professor did not cavort when this statement came from his daughter. He nodded and then passed into a period of reflection. Finally he asked: "But when? That is the point. When?"

The girl made a sad gesture. "I don't know. I don't know. Perhaps when you come to know Rufus better——"

"Know him better. Know that rapscallion better? Why, I know him much better than he knows himself. I know him too well. Do you think I am talking off-hand about this affair? Do you think I am talking without proper information?"

Marjory made no reply.

"Well," said the professor, "you may see Coleman on condition that you inform him at once that I forbid your marriage to him. I don't understand at all how to manage these situations. I don't know what to do. I suppose I should go myself and——No, you can't see him, Marjory."

Still the girl made no reply. Her head sank forward and she breathed a trifle heavily.

"Marjory," cried the professor, "it is impossible that you should think so much of this man." He arose and went to his daughter. "Marjory, many wise children have been guided by foolish fathers, but we both suspect that no foolish child has ever been guided by a wise father. Let us change it. I present myself to you as a wise father. Follow my wishes in this affair and you will be at least happier than if you marry this wretched Coleman."

She answered: "He is waiting for me."

The professor turned abruptly from her and dropped into his chair at the table. He resumed a grip on his pen. "Go," he said, wearily. "Go. But if you have a remnant of sense, remember what I have said to you. Go." He waved his hand in a dismissal that was slightly scornful. "I hoped you would have a minor conception of what you were doing. It seems a pity." Drooping in tears, the girl slowly left the room.

Coleman had an idea that he had occupied the chair for several months. He gazed about at the pictures and the odds and ends of a drawing-room in an attempt to take an interest in them. The great garlanded paper shade over the piano lamp consoled his impatience in a mild degree because he knew that Marjory had made it. He noted the clusters of cloth violets which she had pinned upon the yellow paper and he dreamed over the fact. He was able to endow this shade with certain qualities of sentiment that caused his stare to become almost a part of an intimacy, a communion. He looked as if he could have unburdened his soul to this shade over the piano lamp.

Upon the appearance of Marjory he sprang up and came forward rapidly. "Dearest," he murmured, stretching out both hands. She gave him one set of fingers with chilling convention. She said something which he understood to be "Good-afternoon." He started as if the woman before him had suddenly drawn a knife. "Marjory," he cried, "what is the matter?" They walked together toward a window. The girl looked at him in polite enquiry. "Why?" she said. "Do I seem strange?" There was a moment's silence while he gazed into her eyes, eyes full of innocence and tranquillity. At last she tapped her foot upon the floor in expression of mild impatience. "People do not like to be asked what is the matter when there is nothing the matter. What do you mean?"

Coleman's face had gradually hardened. "Well, what is wrong?" he demanded, abruptly. "What has happened? What is it, Marjory?"

She raised her glance in a perfect reality of wonder. "What is wrong? What has happened? How absurd! Why nothing, of course." She gazed out of the window. "Look," she added, brightly, "the students are rolling somebody in a drift. Oh, the poor man!"

Coleman, now wearing a bewildered air, made some pretense of being occupied with the scene. "Yes," he said, ironically. "Very interesting, indeed."

"Oh," said Marjory, suddenly, "I forgot to tell you. Father is going to take mother and me to Greece this winter with him and the class."

Coleman replied at once. "Ah, indeed? That will be jolly."

"Yes. Won't it be charming?"

"I don't doubt it," he replied. His composure may have displeased her, for she glanced at him furtively and in a way that denoted surprise, perhaps.

"Oh, of course," she said in a glad voice. "It will be more fun. We expect to have a fine time. There is such a nice lot of boys going. Sometimes father chooses these dreadfully studious ones. But this time he acts as if he knew precisely how to make up a party."

He reached for her hand and grasped it vise-like. "Marjory," he breathed, passionately, "don't treat me so. Don't treat me——"

She wrenched her hand from him in regal indignation. "One or two rings make it uncomfortable for the hand that is grasped by an angry gentleman." She held her fingers and gazed as if she expected to find them mere debris. "I am sorry that you are not interested in the students rolling that man in the snow. It is the greatest scene our quiet life can afford."

He was regarding her as a judge faces a lying culprit. "I know," he said, after a pause. "Somebody has been telling you some stories. You have been hearing something about me."

"Some stories?" she enquired. "Some stories about you? What do you mean? Do you mean that I remember stories I may happen to hear about people?"

There was another pause and then Coleman's face flared red. He beat his hand violently upon a table. "Good God, Marjory! Don't make a fool of me. Don't make this kind of a fool of me, at any rate. Tell me what you mean. Explain——"

She laughed at him. "Explain? Really, your vocabulary is getting extensive, but it is dreadfully awkward to ask people to explain when there is nothing to explain."

He glanced at her. "I know as well as you do that your father is taking you to Greece in order to get rid of me."

"And do people have to go to Greece in order to get rid of you?" she asked, civilly. "I think you are getting excited."

"Marjory," he began, stormily.

She raised her hand. "Hush," she said, "there is somebody coming." A bell had rung. A maid entered the room. "Mr. Coke," she said. Marjory nodded. In the interval of waiting, Coleman gave the girl a glance that mingled despair with rage and pride. Then Coke burst with half-tamed rapture into the room. "Oh, Miss Wainwright," he almost shouted, "I can't tell you how glad I am. I just heard to-day you were going. Imagine it. It will be more—oh, how are you Coleman, how are you?"

Marjory welcomed the new-comer with a cordiality that might not have thrilled Coleman with pleasure. They took chairs that formed a triangle and one side of it vibrated with talk. Coke and Marjory engaged in a tumultuous conversation concerning the prospective trip to Greece. The Sunday editor, as remote as if the apex of his angle was the top of a hill, could only study the girl's clear profile. The youthful voices of the two others rang like bells. He did not scowl at Coke; he merely looked at him as if he gently disdained his mental calibre. In fact all the talk seemed to tire him; it was childish; as for him, he apparently found this babble almost insupportable.

"And, just think of the camel rides we'll have," cried Coke.

"Camel rides," repeated Coleman, dejectedly. "My dear Coke."

Finally he arose like an old man climbing from a sick bed. "Well, I am afraid I must go, Miss Wainwright." Then he said affectionately to Coke: "Good-bye, old boy. I hope you will have a good time."

Marjory walked with him to the door. He shook her hand in a friendly fashion. "Good-bye, Marjory," he said. "Perhaps it may happen that I shan't see you again before you start for Greece and so I had best bid you God-speed—or whatever the term is—now. You will have a charming time; Greece must be a delightful place. Really, I envy you, Marjory. And now my dear child"—his voice grew brotherly, filled with the patronage of generous fraternal love,— "although I may never see you again let me wish you fifty as happy years as this last one has been for me." He smiled frankly into her eyes; then dropping her hand, he went away.

Coke renewed his tempest of talk as Marjory turned toward him. But after a series of splendid eruptions, whose red fire illumined all of ancient and modern Greece, he too went away.

The professor was in his library apparently absorbed in a book when a tottering pale-faced woman appeared to him and, in her course toward a couch in a corner of the room, described almost a semi-circle. She flung herself face downward. A thick strand of hair swept over her shoulder. "Oh, my heart is broken! My heart is broken!"

The professor arose, grizzled and thrice-old with pain. He went to the couch, but he found himself a handless, fetless man. "My poor child," he said. "My poor child." He remained listening stupidly to her convulsive sobbing. A ghastly kind of solemnity came upon the room.

Suddenly the girl lifted herself and swept the strand of hair away from her face. She looked at the professor with the wide-open dilated eyes of one who still sleeps. "Father," she said in a hollow voice, "he don't love me. He don't love me. He don't love me at all. You were right, father." She began to laugh.

"Marjory," said the professor, trembling. "Be quiet, child. Be quiet."

"But," she said, "I thought he loved me—I was sure of it. But it don't— don't matter. I—I can't get over it. Women—women, the—but it don't matter."

"Marjory," said the professor. "Marjory, my poor daughter."

She did not heed his appeal, but continued in a dull whisper. "He was playing with me. He was—was—was flirting with me. He didn't care when I told him—I told him—I was going—going away." She turned her face wildly to the cushions again. Her young shoulders shook as if they might break. "Women— women—they always——"

Chapter 5

By a strange mishap of management, the train which bore Coleman back toward New York was fetched into an obscure side-track of some lonely region and there compelled to bide a change of fate. The engine wheezed and sneezed like a paused fat man. The lamps in the cars pervaded a stuffy odor of smoke and oil. Coleman examined his case and found only one cigar. Important brakemen proceeded rapidly along the aisles, and when they swung open the doors, a polar wind circled the legs of the passengers. "Well, now, what is all this for?" demanded Coleman, furiously. "I want to get back to New York."

The conductor replied with sarcasm, "Maybe you think I'm stuck on it? I ain't running the road. I'm running this train, and I run it according to orders." Amid the dismal comforts of the waiting cars, Coleman felt all the profound misery of the rebuffed true lover. He had been sentenced, he thought, to a penal servitude of the heart, as he watched the dusky, vague ribbons of smoke come from the lamps and felt to his knees the cold winds from the brakemen's busy flights. When the train started with a whistle and a jolt, he was elate as if in his abjection his beloved's hand had reached to him from the clouds.

When he had arrived in New York, a cab rattled him to an uptown hotel with speed. In the restaurant he first ordered a large bottle of champagne. The last of the wine he finished in sombre mood like an unbroken and defiant man who chews the straw that litters his prison house. During his dinner he was continually sending out messenger boys. He was arranging a poker party. Through a window he watched the beautiful moving life of upper Broadway at night, with its crowds and clanging cable cars and its electric signs, mammoth and glittering like the jewels of a giantess.

Word was brought to him that the poker players were arriving. He arose joyfully, leaving his cheese. In the broad hall, occupied mainly by miscellaneous people and actors, all deep in leather chairs, he found some of his friends waiting. They trooped up stairs to Coleman's rooms, where as a preliminary, Coleman began to hurl books and papers from the table to the floor. A boy came with drinks. Most of the men, in order to prepare for the game, removed their coats and cuffs and drew up the sleeves of their shirts. The electric globes shed a blinding light upon the table. The sound of clinking chips arose; the elected

280

banker spun the cards, careless and dexterous.

Later, during a pause of dealing, Coleman said: "Billie, what kind of a lad is that young Coke up at Washurst?" He addressed an old college friend.

'Oh, you mean the Sophomore Coke?" asked the friend. "Seems a decent sort of a fellow. I don't know. Why?"

"Well, who is he? Where does he come from? What do you know about him?"

"He's one of those Ohio Cokes—regular thing—father millionaire—used to be a barber—good old boy—why?"

"Nothin,'" said Coleman, looking at his cards. "I know the lad. I thought he was a good deal of an ass. I wondered who his people were."

"Oh, his people are all right—in one way. Father owns rolling mills. Do you raise it, Henry? Well, in order to make vice abhorrent to the young, I'm obliged to raise back."

"I'll see it," observed Coleman, slowly pushing forward two blue chips. Afterward he reached behind him and took another glass of wine.

To the others Coleman seemed to have something bitter upon his mind. He played poker quietly, steadfastly, and, without change of eye, following the mathematical religion of the game. Outside of the play he was savage, almost insupportable.

"What's the matter with you, Rufus?" said his old college friend. "Lost your job? Girl gone back on you? You're a hell of a host. We don't get anything but insults and drinks."

Late at night Coleman began to lose steadily. In the meantime he drank glass after glass of wine. Finally he made reckless bets on a mediocre hand and an opponent followed him thoughtfully bet by bet, undaunted, calm, absolutely without emotion. Coleman lost; he hurled down his cards. "Nobody but a damned fool would have seen that last raise on anything less than a full hand."

"Steady. Come off. What's wrong with you, Rufus?" cried his guests.

"You're not drunk, are you?" said his old college friend, puritanically.

"'Drunk'?" repeated Coleman.

"Oh, say," cried a man, "let's play cards. What's all this gabbling?"

It was when a grey, dirty light of dawn evaded the thick curtains and fought on the floor with the feebled electric glow that Coleman, in the midst of play, lurched his chest heavily upon the table. Some chips rattled to the floor. "I'll call you," he murmured, sleepily.

"Well," replied a man, sternly, "three kings."

The other players with difficulty extracted five cards from beneath Coleman's pillowed head. "Not a pair! Come, come, this won't do. Oh, let's stop playing. This is the rottenest game I ever sat in. Let's go home. Why don't you put him to bed, Billie?"

When Coleman awoke next morning, he looked back upon the poker game as something that had transpired in previous years. He dressed and went down to the grill-room. For his breakfast he ordered some eggs on toast and a pint of champagne. A privilege of liberty belonged to a certain Irish waiter, and this waiter looked at him, grinning. "Maybe you had a pretty lively time last night, Mr. Coleman?"

"Yes, Pat," answered Coleman, "I did. It was all because of an unrequited affection, Patrick." The man stood near, a napkin over his arm. Coleman went on impressively. "The ways of the modern lover are strange. Now, I, Patrick, am a modern lover, and when, yesterday, the dagger of disappointment was driven deep into my heart, I immediately played poker as hard as I could and incidentally got loaded. This is the modern point of view. I understand on good authority that in old times lovers used to languish. That is probably a lie, but at any rate we do not, in these times, languish to any great extent. We get drunk. Do you understand, Patrick?"

The waiter was used to a harangue at Coleman's breakfast time. He placed his hand over his mouth and giggled. "Yessir."

"Of course," continued Coleman, thoughtfully. "It might be pointed out by uneducated persons that it is difficult to maintain a high standard of drunkenness for the adequate length of time, but in the series of experiments which I am about to make I am sure I can easily prove them to be in the wrong."

"I am sure, sir," said the waiter, "the young ladies would not like to be hearing you talk this way."

"Yes; no doubt, no doubt. The young ladies have still quite medieval ideas. They don't understand. They still prefer lovers to languish."

"At any rate, sir, I don't see that your heart is sure enough broken. You seem to take it very easy."

"Broken!" cried Coleman. "Easy? Man, my heart is in fragments. Bring me another small bottle."

Chapter 6

ix weeks later, Coleman went to the office of the proprietor of the *Eclipse*. Coleman was one of those smooth-shaven old-young men who wear upon some occasions a singular air of temperance and purity. At these times, his features lost their quality of worldly shrewdness and endless suspicion and bloomed as the face of some innocent boy. It then would be hard to tell that he had ever encountered even such a crime as a lie or a cigarette. As he walked into the proprietor's office he was a perfect semblance of a fine, inexperienced youth. People usually concluded this change was due to a Turkish bath or some other expedient of recuperation, but it was due probably to the power of a physical characteristic.

"Boss in?" said Coleman.

"Yeh," said the secretary, jerking his thumb toward an inner door. In his private office, Sturgeon sat on the edge of the table dangling one leg and dreamily surveying the wall. As Coleman entered he looked up quickly. "Rufus," he cried, "you're just the man I wanted to see. I've got a scheme. A great scheme." He slid from the table and began to pace briskly to and fro, his hands deep in his trousers' pockets, his chin sunk in his collar, his light blue eyes afire with interest. "Now listen. This is immense. The *Eclipse* enlists a battalion of men to go to Cuba and fight the Spaniards under its own flag—the *Eclipse* flag. Collect trained officers from here and there—enlist every young devil we see—drill'em—best rifles—loads of ammunition—provisions—staff of doctors and nurses—a couple of dynamite guns—everything complete—best in the world. Now, isn't that great? What's the matter with that now? Eh? Eh? Isn't that great? It's great, isn't it? Eh? Why, my boy, we'll free——"

Coleman did not seem to ignite. "I have been arrested four or five times already on fool matters connected with the newspaper business," he observed, gloomily, "but I've never yet been hung. I think your scheme is a beauty."

Sturgeon paused in astonishment. "Why, what happens to be the matter with you? What are you kicking about?"

Coleman made a slow gesture. "I'm tired," he answered. "I need a vacation."

"Vacation!" cried Sturgeon. "Why don't you take one then?"

"That's what I've come to see you about. I've had a pretty heavy strain on

283

me for three years now, and I want to get a little rest."

"Well, who in thunder has been keeping you from it? It hasn't been me."

"I know it hasn't been you, but, of course, I wanted the paper to go and I wanted to have my share in its success, but now that everything is all right I think I might go away for a time if you don't mind."

"Mind!" exclaimed Sturgeon falling into his chair and reaching for his check book. "Where do you want to go? How long do you want to be gone? How much money do you want?"

"I don't want very much. And as for where I want to go, I thought I might like to go to Greece for a while."

Sturgeon had been writing a check. He poised his pen in the air and began to laugh. "That's a queer place to go for a rest. Why, the biggest war of modern times—a war that may involve all Europe—is likely to start there at any moment. You are not likely to get any rest in Greece."

"I know that," answered Coleman. "I know there is likely to be a war there. But I think that is exactly what would rest me. I would like to report the war."

"You are a queer bird," answered Sturgeon deeply fascinated with this new idea. He had apparently forgotten his vision of a Cuban volunteer battalion. "War correspondence is about the most original medium for a rest I ever heard of."

"Oh, it may seem funny, but really, any change will be good for me now. I've been whacking at this old Sunday edition until I'm sick of it, and sometimes I wish the *Eclipse* was in hell."

"That's all right," laughed the proprietor of the *Eclipse*. "But I still don't see how you are going to get any vacation out of a war that will upset the whole of Europe. But that's your affair. If you want to become the chief correspondent in the field in case of any such war, why, of course, I would be glad to have you. I couldn't get anybody better. But I don't see where your vacation comes in."

"I'll take care of that," answered Coleman. "When I take a vacation I want to take it my own way, and I think this will be a vacation because it will be different—don't you see—different?"

"No, I don't see any sense in it, but if you think that is the way that suits you, why, go ahead. How much money do you want?"

"I don't want much. Just enough to see me through nicely."

Sturgeon scribbled on his check book and then ripped a check from it. "Here's a thousand dollars. Will that do you to start with?"

"That's plenty."

"When do you want to start?"

"To-morrow."

"Oho," said Sturgeon. 'You're in a hurry." This impetuous manner of exit from business seemed to appeal to him. "To-morrow," he repeated smiling. In reality he was some kind of a poet using his millions romantically, spending wildly on a sentiment that might be with beauty or without beauty, according to the momentary vacillation. The vaguely-defined desperation in Coleman's last announcement appeared to delight him. He grinned and placed the points of his fingers together stretching out his legs in a careful attitude of indifference which might even mean disapproval. "To-morrow," he murmured teasingly.

"By jiminy," exclaimed Coleman, ignoring the other man's mood, "I'm sick of the whole business. I've got out a Sunday paper once a week for three years and I feel absolutely incapable of getting out another edition. It would be all right if we were running on ordinary lines, but when each issue is more or less of an attempt to beat the previous issue, it becomes rather wearing, you know. If I can't get a vacation now I take one later in a lunatic asylum."

"Why, I'm not objecting to your having a vacation. I'm simply marvelling at the kind of vacation you want to take. And 'to-morrow,' too, eh?"

"Well, it suits me," muttered Coleman, sulkily.

"Well, if it suits you, that's enough. Here's your check. Clear out now and don't let me see you again until you are thoroughly rested, even if it takes a year." He arose and stood smiling. He was mightily pleased with himself. He liked to perform in this way. He was almost seraphic as he thrust the check for a thousand dollars toward Coleman.

Then his manner changed abruptly. "Hold on a minute. I must think a little about this thing if you are going to manage the correspondence. Of course it will be a long and bloody war."

"You bet."

"The big chance is that all Europe will be dragged into it. Of course then you would have to come out of Greece and take up a better position—say Vienna."

"No, I wouldn't care to do that," said Coleman positively. "I just want to take care of the Greek end of it."

"It will be an idiotic way to take a vacation," observed Sturgeon.

"Well, it suits me," muttered Coleman again. "I tell you what it is—" he added suddenly. "I've got some private reasons—see?"

Sturgeon was radiant with joy. "Private reasons." He was charmed by the sombre pain in Coleman's eyes and his own ability to eject it. "Good. Go now and be blowed. I will cable final instruction to meet you in London. As soon as you get to Greece, cable me an account of the situation there and we will arrange our plans." He began to laugh. "Private reasons. Come out to dinner with me."

"I can't very well," said Coleman. "If I go to-morrow, I've got to pack——"

But here the real tyrant appeared, emerging suddenly from behind the curtain of sentiment, appearing like a red devil in a pantomine. "You can't?" snapped Sturgeon. "Nonsense——"

Chapter 7

S weeping out from between two remote, half-submerged dunes on which stood slender sentry lighthouses, the steamer began to roll with a gentle insinuating motion. Passengers in their staterooms saw at rhythmical intervals the spray racing fleetly past the portholes. The waves grappled hurriedly at the sides of the great flying steamer and boiled discomfited astern in a turmoil of green and white. From the tops of the enormous funnels streamed level masses of smoke which were immediately torn to nothing by the headlong wind. Meanwhile as the steamer rushed into the northeast, men in caps and ulsters comfortably paraded the decks and stewards arranged deck chairs for the reception of various women who were coming from their cabins with rugs.

In the smoking room, old voyagers were settling down comfortably while new voyagers were regarding them with a diffident respect. Among the passengers Coleman found a number of people whom he knew, including a wholesale wine merchant, a Chicago railway magnate and a New York millionaire. They lived practically in the smoking room. Necessity drove them from time to time to the salon, or to their berths. Once indeed the millionaire was absent from the group while penning a short note to his wife.

When the Irish coast was sighted Coleman came on deck to look at it. A tall young woman immediately halted in her walk until he had stepped up to her. "Well, of all ungallant men, Rufus Coleman, you are the star," she cried laughing and held out her hand.

"Awfully sorry, I'm sure," he murmured. "Been playing poker in the smoking room all voyage. Didn't have a look at the passenger list until just now. Why didn't you send me word?" These lies were told so modestly and sincerely that when the girl flashed her brilliant eyes full upon their author there was a mixture of admiration in the indignation.

"Send you a card? I don't believe you can read, Rufus, else you would have known I was to sail on this steamer. If I hadn't been ill until to-day you would have seen me in the salon. I open at the Folly Theatre next week. Dear ol' Lunnon, y'know."

"Of course, I knew you were going," said Coleman. "But I thought you were to go later. What do you open in?"

"Fly by Night. Come walk along with me. See those two old ladies? They've been watching for me like hawks ever since we left New York. They expected me to flirt with every man on board. But I've fooled them. I've been just as g-o-o-d. I had to be."

As the pair moved toward the stern, enormous and radiant green waves were crashing futilely after the steamer. Ireland showed a dreary coast line to the north. A wretched man who had crossed the Atlantic eighty-four times was declaiming to a group of novices. A venerable banker, bundled in rugs, was asleep in his deck chair.

"Well, Nora," said Coleman, "I hope you make a hit in London. You deserve it if anybody does. You've worked hard."

"Worked hard," cried the girl. "I should think so. Eight years ago I was in the rear row. Now I have the centre of the stage whenever I want it. I made Chalmers cut out that great scene in the second act between the queen and Rodolfo. The idea! Did he think I would stand that? And just because he was in love with Clara Trotwood, too."

Coleman was dreamy. "Remember when I was dramatic man for the *Gazette* and wrote the first notice?"

"Indeed, I do," answered the girl affectionately. "Indeed, I do, Rufus. Ah, that was a great lift. I believe that was the first thing that had an effect on old Oliver. Before that, he never would believe that I was any good. Give me your arm, Rufus. Let's parade before the two old women." Coleman glanced at her keenly. Her voice had trembled slightly. Her eyes were lustrous as if she were about to weep.

"Good heavens," he said. "You are the same old Nora Black. I thought you would be proud and 'aughty by this time."

"Not to my friends," she murmured. "Not to my friends. I'm always the same and I never forget, Rufus."

"Never forget what?" asked Coleman.

"If anybody does me a favour I never forget it as long as I live," she answered fervently.

"Oh, you mustn't be so sentimental, Nora. You remember that play you bought from little Ben Whipple just because he had once sent you some flowers in the old days when you were poor and happened to be sick. A sense of gratitude cost you over eight thousand dollars that time, didn't it?" Coleman laughed heartily.

"Oh, it wasn't the flowers at all," she interrupted seriously. "Of course Ben was always a nice boy, but then his play was worth a thousad dollars. That's all I gave him. I lost some more in trying to make it go. But it was too good. That was what was the matter. It was altogether too good for the public. I felt awfully sorry for poor little Ben."

"Too good?" sneered Coleman. "Too good? Too indifferently bad, you mean. My dear girl, you mustn't imagine that you know a good play. You don't, at all."

She paused abruptly and faced him. This regal creature was looking at him so sternly that Coleman felt awed for a moment as if he were in the presence of a great mind. "Do you mean to say that I'm not an artist?" she asked.

Coleman remained cool. "I've never been decorated for informing people of their own affairs," he observed, "but I should say that you were about as much of an artist as I am."

Frowning slightly, she reflected upon this reply. Then, of a sudden, she laughed. "There is no use in being angry with you, Rufus. You always were a hopeless scamp. But," she added, childishly wistful, "have you ever seen Fly by Night? Don't you think my dance in the second act is artistic?"

"No," said Coleman, "I haven't seen Fly by Night yet, but of course I know that you are the most beautiful dancer on the stage. Everybody knows that."

It seemed that her hand tightened on his arm. Her face was radiant. "There," she exclaimed. "Now you are forgiven. You are a nice boy, Rufus—sometimes."

When Miss Black went to her cabin, Coleman strolled into the smoking room. Every man there covertly or openly surveyed him. He dropped lazily into a chair at a table where the wine merchant, the Chicago railway king and the New York millionaire were playing cards. They made a noble pretense of not being aware of him. On the oilcloth top of the table the cards were snapped down, turn by turn.

Finally the wine merchant, without lifting his head to address a particular person, said: "New conquest."

Hailing a steward Coleman asked for a brandy and soda.

The millionaire said: "He's a sly cuss, anyhow." The railway man grinned. After an elaborate silence the wine merchant asked: "Know Miss Black long, Rufus?" Coleman looked scornfully at his friends. "What's wrong with you there, fellows, anyhow?" The Chicago man answered airily. "Oh, nothin'. Nothin', whatever."

At dinner in the crowded salon. Coleman was aware that more than one passenger glanced first at Nora Black and then at him, as if connecting them in some train of thought, moved to it by the narrow horizon of shipboard and by a sense of the mystery that surrounds the lives of the beauties of the stage. Near the captain's right hand sat the glowing and splendid Nora, exhibiting under the gaze of the persistent eyes of many meanings, a practiced and profound composure that to the populace was terrifying dignity.

Strolling toward the smoking room after dinner, Coleman met the New York millionaire, who seemed agitated. He took Coleman fraternally by the arm. "Say, old man, introduce me, won't you? I'm crazy to know her."

"Do you mean Miss Black?" asked Coleman. "Why, I don't know that I have a right. Of course, you know, she hasn't been meeting anybody aboard. I'll ask her, though—certainly."

"Thanks, old man, thanks. I'd be tickled to death. Come along and have a drink. When will you ask her?"

"Why, I don't know when I'll see her. To-morrow, I suppose——"

They had not been long in the smoking room, however, when the deck steward came with a card to Coleman. Upon it was written: 'Come for a stroll?" Everybody saw Coleman read this card and then look up and whisper to the deck steward. The deck steward bent his head and whispered discreetly in reply. There was an abrupt pause in the hum of conversation. The interest was acute.

Coleman leaned carelessly back in his chair, puffing at his cigar. He mingled calmly in a discussion of the comparative merits of certain trans-Atlantic lines. After a time he threw away his cigar and arose. Men nodded. "Didn't I tell you?" His studiously languid exit was made dramatic by the eagle-eyed attention of the smoking room.

On deck, he found Nora pacing to and fro. "You didn't hurry yourself," she said, as he joined her. The lights of Queenstown were twinkling. A warm wind, wet with the moisture of rain-stricken sod, was coming from the land.

"Why," said Coleman, "we've got all these duffers very much excited."

"Well, what do you care?" asked the girl. "You don't care, do you?"

"No, I don't care. Only it's rather absurd to be watched all the time." He said this precisely as if he abhorred being watched in this case. "Oh, by the way," he added. Then he paused for a moment. "Aw—a friend of mine—not a bad fellow—he asked me for an introduction. Of course, I told him I'd ask you."

She made a contemptuous gesture. "Oh, another Willie. Tell him no. Tell him to go home to his family. Tell him to run away."

"He isn't a bad fellow. He—" said Coleman diffidently, "he would probably be at the theatre every night in a box."

"Yes, and get drunk and throw a wine bottle on the stage instead of a bouquet. No," she declared positively, "I won't see him."

Coleman did not seem to be oppressed by this ultimatum. "Oh, all right. I promised him—that was all."

"Besides, are you in a great hurry to get rid of me?"

"Rid of you? Nonsense."

They walked in the shadows. "How long are you going to be in London, Rufus?" asked Nora softly.

"Who? I? Oh, I'm going right off to Greece. First train. There's going to be a war, you know."

"A war? Why, who is going to fight? The Greeks and the—the—the what?"

"The Turks. I'm going right over there."

"Why, that's dreadful, Rufus," said the girl, mournful and shocked. "You might get hurt or something." Presently she asked: "And aren't you going to be in London any time at all?"

"Oh," he answered puffing out his lips, "I may stop in London for three or four days on my way home. I'm not sure of it."

"And when will that be?"

"Oh, I can't tell. It may be in three or four months, or it may be a year from now. When the war stops."

There was a long silence as they walked up and down the swaying deck.

"Do you know," said Nora at last, "I like you, Rufus Coleman. I don't know any good reason for it, either, unless it is because you are such a brute. Now, when I was asking you if you were to be in London, you were perfectly detestable. You knew I was anxious."

"I—detestable?" cried Coleman, feigning amazement. "Why, what did I say?"

"It isn't so much what you said——" began Nora slowly. Then she suddenly changed her manner. "Oh, well, don't let's talk about it any more. It's too foolish. Only—you are a disagreeable person sometimes."

In the morning, as the vessel steamed up the Irish channel, Coleman was on deck, keeping furtive watch on the cabin stairs. After two hours of waiting, he scribbled a message on a card and sent it below. He received an answer that Miss Black had a headache, and felt too ill to come on deck. He went to the smoking room. The three card-players glanced up, grinning. "What's the matter?" asked the wine merchant. "You look angry." As a matter of fact,

Coleman had purposely wreathed his features in a pleasant and satisfied expression, so he was for a moment furious at the wine merchant.

"Confound the girl," he thought to himself. "She has succeeded in making all these beggars laugh at me." He mused that if he had another chance he would show her how disagreeable or detestable or scampish he was under some circumstances. He reflected ruefully that the complacence with which he had accepted the comradeship of the belle of the voyage might have been somewhat overdone. Perhaps he had got a little out of proportion. He was annoyed at the stares of the other men in the smoking room, who seemed now to be reading his discomfiture. As for Nora Black he thought of her wistfully and angrily as a superb woman whose company was honour and joy, a payment for any sacrifices.

"What's the matter?" persisted the wine merchant. "You look grumpy."

Coleman laughed. "Do I?"

At Liverpool, as the steamer was being slowly warped to the landing stage by some tugs, the passengers crowded the deck with their hand-bags. Adieus were falling as dead leaves fall from a great tree. The stewards were handling small hills of luggage marked with flaming red labels. The ship was firmly against the dock before Miss Black came from her cabin. Coleman was at the time gazing shoreward, but his three particular friends instantly nudged him. "What?" "There she is?" "Oh, Miss Black?" He composedly walked toward her. It was impossible to tell whether she saw him coming or whether it was accident, but at any rate she suddenly turned and moved toward the stern of the ship. Ten watchful gossips had noted Coleman's travel in her direction and more than half the passengers noted his defeat. He wheeled casually and returned to his three friends. They were colic-stricken with a coarse and yet silent merriment. Coleman was glad that the voyage was over.

After the polite business of an English custom house, the travellers passed out to the waiting train. A nimble little theatrical agent of some kind, sent from London, dashed forward to receive Miss Black. He had a first-class compartment engaged for her and he bundled her and her maid into it in an exuberance of enthusiasm and admiration. Coleman passing moodily along the line of coaches heard Nora's voice hailing him.

"Rufus." There she was, framed in a carriage window, beautiful and smiling brightly. Every nearby person turned to contemplate this vision.

"Oh," said Coleman advancing, "I thought I was not going to get a chance to say good-bye to you." He held out his hand. "Good-bye."

She pouted. "Why, there's plenty of room in this compartment." Seeing that some forty people were transfixed in observation of her, she moved a short way back. "Come on in this compartment, Rufus," she said.

"Thanks. I prefer to smoke," said Coleman. He went off abruptly.

On the way to London, he brooded in his corner on the two divergent emotions he had experienced when refusing her invitation. At Euston Station in London, he was directing a porter, who had his luggage, when he heard Nora speak at his shoulder. "Well, Rufus, you sulky boy," she said, "I shall be at the Cecil. If you have time, come and see me."

"Thanks, I'm sure, my dear Nora," answered Coleman effusively. "But honestly, I'm off for Greece."

A brougham was drawn up near them and the nimble little agent was waiting. The maid was directing the establishment of a mass of luggage on and in a four-wheeler cab. "Well, put me into my carriage, anyhow," said Nora. "You will have time for that."

Afterwards she addressed him from the dark interior. "Now, Rufus, you must come to see me the minute you strike London again—" She hesitated a moment, and then smiling gorgeously upon him, she said: "Brute!"

Chapter 8

As soon as Coleman had planted his belongings in a hotel he was bowled in a hansom briskly along the smoky Strand, through a dark city whose walls dripped like the walls of a cave and whose passages were only illuminated by flaring yellow and red signs.

Walkley the London correspondent of the *Eclipse*, whirled from his chair with a shout of joy and relief at sight of Coleman. "Cables," he cried. "Nothin' but cables! All the people in New York are writing cables to you. The wires groan with them. And we groan with them too. They come in here in bales. However, there is no reason why you should read them all. Many are similar in words and many more are similar in spirit. The sense of the whole thing is that you get to Greece quickly, taking with you immense sums of money and enormous powers over nations."

"Well, when does the row begin?"

"The most astute journalists in Europe have been predicting a general European smash-up every year since 1878," said Walkley, "and the prophets weep. The English are the only people who can pull off wars on schedule time, and they have to do it in odd corners of the globe. I fear the war business is getting tuckered. There is sorrow in the lodges of the lone wolves, the war correspondents. However, my boy, don't bury your face in your blanket. This Greek business looks very promising, very promising." He then began to proclaim trains and connections. "Dover, Calais, Paris, Brindisi, Corfu, Patras, Athens. That is your game. You are supposed to sky-rocket yourself over that route in the shortest possible time, but you would gain no time by starting before to-morrow, so you can cool your heels here in London until then. I wish I was going along."

Coleman returned to his hotel, a knight impatient and savage at being kept for a time out of the saddle. He went for a late supper to the grill room and as he was seated there alone, a party of four or five people came to occupy the table directly behind him. They talked a great deal even before they arrayed themselves at the table, and he at once recognised the voice of Nora Black. She was queening it, apparently, over a little band of awed masculine worshippers.

Either by accident or for some curious reason she took a chair back to back with Coleman's chair. Her sleeve of fragrant stuff almost touched his shoulder and he felt appealing to him seductively a perfume of orris root and violet. He was drinking bottled stout with his chop; he sat with a face of wood.

"Oh, the little lord?" Nora was crying to some slave. "Now, do you know, he won't do at all. He is too awfully charming. He sits and ruminates for fifteen minutes and then he pays me a lovely compliment. Then he ruminates for another fifteen minutes and cooks up another fine thing. It is too tiresome. Do you know what kind of man I like?" she asked softly and confidentially. And here she sank back in her chair until Coleman knew from the tingle that her head was but a few inches from his head. Her sleeve touched him. He turned more wooden under the spell of the orris root and violet. Her courtiers thought it all a graceful pose, but Coleman believed otherwise. Her voice sank to the liquid siren note of a succubus. "Do you know what kind of a man I like? Really like? I like a man that a woman can't bend in a thousand different ways in five minutes. He must have some steel in him. He obliges me to admire him the most when he remains stolid; stolid to me lures. Ah, that is the only kind of a man who can ever break a heart among us women of the world. His stolidity is not real; no; it is mere art, but it is a highly finished art and often enough we can't cut through it. Really we can't. And then we may actually come to—er—care for the man. Really we may. Isn't it funny?"

At the end Coleman arose and strolled out of the room, smoking a cigarette. He did not betray a sign. Before the door clashed softly behind him, Nora laughed a little defiantly, perhaps a little loudly. It made every man in the grill-room perk up his ears. As for her courtiers, they were entranced. In her description of the conquering man, she had easily contrived that each one of them wondered if she might not mean him. Each man was perfectly sure that he had plenty of steel in his composition and that seemed to be a main point.

Coleman delayed for a time in the smoking room and then went to his own quarters. In reality he was somewhat puzzled in his mind by a projection of the beauties of Nora Black upon his desire for Greece and Marjory. His thoughts formed a duality. Once he was on the point of sending his card to Nora Black's parlour, inasmuch as Greece was very distant and he could not start until the morrow. But he suspected that he was holding the interest of the actress because of his recent appearance of impregnable serenity in the presence of her fascinations. If he now sent his card, it was a form of surrender and he knew her to be one to take a merciless advantage. He would not make this tactical mistake. On the contrary he would go to bed and think of war.

In reality he found it easy to fasten his mind upon the prospective war. He regarded himself cynically in most affairs, but he could not be cynical of war, because had he seen none of it. His rejuvenated imagination began to thrill to the roll of battle, through his thought passing all the lightning in the pictures of Detaille, de Neuville and Morot; lashed battery horse roaring over bridges; grand cuirassiers dashing headlong against stolid invincible red-faced lines of German infantry; furious and bloody grapplings in the streets of little villages of northeastern France. There was one thing at least of which he could still feel the spirit of a debutante. In this matter of war he was not, too, unlike a young girl embarking upon her first season of opera. Walkely, the next morning, saw this mood sitting quaintly upon Coleman and cackled with astonishment and glee. Coleman's usual manner did not return until he detected Walkely's appreciation of his state and then he snubbed him according to the ritual of the Sunday editor

of the *New York Eclipse*. Parenthetically, it might be said that if Coleman now
recalled Nora Black to his mind at all, it was only to think of her for a moment
with ironical complacence. He had beaten her.

When the train drew out of the station, Coleman felt himself thrill. Was ever
fate less perverse? War and love—war and Marjory—were in conjunction—both
in Greece—and he could tilt with one lance at both gods. It was a great fine
game to play and no man was ever so blessed in vacations. He was smiling
continually to himself and sometimes actually on the point of talking aloud. This
was despite the presence in the compartment of two fellow passengers who
preserved in their uncomfortably rigid, icy and uncompromising manners many
of the more or less ridiculous traditions of the English first class carriage.
Coleman's fine humour betrayed him once into addressing one of these
passengers and the man responded simply with a wide look of incredulity, as if
he discovered that he was travelling in the same compartment with a zebu. It
turned Coleman suddenly to evil temper and he wanted to ask the man
questions concerning his education and his present mental condition: and so
until the train arrived at Dover, his ballooning soul was in danger of collapsing.
On the packet crossing the channel, too, he almost returned to the usual Rufus
Coleman since all the world was seasick and he could not get a cabin in which to
hide himself from it. However he reaped much consolation by ordering a bottle
of champagne and drinking it in sight of the people, which made them still more
seasick. From Calais to Brindisi really nothing met his disapproval save the
speed of the train, the conduct of some of the passengers, the quality of the food
served, the manners of the guards, the temperature of the carriages, the prices
charged and the length of the journey.

In time he passed as in a vision from wretched Brindisi to charming Corfu,
from Corfu to the little war-bitten city of Patras and from Patras by rail at the
speed of an ox-cart to Athens.

With a smile of grim content and surrounded in his carriage with all his
beautiful brown luggage, he swept through the dusty streets of the Greek
capital. Even as the vehicle arrived in a great terraced square in front of the
yellow palace, Greek recruits in garments representing many trades and many
characters were marching up cheering for Greece and the king. Officers stood
upon the little iron chairs in front of the cafes; all the urchins came running and
shouting; ladies waved their handkerchiefs from the balconies; the whole city
was vivified with a leaping and joyous enthusiasm. The Athenians—as
dragomen or otherwise—had preserved an ardor for their glorious traditions,
and it was as if that in the white dust which lifted from the plaza and floated
across the old-ivory face of the palace, there were the souls of the capable
soldiers of the past. Coleman was almost intoxicated with it. It seemed to
celebrate his own reasons, his reasons of love and ambition to conquer in love.

When the carriage arrived in front of the Hotel D'Angleterre, Coleman
found the servants of the place with more than one eye upon the scene in the
plaza, but they soon paid heed to the arrival of a gentleman with such an
amount of beautiful leather luggage, all marked boldly with the initials "R.C."
Coleman let them lead him and follow him and conduct him and use bad English
upon him without noting either their words, their salaams or their work. His
mind had quickly fixed upon the fact that here was the probable headquarters of
the Wainwright party and, with the rush of his western race fleeting through his

veins, he felt that he would choke and die if he did not learn of the Wainwrights in the first two minutes. It was a tragic venture to attempt to make the Levantine mind understand something off the course, that the new arrival's first thought was to establish a knowledge of the whereabouts of some of his friends rather than to swarm helter-skelter into that part of the hotel for which he was willing to pay rent. In fact he failed to thus impress them; failed in dark wrath, but, nevertheless, failed. At last he was simply forced to concede the travel of files of men up the broad, red-carpeted stair-case, each man being loaded with Coleman's luggage. The men in the hotel-bureau were then able to comprehend that the foreign gentleman might have something else on his mind. They raised their eye-brows languidly when he spoke of the Wainwright party in gentle surprise that he had not yet learned that they were gone some time. They were departed on some excursion. Where? Oh, really—it was almost laughable, indeed—they didn't know. Were they sure? Why, yes—it was almost laughable, indeed—they were quite sure. Where could the gentleman find out about them? Well, they—as they had explained—did not know, but—it was possible—the American minister might know. Where was he to be found? Oh, that was very simple. It was well known that the American minister had apartments in the hotel. Was he in? Ah, that they could not say.

So Coleman, rejoicing at his final emancipation and with the grime of travel still upon him, burst in somewhat violently upon the secretary of the Hon. Thomas M. Gordner of Nebraska, the United States minister to Greece. From his desk the secretary arose from behind an accidental bulwark of books and governmental pamphlets. "Yes, certainly. Mr. Gordner is in. If you would give me your card——"

Directly, Coleman was introduced into another room where a quiet man who was rolling a cigarette looked him frankly but carefully in the eye. "The Wainwrights?" said the minister immediately after the question. "Why, I myself am immensely concerned about them at present. I'm afraid they've gotten themselves into trouble.'

"Really?" said Coleman.

"Yes. That little professor is rather—er—stubborn; Isn't he? He wanted to make an expedition to Nikopolis and I explained to him all the possibilities of war and begged him to at least not take his wife and daughter with him."

"Daughter," murmured Coleman, as if in his sleep.

"But that little old man had a head like a stone and only laughed at me. Of course those villainous young students were only too delighted at a prospect of war, but it was a stupid and absurd thing for the man to take his wife and daughter there. They are up there now. I can't get a word from them or get a word to them."

Coleman had been choking. "Where is Nikopolis?" he asked.

The minister gazed suddenly in comprehension of the man before him. "Nikopolis is in Turkey," he answered gently.

Turkey at that time was believed to be a country of delay, corruption, turbulence and massacre. It meant everything. More than a half of the Christians of the world shuddered at the name of Turkey. Coleman's lips tightened and perhaps blanched, and his chin moved out strangely, once, twice, thrice. "How can I get to Nikopolis?" he said.

The minister smiled. "It would take you the better part of four days if you could get there, but as a matter of fact you can't get there at the present time. A Greek army and a Turkish army are looking at each other from the sides of the river at Arta—the river is there the frontier—and Nikopolis happens to be on the wrong side. You can't reach them. The forces at Arta will fight within three days. I know it. Of course I've notified our legation at Constantinople, but, with Turkish methods of communication, Nikopolis is about as far from Constantinople as New York is from Pekin."

Coleman arose. "They've run themselves into a nice mess," he said crossly. "Well, I'm a thousand times obliged to you, I'm sure."

The minister opened his eyes a trifle. "You are not going to try to reach them, are you?"

"Yes," answered Coleman, abstractedly. "I'm going to have a try at it. Friends of mine, you know——"

At the bureau of the hotel, the correspondent found several cables awaiting him from the alert office of the *New York Eclipse.* One of them read: "State Department gives out bad plight of Wainwright party lost somewhere; find them. *Eclipse.*" When Coleman perused the message he began to smile with seraphic bliss. Could fate have ever been less perverse.

Whereupon he whirled himself in Athens. And it was to the considerable astonishment of some Athenians. He discovered and instantly subsidised a young Englishman who, during his absence at the front, would act as correspondent for the *Eclipse* at the capital. He took unto himself a dragoman and then bought three horses and hired a groom at a speed that caused a little crowd at the horse dealer's place to come out upon the pavement and watch this surprising young man ride back toward his hotel. He had already driven his dragoman into a curious state of Oriental bewilderment and panic in which he could only lumber hastily and helplessly here and there, with his face in the meantime marked with agony. Coleman's own field equipment had been ordered by cable from New York to London, but it was necessary to buy much tinned meats, chocolate, coffee, candles, patent food, brandy, tobaccos, medicine and other things.

He went to bed that night feeling more placid. The train back to Patras was to start in the early morning, and he felt the satisfaction of a man who is at last about to start on his own great quest. Before he dropped off to slumber, he heard crowds cheering exultantly in the streets, and the cheering moved him as it had done in the morning. He felt that the celebration of the people was really an accompaniment to his primal reason, a reason of love and ambition to conquer in love—even as in the theatre, the music accompanies the hero in his progress. He arose once during the night to study a map of the Balkan peninsula and get nailed into his mind the exact position of Nikopolis. It was important.

Chapter 9

Coleman's dragoman aroused him in the blue before dawn. The correspondent arrayed himself in one of his new khaki suits—riding breeches and a tunic well marked with buttoned pockets—and accompanied by some of his beautiful brown luggage, they departed for the station.

The ride to Patras is a terror under ordinary circumstances. It begins in the early morning and ends in the twilight. To Coleman, having just come from Patras to Athens, this journey from Athens to Patras had all the exasperating elements of a forced recantation. Moreover, he had not come prepared to view with awe the ancient city of Corinth nor to view with admiration the limpid beauties of the gulf of that name with its olive grove shore. He was not stirred by Parnassus, a far-away snow-field high on the black shoulders of the mountains across the gulf. No; he wished to go to Nikopolis. He passed over the graves of an ancient race the gleam of whose mighty minds shot, hardly dimmed, through the clouding ages. No; he wished to go to Nikopolis. The train went at a snail's pace, and if Coleman had an interest it was in the people who lined the route and cheered the soldiers on the train. In Coleman's compartment there was a greasy person who spoke a little English. He explained that he was a poet, a poet who now wrote of nothing but war. When a man is in pursuit of his love and success is known to be at least remote, it often relieves his strain if he is deeply bored from time to time.

The train was really obliged to arrive finally at Patras even if it was a tortoise, and when this happened, a hotel runner appeared, who lied for the benefit of the hotel in saying that there was no boat over to Mesalonghi that night. When, all too late, Coleman discovered the truth of the matter his wretched dragoman came in for a period of infamy and suffering. However, while strolling in the plaza at Patras, amid newsboys from every side, by rumour and truth, Coleman learned things to his advantage. A Greek fleet was bombarding Prevasa. Prevasa was near Nikopolis. The opposing armies at Arta were engaged, principally in an artillery duel. Arta was on the road from Nikopolis into Greece. Hearing this news in the sunlit square made him betray no weakness, but in the darkness of his room at the hotel, he seemed to behold Marjory encircled by insurmountable walls of flame. He could look out of his window into the black night of the north and feel every ounce of a hideous

297

circumstance. It appalled him; here was no power of calling up a score of reporters and sending them scampering to accomplish everything. He even might as well have been without a tongue as far as it could serve him in goodly speech. He was alone, confronting the black ominous Turkish north behind which were the deadly flames; behind the flames was Marjory. It worked upon him until he felt obliged to call in his dragoman, and then, seated upon the edge of his bed and waving his pipe eloquently, he described the plight of some very dear friends who were cut off at Nikopolis in Epirus. Some of his talk was almost wistful in its wish for sympathy from his servant, but at the end he bade the dragoman understand that he, Coleman, was going to their rescue, and he defiantly asked the hireling if he was prepared to go with him. But he did not know the Greek nature. In two minutes the dragoman was weeping tears of enthusiasm, and, for these tears, Coleman was over-grateful, because he had not been told that any of the more crude forms of sentiment arouse the common Greek to the highest pitch, but sometimes, when it comes to what the Americans call a "show down," when he gets backed toward his last corner with a solitary privilege of dying for these sentiments, perhaps he does not always exhibit those talents which are supposed to be possessed by the bulldog. He often then, goes into the cafes and takes it all out in oration, like any common Parisian.

In the morning a steamer carried them across the strait and landed them near Mesalonghi at the foot of the railroad that leads to Agrinion. At Agrinion Coleman at last began to feel that he was nearing his goal. There were plenty of soldiers in the town, who received with delight and applause this gentleman in the distinguished-looking khaki clothes with his revolver and his field glasses and his canteen and his dragoman. The dragoman lied, of course, and vociferated that the gentleman in the distinguished-looking khaki clothes was an English soldier of reputation, who had, naturally, come to help the cross in its fight against the crescent. He also said that his master had three superb horses coming from Athens in charge of a groom, and was undoubtedly going to join the cavalry. Whereupon the soldiers wished to embrace and kiss the gentleman in the distinguished-looking khaki clothes.

There was more or less a scuffle. Coleman would have taken to kicking and punching, but he found that by a series of elusive movements he could dodge the demonstrations of affection without losing his popularity. Escorted by the soldiers, citizens, children and dogs, he went to the diligence which was to take him and others the next stage of the journey. As the diligence proceeded, Coleman's mind suffered another little inroad of ill-fate as to the success of his expedition. In the first place it appeared foolish to expect that this diligence would ever arrive anywhere. Moreover, the accommodations were about equal to what one would endure if one undertook to sleep for a night in a tree. Then there was a devil-dog, a little black-and-tan terrier in a blanket gorgeous and belled, whose duty it was to stand on the top of the coach and bark incessantly to keep the driver fully aroused to the enormity of his occupation. To have this cur silenced either by strangulation or ordinary clubbing, Coleman struggled with his dragoman as Jacob struggled with the angel, but in the first place, the dragoman was a Greek whose tongue could go quite drunk, a Greek who became a slave to the heralding and establishment of one certain fact, or lie, and now he was engaged in describing to every village and to all the country side the prowess of the gentleman in the distinguished-looking khaki clothes. It was the general absurdity of this advance to the frontier and the fighting, to the crucial place where he was resolved to make an attempt to rescue his sweetheart; it was this ridiculous aspect that caused to come to Coleman a premonition of failure. No knight ever went out to recover a lost love in such a diligence and with such a devil-dog, tinkling his little bells and yelping insanely to keep the driver awake.

After night-fall they arrived at a town on the southern coast of the Gulf of Arta and the goaded dragoman was thrust forth from the little inn into the street to find the first possible means of getting on to Arta. He returned at last to tremulously say that there was no single chance of starting for Arta that night. Whereupon he was again thrust into the street with orders, strict orders. In due time, Coleman spread his rugs upon the floor of his little room and thought himself almost asleep, when the dragoman entered with a really intelligent man who, for some reason, had agreed to consort with him in the business of getting the stranger off to Arta. They announced that there was a brigantine about to sail with a load of soldiers for a little port near Arta, and if Coleman hurried he could catch it, permission from an officer having already been obtained. He was up at once, and the dragoman and the unaccountably intelligent person hastily gathered his chattels. Stepping out into a black street and moving to the edge of black water and embarking in a black boat filled with soldiers whose rifles dimly shone, was as impressive to Coleman as if, really, it had been the first start. He had endured many starts, it was true, but the latest one always touched him as being conclusive.

There were no lights on the brigantine and the men swung precariously up her sides to the deck which was already occupied by a babbling multitude. The dragoman judiciously found a place for his master where during the night the latter had to move quickly everytime the tiller was shifted to starboard. The craft raised her shadowy sails and swung slowly off into the deep gloom. Forward, some of the soldiers began to sing weird minor melodies. Coleman, enveloped in his rugs, smoked three or four cigars. He was content and miserable, lying there, hearing these melodies which defined to him his own affairs.

At dawn they were at the little port. First, in the carmine and grey tints from a sleepy sun, they could see little mobs of soldiers working amid boxes of stores. And then from the back in some dun and green hills sounded a deep-throated thunder of artillery. An officer gave Coleman and his dragoman positions in one of the first boats, but of course it could not be done without an almost endless amount of palaver. Eventually they landed with their traps. Coleman felt through the sole of his boot his foot upon the shore. He was within striking distance.

But here it was smitten into the head of Coleman's servant to turn into the most inefficient dragoman, probably in the entire East. Coleman discerned it immediately, before any blunder could tell him. He at first thought that it was the voices of the guns which had made a chilly inside for the man, but when he reflected upon the incompetency, or childish courier's falsity, at Patras and his discernible lack of sense from Agrinion onward, he felt that the fault was elemental in his nature. It was a mere basic inability to front novel situations which was somehow in the dragoman; he retrated from everything difficult in a smoke of gibberish and gesticulation. Coleman glared at him with the hatred that sometimes ensues when breed meets breed, but he saw that this man was indeed a golden link in his possible success. This man connected him with Greece and its language. If he destroyed him he delayed what was now his main desire in life. However, this truth did not prevent him from addressing the man in elegant speech.

The two little men who were induced to carry Coleman's luggage as far as the Greek camp were really procured by the correspondent himself, who pantomined vigourously and with unmistakable vividness. Followed by his dragoman and the two little men, he strode off along a road which led straight as a stick to where the guns were at intervals booming. Meanwhile the dragoman and the two little men talked, talked, talked.—Coleman was silent, puffing his cigar and reflecting upon the odd things which happen to chivalry in the modern age.

He knew of many men who would have been astonished if they could have seen into his mind at that time, and he knew of many more men who would have laughed if they had the same privilege of sight. He made no attempt to conceal from himself that the whole thing was romantic, romantic despite the little tinkling dog, the decrepit diligence, the palavering natives, the super-idiotic dragoman. It was fine. It was from another age and even the actors could not deface the purity of the picture. However it was true that upon the brigantine the previous night he had unaccountably wetted all his available matches. This was momentous, important, cruel truth, but Coleman, after all, was taking—as well as he could forget—a solemn and knightly joy of this adventure and there were as many portraits of his lady envisioning before him as ever held the heart of an armour-encased young gentleman of medieval poetry. If he had been travelling in this region as an ordinary tourist, he would have been apparent mainly for his lofty impatience over trifles, but now there was in him a positive assertion of direction which was undoubtedly one of the reasons for the despair of the accomplished dragoman.

Before them the country slowly opened and opened, the straight white road always piercing it like a lanceshaft. Soon they could see black masses of men marking the green knolls. The artillery thundered loudly and now vibrated augustly through the air. Coleman quickened his pace, to the despair of the little men carrying the traps. They finally came up with one of these black bodies of men and found it to be composed of a considerable number of soldiers who were idly watching some hospital people bury a dead Turk. The dragoman at once dashed forward to peer through the throng and see the face of the corpse. Then he came and supplicated Coleman as if he were hawking him to look at a relic and Coleman moved by a strong, mysterious impulse, went forward to look at the poor little clay-coloured body. At that moment a snake ran out from a tuft of grass at his feet and wriggled wildly over the sod. The dragoman shrieked, of course, but one of the soldiers put his heel upon the head of the reptile and it flung itself into the agonising knot of death. Then the whole crowd pow-wowed, turning from the dead man to the dead snake. Coleman signaled his contingent and proceeded along the road.

This incident, this paragraph, had seemed a strange introduction to war. The snake, the dead man, the entire sketch, made him shudder of itself, but more than anything he felt an uncanny symbolism. It was no doubt a mere occurrence; nothing but an occurrence; but inasmuch as all the detail of this daily life associated itself with Marjory, he felt a different horror. He had thought of the little devil-dog and Marjory in an interwoven way. Supposing Marjory had been riding in the diligence with the devil-dog-a-top? What would she have said? Of her fund of expressions, a fund uncountable, which would she have innocently projected against the background of the Greek hills? Would it have smitten her nerves badly or would she have laughed? And supposing Marjory could have seen him in his new khaki clothes cursing his dragoman as he listened to the devil-dog?

And now he interwove his memory of Marjory with a dead man and with a snake in the throes of the end of life. They crossed, intersected, tangled, these two thoughts. He perceived it clearly; the incongruity of it. He academically reflected upon the mysteries of the human mind, this homeless machine which lives here and then there and often lives in two or three opposing places at the same instant. He decided that the incident of the snake and the dead man had no more meaning than the greater number of the things which happen to us in our daily lives. Nevertheless it bore upon him.

On a spread of plain they saw a force drawn up in a long line. It was a flagrant inky streak on the verdant prairie. From somewhere near it sounded the timed reverberations of guns. The brisk walk of the next ten minutes was actually exciting to Coleman. He could not but reflect that those guns were being fired with serious purpose at certain human bodies much like his own.

As they drew nearer they saw that the inky streak was composed of cavalry, the troopers standing at their bridles. The sunlight flicked upon their bright weapons. Now the dragoman developed in one of his extraordinary directions. He announced forsooth that an intimate friend was a captain of cavalry in this command. Coleman at first thought that this was some kind of mysterious lie, but when he arrived where they could hear the stamping of hoofs, the clank of weapons, and the murmur of men, behold, a most dashing young officer gave a shout of joy and he and the dragoman hurled themselves into a mad embrace. After this first ecstacy was over, the dragoman bethought him of his employer, and looking toward Coleman hastily explained him to the officer. The latter, it appeared, was very affable indeed. Much had happened. The Greeks and the Turks had been fighting over a shallow part of the river nearly opposite this point and the Greeks had driven back the Turks and succeeded in throwing a bridge of casks and planking across the stream. It was now the duty and the delight of this force of cavalry to cross the bridge and, passing the little force of covering Greek infantry, to proceed into Turkey until they came in touch with the enemy.

Coleman's eyes dilated. Was ever fate less perverse? Partly in wretched French to the officer and partly in idiomatic English to the dragoman, he proclaimed his fiery desire to accompany the expedition. The officer immediately beamed upon him. In fact, he was delighted. The dragoman had naturally told him many falsehoods concerning Coleman, incidentally referring to himself more as a philanthropic guardian and valuable friend of the correspondent than as a plain, unvarnished dragoman with an exceedingly good eye for the financial possibilities of his position.

Coleman wanted to ask his servant if there was any chance of the scout taking them near Nikopolis, but he delayed being informed upon this point until such time as he could find out, secretly, for himself. To ask the dragoman would be mere stupid questioning which would surely make the animal shy. He tried to be content that fate had given him this early opportunity of dealing with a medieval situation with some show of proper form; that is to say, armed, a-horseback, and in danger. Then he could feel that to the gods of the game he was not laughable, as when he rode to rescue his love in a diligence with a devil-dog yelping a-top.

With some flourish, the young captain presented him to the major who commanded the cavalry. This officer stood with his legs wide apart, eating the rind of a fresh lemon and talking betimes to some of his officers. The major also beamed upon Coleman when the captain explained that the gentleman in the distinguished-looking khaki clothes wished to accompany the expedition. He at once said that he would provide two troop horses for Coleman and the dragoman. Coleman thanked fate for his behaviour and his satisfaction was not without a vestige of surprise. At that time he judged it to be a remarkable amiability of individuals, but in later years he came to believe in certain laws which he deemed existent solely for the benefit of war correspondents. In the minds of governments, war offices and generals they have no function save one of disturbance, but Coleman deemed it proven that the common men, and many uncommon men, when they go away to the fighting ground, out of the sight, out of the hearing of the world known to them, and are eager to perform feats of war in this new place, they feel an absolute longing for a spectator. It is indeed the veritable coronation of this world. There is not too much vanity of the street in this desire of men to have some disinterested fellows perceive their deeds. It is merely that a man doing his best in the middle of a sea of war, longs to have people see him doing his best. This feeling is often notably serious if, in peace, a man has done his worst, or part of his worst. Coleman believed that, above everybody, young, proud and brave subalterns had this itch, but it existed, truly enough, from lieutenants to colonels. None wanted to conceal from his left hand that his right hand was performing a manly and valiant thing, although there might be times when an application of the principle would be immensely convenient. The war correspondent arises, then, to become a sort of a cheap telescope for the people at home; further still, there have been fights where the eyes of a solitary man were the eyes of the world; one spectator, whose business it was to transfer, according to his ability, his visual impressions to other minds.

Coleman and his servant were conducted to two saddled troop horses, and beside them, waited decently in the rear of the ranks. The uniform of the troopers was of plain, dark green cloth and they were well and sensibly equipped. The mounts, however, had in no way been picked; there were little horses and big horses, fat horses and thin horses. They looked the result of a wild conscription. Coleman noted the faces of the troopers, and they were calm enough save when a man betrayed himself by perhaps a disproportionate angry jerk at the bridle of his restive horse.

The major, artistically drooping his cloak from his left shoulder and tenderly and musingly fingering his long yellow moustache, rode slowly to the middle of the line and wheeled his horse to face his men. A bugle called attention, and then he addressed them in a loud and rapid speech, which did not seem to have an end. Coleman imagined that the major was paying tribute to the Greek tradition of the power of oratory. Again the trumpet rang out, and this parade front swung off into column formation. Then Coleman and the dragoman trotted at the tail of the squadron, restraining with difficulty their horses, who could not understand their new places in the procession, and worked feverishly to regain what they considered their positions in life.

The column jangled musically over the sod, passing between two hills on one of which a Greek light battery was posted. Its men climbed to the tops of their intrenchments to witness the going of the cavalry. Then the column curved along over ditch and through hedge to the shallows of the river. Across this narrow stream was Turkey. Turkey, however, presented nothing to the eye but a muddy bank with fringes of trees back of it. It seemed to be a great plain with sparse collections of foliage marking it, whereas the Greek side presented in the main a vista of high, gaunt rocks. Perhaps one of the first effects of war upon the mind is a new recognition and fear of the circumscribed ability of the eye, making all landscape seem inscrutable. The cavalry drew up in platoon formation on their own bank of the stream and waited. If Coleman had known anything of war, he would have known, from appearances, that there was nothing in the immediate vicinity to cause heart-jumping, but as a matter of truth he was deeply moved and wondered what was hidden, what was veiled by those trees. Moreover, the squadrons resembled an old picture of a body of horse awaiting Napoleon's order to charge. In the meantime his mount fumed at the bit, plunging to get back to the ranks. The sky was without a cloud, and the sun rays swept down upon them. Sometimes Coleman was on the verge of addressing the dragoman, according to his anxiety, but in the end he simply told him to go to the river and fill the canteens.

At last an order came, and the first troop moved with muffled tumult across the bridge. Coleman and his dragoman followed the last troop. The horses scrambled up the muddy bank much as if they were merely breaking out of a pasture, but probably all the men felt a sudden tightening of their muscles. Coleman, in his excitement, felt, more than he saw, glossy horse flanks, green-clothed men chumping in their saddles, banging sabres and canteens, and carbines slanted in line.

There were some Greek infantry in a trench. They were heavily overcoated, despite the heat, and some were engaged in eating loaves of round, thick bread. They called out lustily as the cavalry passed them. The troopers smiled slowly, somewhat proudly in response.

Presently there was another halt and Coleman saw the major trotting busily here and there, while troop commanders rode out to meet him. Spreading groups of scouts and flankers moved off and disappeared. Their dashing young officer friend cantered past them with his troop at his heels. He waved a joyful good-bye. It was the doings of cavalry in actual service, horsemen fanning out in all forward directions. There were two troops held in reserve, and as they jangled ahead at a foot pace, Coleman and his dragoman followed them.

The dragoman was now moved to erect many reasons for an immediate return. It was plain that he had no stomach at all for this business, and that he wished himself safely back on the other side of the river. Coleman looked at him askance. When these men talked together Coleman might as well have been a polar bear for all he understood of it. When he saw the trepidation of his dragoman, he did not know what it foreboded. In this situation it was not for him to say that the dragoman's fears were founded on nothing. And ever the dragoman raised his reasons for a retreat. Coleman spoke to himself. "I am just a trifle rattled," he said to his heart, and after he had communed for a time upon the duty of steadiness, he addressed the dragoman in cool language. "Now, my persuasive friend, just quit all that, because business is business, and it may be rather annoying business, but you will have to go through with it." Long afterward, when ruminating over the feelings of that morning, he saw with some astonishment that there was not a single thing within sound or sight to cause a rational being any quaking. He was simply riding with some soldiers over a vast tree-dotted prairie.

Presently the commanding officer turned in his saddle and told the dragoman that he was going to ride forward with his orderly to where he could see the flanking parties and the scouts, and courteously, with the manner of a gentleman entertaining two guests, he asked if the civilians cared to accompany him. The dragoman would not have passed this question correctly on to Coleman if he had thought he could have avoided it, but, with both men regarding him, he considered that a lie probably meant instant detection. He spoke almost the truth, contenting himself with merely communicating to Coleman in a subtle way his sense that a ride forward with the commanding officer and his orderly would be depressing and dangerous occupation. But Coleman immediately accepted the invitation mainly because it was the invitation of the major, and in war it is a brave man who can refuse the invitation of a commanding officer. The little party of four trotted away from the reserves, curving in single file about the water-holes. In time they arrived at where the plain lacked trees and was one great green lake of grass; grass and scrubs. On this expanse they could see the Greek horsemen riding, mainly appearing as little black dots. Far to the left there was a squad said to be composed of only twenty troopers, but in the distance their black mass seemed to be a regiment.

As the officer and his guests advanced they came in view of what one may call the shore of the plain. The rise of ground was heavily clad with trees, and over the tops of them appeared the cupola and part of the walls of a large white house, and there were glimpses of huts near it as if a village was marked. The black specks seemed to be almost to it. The major galloped forward and the others followed at his pace. The house grew larger and larger and they came nearly to the advance scouts who they could now see were not quite close to the village. There had been a deception of the eye precisely as occurs at sea. Herds of unguarded sheep drifted over the plain and little ownerless horses, still cruelly hobbled, leaped painfully away, frightened, as if they understood that an anarchy had come upon them. The party rode until they were very nearly up with the scouts, and then from low down at the very edge of the plain there came a long rattling noise which endured as if some kind of grinding machine had been put in motion. Smoke arose, faintly marking the position of an intrenchment. Sometimes a swift spitting could be heard from the air over the party.

It was Coleman's fortune to think at first that the Turks were not firing in his direction, but as soon as he heard the weird voices in the air he knew that war was upon him. But it was plain that the range was almost excessive, plain even to his ignorance. The major looked at him and laughed; he found no difficulty in smiling in response. If this was war, it could be withstood somehow. He could not at this time understand what a mere trifle was the present incident. He felt upon his cheek a little breeze which was moving the grass-blades. He had tied his canteen in a wrong place on the saddle and every time the horse moved quickly the canteen banged the correspondent, to his annoyance and distress, forcibly on the knee. He had forgotten about his dragoman, but happening to look upon that faithful servitor, he saw him gone white with horror. A bullet at that moment twanged near his head and the slave to fear ducked in a spasm. Coleman called the orderly's attention and they both laughed discreetly. They made no pretension of being heroes, but they saw plainly that they were better than this man.

Coleman said to him: "How far is it now to Nikopolis?" The dragoman replied only with a look of agonized impatience.

But of course there was no going to Nikopolis that day. The officer had advanced his men as far as was intended by his superiors, and presently they were all recalled and trotted back to the bridge. They crossed it to their old camp.

An important part of Coleman's traps was back with his Athenian horses and their groom, but with his present equipment he could at least lie smoking on his blankets and watch the dragoman prepare food. But he reflected that for that day he had only attained the simple discovery that the approach to Nikopolis was surrounded with difficulties.

Chapter 10

The same afternoon Coleman and the dragoman rode up to Arta on their borrowed troop horses. The correspondent first went to the telegraph office and found there the usual number of despairing clerks. They were outraged when they found he was going to send messages and thought it preposterous that he insisted upon learning if there were any in the office for him. They had trouble enough with endless official communications without being hounded about private affairs by a confident young man in khaki. But Coleman at last unearthed six cablegrams which collectively said that the *Eclipse* wondered why they did not hear from him, that Walkley had been relieved from duty in London and sent to join the army of the crown prince, that young Point, the artist, had been shipped to Greece, that if he, Coleman, succeeded in finding the Wainwright party the paper was prepared to make a tremendous uproar of a celebration over it and, finally, the paper wondered twice more why they did not hear from him.

When Coleman went forth to enquire if anybody knew of the whereabouts of the Wainwright party he thought first of his fellow correspondents. He found most of them in a cafe where was to be had about the only food in the soldier-laden town. It was a slothful den where even an ordinary boiled egg could be made unpalatable. Such a common matter as the salt men watched with greed and suspicion as if they were always about to grab it from each other. The proprietor, in a dirty shirt, could always be heard whining, evidently telling the world that he was being abused, but he had spirit enough remaining to charge three prices for everything with an almost Jewish fluency.

The correspondents consoled themselves largely upon black bread and the native wines. Also there were certain little oiled fishes, and some green odds and ends for salads. The correspondents were practically all Englishmen. Some of them were veterans of journalism in the Sudan, in India, in South Africa; and there were others who knew as much of war as they could learn by sitting at a desk and editing the London stock reports. Some were on their own hook; some had horses and dragomen and some had neither the one nor the other; many knew how to write and a few had it yet to learn. The thing in common was a spirit of adventure which found pleasure in the extraordinary business of seeing how men kill each other.

They were talking of an artillery duel which had been fought the previous day between the Greek batteries above the town and the Turkish batteries across the river. Coleman took seat at one of the long tables, and the astute dragoman got somebody in the street to hold the horses in order that he might be present at any feasting.

One of the experienced correspondents was remarking that the fire of the Greek batteries in the engagement had been the finest artillery practice of the century. He spoke a little loudly, perhaps, in the wistful hope that some of the Greek officers would understand enough English to follow his meaning, for it is always good for a correspondent to admire the prowess on his own side of the battlefield. After a time Coleman spoke in a lull, and describing the supposed misfortunes of the Wainwright party, asked if any one had news of them. The correspondents were surprised; they had none of them heard even of the existence of a Wainwright party. Also none of them seemed to care exceedingly. The conversation soon changed to a discussion of the probable result of the general Greek advance announced for the morrow.

Coleman silently commented that this remarkable appearance of indifference to the mishap of the Wainwrights, a little party, a single group, was a better definition of a real condition of war than that bit of long-range musketry of the morning. He took a certain despatch out of his pocket and again read it. "Find Wainwright party at all hazards; much talk here; success means red fire by ton. *Eclipse*." It was an important matter. He could imagine how the American people, vibrating for years to stories of the cruelty of the Turk, would tremble— indeed, was now trembling—while the newspapers howled out the dire possibilities. He saw all the kinds of people, from those who would read the Wainwright chapters from day to day as a sort of sensational novel, to those who would work up a gentle sympathy for the woe of others around the table in the evenings. He saw barkeepers and policemen taking a high gallery thrill out of this kind of romance. He saw even the emotion among American colleges over the tragedy of a professor and some students. It certainly was a big affair. Marjory of course was everything in one way, but that, to the world, was not a big affair. It was the romance of the Wainwright party in its simplicity that to the American world was arousing great sensation; one that in the old days would have made his heart leap like a colt.

Still, when batteries had fought each other savagely, and horse, foot and guns were now about to make a general advance, it was difficult, he could see, to stir men to think and feel out of the present zone of action; to adopt for a time in fact the thoughts and feelings of the other side of the world. It made Coleman dejected as he saw clearly that the task was wholly on his own shoulders.

Of course they were men who when at home manifested the most gentle and wide-reaching feelings; most of them could not by any possibility have slapped a kitten merely for the prank and yet all of them who had seen an unknown man shot through the head in battle had little more to think of it than if the man had been a rag-baby. Tender they might be; poets they might be; but they were all horned with a provisional, temporary, but absolutely essential callouse which was formed by their existence amid war with its quality of making them always think of the sights and sounds concealed in their own direct future.

They had been simply polite. "Yes?" said one to Coleman. "How many

people in the party? Are they all Americans? Oh, I suppose it will be quite right.
Your minister in Constantinople will arrange that easily. Where did you say? At
Nikopolis? Well, we conclude that the Turks will make no stand between here
and Pentepigadia. In that case your Nikopolis will be uncovered unless the
garrison at Prevasa intervenes. That garrison at Prevasa, by the way, may make
a deal of trouble. Remember Plevna."

"Exactly how far is it to Nikopolis?" asked Coleman.

"Oh, I think it is about thirty kilometers," replied the others. "There is a
good military road as soon as you cross the Louros river. I've got the map of the
Austrian general staff. Would you like to look at it?"

Coleman studied the map, speeding with his eye rapidly to and fro between
Arta and Nikopolis. To him it was merely a brown lithograph of mystery, but he
could study the distances.

He had received a cordial invitation from the commander of the cavalry to
go with him for another ride into Turkey, and he inclined to believe that his
project would be furthered if he stuck close to the cavalry. So he rode back to the
cavalry camp and went peacefully to sleep on the sod. He awoke in the morning
with chattering teeth to find his dragoman saying that the major had
unaccountably withdrawn his loan of the two troop horses. Coleman of course
immediately said to himself that the dragoman was lying again in order to
prevent another expedition into ominous Turkey, but after all if the commander
of the cavalry had suddenly turned the light of his favour from the correspondent it was only a proceeding consistent with the nature which Coleman
now thought he was beginning to discern, a nature which can never think twice
in the same place, a gaseous mind which drifts, dissolves, combines, vanishes
with the ability of an aerial thing until the man of the north feels that when he
clutches it with full knowledge of his senses he is only the victim of his ardent
imagination. It is the difference in standards, in creeds, which is the more
luminous when men call out that they are all alike.

So Coleman and his dragoman loaded their traps and moved out to again
invade Turkey. It was not yet clear daylight, but they felt that they might well
start early since they were no longer mounted men.

On the way to the bridge, the dragoman, although he was curiously in love
with his forty francs a day and his opportunities, ventured a stout protest, based
apparently upon the fact that after all this foreigner, four days out from Athens
was somewhat at his mercy. "Meester Coleman," he said, stopping suddenly, "I
think we make no good if we go there. Much better we wait Arta for our horse.
Much better. I think this no good. There is coming one big fight and I think
much better we go stay Arta. Much better."

"Oh, come off," said Coleman. And in clear language he began to labour
with the man. "Look here, now, if you think you are engaged in steering a
bunch of wooden-headed guys about the Acropolis, my dear partner of my joys
and sorrows, you are extremely mistaken. As a matter of fact you are now the
dragoman of a war correspondent and you were engaged and are paid to be one.
It becomes necessary that you make good. Make good, do you understand? I'm
not out here to be buncoed by this sort of game." He continued indefinitely in
this strain and at intervals he asked sharply: "Do you understand?"

Perhaps the dragoman was dumbfounded that the laconic Coleman could
on occasion talk so much, or perhaps he understood everything and was

impressed by the argumentative power. At any rate he suddenly wilted. He made a gesture which was a protestation of martyrdom and picking up his burden proceeded on his way.

Whey they reached the bridge, they saw strong columns of Greek infantry, dead black in the dim light, crossing the stream and slowly deploying on the other shore. It was a bracing sight to the dragoman, who then went into one of his absurd babbling moods, in which he would have talked the head off any man who was not born in a country laved by the childish Mediterranean. Coleman could not understand what he said to the soldiers as they passed, but it was evidently all grandiose nonsense.

Two light batteries had precariously crossed the rickety bridge during the night, and now this force of several thousand infantry, with the two batteries, was moving out over the territory which the cavalry had reconnoitered on the previous day. The ground being familiar to Coleman, he no longer knew a tremour, and, regarding his dragoman, he saw that that invaluable servitor was also in better form. They marched until they found one of the light batteries unlimbered and aligned on the lake of grass about a mile from where parts of the white house appeared above the tree-tops. Here the dragoman talked with the captain of artillery, a tiny man on an immense horse, who for some unknown reason told him that this force was going to raid into Turkey and try to swing around the opposing army's right flank. He announced, as he showed his teeth in a smile, that it would be very, very dangerous work. The dragoman precipitated himself upon Coleman.

"This is much danger. The copten he tells me the trups go now in back of the Turks. It will be much danger. I think much better we go Arta wait for horse. Much better." Coleman, although he believed he despised the dragoman, could not help but be influenced by his fears. They were, so to speak, in a room with one window, and only the dragoman looked forth from the window, so if he said that what he saw outside frightened him, Coleman was perforce frightened also in a meaure. But when the correspondent raised his eyes he saw the captain of the battery looking at him, his teeth still showing in a smile, as if his information, whether true or false, had been given to convince the foreigner that the Greeks were a very superior and brave people, notably one little officer of artillery. He had apparently assumed that Coleman would balk from venturing with such a force upon an excursion to trifle with the rear of a hard-fighting Ottoman army. He exceedingly disliked that man, sitting up there on his tall horse and grinning like a cruel little ape with a secret. In truth, Coleman was taken back at the outlook, but he could no more refrain from instantly accepting this half-concealed challenge than he could have refrained from resenting an ordinary form of insult. His mind was not at peace, but the small vanities are very large. He was perfectly aware that he was being misled into the thing by an odd pride, but anyhow, it easily might turn out to be a stroke upon the doors of Nikopolis. He nodded and smiled at the officer in grateful acknowledgment of his service.

The infantry was moving steadily a-field. Black blocks of men were trailing in column slowly over the plain. They were not unlike the backs of dominoes on a green baize table; they were so vivid, so startling. The correspondent and his servant followed them. Eventually they overtook two companies in command of a captain, who seemed immensely glad to have the strangers with him. As they marched, the captain spoke through the dragoman upon the virtues of his men, announcing with other news the fact that his first sergeant was the bravest man in the world.

A number of columns were moving across the plain parallel to their line of march, and the whole force seemed to have orders to halt when they reached a long ditch about four hundred yards from where the shore of the plain arose to the luxuriant groves with the cupola of the big white house sticking above them. The soldiers lay along the ditch, and the bravest man in the world spread his blanket on the ground for the captain, Coleman and himself. During a long pause Coleman tried to elucidate the question of why the Greek soldiers wore heavy overcoats, even in the bitter heat of midday, but he could only learn that the dews, when they came, were very destructive to the lungs. Further, he convinced himself anew that talking through an interpreter to the minds of other men was as satisfactory as looking at landscape through a stained glass window.

After a time there was, in front, a stir near where a curious hedge of dry brambles seemed to outline some sort of a garden patch. Many of the soldiers exclaimed and raised their guns. But there seemed to come a general understanding to the line that it was wrong to fire. Then presently into the open came a dirty brown figure, and Coleman could see through his glasses that its head was crowned with a dirty fez which had once been white. This indicated that the figure was that of one of the Christian peasants of Epirus. Obedient to the captain, the sergeant arose and waved invitation. The peasant wavered, changed his mind, was obviously terror-stricken, regained confidence and then began to advance circuitously toward the Greek lines. When he arrived within hailing distance, the captain, the sergeant, Coleman's dragoman and many of the soldiers yelled human messages, and a moment later he was seen to be a poor, yellow-faced stripling with a body which seemed to have been first twisted by an ill-birth and afterward maimed by either labour or oppression, these being often identical in their effects.

His reception of the Greek soldiery was no less fervid than their welcome of him to their protection. He threw his grimy fez in the air and croaked out cheers, while tears wet his cheeks. When he had come upon the right side of the ditch he ran capering among them and the captain, the sergeant, the dragoman and a number of soldiers received wild embraces and kisses. He made a dash at Coleman, but Coleman was now wary in the game, and retired dexterously behind different groups with a finished appearance of not noting that the young man wished to greet him.

Behind the hedge of dry brambles there were more indications of life, and the peasant stood up and made beseeching gestures. Soon a whole flock of miserable people had come out to the Greeks, men, women and children, in crude and comic smocks, prancing here and there, uproariously embracing and kissing their deliverers. An old, tearful, toothless hag flung herself rapturously into the arms of the captain, and Coleman's brick-and-iron soul was moved to admiration at the way in which the officer administered a chaste salute upon the furrowed cheek. The dragoman told the correspondent that the Turks had run away from the village on up a valley toward Jannina. Everybody was proud and happy.

A major of infantry came from the rear at this time and asked the captain in sharp tones who were the two strangers in civilian attire. When the captain had

answered correctly the major was immediately mollified, and had it announced
to the correspondent that his battalion was going to move immediately into the
village, and that he would be delighted to have his company.

The major strode at the head of his men with the group of villagers singing
and dancing about him and looking upon him as if he were a god. Coleman and
the dragoman, at the officer's request, marched one on either side of him, and in
this manner they entered the village. From all sorts of hedges and thickets,
people came creeping out to pass into a delirium of joy. The major borrowed
three little pack horses with rope-bridles, and thus mounted and followed by the
clanking column, they rode on in triumph.

It was probably more of a true festival than most men experience even in
the longest life time. The major with his Greek instinct of drama was a splendid
personification of poetic quality; in fact he was himself almost a lyric. From time
to time he glanced back at Coleman with eyes half dimmed with appreciation.
The people gathered flowers, great blossoms of purple and corn colour. They
sprinkled them over the three horsemen and flung them deliriously under the
feet of the little nags. Being now mounted Coleman had no difficulty in avoiding
the embraces of the peasants, but he felt to the tips of his toes an abandonment
to a kind of pleasure with which he was not at all familiar. Riding thus amid
cries of thanksgiving addressed at him equally with the others, he felt a burning
virtue and quite lost his old self in an illusion of noble benignity. And there
continued the fragrant hail of blossoms.

Miserable little huts straggled along the sides of the village streets as if they
were following at the heels of the great white house of the bey. The column
proceeded northward, announcing laughingly to the glad villagers that they
would never see another Turk. Before them on the road was here and there a fez
from the head of a fled Turkish soldier and they lay like drops of blood from
some wounded leviathan. Ultimately it grew cloudy. It even rained slightly. In
the misty downfall the column of soldiers in blue was dim as if it were merely a
long trail of low-hung smoke.

They came to the ruins of a church and there the major halted his battalion.
Coleman worried at his dragoman to learn if the halt was only temporary. It was
a long time before there was answer from the major, for he had drawn up his
men in platoons and was addressing them in a speech as interminable as any
that Coleman had heard in Greece. The officer waved his arms and roared out
evidently the glories of patriotism and soldierly honour, the glories of their
ancient people, and he may have included any subject in this wonderful speech,
for the reason that he had plenty of time in which to do it. It was impossible to
tell whether the oration was a good one or bad one, because the men stood in
their loose platoons without discernible feelings as if to them this appeared
merely as one of the inevitable consequences of a campaign, an established rule
of warfare. Coleman ate black bread and chocolate tablets while the dragoman
hovered near the major with the intention of pouncing upon him for information
as soon as his lungs yielded to the strain upon them.

The dragoman at last returned with a very long verbal treatise from the
major, who apparently had not been as exhausted after his speech to the men as
one would think. The major had said that he had been ordered to halt here to
form a junction with some of the troops coming direct from Arta, and that he
expected that in the morning the army would be divided and one wing would

chase the retreating Turks on toward Jannina, while the other wing would advance upon Prevasa because the enemy had a garrison there which had not retreated an inch, and, although it was cut off, it was necessary to send either a force to hold it in its place or a larger force to go through with the business of capturing it. Else there would be left in the rear of the left flank of a Greek advance upon Jannina a body of the enemy which at any moment might become active. The major said that his battalion would probably form part of the force to advance upon Prevasa. Nikopolis was on the road to Prevasa and only three miles away from it.

Chapter 11

Coleman spent a long afternoon in the drizzle. Enveloped in his macintosh he sat on a boulder in the lee of one of the old walls and moodily smoked cigars and listened to the ceaseless clatter of tongues. A ray of light penetrated the mind of the dragoman and he laboured assiduously with wet fuel until he had accomplished a tin mug of coffee. Bits of cinder floated in it, but Coleman rejoiced and was kind to the dragoman.

The night was of cruel monotony. Afflicted by the wind and the darkness, the correspondent sat with nerves keyed high waiting to hear the pickets open fire on a night attack. He was so unaccountably sure that there would be a tumult and panic of this kind at some time of the night that he prevented himself from getting a reasonable amount of rest. He could hear the soldiers breathing in sleep all about him. He wished to arouse them from this slumber which, to his ignorance, seemed stupid. The quality of mysterious menace in the great gloom and the silence would have caused him to pray if prayer would have transported him magically to New York and made him a young man with no coat playing billiards at his club.

The chill dawn came at last and with a fine elation which ever follows a dismal night in war; an elation which bounds in the bosom as soon as day has knocked the shackles from a trembling mind. Although Coleman had slept but a short time he was now as fresh as a total abstainer coming from the bath. He heard the creak of battery wheels; he saw crawling bodies of infantry moving in the dim light like ghostly processions. He felt a tremendous virility come with this new hope in the daylight. He again took satisfaction in his sentimental journey. It was a shining affair. He was on active service, an active service of the heart, and he felt that he was a strong man ready to conquer difficulty even as the olden heroes conquered difficulty. He imagined himself in a way like them. He, too, had come out to fight for love with giants, dragons and witches. He had never known that he could be so pleased with that kind of a parallel.

The dragoman announced that the major had suddenly lent their horses to some other people, and after cursing this versatility of interest, he summoned his henchmen and they moved out on foot, following the sound of the creaking wheels. They came in time to a bridge, and on the side of this bridge was a hard military road which sprang away in two directions, north and west. Some troops

313

were creeping out the westward way and the dragoman pointing at them said: "They going Prevasa. That is road to Nikopolis." Coleman grinned from ear to ear and slapped his dragoman violently on the shoulder. For a moment he intended to hand the man a louis of reward, but he changed his mind.

Their traps were in the way of being heavy, but they minded little since the dragoman was now a victim of the influence of Coleman's enthusiasm. The road wound along the base of the mountain range, sheering around the abutments in wide white curves and then circling into glens where immense trees spread their shade over it. Some of the great trunks were oppressed with vines green as garlands, and these vines even ran like verdant foam over the rocks. Streams of translucent water showered down from the hills, and made pools in which every pebble, every leaf of a water plant shone with magic lustre, and if the bottom of a pool was only of clay, the clay glowed with sapphire light. The day was fair. The country was part of that land which turned the minds of its ancient poets toward a more tender dreaming, so that indeed their nymphs would die, one is sure, in the cold mythology of the north with its storms amid the gloom of pine forests. It was all wine to Coleman's spirit. It enlivened him to think of success with absolute surety. To be sure one of his boots began soon to rasp his toes, but he gave it no share of his attention. They passed at a much faster pace than the troops, and everywhere they met laughter and confidence and the cry: "On to Prevasa!"

At midday they were at the heels of the advance battalion, among its stragglers, taking its white dust into their throats and eyes. The dragoman was waning and he made a number of attempts to stay Coleman, but no one could have had influence upon Coleman's steady rush with his eyes always straight to the front as if thus to symbolize his steadiness of purpose. Rivulets of sweat marked the dust on his face, and two of his toes were now paining as if they were being burned off. He was obliged to concede a privilege of limping, but he would not stop.

At nightfall they halted with the outpost batallion of the infantry. All the cavalry had in the meantime come up and they saw their old friends. There was a village from which the Christian peasants came and cheered like a trained chorus. Soldiers were driving a great flock of fat sheep into a corral. They had belonged to a Turkish bey and they bleated as if they knew that they were now mere spoils of war. Coleman lay on the steps of the bey's house smoking with his head on his blanket roll. Camp fires glowed off in the fields. He was now about four miles from Nikopolis.

Within the house, the commander of the cavalry was writing dispatches. Officers clanked up and down the stairs. The dashing young captain came and said that there would be a general assault on Prevasa at the dawn of the next day. Afterward the dragoman descended upon the village and in some way wrenched a little grey horse from an inhabitant. Its pack saddle was on its back and it would very handily carry the traps. In this matter the dragoman did not consider his master; he considered his own sore back.

Coleman ate more bread and chocolate tablets and also some tinned sardines. He was content with the day's work. He did not see how he could have improved it. There was only one route by which the Wainwright party could avoid him, and that was by going to Prevasa and thence taking ship. But since Prevasa was blockaded by a Greek fleet, he conceived that event to be impossible. Hence, he had them hedged on this peninsula and they must be either at Nikopolis or Prevasa. He would probably know all early in the morning. He reflected that he was too tired to care if there might be a night attack and then wrapped in his blankets he went peacefully to sleep in the grass under a big tree with the crooning of some soldiers around their fire blending into his slumber.

And now, although the dragoman had performed a number of feats of incapacity, he achieved during the one hour of Coleman's sleeping a blunder which for real finish was simply a perfection of art. When Coleman, much later, extracted the full story, it appeared that ringing events happened during that single hour of sleep. Ten minutes after he had lain down for a night of oblivion, the battalion of infantry, which had advanced a little beyond the village, was recalled and began a hurried night march back on the way it had so festively come. It was significant enough to appeal to almost any mind, but the dragoman was able to not understand it. He remained jabbering to some acquaintances among the troopers. Coleman had been asleep his hour when the dashing young captain perceived the dragoman, and completely horrified by his presence at that place, ran to him and whispered to him swiftly that the game was to flee, flee, flee. The wing of the army which had advanced northward upon Jannina had already been tumbled back by the Turks and all the other wing had been recalled to the Louros river and there was now nothing practically between him and his sleeping master and the enemy but a cavalry picket. The cavalry was immediately going to make a forced march to the rear. The stricken dragoman could even then see troopers getting into their saddles. He rushed to the tree, and in a panic simply bundled Coleman upon his feet before he was awake. He stuttered out his tale, and the dazed correspondent heard it punctuated by the steady trample of the retiring cavalry. The dragoman saw a man's face then turn in a flash from an expression of luxurious drowsiness to an expression of utter malignancy. However, he was in too much of a hurry to be afraid of it; he ran off to the little grey horse and frenziedly but skilfully began to bind the traps upon the pack-saddle. He appeared in a moment tugging at the halter. He could only say: "Come! Come! Come! Queek! Queek!" They slid hurriedly down a bank to the road and started to do again that which they had accomplished with considerable expenditure of physical power during the day. The hoof beats of the cavalry had already died away and the mountains shadowed them in lonely silence. They were the rear guard after the rear guard.

The dragoman muttered hastily his last dire rumours. Five hundred Circassian cavalry were comng. The mountains were now infested with the dread Albanian irregulars. Coleman had thought in his daylight tramp that he had appreciated the noble distances, but he found that he knew nothing of their nobility until he tried this night stumbling. And the hoofs of the little horse made on the hard road more noise than could be made by men beating with hammers upon brazen cylinders. The correspondent glanced continually up at the crags. From the other side he could sometimes hear the metallic clink of water deep down in a glen. For the first time in his life he seriously opened the flap of his holster and let his fingers remain on the handle of his revolver. From just in front of him he could hear the chattering of the dragoman's teeth which no attempt at more coolness could seem to prevent. In the meantime the casual manner of the little grey horse struck Coleman with maddening vividness. If the blank darkness was simply filled with ferocious Albanians, the horse did not care a button; he leisurely put his feet down with a resounding ring. Coleman whispered hastily to the dragoman. "If they rush us, jump down the bank, no matter how deep it is. That's our only chance. And try to keep together."

All they saw of the universe was, in front of them, a place faintly luminous near their feet, but fading in six yards to the darkness of a dungeon. This represented the bright white road of the day time. It had no end. Coleman had thought that he could tell from the very feel of the air some of the landmarks of his daytime journey, but he had now no sense of location at all. He would not have denied that he was squirming on his belly like a worm through black mud.

They went on and on. Visions of his past were sweeping through Coleman's mind precisely as they are said to sweep through the mind of a drowning person. But he had no regret for any bad deeds; he regretted merely distant hours of peace and protection. He was no longer a hero going to rescue his love. He was a slave making a gasping attempt to escape from the most incredible tyranny of circumstances. He half vowed to himself that if the God whom he had in no wise heeded, would permit him to crawl out of this slavery he would never again venture a yard toward a danger any greater than may be incurred from the police of a most proper metropolis. If his juvenile and uplifting thoughts of other days had reproached him he would simply have repeated and repeated: "Adventure be damned."

It became known to them that the horse had to be led. The debased creature was asserting its right to do as it had been trained, to follow its customs; it was asserting this right during a situation which required conduct superior to all training and custom. It was so grossly conventional that Coleman would have understood that demoniac form of anger which sometimes leads men to jab knives into warm bodies. Coleman from cowardice tried to induce the dragoman to go ahead leading the horse, and the dragoman from cowardice tried to induce Coleman to go ahead leading the horse. Coleman of course had to succumb. The dragoman was only good to walk behind and tearfully whisper maledictions as he prodded the flanks of their tranquil beast.

In the absolute black of the frequent forests, Coleman could not see his feet and he often felt like a man walking forward to fall at any moment down a thousand yards of chasm. He heard whispers; he saw skulking figures, and these frights turned out to be the voice of a little trickle of water or the effects of wind among the leaves, but they were replaced by the same terrors in slightly different forms.

Then the poignant thing interpolated. A volley crashed ahead of them some half of a mile away and another volley answered from a still nearer point. Swishing noises which the correspondent had heard in the air he now knew to have been from the passing of bullets. He and the dragoman came stock still. They heard three other volleys sounding with the abrupt clamour of a hail of little stones upon a hollow surface. Coleman and the dragoman came close together and looked into the whites of each other's eyes. The ghastly horse at that moment stretched down his neck and began placidly to pluck the grass at the roadside. The two men were equally blank with fear and each seemed to seek in the other some newly rampant manhood upon which he could lean at this time. Behind them were the Turks. In front of them was a fight in the darkness. In front it was mathematic to suppose in fact were also the Turks.

They were barred; enclosed; cut off. The end was come.

Even at that moment they heard from behind them the sound of slow, stealthy footsteps. They both wheeled instantly, choking with this additional terror. Coleman saw the dragoman move swiftly to the side of the road, ready to jump into whatever abyss happened to be there. Coleman still gripped the halter as if it were in truth a straw. The stealthy footsteps were much nearer. Then it was that an insanity came upon him as if fear had flamed up within him until it gave him all the magnificent desperation of a madman. He jerked the grey horse broadside to the approaching mystery, and grabbing out his revolver aimed it from the top of his improvised bulwark. He hailed the darkness.

"Halt. Who's there?" He had expected his voice to sound like a groan, but instead it happened to sound clear, stern, commanding, like the voice of a young sentry at an encampment of volunteers. He did not seem to have any privilege of selection as to the words. They were born of themselves.

He waited then, blanched and hopeless, for death to wing out of the darkness and strike him down. He heard a voice. The voice said: "Do you speak English?" For one or two seconds he could not even understand English, and then the great fact swelled up and within him. This voice with all its new quavers was still undoubtedly the voice of Prof. Harrison B. Wainwright of Washurst College.

Chapter 12

A change flashed over Coleman as if it had come from an electric storage. He had known the professor long, but he had never before heard a quaver in his voice, and it was this little quaver that seemed to impel him to supreme disregard of the dangers which he looked upon as being the final dangers. His own voice had not quavered.

When he spoke, he spoke in a low tone, it was the voice of the master of the situation. He could hear his dupes fluttering there in the darkness. "Yes," he said, "I speak English. There is some danger. Stay where you are and make no noise." He was as cool as an iced drink. To be sure the circumstances had in no wise changed as to his personal danger, but beyond the important fact that there were now others to endure it with him, he seemed able to forget it in a strange, unauthorized sense of victory. It came from the professor's quavers.

Meanwhile he had forgotten the dragoman, but he recalled him in time to bid him wait. Then, as well concealed as a monk hiding in his cowl, he tip-toed back into a group of people who knew him intimately. He discerned two women mounted on little horses and about them were dim men. He could hear them breathing hard. "It is all right" he began smoothly. "You only need to be very careful——"

Suddenly out of the blackness projected a half phosphorescent face. It was the face of the little professor. He stammered. "We—we—do you really speak English?" Coleman in his feeling of superb triumph could almost have laughed. His nerves were as steady as hemp, but he was in haste and his haste allowed him to administer rebuke to his old professor. "Didn't you hear me?" he hissed through his tightening lips. "They are fighting just ahead of us on the road and if you want to save yourselves don't waste time."

Another face loomed faintly like a mask painted in dark grey. It belonged to Coke, and it was a mask figured in profound stupefaction. The lips opened and tensely breathed out the name: "Coleman." Instantly the correspondent felt about him that kind of a tumult which tries to suppress itself. He knew that it was the most theatric moment of his life. He glanced quickly toward the two figures on horseback. He believed that one was making foolish gesticulation while the other sat rigid and silent. This latter one he knew to be Marjory. He was content that she did not move. Only a woman who was glad he had come

318

but did not care for him would have moved. This applied directly to what he thought he knew of Marjory's nature.

There was confusion among the students, but Coleman suppressed it as in such situation might a centurion. "S-s-steady!" He seized the arm of the professor and drew him forcibly close. "The condition is this," he whispered rapidly. "We are in a fix with this fight on up the road. I was sent after you, but I can't get you into the Greek lines to-night. Mrs. Wainwright and Marjory must dismount and I and my man will take the horses on and hide them. All the rest of you must go up about a hundred feet into the woods and hide. When I come back, I'll hail you and you answer low." The professor was like pulp in his grasp. He choked out the word "Coleman" in agony and wonder, but he obeyed with a palpable gratitude. Coleman sprang to the side of the shadowy figure of Marjory. "Come," he said authoritatively. She laid in his palm a little icy cold hand and dropped from her horse. He had an impulse to cling to the small fingers, but he loosened them immediately, imparting to his manner, as well as the darkness permitted him, a kind of casual politeness as if he were too intent upon the business in hand. He bunched the crowd and pushed them into the wood. Then he and the dragoman took the horses a hundred yards onward and tethered them. No one would care if they were stolen; the great point was to get them where their noise would have no power of revealing the whole party. There had been no further firing.

After he had tied the little grey horse to a tree he unroped his luggage and carried the most of it back to the point where the others had left the road. He called out cautiously and received a sibilant answer. He and the dragoman bunted among the trees until they came to where a forlorn company was seated awaiting them, lifting their faces like frogs out of a pond. His first question did not give them any assurance. He said at once: "Are any of you armed?" Unanimously they lowly breathed: "No." He searched them out one by one and finally sank down by the professor. He kept sort of a hypnotic handcuff upon the dragoman, because he foresaw that this man was really going to be the key to the best means of escape. To a large neutral party wandering between hostile lines there was technically no danger, but actually there was a great deal. Both armies had too many irregulars, lawless hillsmen come out to fight in their own way, and if they were encountered in the dead of night on such hazardous ground the Greek hillsmen with their white cross on a blue field would be precisely as dangerous as the blood-hungry Albanians. Coleman knew that the rational way was to reach the Greek lines, and he had no intention of reaching the Greek lines without a tongue, and the only tongue was in the mouth of the dragoman. He was correct in thinking that the professor's deep knowledge of the ancient language would give him small clue to the speech of the modern Greek.

As he settled himself by the professor the band of students, eight in number, pushed their faces close.

He did not see any reason for speaking. There were thirty seconds of deep silence in which he felt that all were bending to hearken to his words of counsel. The professor huskily broke the stillness. "Well * * * what are we to do now?"

Coleman was decisive, indeed absolute. "We'll stay here until daylight unless you care to get shot."

"All right," answered the professor. He turned and made a useless remark to his flock. "Stay here."

Coleman asked civilly, "Have you had anything to eat? Have you got anything to wrap around you?"

"We have absolutely nothing," answered the professor. "Our servants ran away and * * and then we left everything behind us and * * I've never been in such a position in my life."

Coleman moved softly in the darkness and unbuckled some of his traps. On his knee he broke the hard cakes of bread and with his fingers he broke the little tablets of chocolate. These he distributed to his people. And at this time he felt fully the appreciation of the conduct of the eight American college students. They had not yet said a word—with the exception of the bewildered exclamation from Coke. They all knew him well. In any circumstance of life which as far as he truly believed, they had yet encountered, they would have been privileged to accost him in every form of their remarkable vocabulary. They were as new to this game as would have been eight newly-caught Apache Indians if such were set to run the elevators in the Tract Society Building. He could see their eyes gazing at him anxiously and he could hear their deep-drawn breaths. But they said no word. He knew that they were looking upon him as their leader, almost as their saviour, and he knew also that they were going to follow him without a murmur in the conviction that he knew ten-fold more than they knew. It occurred to him that his position was ludicrously false, but, anyhow, he was glad. Surely it would be a very easy thing to lead them to safety in the morning and he foresaw the credit which would come to him. He concluded that it was beneath his dignity as preserver to vouchsafe them many words. His business was to be the cold, masterful, enigmatic man. It might be said that these reflections were only half-thoughts in his mind. Meanwhile a section of his intellect was flying hither and thither, speculating upon the Circassian cavalry and the Albanian guerillas and even the Greek outposts.

He unbuckled his blanket roll and taking one blanket placed it about the shoulders of the shadow which was Mrs. Wainwright. The shadow protested incoherently, but he muttered: "Oh, that's all right." Then he took his other blanket and went to the shadow which was Marjory. It was something like putting a wrap about the shoulders of a statue. He was base enough to linger in the hopes that he could detect some slight trembling, but as far as he knew she was of stone. His macintosh he folded around the body of the professor amid quite senile protest, so senile that the professor seemed suddenly proven to him as an old, old man, a fact which had never occurred to Washurst or her children. Then he went to the dragoman and pre-empted half of his blankets. The dragoman grunted, but Coleman was panther-fashion with him. It would not do to have this dragoman develop a luxurious temperament when eight American college students were, without speech, shivering in the cold night.

Coleman really begun to ruminate upon his glory, but he found that he could not do this well without smoking, so he crept away some distance from this fireless encampment, and bending his face to the ground at the foot of a tree he struck a match and lit a cigar. His return to the others would have been somewhat in the manner of coolness as displayed on the stage if he had not been prevented by the necessity of making no noise. He saw regarding him as before the dimly visible eyes of the eight students and Marjory and her father and mother. Then he whispered the conventional words. "Go to sleep if you can.

You'll need your strength in the morning. I and this man here will keep watch."
Three of the college students of course crawled up to him and each said: "I'll
keep watch, old man."

"No. We'll keep watch. You people try to sleep."

He deemed that it might be better to yield the dragoman his blanket, and so
he got up and leaned against a tree, holding his hand to cover the brilliant point
of his cigar. He knew perfectly well that none of them could sleep. But he stood
there somewhat like a sentry without the attitude, but with all the effect of
responsibility.

He had no doubt but what escape to civilisation would be easy, but anyhow
his heroism should be preserved. He was the rescuer. His thoughts of Marjory
were somewhat in a puzzle. The meeting had placed him in such a position that
he had expected a lot of condescension on his own part. Instead she had
exhibited about as much recognition of him as would a stone fountain on his
grandfather's place in Connecticut. This in his opinion was not the way to greet
the knight who had come to the rescue of his lady. He had not expected it so to
happen. In fact from Athens to this place he had engaged himself with imagery
of possible meetings. He was vexed, certainly, but, far beyond that, he knew a
deeper admiration for this girl. To him she represented the sex, and so the sex as
embodied in her seemed a mystery to be feared. He wondered if safety came on
the morrow he would not surrender to this feminine invulnerability. She had not
done anything that he had expected of her and so inasmuch as he loved her he
loved her more. It was bewitching. He half considered himself a fool. But at any
rate he thought resentfully she should be thankful to him for having rendered
her a great service. However, when he came to consider this proposition he
knew that on a basis of absolute manly endeavour he had rendered her little or
no service.

The night was long.

Chapter 13

Coleman suddenly found himself looking upon his pallid dragoman. He saw that he had been asleep crouched at the foot of the tree. Without any exchange of speech at all he knew there had been alarming noises. Then shots sounded from near by. Some were from rifles aimed in that direction and some were from rifles opposed to them. This was distinguishable to the experienced man, but all that Coleman knew was that the conditions of danger were now triplicated. Unconsciously he stretched his hands in supplication over his charges. "Don't move! Don't move! And keep close to the ground!" All heeded him but Marjory. She still sat straight. He himself was on his feet, but he now knew the sound of bullets, and he knew that no bullets had spun through the trees. He could not see her distinctly, but it was known to him in some way that she was mutinous. He leaned toward her and spoke as harshly as possible. "Marjory, get down!" She wavered for a moment as if resolved to defy him. As he turned again to peer in the direction of the firing it went through his mind that she must love him very much indeed. He was assured of it.

It must have been some small outpour between nervous pickets and eager hillsmen, for it ended in a moment. The party waited in abasement for what seemed to them a long time, and the blue dawn began to laggardly shift the night as they waited. The dawn itself seemed prodigiously long in arriving at anything like discernible landscape. When this was consummated, Coleman, in somewhat the manner of the father of a church, dealt bits of chocolate out to the others. He had already taken the precaution to confer with the dragoman, so he said: "Well, come ahead. We'll make a try for it." They arose at his bidding and followed him to the road. It was the same broad, white road, only that the white was in the dawning something like the grey of a veil. It took some courage to venture upon this thoroughfare, but Coleman stepped out after looking quickly in both directions. The party tramped to where the horses had been left, and there they were found without change of a rope. Coleman rejoiced to see that his dragoman now followed him in the way of a good lieutenant. They both dashed in among the trees and had the horses out into the road in a twinkle. When Coleman turned to direct that utterly subservient group he knew that his face was drawn from hardship and anxiety, but he saw everywhere the same style of face with the exception of the face of Marjory, who looked simply of lovely marble. He noted with a curious satisfaction, as if the thing was a tribute to himself, that his macintosh was over the professor's shoulder, that Marjory and her mother were each carrying a blanket, and that the corps of students had dutifully brought all the traps which his dragoman had forgotten. It was grand.

He addressed them to say: "Now, approaching outposts is very dangerous business at this time in the morning. So my man, who can talk both Greek and Turkish, will go ahead forty yards, and I will follow somewhere between him and you. Try not to crowd forward."

He directed the ladies upon their horses and placed the professor upon the little grey nag. Then they took up their line of march. The dragoman had looked somewhat dubiously upon this plan of having him go forty yards in advance, but he had the utmost confidence in this new Coleman, whom yesterday he had not known. Besides, he himself was a very gallant man indeed, and it befitted him to take the post of danger before the eyes of all these foreigners. In his new position he was as proud and unreasonable as a rooster. He was continually turning his head to scowl back at them, when only the clank of hoofs was sounding. An impenetrable mist lay on the valley and the hill-tops were shrouded. As for the people, they were like mice. Coleman paid no attention to the Wainwright party, but walked steadily along near the dragoman.

Perhaps the whole thing was a trifle absurd, but to a great percentage of the party it was terrible. For instance, those eight boys, fresh from a school, could in no wise gauge the dimensions. And if this was true of the students, it was more distinctly true of Marjory and her mother. As for the professor, he seemed weighted to the earth by his love and his responsibility.

Suddenly the dragoman wheeled and made demoniac signs. Coleman half-turned to survey the main body, and then paid his attention swiftly to the front. The white road sped to the top of a hill where it seemed to make a rotund swing into oblivion. The top of the curve was framed in foliage, and therein was a horseman. He had his carbine slanted on his thigh, and his bridle-reins taut. Upon sight of them he immediately wheeled and galloped down the other slope and vanished.

The dragoman was throwing wild gestures into the air. As Coleman looked back at the Wainwright party he saw plainly that to an ordinary eye they might easily appear as a strong advance of troops. The peculiar light would emphasize such theory. The dragoman ran to him jubilantly, but he contained now a form of intelligence which caused him to whisper: "That was one Greek. That was one Greek—what do you call—sentree?"

Coleman addressed the others. He said: "It's all right. Come ahead. That was a Greek picket. There is only one trouble now, and that is to approach them easy—do you see—easy."

His obedient charges came forward at his word. When they arrived at the top of this rise they saw nothing. Coleman was very uncertain. He was not sure that this picket had not carried with him a general alarm, and in that case there would soon occur a certain amount of shooting. However, as far as he understood the business, there was no way but forward. Inasmuch as he did not indicate to the Wainwright party that he wished them to do differently, they followed on doggedly after him and the dragoman. He knew now that the dragoman's heart had for the tenth time turned to dog-biscuit, so he kept abreast of him. And soon together they walked into a cavalry outpost, commanded by no less a person than the dashing young captain, who came laughing out to meet them.

Suddenly losing all colour of war, the condition was now such as might occur in a drawing room. Coleman felt the importance of establishing highly conventional relations between the captain and the Wainwright party. To compass this he first seized his dragoman, and the dragoman, enlightened immediately, spun a series of lies which must have led the captain to believe that the entire heart of the American republic had been taken out of that western continent and transported to Greece. Coleman was proud of the captain. The latter immediately went and bowed in the manner of the French school and asked everybody to have a cup of coffee, although acceptation would have proved his ruin and disgrace. Coleman refused in the name of courtesy. He called his party forward, and now they proceeded merely as one crowd. Marjory had dismounted in the meantime.

The moment was come. Coleman felt it. The first rush was from the students. Immediately he was buried in a thrashing mob of them. "Good boy! Good boy! Great man! Oh, isn't he a peach? How did he do it? He came in strong at the finish! Good boy, Coleman!" Through this mist of glowing youthful congratulation he saw the professor standing at the outskirts with · direct formal thanks already moving on his lips, while near him his wife wept joyfully. Marjory was evidently enduring some inscrutable emotion.

After all, it did penetrate his mind that it was indecent to accept all this wild gratitude, but there was built within him no intention of positively declaring himself lacking in all credit, or at least, lacking in all credit in the way their praises defined it. In truth he had assisted them, but he had been at the time largely engaged in assisting himself, and their coming had been more of a boon to his loneliness than an addition to his care. However, he soon had no difficulty in making his conscience appropriate every line in these hymns sung in his honour. The students, curiously wise of men, thought his conduct quite perfect. "Oh, say, come off!" he protested. "Why, I didn't do anything. You fellows are crazy. You would have gotten in all right by yourselves. Don't act like asses—"

As soon as the professor had opportunity he came to Coleman. He was a changed little man and his extraordinary bewilderment showed in his face. It was the disillusion and amazement of a stubborn mind that had gone implacably in its one direction and found in the end that the direction was all wrong, and that really a certain mental machine had not been infallible. Coleman remembered what the American minister in Athens had described of his protests against the starting of the professor's party on this journey, and of the complete refusal of the professor to recognise any value in the advice. And here now was the consequent defeat. It was mirrored in the professor's astonished eyes. Coleman went directly to his dazed old teacher. "Well, you're out of it now, professor," he said warmly. "I congratulate you on your escape, sir." The professor looked at him, helpless to express himself, but the correspondent was at that time suddenly enveloped in the hysterical gratitude of Mrs. Wainwright, who hurled herself upon him with extravagant manifestations. Coleman played his part with skill. To both the professor and Mrs. Wainwright his manner was a combination of modestly filial affection and a pretentious disavowal of his having done anything at all. It seemed to charm everybody but Marjory. It irritated him to see that she was apparently incapable of acknowledging that he was a grand man.

He was actually compelled to go to her and offer congratulations upon her escape, as he had congratulated the professor.

If his manner to her parents had been filial, his manner to her was parental. "Well, Marjory," he said kindly, "you have been in considerable danger. I suppose you're glad to be through with it." She at that time made no reply, but by her casual turn he knew that he was expected to walk along by her side. The others knew it, too, and the rest of the party left them free to walk side by side in the rear.

"This is a beautiful country here-abouts if one gets a good chance to see it," he remarked. Then he added: "But I suppose you had a view of it when you were going out to Nikopolis?"

She answered in muffled tones. "Yes, we thought it very beautiful."

"Did you note those streams from the mountains? That seemed to me the purest water I'd ever seen, but I bet it would make one ill to drink it. There is, you know, a prominent German chemist who has almost proven that really pure water is practical poison to the human stomach."

"Yes?" she said.

There was a period of silence, during which he was perfectly comfortable because he knew that she was ill at ease. If the silence was awkward, she was suffering from it. As for himself, he had no inclination to break it. His position was, as far as the entire Wainwright party was concerned, a place where he could afford to wait. She turned to him at last. "Of course, I know how much you have done for us, and I want you to feel that we all appreciate it deeply— deeply." There was discernible to the ear a certain note of desperation.

"Oh, not at all," he said generously. "Not at all. I didn't do anything. It was quite an accident. Don't let that trouble you for a moment."

"Well, of course you would say that," she said more steadily. "But I—we— we know how good and how—brave it was in you to come for us, and I—we must never forget it."

"As a matter of fact," replied Coleman, with an appearance of ingenuous candor, "I was sent out here by the *Eclipse* to find you people, and of course I worked rather hard to reach you, but the final meeting was purely accidental and does not redound to my credit in the least."

As he had anticipated, Marjory shot him a little glance of disbelief. "Of course you would say that," she repeated with gloomy but flattering conviction.

"Oh, if I had been a great hero," he said smiling, "no doubt I would have kept up this same manner which now sets so well upon me, but I am telling you the truth when I say that I had no part in your rescue at all."

She became slightly indignant. "Oh, if you care to tell us constantly that you were of no service to us, I don't see what we can do but continue to declare that you were."

Suddenly he felt vulgar. He spoke to her this time with real meaning. "I beg of you never to mention it again. That will be the best way."

But to this she would not accede. "No, we will often want to speak of it."

He replied: "How do you like Greece? Don't you think that some of these ruins are rather out of shape in the popular mind? Now, for my part, I would rather look at a good strong finish at a horserace than to see ten thousand Parthenons in a bunch."

She was immediately in the position of defending him from himself. "You would rather see no such thing. You shouldn't talk in that utterly trivial way. I like the Parthenon, of course, but I can't think of it now because my head is too full of my escape from where I was so—so frightened."

Coleman grinned. "Were you really frightened?"

"Naturally," she answered. "I suppose I was more frightened for mother and father, but I was frightened enough for myself. It was not—not a nice thing."

"No, it wasn't," said Coleman. "I could hardly believe my senses when the minister at Athens told me that you all ventured into such a trap, and there is no doubt but what you can be glad that you are well out of it."

She seemed to have some struggle with herself and then she deliberately said: "Thanks to you."

Coleman embarked on what he intended to make a series of high-minded protests. "Not at all—" but at that moment the dragoman whirled back from the van-guard with a great collection of the difficulties which had been gathering upon him. Coleman was obliged to resign Marjory and again take up the active leadership. He disposed of the dragoman's difficulties mainly by declaring that they were not difficulties at all. He had learned that this was the way to deal with dragomen.

The fog had already lifted from the valley and as they passed along the wooded mountain-side the fragance of leaves and earth came to them. Ahead, along the hooded road, they could see the blue clad figures of Greek infantry-men. Finally they passed an encampment of a battalion whose line was at a right angle to the highway. A hundred yards in advance was the bridge across the Louros river. And there a battery of artillery was encamped. The dragoman became involved in all sorts of discussions with other Greeks, but Coleman stuck to his elbow and stifled all aimless oration. The Wainwright party waited for them in the rear in an observant but patient group.

Across a plain, the hills directly behind Arta loomed up showing the straight yellow scar of a modern entrenchment. To the north of Arta were some grey mountains with a dimly marked road winding to the summit. On one side of this road were two shadows. It took a moment for the eye to find these shadows, but when this was accomplished it was plain that they were men. The captain of the battery explained to the dragoman that he did not know that they were not also Turks. In which case the road to Arta was a dangerous path. It was no good news to Coleman. He waited a moment in order to gain composure and then walked back to the Wainwright party. They must have known at once from his peculiar gravity that all was not well. Five of the students and the professor immediately asked: "What is it?"

He had at first some old-fashioned idea of concealing the ill tidings from the ladies, but he perceived what flagrant nonsense this would be in circumstances in which all were fairly likely to incur equal dangers, and at any rate he did not see his way clear to allow their imagination to run riot over a situation which might not turn out to be too bad. He said slowly: "You see those mountains over there? Well, troops have been seen there and the captain of this battery thinks they are Turks. If they are Turks the road to Arta is distinctly—er—unsafe."

This new blow first affected the Wainwright party as being too much to endure. They thought they had gone through enough. This was a general sentiment. Afterward the emotion took colour according to the individual character. One student laughed and said: "Well, I see our finish."

Another student piped out: "How do they know they are Turks? What makes them think they are Turks?"

Another student expressed himself with a sigh. "This is a long way from the Bowery."

The professor said nothing but looked annihilated; Mrs. Wainwright wept profoundly; Marjory looked expectantly toward Coleman.

As for the correspondent he was adamantine and reliable and stern, for he had not the slightest idea that those men on the distant hill were Turks at all.

Chapter 14

O
h," said a student, "this game ought to quit. I feel like thirty cents. We didn't come out here to be pursued about the country by these Turks. Why don't they stop it?"

Coleman was remarking: "Really, the only sensible thing to do now is to have breakfast. There is no use in worrying ourselves silly over this thing until we've got to."

They spread the blankets on the ground and sat about a feast of bread, water cress and tinned beef. Coleman was the real host, but he contrived to make the professor appear as that honourable person. They ate, casting their eyes from time to time at the distant mountain with its two shadows. People began to fly down the road from Jannina, peasants hurriedly driving little flocks, women and children on donkeys and little horses which they clubbed unceasingly. One man rode at a gallop, shrieking and flailing his arms in the air. They were all Christain peasants of Turkey, but they were in flight now because they did not wish to be at home if the Turk was going to return and reap revenge for his mortification. The Wainwright party looked at Coleman in abrupt questioning. "Oh, it's all right," he said, easily. "They are always taking on that way."

Suddenly the dragoman gave a shout and dashed up the road to the scene of a mêlée, where a little rat-faced groom was vociferously defending three horses from some Greek officers, who as vociferously were stating their right to requisition them. Coleman ran after his dragoman. There was a sickening pow-wow, but in the end Coleman, straight and easy in the saddle, came cantering back on a superb open-mouthed snorting bay horse. He did not mind if the half-wild animal plunged crazily. It was part of his role. "They were trying to steal my horses," he explained. He leaped to the ground, and holding the horse by the bridle, he addressed his admiring companions. "The groom—the man who has charge of the horses—says that he thinks that the people on the mountain-side are Turks, but I don't see how that is possible. You see—" he pointed wisely—"that road leads directly south to Arta, and it is hardly possible that the Greek army would come over here and leave that approach to Arta utterly unguarded. It would be too foolish. They must have left some men to cover it, and that is certainly what those troops are. If you are ready and willing, I don't see anything to do but make a good, stout-hearted dash for Arta. It would be no more dangerous than to sit here."

The professor was at last able to make his formal speech. "Mr. Coleman," he said distinctly, "we place ourselves entirely in your hands." It was somehow pitiful. This man who, for years and years had reigned in a little college town almost as a monarch, passing judgment with the air of one who words the law, dealing criticism upon the universe as one to whom all things are plain, publicly disdaining defeat as one to whom all things are easy—this man was now veritably appealing to Coleman to save his wife, his daughter and himself, and really declared himself dependent for safety upon the ingenuity and courage of the correspondent.

The attitude of the students was utterly indifferent. They did not consider themselves helpless at all. They were evidently quite ready to withstand anything but they looked frankly up to Coleman as their intelligent leader. If they suffered any, their own expression of it was in the simple grim slang of their period.

"I wish I was at Coney Island."

"This is not so bad as trigonometry, but it's worse than playing billiards for the beers."

And Coke said privately to Coleman: "Say, what in hell are these two damn peoples fighting for, anyhow?"

When he saw that all opinions were in favour of following him loyally, Coleman was impelled to feel a responsibility. He was now no errant rescuer, but a properly elected leader of fellow beings in distress. While one of the students held his horse, he took the dragoman for another consultation with the captain of the battery. The officer was sitting on a large stone, with his eyes fixed into his field glasses. When again questioned he could give no satisfaction as to the identity of the troops on the distant mountain. He merely shrugged his shoulders and said that if they were Greeks it was very good, but if they were Turks it was very bad. He seemed more occupied in trying to impress the correspondent that it was a matter of soldierly indifference to himself. Coleman, after loathing him sufficiently in silence, returned to the others and said: "Well, we'll chance it."

They looked to him to arrange the caravan. Speaking to the men of the party he said: "Of course, any one of you is welcome to my horse if you can ride it, but—if you're not too tired—I think I had myself better ride, so that I can go ahead at times."

His manner was so fine as he said this that the students seemed fairly to worship him. Of course it had been most improbable that any of them could have ridden that volcanic animal even if one of them had tried it.

He saw Mrs. Wainwright and Marjory upon the backs of their two little natives, and hoisted the professor into the saddle of the groom's horse, leaving instructions with the servant to lead the animal always and carefully. He and the dragoman then mounted at the head of the procession, and amid curious questionings from the soldiery they crossed the bridge and started on the trail to Arta. The rear was brought up by the little grey horse with the luggage, led by one student and flogged by another.

Coleman, checking with difficulty the battling disposition of his horse, was very uneasy in his mind because the last words of the captain of the battery had made him feel that perhaps on this ride he would be placed in a position where only the best courage would count, and he did not see his way clear to feeling very confident about his conduct in such a case. Looking back upon the caravan, he saw it as a most unwieldy thing, not even capable of running away. He hurried it with sudden, sharp contemptuous phrases.

On the march there incidentally flashed upon him a new truth. More than half of that student band were deeply in love with Marjory. Of course, when he had been distant from her he had had an eternal jealous reflection to that effect. It was natural that he should have thought of the intimate camping relations between Marjory and these young students with a great deal of bitterness, grinding his teeth when picturing their opportunities to make Marjory fall in love with some one of them. He had raged particularly about Coke, whose father had millions of dollars. But he had forgotten all these jealousies in the general splendour of his exploits. Now, when he saw the truth, it seemed to bring him back to his common life, and he saw himself suddenly as not being frantically superior in any way to those other young men. The more closely he looked at this last fact, the more convinced he was of its truth. He seemed to see that he had been improperly elated over his services to the Wainwrights, and that in the end the girl might fancy a man because the man had done her no service at all. He saw his proud position lower itself to be a pawn in the game. Looking back over the students, he wondered which one Marjory might love. This hideous Nikopolis had given eight men a chance to win her. His scorn and his malice quite centered upon Coke, for he could never forget that the man's father had millions of dollars. The unfortunate Coke chose that moment to address him querulously: "Look here, Coleman, can't you tell us how far it is to Arta?"

"Coke," said Coleman, "I don't suppose you take me for a tourist agency, but if you can only try to distinguish between me and a map with the scale of miles printed in the lower left-hand corner, you will not contribute so much to the sufferings of the party which you now adorn."

The students within hearing guffawed and Coke retired in confusion.

The march was not rapid. Coleman almost wore out his arms holding in check his impetuous horse. Often the caravan floundered through mud, while at the same time a hot, yellow dust came from the north.

They were perhaps half way to Arta when Coleman decided that a rest and luncheon were the things to be considered. He halted his troop then in the shade of some great trees, and privately he bade his dragoman prepare the best feast which could come out of those saddle-bags fresh from Athens. The result was rather gorgeous in the eyes of the poor wanderers. First of all there were three knives, three forks, three spoons, three tin cups and three tin plates, which the entire party of twelve used on a most amiable socialistic principle. There were crisp, salty biscuits and olives, for which they speared in the bottle. There was potted turkey, and potted ham, and potted tongue, all tasting precisely alike. There were sardines and the ordinary tinned beef, disguised sometimes with onions, carrots and potatoes. Out of the saddle-bags came pepper and salt and even mustard. The dragoman made coffee over a little fire of sticks that blazed with a white light. The whole thing was prodigal, but any philanthropist would have approved of it if he could have seen the way in which the eight students laid into the spread. When there came a polite remonstrance—notably from Mrs. Wainwright—Coleman merely pointed to a large bundle strapped back of the groom's saddle. During the coffee he was considering how best to get the students one by one out of the sight of the Wainwrights where he could give them goods drinks of whisky.

There was an agitation on the road toward Arta. Some people were coming on horses. He paid small heed until he heard a thump of pausing hoofs near him, and a musical voice say: "Rufus!"

He looked up quickly, and then all present saw his eyes really bulge. There on a fat and glossy horse sat Nora Black, dressed in probably one of the most correct riding habits which had ever been seen in the East. She was smiling a radiant smile, which held the eight students simply spell-bound. They would have recognised her if it had not been for this apparitional coming in the wilds of southeastern Europe. Behind her were her people—some servants and an old lady on a very little pony. "Well, Rufus?" she said.

Coleman made the mistake of hesitating. For a fraction of a moment he had acted as if he were embarrassed, and was only going to nod and say: "How d'do?"

He arose and came forward too late. She was looking at him with a menacing glance which meant difficulties for him if he was not skilful. Keen as an eagle, she swept her glance over the face and figure of Marjory. Without further introduction, the girls seemed to understand that they were enemies.

Despite his feeling of awkwardness, Coleman's mind was mainly occupied by pure astonishment. "Nora Black?" he said, as if even then he could not believe his senses. "How in the world did you get down here?"

She was not too amiable, evidently, over his reception, and she seemed to know perfectly that it was in her power to make him feel extremely unpleasant. "Oh, it's not so far," she answered. "I don't see where you come in to ask what I'm doing here. What are you doing here?" She lifted her eyes and shot the half of a glance at Marjory. Into her last question she had interjected a spirit of ownership in which he saw future woe. It turned him cowardly. "Why, you know I was sent up here by the paper to rescue the Wainwright party, and I've got them. I'm taking them to Arta. But why are you here?"

"I am here," she said, giving him the most defiant of glances, "principally to look for you."

Even the horse she rode betrayed an intention of abiding upon that spot forever. She had made her communication with Coleman appear to the Wainwright party as a sort of tender reunion.

Coleman looked at her with a steely eye. "Nora, you can certainly be a devil when you choose."

"Why don't you present me to your friends? Miss Nora Black, special correspondent of the *New York Daylight*, if you please. I belong to your opposition. I am your rival, Rufus, and I draw a bigger salary—see? Funny looking gang, that. Who is the old Johnnie in the white wig?"

"Er—where you goin'—you can't"—blundered Coleman miserably. "Aw—the army is in retreat and you must go back to—don't you see?"

"Is it?" she asked. After a pause she added coolly: "Then I shall go back to Arta with you and your precious Wainwrights."

Chapter 15

Giving Coleman another glance of subtle menace Nora repeated: "Why don't you present me to your friends?" Coleman had been swiftly searching the whole world for a way clear of this unhappiness, but he knew at last that he could only die at his guns. "Why, certainly," he said quickly, "if you wish it." He sauntered easily back to the luncheon blanket. "This is Miss Black of the *New York Daylight* and she says that those people on the mountain are Greeks." The students were gaping at him, and Marjory and her father sat in the same silence. But to the relief of Coleman and to the high edification of the students, Mrs Wainwright cried out: "Why, is she an American woman?" And seeing Coleman's nod of assent she rustled to her feet and advanced hastily upon the complacent horsewoman. "I'm delighted to see you. Who would think of seeing an American woman way over here. Have you been here long? Are you going on further? Oh, we've had such a dreadful time." Coleman remained long enough to hear Nora say: "Thank you very much, but I shan't dismount. I am going to ride back to Arta presently."

Then he heard Mrs. Wainwright cry: 'Oh, are you indeed? Why we, too, are going at once to Arta. We can all go together." Coleman fled then to the bosom of the students, who all looked at him with eyes of cynical penetration. He cast a glance at Marjory more than fearing a glare which denoted an implacable resolution never to forgive this thing. On the contrary he had never seen her so content and serene. "You have allowed your coffee to get chilled," she said considerately. "Won't you have the man warm you some more?"

"Thanks, no," he answered with gratitude.

Nora, changing her mind, had dismounted and was coming with Mrs. Wainwright. That worthy lady had long had a fund of information and anecdote the sound of which neither her husband nor her daughter would endure for a moment. Of course the rascally students were out of the question. Here, then, was really the first ear amiably and cheerfully open, and she was talking at what the students called her "thirty knot gait."

"Lost everything. Absolutely everything. Neither of us have even a brush and comb, or a cake of soap, or enough hairpins to hold up our hair. I'm going to take Marjory's away from her and let her braid her hair down her back. You can imagine how dreadful it is——"

332

From time to time the cool voice of Nora sounded without effort through this clamour. "Oh, it will be no trouble at all. I have more than enough of everything. We can divide very nicely."

Coleman broke somewhat imperiously into this feminine chat. "Well, we must be moving, you know," and his voice started the men into activity. When the traps were all packed again on the horse Coleman looked back surprised to see the three women engaged in the most friendly discussion. The combined parties now made a very respectable squadron. Coleman rode off at its head without glancing behind at all. He knew that they were following from the soft pounding of the horses hoofs on the sod and from the mellow hum of human voices.

For a long time he did not think to look upon himself as anything but a man much injured by circumstances. Among his friends he could count numbers who had lived long lives without having this peculiar class of misfortune come to them. In fact it was so unusual a misfortune that men of the world had not found it necessary to pass from mind to mind a perfect formula for dealing with it. But he soon began to consider himself an extraordinarily lucky person inasmuch as Nora Black had come upon him with her saddle bags packed with inflammable substances, so to speak, and there had been as yet only enough fire to boil coffee for luncheon. He laughed tenderly when he thought of the innocence of Mrs. Wainwright, but his face and back flushed with heat when he thought of the canniness of the eight American college students.

He heard a horse cantering up on his left side and looking he saw Nora Black. She was beaming with satisfaction and good nature. "Well, Rufus," she cried flippantly, "how goes it with the gallant rescuer? You've made a hit, my boy. You are the success of the season."

Coleman reflected upon the probable result of a direct appeal to Nora. He knew of course that such appeals were usually idle, but he did not consider Nora an ordinary person. His decision was to venture it. He drew his horse close to hers. "Nora," he said, "do you know that you are raising the very devil?"

She lifted her finely penciled eyebrows and looked at him with the baby-stare. "How?" she enquired.

"You know well enough," he gritted out wrathfully.

"Raising the very devil?" she asked. "How do you mean?" She was palpably interested for his answer. She waited for his reply for an interval, and then she asked him outright. "Rufus Coleman do you mean that I am not a respectable woman?"

In reality he had meant nothing of the kind, but this direct throttling of a great question stupified him utterly, for he saw now that she would probably never understand him in the least and that she would at any rate always pretend not to understand him and that the more he said the more harm he manufactured. She studied him over carefully and then wheeled her horse towards the rear with some parting remarks. "I suppose you should attend more strictly to your own affairs, Rufus. Instead of raising the devil I am lending hairpins. I have seen you insult people, but I have never seen you insult any one quite for the whim of the thing. Go soak your head."

Not considering it advisable to then indulge in such immersion Coleman rode moodily onward. The hot dust continued to sting the cheeks of the travellers and in some places great clouds of dead leaves roared in circles about them. All of the Wainwright party were utterly fagged. Coleman felt his skin crackle and his throat seemed to be coated with the white dust. He worried his dragoman as to the distance to Arta until the dragoman lied to the point where he always declared that Arta was only off some hundreds of yards.

At their places in the procession Mrs. Wainwright and Marjory were animatedly talking to Nora and the old lady on the little pony. They had at first suffered great amazement at the voluntary presence of the old lady, but she was there really because she knew no better. Her colossal ignorance took the form, mainly, of a most obstreperous patriotism, and indeed she always acted in a foreign country as if she were the special commissioner of the President, or perhaps as a special commissioner could not act at all. She was very aggressive, and when any of the travelling arrangements in Europe did not suit her ideas she was won't to shrilly exclaim: "Well! New York is good enough for me." Nora, morbidly afraid that her expense bill to the *Daylight* would not be large enough, had dragged her bodily off to Greece as her companion, friend and protection. At Arta they had heard of the grand success of the Greek army. The Turks had not stood for a moment before that gallant and terrible advance; no; they had scampered howling with fear into the north. Jannina would fall—well, Jannina would fall as soon as the Greeks arrived. There was no doubt of it. The correspondent and her friend, deluded and hurried by the light-hearted confidence of the Greeks in Arta, had hastened out then on a regular tourist's excursion to see Jannina after its capture. Nora concealed from her friend the fact that the editor of the *Daylight* particularly wished her to see a battle so that she might write an article on actual warfare from a woman's point of view. With her name as a queen of comic opera, such an article from her pen would be a burning sensation.

Coleman had been the first to point out to Nora that instead of going on a picnic to Jannina, she had better run back to Arta. When the old lady heard that they had not been entirely safe, she was furious with Nora. "The idea!" she exclaimed to Mrs. Wainwright. "They might have caught us! They might have caught us!"

"Well," said Mrs. Wainwright. "I verily believe they would have caught us if it had not been for Mr. Coleman."

"Is he the gentleman on the fine horse?"

"Yes; that's him. Oh, he has been sim-plee splendid. I confess I was a little bit—er—surprised. He was in college under my husband. I don't know that we thought very great things of him, but if ever a man won golden opinions he has done so from us."

"Oh, that must be the Coleman who is such a great friend of Nora's."

"Yes?" said Mrs. Wainwright insidiously. "Is he? I didn't know. Of course he knows so many people." Her mind had been suddenly illumined by the old lady and she thought extravagantly of the arrival of Nora upon the scene. She remained all sweetness to the old lady. "Did you know he was here? Did you expect to meet him? It seemed such a delightful coincidence." In truth she was being subterraneously clever.

"Oh, no; I don't think so. I didn't hear Nora mention it. Of course she would have told me. You know, our coming to Greece was such a surprise. Nora had an engagement in London at the Folly Theatre in *Fly by Night*, but the manager was insufferable, oh, insufferable. So, of course, Nora wouldn't stand it a minute, and then these newspaper people came along and asked her to go to Greece for them and she accepted. I am sure I never expected to find us—aw—fleeing from the Turks or I shouldn't have come."

Mrs. Wainwright was gasping. "You don't mean that she is—she is Nora Black, the actress."

"Of course, she is," said the old lady jubilantly.

"Why, how strange," choked Mrs. Wainwright. Nothing she knew of Nora could account for her stupefaction and grief. What happened glaringly to her was the duplicity of man. Coleman was a ribald deceiver. He must have known and yet he had pretended throughout that the meeting was a pure accident. She turned with a nervous impulse to sympathise with her daughter, but despite the lovely tranquillity of the girl's face there was something about her which forbade the mother to meddle. Anyhow Mrs. Wainwright was sorry that she had told nice things of Coleman's behaviour, so she said to the old lady: "Young men of these times get a false age so quickly. We have always thought it a great pity about Mr. Coleman."

"Why, how so?" asked the old lady.

"Oh, really nothing. Only, to us he seemed rather—er—prematurely experienced or something of that kind."

The old lady did not catch the meaning of the phrase. She seemed surprised. "Why, I've never seen any full-grown person in this world who got experience any too quick for his own good."

At the tail of the procession there was talk between the two students who had in charge the little grey horse—one to lead and one to flog. "Billie," said one, "it now becomes necessary to lose this hobby into the hands of some of the other fellows. Whereby we will gain opportunity to pay homage to the great Nora. Why, you egregious thick-head, this is the chance of a life-time. I'm damned if I'm going to tow this beast of burden much further."

"You wouldn't stand a show," said Billie pessimistically. "Look at Coleman."

"That's all right. Do you mean to say that you prefer to continue towing pack horses in the presence of this queen of song and the dance just because you think Coleman can throw out his chest a little more than you. Not so. Think of your bright and sparkling youth. There's Coke and Pete Tounley near Marjory. We'll call 'em." Whereupon he set up a cry. "Say, you people, we're not getting a salary for this. Supposin' you try for a time. It'll do you good." When the two addressed had halted to await the arrival of the little grey horse, they took on glum expressions. "You look like poisoned pups," said the student who led the horse. "Too strong for light work. Grab onto the halter, now, Peter, and tow. We are going ahead to talk to Nora Black."

"Good time you'll have," answered Peter Tounley. "Coleman is cuttin' up scandalous. You won't stand a show."

"What do you think of him?" said Coke. "Seems curious, all 'round. Do you suppose he knew she would show up? It was nervy to—"

"Nervy to what?" asked Billie.

"Well," said Coke, "seems to me he is playing both ends against the middle. I don't know anything about Nora Black, but—"

The three other students expressed themselves with conviction and in chorus. "Coleman's all right."

"Well, anyhow," continued Coke, "I don't see my way free to admiring him introducing Nora Black to the Wainwrights."

"He didn't," said the others, still in chorus.

"Queer game," said Peter Tounley. "He seems to know her pretty well."

"Pretty damn well," said Billie.

"Anyhow he's a brick," said Peter Tounley. "We mustn't forget that. Lo, I begin to feel that our Rufus is a fly guy of many different kinds. Any play that he is in commands my respect. He won't be hit by a chimney in the daytime, for unto him has come much wisdom, I don't think I'll worry."

"Is he stuck on Nora Black, do you know?" asked Billie.

"One thing is plain," replied Coke. "She has got him somehow by the short hair and she intends him to holler murder. Anybody can see that."

"Well, he won't holler murder," said one of them with conviction. "I'll bet you he won't. He'll hammer the war-post and beat the tom-tom until he drops, but he won't holler murder."

"Old Mother Wainwright will be in his wool presently," quoth Peter Tounley musingly. "I could see it coming in her eye. Somebody has given his snap away, or something."

"Aw, he had no snap," said Billie. "Couldn't you see how rattled he was? He would have given a lac if dear Nora hadn't turned up."

"Of course," the others assented. "He was rattled."

"Looks queer. And nasty," said Coke.

"Nora herself had an axe ready for him."

They began to laugh. "If she had had an umbrella she would have basted him over the head with it. Oh, my! He was green."

"Nevertheless," said Peter Tounley, "I refuse to worry over our Rufus. When he can't take care of himself the rest of us want to hung cover. He is a fly guy."

Coleman in the meantime had become aware that the light of Mrs. Wainwright's countenance was turned from him. The party stopped at a well, and when he offered her a drink from his cup he thought she accepted it with scant thanks. Marjory was still gracious, always gracious, but this did not reassure him, because he felt there was much unfathomable deception in it. When he turned to seek consolation in the manner of the professor he found him as before, stunned with surprise, and the only idea he had was to be as tractable as a child.

When he returned to the head of the column, Nora again cantered forward to join him. "Well, me gay Lochinvar," she cried, "and has your disposition improved?"

"You are very fresh," he said.

She laughed loud enough to be heard the full length of the caravan. It was a beautiful laugh, but full of insolence and confidence. He flashed his eyes malignantly upon her, but then she only laughed more. She could see that he wished to strangle her. "What a disposition!" she said. "What a disposition! You are not nearly so nice as your friends. Now, they are charming, but you—Rufus, I wish you would get that temper mended. Dear Rufus, do it to please me. You know you like to please me. Don't you now, dear?"

He finally laughed. "Confound you, Nora, I would like to kill you."

But at his laugh she was all sunshine. It was as if she had been trying to taunt him into good humour with her. "Aw, now, Rufus, don't be angry. I'll be good, Rufus. Really, I will. Listen. I want to tell you something. Do you know what I did? Well, you know, I never was cut out for this business, and, back there, when you told me about the Turks being near and all that sort of thing, I was frightened almost to death. Really, I was. So, when nobody was looking, I sneaked two or three little drinks out of my flask. Two or three little drinks——"

Chapter 16

Good God!'' said Coleman. "You don't mean——"

Nora smiled rosily at him. "Oh, I'm all right," she answered. "Don't worry about your Aunt Nora, my precious boy. Not for a minute."

Coleman was horrified. "But you are not going to—you are not going to——"

"Not at all, me son. Not at all," she answered. "I'm not going to prance. I'm going to be as nice as pie, and just ride quietly along here with dear little Rufus. Only * * you know what I can do when I get started, so you had better be a very good boy. I might take it into my head to say some things, you know."

Bound hand and foot at his stake, he could not even chant his defiant torture song. It might precipitate—in fact, he was sure it would precipitate the grand smash. But to the very core of his soul, he for the time hated Nora Black. He did not dare to remind her that he would revenge himself; he dared only to dream of this revenge, but it fairly made his thoughts flame, and deep in his throat he was swearing an inflexible persecution of Nora Black. The old expression of his sex came to him, "Oh, if she were only a man!" If she had been a man, he would have fallen upon her tooth and nail. Her motives for all this impressed him not at all; she was simply a witch who bound him helpless with the power of her femininity, and made him eat cinders. He was so sure that his face betrayed him that he did not dare let her see it. "Well, what are you going to do about it?" he asked, over his shoulder.

"O-o-oh," she drawled, impudently. "Nothing." He could see that she was determined not to be confessed. "I may do this or I may do that. It all depends upon your behaviour, my dear Rufus."

As they rode on, he deliberated as to the best means of dealing with this condition. Suddenly he resolved to go with the whole tale direct to Marjory, and to this end he half wheeled his horse. He would reiterate that he loved her and then explain—explain! He groaned when he came to the word, and ceased formulation.

The cavalcade reached at last the bank of the Aracthus river, with its lemon groves and lush grass. A battery wheeled before them over the ancient bridge—a flight of short, broad cobbled steps up as far as the centre of the stream and a similar flight down to the other bank. The returning aplomb of the travellers was well illustrated by the professor who, upon sighting this bridge, murmured:

"Byzantine." This was the first indication that he had still within him a power to resume the normal.

The steep and narrow street was crowded with soldiers; the smoky little coffee shops were a-babble with people discussing the news from the front. None seemed to heed the remarkable procession that wended its way to the cable office. Here Coleman resolutely took precedence. He knew that there was no good in expecting intelligence out of the chaotic clerks, but he managed to get upon the wires this message: "*Eclipse*, New York: Got Wainwright party; all well. Coleman." The students had struggled to send messages to their people in America, but they had only succeeded in deepening the tragic boredom of the clerks.

When Coleman returned to the street he thought that he had seldom looked upon a more moving spectacle than the Wainwright party presented at that moment. Most of the students were seated in a row, dejectedly, upon the kerb. The professor and Mrs. Wainwright looked like two old pictures, which, after an existence in a considerable gloom, had been brought out in their tawdriness to the clear light. Hot white dust covered everybody, and from out the grimy faces the eyes blinked, red-fringed with sleeplessness. Desolation sat upon all, save Marjory. She possessed some marvellous power of looking always fresh. This quality had indeed impressed the old lady on the little pony until she had said to Nora Black: "That girl would look well anywhere." Nora Black had not been amiable in her reply.

Coleman called the professor and the dragoman for a durbar. The dragoman said: "Well, I can get one carriage, and we can go immediate-lee."

"Carriage be blowed!" said Coleman. "What these people need is rest, sleep. You must find a place at once. These people can't remain in the street." He spoke in anger, as if he had previously told the dragoman and the latter had been inattentive. The man immediately departed.

Coleman remarked that there was no course but to remain in the street until his dragoman had found them a habitation. It was a mournful waiting. The students sat on the kerb. Once they whispered to Coleman, suggesting a drink, but he told them that he knew only one cafe, the entrance of which would be in plain sight of the rest of the party. The ladies talked together in a group of four. Nora Black was bursting with the fact that her servant had hired rooms in Arta on their outcoming journey, and she wished Mrs. Wainwright and Marjory to come to them, at least for a time, but she dared not risk a refusal, and she felt something in Mrs. Wainwright's manner which led her to be certain that such would be the answer to her invitation. Coleman and the professor strolled slowly up and down the walk.

"Well, my work is over, sir," said Coleman. "My paper told me to find you, and, through no virtue of my own, I found you. I am very glad of it. I don't know of anything in my life that has given me greater pleasure."

The professor was himself again in so far as he had lost all manner of dependence. But still he could not yet be bumptious. "Mr. Coleman," he said, "I am placed under life-long obligation to you. * * * I am not thinking of myself so much. * * * My wife and daughter——" His gratitude was so genuine that he could not finish its expression.

"Oh, don't speak of it," said Coleman. "I really didn't do anything at all."

The dragoman finally returned and led them all to a house which he had rented for gold. In the great, bare, upper chamber the students dropped wearily to the floor, while the woman of the house took the Wainwrights to a more secluded apartment. As the door closed on them, Coleman turned like a flash. "Have a drink," he said. The students arose around him like the wave of a flood. "You bet." In the absence of changes of clothing, ordinary food, the possibility of a bath, and in the presence of great weariness and dust, Coleman's whisky seemed to them a glistening luxury. Afterward they laid down as if to sleep, but in reality they were too dirty and too fagged to sleep. They simply lay murmuring. Peter Tounley even developed a small fever.

It was at this time that Coleman suddenly discovered his acute interest in the progressive troubles of his affair of the heart had placed the business of his newspaper in the rear of his mind. The greater part of the next hour he spent in getting off to New York that dispatch which created so much excitement for him later. Afterward he was free to reflect moodily upon the ability of Nora Black to distress him. She, with her retinue, had disappeared toward her own rooms. At dusk he went into the street, and was edified to see Nora's dragoman dodging along in his wake. He thought that this was simply another manifestation of Nora's interest in his movements, and so he turned a corner, and there pausing, waited until the dragoman spun around directly into his arms. But it seemed that the man had a note to deliver, and this was only his Oriental way of doing it.

The note read: "Come and dine with me to-night." It was not a request. It was peremptory. "All right," he said, scowling at the man.

He did not go at once, for he wished to reflect for a time and find if he could not evolve some weapons of his own. It seemed to him that all the others were liberally supplied with weapons.

A clear, cold night had come upon the earth when he signified to the lurking dragoman that he was in readiness to depart with him to Nora's abode. They passed finally into a dark court-yard, up a winding staircase, across an embowered balcony, and Coleman entered alone a room where there were lights.

His feet were scarcely over the threshold before he had concluded that the tigress was now going to try some velvet purring. He noted that the arts of the stage had not been thought too cheaply obvious for use. Nora sat facing the door. A bit of yellow silk had been twisted about the crude shape of the lamp, and it made the play of light, amber-like, shadowy and yet perfectly clear, the light which women love. She was arrayed in a puzzling gown of that kind of Grecian silk which is so docile that one can pull yards of it through a ring. It was of the colour of new straw. Her chin was leaned pensively upon her palm and the light fell on a pearly rounded forearm. She was looking at him with a pair of famous eyes, azure, perhaps—certainly purple at times—and it may be, black at odd moments—a pair of eyes that had made many an honest man's heart jump if he thought they were looking at him. It was a vision, yes, but Coleman's cynical knowledge of drama overpowered his sense of its beauty. He broke out brutally, in the phrases of the American street. "Your dragoman is a rubberneck. If he keeps darking me I will simply have to kick the stuffing out of him."

She was alone in the room. Her old lady had been instructed to have a headache and send apologies. She was not disturbed by Coleman's words. "Sit down, Rufus, and have a cigarette, and don't be cross, because I won't stand it."

He obeyed her glumly. She had placed his chair where not a charm of her could be lost upon an observant man. Evidently she did not purpose to allow him to irritate her away from her original plan. Purring was now her method, and none of his insolence could achieve a growl from the tigress. She arose, saying softly: "You look tired, almost ill, poor boy. I will give you some brandy. I have almost everything that I could think to make those *Daylight* people buy." With a sweep of her hand she indicated the astonishing opulence of the possessions in different parts of the room.

As she stood over him with the brandy there came through the smoke of his cigarette the perfume of orris-root and violet.

A servant began to arrange the little cold dinner on a camp table, and Coleman saw with an enthusiasm which he could not fully master, four quart bottles of a notable brand of champagne placed in a rank on the floor.

At dinner Nora was sisterly. She watched him, waited upon him, treated him to an affectionate intimacy for which he knew a thousand men who would have hated him. The champagne was cold.

Slowly he melted. By the time that the boy came with little cups of Turkish coffee he was at least amiable. Nora talked dreamily. "The dragoman says this room used to be part of the harem long ago." She shot him a watchful glance, as if she had expected the fact to affect him. "Seems curious, doesn't it? A harem. Fancy that." He smoked one cigar and then discarded tobacco, for the perfume of orris-root and violet was making him meditate. Nora talked on in a low voice. She knew that, through half-closed lids, he was looking at her in steady speculation. She knew that she was conquering, but no movement of hers betrayed an elation. With the most exquisite art she aided his contemplation, baring to him, for instance, the glories of a statuesque neck, doing it all with the manner of a splendid and fabulous virgin who knew not that there was such a thing as shame. Her stockings were of black silk.

Coleman presently answered her only in monosyllable, making small distinction between yes and no. He simply sat watching her with eyes in which there were two little covetous steel-coloured flames.

He was thinking, "To go to the devil—to go to the devil—to go to the devil with this girl is not a bad fate—not a bad fate—not a bad fate."

Chapter 17

"Come out on the balcony," cooed Nora. "There are some funny old storks on top of some chimneys near here and they clatter like mad all day and night."

They moved together out to the balcony, but Nora retreated with a little cry when she felt the coldness of the night. She said that she would get a cloak. Coleman was not unlike a man in a dream. He walked to the rail of the balcony where a great vine climbed toward the roof. He noted that it was dotted with blossoms, which in the deep purple of the Oriental night were coloured in strange shades of maroon. This truth penetrated his abstraction until when Nora came she found him staring at them as if their colour was a revelation which affected him vitally. She moved to his side without sound and he first knew of her presence from the damning fragrance. She spoke just above her breath. "It's a beautiful evening."

"Yes," he answered. She was at his shoulder. If he moved two inches he must come in contact. They remained in silence leaning upon the rail. Finally he began to mutter some commonplaces which meant nothing particularly, but into his tone as he mouthed them was the note of a forlorn and passionate lover. Then as if by accident he traversed the two inches and his shoulder was against the soft and yet firm shoulder of Nora Black. There was something in his throat at this time which changed his voice into a mere choking noise. She did not move. He could see her eyes glowing innocently out of the pallour which the darkness gave to her face. If he was touching her, she did not seem to know it.

"I am awfully tired," said Coleman, thickly. "I think I will go home and turn in."

"You must be, poor boy," said Nora tenderly. "Wouldn't you like a little more of that champagne?"

"Well, I don't mind another glass."

She left him again and his galloping thought pounded to the old refrain. "To go to the devil—to go to the devil—to go to the devil with this girl is not a bad fate—not a bad fate—not a bad fate." When she returned he drank his glass of champagne. Then he mumbled: "You must be cold. Let me put your cape around you better. It won't do to catch cold here, you know."

She made a sweet pretence of rendering herself to his care. "Oh, thanks * * *

342

I am not really cold * * * There that's better."

Of course all his manipulation of the cloak had been a fervid caress, and although her acting up to this point had remained in the role of the splendid and fabulous virgin she now turned her liquid eyes to his with a look that expressed knowledge, triumph and delight. She was sure of her victory. And she said: "Sweetheart * * * don't you think I am as nice as Marjory?" The impulse had been airily confident.

It was as if the silken cords had been parted by the sweep of a sword. Coleman's face had instantly stiffened and he looked like a man suddenly recalled to the ways of light. It may easily have been that in a moment he would have lapsed again to his luxurious dreaming. But in his face the girl had read a fatal character to her blunder and her resentment against him took precedence of any other emotion. She wheeled abruptly from him and said with great contempt: "Rufus, you had better go home. You're tired and sleepy, and more or less drunk."

He knew that the grand tumble of all their little embowered incident could be neither stayed or mended. "Yes," he answered sulkily, "I think so too." They shook hands huffily and he went away.

When he arrived among the students he found that they had appropriated everything of his which would conduce to their comfort. He was furious over it. But to his bitter speeches they replied in jibes.

"Rufus is himself again. Admire his angelic disposition. See him smile. Gentle soul."

A sleepy voice said from a corner: "I know what pinches him."

"What?" asked several.

"He's been to see Nora and she flung him out bodily."

"Yes?" sneered Coleman. "At times I seem to see in you, Coke, the fermentation of some primeval form of sensation, as if it were possible for you to develop a mind in two or three thousand years, and then at other times you appear * * * much as you are now."

As soon as they had well measured Coleman's temper all of the students save Coke kept their mouths tightly closed. Coke either did not understand or his mood was too vindictive for silence. "Well, I know you got a throw-down all right," he muttered.

"And how would you know when I got a throw-down? You pimply, milk-fed sophomore."

The others perked up their ears in mirthful appreciation of this language.

"Of course," continued Coleman, "no one would protest against your continued existence, Coke, unless you insist on recalling yourself violently to people's attention in this way. The mere fact of your living would not usually be offensive to people if you weren't eternally turning a sort of calcium light on your prehensile attributes."

Coke was suddenly angry, angry much like a peasant, and his anger first evinced itself in a mere sputtering and spluttering. Finally he got out a rather long speech, full of grumbling noises, but he was understood by all to declare that his prehensile attributes had not led him to cart a notorious woman about the world with him. When they quickly looked at Coleman they saw that he was livid. "You——"

But, of course, there immediately arose all sorts of protesting cries from the seven non-combatants. Coleman, as he took two strides toward Coke's corner, looked fully able to break him across his knee, but for this Coke did not seem to care at all. He was on his feet with a challenge in his eye. Upon each cheek burned a sudden hectic spot. The others were clamouring, "Oh, say, this won't do. Quit it. Oh, we mustn't have a fight. He didn't mean it, Coleman." Peter Tounley pressed Coke to the wall saying: "You damned young jackass, be quiet."

They were in the midst of these festivities when a door opened and disclosed the professor. He might have been coming into the middle of a row in one of the corridors of the college at home only this time he carried a candle. His speech, however, was a Washurst speech: "Gentlemen, gentlemen, what does this mean?" All seemed to expect Coleman to make the answer. He was suddenly very cool. "Nothing, professor," he said, "only that this—only that Coke has insulted me. I suppose that it was only the irresponsibility of a boy, and I beg that you will not trouble over it."

"Mr. Coke," said the professor, indignantly, "what have you to say to this?" Evidently he could not clearly see Coke, and he peered around his candle at where the virtuous Peter Tounley was expostulating with the young man. The figures of all the excited group moving in the candle light caused vast and uncouth shadows to have conflicts in the end of the room.

Peter Tounley's task was not light, and beyond that he had the conviction that his struggle with Coke was making him also to appear as a rowdy. This conviction was proven to be true by a sudden thunder from the old professor, "Mr. Tounley, desist!"

In wrath he desisted and Coke flung himself forward. He paid less attention to the professor than if the latter had been a jack-rabbit. "You say I insulted you?" he shouted crazily in Coleman's face. "Well * * * I meant to, do you see?"

Coleman was glacial and lofty beyond everything. "I am glad to have you admit the truth of what I have said."

Coke was still suffocating with his peasant rage, which would not allow him to meet the clear, calm expressions of Coleman. "Yes * * * I insulted you * * * I insulted you because what I said was correct ** my prehensile attributes ** yes ** but I have never——"

He was interrupted by a chorus from the other students. "Oh, no, that won't do. Don't say that. Don't repeat that, Coke."

Coleman remembered the weak bewilderment of the little professor in hours that had not long passed, and it was with something of an impersonal satisfaction that he said to himself: "The old boy's got his war-paint on again." The professor had stepped sharply up to Coke and looked at him with eyes that seemed to throw out flame and heat. There was a moment's pause, and then the old scholar spoke, biting his words as if they were each a short section of steel wire. "Mr. Coke, your behaviour will end your college career abruptly and in gloom, I promise you. You have been drinking."

Coke, his head simply floating in a sea of universal defiance, at once blurted out: "Yes, sir."

"You have been drinking?" cried the professor, ferociously. "Retire to your—retire to your—retire—" And then in a voice of thunder he shouted: "Retire."

Whereupon seven hoodlum students waited a decent moment, then shrieked with laughter. But the old professor would have none of their nonsense. He quelled them all with force and finish.

Coleman now spoke a few words. "Professor, I can't tell you how sorry I am that I should be concerned in any such riot as this, and since we are doomed to be bound so closely into each other's society I offer myself without reservation as being willing to repair the damage as well as may be done. I don't see how I can forget at once that Coke's conduct was insolently unwarranted, but * * * if he has anything to say * * * of a nature that might heal the breach * * * I would be willing to * * * to meet him in the openest manner." As he made these remarks Coleman's dignity was something grand, and, morever, there was now upon his face that curious look of temperance and purity which had been noted in New York as a singular physical characteristic. If he was guilty of anything in this affair at all—in fact, if he had ever at any time been guilty of anything—no mark had come to stain that bloom of innocence. The professor nodded in the fullest appreciation and sympathy. "Of course * * * really there is no other sleeping place * * * I suppose it would be better——" Then he again attacked Coke. "Young man, you have chosen an unfortunate moment to fill us with a suspicion that you may not be a gentleman. For the time there is nothing to be done with you." He addressed the other students. "There is nothing for me to do, young gentlemen, but to leave Mr. Coke in your care. Good-night, sirs. Good-night, Coleman." He left the room with his candle.

When Coke was bade to "Retire" he had, of course, simply retreated fuming to a corner of the room where he remained looking with yellow eyes like an animal from a cave. When the others were able to see through the haze of mental confusion they found that Coleman was with deliberation taking off his boots. Afterward, when he removed his waist-coat, he took great care to wind his large gold watch.

The students, much subdued, lay again in their places, and when there was any talking it was of an extremely local nature, referring principally to the floor as being unsuitable for beds and also referring from time to time to a real or an alleged selfishness on the part of some one of the recumbent men. Soon there was only the sound of heavy breathing.

When the professor had returned to what he called the Wainwright part of the house he was greeted instantly with the question: "What was it?" His wife and daughter were up in alarm. "What was it?" they repeated, wildly.

He was peevish. "Oh, nothing, nothing. But that young Coke is a regular ruffian. He had gotten himself into some tremendous uproar with Coleman. When I arrived he seemed actually trying to assault him. Revolting! He had been drinking. Coleman's behaviour, I must say, was splendid. Recognised at once the delicacy of my position—he not being a student. If I had found him in the wrong it would have been simpler than finding him in the right. Confound that rascal of a Coke." Then, as he began a partial disrobing, he treated them to grunted scraps of information. "Coke was quite insane * * * I feared that I couldn't control him * * * Coleman was like ice * * * and as much as I have seen to admire in him during the last few days, this quiet beat it all. If he had not recognised my helplessness as far as he was concerned the whole thing might have been a most miserable business. He is a very fine young man." The dissenting voice to this last tribute was the voice of Mrs. Wainwright. She said: "Well, Coleman drinks, too—everybody knows that."

"I know," responded the professor, rather bashfully, "but I am confident that he had not touched a drop."

Marjory said nothing.

The earlier artillery battles had frightened most of the furniture out of the houses of Arta, and there was left in this room only a few old red cushions, and the Wainwrights were camping upon the floor. Marjory was enwrapped in Coleman's macintosh, and while the professor and his wife maintained some low talk of the recent incident she in silence had turned her cheek into the yellow velvet collar of the coat. She felt something against her bosom, and putting her hand carefully into the top pocket of the coat she found three cigars. These she took in the darkness and laid aside, telling herself to remember their position in the morning. She had no doubt that Coleman would rejoice over them, before he could get back to Athens where there were other good cigars.

Chapter 18

The ladies of the Wainwright party had not complained at all when deprived of even such civilised advantages as a shelter and a knife and fork and soap and water, but Mrs. Wainwright complained bitterly amid the half-civilisation of Arta. She could see here no excuse for the absence of several hundred things which she had always regarded as essential to life. She began at 8.30 A.M. to make both the professor and Marjory woeful with an endless dissertation upon the beds in the hotel at Athens. Of course she had not regarded them at the time as being exceptional beds * * * that was quite true, * * * but then one really never knew what one was really missing until one really missed it * * * She would never have thought that she would come to consider those Athenian beds as excellent * * * but experience is a great teacher * * * makes one reflect upon the people who year in and year out have no beds at all, poor things. * * * Well, it made one glad if one did have a good bed, even if it was at the time on the other side of the world. * * * If she ever reached it she did not know what could ever induce her to leave it again. * * * She would never be induced——

"'Induced!'" snarled the professor. The word represented to him a practical feminine misusage of truth, and at such his white warlock always arose. "'Induced!'" Out of four American women I have seen lately, you seem to be the only one who would say that you had endured this thing because you had been 'induced' by others to come over here. How absurd!"

Mrs. Wainwright fixed her husband with a steely eye. She saw opportunity for a shattering retort. "You don't mean, Harrison, to include Marjory and I in the same breath with those two women?"

The professor saw no danger ahead for himself. He merely answered: "I had no thought either way. It did not seem important."

"Well, it is important," snapped Mrs. Wainwright. "Do you know that you are speaking in the same breath of Marjory and Nora Black, the actress?"

"No," said the professor. "Is that so?" He was astonished, but he was not aghast at all. "Do you mean to say that is Nora Black, the comic opera star?"

"That's exactly who she is," said Mrs. Wainwright, dramatically. "And I consider that—I consider that Rufus Coleman has done no less than—misled us."

This last declaration seemed to have no effect upon the professor's pure astonishment, but Marjory looked at her mother suddenly. However, she said no word, exhibiting again that strange and inscrutable countenance which masked even the tiniest of her maidenly emotions.

Mrs. Wainwright was triumphant, and she immediately set about celebrating her victory. "Men never see those things," she said to her husband. "Men never see those things. You would have gone on forever without finding out that your—your—hospitality was being abused by that Rufus Coleman."

The professor woke up. "Hospitality?" he said, indignantly. "Hospitality? I have not had any hospitality to be abused. Why don't you talk sense? It is not that, but—it might——" He hesitated and then spoke slowly. "It might be very awkward. Of course one never knows anything definite about such people, but I suppose * * * Anyhow, it was strange in Coleman to allow her to meet us."

"It was all a pre-arranged plan," announced the triumphant Mrs. Wainwright. "She came here on purpose to meet Rufus Coleman, and he knew it, and I should not wonder if they had not the exact spot picked out where they were going to meet."

"I can hardly believe that," said the professor, in distress. "I can hardly believe that. It does not seem to me that Coleman——"

"Oh, yes. Your dear Rufus Coleman," cried Mrs. Wainwright. "You think he is very fine now. But I can remember when you didn't think——"

And the parents turned together an abashed look at their daughter. The professor actually flushed with shame. It seemed to him that he had just committed an atrocity upon the heart of his child. The instinct of each of them was to go to her and console her in their arms. She noted it immediately, and seemed to fear it. She spoke in a clear and even voice. "I don't think, father, that you should distress me by supposing that I am concerned at all if Mr. Coleman cares to get Nora Black over here."

"Not at all," stuttered the professor. "I——'

Mrs. Wainwright's consternation turned suddenly to anger. "He is a scapegrace. A rascal. A—a—"

"Oh," said Marjory, coolly, "I don't see why it isn't his own affair. He didn't really present her to you, mother, you remember? She seemed quite to force her way at first, and then you—you did the rest. It should be very easy to avoid her, now that we are out of the wilderness. And then it becomes a private matter of Mr. Coleman's. For my part, I rather liked her. I don't see such a dreadful calamity."

"Marjory!" screamed her mother. "How dreadful. Liked her! Don't let me hear you say such shocking things."

"I fail to see anything shocking," answered Marjory, stolidly.

The professor was looking helplessly from his daughter to his wife, and from his wife to his daughter, like a man who was convinced that his troubles would never end. This new catastrophe created a different kind of difficulty, but he considered that the difficulties were as robust as had been the preceding ones. He put on his hat and went out of the room. He felt an impossibility of saying anything to Coleman, but he felt that he must look upon him. He must look upon this man and try to know from his manner the measure of guilt. And incidentally he longed for the machinery of a finished society which prevents its parts from clashing, prevents it with its great series of law upon law, easily operative but relentless. Here he felt as a man flung into the jungle with his wife and daughter, where they could become the victims of any sort of savagery. His thought referred once more to what he considered the invaluable services of Coleman, and as he observed them in conjunction with the present accusation, he was simply dazed. It was then possible that one man could play two such divergent parts. He had not learned this at Washurst. But no; the world was not such a bed of putrefaction. He would not believe it; he would not believe it.

After adventures which require great nervous endurance, it is only upon the second or third night that the common man sleeps hard. The students had expected to slumber like dogs on the first night after their trials, but none slept long, and few slept soundly.

Coleman was the first man to arise. When he left the room the students were just beginning to blink. He took his dragoman among the shops and he bought there all the little odds and ends which might go to make up the best breakfast in Arta. If he had had news of certain talk he probably would not have been playing dragoman for eleven people. Instead, he would have been buying breakfast for one. During his absence the students arose and performed their frugal toilets. Considerable attention was paid to Coke by the others. "He made a monkey of you," said Peter Tounley with unction. "He twisted you until you looked like a wet, grey rag. You had better leave this wise guy alone."

It was not the night nor was it meditation that had taught Coke anything, but he seemed to have learned something from the mere lapse of time. In appearance he was subdued, but he managed to make a temporary jauntiness as he said: "Oh, I don't know."

"Well, you ought to know," said he who was called Billie. 'You ought to know. You made an egregious snark of yourself. Indeed, you sometimes resembled a boojum. Anyhow, you were a plain chump. You exploded your face about something of which you knew nothing, and I'm damned if I believe you'd make even a good retriever."

"You're a half-bred water-spaniel," blurted Peter Tounley. "And," he added, musingly, "that is a pretty low animal."

Coke was argumentative. "Why am I?" he asked, turning his head from side to side. "I don't see where I was so wrong."

"Oh, dances, balloons, picnics, parades and ascensions," they retorted, profanely. "You swam voluntarily into water that was too deep for you. Swim out. Get dry. Here's a towel."

Coke, smitten in the face with a wet cloth rolled into a ball, grabbed it and flung it futilely at a well-dodging companion. "No," he cried, "I don't see it. Now look here. I don't see why we shouldn't all resent this Nora Black business."

One student said: "Well, what's the matter with Nora Black, anyhow?"

Another student said: "I don't see how you've been issued any license to say things about Nora Black."

Another student said dubiously: "Well, he knows her well."

And then three or four spoke at once. "He was very badly rattled when she appeared upon the scene."

Peter Tounley asked: "Well, which of you people know anything wrong about Nora Black?"

There was a pause, and then Coke said: "Oh, of course—I don't know—but——"

He who was called Billie then addressed his companions. "It wouldn't be right to repeat any old lie about Nora Black, and by the same token it wouldn't be right to see old Mother Wainwright chummin' with her. There is no wisdom in going further than that. Old Mother Wainwright don't know that her fair companion of yesterday is the famous comic opera star. For my part, I believe that Coleman is simply afraid to tell her. I don't think he wished to see Nora Black yesterday any more than he wished to see the devil. The discussion, as I understand it—concerned itself only with what Coleman had to do with the thing, and yesterday anybody could see that he was in a panic."

They heard a step on the stair, and directly Coleman entered, followed by his dragoman. They were laden with the raw material for breakfast. The correspondent looked keenly among the students, for it was plain that they had been talking of him. It filled him with rage, and for a stifling moment he could not think why he failed to immediately decamp in chagrin and leave eleven orphans to whatever fate their general incompetence might lead them. It struck him as a deep shame that even then he and his paid man were carrying in the breakfast. He wanted to fling it all on the floor and walk out. Then he remembered Marjory. She was the reason. She was the reason for everything.

But he could not repress certain of his thoughts. "Say, you people," he said, icily, "you had better soon learn to hustle for yourselves. I may be a dragoman, and a butler, and a cook, and a housemaid, but I'm blowed if I'm a wet nurse." In reality, he had taken the most generous pleasure in working for the others before their eyes had even been opened from sleep, but it was now all turned to wormwood. It is certain that even this could not have deviated this executive man from labour and management, because these were his life. But he felt that he was about to walk out of the room, consigning them all to Hades. His glance of angry reproach fastened itself mainly upon Peter Tounley, because he knew that of all, Peter was the most innocent.

Peter Tounley was abashed by this glance. "So you've brought us something to eat, old man. That is tremendously nice of you—we—appreciate it like—everything."

Coleman was mollified by Peter's tone. Peter had had that emotion which is equivalent to a sense of guilt, although in reality he was speckless. Two or three of the other students bobbed up to a sense of the situation. They ran to Coleman, and with polite cries took his provisions from him. One dropped a bunch of lettuce on the floor, and others reproached him with scholastic curses. Coke was seated near the window, half militant, half conciliatory. It was impossible for him to keep up a manner of deadly enmity while Coleman was bringing in his breakfast. He would have much preferred that Coleman had not brought in his breakfast. He would have much preferred to have foregone breakfast altogether. He would have much preferred anything. There seemed to be a conspiracy of circumstance to put him in the wrong and make him appear as a ridiculous young peasant. He was the victim of a benefaction, and he hated Coleman harder now than at any previous time. He saw that if he stalked out and took his breakfast alone in a cafe, the others would consider him still more of an outsider. Coleman had expressed himself like a man of the world and a gentleman, and Coke was convinced that he was a superior man of the world and a superior gentleman, but that he simply had not had words to express his position at the proper time. Coleman was glib. Therefore, Coke had been the victim of an attitude as well as of a benefaction. And so he deeply hated Coleman.

The others were talking cheerfully. "What the deuce are these, Coleman? Sausages? Oh, my. And look at these burlesque fishes. Say, these Greeks don't care what they eat. Them thar things am sardines in the crude state. No? Great God, look at those things. Look. What? Yes, they are. Radishes. Greek synonym for radishes."

The professor entered. "Oh," he said apologetically, as if he were intruding in a boudoir. All his serious desire to probe Coleman to the bottom ended in embarrassment. Mayhap it was not a law of feeling, but it happened at any rate. He had come in a puzzled frame of mind, even an accusative frame of mind, and almost immediately he found himself suffering like a culprit before his judge. It is a phenomenon of what we call guilt and innocence.

Coleman welcomed him cordially. "Well, professor, good-morning. I've rounded up some things that at least may be eaten."

"You are very good; very considerate, Mr. Coleman," answered the professor, hastily. "I am sure we are much indebted to you." He had scanned the correspondent's face, and it had been so devoid of guile that he was fearful that his suspicion, a base suspicion, of this noble soul would be detected. "No, no, we can never thank you enough.

Some of the students began to caper with a sort of decorous hilarity before their teacher. "Look at the sausage, professor. Did you ever see such sausage? Isn't it salubrious? And see these other things, sir. Aren't they curious? I shouldn't wonder if they were alive. Turnips, sir? No, sir. I think they are Pharisees. I have seen a Pharisee look like a pelican, but I have never seen a Pharisee look like a turnip, so I think these turnips must be Pharisees, sir. Yes, they may be walrus. We're not sure. Anyhow, their angles are geometrically all wrong. Peter, look out." Some green stuff was flung across the room. The professor laughed; Coleman laughed. Despite Coke, dark-browed, sulking, and yet desirous of reinstating himself, the room had waxed warm with the old college feeling, the feeling of lads who seemed never to treat anything respectfully, and yet at the same time managed to treat the real things with respect. The professor himself contributed to their wild carouse over the strange Greek viands. It was a vivacious moment common to this class in times of relaxation, and it was understood perfectly.

Coke arose. "I don't see that I have any friends here," he said, hoarsely, "and in consequence I don't see why I should remain here."

All looked at him. At the same moment Mrs. Wainwright and Marjory entered the room.

Chapter 19

G ood-morning," said Mrs. Wainwright jovially to the students and then she stared at Coleman as if he were a sweep at a wedding.

"Good-morning," said Marjory.

Coleman and the students made reply. "Good-morning. Good-morning. Good-morning. Good-morning——"

It was curious to see this greeting, this common phrase, this bit of old ware, this antique, come upon a dramatic scene and pulverise it. Nothing remained but a ridiculous dust. Coke, glowering, with his lips still trembling from heroic speech, was an angry clown, a pantaloon in rage. Nothing was to be done to keep him from looking like an ass. He strode toward the door mumbling about a walk before breakfast.

Mrs. Wainwright beamed upon him. "Why, Mr. Coke, not before breakfast? You surely won't have time." It was grim punishment. He appeared to go blind, and he fairly staggered out of the door mumbling again, mumbling thanks or apologies or explanations. About the mouth of Coleman played a sinister smile. The professor cast upon his wife a glance expressing weariness. It was as if he said: "There you go again. You can't keep your foot out of it." She understood the glance, and so she asked blankly: "Why. What's the matter? Oh." Her belated mind grasped that it was an aftermath of the quarrel of Coleman and Coke. Marjory looked as if she was distressed in the belief that her mother had been stupid. Coleman was outwardly serene. It was Peter Tounley who finally laughed a cheery, healthy laugh and they all looked at him with gratitude as if his sudden mirth had been a real statement of reconciliation and consequent peace.

The dragoman and others disported themselves until a breakfast was laid upon the floor. The adventurers squatted upon the floor. They made a large company. The professor and Coleman discussed the means of getting to Athens. Peter Tounley sat next to Marjory. "Peter," she said, privately, "what was all this trouble between Coleman and Coke?"

Peter answered blandly: "Oh, nothing at all. Nothing at all."

"Well, but——" she persisted, "what was the cause of it?"

He looked at her quaintly. He was not one of those in love with her, but he was interested in the affair. "Don't you know?" he asked.

She understood from his manner that she had been some kind of an issue in the quarrel. "No," she answered, hastily. "I don't."

"Oh, I don't mean that," said Peter. "I only meant—I only meant—oh, well, it was nothing—really."

"It must have been about something," continued Marjory. She continued, because Peter had denied that she was concerned in it. "Whose fault?"

"I really don't know. It was all rather confusing," lied Peter, tranquilly.

Coleman and the professor decided to accept a plan of the correspondent's dragoman to start soon on the first stages of the journey to Athens. The dragoman had said that he had found two large carriages rentable.

Coke, the outcast, walked alone in the narrow streets. The flight of the crown prince's army from Larissa had just been announced in Arta, but Coke was probably the most woebegone object on the Greek peninsula.

He encountered a strange sight on the streets. A woman garbed in the style for walking of an afternoon on upper Broadway was approaching him through a mass of kilted mountaineers and soldiers in soiled overcoats. Of course he recognised Nora Black.

In his conviction that everybody in the world was at this time considering him a mere worm, he was sure that she would not heed him. Beyond that he had been presented to her notice in but a transient and cursory fashion. But contrary to his conviction, she turned a radiant smile upon him. "Oh," she said, brusquely, "you are one of the students. Good-morning." In her manner was all the confidence of an old warrior, a veteran, who addresses the universe with assurance because of his past battles.

Coke grinned at this strange greeting. "Yes, Miss Black," he answered, "I am one of the students."

She did not seem to quite know how to formulate her next speech. "Er—I suppose you're going to Athens at once? You must be glad after your horrid experiences."

"I believe they are going to start for Athens today," said Coke.

Nora was all attention. "'They?'" she repeated. "Aren't you going with them?"

"Well," he said, "** Well——"

She saw of course that there had been some kind of trouble. She laughed. "You look as if somebody had kicked you down stairs," she said, candidly. She at once assumed an intimate manner toward him which was like a temporary motherhood. "Come, walk with me and tell me all about it." There was in her tone a most artistic suggestion that whatever had happened she was on his side. He was not loath. The street was full of soldiers whose tongues clattered so loudly that the two foreigners might have been wandering in a great cave of the winds. "Well, what was the row about?" asked Nora. "And who was in it?"

It would have been no solace to Coke to pour out his tale even if it had been a story that he could have told Nora. He was not stopped by the fact that he had gotten himself in the quarrel because he had insulted the name of the girl at his side. He did not think of it at that time. The whole thing was now extremely vague in outline to him and he only had a dull feeling of misery and loneliness. He wanted her to cheer him.

Nora laughed again. "Why, you're a regular little kid. Do you mean to say you've come out here sulking alone because of some nursery quarrel?" He was ruffled by her manner. It did not contain the cheering he required. "Oh, I don't know that I'm such a regular little kid," he said, sullenly. "The quarrel was not a nursery quarrel."

"Why don't you challenge him to a duel?" asked Nora, suddenly. She was watching him closely.

"Who?" said Coke.

"Coleman, you stupid," answered Nora.

They stared at each other, Coke paying her first the tribute of astonishment and then the tribute of admiration. "Why, how did you guess that?" he demanded.

"Oh," said Nora, "I've known Rufus Coleman for years, and he is always rowing with people."

"That is just it," cried Coke eagerly. "That is just it. I fairly hate the man. Almost all of the other fellows will stand his abuse, but it riles me, I tell you. I think he is a beast. And, of course, if you seriously meant what you said about challenging him to a duel—I mean if there is any sense in that sort of thing—I would challenge Coleman. I swear I would. I think he's a great bluffer, anyhow. Shouldn't wonder if he would back out. Really, I shouldn't.

Nora smiled humourously at a house on her side of the narrow way. "I wouldn't wonder if he did either," she answered. After a time she said: "Well, do you mean to say that you have definitely shaken them? Aren't you going back to Athens with them or anything?"

"I—I don't see how I can," he said, morosely.

"Oh," she said. She reflected for a time. At last she turned to him archly and asked: "Some words over a lady?"

Coke looked at her blankly. He suddenly remembered the horrible facts. "No—no—not over a lady."

"My dear boy, you are a liar," said Nora, freely. "You are a little unskilful liar. It was some words over a lady, and the lady's name is Marjory Wainwright."

Coke felt as though he had suddenly been let out of a cell, but he continued a mechanical denial. "No, no * * It wasn't truly * * upon my word * *"

"Nonsense," said Nora. "I know better. Don't you think you can fool me, you little cub. I know you're in love with Marjory Wainwright, and you think Coleman is your rival. What a blockhead you are. Can't you understand that people see these things?"

"Well—" stammered Coke.

"Nonsense," said Nora again. "Don't try to fool me, you may as well understand that it's useless. I am too wise."

"Well—" stammered Coke.

"Go ahead," urged Nora. "Tell me about it. Have it out."

He began with great importance and solemnity. "Now, to tell you the truth * * that is why I hate him * * I hate him like anything. * * I can't see why everybody admires him so. I don't see anything to him myself. I don't believe he's got any more principle than a wolf. I wouldn't trust him with two dollars. Why, I know stories about him that would make your hair curl. When I think of a girl like Marjory——"

His speech had become a torrent. But here Nora raised her hand. "Oh! Oh! Oh! That will do. That will do. Don't lose your senses. I don't see why this girl

Marjory is any too good. She is no chicken, I'll bet. Don't let yourself get fooled with that sort of thing."

Coke was unaware of his incautious expressions. He floundered on, while Nora looked at him as if she wanted to wring his neck. "No—she's too fine and too good—for him or anybody like him—she's too fine and too good——"

"Aw, rats," interrupted Nora, furiously. "You make me tired."

Coke had a wooden-headed conviction that he must make Nora understand Marjory's infinite superiority to all others of her sex, and so he passed into a panegyric, each word of which was a hot coal to the girl addressed. Nothing would stop him, apparently. He even made the most stupid repetitions. Nora finally stamped her foot formidably. "Will you stop? Will you stop?" she said through her clenched teeth. "Do you think I want to listen to your everlasting twaddle about her? Why, she's—she's no better than other people, you ignorant little mamma's boy. She's no better than other people, you swab!"

Coke looked at her with the eyes of a fish. He did not understand. "But she is better than other people," he persisted.

Nora seemed to decide suddenly that there would be no accomplishment in flying desperately against this rock-walled conviction. "Oh, well," she said, with marvellous good nature, "perhaps you are right, numbskull. But, look here; do you think she cares for him?"

In his heart, his jealous heart, he believed that Marjory loved Coleman, but he reiterated eternally to himself that it was not true. As for speaking it to another, that was out of the question. "No," he said, stoutly, "she doesn't care a snap for him." If he had admitted it, it would have seemed to him that he was somehow advancing Coleman's chances.

"Oh, she doesn't, eh?" said Nora enigmatically. "She doesn't?" He studied her face with an abrupt, miserable suspicion, but he repeated doggedly: "No, she doesn't."

"Ahem," replied Nora. "Why, she's set her cap for him all right. She's after him for certain. It's as plain as day. Can't you see that, stupidity?"

"No," he said hoarsely.

"You are a fool," said Nora. "It isn't Coleman that's after her. It is she that is after Coleman."

Coke was mulish. "No such thing. Coleman's crazy about her. Everybody has known it ever since he was in college. You ask any of the other fellows."

Nora was now very serious, almost doleful. She remained still for a time, casting at Coke little glances of hatred. "I don't see my way clear to ask any of the other fellows," she said at last, with considerable bitterness. "I'm not in the habit of conducting such enquiries."

Coke felt now that he disliked her, and he read plainly her dislike of him. If they were the two villains of the play, they were not having fun together at all. Each had some kind of a deep knowledge that their aspirations, far from colliding, were of such character that the success of one would mean at least assistance to the other, but neither could see how to confess it. Perhaps it was from shame; perhaps it was because Nora thought Coke to have little wit; perhaps it was because Coke thought Nora to have little conscience. Their talk was mainly rudderless. From time to time Nora had an inspiration to come boldly to the point, but this inspiration was commonly defeated by some extraordinary manifestation of Coke's incapacity. To her mind, then, it seemed like a proposition to ally herself to a butcher-boy in a matter purely sentimental. She wondered indignantly how she was going to conspire with this lad, who puffed out his infantile cheeks in order to conceitedly demonstrate that he did not understand the game at all. She hated Marjory for it. Evidently it was only the weaklings who fell in love with that girl. Coleman was an exception, but then, Coleman was misled by extraordinary artifices. She meditated for a moment if she should tell Coke to go home and not bother her. What at last decided the question was his unhappiness. She clung to this unhappiness for its value as it stood alone, and because its reason for existence was related to her own unhappiness. "You say you are not going back to Athens with your party. I don't suppose you're going to stay here. I'm going back to Athens to-day. I came up here to see a battle, but it doesn't seem that there are to be any more battles. The fighting will now all be on the other side of the mountains." Apparently she had learned in some haphazard way that the Greek peninsula was divided by a spine of almost inaccessible mountains, and the war was thus split into two simultaneous campaigns. The Arta campaign was known to be ended. "If you want to go back to Athens without consorting with your friends, you had better go back with me. I can take you in my carriage as far as the beginning of the railroad. Don't you worry. You've got money enough, haven't you? The professor isn't keeping your money?"

"Yes," he said slowly, "I've got money enough." He was apparently dubious over the proposal.

In their abstracted walk they had arrived in front of the house occupied by Coleman and the Wainwright party. Two carriages, forlorn in dusty age, stood before the door. Men were carrying out new leather luggage and flinging it into the traps amid a great deal of talk which seemed to refer to nothing. Nora and Coke stood looking at the scene without either thinking of the importance of running away, when out tumbled seven students, followed immediately but in more decorous fashion by the Wainwrights and Coleman.

Some student set up a whoop. "Oh, there he is. There's Coke. Hey, Coke, where you been? Here he is, professor."

For a moment after the hoodlum had subsided, the two camps stared at each other in silence.

Chapter 20

Nora and Coke were an odd looking pair at the time. They stood indeed as if rooted to the spot, staring vacuously, like two villagers, at the surprising travellers. It was not an eternity before the practiced girl of the stage recovered her poise, but to the end of the incident the green youth looked like a culprit and a fool. Mrs. Wainwright's glower of offensive incredulity was a masterpiece. Marjory nodded pleasantly; the professor nodded. The seven students clambered boisterously into the forward carriage making it clang with noise like a rook's nest. They shouted to Coke. "Come on; all aboard; come on, Coke; we're off. Hey, there, Cokey, hurry up." The professor, as soon as he had seated himself on the forward seat of the second carriage, turned in Coke's general direction and asked formally: "Mr. Coke, you are coming with us?" He felt seemingly much in doubt as to the propriety of abandoning the headstrong young man, and this doubt was not at all decreased by Coke's appearance with Nora Black. As far as he could tell, any assertion of authority on his part would end only in a scene in which Coke would probably insult him with some gross violation of collegiate conduct. As at first the young man made no reply, the professor after waiting spoke again. "You understand, Mr. Coke, that if you separate yourself from the party you encounter my strongest disapproval, and if I did not feel responsible to the college and your father for your safe journey to New York I—I don't know but what I would have you expelled by cable if that were possible."

Although Coke had been silent, and Nora Black had had the appearance of being silent, in reality she had lowered her chin and whispered sideways and swiftly. She had said: "Now, here's your time. Decide quickly, and don't look such a wooden Indian."

Coke pulled himself together with a visible effort, and spoke to the professor from an inspiration in which he had no faith. "I understand my duties to you, sir, perfectly. I also understand my duty to the college. But I fail to see where either of these obligations require me to accept the introduction of objectionable people into the party. If I owe a duty to the college and to you, I don't owe any to Coleman, and, as I understand it, Coleman was not in the original plan of this expedition. If such had been the case, I would not have been here. I can't tell what the college may see fit to do, but as for my father I have no

357

doubt of how he will view it.''

The first one to be electrified by the speech was Coke himself. He saw with a kind of sub-conscious amazement this volley of bird-shot take effect upon the face of the old professor. The face of Marjory flushed crimson as if her mind had sprung to a fear that if Coke could develop ability in this singular fashion he might succeed in humiliating her father in the street in the presence of the seven students, her mother, Coleman and—herself. She had felt the birdshot sting her father.

When Coke had launched forth, Coleman with his legs stretched far apart had just struck a match on the wall of the house and was about to light a cigar. His groom was leading up his horse. He saw the value of Coke's argument more appreciatively and sooner perhaps than did Coke. The match dropped from his fingers, and in the white sunshine and still air it burnt on the pavement orange coloured and with langour. Coleman held his cigar with all five fingers—in a manner out of all the laws of smoking. He turned toward Coke. There was danger in the moment, but then in a flash it came upon him that his role was not of squabbling with Coke, far less of punching him. On the contrary, he was to act the part of a cool and instructed man who refused to be waylaid into foolishness by the outcries of this pouting youngster and who placed himself in complete deference to the wishes of the professor. Before the professor had time to embark upon any reply to Coke, Coleman was at the side of the carriage and, with a fine assumption of distress, was saying: "Professor, I could very easily ride back to Agrinion alone. It would be all right. I don't want to——"

To his surprise the professor waved at him to be silent as if he were a mere child. The old man's face was set with the resolution of exactly what he was going to say to Coke. He began in measured tone, speaking with feeling, but with no trace of anger. "Mr. Coke, it has probably escaped your attention that Mr. Coleman, at what I consider a great deal of peril to himself, came out to rescue this party—you and others—and although he studiously disclaims all merit in his finding us and bringing us in, I do not regard it in that way, and I am surprised that any member of this party should conduct himself in this manner toward a man who has been most devotedly and generously at our service." It was at this time that the professor raised himself and shook his finger at Coke, his voice now ringing with scorn. In such moments words came to him and formed themselves into sentences almost too rapidly for him to speak them. "You are one of the most remarkable products of our civilisation which I have yet come upon. What do you mean, sir? Where are your senses? Do you think that all this pulling and pucking is manhood? I will tell you what I will do with you. I thought I brought out eight students to Greece, but when I find that I brought out seven students and—er—an—ourang-outang—don't get angry, sir—I don't care for your anger—I say when I discover this I am naturally puzzled for a moment. I will leave you to the judgment of your peers. Young gentlemen!"

Of the seven heads of the forward carriage none had to be turned. All had been turned since the beginning of the talk. If the professor's speech had been delivered in one of the class-rooms of Washurst they would have glowed with delight over the butchery of Coke, but they felt its portentous aspect. Butchery here in Greece thousands of miles from home presented to them more of the emphasis of downright death and destruction. The professor called out: "Young gentlemen, I have done all that I can do without using force, which, much to my regret, is impracticable. If you will persuade your fellow student to accompany you I think our consciences will be the better for not having left a weak minded brother alone among the by-paths."

The valuable aggregation of intelligence and refinement which decorated the interior of the first carriage did not hesitate over answering this appeal. In fact, his fellow students had worried among themselves over Coke, and their desire to see him come out of his troubles in fair condition was intensified by the fact that they had lately concentrated much thought upon him. There was a somewhat comic pretense of speaking so that only Coke could hear. Their chorus was low sung. 'Oh, cheese it, Coke, Let up on yourself, you blind ass. Wait till you get to Athens and then go and act like a monkey. All this is no good——"

The advice which came from the carriage was all in one direction, and there was so much of it that the hum of voices sounded like a wind blowing through a forest.

Coke spun suddenly and said something to Nora Black. Nora laughed rather loudly, and then the two turned squarely and the Wainwright party contemplated what were surely at that time the two most insolent backs in the world.

The professor looked as if he might be going to have a fit. Mrs. Wainwright lifted her eyes toward heaven, and flinging out her trembling hands, cried: "Oh, what an outrage. What an outrage! That minx——" The concensus of opinion in the first carriage was perfectly expressed by Peter Tounley, who with a deep drawn breath, said: "Well, I'm damned!" Marjory had moaned and lowered her head as from a sense of complete personal shame. Coleman lit his cigar and mounted his horse. "Well, I suppose there is nothing for it but to be off, professor?" His tone was full of regret, with sort of poetic regret. For a moment the professor looked at him blankly, and then gradually recovered part of his usual manner. "Yes," he said sadly, "there is nothing for it but to go on." At a word from the dragoman, the two impatient drivers spoke gutturally to their horses and the carriages whirled out of Arta. Coleman, his dragoman and the groom trotted in the dust from the wheels of the Wainwright carriage. The correspondent always found his reflective faculties improved by the constant pounding of a horse on the trot, and he was not sorry to have now a period for reflection, as well as this artificial stimulant. As he viewed the game he had in his hand about all the cards that were valuable. In fact, he considered that the only ace against him was Mrs. Wainwright. He had always regarded her as a stupid person, concealing herself behind a mass of trivialities which were all conventional, but he thought now that the more stupid she was and the more conventional in her triviality the more she approached to being the very ace of trumps itself. She was just the sort of a card that would come upon the table mid the neat play of experts and by some inexplicable arrangement of circumstance, lose a whole game for the wrong man.

After Mrs. Wainwright he worried over the students. He believed them to be reasonable enough; in fact, he honoured them distinctly in regard to their powers of reason, but he knew that people generally hated a row. It put them off their balance, made them sweat over a lot of pros and cons, and prevented them from thinking for a time at least only of themselves. Then they came to resent the principals in a row. Of course the principal, who was thought to be in the wrong, was the most resented, but Coleman believed that, after all, people always came to resent the other principal, or at least be impatient and suspicious of him. If he was a correct person, why was he in a row at all? The principal who had been in the right often brought this impatience and suspicion upon himself, no doubt, by never letting the matter end, continuing to yawp about his virtuous suffering, and not allowing people to return to the steady contemplation of their own affairs. As a precautionary measure he decided to say nothing at all about the late trouble, unless some one addressed him upon it. Even then he would be serenely laconic. He felt that he must be popular with the seven students. In the first place, it was nice that in the presence of Marjory they should like him, and in the second place he feared to displease them as a body because he believed that he had some dignity. Hoodlums are seldom dangerous to other hoodlums, but if they catch pomposity alone in the field, pomposity is their prey. They tear him to mere bloody ribbons, amid heartless shrieks. When Coleman put himself on the same basis with the students, he could cope with them easily, but he did not want the wild pack after him when Marjory could see the chase. And so he reasoned that his best attitude was to be one of rather taciturn serenity.

On the hard military road the hoofs of the horses made such clatter that it was practically impossible to hold talk between the carriages and the horsemen without all parties bellowing. The professor, however, strove to overcome the difficulties. He was apparently undergoing a great amiability toward Coleman. Frequently he turned with a bright face, and pointing to some object in the landscape, obviously tried to convey something entertaining to Coleman's mind. Coleman could see his lips mouth the words. He always nodded cheerily in answer and yelled.

The road ultimately became that straight lance-handle which Coleman—it seemed as if many years had passed—had traversed with his dragoman and the funny little carriers. He was fixing in his mind a possible story to the Wainwrights about the snake and his first dead Turk. But suddenly the carriages left this road and began a circuit of the Gulf of Arta, winding about an endless series of promontories. The journey developed into an excess of dust whirling from a road, which half circled the waist of cape after cape. All dramatics were lost in the rumble of wheels and in the click of hoofs. They passed a little soldier leading a prisoner by a string. They passed more frightened peasants, who seemed resolved to flee down into the very boots of Greece. And people looked at them with scowls, envying them their speed. At the little town from which Coleman embarked at one stage of the upward journey, they found crowds in the streets. There was no longer any laughter, any confidence, any vim. All the spirit of the visible Greek nation seemed to have been knocked out of it in two blows. But still they talked and never ceased talking. Coleman noticed that the most curious changes had come upon them since his journey to the frontier. They no longer approved of foreigners. They seemed to blame the travellers for something which had transpired in the past few days. It was not that they really blamed the travellers for the nation's calamity: It was simply that their minds were half stunned by the news of defeats, and, not thinking for a moment to blame themselves, or even not thinking to attribute the defeats to mere numbers and skill, they were savagely eager to fasten it upon something near enough at hand for the operation of vengeance.

Coleman perceived that the dragoman, all his former plumage gone, was whining and snivelling as he argued to a dark-browed crowd that was running beside the cavalcade. The groom, who always had been a miraculously laconic man, was suddenly launched forth garrulously. The drivers, from their high seats, palavered like mad men, driving with one hand and gesturing with the other, explaining evidently their own great innocence.

Coleman saw that there was trouble, but he only sat more stiffly in his saddle. The eternal gabble moved him to despise the situation. At any rate, the travellers would soon be out of this town and on to a more sensible region.

However, he saw the driver of the first carriage suddenly pull up before a little blackened coffee shop and inn. The dragoman spurred forward and began wild expostulation. The second carriage pulled close behind the other. The crowd, murmuring like a Roman mob in Nero's time, closed around them.

Chapter 21

Coleman pushed his horse coolly through to the dragoman's side. "What is it?" he demanded. The dragoman was broken-voiced. "These peoples, they say you are Germans, all Germans, and they are angry," he wailed. "I can do nossing—nossing."

"Well, tell these men to drive on," said Coleman, "tell them they must drive on."

"They will not drive on," wailed the dragoman, still more loudly. "I can do nossing. They say here is place for feed the horse. It is the custom and they will note drive on."

"Make them drive on."

"They will note," shrieked the agonised servitor.

Coleman looked from the men waving their arms and chattering on the box-seats to the men of the crowd who also waved their arms and chattered. In this throng far to the rear of the fighting armies there did not seem to be a single man who was not able-bodied, who had not been free to enlist as a soldier. They were of that scurvy behind-the-rear-guard which every nation has in degree proportionate to its worth. The manhood of Greece had gone to the frontier, leaving at home this rabble of talkers, most of whom were armed with rifles for mere pretention. Coleman loathed them to the end of his soul. He thought them a lot of infants who would like to prove their courage upon eleven innocent travellers, all but unarmed, and in this fact he was quick to see a great danger to the Wainwright party. One could deal with soldiers; soldiers would have been ashamed to bait helpless people; but this rabble——

The fighting blood of the correspondent began to boil, and he really longed for the privilege to run amuck through the multitude. But a look at the Wainwrights kept him in his senses. The professor had turned pale as a dead man. He sat very stiff and still while his wife clung to him, hysterically beseeching him to do something, do something, although what he was to do she could not have even imagined.

Coleman took the dilemma by its beard. He dismounted from his horse into the depths of the crowd and addressed the Wainwrights. "I suppose we had better go into this place and have some coffee while the men feed their horses. There is no use in trying to make them go on." His manner was fairly casual, but they looked at him in glazed horror. "It is the only thing to do. This crowd is not nearly so bad as they think they are. But we've got to look as if we felt confident." He himself had no confidence with this angry buzz in his ears, but he felt certain that the only correct move was to get everybody as quickly as possible within the shelter of the inn. It might not be much of a shelter for them, but it was better than the carriages in the street.

The professor and Mrs. Wainwright seemed to be considering their carriage as a castle, and they looked as if their terror had made them physically incapable of leaving it. Coleman stood waiting. Behind him the clapper-tongued crowd was moving ominously. Marjory arose and stepped calmly down to him.

He thrilled to the end of every nerve. It was as if she had said: "I don't think there is great danger, but if there is great danger, why * * here I am * ready * with you." It conceded everything, admitted everything. It was a surrender without a blush, and it was only possible in the shadow of the crisis when they did not know what the next moments might contain for them. As he took her hand and she stepped past him he whispered swiftly and fiercely in her ear, "I love you." She did not look up, but he felt that in this quick incident they had claimed each other, accepted each other with a far deeper meaning and understanding than could be possible in a mere drawing-room. She laid her hand on his arm, and with the strength of four men he twisted his horse into the making of furious prancing side-steps toward the door of the inn, clanking side-steps which mowed a wide lane through the crowd for Marjory, his Marjory. He was as haughty as a new German lieutenant, and although he held the fuming horse with only his left hand, he seemed perfectly capable of hurling the animal over a house without calling into service the arm which was devoted to Marjory.

It was not an exhibition of coolness such as wins applause on the stage when the hero placidly lights a cigarette before the mob which is clamouring for his death. It was, on the contrary, an exhibition of downright classic disdain, a disdain which with the highest arrogance declared itself in every glance of his eye into the faces about him. "Very good * * attack me if you like * * there is nothing to prevent it * * you mongrels." Every step of his progress was made a renewed insult to them. The very air was charged with what this lone man was thinking of this threatening crowd.

His audacity was invincible. They actually made way for it as quickly as children would flee from a ghost. The horse, dancing with ringing steps, with his glistening neck arched toward the iron hand at his bit, this powerful, quivering animal was a regular engine of destruction, and they gave room until Coleman halted him at an exclamation from Marjory. "My mother and father." But they were coming close behind and Coleman resumed this contemptuous journey to the door of the inn. The groom, with his new-born tongue, was clattering there to the populace. Coleman gave him the horse and passed after the Wainwrights into the public room of the inn. He was smiling. What simpletons!

A new actor suddenly appeared in the person of the keeper of the inn. He too had a rifle and a prodigious belt of cartridges, but it was plain at once that he had elected to be a friend of the worried travellers. A large part of the crowd were thinking it necessary to enter the inn and pow-wow more. But the innkeeper stayed at the door with the dragoman, and together they vociferously held back the tide. The spirit of the mob had subsided to a more reasonable feeling. They no longer wished to tear the strangers limb from limb on the suspicion that they were Germans. They now were frantic to talk as if some inexorable law had kept them silent for ten years and this was the very moment of their release. Whereas, their simultaneous and interpolating orations had throughout made noise much like a coal-breaker.

Coleman led the Wainwrights to a table in a far part of the room. They took chairs as if he had commanded them. "What an outrage," he said jubilantly. "The apes." He was keeping more than half an eye upon the door, because he knew that the quick coming of the students was important.

Then suddenly the storm broke in wrath. Something had happened in the street. The jabbering crowd at the door had turned and were hurrying upon some central tumult. The dragoman screamed to Coleman. Coleman jumped and grabbed the dragoman. "Tell this man to take them somewhere up stairs," he cried, indicating the Wainwrights with a sweep of his arm. The innkeeper seemed to understand sooner than the dragoman, and he nodded eagerly. The professor was crying: "What is it, Mr. Coleman? What is it?" An instant later, the correspondent was out in the street, buffeting toward a scuffle. Of course it was the students. It appeared, afterward, that those seven young men, with their feelings much ruffled, had been making the best of their way toward the door of the inn, when a large man in the crowd, during a speech which was surely most offensive, had laid an arresting hand on the shoulder of Peter Tounley. Whereupon the excellent Peter Tounley had hit the large man on the jaw in such a swift and skilful manner that the large man had gone spinning through a group of his countrymen to the hard earth, where he lay holding his face together and howling. Instantly, of course, there had been a riot. It might well be said that even then the affair could have ended in a lot of talking, but in the first place the students did not talk modern Greek, and in the second place they were now past all thought of talking. They regarded this affair seriously as a fight, and now that they at last were in it, they were in it for every pint of blood in their bodies. Such a pack of famished wolves had never before been let loose upon men armed with Gras rifles.

They all had been expecting the row, and when Peter Tounley had found it expedient to knock over the man, they had counted it a signal: their arms immediately begun to swing out as if they had been wound up. It was at this time that Coleman swam brutally through the Greeks and joined his country-men. He was more frightened than any of those novices. When he saw Peter Tounley overthrow a dreadful looking brigand whose belt was full of knives, and who crashed to the ground amid a clang of cartridges, he was appalled by the utter simplicity with which the lads were treating the crisis. It was to them no common scrimmage at Washurst, of course, but it flashed through Coleman's mind that they had not the slightest sense of the size of the thing. He expected every instant to see the flash of knives or to hear the deafening intonation of a rifle fired against his ear. It seemed to him miraculous that the tragedy was so long delayed.

In the meantime he was in the affray. He jilted one man under the chin with his elbow in a way that reeled him off from Peter Tounley's back; a little person in checked clothes he smote between the eyes; he received a gun-butt emphatically on the side of the neck; he felt hands tearing at him; he kicked the pins out from under three men in rapid succession. He was always yelling. "Try to get to the inn, boys, try to get to the inn. Look out, Peter. Take care for his knife, Peter—'' Suddenly he whipped a rifle out of the hands of a man and swung it, whistling. He had gone stark mad with the others.

The boy Billy, drunk from some blows and bleeding, was already staggering toward the inn over the clearage which the wild Coleman made with the clubbed rifle. The others followed as well as they might while beating off a discouraged enemy. The remarkable innkeeper had barred his windows with strong wood shutters. He held the door by the crack for them, and they stumbled one by one through the portal. Coleman did not know why they were not all dead, nor did he understand the intrepid and generous behaviour of the innkeeper, but at any rate he felt that the fighting was suspended, and he wanted to see Marjory. The innkeeper was doing a great pantomime in the middle of the darkened room, pointing to the outer door and then aiming his rifle at it to explain his intention of defending them at all costs. Some of the students moved to a billiard table and spread themselves wearily upon it. Others sank down where they stood. Outside the crowd was beginning to roar. Coleman's groom crept out from under the little coffee bar and comically saluted his master. The dragoman was not present. Coleman felt that he must see Marjory, and he made signs to the innkeeper. The latter understood quickly, and motioned that Coleman should follow him. They passed together through a dark hall and up a darker stairway, whereafter Coleman stepped out into a sun-lit room, saying loudly: "Oh, it's all right. It's all over. Don't worry."

Three wild people were instantly upon him. "Oh, what was it? What did happen? Is anybody hurt? Oh, tell us quick!" It seemed at the time that it was an avalanche of three of them, and it was not until later that he recognised that Mrs. Wainwright had tumbled the largest number of questions upon him. As for Marjory, she had said nothing until the time when she cried: "Oh—he is bleeding—he is bleeding. Oh, come, quick!" She fairly dragged him out of one room into another room, where there was a jug of water. She wet her handkerchief and softly smote his wounds. "Bruises," she said, piteously, tearfully. "Bruises. Oh, dear! How they must hurt you." The handkerchief was soon stained crimson.

When Coleman spoke his voice quavered. "It isn't anything. Really, it isn't anything." He had not known of these wonderful wounds, but he almost choked in the joy of Marjory's ministry and her half-coherent exclamations. This proud and beautiful girl, this superlative creature, was reddening her handkerchief with his blood, and no word of his could have prevented her from thus attending him. He could hear the professor and Mrs. Wainwright fussing near him, trying to be of use. He would have liked to have been able to order them out of the room. Marjory's cool fingers on his face and neck had conjured within him a vision of an intimacy that was even sweeter than anything which he had imagined, and he longed to pour out to her the bubbling, impassioned speech which came to his lips. But, always doddering behind him, were the two old people, strenuous to be of help to him.

Suddenly a door opened and a youth appeared, simply red with blood. It was Peter Tounley. His first remark was cheerful. "Well, I don't suppose those people will be any too quick to look for more trouble."

Coleman felt a swift pang because he had forgotten to announce the dilapidated state of all the students. He had been so submerged by Marjory's tenderness that all else had been drowned from his mind. His heart beat quickly as he waited for Marjory to leave him and rush to Peter Tounley.

But she did nothing of the sort. "Oh, Peter," she cried in distress, and then she turned back to Coleman. It was the professor and Mrs. Wainwright who, at last finding a field for their kindly ambitions, flung themselves upon Tounley and carried him off to another place. Peter was removed, crying: "Oh, now, look here, professor, I'm not dying or anything of that sort——"

Coleman and Marjory were left alone. He suddenly and forcibly took one of her hands and the bloodstained handkerchief dropped to the floor.

Chapter 22

From below they could hear the thunder of weapons and fists upon the door of the inn amid a great clamour of tongues. Sometimes there arose the argumentative howl of the innkeeper. Above this roar, Coleman's quick words sounded in Marjory's ear. "I've got to go. I've got to go back to the boys, but—I love you."

"Yes, go, go," she whispered hastily. "You should be there, but—come back."

He held her close to him. "But you are mine, remember," he said fiercely and sternly. "You are mine—forever—as I am yours—remember."

Her eyes half closed. She made intensely solemn answer. "Yes." He released her and was gone.

In the glooming coffee room of the inn he found the students, the dragoman, the groom and the innkeeper armed with a motley collection of weapons which ranged from the rifle of the innkeeper to the table leg in the hands of Peter Tounley. The last named young student of archæology was in a position of temporary leadership and holding a great pow-bow with the innkeeper through the medium of piercing outcries by the dragoman. Coleman had not yet understood why none of them had been either stabbed or shot in the fight in the street, but it seemed to him now that affairs were leading toward a crisis of tragedy. He thought of the possibilities of having the dragoman go to an upper window and harangue the people, but he saw no chance of success in such a plan. He saw that the crowd would merely howl at the dragoman while the dragoman howled at the crowd. He then asked if there was any other exit from the inn by which they could secretly escape. He learned that the door into the coffee room was the only door which pierced the four great walls. All he could then do was to find out from the innkeeper how much of a siege the place could stand, and to this the innkeeper answered volubly and with smiles that this hostelry would easily endure until the mercurial temper of the crowd had darted off in a new direction. It may be curious to note here that all of Peter Tounley's impassioned communication with the innkeeper had been devoted to an endeavour to learn what in the devil was the matter with these people, as a man about to be bitten by poisonous snakes should, first of all, furiously insist upon learning their exact species before deciding upon either his route, if he intended to run away, or his weapon if he intended to fight them.

The innkeeper was evidently convinced that this house would withstand the rage of the populace, and he was such an unaccountably gallant little chap that Coleman trusted entirely to his word. His only fear or suspicion was an occasional one as to the purity of the dragoman's translation.

Suddenly there was half a silence on the mob without the door. It is inconceivable that it could become altogether silent, but it was as near to a rational stillness of tongues as it was able. Then there was a loud knocking by a single fist and a new voice began to spin Greek, a voice that was somewhat like the rattle of pebbles in a tin box. Then a startling voice called out in English. "Are you in there, Rufus?"

Answers came from every English speaking person in the room in one great outburst. "Yes."

"Well, let us in," called Nora Black. "It is all right. We've got an officer with us."

"Opon the door," said Coleman with speed. The little innkeeper labouriously unfastened the great bars, and when the door finally opened there appeared on the threshold Nora Black with Coke and an officer of infantry, Nora's little old companion, and Nora's dragoman.

"We saw your carriage in the street," cried the queen of comic opera as she swept into the room. She was beaming with delight. "What is all the row, anyway? O-o-o, look at that student's nose. Who hit him? And look at Rufus. What have you boys been doing?"

Her little Greek officer of infantry had stopped the mob from flowing into the room. Coleman looked toward the door at times with some anxiety. Nora, noting it, waved her hand in careless reassurance. "Oh, it's all right. Don't worry about them any more. He is perfectly devoted to me. He would die there on the threshold if I told him it would please me. Speaks splendid French. I found him limping along the road and gave him a lift. And now do hurry up and tell me exactly what happened.

They all told what had happened, while Nora and Coke listened agape. Coke, by the way, had quite floated back to his old position with the students. It had been easy in the stress of excitement and wonder. Nobody had any time to think of the excessively remote incidents of the early morning. All minor interests were lost in the marvel of the present situation.

"Who landed you in the eye, Billie?" asked the awed Coke. "That was a bad one."

"Oh, I don't know," said Billie. "You really couldn't tell who hit you, you know. It was a football rush. They had guns and knives, but they didn't use 'em. I don't know why. Jinks! I'm getting pretty stiff. My face feels as if it were made of tin. Did they give you people a row, too?"

"No; only talk. That little officer managed them. Out-talked them, I suppose. Hear him buzz, now.

The Wainwrights came down stairs. Nora Black went confidently forward to meet them. "You've added one more to your list of rescuers," she cried, with her glowing, triumphant smile. "Miss Black of the *New York Daylight*—at your service. How in the world do you manage to get yourselves into such dreadful scrapes? You are the most remarkable people. You need a guardian. Why, you might have all been killed. How exciting it must seem to be regularly of your party." She had shaken cordially one of Mrs. Wainwright's hands without that lady indicating assent to the proceeding, but Mrs. Wainwright had not felt repulsion. In fact she had had no emotion springing directly from it. Here again the marvel of the situation came to deny Mrs. Wainwright the right to resume a state of mind which had been so painfully interesting to her a few hours earlier.

The professor, Coleman and all the students were talking together. Coke had addressed Coleman civilly and Coleman had made a civil reply. Peace was upon them.

Nora slipped her arm lovingly through Marjory's arm. "That Rufus! Oh, that Rufus," she cried joyously. "I'll give him a good scolding as soon as I see him alone. I might have foreseen that he would get you all into trouble. The old stupid!"

Marjory did not appear to resent anything. "Oh, I don't think it was Mr. Coleman's fault at all," she answered calmly. "I think it was more the fault of Peter Tounley, poor boy."

"Well, I'd be glad to believe it, I'd be glad to believe it," said Nora. "I want Rufus to keep out of that sort of thing, but he is so hot-headed and foolish." If she had pointed out her proprietary stamp on Coleman's cheek she could not have conveyed what she wanted with more clearness.

"Oh," said the impassive Marjory, "I don't think you need have any doubts as to whose fault it was, if there were any of our boys at fault. Mr. Coleman was inside when the fighting commenced, and only ran out to help the boys. He had just brought us safely through the mob, and, far from being hot-headed and foolish, he was utterly cool in manner, impressively cool, I thought. I am glad to be able to reassure you on these points, for I see that they worry you."

"Yes, they do worry me," said Nora, densely. "They worry me night and day when he is away from me."

'Oh," responded Marjory, "I have never thought of Mr. Coleman as a man that one would worry about much. We consider him very self-reliant, able to take care of himself under almost any conditions, but then, of course, we do not know him at all in the way that you know him. I should think you would find that he came off rather better than you expected from most of his difficulties. But then, of course, as I said, you know him so much better than we do." Her easy indifference was a tacit dismissal of Coleman as a topic.

Nora, now thoroughly alert, glanced keenly into the other girl's face, but it was inscrutable. The actress had intended to go careering through a whole circle of daring illusions to an intimacy with Coleman, but here, before she had really developed her attack, Marjory, with a few conventional and indifferent sentences, almost expressive of boredom, had made the subject of Coleman impossible. An effect was left upon Nora's mind that Marjory had been extremely polite in listening to much nervous talk about a person in whom she had no interest.

The actress was dazed. She did not know how it had all been done. Where was the head of this thing? And where was the tail? A fog had mysteriously come upon all her brilliant prospects of seeing Marjory Wainwright suffer, and this fog was the product of a kind of magic with which she was not familiar. She could not think how to fight it. After being simply dubious throughout a long pause, she in the end went into a great rage. She glared furiously at Marjory, dropped her arm as if it had burned her and moved down upon Coleman. She must have reflected that at any rate she could make him wriggle. When she was come near to him, she called out: "Rufus!" In her tone was all the old insolent statement of ownership. Coleman might have been a poodle. She knew how to call his name in a way that was nothing less than a public scandal. On this occasion everybody looked at him and then went silent, as people awaiting the startling denouement of a drama. "Rufus!" She was baring his shoulder to show the fleur-de-lis of the criminal. The students gaped.

Coleman's temper was, if one may be allowed to speak in that way, broken loose inside of him. He could hardly breathe; he felt that his body was about to explode into a thousand fragments. He simply snarled out "What?" Almost at once he saw that she had at last goaded him into making a serious tactical mistake. It must be admitted that it is only when the relations between a man and a woman are the relations of wedlock, or at least an intimate resemblance to it, that the man snarls out "What?" to the woman. Mere lovers say "I beg your pardon?" It is only Cupid's finished product that spits like a cat. Nora Black had called him like a wife, and he had answered like a husband. For his cause, his manner could not possibly have been worse. He saw the professor stare at him in surprise and alarm, and felt the excitement of the eight students. These latter were diabolic in the celerity with which they picked out meanings. It was as plain to them as if Nora Black had said: "He is my property."

Coleman would have given his nose to have been able to recall that single reverberating word. But he saw that the scene was spelling downfall for him, and he went still more blind and desperate of it. His despair made him burn to make matters worse. He did not want to improve anything at all. "What?" he demanded. "What do ye' want?"

Nora was sweetly reproachful. "I left my jacket in the carriage, and I want you to get it for me."

"Well, get it for yourself, do you see? Get it for yourself."

Now it is plainly to be seen that no one of the people listening there had ever heard a man speak thus to a woman who was not his wife. Whenever they had heard that form of spirited repartee it had come from the lips of a husband. Coleman's rude speech was to their ears a flat announcement of an extra-ordinary intimacy between Nora Black and the correspondent. Any other interpretation would not have occurred to them. It was so palpable that it greatly distressed them with its arrogance and boldness. The professor had blushed. The very milkiest word in his mind at the time was the word vulgarity.

Nora Black had won a great battle. It was her Agincourt. She had beaten the clever Coleman in a way that left little of him but rags. However, she could have lost it all again if she had shown her feeling of elation. At Coleman's rudeness her manner indicated a mixture of sadness and embarrassment. Her suffering was so plain to the eye that Peter Tounley was instantly moved. "Can't I get your jacket for you, Miss Black?" he asked hastily, and at her grateful nod he was off at once.

Coleman was resolved to improve nothing. His overthrow seemed to him to be so complete that he could not in any way mend it without a sacrifice of his dearest prides. He turned away from them all and walked to an isolated corner of the room. He would abide no longer with them. He had been made an outcast by Nora Black, and he intended to be an outcast. There was no sense in attempting to stem this extraordinary deluge. It was better to acquiesce.

Then suddenly he was angry with Marjory. He did not exactly see why he was angry at Marjory, but he was angry at her nevertheless. He thought of how he could revenge himself upon her. He decided to take horse with his groom and dragoman and proceed forthwith on the road, leaving the jumble as it stood. This would pain Marjory, anyhow, he hoped. She would feel it deeply, he hoped.

Acting upon this plan, he went to the professor. "Well, of course you are all right now, professor, and if you don't mind, I would like to leave you—go on ahead. I've got a considerable pressure of business on my mind, and I think I should hurry on to Athens, if you don't mind."

The professor did not seem to know what to say. "Of course, if you wish it—sorry, I'm sure—of course it is as you please—but you have been such a power in our favour—it seems too bad to lose you—but—if you wish it—if you insist——"

"Oh, yes, I quite insist," said Coleman, calmly. "I quite insist. Make your mind easy on that score, professor. I insist."

"Well, Mr. Coleman," stammered the old man. "Well, it seems a great pity to lose you—you have been such a power in our favour——"

"Oh, you are now only eight hours from the railway. It is very easy. You would not need my assistance, even if it were a benefit!"

"But——" said the professor.

Coleman's dragoman came to him then and said: "There is one man here who says you made to take one rifle in the fight and was break his head. He was say he wants sunthing for you was break his head. He says hurt."

"How much does he want?" asked Coleman, impatiently.

The dragoman wrestled then evidently with a desire to protect this mine from outside fingers. "I—I think two gold piece plenty."

"Take them," said Coleman. It seemed to him preposterous that this idiot with a broken head should interpolate upon his tragedy. "Afterward, you and the groom get the three horses and we will start for Athens at once."

"For Athens? At once?" said Marjory's voice in his ear.

Chapter 23

Oh," said Coleman, "I was thinking of starting."

"Why?" asked Marjory, unconcernedly.

Coleman shot her a quick glance. "I believe my period of usefulness is quite ended," he said with just a small betrayal of bitter feeling.

"It is certainly true that you have had a remarkable period of usefulness to us," said Marjory with a slow smile, "but if it is ended, you should not run away from us."

Coleman looked at her to see what she could mean. From many women, these words would have been equal, under the circumstances, to a command to stay, but he felt that none might know what impulses moved the mind behind that beautiful mask. In his misery he thought to hurt her into an expression of feeling by a rough speech. "I'm so in love with Nora Black, you know, that I have to be very careful of myself."

"Oh," said Marjory, "I never thought of that. I should think you would have to be careful of yourself." She did not seem moved in any way. Coleman despaired of finding her weak spot. She was adamantine, this girl. He searched his mind for something to say which would be still more gross than his last outbreak, but when he felt that he was about to hit upon it, the professor interrupted with an agitated speech to Marjory. "You had better go to your mother, my child, and see that you are all ready to leave here as soon as the carriages come up."

"We have absolutely nothing to make ready," said Marjory, laughing. "But I'll go and see if mother needs anything before we start that I can get for her." She went away without bidding good-bye to Coleman. The sole maddening impression to him was that the matter of his going had not been of sufficient importance to remain longer than a moment upon her mind. At the same time he decided that he would go, irretrievably go.

Even then the dragoman entered the room. "We will pack everything upon the horse?"

"Everything—yes."

Peter Tounley came afterward. "You are not going to bolt?"

"Yes, I'm off," answered Coleman recovering himself for Peter's benefit. "See you in Athens, probably."

372

Presently the dragoman announced the readiness of the horses. Coleman shook hands with the students and the Professor amid cries of surprise and polite regret. "What? Going, old man? Really? What for? Oh, wait for us. We're off in a few minutes. Sorry as the devil, old boy, to see you go." He accepted their protestations with a somewhat sour face. He knew perfectly well that they were thinking of his departure as something that related to Nora Black. At the last, he bowed to the ladies as a collection. Marjory's answering bow was affable; the bow of Mrs. Wainwright spoke a resentment for something; and Nora's bow was triumphant mockery. As he swung into the saddle an idea struck him with overwhelming force. The idea was that he was a fool. He was a colossal imbecile. He touched the spur to his horse and the animal leaped superbly, making the Greeks hasten for safety in all directions. He was off; he could no more return to retract his devious idiocy than he could make his horse fly to Athens. What was done was done. He could not mend it. And he felt like a man that had broken his own heart; perversely, childishly, stupidly broken his own heart.

He was sure that Marjory was lost to him. No man could be degraded so publicly and resent it so crudely and still retain a Marjory. In his abasement from his defeat at the hands of Nora Black he had performed every imaginable block-headish act and had finally climaxed it all by a departure which left the tongue of Nora to speak unmolested into the ear of Marjory. Nora's victory had been a serious blow to his fortunes, but it had not been so serious as his own subsequent folly. He had generously muddled his own affairs until he could read nothing out of them but despair.

He was in the mood for hatred. He hated many people. Nora Black was the principal item, but he did not hesitate to detest the professor, Mrs. Wainwright, Coke and all the students. As for Marjory, he would revenge himself upon her. She had done nothing that he defined clearly but, at any rate, he would take revenge for it. As much as was possible, he would make her suffer. He would convince her that he was a tremendous and inexorable person. But it came upon his mind that he was powerless in all ways. If he hated many people they probably would not be even interested in his emotion and, as for his revenge upon Marjory, it was beyond his strength. He was nothing but the complaining victim of Nora Black and himself.

He felt that he would never again see Marjory, and while feeling it he began to plan his attitude when next they met. He would be very cold and reserved.

At Agrinion he found that there would be no train until the next daybreak. The dragoman was excessively annoyed over it, but Coleman did not scold at all. As a matter of fact his heart had given a great joyous bound. He could not now prevent his being overtaken. They were only a few leagues away, and while he was waiting for the train they would easily cover the distance. If anybody expressed surprise at seeing him he could exhibit the logical reasons.

If there had been a train starting at once he would have taken it. His pride would have put up with no subterfuge. If the Wainwrights overtook him it was because he could not help it. But he was delighted that he could not help it. There had been an interposition by some specially beneficent fate. He felt like whistling. He spent the early half of the night in blissful smoke, striding the room which the dragoman had found for him. His head was full of plans and detached impressive scenes in which he figured before Marjory. The simple fact that there was no train away from Agrinion until the next daybreak had wrought a stupendous change in his outlook. He unhesitatingly considered it an omen of a good future.

He was up before the darkness even contained presage of coming light, but near the railway station was a litle hut where coffee was being served to several prospective travellers who had come even earlier to the rendezvous. There was no evidence of the Wainwrights.

Coleman sat in the hut and listened for the rumble of wheels. He was suddenly appalled that the Wainwrights were going to miss the train. Perhaps they had decided against travelling during the night. Perhaps this thing and perhaps that thing. The morning was very cold. Closely muffled in his cloak, he went to the door and stared at where the road was whitening out of night. At the station stood a little spectral train, and the engine at intervals emitted a long, piercing scream which informed the echoing land that, in all probability, it was going to start after a time for the south. The Greeks in the coffee room were, of course, talking.

At last Coleman did hear the sound of hoofs and wheels. The three carriages swept up in grand procession. The first was laden with students; in the second was the professor, the Greek officer, Nora Black's old lady and other persons, all looking marvellously unimportant and shelved. It was the third carriage at which Coleman stared. At first he thought the dim light deceived his vision, but in a moment he knew that his first leaping conception of the arrangement of the people in this vehicle had been perfectly correct. Nora Black and Mrs Wainwright sat side by side on the back seat, while facing them were Coke and Marjory.

They looked cold but intimate.

The oddity of the grouping stupefied Coleman. It was anarchy, naked and unashamed. He could not imagine how such changes could have been consummated in the short time he had been away from them, but he laid it all to some startling necromancy on the part of Nora Black, some wondrous play which had captured them all because of its surpassing skill and because they were, in the main, rather gullible people. He was wrong. The magic had been wrought by the unaided foolishness of Mrs. Wainwright. As soon as Nora Black had succeeded in creating an effect of intimacy and dependence between herself and Coleman, the professor had flatly stated to his wife that the presence of Nora Black in the party, in the inn, in the world, was a thing that did not meet his approval in any way. She should be abolished. As for Coleman, he would not defend him. He preferred not to talk to him. It made him sad. Coleman at least had been very indiscreet, very indiscreet. It was a great pity. But as for this blatant woman, the sooner they rid themselves of her, the sooner he would feel that all the world was not evil.

Whereupon Mrs. Wainwright had changed front with the speed of light and attacked with horse, foot and guns. She failed to see, she had declared, where this poor, lone girl was in great fault. Of course it was probable that she had listened to this snaky-tongued Rufus Coleman, but that was ever the mistake that women made. Oh, certainly; the professor would like to let Rufus Coleman off scot-free. That was the way with men. They defended each other in all cases. If wrong were done it was the woman who suffered. Now, since this poor girl was alone far off here in Greece, Mrs. Wainwright announced that she had such full sense of her duty to her sex that her conscience would not allow her to scorn and desert a sister, even if that sister was, approximately, the victim of a creature like Rufus Coleman. Perhaps the poor thing loved this wretched man, although it was hard to imagine any woman giving her heart to such a monster.

The professor had then asked with considerable spirit for the proofs upon which Mrs. Wainwright named Coleman a monster, and had made a wry face over her completely conventional reply. He had told her categorically his opinion of her erudition in such matters.

But Mrs. Wainwright was not to be deterred from an exciting espousal of the cause of her sex. Upon the instant that the professor strenuously opposed her she became an apostle, an enlightened, uplifted apostle to the world on the wrongs of her sex. She had come down with this thing as if it were a disease. Nothing could stop her. Her husband, her daughter, all influences in other directions, had been overturned with a roar, and the first thing fully clear to the professor's mind had been that his wife was riding affably in the carriage with Nora Black.

Coleman aroused when he heard one of the students cry out: "Why, there is Rufus Coleman's dragoman. He must be here." A moment later they thronged upon him. "Hi, old man, caught you again! Where did you break to? Glad to catch you, old boy. How are you making it? Where's your horse?"

"Sent the horses on to Athens," said Coleman. He had not yet recovered his composure, and he was glad to find available this commonplace return to their exuberant greetings and questions. "Sent 'em on to Athens with the groom."

In the meantime the engine of the little train was screaming to heaven that its intention of starting was most serious. The diligencia careered to the station platform and unburdened. Coleman had had his dragoman place his luggage in a little first-class carriage and he defiantly entered it and closed the door. He had a sudden return to the old sense of downfall, and with it came the original rebellious desires. However, he hoped that somebody would intrude upon him.

It was Peter Tounley. The student flung open the door and then yelled to the distance: "Here's an empty one." He clattered into the compartment. "Hello, Coleman! Didn't know you were in here!" At his heels came Nora Black, Coke and Marjory.

"Oh!" they said, when they saw the occupant of the carriage. "Oh!" Coleman was furious. He could have distributed some of his traps in a way to create more room, but he did not move.

Chapter 24

There was a demonstration of the unequalled facilities of a European railway carriage for rendering unpleasant things almost intolerable. These people could find no way to alleviate the poignancy of their position. Coleman did not know where to look. Every personal mannerism becomes accentuated in a European railway carriage. If you glance at a man, your glance defines itself as a stare. If you carefully look at nothing, you create for yourself a resemblance to all wooden-headed things. A newspaper is, then, in the nature of a preservative, and Coleman longed for a newspaper.

It was this abominable railway carriage which exacted the first display of agitation from Marjory. She flushed rosily, and her eyes wavered over the compartment. Nora Black laughed in a way that was a shock to the nerves. Coke seemed very angry, indeed, and Peter Tounley was in pitiful distress. Everything was acutely, painfully vivid, bald, painted as glaringly as a grocer's new wagon. It fulfilled those traditions which the artists deplore when they use their pet phrase on a picture, "It hurts." The damnable power of accentuation of the European railway carriage seemed, to Coleman's amazed mind, to be redoubled and redoubled.

It was Peter Tounley who seemed to be in the greatest agony. He looked at the correspondent beseechingly and said: "It's a very cold morning, Coleman." This was an actual appeal in the name of humanity.

Coleman came squarely to the front and even grinned a little at poor Peter Tounley's misery. "Yes, it is a cold morning, Peter. I should say it is one of the coldest mornings in my recollection."

Peter Tounley had not intended a typical American emphasis on the polar conditions which obtained in the compartment at this time, but Coleman had given the word this meaning. Spontaneously everybody smiled, and at once the tension was relieved. But of course the satanic powers of the railway carriage could not be altogether set at naught. Of course it fell to the lot of Coke to get the seat directly in front of Coleman, and thus, face to face, they were doomed to stare at each other.

Peter Tounley was inspired to begin conventional babble, in which he took great care to make an appearance of talking to all in the carriage. "Funny thing. I never knew these mornings in Greece were so cold. I thought the climate here was quite tropical. It must have been inconvenient in the ancient times, when, I

376

am told, people didn't wear near so many—er—clothes. Really, I don't see how they stood it. For my part, I would like nothing so much as a buffalo robe. I suppose when those great sculptors were doing their masterpieces, they had to wear gloves. Ever think of that? Funny, isn't it? Aren't you cold, Marjory? I am. Jingo! Imagine the Spartans in ulsters, going out to meet an enemy in cape-overcoats, and being desired by their mothers to return with their ulsters or wrapped in them."

It was rather hard work for Peter Tounley. Both Marjory and Coleman tried to display an interest in his labours, and they laughed not at what he said, but because they believed it assisted him. The little train, meanwhile, wandered up a great green slope, and the day rapidly coloured the land.

At first Nora Black did not display a militant mood, but as time passed Coleman saw clearly that she was considering the advisability of a new attack. She had Coleman and Marjory in conjunction and where they were unable to escape from her. The opportunities were great. To Coleman, she seemed to be gloating over the possibilities of making more mischief. She was looking at him speculatively, as if considering the best place to hit him first. Presently she drawled: "Rufus, I wish you would fix my rug about me a little better." Coleman saw that this was a beginning.

Peter Tounley sprang to his feet with speed and enthusiasm. "Oh, let me do it for you." He had her well muffled in the rug before she could protest, even if a protest had been rational. The young man had no idea of defending Coleman. He had no knowledge of the necessity for it. It had been merely the exercise of his habit of amiability, his chronic desire to see everybody comfortable. His passion in this direction was well known in Washurst, where the students had borrowed a phrase from the photographers in order to describe him fully in a nickname. They called him "Look-pleasant Tounley." This did not in any way antagonise his perfect willingness to fight on occasions with a singular desperation, which usually has a small stool in every mind where good nature has a throne.

"Oh, thank you very much, Mr. Tounley," said Nora Black, without gratitude. "Rufus is always so lax in these matters."

"I don't know how you know it," said Coleman boldly, and he looked her fearlessly in the eye. The battle had begun.

"Oh," responded Nora, airily, "I have had opportunity enough to know it, I should think, by this time."

"No," said Coleman, "since I have never paid you particular and direct attention, you cannot possibly know what I am lax in and what I am not lax in. I would be obliged to be of service at any time, Nora, but surely you do not consider that you have a right to my services superior to any other right."

Nora Black simply went mad, but fortunately part of her madness was in the form of speechlessness. Otherwise there might have been heard something approaching to billingsgate.

Marjory and Peter Tounley turned first hot and then cold, and looked as if they wanted to fly away; and even Coke, penned helplessly in with this unpleasant incident, seemed to have a sudden attack of distress. The only frigid person was Coleman. He had made his declaration of independence, and he saw with glee that the victory was complete. Nora Black might storm and rage, but he had announced his position in an unconventional blunt way which nobody in the carriage could fail to understand. He felt somewhat like smiling with confidence and defiance in Nora's face, but he still had the fear for Marjory.

Unexpectedly, the fight was all out of Nora Black. She had the fury of a woman scorned, but evidently she had perceived that all was over and lost. The remainder of her wrath dispensed itself in glares which Coleman withstood with great composure.

A strained silence fell upon the group which lasted until they arrived at the little port of Mesalonghi, whence they were to take ship for Patras. Coleman found himself wondering why he had not gone flatly at the great question at a much earlier period, indeed at the first moment when the great question began to make life exciting for him. He thought that if he had charged Nora's guns in the beginning they would have turned out to be the same incapable artillery. Instead of that he had run away and continued to run away until he was actually cornered and made to fight, and his easy victory had defined him as a person who had, earlier, indulged in much stupidity and cowardice.

Everything had worked out so simply, his terrors had been dispelled so easily, that he probably was led to overestimate his success. And it occurred suddenly to him. He foresaw a fine occasion to talk privately to Marjory when all had boarded the steamer for Patras and he resolved to make use of it. This he believed would end the strife and conclusively laurel him.

The train finally drew up on a little stone pier and some boatmen began to scream like gulls. The steamer lay at anchor in the placid blue cove. The embarkation was chaotic in the Oriental fashion and there was the customary misery which was only relieved when the travellers had set foot on the deck of the steamer. Coleman did not devote any premature attention to finding Marjory, but when the steamer was fairly out on the calm waters of the Gulf of Corinth, he saw her pacing to and fro with Peter Tounley. At first he lurked in the distance waiting for an opportunity, but ultimately he decided to make his own opportunity. He approached them. "Marjory, would you let me speak to you alone for a few moments? You won't mind, will you, Peter?"

"Oh, no, certainly not," said Peter Tounley.

"Of course. It is not some dreadful revelation, is it?" said Marjory, bantering him coolly.

"No," answered Coleman, abstractedly. He was thinking of what he was going to say. Peter Tounley vanished around the corner of a deck-house and Marjory and Coleman began to pace to and fro even as Marjory and Peter Tounley had done. Coleman had thought to speak his mind frankly and once for all, and on the train he had invented many clear expressions of his feelings. It did not appear that he had forgotten them. It seemed, more, that they had become entangled in his mind in such a way that he could not unravel the end of his discourse.

In the pause, Marjory began to speak in admiration of the scenery. "I never imagined that Greece was so full of mountains. One reads so much of the Attic Plains, but aren't these mountains royal? They look so rugged and cold, whereas the bay is absolutely is blue as the old descriptions of a summer sea."

"I wanted to speak to you about Nora Black," said Coleman.

"Nora Black? Why?" said Marjory, lifting her eyebrows.

"You know well enough," said Coleman, in a headlong fashion. "You must know, you must have seen it. She knows I care for you and she wants to stop it.

And she has no right to—to interfere. She is a fiend, a perfect fiend. She is trying to make you feel that I care for her."

"And don't you care for her?" asked Marjory.

"No," said Coleman, vehemently. "I don't care for her at all."

"Very well," answered Marjory, simply. "I believe you." She managed to give the words the effect of a mere announcement that she believed him and it was in no way plain that she was glad or that she esteemed the matter as being of consequence.

He scowled at her in dark resentment. "You mean by that, I suppose, that you don't believe me?"

"Oh," answered Marjory, wearily, "I believe you. I said so. Don't talk about it any more."

"Then," said Coleman, slowly, "you mean that you do not care whether I'm telling the truth or not?"

"Why, of course I care," she said. "Lying is not nice."

He did not know, apparently, exactly how to deal with her manner, which was actually so pliable that it was marble, if one may speak in that way. He looked ruefully at the sea. He had expected a far easier time. "Well—" he began.

"Really," interrupted Marjory, "this is something which I do not care to discuss. I would rather you would not speak to me at all about it. It seems too—too—bad. I can readily give you my word that I believe you, but I would prefer you not to try to talk to me about it or—anything of that sort. Mother!"

Mrs. Wainwright was hovering anxiously in the vicinity, and she now bore down rapidly upon the pair. "You are very nearly to Patras," she said reproachfully to her daughter, as if the fact had some fault of Marjory's concealed in it. She in no way acknowledged the presence of Coleman.

"Oh, are we?" cried Marjory.

"Yes," said Mrs. Wainwright. "We are."

She stood waiting as if she expected Marjory to instantly quit Coleman. The girl wavered a moment and then followed her mother. "Good-bye," she said. "I hope we may see you again in Athens." It was a command to him to travel alone with his servant on the long railway journey from Patras to Athens. It was a dismissal of a casual acquaintance given so graciously that it stung him to the depths of his pride. He bowed his adieu and his thanks. When the yelling boatmen came again, he and his man proceeded to the shore in an early boat without looking in any way after the welfare of the others.

At the train, the party split into three sections. Coleman and his man had one compartment, Nora Black and her squad had another, and the Wainwrights and students occupied two more.

The little officer was still in tow of Nora Black. He was very enthusiastic. In French she directed him to remain silent, but he did not appear to understand. "You tell him," she then said to her dragoman, "to sit in a corner and not to speak until I tell him to, or I won't have him in here." She seemed anxious to unburden herself to the old lady companion. "Do you know," she said, "that girl has a nerve like steel. I tried to break it there in that inn, but I couldn't budge her. If I am going to have her beaten I must prove myself to be a very, very artful person."

"Why did you try to break her nerve?" asked the old lady, yawning. "Why do you want to have her beaten?"

"Because I do, old stupid," answered Nora. "You should have heard the things I said to her."

"About what?"

"About Coleman. Can't you understand anything at all?"

"And why should you say anything about Coleman to her?" queried the old lady, still hopelessly befogged.

"Because," cried Nora, darting a look of wrath at her companion, "I want to prevent that marriage." She had been betrayed into this avowal by the singularly opaque mind of the old lady. The latter at once sat erect. "Oh, ho," she said, as if a ray of light had been let into her head. "Oh, ho. So that's it, is it?"

"Yes, that's it," rejoined Nora, shortly.

The old lady was amazed into a long period of meditation. At last she spoke depressingly. "Well, how are you going to prevent it? Those things can't be done in these days at all. If they care for each other——"

Nora burst out furiously. "Don't venture opinions until you know what you are talking about, please. They don't care for each other, do you see? She cares for him, but he don't give a snap of his fingers for her."

"But," cried the bewildered lady, "if he don't care for her, there will be nothing to prevent. If he don't care for her, he won't ask her to marry him, and so there won't be anything to prevent."

Nora made a broad gesture of impatience. "Oh, can't you get anything through your head? Haven't you seen that the girl has been the only young woman in that whole party lost up there in the mountains, and that naturally more than half of the men still think they are in love with her? That's what it is. Can't you see? It always happens that way. Then Coleman comes along and makes a fool of himself with the others.

The old lady spoke up brightly as if at last feeling able to contribute something intelligent to the talk. "Oh, then, he does care for her."

Nora's eyes looked as if their glance might shrivel the old lady's hair. "Don't I keep telling you that it is no such thing? Can't you understand? It is all glamour! Fascination! 'Way up there in the wilderness! Only one even passable woman in sight."

"I don't say that I am so very keen," said the old lady, somewhat offended, "but I fail to see where I could improve when first you tell me he don't care for her, and then you tell me that he does care for her."

"'Glamour,' 'Fascination,'" quoted Nora. "Don't you understand the meaning of the words?"

"Well," asked the other, "didn't he know her, then, before he came over here?"

Nora was silent for a time, while a gloom upon her face deepened. It had struck her that the theories for which she protested so energetically might not be of such great value. Spoken aloud, they had a sudden new flimsiness. Perhaps she had reiterated to herself that Coleman was the victim of glamour only because she wished it to be true. One theory, however, remained unshaken. Marjory was an artful minx, with no truth in her.

She presently felt the necessity of replying to the question of her companion. "Oh," she said, carelessly, "I suppose they were acquainted—in a way."

The old lady was giving the best of her mind to the subject. "If that's the case—" she observed, musingly, "if that's the case, you can't tell what is between 'em."

The talk had so slackened that Nora's unfortunate Greek admirer felt that here was a good opportunity to present himself again to the notice of the actress. The means was a smile and a French sentence, but his reception would have frightened a man in armour. His face blanched with horror at the storm he had invoked, and he dropped limply back as if some one had shot him. "You tell this little snipe to let me alone!" cried Nora, to the dragoman. "If he dares to come around me with any more of those Parisian dude speeches, I—I don't know what I'll do! I won't have it, I say." The impression upon the dragoman was hardly less in effect. He looked with bulging eyes at Nora, and then began to stammer at the officer. The latter's voice could sometimes be heard in awed whispers for the more elaborate explanation of some detail of the tragedy. Afterward, he remained meek and silent in his corner, barely more than a shadow, like the proverbial husband of imperious beauty.

"Well," said the old lady, after a long and thoughtful pause, "I don't know, I'm sure, but it seems to me that if Rufus Coleman really cares for that girl, there isn't much use in trying to stop him from getting her. He isn't that kind of a man."

"For heaven's sake, will you stop assuming that he does care for her?" demanded Nora, breathlessly.

"And I don't see," continued the old lady, "what you want to prevent him for, anyhow."

Chapter 25

"I feel in this radiant atmosphere that there could be no such thing as war—men striving together in black and passionate hatred." The professor's words were for the benefit of his wife and daughter. He was viewing the sky-blue waters of the Gulf of Corinth with its background of mountains that in the sunshine were touched here and there with a copperish glare. The train was slowly sweeping along the southern shore. "It is strange to think of those men fighting up there in the north. And it is strange to think that we ourselves are but just returning from it."

"I cannot begin to realise it yet," said Mrs. Wainwright, in a high voice.

"Quite so," responded the professor, reflectively. "I do not suppose any of us will realise it fully for some time. It is altogether too odd, too very odd."

"To think of it!" cried Mrs. Wainwright. "To think of it! Supposing those dreadful Albanians or those awful men from the Greek mountains had caught us! Why, years from now I'll wake up in the night and think of it!"

The professor mused. "Strange that we cannot feel it strongly now. My logic tells me to be aghast that we ever got into such a place, but my nerves at present refuse to thrill. I am very much afraid that this singular apathy of ours has led us to be unjust to poor Coleman."

Here Mrs. Wainwright objected. "'Poor Coleman!' I don't see why you call him 'poor Coleman.'"

"Well," answered the professor, slowly, "I am in doubt about our behaviour. It——"

"Oh," cried the wife, gleefully, "in doubt about our behaviour! I'm in doubt about his behaviour."

"So, then, you do have a doubt of his behaviour?"

"Oh, no," responded Mrs. Wainwright, hastily, "not about its badness. What I meant to say was that in the face of his outrageous conduct with that—that woman, it is curious that you should worry about our behaviour. It surprises me, Harrison."

The professor was wagging his head sadly. "I don't know ** I don't know ** It seems hard to judge ** I hesitate to——"

Mrs. Wainwright treated this attitude with disdain. "It is not hard to judge," she scoffed, "and I fail to see why you have any reason for hesitation at

382

all. Here he brings this woman——"

The professor got angry. "Nonsense! Nonsense! I do not believe that he brought her. If I ever saw a spectacle of a woman bringing herself, it was then. You keep chanting that thing like an outright parrot."

"Well," retorted Mrs. Wainwright, bridling, "I suppose you imagine that you understand such things. Men usually think that, but I want to tell you that you seem to me utterly blind."

"Blind or not, do stop the everlasting reiteration of that sentence."

Mrs. Wainwright passed into an offended silence, and the professor, also silent, looked with a gradually dwindling indignation at the scenery.

Night was suggested in the sky before the train was near to Athens. "My trunks," sighed Mrs. Wainwright. "How glad I will be to get back to my trunks! Oh, the dust! Oh, the misery! Do find out when we will get there, Harrison. Maybe the train is late."

But, at last, they arrived in Athens, amid a darkness which was confusing, and, after no more than the common amount of trouble, they procured carriages and were taken to the hotel. Mrs. Wainwright's impulses now dominated the others in the family. She had one passion after another. The majority of the servants in the hotel pretended that they spoke English, but, in three minutes, she drove them distracted with the abundance and violence of her requests. It came to pass in the excitement the old couple quite forgot Marjory. It was not until Mrs. Wainwright, then feeling splendidly, was dressed for dinner, that she thought to open Marjory's door and go to render a usual motherly supervision of the girl's toilet.

There was no light: there did not seem to be anybody in the room. "Marjory!" called the mother, in alarm. She listened for a moment and then ran hastily out again. "Harrison!" she cried. "I can't find Marjory!" The professor had been tying his cravat. He let the loose ends fly. "What?" he ejaculated, opening his mouth wide. Then they both rushed into Marjory's room. "Marjory!" beseeched the old man in a voice which would have invoked the grave.

The answer was from the bed. "Yes?" It was low, weary, tearful. It was not like Marjory. It was dangerously the voice of a heart-broken woman. They hurried forward with outcries. "Why, Marjory! Are you ill, child? How long have you been lying in the dark? Why didn't you call us? Are you ill?"

"No," answered this changed voice, "I am not ill. I only thought I'd rest for a time. Don't bother."

The professor hastily lit the gas and then father and mother turned hurriedly to the bed. In the first of the illumination they saw that tears were flowing unchecked down Marjory's face.

The effect of this grief upon the professor was, in part, an effect of fear. He seemed afraid to touch it, to go near it. He could, evidently, only remain in the outskirts, a horrified spectator. The mother, however, flung her arms about her daughter. "Oh, Marjory!" She, too, was weeping.

The girl turned her face to the pillow and held out a hand of protest. "Don't, mother! Don't!"

"Oh, Marjory! Oh, Marjory!"

"Don't mother. Please go away. Please go away. Don't speak at all, I beg of you."

"Oh, Marjory! Oh, Marjory!"

"Don't." The girl lifted a face which appalled them. It had something entirely new in it. "Please go away, mother. I will speak to father, but I won't—I can't—I can't be pitied."

Mrs. Wainwright looked at her husband. "Yes," said the old man, trembling. "Go!" She threw up her hands in a sorrowing gesture that was not without its suggestion that her exclusion would be a mistake. She left the room.

The professor dropped on his knees at the bedside and took one of Marjory's hands. His voice dropped to its tenderest note. "Well, my Marjory?"

She had turned her face again to the pillow. At last she answered in muffled tones, "You know."

Thereafter came a long silence full of sharpened pain. It was Marjory who spoke first. "I have saved my pride, daddy, but—I have—lost—everything—else." Even her sudden resumption of the old epithet of her childhood was an additional misery to the old man. He still said no word. He knelt, gripping her fingers and staring at the wall.

"Yes, I have lost—everything—else."

The father gave a low groan. He was thinking deeply, bitterly. Since one was only a human being, how was one going to protect beloved hearts assailed with sinister fury from the inexplicable zenith? In this tragedy he felt as helpless as an old grey ape. He did not see a possible weapon with which he could defend his child from the calamity which was upon her. There was no wall, no shield which could turn this sorrow from the heart of his child. If one of his hands' loss could have spared her, there would have been a sacrifice of his hand, but he was potent for nothing. He could only groan and stare at the wall.

He reviewed the past half in fear that he would suddenly come upon his error which was now the cause of Marjory's tears. He dwelt long upon the fact that in Washurst he had refused his consent to Marjory's marriage with Coleman, but even now he could not say that his judgment was not correct. It was simply that the doom of woman's woe was upon Marjory, this ancient woe of the silent tongue and the governed will, and he could only kneel at the bedside and stare at the wall.

Marjory raised her voice in a laugh. "Did I betray myself? Did I become the maiden all forlorn? Did I giggle to show people that I did not care? No—I did not—I did not. And it was such a long time, daddy! Oh, such a long time! I thought we would never get here. I thought I would never get where I could be alone like this, where I could—cry—if I wanted to. I am not much of a crier, am I, daddy? But this time—this time——"

She suddenly drew herself over near to her father and looked at him. "Oh, daddy, I want to tell you one thing. Just one simple little thing." She waited then, and while she waited her father's head went lower and lower. "Of course, you know—I told you once. I love him! I love him! Yes, probably he is a rascal, but, do you know, I don't think I would mind if he was a—an assassin. This morning I sent him away, but, daddy, he didn't want to go at all. I know he didn't. This Nora Black is nothing to him. I know she is not. I am sure of it. Yes—I am sure of it. * * * I never expected to talk this way to any living creature, but—you are so good, daddy. * * * Dear old daddy——"

She ceased, for she saw that her father was praying.

The sight brought to her a new outburst of sobbing, for her sorrow now had dignity and solemnity from the bowed white head of her old father, and she felt that her heart was dying amid the pomp of the church. It was the last rites being performed at the death-bed. Into her ears came some imagining of the low melancholy chant of monks in a gloom.

Finally, her father arose. He kissed her on the brow. "Try to sleep, dear," he said. He turned out the gas and left the room. His thought was full of chastened emotion.

But if his thought was full of chastened emotion, it received some degree of shock when he arrived in the presence of Mrs. Wainwright. "Well, what is all this about?" she demanded, irascibly. "Do you mean to say that Marjory is breaking her heart over that man Coleman? It is all your fault——" She was apparently still ruffled over her exclusion.

When the professor interrupted her he did not speak with his accustomed spirit, but from something novel in his manner she recognised a danger signal.

"Please do not burst out at it in that way."

"Then it is true?" she asked. Her voice was a mere awed whisper.

"It is true," answered the professor.

"Well," she said, after reflection, "I knew it. I always knew it. If you hadn't been so blind! You turned like a weather-cock in your opinions of Coleman. You never could keep your opinion about him for more than an hour. Nobody could imagine what you might think next. And now you see the result of it! I warned you! I told you what this Coleman was, and if Marjory is suffering now, you have only yourself to blame for it. I warned you!"

"If it is my fault," said the professor, drearily, "I hope God may forgive me, for here is a great wrong to my daughter."

"Well, if you had done as I told you——" she began.

Here the professor revolted. "Oh, now, do not begin on that," he snarled, peevishly. "Do not begin on that."

"Anyhow," said Mrs. Wainwright, "it is time that we should be going down to dinner. Is Marjory coming?"

"No, she is not," answered the professor, "and I do not know as I shall go myself."

"But you must go. Think how it would look! All the students down there dining without us, and cutting up capers! You must come."

"Yes," he said, dubiously, "but who will look after Marjory?"

"She wants to be left alone," announced Mrs. Wainwright, as if she was the particular herald of this news. "She wants to be left alone."

"Well, I suppose we may as well go down."

Before they went, the professor tiptoed into his daughter's room. In the darkness he could only see her waxen face on the pillow, and her two eyes gazing fixedly at the ceiling. He did not speak, but immediately withdrew, closing the door noiselessly behind him.

Chapter 26

If the professor and Mrs. Wainwright had descended sooner to a lower floor of the hotel, they would have found reigning there a form of anarchy. The students were in a smoking room which was also an entrance hall to the dining room, and because there was in the middle of this apartment a fountain containing gold fish, they had been moved to license and sin. They had all been tubbed and polished and brushed and dressed until they were exuberantly beyond themselves. The proprietor of the hotel brought in his dignity and showed it to them, but they minded it no more than if he had been only a common man. He drew himself to his height and looked gravely at them and they jovially said: "Hello, Whiskers." American college students are notorious in their country for their inclination to scoff at robed and crowned authority, and, far from being awed by the dignity of the hotel-keeper, they were delighted with it. It was something with which to sport. With immeasurable impudence, they copied his attitude, and, standing before him, made comic speeches, always alluding with blinding vividness to his beard. His exit disappointed them. He had not remained long under fire. They felt that they could have interested themselves with him an entire evening. "Come back, Whiskers! Oh, come back!" Out in the main hall he made a gesture of despair to some of his gaping minions and then fled to seclusion.

A formidable majority then decided that Coke was a gold fish, and that therefore his proper place was in the fountain. They carried him to it while he struggled madly. This quiet room with its crimson rugs and gilded mirrors seemed suddenly to have become an important apartment in hell. There being as yet no traffic in the dining room, the waiters were all at liberty to come to the open doors, where they stood as men turned to stone. To them, it was no less than incendiarism.

Coke, standing with one foot on the floor and the other on the bottom of the shallow fountain, blasphemed his comrades in a low tone, but with intention. He was certainly desirous of lifting his foot out of the water, but it seemed that all movement to that end would have to wait until he had successfully expressed his opinions. In the meantime, there was heard slow footsteps and the rustle of skirts, and then some people entered the smoking room on their way to dine. Coke took his foot hastily out of the fountain.

The faces of the men of the arriving party went blank, and they turned their cold and pebbly eyes straight to the front, while the ladies, after little expressions of alarm, looked as if they wanted to run. In fact, the whole crowd rather bolted from this extraordinary scene.

"There, now," said Coke bitterly to his companions. "You see? We looked like little schoolboys——"

"Oh, never mind, old man," said Peter Tounley. "We'll forgive you, although you did embarrass us. But, above everything, don't drip. Whatever you do, don't drip."

The students took this question of dripping and played upon it until they would have made quite insane anybody but another student. They worked it into all manner of forms, and hacked and haggled at Coke until he was driven to his room to seek other apparel. "Be sure and change both legs," they told him. "Remember you can't change one leg without changing both legs."

After Coke's departure, the United States minister entered the room, and instantly they were subdued. It was not his lofty station that affected them. There are probably few stations that would have at all affected them. They became subdued because they unfeignedly liked the United States minister. They were suddenly a group of well-bred, correctly attired young men who had not put Coke's foot in the fountain. Nor had they desecrated the majesty of the hotelkeeper.

"Well, I am delighted," said the minister, laughing as he shook hands with them all. "I was not sure I would ever see you again. You are not to be trusted, and, good boys as you are, I'll be glad to see you once and forever over the boundary of my jurisdiction. Leave Greece, you vagabonds. However, I am truly delighted to see you all safe."

"Thank you, sir," they said.

"How in the world did you get out of it? You must be remarkable chaps. I thought you were in a hopeless position. I wired and cabled everywhere I could, but I could find out nothing."

"A correspondent," said Peter Tounley. "I don't know if you have met him. His name is Coleman. He found us."

"Coleman?" asked the minister, quickly.

"Yes, sir. He found us and brought us out safely."

"Well, glory be to Coleman," exclaimed the minister, after a long sigh of surprise. "Glory be to Coleman! I never thought he could do it."

The students were alert immediately. "Why, did you know about it, sir? Did he tell you he was coming after us?"

"Of course. He came to me here in Athens and asked where you were. I told him you were in a peck of trouble. He acted quietly and somewhat queerly, and said that he would try to look you up. He said you were friends of his. I warned him against trying it. Yes, I said it was impossible. I had no idea that he would really carry the thing out. But didn't he tell you anything about this himself?"

"No, sir," answered Peter Tounley. "He never said much about it. I think he usually contended that it was mainly an accident."

"It was no accident," said the minister, sharply. "When a man starts out to do a thing and does it, you can't say it is an accident."

"I didn't say so, sir," said Peter Tounley diffidently.

"Quite true, quite true! You didn't, but—this Coleman must be a man!"

"We think so, sir," said he who was called Billie. "He certainly brought us through in style."

"But how did he manage it?" cried the minister, keenly interested. "How did he do it?"

"It is hard to say, sir. But he did it. He met us in the dead of night out near Nikopolis——"

"Near Nikopolis?"

"Yes, sir. And he hid us in a forest while a fight was going on, and then in the morning he brought us inside the Greek lines. Oh, there is a lot to tell——"

Whereupon they told it, or as much as they could of it. In the end, the minister said: "Well, where are the professor and Mrs. Wainwright? I want you all to dine with me to-night. I am dining in the public room, but you won't mind that after Epirus."

"They should be down now, sir," answered a student.

People were now coming rapidly to dinner and presently the professor and Mrs. Wainwright appeared. The old man looked haggard and white. He accepted the minister's warm greeting with a strained pathetic smile. "Thank you. We are glad to return safely."

Once at dinner the minister launched immediately into the subject of Coleman. "He must be altogether a most remarkable man. When he told me, very quietly, that he was going to try to rescue you, I frankly warned him against any such attempt. I thought he would merely add one more to a party of suffering people. But the boys tell me that he did actually rescue you."

"Yes, he did," said the professor. "It was a very gallant performance, and we are very grateful."

"Of course," spoke Mrs. Wainwright, "we might have rescued ourselves. We were on the right road, and all we had to do was to keep going on."

"Yes, but I understand—" said the minister. "I understand he took you into a wood to protect you from that fight, and generally protected you from all kinds of trouble. It seems wonderful to me, not so much because it was done as because it was done by the man who, some time ago, calmly announced to me that he was going to do it. Extraordinary."

"Of course," said Mrs. Wainwright. "Oh, of course."

"And where is he now?" asked the minister suddenly. "Has he now left you to the mercies of civilisation?"

There was a moment's curious stillness, and then Mrs. Wainwright used that high voice which—the students believed—could only come to her when she was about to say something peculiarly destructive to the sensibilities. "Oh, of course, Mr. Coleman rendered us a great service, but in his private character he is not a man whom we exactly care to associate with."

"Indeed!" said the minister staring. Then he hastily addressed the students. "Well, isn't this a comic war? Did you ever imagine war could be like this?" The professor remained looking at his wife with an air of stupefaction, as if she had opened up to him visions of imbecility of which he had not even dreamed. The students loyally began to chatter at the minister. "Yes, sir, it is a queer war. After all their bragging, it is funny to hear that they are running away with such agility. We thought, of course, of the old Greek wars."

Later, the minister asked them all to his rooms for coffee and cigarettes, but the professor and Mrs. Wainwright apologetically retired to their own quarters.

The minister and the students made clouds of smoke, through which sang the eloquent descriptions of late adventures.

The minister had spent days of listening to questions from the State Department at Washington as to the whereabouts of the Wainwright party. "I suppose you know that you are very prominent people in the United States just now? Your pictures must have been in all the papers, and there must have been columns printed about you. My life here was made almost insupportable by your friends, who consist, I should think, of about half the population of the country. Of course they laid regular siege to the department. I am angry at Coleman for only one thing. When he cabled the news of your rescue to his newspaper from Arta, he should have also wired me, if only to relieve my failing mind. My first news of your escape was from Washington—think of that."

"Coleman had us all on his hands at Arta," said Peter Tounley. "He was a fairly busy man."

"I suppose so," said the minister. "By the way," he asked bluntly, "what is wrong with him? What did Mrs. Wainwright mean?"

They were silent for a time, but it seemed plain to him that it was not evidence that his question had demoralised them. They seemed to be deliberating upon the form of answer. Ultimately Peter Tounley coughed behind his hand. "You see, sir," he began, "there is—well, there is a woman in the case. Not that anybody would care to speak of it excepting to you. But that is what is the cause of things, and then, you see, Mrs. Wainwright is—well——" He hesitated a moment and then completed his sentence in the ingenuous profanity of his age and condition. "She is rather an extraordinary old bird."

"But who is the woman?"

"Why, it is Nora Black, the actress."

"Oh," cried the minister, enlightened. "Her? Why, I saw here here. She was very beautiful, but she seemed harmless enough. She was somewhat—er—confident, perhaps, but she did not alarm me. She called upon me, and I confess I—why, she seemed charming."

"She's sweet on little Rufus. That's the point," said an oracular voice.

"Oh," cried the host, suddenly. "I remember. She asked me where he was. She said she had heard he was in Greece, and I told her he had gone knight-erranting off after you people. I remember now. I suppose she posted after him up to Arta, eh?"

"That's it. And so she asked you where he was?"

"Yes."

"Why, that old flamingo—Mrs. Wainwright—insists that it was a rendez-vous."

Every one exchanged glances and laughed a little.

"And did you see any actual fighting?" asked the minister.

"No. We only heard it——"

Afterward, as they were trooping up to their rooms, Peter Tounley spoke musingly. "Well, it looks to me now as if Old Mother Wainwright was just a bad-minded old hen."

"Oh, I don't know. How is one going to tell what the truth is?"

"At any rate, we are sure now that Coleman had nothing to do with Nora's debut in Epirus."

They had talked much of Coleman, but in their tones there always had been a note of indifference or carelessness. This matter, which to some people was as vital and fundamental as existence, remained to others who knew of it only a harmless detail of life, with no terrible powers, and its significance had faded greatly when had ended the close associations of the late adventure.

After dinner the professor had gone directly to his daughter's room. Apparently she had not moved. He knelt by the bedside again and took one of her hands. She was not weeping. She looked at him and smiled through the darkness. "Daddy, I would like to die," she said. "I think—yes—I would like to die."

For a long time the old man was silent, but he arose at last with a definite abruptness and said hoarsely: "Wait!"

Mrs. Wainwright was standing before her mirror with her elbows thrust out at angles above her head, while her fingers moved in a disarrangement of her hair. In the glass she saw a reflection of her husband coming from Marjory's room, and his face was set with some kind of alarming purpose. She turned to watch him actually, but he walked towards the door into the corridor and did not in any wise heed her. "Harrison!" she called. "Where are you going?"

He turned a troubled face upon her, and, as if she had hailed him in his sleep, he vacantly said: "What?"

"Where are you going?" she demanded with increasing trepidation.

He dropped heavily into a chair. "Going?" he repeated.

She was angry. "Yes! Going? Where are you going?"

"I am going——" he answered, "I am going to see Rufus Coleman."

Mrs. Wainwright gave voice to a muffled scream. "Not about Marjory?"

"Yes," he said, "about Marjory."

It was now Mrs. Wainwright's turn to look at her husband with an air of stupefaction as if he had opened up to her visions of imbecility of which she had not even dreamed. "About Marjory!" she gurgled. Then suddenly her wrath flamed out. "Well, upon my word, Harrison Wainwright, you are, of all men in the world, the most silly and stupid. You are absolutely beyond belief. Of all projects! And what do you think Marjory would have to say of it if she knew it? I suppose you think she would like it? Well, I tell you she would keep her right hand in the fire until it was burned off before she would allow you to do such a thing."

"She must never know it," responded the professor, in dull misery.

"Then think of yourself! Think of the shame of it! The shame of it!"

The professor raised his eyes for an ironical glance at his wife. "Oh * * I have thought of the shame of it!"

"And you'll accomplish nothing," cried Mrs. Wainwright. "You'll accomplish nothing. He'll only laugh at you."

"If he laughs at me, he will laugh at nothing but a poor, weak, unworldly old man. It is my duty to go."

Mrs. Wainwright opened her mouth as if she was about to shriek. After choking a moment she said: "Your duty? Your duty to go and bend the knee to that man? Your duty?"

"'It is my duty to go,'" he repeated humbly. "If I can find even one chance for my daughter's happiness in a personal sacrifice. He can do no more than—he can do no more than make me a little sadder."

His wife evidently understood his humility as a tribute to her arguments and a clear indication that she had fatally undermined his original intention. "Oh, he would have made you sadder," she quoth grimly. "No fear! Why, it was the most insane idea I ever heard of."

The professor arose wearily. "Well, I must be going to this work. It is a thing to have ended quickly." There was something almost biblical in his manner.

"Harrison!" burst out his wife in amazed lamentation. "You are not really going to do it? Not really!"

"I am going to do it," he answered.

"Well, there!" ejaculated Mrs. Wainwright to the heavens. She was, so to speak, prostrate. "Well, there!"

As the professor passed out of the door she cried beseechingly but futilely after him. "Harrison." In a mechanical way she turned then back to the mirror and resumed the disarrangement of her hair. She addressed her image. "Well, of all stupid creatures under the sun, men are the very worst!" And her image said this to her even as she informed it, and afterward they stared at each other in a profound and tragic reception and acceptance of this great truth.

Presently she began to consider the advisability of going to Marjory with the whole story. Really, Harrison must not be allowed to go on blundering until the whole world heard that Marjory was trying to break her heart over that common scamp of a Coleman. It seemed to be about time for her, Mrs. Wainwright, to come into the situation and mend matters.

Chapter 27

When the professor arrived before Coleman's door, he paused a moment and looked at it. Previously, he could not have imagined that a simple door would ever so affect him. Every line of it seemed to express cold superiority and disdain. It was only the door of a former student, one of his old boys, whom, as the need arrived, he had whipped with his satire in the class rooms at Washurst until the mental blood had come, and all without a conception of his ultimately arriving before the door of this boy in the attitude of a supplicant. He would not say it; Coleman probably would not say it; but—they would both know it. A single thought of it, made him feel like running away. He would never dare to knock on that door. It would be too monstrous. And even as he decided that he was afraid to knock, he knocked.

Coleman's voice said: "Come in." The professor opened the door. The correspondent, without a coat, was seated at a paper-littered table. Near his elbow, upon another table, was a tray from which he had evidently dined and also a brandy bottle with several recumbent bottles of soda. Although he had so lately arrived at the hotel he had contrived to diffuse his traps over the room in an organised disarray which represented a long and careless occupation if it did not represent the scene of a scuffle. His pipe was in his mouth.

After a first murmur of surprise, he arose and reached in some haste for his coat. "Come in, professor, come in," he cried, wriggling deeper into his jacket as he held out his hand. He had laid aside his pipe and had also been very successful in flinging a newspaper so that it hid the brandy and soda. This act was a feat of deference to the professor's well known principles.

"Won't you sit down, sir?" said Coleman cordially. His quick glance of surprise had been immediately suppressed and his manner was now as if the professor's call was a common matter.

"Thank you, Mr. Coleman, I—yes, I will sit down," replied the old man. His hand shook as he laid it on the back of the chair and steadied himself down into it. "Thank you!"

Coleman looked at him with a great deal of expectation.

"Mr. Coleman!"

'Yes, sir."

"I——"

He halted then and passed his hand over his face. His eyes did not seem to rest once upon Coleman, but they occupied themselves in furtive and frightened glances over the room. Coleman could make neither head nor tail of the affair. He would not have believed any man's statement that the professor could act in such an extraordinary fashion. "Yes, sir," he said again suggestively. The simple strategy resulted in a silence that was actually awkward. Coleman, despite his bewilderment, hastened into a preserving gossip. "I've had a great many cables waiting for me for heaven knows how long and others have been arriving in flocks to-night. You have no idea of the row in America, professor. Why, everybody must have gone wild over the lost sheep. My paper has cabled some things that are evidently for you. For instance, here is one that says a new puzzle-game called Find the Wainwright Party has had a big success. Think of that, would you." Coleman grinned at the professor. "Find the Wainwright Party, a new puzzle-game."

The professor had seemed grateful for Coleman's tangent off into matters of a light vein. "Yes?" he said, almost eagerly. "Are they selling a game really called that?"

"Yes, really," replied Coleman. "And of course you know that—er—well, all the Sunday papers would of course have big illustrated articles—full pages— with your photographs and general private histories pertaining mostly to things which are none of their business."

"Yes, I suppose they would do that," admitted the professor. "But I dare say it may not be as bad as you suggest."

"Very like not," said Coleman. "I put it to you forcibly so that in the future the blow will not be too cruel. They are often a weird lot."

"Perhaps they can't find anything very bad about us."

"Oh, no. And besides the whole episode will probably be forgotten by the time you return to the United States."

They talked on in this way slowly, strainedly, until they each found that the situation would soon become insupportable. The professor had come for a distinct purpose and Coleman knew it; they could not sit there lying at each other forever. Yet when he saw the pain deepening in the professor's eyes, the correspondent again ordered up his trivialities. "Funny thing. My paper has been congratulating me, you know, sir, in a wholesale fashion, and I think—I feel sure—that they have been exploiting my name all over the country as the Heroic Rescuer. There is no sense in trying to stop them, because they don't care whether it is true or not true. All they want is the privilege of howling out that their correspondent rescued you, and they would take that privilege without in any ways worrying if I refused my consent. You see, sir? I wouldn't like you to feel that I was such a strident idiot as I doubtless am appearing now before the public."

"No," said the professor absently. It was plain that he had been a very slack listener. "I—Mr. Coleman—" he began.

"Yes, sir," answered Coleman promptly and gently.

It was obviously only a recognition of the futility of further dallying that was driving the old man onward. He knew, of course, that if he was resolved to take this step, a longer delay would simply make it harder for him. The correspondent, leaning forward, was watching him almost breathlessly.

"Mr. Coleman, I understand—or at least I am led to believe—that you—at one time, proposed marriage to my daughter?"

The faltering words did not sound as if either man had aught to do with them. They were an expression by the tragic muse herself. Coleman's jaw fell and he looked glassily at the professor. He said: "Yes!" But already his blood was leaping as his mind flashed everywhere in speculation.

"I refused my consent to that marriage," said the old man more easily. "I do not know if the matter has remained important to you, but at any rate, I—I retract my refusal."

Suddenly the blank expression left Coleman's face and he smiled with sudden intelligence, as if information of what the professor had been saying had just reached him. In this smile there was a sudden betrayal, too, of something keen and bitter which had lain hidden in the man's mind. He arose and made a step towards the professor and held out his hand. "Sir, I thank you from the bottom of my heart!" And they both seemed to note with surprise that Coleman's voice had broken.

The professor had arisen to receive Coleman's hand. His nerve was now of iron and he was very formal. "I judge from your tone that I have not made a mistake—something which I feared."

Coleman did not seem to mind the professor's formality. "Don't fear anything. Won't you sit down again? Will you have a cigar. * * No, I couldn't tell you how glad I am. How glad I am. I feel like a fool. * * It——"

But the professor fixed him with an Arctic eye and bluntly said: "You love her?"

The question steadied Coleman at once. He looked undauntedly straight into the professor's face. He simply said: "I love her!"

"You love her?" repeated the professor.

"I love her," repeated Coleman.

After some seconds of pregnant silence, the professor arose. "Well, if she cares to give her life to you, I will allow it, but I must say that I do not consider you nearly good enough. Good-night." He smiled faintly as he held out his hand.

"Good-night, sir," said Coleman. "And I can't tell you now——"

Mrs. Wainwright, in her room was languishing in a chair and applying to her brow a handkerchief wet with cologne water. She kept her feverish glance upon the door. Remembering well the manner of her husband when he went out she could hardly identify him when he came in. Serenity, composure, even self-satisfaction, was written upon him. He paid no attention to her, but going to a chair sat down with a groan of contentment.

"Well?" cried Mrs. Wainwright, starting up. "Well?"

"Well—what?" he asked.

She waved her hand impatiently. "Harrison, don't be absurd. You know perfectly well what I mean. It is a pity you couldn't think of the anxiety I have been in." She was going to weep.

"Oh, I'll tell you after awhile," he said stretching out his legs with the complacency of a rich merchant after a successful day.

"No! Tell me now," she implored him. "Can't you see I've worried myself nearly to death?" She was not going to weep, she was going to wax angry.

"Well, to tell the truth," said the professor with considerable pomposity, "I've arranged it. Didn't think I could do it at first, but it turned out——"

"Arranged it," wailed Mrs. Wainwright. "Arranged what?"

It here seemed to strike the professor suddenly that he was not such a flaming example for diplomatists as he might have imagined. "Arranged," he stammered. "Arranged——"

"Arranged what?"

"Why, I fixed—I fixed it up."

"Fixed what up?"

"It—it——" began the professor. Then he swelled with indignation. "Why, can't you understand anything at all? I—I fixed it."

"Fixed what?"

"Fixed it. Fixed it with Coleman."

"Fixed what with Coleman?"

The professor's wrath now took control of him. "Thunder and lightenin'! You seem to jump at the conclusion that I've made some horrible mistake. For goodness' sake, give me credit for a particle of sense."

"What did you do?" she asked in a sepulchral voice.

"Well," said the professor in a burning defiance, "I'll tell you what I did. I went to Coleman and told him that once—as he of course knew—I had refused his marriage with my daughter, but that now——"

"Grrr," said Mrs. Wainwright.

"But that now——" continued the professor, "I retracted that refusal."

'Mercy on us!" cried Mrs. Wainwright, throwing herself back in the chair. "Mercy on us! What fools men are!"

"Now, wait a minute——"

But Mrs. Wainwright began to croon: "Oh, if Marjory should hear of this! Oh, if she should hear of it! Just let her hear——"

"But she must not," cried the professor, tigerishly. "Just you dare!" And the woman saw before her a man whose eyes were lit with a flame which almost expressed a temporary hatred.

* * *

The professor had left Coleman so abruptly that the correspondent found himself murmuring half-coherent gratitude to the closed door of his room. Amazement soon began to be mastered by exultation. He flung himself upon the brandy and soda and negotiated a strong glass. Pacing the room with nervous steps, he caught a vision of himself in a tall mirror. He halted before it. "Well, well," he said. "Rufus, you're a grand man. There is not your equal anywhere. You are a great, bold, strong player, fit to sit down to a game with the best."

A moment later it struck him that he had appropriated too much. If the professor had paid him a visit and made a wonderful announcement, he, Coleman, had not been the engine of it. And then he enunciated clearly something in his mind which, even in a vague form, had been responsible for much of his early elation. Marjory herself had compassed this thing. With shame he rejected a first wild and preposterous idea that she had sent her father to him. He reflected that a man who for an instant could conceive such a thing was a natural-born idiot. With an equal feeling, he rejected also an idea that she could have known anything of her father's purpose. If she had known of his purpose, there would have been no visit.

What, then, was the cause? Coleman soon decided that the professor had witnessed some demonstration of Marjory's emotion which had been sufficiently severe in its character to force him to the extraordinary visit. But then this also was wild and preposterous. That coldly beautiful goddess would not have given a demonstration of emotion over Rufus Coleman sufficiently alarming to have forced her father on such an errand. That was impossible. No, he was wrong; Marjory even indirectly, could not be connected with the visit. As he arrived at this decision, the enthusiasm passed out of him and he wore a doleful, monkish face.

"Well, what, then, was the cause?" After eliminating Marjory from the discussion waging in his mind, he found it hard to hit upon anything rational. The only remaining theory was to the effect that the professor, having a very high sense of the correspondent's help in the escape of the Wainwright party, had decided that the only way to express his gratitude was to revoke a certain decision which he now could see had been unfair. The retort to this theory seemed to be that if the professor had had such a fine conception of the services rendered by Coleman, he had had ample time to display his appreciation on the road to Arta and on the road down from Arta. There was no necessity for his waiting until their arrival in Athens. It was impossible to concede that the professor's emotion could be a new one; if he had it now, he must have had it in far stronger measure directly after he had been hauled out of danger.

So, it may be seen that after Coleman had eliminated Marjory from the discussion that was waging in his mind, he had practically succeeded in eliminating the professor as well. This, he thought, mournfully, was eliminating with a vengeance. If he dissolved all the factors he could hardly proceed.

The mind of a lover moves in a circle, or at least on a more circular course than other minds, some of which at times even seem to move almost in a straight line. Presently, Coleman was at the point where he had started, and he did not pause until he reached that theory which asserted that the professor had been inspired to his visit by some sight or knowledge of Marjory in distress. Of course, Coleman was wistfully desirous of proving to himself the truth of this theory.

The palpable agitation of the professor during the interview seemed to support it. If he had come on a mere journey of conscience, he would have hardly appeared as a white and trembling old man. But then, said Coleman, he himself probably exaggerated this idea of the professor's appearance. It might have been that he was only sour and distressed over the performance of a very disagreeable duty.

The correspondent paced his room and smoked. Sometimes he halted at the little table where was the brandy and soda. He thought so hard that sometimes it seemed that Marjory had been to him to propose marriage, and at other times it seemed that there had been no visit from any one at all.

A desire to talk to somebody was upon him. He strolled down stairs and into the smoking and reading rooms, hoping to see a man he knew, even if it were Coke. But the only occupants were two strangers, furiously debating the war. Passing the minister's room, Coleman saw that there was a light within, and he could not forbear knocking. He was bidden to enter, and opened the door upon the minister, carefully reading his *Spectator* fresh from London.

He looked up and seemed very glad. "How are you?" he cried. "I was tremendously anxious to see you, do you know! I looked for you to dine with me to-night, but you were not down?"

"No; I had a great deal of work."

"Over the Wainwright affair? By the way, I want you to accept my personal thanks for that work. In a week more I would have gone demented and spent the rest of my life in some kind of a cage, shaking the bars and howling out State Department messages about the Wainwrights. You see, in my territory there are no missionaries to get into trouble, and I was living a life of undisturbed and innocent calm, ridiculing the sentiments of men from Smyrna and other interesting towns who maintained that the diplomatic service was exciting. However, when the Wainwright party got lost, my life at once became active. I was all but helpless, too, which was the worst of it. I suppose Terry at Constantinople must have got grandly stirred up, also. Pity he can't see you to thank you for saving him from probably going mad. By the way," he added, while looking keenly at Coleman, "the Wainwrights don't seem to be smothering you with gratitude?"

"Oh, as much as I deserve—sometimes more," answered Coleman. "My exploit was more or less of a fake, you know. I was between the lines by accident, or through the efforts of that blockhead of a dragoman. I didn't intend it. And then, in the night, when we were waiting in the road because of a fight, they almost bunked into us. That's all."

"They tell it better," said the minister, severely. "Especially the youngsters."

"Those kids got into a high old fight at a town up there beyond Agrinion. Tell you about that, did they? I thought not. Clever kids. You have noted that there are signs of a few bruises and scratches?"

"Yes, but I didn't ask——"

"Well, they are from the fight. It seems the people took us for Germans, and there was an awful palaver, which ended in a proper and handsome shindig. It raised the town, I tell you."

The minister sighed in mock despair. "Take these people home, will you? Or at any rate, conduct them out of the field of my responsibility. Now, they would like Italy immensely, I am sure."

Coleman laughed, and they smoked for a time. "That's a charming girl— Miss Wainwright," said the minister, musingly. "And what a beauty! It does my exiled eyes good to see her. I suppose all those youngsters are madly in love with her? I don't see how they could help it."

"Yes," said Coleman, glumly. "More than half of 'em."

The minister seemed struck with a sudden thought. "You ought to try to win that splendid prize yourself. The rescuer! Perseus! What more fitting?"

Coleman answered calmly: "Well * * * I think I'll take your advice."

Chapter 28

The next morning Coleman awoke with a sign of a resolute decision on his face, as if it had been a development of his sleep. He would see Marjory as soon as possible, see her despite any barbed-wire entanglements which might be placed in the way by her mother, whom he regarded as his strenuous enemy. And he would ask Marjory's hand in the presence of all Athens if it became necessary.

He sat a long time at his breakfast in order to see the Wainwrights enter the dining room, and as he was about to surrender to the will of time, they came in, the professor placid and self-satisfied, Mrs. Wainwright worried and injured and Marjory cool, beautiful, serene. If there had been any kind of a storm there was no trace of it on the white brow of the girl. Coleman studied her closely but furtively while his mind spun around his circle of speculation.

Finally he noted the waiter who was observing him with a pained air as if it was on the tip of his tongue to ask this guest if he was going to remain at breakfast forever. Coleman passed out to the reading room where upon the table a multitude of great red guide books were crushing the fragile magazines of London and Paris. On the walls were various depressing maps with the name of a tourist agency luridly upon them, and there were also some pictures of hotels with their rates—in francs—printed beneath. The room was cold, dark, empty, with the trail of the tourist upon it.

Coleman went to the picture of a hotel in Corfu and stared at it precisely as if he was interested. He was standing before it when he heard Marjory's voice just without the door. "All right! I'll wait." He did not move for the reason that the hunter moves not when the unsuspecting deer approaches his hiding place. She entered rather quickly and was well toward the centre of the room before she perceived Coleman. "Oh," she said and stopped. Then she spoke the immortal sentence, a sentence which, curiously enough is common to the drama, to the novel, and to life. "I thought no one was here." She looked as if she was going to retreat, but it would have been hard to make such retreat graceful, and probably for this reason she stood her ground.

Coleman immediately moved to a point between her and the door. "You are not going to run away from me, Marjory Wainwright," he cried, angrily. "You at least owe it to me to tell me definitely that you don't love me—that you can't love me—"

398

She did not face him with all of her old spirit, but she faced him, and in her answer there was the old Marjory. "A most common question. Do you ask all your feminine acquaintances that?"

"I mean—" he said. "I mean that I love you and——"

"Yesterday—no. To-day—yes. To-morrow—who knows. Really, you ought to take some steps to know your own mind."

"Know my own mind," he retorted in a burst of indignation. "You mean you ought to take steps to know your own mind."

"My own mind! You—" Then she halted in acute confusion and all her face went pink. She had been far quicker than the man to define the scene. She lowered her head. "Let me past, please——"

But Coleman sturdily blocked the way and even took one of her struggling hands. "Marjory——" And then his brain must have roared with a thousand quick sentences for they came tumbling out, one over the other. * * Her resistance to the grip of his fingers grew somewhat feeble. Once she raised her eyes in a quick glance at him. * * Then suddenly she wilted. She surrendered, she confessed without words. "Oh, Marjory, thank God, thank God——"

Peter Tounley made a dramatic entrance on the gallop. He stopped, petrified. "Whoo!" he cried. "My stars!" He turned and fled. But Coleman called after him in a low voice, intense with agitation. "Come back here, you young scoundrel! Come back here!"

Peter returned, looking very sheepish. "I hadn't the slightest idea you——"

"Never mind that now. But look here, if you tell a single soul—particularly those other young scoundrels—I'll break——"

"I won't, Coleman. Honest, I won't." He was far more embarrassed than Coleman and almost equally so with Marjory. He was like a horse tugging at a tether. "I won't, Coleman! Honest!"

"Well, all right, then." Peter escaped.

* * *

The professor and his wife were in their sitting room writing letters. The cablegrams had all been answered, but as the professor intended to prolong his journey homeward into a month of Paris and London, there remained the arduous duty of telling their friends at length exactly what had happened. There was considerable of the lore of olden Greece in the professor's descriptions of their escape, and in those of Mrs. Wainwright there was much about the lack of hair-pins and soap.

Their heads were lowered over their writing when the door into the corridor opened and shut quickly, and upon looking up they saw in the room a radiant girl, a new Marjory. She dropped to her knees by her father's chair and reached her arms to his neck. "Oh, daddy! I'm happy! I'm so happy!"

"Why—what——" began the professor stupidly.

"Oh, I am so happy, daddy!"

Or course he could not be long in making his conclusion. The one who could give such joy to Marjory was the one who, last night, gave her such grief. The professor was only a moment in understanding. He laid his hand tenderly upon her head. "Bless my soul," he murmured. "And so—and so—he——"

At the personal pronoun, Mrs. Wainwright lumbered frantically to her feet. "What?" she shouted. "Coleman?"

"Yes," answered Marjory. "Coleman." As she spoke the name her eyes were shot with soft yet tropic flashes of light.

Mrs. Wainwright dropped suddenly back into her chair. "Well—of—all—things!"

The professor was stroking his daughter's hair and although for a time after Mrs. Wainwright's outbreak there was little said, the old man and the girl seemed in gentle communion, she making him feel her happiness, he making her feel his appreciation. Providentially Mrs. Wainwright had been so stunned by the first blow that she was evidently rendered incapable of speech.

"And are you sure you will be happy with him?" asked her father gently.

"All my life long," she answered.

"I am glad! I am glad!" said the father, but even as he spoke a great sadness came to blend with his joy. The hour when he was to give this beautiful and beloved life into the keeping of another had been heralded by the god of the sexes, the ruthless god that devotes itself to the tearing of children from the parental arms and casting them amid the mysteries of an irretrievable wedlock. The thought filled him with solemnity.

But in the dewy eyes of the girl there was no question. The world to her was a land of glowing promise.

"I am glad," repeated the professor.

The girl arose from her knees. "I must go away and—think all about it," she said, smiling. When the door of her room closed upon her, the mother arose in majesty.

"Harrison Wainwright," she declaimed, "you are not going to allow this monstrous thing!"

The professor was aroused from a reverie by these words. "What monstrous thing?" he growled.

"Why, this between Coleman and Marjory."

"Yes," he answered boldly.

"Harrison! That man who——"

The professor crashed his hand down on the table. "Mary! I will not hear another word of it!"

"Well," said Mrs. Wainwright, sullen and ominous, "time will tell! Time will tell!"

* * *

When Coleman had turned from the fleeing Peter Tounley again to Marjory, he found her making the preliminary movements of a flight. "What's the matter?" he demanded anxiously.

"Oh, it's too dreadful!"

"Nonsense," he retorted stoutly. "Only Peter Tounley! He don't count. What of that?"

"Oh, dear!" She pressed her palm to a burning cheek. She gave him a star-like, beseeching glance. "Let me go now—please."

"Well," he answered, somewhat affronted, "if you like——"

At the door she turned to look at him, and this glance expressed in its elusive way a score of things which she had not yet been able to speak. It explained that she was loth to leave him, that she asked forgiveness for leaving him, that even for a short absence she wished to take his image in her eyes, that he must not bully her, that there was something now in her heart which frightened her, that she loved him, that she was happy——

When she had gone, Coleman went to the rooms of the American minister. A Greek was there who talked wildly as he waved his cigarette. Coleman waited in well-concealed impatience for the evaporation of this man. Once the minister, regarding the correspondent hurriedly, interpolated a comment. "You look very cheerful?"

"Yes," answered Coleman, "I've been taking your advice."

"Oh, ho!" said the minister.

The Greek with the cigarette jawed endlessly. Coleman began to marvel at the enduring good manners of the minister, who continued to nod and nod in polite appreciation of the Greek's harangue, which, Coleman firmly believed, had no point of interest whatever. But at last the man, after an effusive farewell, went his way.

"Now," said the minister, wheeling in his chair, "tell me all about it."

Coleman arose, and thrusting his hands deep in his trousers' pockets, began to pace the room with long strides. He said nothing, but kept his eyes on the floor.

"Can I have a drink?" he asked, abruptly pausing.

"What would you like?" asked the minister, benevolently, as he touched the bell.

"A brandy and soda. I'd like it very much. You see," he said, as he resumed his walk, "I have no kind of right to burden you with my affairs, but, to tell the truth, if I don't get this news off my mind and into somebody's ear, I'll die. It's this—I asked Marjory Wainwright to marry me, and—she accepted, and—that's all."

"Well, I am very glad," cried the minister, arising and giving his hand. "And as for burdening me with your affairs, no one has a better right, you know, since you released me from the persecution of Washington and the friends of the Wainwrights. May good luck follow you both forever. You, in my opinion, are a very, very fortunate man. And, for her part—she has not done too badly."

Seeing that it was important that Coleman should have his spirits pacified in part, the minister continued: "Now, I have got to write an official letter, so you just walk up and down here and use up this surplus steam. Else you'll explode."

But Coleman was not to be detained. Now that he had informed the minister, he must rush off somewhere, anywhere, and do—he knew not what.

"All right," said the minister, laughing. "You have a wilder head than I thought. But look here," he called, as Coleman was making for the door. "Am I to keep this news a secret?"

Coleman with his hand on the knob, turned impressively. He spoke with deliberation. "As far as I am concerned, I would be glad to see a man paint it in red letters, eight feet high, on the front of the king's palace."

The minister, left alone, wrote steadily and did not even look up when Peter Tounley and two others entered, in response to his cry of permission. However, he presently found time to speak over his shoulder to them. "Hear the news?"

"No, sir," they answered.

"Well, be good boys, now, and read the papers and look at pictures until I finish this letter. Then I'll tell you."

They surveyed him keenly. They evidently judged that the news was worth hearing, but, obediently, they said nothing. Ultimately the minister affixed a rapid signature to the letter, and turning, looked at the students with a smile.

"Haven't heard the news, eh?"

"No, sir."

"Well, Marjory Wainwright is engaged to marry Coleman."

The minister was amazed to see the effect of this announcement upon the three students. He had expected the crows and cackles of rather absurd merriment with which unbearded youth often greets such news. But there was no crow or cackle. One young man blushed scarlet and looked guiltily at the floor. With a great effort he muttered: "She's too good for him." Another student had turned ghastly pale and was staring. It was Peter Tounley who relieved the minister's mind, for upon that young man's face was a broad jack-o'-lantern grin, and the minister saw that, at any rate, he had not made a complete massacre.

Peter Tounley said triumphantly: "I knew it!"

The minister was anxious over the havoc he had wrought with the two other students, but slowly the colour abated in one face and grew in the other. To give them opportunity, the minister talked busily to Peter Tounley. "And how did you know it, you young scamp?"

Peter was jubilant. "Oh, I knew it! I knew it! I am very clever."

The student who had blushed now addressed the minister in a slightly strained voice. "Are you positive that it is true, Mr. Gordner?"

"I had it on the best authority," replied the minister gravely.

The student who had turned pale said: "Oh, it's true, of course."

"Well," said crudely the one who had blushed, "she's a great sight too good for Coleman or anybody like him. That's all I've got to say."

"Oh, Coleman is a good fellow," said Peter Tounley, reproachfully. "You've no right to say that—exactly. You don't know where you'd be now if it were not for Coleman."

The response was, first, an angry gesture. "Oh, don't keep everlasting rubbing that in. For heaven's sake, let up. Supposing I don't know where I'd be now if it were not for Rufus Coleman? What of it? For the rest of my life have I got to——"

The minister saw that this was the embittered speech of a really defeated youth, so, to save scenes, he gently ejected the trio. "There, there, now! Run along home like good boys. I'll be busy until luncheon. And I dare say you won't find Coleman such a bad chap."

In the corridor, one of the students said offensively to Peter Tounley: "Say, how in hell did you find out all this so early?"

Peter's reply was amiable in tone. "You are a damned bleating little kid and you made a holy show of yourself before Mr. Gordner. There's where you stand. Didn't you see that he turned us out because he didn't know but what you were going to blubber or something. You are a sucking pig, and if you want to know how I find out things go ask the Delphic Oracle, you blind ass."

"You better look out or you may get a punch in the eye!"

"You take one punch in the general direction of my eye, me son," said Peter cheerfully, "and I'll distribute your remains over this hotel in a way that will cause your friends years of trouble to collect you. Instead of anticipating an attack upon my eye, you had much better be engaged in improving your mind, which is at present not a fit machine to cope with exciting situations. There's Coke! Hello, Coke, hear the news? Well, Marjory Wainwright and Rufus Coleman are engaged. Straight? Certainly! go ask the minister."

Coke did not take Peter's word. "Is that so?" he asked the others.

"So the minister told us," they answered, and then these two, who seemed so unhappy, watched Coke's face to see if they could not find surprised misery there. But Coke coolly said: "Well, then, I suppose it's true."

It soon became evident that the students did not care for each other's society. Peter Tounley was probably an exception, but the others seemed to long for quiet corners. They were distrusting each other, and, in a boyish way, they were even capable of malignant things. Their excuses for separation were badly made.

"I—I think I'll go for a walk."

"I'm going up stairs to read."

"Well, so long, old man." "So long." There was no heart to it.

Peter Tounley went to Coleman's door, where he knocked with noisy hilarity. "Come in!" The correspondent apparently had just come from the street, for his hat was on his head and a light top-coat was on his back. He was searching hurriedly through some papers. "Hello, you young devil. What are you doing here?"

Peter's entrance was a somewhat elaborate comedy which Coleman watched in icy silence. Peter, after a long and impudent pantomime halted abruptly and fixing Coleman with his eye demanded: "Well?"

"Well—what?" said Coleman, bristling a trifle.

"Is it true?"

"Is what true?"

"Is it true?" Peter was extremely solemn.

"Say, me bucko," said Coleman suddenly, "if you've come up here to twist the beard of the patriarch, don't you think you are running a chance?"

"All right. I'll be good," said Peter, and he sat on the bed. "But—is it true?"

"Is what true?"

"What the whole hotel is saying."

"I haven't heard the hotel making any remarks lately. Been talking to the other buildings, I suppose."

"Well, I want to tell you that everybody knows that you and Marjory have done gone and got yourselves engaged," said Peter bluntly.

"And well?" asked Coleman imperturbably.

"Oh, nothing," replied Peter, waving his hand. "Only—I thought it might interest you."

Coleman was silent for some time. He fingered his papers. At last he burst out joyously. "And so they know it already, do they? Well—damn them—let them know it. But you didn't tell them yourself?"

"I!" quoth Peter wrathfully. "No! The minister told us."

Then Coleman was again silent for a time and Peter Tounley sat on the bed reflectively looking at the ceiling. "Funny thing, Marjory 'way over here in Greece, and then you happening over here the way you did."

"It isn't funny at all."

"Why isn't it?"

"Because," said Coleman impressively, "that is why I came to Greece. It was all planned. See?"

"Whirroo," exclaimed Peter. "This here is magic."

"No magic at all." Coleman displayed some complacence. "No magic at all. Just pure, plain—whatever you choose to call it."

"Holy smoke," said Peter, admiring the situation. "Why, this is plum romance, Coleman. I'm blowed if it isn't."

Coleman was grinning with delight. He took a fresh cigar and his bright eyes looked at Peter through the smoke. "Seems like it, don't it? Yes. Regular romance. Have a drink, my boy, just to celebrate my good luck. And be patient if I talk a great deal of my—my—future. My head spins with it." He arose to pace the room flinging out his arms in a great gesture. "God! When I think yesterday was not like to-day I wonder how I stood it." There was a knock at the door and a waiter left a note in Coleman's hand.

"Dear Rufus:—We are going for a drive this afternoon at three, and mother wishes you to come, if you care to. I too wish it, if you care to. Yours,

"MARJORY."

With a radiant face, Coleman gave the note a little crackling flourish in the air. "Oh, you don't know what life is, kid."

"S-steady the Blues," said Peter Tounley seriously. "You'll lose your head if you don't watch out."

"Not I," cried Coleman with irritation. "But a man must turn loose some times, mustn't he?"

* * *

When the four students had separated in the corridor, Coke had posted at once to Nora Black's sitting room. His entrance was somewhat precipitate, but he cooled down almost at once, for he reflected that he was not bearing good news. He ended by perching in awkward fashion on the brink of his chair and fumbling his hat uneasily. Nora floated to him in a cloud of a white dressing gown. She gave him a plump hand. "Well, young man?" she said, with a glowing smile. She took a chair, and the stuff of her gown fell in curves over the arms of it.

Coke looked hot and bothered, as if he could have more than half wanted to retract his visit. "I—aw—we haven't seen much of you lately," he began, sparring. He had expected to tell his news at once.

"No," said Nora, languidly. "I have been resting after that horrible journey—that horrible journey. Dear, dear! Nothing will ever induce me to leave London, New York and Paris. I am at home there. But here! Why, it is worse than living in Brooklyn. And that journey into the wilds! No, no; not for me!"

"I suppose we'll all be glad to get home," said Coke, aimlessly.

At the moment a waiter entered the room and began to lay the table for luncheon. He kept open the door to the corridor, and he had the luncheon at a point just outside the door. His excursions to the trays were flying ones, so that, as far as Coke's purpose was concerned, the waiter was always in the room. Moreover, Coke was obliged, naturally, to depart at once. He had bungled everything.

As he arose he whispered hastily: "Does this waiter understand English?"

"Yes," answered Nora. "Why?"

"Because I have something to tell you—important."

"What is it?" whispered Nora, eagerly.

He leaned toward her and replied: "Marjory Wainwright and Coleman are engaged."

To his unfeigned astonishment, Nora Black burst into peals of silvery laughter. "Oh, indeed? And so this is your tragic story, poor, innocent lambkin? And what did you expect? That I would faint?"

"I thought—I don't know——" murmured Coke in confusion.

Nora became suddenly business-like. "But how do you know? Are you sure? Who told you? Anyhow, stay to luncheon. Do—like a good boy. Oh, you must."

Coke dropped again into his chair. He studied her in some wonder. "I thought you'd be surprised," he said, ingenuously.

"Oh, you did, did you? Well, you see I'm not. And now tell me all about it."

"There's really nothing to tell but the plain fact. Some of the boys dropped in at the minister's rooms a little while ago, and he told them of it. That's all."

"Well, how did he know?"

"I am sure I can't tell you. Got it first hand, I suppose. He likes Coleman, and Coleman is always hanging up there."

"Oh, perhaps Coleman was lying," said Nora easily. Then suddenly her face brightened and she spoke with animation. "Oh, I haven't told you how my little Greek officer has turned out. Have I? No? Well, it is simply lovely. Do you know, he belongs to one of the best families in Athens? He does. And they're rich—rich as can be. My courier tells me that the marble palace where they live is enough to blind you, and that if titles hadn't gone out of style—or something—here in Greece, my little officer would be a prince! Think of that! The courier didn't know it until we got to Athens, and the little officer—the prince—gave me his card, of course. One of the oldest, noblest and richest families in Greece. Think of that! There I thought he was only a bothersome little officer who came in handy at times, and there he turns out to be a prince. I could hardly keep myself from rushing right off to find him and apologise to him for the way I treated him. It was awful! And——" added the fair Nora, pensively, "if he does meet me in Paris, I'll make him wear that title down to a shred, you can bet. What's the good of having a title unless you make it work?"

Chapter 29

Coke did not stay to luncheon with Nora Black. He went away saying to himself: "Either that girl don't care a straw for Coleman or she has got a heart absolutely of flint, or she is the greatest actress on earth or—there is some other reason."

At his departure, Nora turned and called into an adjoining room. "Maude!" The voice of her companion and friend answered her peevishly. "What? Don't bother me. I'm reading."

"Well, anyhow, luncheon is ready, so you will have to stir your precious self," responded Nora. "You're lazy."

"I don't want any luncheon. Don't brother me. I've got a headache."

"Well, if you don't come out, you'll miss the news. That's all I've got to say."

There was a rustle in the adjoining room, and immediately the companion appeared, seeming much annoyed but curious. "Well, what is it?"

"Rufus Coleman is engaged to be married to that Wainwright girl, after all."

"Well, I declare!" ejaculated the little old lady. "Well, I declare." She meditated for a moment, and then continued in a tone of satisfaction. "I told you that you couldn't stop that man Coleman if he had really made up his mind to ——"

"You're a fool," said Nora, pleasantly.

"Why?" said the old lady.

"Because you are. Don't talk to me about it. I want to think of Marco."

"'Marco,'" quoted the old lady startled.

"The prince. The prince. Can't you understand? I mean the prince."

"'Marco!'" again quoted the old lady, under her breath.

"Yes, 'Marco,'" cried Nora, belligerently. "'Marco.' Do you object to the name? What's the matter with you, anyhow?"

"Well," rejoined the other, nodding her head wisely, "he may be a prince, but I've always heard that these continental titles are no good in comparison to the English titles."

"Yes, but who told you so, eh?" demanded Nora, noisily. She herself answered the question. "The English!"

"Anyhow, that little marquis who tagged after you in London is a much

406

bigger man in every way, I'll bet, than this little prince of yours."

"But—good heavens—he didn't mean it. Why, he was only one of the regular rounders. But Marco, he is serious! He means it. He'd go through fire and water for me and be glad of the chance."

"Well," proclaimed the old lady, "if you are not the strangest woman in the world, I'd like to know! Here I thought——"

"What did you think?" demanded Nora, suspiciously.

"I thought that Coleman——"

"Bosh!" interrupted the graceful Nora. "I tell you what, Maude; you'd better try to think as little as possible. It will suit your style of beauty better. And above all, don't think of my affairs. I myself am taking pains not to think of them. It's easier."

* * *

Mrs. Wainwright, with no spirit of intention whatever, had set about readjusting her opinions. It is certain that she was unconscious of any evolution. If some one had said to her that she was surrendering to the inevitable, she would have been immediately on her guard, and would have opposed forever all suggestions of a match between Marjory and Coleman. On the other hand, if some one had said to her that her daughter was going to marry a human serpent, and that there were people in Athens who would be glad to explain his treacherous character, she would have haughtily scorned the tale-bearing and would have gone with more haste into the professor's way of thinking. In fact, she was in process of undermining herself, and the work could have been retarded or advanced by any irresponsible, gossipy tongue.

The professor, from the depths of his experience with her, arranged a course of conduct. "If I just leave her to herself she will come around all right, but if I go 'striking while the iron is hot,' or any of those things, I'll bungle it surely."

As they were making ready to go down to luncheon, Mrs. Wainwright made her speech which first indicated a changing mind. "Well, what will be, will be," she murmured with a prolonged sigh of resignation. "What will be, will be. Girls are very headstrong in these days, and there is nothing much to be done with them. They go their own roads. It wasn't so in my girlhood. We were obliged to pay attention to our mothers' wishes."

"I did not notice that you paid much attention to your mother's wishes when you married me," remarked the professor. "In fact, I thought——"

"That was another thing," retorted Mrs. Wainwright with severity. "You were a steady young man who had taken the highest honours all through your college course, and my mother's sole objection was that we were too hasty. She thought we ought to wait until you had a penny to bless yourself with, and I can see now where she was quite right."

"Well, you married me, anyhow," said the professor, victoriously.

Mrs. Wainwright allowed her husband's retort to pass over her thoughtful mood. "They say * * they say Rufus Coleman makes as much as fifteen thousand dollars a year. That's more than three times your income * * I don't know. * * It all depends on whether they try to save or not. His manner of life is, no doubt, very luxurious. I don't suppose he knows how to economise at all. That kind of a man usually doesn't. And then, in the newspaper world positions are so very precarious. Men may have valuable positions one minute and be penniless in the street the next minute. It isn't as if he had any real income, and of course he has no real ability. If he was suddenly thrown out of his position, goodness knows what would become of him. Still * * still * * fifteen thousand dollars a year is a big income * * while it lasts. I suppose he is very extravagant. That kind of a man usually is. And I wouldn't be surprised if he was heavily in debt; very heavily in debt. Still * * if Marjory has set her heart there is nothing to be done, I suppose. It wouldn't have happened if you had been as wise as you thought you were * * I suppose he thinks I have been very rude to him. Well, sometimes I wasn't nearly so rude as I felt like being. Feeling as I did, I could hardly be very amiable. * * Of course this drive this afternoon was all your affair and Marjory's. But, of course, I shall be nice to him."

"And what of all this Nora Black business?" asked the professor, with a display of valour, but really with much trepidation.

"She is a hussy," responded Mrs. Wainwright with energy. "Her conversation in the carriage on the way down to Agrinion sickened me!"

"I really believe that her plan was simply to break everything off between Marjory and Coleman," said the professor, "and I don't believe she had any grounds for all that appearance of owning Coleman and the rest of it."

"Of course she didn't," assented Mrs. Wainwright. "The vicious thing!"

"On the other hand," said the professor, "there might be some truth in it."

"I don't think so," said Mrs. Wainwright seriously. "I don't believe a word of it."

"You do not mean to say that you think Coleman a model man?" demanded the professor.

"Not at all! Not at all!" she hastily answered, "But * * one doesn't look for model men these days."

"Who told you he made fifteen thousand a year?" asked the professor.

"It was Peter Tounley this morning. We were talking upstairs after breakfast, and he remarked that he if could make fifteen thousand a year like Coleman, he'd—I've forgotten what—some fanciful thing."

"I doubt if it is true," muttered the old man wagging his head.

"Of course it's true," said his wife emphatically. "Peter Tounley says everybody knows it."

"Well * anyhow * money is not everything."

"But it's a great deal, you know well enough. You know you are always speaking of poverty as an evil, as a grand resultant, a collaboration of many lesser evils. Well, then?"

"But," began the professor meekly, "when I say that I mean——"

"Well, money is money and poverty is poverty," interrupted his wife. "You don't have to be very learned to know that."

"I do not say that Coleman has not a very nice thing of it, but I must say it is hard to think of his getting any such sum as you mention."

"Isn't he known as the most brilliant journalist in New York?" she demanded harshly.

"Y-yes, as long as it lasts, but then one never knows when he will be out in the street penniless. Of course he has no particular ability which would be marketable if he suddenly lost his present employment. Of course it is not as if he was a really talented young man. He might not be able to make his way at all in any new direction."

"I don't know about that," said Mrs. Wainwright in reflective protestation. "I don't know about that. I think he would."

"I thought you said a moment ago—" The professor spoke with an air of puzzled hesitancy. "I thought you said a moment ago that he wouldn't succeed in anything but journalism."

Mrs. Wainwright swam over the situation with a fine tranquility. "Well-l-l," she answered musingly, "if I did say that, I didn't mean it exactly."

"No, I suppose not," spoke the professor, and despite the necessity for caution he could not keep out of his voice a faint note of annoyance.

"Of course," continued the wife, "Rufus Coleman is known everywhere as a brilliant man, a very brilliant man, and he even might do well in—in politics or something of that sort."

"I have a very poor opinion of that kind of a mind which does well in American politics," said the professor, speaking as a collegian, "but I suppose there may be something in it."

"Well, at any rate," decided Mrs. Wainwright. "At any rate——"

At that moment, Marjory attired for luncheon and the drive entered from her room, and Mrs. Wainwright checked the expression of her important conclusion. Neither father or mother had ever seen her so glowing with triumphant beauty, a beauty which would carry the mind of a spectator far above physical appreciation into that realm of poetry where creatures of light move and are beautiful because they cannot know pain or a burden. It carried tears to the old father's eyes. He took her hands. "Don't be too happy, my child, don't be too happy," he admonished her tremulously. "It makes me afraid—it makes me afraid."

Chapter 30

It seems strange that the one who was the most hilarious over the engagement of Marjory and Coleman should be Coleman's dragoman who was indeed in a state bordering on transport. It is not known how he learned the glad tidings, but it is certain that he learned them before luncheon. He told all the visible employees of the hotel and allowed them to know that the betrothal really had been his handiwork. He had arranged it. He did not make quite clear how he had performed this feat, but at least he was perfectly frank in acknowledging it.

When some of the students came down to luncheon, they saw him but could not decide what ailed him. He was in the main corridor of the hotel, grinning from ear to ear, and when he perceived the students he made signs to intimate that they possessed in common a joyous secret. "What's the matter with that idiot?" asked Coke morosely. "Looks as if his wheels were going around too fast."

Peter Tounley walked close to him and scanned him imperturbably, but with care. "What's up, Phidias?" The man made no articulate reply. He continued to grin and gesture. "Pain in oo tummy? Mother dead? Caught the cholera? Found out that you've swallowed a pair of hammered brass and irons in your beer? Say, who are you, anyhow?" But he could not shake this invincible glee, so he went away.

The dragoman's rapture reached its zenith when Coleman lent him to the professor and he was commissioned to bring a carriage for four people to the door at three o'clock. He himself was to sit on the box and tell the driver what was required of him. He dashed off, his hat in his hand, his hair flying, puffing, important beyond everything, and apparently babbling his mission to half the people he met on the street. In most countries he would have landed speedily in jail, but among a people who exist on a basis of jibbering, his violent gabble aroused no suspicions as to his sanity. However, he stirred several livery stables to their depths and set men running here and there wildly and for the most part futilely.

At fifteen minutes to three o'clock, a carriage with its horses on a gallop tore around the corner and up to the front of the hotel, where it halted with the pomp and excitement of a fire engine. The dragoman jumped down from his seat beside the driver and scrambled hurriedly into the hotel, in the gloom of which he met a serene stillness which was punctuated only by the leisurely tinkle of silver and glass in the dining room. For a moment the dragoman seemed really astounded out of speech. Then he plunged into the manager's room. Was it conceivable that Monsieur Coleman was still at luncheon? Yes; in fact, it was true. But the carriage was at the door! The carriage was at the door! The manager, undisturbed, asked for what hour Monsieur Coleman had been pleased to order a carriage. Three o'clock! Three o'clock? The manager pointed calmly at the clock. Very well. It was now only thirteen minutes of three o'clock. Monsieur Coleman doubtless would appear at three. Until that hour the manager would not disturb Monsieur Coleman! The dragoman clutched both his hands in his hair and cast a look of agony to the ceiling. Great God! Had he accomplished the herculean task of getting a carriage for four people to the door of the hotel in time for a drive at three o'clock, only to meet with this stoniness, this inhumanity? Ah, it was unendurable? He begged the manager; he implored him. But at every word the manager seemed to grow more indifferent, more callous. He pointed with a wooden finger at the clock-face. In reality, it is thus that Greek meets Greek.

Professor Wainwright and Coleman strolled together out of the dining room. The dragoman rushed ecstatically upon the correspondent. "Oh, Meester Coleman! The carge is ready!"

"Well, all right," said Coleman, knocking ashes from his cigar. "Don't be in a hurry. I suppose we'll be ready presently." The man was in despair.

The departure of the Wainwrights and Coleman on this ordinary drive was of a somewhat dramatic and public nature. No one seemed to know how to prevent its being so. In the first place, the attendants thronged out en masse for a reason which was plain at the time only to Coleman's dragoman. And, rather in the background, lurked the interested students. The professor was surprised and nervous. Coleman was rigid and angry. Marjory was flushed and somewhat hurried, and Mrs. Wainwright was as proud as an old turkey-hen.

As the carriage rolled away, Peter Tounley turned to his companions and said: "Now, that's official! That is the official announcement! Did you see Old Mother Wainwright? Oh, my eye, wasn't she puffed up! Say, what in hell do you suppose all these jay-hawking bell-boys poured out to the kerb for? Go back to your cages, my good people——"

As soon as the carriage wheeled into another street, its occupants exchanged easier smiles, and they must have confessed in some subtle way of glances that now at last they were upon their own mission, a mission undefined but earnest to them all. Coleman had a glad feeling of being let into the family, or becoming one of them.

The professor looked sideways at him and smiled gently. "You know, I thought of driving you to some ruins, but Marjory would not have it. She flatly objected to any more ruins. So I thought we would drive down to New Phalerum."

Coleman nodded and smiled as if he were immensely pleased, but of course New Phalerum was to him no more nor less than Vladivostok or Khartoum. Neither place nor distance had interest for him. They swept along a shaded avenue where the dust lay thick on the leaves; they passed cafes where crowds were angrily shouting over the news in the little papers; they passed a hospital before which wounded men, white with bandages, were taking the sun; then came soon to the arid valley flanked by gaunt naked mountains, which would lead them to the sea. Sometimes to accentuate the dry nakedness of this valley, there would be a patch of grass upon which poppies burned crimson spots. The dust writhed out from under the wheels of the carriage; in the distance the sea appeared, a blue half-disc set between shoulders of barren land. It would be common to say that Coleman was oblivious to all about him but Marjory. On the contrary, the parched land, the isolated flame of poppies, the cool air from the sea, all were keenly known to him, and they had developed an extraordinary power of blending sympathetically into his mood. Meanwhile the professor talked a great deal. And as a somewhat exhilarating detail, Coleman perceived that Mrs. Wainwright was beaming upon him.

At New Phalerum—a small collection of pale square villas—they left the carriage and strolled by the sea. The waves were snarling together like wolves amid the honeycomb rocks and from where the blue plane sprang level to the horizon, came a strong cold breeze, the kind of a breeze which moves an exulting man or a parson to take off his hat and let his locks flutter and tug back from his brow.

The professor and Mrs. Wainwright were left to themselves.

Marjory and Coleman did not speak for a time. It might have been that they did not quite know where to make a beginning. At last Marjory asked:

"What has become of your splendid horse?"

"Oh, I've told the dragoman to have him sold as soon as he arrives," said Coleman absently.

"Oh, I'm sorry * * I liked that horse."

"Why?"

"Oh, because——"

"Well, he was a fine——" Then he, too, interrupted himself, for he saw plainly that they had not come to this place to talk about a horse. Thereat he made speeches of matters which at least did not afford as many opportunities for coherency as would the horse. "Marjory, it can't be true * * * Is it true, dearest?" * * I can hardly believe it. —I——"

* * *

"Oh, I know I'm not nearly good enough for you."

"Good enough for me, dear?"

"They all told me so, and they were right! Why, even the American minister said it. Everybody thinks it."

"Why, aren't they wretches! To think of them saying such a thing! As if—as if anybody could be too——"

* * *

"Do you know——" She paused and looked at him with a certain timid challenge. "I don't know why I feel it, but—sometimes I feel that I've been—I've been flung at your head."

He opened his mouth in astonishment. "Flung at my head!"

She held up her finger. "And if I thought you could ever believe it!"

"Is a girl flung at a man's head when her father carries her thousands of miles away and the man follows her all these miles, and at last——"

Her eyes were shining. "And you really came to Greece—on purpose to—to——"

* * *

"Confess you knew it all the time! Confess!"

The answer was muffled. "Well, sometimes I thought you did, and at other times I thought you—didn't."

* * *

In a secluded cove, in which the sea-maids once had played, no doubt, Marjory and Coleman sat in silence. He was below her, and if he looked at her he had to turn his glance obliquely upward. She was staring at the sea with woman's mystic gaze, a gaze which men at once reverence and fear since it seems to look into the deep, simple heart of nature, and men begin to feel that their petty wisdoms are futile to control these strange spirits, as wayward as nature and as pure as nature, wild as the play of waves, sometimes as unalterable as the mountain amid the winds; and to measure them, man must perforce use a mathematical formula.

* * *

He wished that she would lay her hand upon his hair. He would be happy then. If she would only, of her own will, touch his hair lightly with her fingers—if she would do it with an unconscious air it would be even better. It would show him that she was thinking of him, even when she did not know she was thinking of him.

Perhaps he dared lay his head softly against her knee. Did he dare?

* * *

As his head touched her knee, she did not move. She seemed to be still gazing at the sea. Presently idly caressing fingers played in his hair near the forehead. He looked up suddenly lifting his arms. He breathed out a cry which was laden with a kind of diffident ferocity. "I haven't kissed you yet——"

CONTENTS

THE BATTLE OF BUNKER HILL

On the 12th of June, 1775, Captain Harris, afterwards Lord Harris, wrote home from the town of Boston, then occupied by British troops:

"I wish the Americans may be brought to a sense of their duty. One good drubbing, which I long to give them, by way of retaliation, might have a good effect towards it. At present they are so elated by the petty advantage they gained the 19th of April, that they despise the powers of Britain. We shall soon take the field on the other side of the Neck."

This very fairly expressed the irritation in the British camp. The troops had been sent to Massachusetts to subdue it, but as yet nothing had been done in that direction.

The ignominious flight of the British regulars from Lexington and Concord was still unavenged. More than that, they had been kept close in Boston ever since by the provincial militia.

"What!" cried General Burgoyne when on his arrival in May he was told this news. "What! Ten thousand peasants keep five thousand King's troops shut up? Let *us* get in, and we'll soon find elbow-room!" "Elbow-room" was the army's name for Burgoyne after that.

A little later General Gage remarked to General Timothy Ruggles, "It is impossible for the rebels to withstand our arms a moment."

Ruggles replied: "Sir, you do not know with whom you have to contend. These are the very men who conquered Canada. I fought with them side by side. I know them well; they will fight bravely. My God, sir, your folly has ruined your cause!"

Besides Burgoyne, the Cerberus brought over Generals Clinton and Howe and large re-enforcements, so that the forces under General Gage, the commander-in-chief, were over ten thousand. By June 12th the army in Boston was actually unable to procure fresh provisions, and Gage proclaimed martial law, designating those who were in arms as rebels and traitors.

The *Essex Gazette* of June 8th says: "We have the pleasure to inform the public that the Grand American Army is nearly completed." This Grand

419

American Army was spread around Boston, its headquarters at Cambridge, under command of General Artemas Ward, who had fought under Abercrombie. The Grand American Army was an army of allies. Ward, its supposed chief, was authorized to command only the Massachusetts and New Hampshire forces, and when the Connecticut and Rhode Island men obeyed him it was purely through courtesy. Each colony supplied its own troops with provisions and ammunition; each had its own officers, appointed by the Committee of Safety.

To this committee, June 13th, came the tidings that Gage proposed to occupy Bunker Hill, in Charlestown, on the 18th, and a council of war was held, which included the savagely bluff, warm-hearted patriot, General Israel Putnam, of the Connecticut troops; General Seth Pomeroy, Colonel William Prescott, the hardy, independent Stark, and Captain Gridley, the engineer—all of whom were veterans of the French and Indian War.

As a result of the meeting, a detachment of nine hundred men of the Massachusetts regiments, under Colonels Prescott, Frye, and Bridge, with two hundred men from Connecticut and Captain Gridley's artillery company of forty-nine men and two field-pieces, were ordered to parade at six o'clock P.M., the 16th, on Cambridge Common. There they appeared with weapons, packs, blankets, and intrenching tools. President Langdon, of Harvard College, made an impressive prayer, and by nine o'clock they had marched, the entire force being under the command of Colonel Prescott.

A uniform of blue turned back with red was worn by some of the men, but for the most part they wore their "Sunday suits" of homespun. Their guns were of all sorts and sizes, and many carried old-fashioned powder-horns and pouches. Prescott walked at their head, with two sergeants carrying dark lanterns, until they reached the Neck.

The Neck was the strip of land leading to the peninsula opposite Boston, where lay the small town of Charlestown. The peninsula is only one mile in length, its greatest breadth but half a mile. The Charles River separates it from Boston on the south, and to the north and east is the Mystic River. Bunker Hill begins at the isthmus and rises gradually to a height of one hundred and ten feet, forming a smooth, round hill.

At Cambridge Common, the night the troops started for Bunker Hill, Israel Putnam had made this eloquent address: "Men, there are enough of you on the Common this evening to fill hell so full of the red-coats to-morrow that the devils will break their shins over them."

At Bunker Hill the expedition halted, and a long discussion ensued between Prescott, Gridley, Major Brooks, and Putnam as to whether it would be better to follow Ward's orders literally and fortify Bunker Hill itself, or to go on to the lesser elevation southeast of it, which is now known as Breed's Hill, but had then no special name. They agreed upon Breed's Hill.

They began to intrench at midnight.

Prescott was consumed with anxiety lest his men should be attacked before some screen could be raised to shelter them. However enthusiastic they might be, he did not think it possible for his raw troops to meet to any advantage a disciplined soldiery in the open field.

So the pickaxe and the spade were busy throughout the night. It was silent work, for the foe was near. In Boston Harbor lay the Lively, the Somerset, the Cerberus, the Glasgow, the Falcon, and the Symmetry, besides the floating batteries. On the Boston shore the sentinels were pacing outside the British encampment. At intervals through the night Prescott and Brooks stole down to the shore of Charles River and listened till the call of "All's well!" rang over the water from the ships and told them that their scheme was still undiscovered.

At dawn the intrenchments were six feet high, and there was a great burst of fire at them from the Lively, which was joined in a few moments by the other men-of-war and the batteries on Copp's Hill, on the Boston shore.

The strange thunder of the cannonade brought forth every man, woman, and child in Boston. Out of their prim houses they rushed under trellises heavy with damask roses and honeysuckle, and soon every belfry and tower, house-top and hill-top, was crowded with them. There the most of them stayed till the thrilling play in which they had so vital an interest was enacted.

Meanwhile Prescott, to inspire his raw men with confidence, mounted the parapet of the redoubt they had raised and deliberately sauntered around it, making jocular speeches, until the men cheered each cannon-ball as it came.

Gage, looking through his field-glasses from the other shore, marked the tall figure with the three-cornered hat and the banyan—a linen blouse—buckled about the waist, and asked of Councillor Willard, who stood near him,—

"Who is the person who appears to command?"

"That is my brother-in-law, Colonel Prescott."

"Will he fight?"

"Yes, sir; he is an old soldier, and will fight as long as a drop of blood remains in his veins."

"The works must be carried," said Gage.

Gage was strongly advised by his generals to land a force at the Neck and attack the Americans in the rear. It was also suggested that they might be bombarded by the fleet from the Mystic and the Charles, and, indeed, might be starved out without any fighting at all. But none of this suited the warlike British temper; the whole army longed to fight—to chase the impudent enemy out of those intrenchments he had so insolently reared. The challenge was a bold one; it must be accepted. The British had the weight in all ways, but they also had the preposterous arrogance of the British army, which always deems itself invincible because it remembers its traditions, and traditions are dubious and improper weapons to fire at a foe.

At noon the watchers on the house-tops saw the lines of smart grenadiers and light infantry embark in barges under command of General Howe, who had with him Brigadier-General Pigot and some of the most distinguished officers in Boston. They landed at the southwestern point of the peninsula.

When the intelligence that the British troops had landed reached Cambridge it caused great excitement. A letter of Captain Chester reads:

"Just after dinner on the 17th ult. I was walking out from my lodgings, quite calm and composed, and all at once the drums beat to arms, and bells rang, and a great noise in Cambridge. Captain Putnam came by on full gallop. 'What is the matter?' says I. 'Have you not heard?' 'No.' 'Why, the regulars are landing at Charlestown,' says he, 'and father says you must all meet and march immediately to Bunker Hill to oppose the enemy.' I waited not, but ran and got my arms and ammunition, and hastened to my company (who were in the church for barracks), and found them nearly ready to march. We soon marched, with our frocks and trousers on over our other clothes (for our company is in uniform wholly blue, turned up with red), for we were loath to expose ourselves by our dress; and down we marched."

After a reconnoissance, Howe sent back to Gage for re-inforcements, and remained passive until they came.

Meanwhile, there were bitter murmurings among the troops on Breed's Hill. They had watched the brilliant pageant,—the crossing over of their adversaries, scarlet-clad, with glittering equipments, with formidable guns in their train,— and were conscious of being themselves exhausted from the night's labor and the hot morning sun. It was two o'clock, and they had had practically nothing to eat that day. Among themselves they accused their officers of treachery. It seemed incredible that after doing all the hard work they should be expected to do the fighting as well. Loud huzzas arose from their lips, however,—these cross and hungry Yankees,—when Doctor—or General—Joseph Warren appeared among them with Seth Pomeroy.

Few men had risen to a higher degree of universal love and confidence in the hearts of the Massachusetts people than Warren. He had been active in every patriotic movement. The councils through which the machinery of the Revolution was put in motion owed much to him. He was president of the Committee of Safety, and probably had been one of the Indians of the Boston Tea Party. But a few days before he had been appointed major-general. In recognition of this, Israel Putnam, who was keeping a squad of men working at intrenchments on Bunker Hill, had offered to take orders from him. But Warren refused, and asked where he might go to be of the greatest service. "Where will the onset be most furious?" he asked, and Putnam sent him to the redoubt. There Prescott also offered him the chief command, but Warren replied, "I came as a volunteer with my musket to serve under you, and shall be happy to learn from a soldier of your experience."

At three o'clock the redoubt was in good working order. About eight yards square, its strongest side, the front, faced the settled part of Charlestown and protected the south side of the hill. The east side commanded a field; the north side had an open passage-way; to the left extended a breastwork for about two hundred yards.

By three o'clock some re-enforcements for General Howe had arrived, so that he now had over three thousand men. Just before action he addressed the officers around him as follows:

"Gentlemen, I am very happy in having the honor of commanding so fine a body of men. I do not in the least doubt that you will behave like Englishmen and as becomes good soldiers. If the enemy will not come out from their intrenchments, we must drive them out at all events; otherwise the town of Boston will be set on fire by them. I shall not desire one of you to go a step farther than where I go myself at your head. Remember, gentlemen, we have no recourse to any resources if we lose Boston but to go on board our ships, which will be very disagreeable to us all."

From the movements of the British, they seemed intending to turn the American left and surround the redoubt. To prevent this, Prescott sent down the artillery with two field-pieces—he had only four altogether—and the Connecticut troops under Captain Knowlton. Putnam met them as they neared the Mystic, shouting,—

"Man the rail fence, for the enemy is flanking of us fast!"

This rail fence—half of which was stone—reached from the shore of the Mystic to within two hundred yards of the breast-works. It was not high, but

Putnam had said:

"If you can shield a Yankee's shins he's not afraid of anything. His head he does not think of."

Captain Knowlton, joined by Colonels Stark and Reid and their regiments, made another parallel fence a short distance in front of this, filling in the space between with new-mown hay from the fields.

A great cannonade was thundering from ships and batteries to cover Howe's advance. His troops, now increased to three thousand, came on in two divisions, the left wing, under Pigot, towards the breastwork and redoubt; the right, led by Howe, to storm the rail fence. The artillery moved heavily through the miry, low ground, and the embarrassing discovery was made that there were only twelve-pound balls for six-pounders. Howe decided to load them with grape. The troops were hindered by a number of fences, as well as the thick, tall grass. Their knapsacks were extraordinarily heavy, and they felt the power of the scorching sun.

Inside the redoubt the Americans waited for them, Prescott assuring his men that the red-coats would never reach the redoubt if they obeyed him and reserved their fire until he gave the word. As the assaulting force drew temptingly near, the American officers only restrained their men from firing by mounting the parapet and kicking up their guns.

But at last the word was given—the stream of fire broke out all along the line. They were wonderful marksmen. The magnificent regulars were staggered, but they returned the fire. They could make no headway against the murderous volleys flashed in quick succession at them. The dead and wounded fell thickly. General Pigot ordered a retreat, while great shouts of triumph arose from the Americans.

At the rail fence Putnam gave his last directions when Howe was nearing him: "Fire low: aim at the waistbands! Wait until you see the whites of their eyes! Aim at the handsome coats! Pick off the commanders!"

The men rested their guns on the rail fence to fire. The officers were used as targets—many of the handsome coats were laid low. So hot was the reception they met that in a few moments Howe's men were obliged to fall back. One of them said afterwards, "It was the strongest post that was ever occupied by any set of men."

There was wild exultation within the American lines, congratulation and praises, for just fifteen minutes; and then Pigot and Howe led the attack again. But the second repulse was so much fiercer than the first that the British broke ranks and ran down hill, some of them getting into the boats.

"The dead," said Stark, "lay in front of us as thick as sheep in a fold."

Meantime Charlestown had been set on fire by Howe's orders, and the spectacle was splendidly terrible to the watchers in Boston. The wooden buildings made a superb blaze, and through the smoke could be seen the British officers striking and pricking their men with their swords in the vain hope of rallying them, while cannon, musketry, crashes of falling houses, and the yells of the victors filled up the measure of excitement to the spectators.

Twice, now, the Americans had met the foe and proved that he was not invincible. The women in Boston thought the last defeat final—that their men-folk had gained the day. But Prescott knew better; he was sure that they would come again, and sure that he could not withstand a third attack.

If at this juncture strong re-enforcements and supplies of ammunition had reached him, he might well have held his own. But such companies as had been sent on would come no farther than Bunker Hill, in spite of Israel Putnam's threats and entreaties. There they straggled about under hay-cocks and apple-trees, demoralized by the sights and sounds of battle, with no authorized leader who could force them to the front.

As for their commander-in-chief, Ward, he would not stir from his house all day, and kept the main body of his forces at Cambridge.

When General Clinton saw the rout of his countrymen from the Boston shore, he rowed over in great haste. With his assistance, and the fine discipline which prevailed, the troops were re-formed within half an hour. Clinton also proprosed a new plan of assault. Accordingly, instead of diffusing their forces across the whole American front, the chief attack was directed on the redoubt. The artillery bombarded the breastwork, and only a small number moved against the rail fence.

"Fight! conquer or die!" was the watchword that passed from mouth to mouth as the tall, commanding figure of Howe led on the third assault. To his soldiers it was a desperate venture—they felt that they were going to certain death. But inside the redoubt few of the men had more than one round of ammunition left, though they shouted bravely,—

"We are ready for the red-coats again!"

Again their first fire was furious and destructive, but although many of the enemy fell, the rest bounded forward without returning it. In a few minutes the columns of Pigot and Clinton had surrounded the redoubt on three sides. The defenders of the breastwork had been driven by the artillery-fire into the redoubt, and balls came whistling through the open passage.

The first rank of red-coats who climbed the parapet was shot down. Major Pitcairn met his death at this time while cheering on his men. But the Americans had come to the end of their ammunition, and they had not fifty bayonets among them, though these were made to do good service as the enemy came swarming over the walls.

Pigot got up by the aid of a tree, and hundreds followed his lead. The American made stout resistance in the hand-to-hand struggle that followed, but there could be only one ending to it, and Prescott ordered a retreat. He was almost the last to leave, and only got away by skilfully parrying with his sword the bayonet thrusts of the foe. His banyan was pierced in many places, but he escaped unhurt.

The men at the rail fence kept firm until they saw the forces leaving the redoubt; they fell back then, but in good order.

A great volley was fired after the Americans. It was then that Warren fell, as he lingered in the rear—a loss that was passionately mourned throughout New England.

During their disordered flight over the little peninsula the Americans lost more men than at any other time of the day, though their list of killed and wounded only amounted to four hundred and forty-nine. The heavy loss of the enemy—ten hundred and fifty-four men—had the effect of checking the eagerness of their pursuit; the Americans passed the Neck without further molestation.

General Howe had maintained his reputation for solid courage, and his long white-silk stockings were soaked in blood.

The speech of Count Vergennes, that "if it won two more such victories as Bunker Hill, there would be no more British Army in America," echoed the general sentiment in England and America as well as in France. So impressed were the British leaders with the indomitable resolution shown by the Provincials in fortifying and defending so desperate a position as Breed's Hill, that they made no attempt to follow up their victory. General Gage admitted that the people of New England were not the despicable rabble they had sometimes been represented.

Among the Grand Army itself many recriminations and courts-martial followed the contest. But Washington soon drilled it into order.

The most important thing to be remembered of Bunker Hill is its effect upon the colonies. The troubles with the mother country had been brewing a long time, but this was the first decisive struggle for supremacy. There was no doubt of the tough soldierly qualities displayed by the Colonials; the thrill of pride that went through the country at the success of their arms welded together the scattered colonies and made a nation of them. The Revolution was an accomplished fact. "England," said Franklin, "has lost her colonies forever."

VITTORIA

The Campaign of 1812, which included the storming of Ciudad Rodrigo and Badajos and the overwhelming victory of Salamanca, had apparently done so much towards destroying the Napoleonic sway in the Peninsula that the defeat of the Allies at Burgos, in October, 1812, came as an embittering disappointment to England; and when Wellington, after his disastrous retreat to Ciudad Rodrigo, reported his losses as amounting to nine thousand, the usual tempest of condemnation against him was raised, and the members of the Cabinet, who were always so free with their oracular advice and so close with the nation's money, wagged their heads despairingly.

But as the whole aspect of affairs was revealed, and as Wellington coolly stated his plans for a new campaign, public opinion changed.

It was a critical juncture: Napoleon had arranged an armistice with Russia, Prussia, and Austria, which was to last until August 16, 1813, and it became known that this armistice might end in peace. Peace on the Continent would mean that Napoleon's unemployed troops might be poured into Spain in such enormous numbers as to overwhelm the Allies. So, to insure Wellington's striking a decisive blow before this could happen, both the English Ministry and the Opposition united in supporting him, and for the first time during the war he felt sure of receiving the supplies for which he had asked.

The winter and spring were spent by Wellington in preparing for his campaign: his troops needed severe discipline after the disorder into which they had fallen during the retreat from Burgos, and the great chief entered into the matter of their equipment with most painstaking attention to detail, removing unnecessary weight from them, and supplying each infantry soldier with three extra pairs of shoes, besides heels and soles for repairs. He drew large re-enforcements from England, and all were drilled to a high state of efficiency.

It is well to quote here from the letter published by Wellington on the 28th of December, 1812. It was addressed to the commanders of divisions and brigades. It created a very pretty storm, as one may readily see. I quote at length, since surely no document could be more illuminative of Wellington's character, and it seems certain that this fearless letter saved the army from the happy-go-lucky feeling, very common in British field forces, that a man is a thorough soldier so long as he is willing at all times to go into action and charge, if ordered, at even the brass gates of Inferno. But Wellington knew that this was not enough. He wrote as follows:

"GENTLEMEN:—I have ordered the army into cantonments, in which I hope that circumstances will enable me to keep them for some time, during which the troops will receive their clothing, necessaries, etc., which are already in progress by different lines of communication to the several divisions and brigades.

"But besides these objects, I must draw your attention in a very particular manner to the state of discipline of the troops. The discipline of every army, after a long and active campaign, becomes in some degree relaxed, and requires the utmost attention on the part of general and other officers to bring it back to the state in which it ought to be for service; but I am concerned to have to observe that the army under my command has fallen off in this respect in the late campaign to a greater degree than any army with which I have ever served, or of which I have ever read.

"It must be obvious, however, to every officer, that from the moment the troops commenced their retreat from the neighborhood of Burgos on the one hand, and from Madrid on the other, the officers lost all command over their men.

"I have no hesitation in attributing these evils to the habitual inattention of the officers of the regiments to their duty as prescribed by the standing regulations of the service and by the orders of this army.

"I am far from questioning the zeal, still less the gallantry and spirit, of the officers of the army; I am quite certain that if their minds can be convinced of the necessity of minute and constant attention to understand, recollect, and carry into execution the orders which have been issued for the performance of their duty, and that the strict performance of this duty is necessary to enable the army to serve the country as it ought to be served, they will in future give their attention to these points.

"Unfortunately, the experience of the officers of the army has induced many to consider that the period during which an army is on service is one of relaxation from all rule, instead of being, as it is, the period during which of all others every rule for the regulation and control of the conduct of the soldier, for the inspection and care of his arms, ammunition, accoutrements, necessaries, and field equipments, and his horse and horse appointments, for the receipt and issue and care of his provisions and the regulation of all that belongs to his food and the forage for his horse, must be most strictly attended to by the officer of his company or troop, if it is intended that an army—a British army in particular—shall be brought into the field of battle in a state of efficiency to meet the enemy on the day of trial.

"These are points, then, to which I most earnestly entreat you to turn your attention, and the attention of the officers of the regiments under your command, Portuguese as well as English, during the period in which it may be in my power to leave the troops in their cantonments.

"In regard to the food of the soldier, I have frequently observed and lamented in the late campaign the facility and celerity with which the French soldiers cooked in comparison with those of our army.

"The cause of this disadvantage is the same with that of every other description, the want of attention of the officers to the orders of the army and the conduct of their men, and the consequent want of authority over their conduct.

"But I repeat that the great object of the attention of the general and field officers must be to get the captains and subalterns of the regiments to understand and perform the duties required from them, as the only mode by which the discipline and efficiency of the army can be restored and maintained during the next campaign."

The British general never refrained from speaking his mind, even if his ideas were certain to be contrary to the spirit of the army. I will quote from "Victories of the British Armies" as follows:

"Colborne marched with the infantry on the right; Head, with the

Thirteenth Light Dragoons and two squadrons of Portuguese, on the left, and the heavy cavalry formed a reserve. Perceiving that their battering train was endangered, the French cavalry, as the ground over which they were retiring was favorable for the movement, charged the Thirteenth. But they were vigorously repulsed; and, failing in breaking the British, the whole, consisting of four regiments, drew up in front, forming an imposing line. The Thirteenth instantly formed and galloped forward—and nothing could have been more splendid than their charge. They rode fairly through the French, overtook and cut down many of the gunners, and at last entirely headed the line of march, keeping up a fierce and straggling encounter with the broken horsemen of the enemy, until some of the English dragoons actually reached the gates of Badajoz."

And now I quote from Wellington's comment to Colborne:

"I wish you would call together the officers of the dragoons and point out to them the mischiefs which must result from the disorder of the troops in action. The undisciplined ardor of the Thirteenth Dragoons and First Regiment of Portuguese cavalry is not of the description of the determined bravery and steadiness of soldiers confident in their discipline and in their officers. Their conduct was that of a rabble, galloping as fast as their horses could carry them over a plain, after an enemy to whom they could do no mischief when they were broken and the pursuit had continued for a limited distance, and sacrificing substantial advantages and all the objects of your operation by their want of discipline. To this description of their conduct I add my entire conviction, that if the enemy could have thrown out of Badajoz only one hundred men regularly formed, they would have driven back these two regiments in equal haste and disorder, and would probably have taken many whose horses would have been knocked up. If the Thirteenth Dragoons are again guilty of this conduct I shall take their horses from them, and send the officers and men to do duty at Lisbon."

The incident of the dragoons' charge happened early in 1811, but it shows how Wellington dealt with the firebrands in the army. However, imagine the feelings of the Thirteenth Dragoons!

As for the Allies, they were for a long time considered quite hopeless by British officers; the Portuguese were commonly known in the ranks as the "Vamosses," from "*vamos,*" "let us be off," which they shouted before they ran away. (The American slang "vamoose" may have had its origin in the Mexican War.)

The Spanish and Portuguese hated each other so cordially that it was with the greatest difficulty that they could be induced to coöperate: they were continually plotting to betray each other, and, incidentally, the English. Wellington had a sufficiently hard task in keeping his English army in order and directing the civil administration of Portugal,—which would otherwise have tumbled to pieces from the corruption of its government,—but hardest of all was the military training of the Spanish and Portuguese. He was now in supreme command of the Spanish army, concerning which he had written:

"There is not in the whole Kingdom of Spain a depot of provisions for the support of a single battalion in operation for one day. Not a shilling of money in any military chest. To move them forward at any point now would be to insure their certain destruction."

After that was written, however, he had been able to equip them with some degree of effectiveness, and had worked them up to a certain standard of discipline: they were brave and patient, and susceptible to improvement under systematic training. Beresford had also accomplished wonders with the Portuguese, and Wellington's army now numbered seventy thousand men, of whom forty thousand were British.

Wellington, with his lean, sharp-featured face, and dry, cold manner, was not the typical Englishman at all. He was more like the genuine Yankee of New England. He made his successes by his resourcefulness, his inability to be overpowered by circumstances. As he said: "The French plan their campaigns just as you might make a splendid set of harness. It answers very well until it gets broken, and then you are done for! Now I made my campaign of ropes; if anything went wrong I tied a knot and went on."

He was always ready, when anything broke or failed him, to "tie a knot and go on." That is the suppleness and adroitness of a great chieftain, whereas the typical English general was too magnificent for the little things; he liked to hurl his men boldly into the abyss—and then, if they perished, it had been magnificently done, at any rate. But Wellington was always practical and ready to take advantage of any opportunity that offered. He had no illusions about the grandeur of getting men killed for nothing.

There were still two hundred and thirty thousand French troops in Spain, but they were scattered across the Peninsula from Asturias to Valencia. To the extreme east was Marshal Suchet with sixty-five thousand men, and an expedition under General Murray was sent against him which kept him there. Clausel was prevented from leaving Biscay with his forty thousand men by the great guerilla warfare with which Wellington enveloped his forces. There remained, then, for Wellington to deal with the centre of the army under Joseph Bonaparte, whose jealous suspicions had been the means of driving from Spain Marshal Soult, a really fine and capable commander. The weak Joseph was now the head of an immense and magnificently equipped army of men and officers in the finest condition for fighting, but who were to prove of how little effect fine soldiers can be when they lack the right chief.

The army of Joseph lay in a curve from Toledo to Zamora, guarding the central valley of the Douro, and covering the great road from Madrid through Burgos and Vittoria to France. Wellington's plan was to move the left wing of his army across the Douro within the Portuguese frontier, to march it up the right bank of the Douro as far as Zamora, and then, crossing the Elsa, to unite it to the Galician forces; while the centre and right, advancing from Agueda by Salamanca, were to force the passage of the Tormes and drive the French entirely from the line of the Douro towards the Carrion.

By constantly threatening them on the flank with the left wing, which was to be always kept in advance, he thus hoped to drive the French back by Burgos into Biscay. He himself expected to establish there a new basis for the war among the numerous and well-fortified seaports on the coast. In this way, forcing the enemy back to his frontier, he would at once better his own position and intercept the whole communication of the enemy. The plan had the obvious objection that in separating his army into two forces, with great mountain ranges and impassable rivers between them, each was exposed to the risk of an attack by the whole force of the enemy.

But Wellington had resolved to take this risk. Sir Thomas Graham, in spite of his sixty-eight years, had the vigor and clear-headedness of youth, and the very genius for the difficult command given him—that of leading the left wing through virgin forests, over rugged mountains, and across deep rivers.

The march of Wellington began May 22nd, and an exalted spirit of enthusiasm pervaded the entire army. Even Wellington became expressive, and as he passed the stream that marks the frontier of Spain he arose in his stirrups, and, waving his hand, exclaimed, "Farewell, Portugal!"

Meanwhile Graham, on May 16th, with forty thousand men, had crossed the Douro and pushed ahead, turning the French right and striking at their communications. Within ten days forty thousand men were transported through two hundred miles of the most broken and rugged country in the Peninsula, with all their artillery and baggage. Soon they were in possession of the whole crest of mountains between the Ebro and the sea. On the 31st Graham reached the Elsa. The French were astounded when Graham appeared upon their flank; they abandoned their strong position on the Douro; then they abandoned Madrid; after that, they hurried out of Burgos and Valladolid.

Wellington had crossed the Douro at Miranda on May 25th, in advance of his troops, by means of a basket slung on a rope from precipice to precipice, at an immense height above the foaming torrent. The rivers were all swollen by floods.

Graham, with the left wing of the Allies, kept up his eager march. Many men were lost while fording the Elsa on May 31st. The water was almost chin-deep and the bottom was covered with shifting stones. Graham hastened with fierce speed to the Ebro, eager to cross it before Joseph and break his communications with France. Joseph had wished to stop his retreat at Burgos and give battle there, but he had been told that incredible numbers of guerillas had joined the English forces, and so he pushed on, leaving the castle at Burgos heavily mined. It was calculated that the explosion would take place just as the English entered the town, but the fuses were too quick—three thousand French soldiers, the last to leave, were crushed by the falling ruins. The allied troops marched triumphantly through the scene of their earlier struggle and defeat.

On abandoning Burgos Joseph took the road to Vittoria and sent pressing orders to Clausel to join him there, but this junction of forces was not effected—Clausel was too late.

Wellington's strategy of turning the French right has been called "the most masterly movement made during the Peninsular War." Its chief merit was that it gave Wellington the advantage of victory with hardly any loss of life. It swept the French back to the Spanish frontier. And Joseph, whose train comprised an incredible number of chariots, carriages, and wagons, bearing a helpless multitude of people of both sexes from Madrid (including the civil functionaries and officers of his court), as well as enormous stores of spoil, began to perceive that this precipitate retreat was his ruin, and that he must risk the chance of a great battle to escape being driven in hopeless confusion through the passes of the Pyrenees.

The sweep of the Allies under Graham around the French right had taken them through the wildest and most enchantingly beautiful regions. At times a hundred men had been needed to drag up one piece of artillery. Again, the guns would be lowered down a precipice by ropes, or forced up the rugged goat-paths. At length, to quote Napier, "the scarlet uniforms were to be seen in every valley, and the stream of war, descending with impetuous force down all the clefts of the mountains, burst in a hundred foaming torrents into the basin of Vittoria."

So accurately had Graham done his work in accordance with Wellington's plans, that he reached the valley just as Joseph's dejected troops were forming themselves in front of Vittoria.

The basin or valley of Vittoria, with the town in its eastern extremity, is a small plain about eight miles by six miles in extent, situated in an elevated plateau among the mountains and guarded on all sides by rugged hills.

The great road from Madrid enters the valley at the Puebla Pass, where too the river Zadora flows through a narrow mountain gorge. This road then runs up the left bank of the Zadora to Vittoria, and from there it goes on towards Bayonne and the Pyrenees. This road was Joseph's line of retreat.

King Joseph, burdened by his treasure, which included the plunder of five years of French occupation in the Peninsula, and consisted largely of priceless works of art, selected with most excellent taste by himself and other French connoisseurs, had dispatched to France two great convoys, a small part of the whole treasure, along the Bayonne road. As these had to be heavily guarded against the Biscay guerillas, some thousands of troops had gone with them. Joseph's remaining forces were estimated at from sixty thousand to sixty-five thousand men.

The French were anxious above all things to keep the road open—the road to Bayonne: there are several rough mountain roads intersecting each other at Vittoria, particularly those to Pampeluna, Bilboa, and Galicia, but the great Bayonne road was the only one capable of receiving the huge train of lumbering carriages without which the army was not to move.

On the afternoon of the 20th Wellington, whose effective force was now sixty-five thousand men, surveyed the place and the enemy from the hill ranges and saw that they were making a stand. He decided then on his tactics. Instead of pushing on his combined forces to a frontal attack, he made up his mind to divide his troops; he would send Graham with the left wing, consisting of eighteen thousand men and twenty guns, around by the northern hills to the rear of the French army, there to seize the road to Bayonne. Sir Rowland Hill with twenty thousand men, including General Murillo with his Spaniards, was to move with the right wing, break through the Puebla Pass, and attack the French left.

The right centre under Wellington himself was to cross the ridges forming the southern boundary of the basin and then move straight forward to the Zadora River and attack the bridges, while the left centre was to move across the bridge of Mendoza in the direction of the town.

The French right, which Graham was to attack, occupied the heights in front of the Zadora River above the village of Abechucho, and covered Vittoria from approach by the Bilboa road; the centre extended along the left bank of the Zadora, commanding the bridges in front of it, and blocking up the great road from Madrid. The left occupied the space from Ariniz to the ridges of Puebla de Arlauzon, and guarded the pass of Puebla, by which Hill was to enter the valley.

The early morning of June 21st was, according to one historian, "rainy and heavy with vapor," while an observer (Leith Hay) said: "The morning was extremely brilliant; a clearer or more beautiful atmosphere never favored the progress of a gigantic conflict."

The valley was a superb spectacle occupied by the French army with the rich uniforms of its officers. Marshal Jourdan, the commander, could be seen riding slowly along the line of his troops. The positions they occupied rose in steps from the centre of the valley, so that all could be seen by the English from the crest of the Morillas as they stood ready for battle. In his "Events of Military Life" Henry says:

"The dark and formidable masses of the French were prepared at all points to repel the meditated attack—the infantry in column with loaded arms, or ambushed thickly in the low woods at the base of their position, the cavalry in lines with drawn swords, and the artillery frowning from the eminences with lighted matches; while on our side all was yet quietness and repose. The chiefs were making their observations and the men walking about in groups amidst the piled arms, chatting and laughing and gazing, and apparently not caring a pin for the fierce hostile array in their front."

At ten o'clock Hill reached the pass of Puebla and forced his way through with extraordinary swiftness. Murillo's Spaniards went swarming up the steep ridges to dislodge the French, but the enemy made a furious resistance, and re-enforcements kept coming to their aid. General Murillo was wounded, but would not be carried from the field. Hill then sent the Seventy-first to help the Spaniards, who were showing high courage, but being terribly mown down by the French musketry. Colonel Cadogan, who led the Seventy-first, had no sooner reached the summit of the height than he fell, mortally wounded. The French were driven from their position, but the loss of Cadogan was keenly felt. The story of his strange state of exaltation the night before the battle is well known—his rapture at the prospect of taking part in it. As he lay dying on the summit he would not be moved, although the dead lay thick about him, but watched the progress of his Highlanders until he could no longer see.

While this conflict was going on, Wellington, with the right centre, had commenced his attack on the bridges over the Zadora. A Spanish peasant brought word that the Bridge of Tres Puentes was negligently guarded, and offered to guide the troops to it. Kempt's Brigade soon reached it; the Fifteenth Hussars galloped over, but a shot from a French battery killed the brave peasant who had guided them.

The forces that crossed at Tres Puentes now formed under the shelter of a hill. One of the officers wrote of this position: "Our post was most extraordinary, as we were isolated from the rest of the army and within one hundred yards of the enemy's advance. As I looked over the bank, I could see El Rey Joseph, surrounded by at least five thousand men, within five hundred yards of us."

It has always seemed an inconceivable thing that the French should not have destroyed the seven narrow bridges across the Zadora before the 21st had dawned. Whether it was from over-confidence or sheer mental confusion, it is impossible to know.

The Third and Seventh Divisions were now moving rapidly down to the bridge of Mendoza, but the enemy's light troops and guns had opened a vigorous fire upon them, until the riflemen of the light division, who had crossed at Tres Puentes, charged the enemy's fire, and the bridge was carried.

Sir Thomas Picton was a picturesque figure in this part of the operations. Through some oversight he and his men, the "Fighting Third," were neglected. Orders came to other troops, bridges were being carried, but no word was sent to Picton. "D—— it!" he cried out to one of his officers, "Lord Wellington must have forgotten us!" He beat the mane of his horse with his stick in his impatience and anger. Finally, an aide-de-camp galloped up and inquired for Lord Dalhousie, who commanded the Seventh Division. In answer to Picton's inquiries he stated that he brought orders for Dalhousie to carry the bridge to the left, while the Fourth and Sixth Divisions were to support the attack. Picton rose in his stirrups, and shouted angrily to the amazed aide-de-camp,—

"You may tell Lord Wellington from me, sir, that the *Third* Division, under my command, shall in less than ten minutes attack the bridge and carry it, and the Fourth and Sixth may support if they choose." Then, addressing his men with his customary blend of affection and profanity, he cried: "Come on, ye rascals! Come on, ye fighting villains!"

They carried the bridge with such fire and speed that the whole British line was animated by the sight.

Maxwell says: "The passage of the river, the movement of glittering masses from right to left as far as the eye could range, the deafening roar of cannon, the sustained fusillade of the artillery, made up a magnificent scene. The British cavalry, drawn up to support the columns, seemed a glittering line of golden helmets and sparkling swords in the keen sunshine which now shone upon the field of battle."

L'Estrange, who was with the Thirty-first, says that the men were marching through standing corn (I suppose some kind of grain that ripens early, certainly not maize) yellow for the sickle and between four and five feet high, and the hissing cannon-balls, as they rent their way through the sea of golden grain, made long furrows in it.

The hill in front of Ariniz was the key of the French line, and Wellington brought up several batteries and hurled Picton's division in a solid mass against it, while the heavy cavalry of the British came up at a gallop from the river to sustain the attack.

This hill had been the scene of a great fight in the wars of the Black Prince, where Sir William Felton, with two hundred archers and swordsmen, had been surrounded by six thousand Spaniards, and all perished, resisting doggedly. It is still called "the Englishmen's hill."

An obstinate fight now raged, for a brief space, on this spot. A long wall was held by several battalions of French infantry, whose fire was so deadly as to check the British for a time. They reached the wall, however, and for a few moments on either side of it was a seething mass of furious soldiers. "Any person," said Kincaid, who was present, "who chose to put his head over from either side, was sure of getting a sword or bayonet up his nostrils."

As the British broke over the wall, the French fell back, abandoning Ariniz for the ridge in front of Gomecha, only to be forced back again.

It was the noise of Graham's guns, booming since mid-day at their rear, that took the heart out of the French soldiery.

Graham had struck the great blow on the left; at eleven he had reached the heights above the village and bridge of Gamara Major, which were strongly occupied by the French under Reille. General Oswald commenced the attack and drove the enemy from the heights; then Major General Robinson, at the head of a brigade of the Fifth Division, formed his men and led them forward on the run to carry the bridge and village of Gamara. But the French fire was so strong that he was compelled to fall back. Again he rallied them and crossed the bridge, but the French drove them back once more. Fresh British troops came up and the bridge was carried again,—and then for the third time it was lost under Reille's murderous fire.

But now the panic from the centre had reached Reille. It was known that the French centre was retreating: the Frenchmen had no longer the moral strength to resist Robinson's attacks, and so the bridge was won by the English and the Bayonne road was lost to the French.

In the centre the battle had become a sort of running fight for six miles; the French were at last all thrown back into the little plain in front of Vittoria, where from the crowded throng cries of despair could be heard.

"At six o'clock," Maxwell says, "the sun was setting, and his last rays fell upon a dreadful spectacle: red masses of infantry were advancing steadily across the plain; the horse artillery came at a gallop to the front to open its fire upon the fugitives; the Hussar Brigade was charging by the Camino Real."

Of the helpless encumbrances of the French army an eyewitness said: "Behind them was the plain in which the city stood, and beyond the city thousands of carriages and animals and non-combatants, men, women, and children, were crowding together in all the madness of terror; and as the English shot went booming overhead the vast crowd started and swerved with a convulsive movement, while a dull and horrid sound of distress arose."

Joseph now ordered the retreat to be conducted by the only road left open, that to Pampeluna, but it was impossible to take away his train of carriages. He, the king, only escaped capture by jumping out of one door of his carriage as his pursuers reached the other: he left his sword of state in it and the beautiful Correggio "Christ in the Garden," now at Apsley House, in England.

Eighty pieces of cannon, jammed close together near Vittoria on the only remaining defensible ridge near the town, had kept up a desperate fire to the last, and Reille had held his ground near the Zadora heroically, but it was useless. The great road to Bayonne was lost, and finally that to Pampeluna was choked with broken-down carriages. The British dragoons were pursuing hotly, and the frantic French soldiers plunged into morasses, over fields and hills, in the wildest rout, leaving their artillery, ammunition-wagons, and the spoil of a kingdom.

The outskirts of Vittoria were strewn with the wreckage. Never before in modern times had such a quantity of spoil fallen into the hands of a victorious army. There were objects of interest from museums, convents, and royal palaces; there were jewels of royal worth and masterpieces of Titian, Raphael, and Correggio.

The marshal's baton belonging to Jourdan had been left, with one hundred and fifty-one brass guns, four hundred and fifteen caissons of ammunition, one million three hundred thousand ball cartridges, fourteen thousand rounds of artillery ammunition, and forty thousand pounds of gunpowder. Joseph's power was gone: he was only a wretched fugitive. Six thousand of his men had been killed and wounded and one thousand were prisoners.

It has not been possible to estimate the value of the private plunder, but five and one-half millions of dollars in the military chest of the army were taken, and untold quantities of private wealth were also lost to their owners; it was all scattered—shining heaps of gold and silver—over the road, and the British soldiers reaped it. Wellington refused to make any effort to induce his men to give up the enormous sums they had absorbed: "They have earned it," he said. But he had reason to regret it. They fell into frightful orgies of intemperance that lasted for days. Wellington wrote Lord Bathurst, June 29th:

"We started with the army in the highest order, and up to the day of the battle nothing could get on better. But that event has, as usual, totally annihilated all order and discipline. The soldiers of the army have got among them about a million sterling in money, with the exception of about one hundred thousand dollars which were got in the military chest. I am convinced that we have now out of our ranks double the amount of our loss in the battle, and have lost more men in the pursuit than the enemy have." It was calculated that seven thousand five hundred men had straggled from the effects of the plunder.

The convoys sent ahead by Joseph had contained some of the choicest works of art; they reached France safely, and are displayed in the museums of Paris. In justice to the Duke of Wellington it must be said that he communicated with Ferdinand, offering to restore the paintings which had fallen into his hands, but Ferdinand desired him to keep them. The wives of the French officers were sent on to Pampeluna the next day by Wellington, who had treated them with great kindness.

As for the rest of the feminine army, the nuns, the actresses, and the superbly arrayed others, they made their escape with greater difficulties and hardships. Alison says: "Rich vestures of all sorts, velvet and silk brocades, gold and silver plate, noble pictures, jewels, laces, cases of claret and champagne, poodles, parrots, monkeys, and trinkets lay scattered about the fields in endless confusion, admidst weeping mothers, wailing infants, and all the unutterable miseries of warlike overthrow."

Napoleon was filled with fury at his brother for the result of Vittoria, but he instructed his ministers to say that "a somewhat brisk engagement with the English took place at Vittoria in which both sides lost equally. The French armies, however, carried out the movements in which they were engaged, but the enemy seized about one hundred guns which were left without teams at Vittoria, and it is these that the English are trying to pass off as artillery captured on the battle-field!"

One of the most important captures of the battle was a mass of documents from the archives of Madrid, including a great part of Napoleon's secret correspondence—an invaluable addition to history.

Napier's summing up of the results of the battle reads:

"Joseph's reign was over; the crown had fallen from his head. And, after years of toils and combats, which had been rather admired than understood, the English general, emerging from the chaos of the Peninsula struggle, stood on the summit of the Pyrenees a recognized conqueror. From these lofty pinnacles the clangor of his trumpets pealed clear and loud, and the splendor of his genius appeared as a flaming beacon to warring nations."

However, Napier always was inclined to be eloquent. Perhaps it was lucky for Wellington that the worthless make-trouble, Joseph Bonaparte, had been in the place of his tremendous brother.

THE SIEGE OF PLEVNA

When the Russian army swarmed through the Shipka Pass of the Balkans there was really nothing before it but a man and an opportunity. Osman Pasha suddenly and with great dexterity took his force into Plevna, a small Bulgarian town near the Russian line of march.

The military importance of Plevna lay in the fact that this mere village of seventeen hundred people was the junction of the roads from Widin, Sophia, Biela, Zimnitza, Nikopolis, and the Shipka Pass. Osman's move was almost entirely on his own initiative. He had no great reputation, and, like Wellington in the early part of the Peninsula campaign, he was obliged to do everything with the strength of his own shoulders. The stupidity of his superiors amounted almost to an oppression.

The Russians recognized the strategic importance of Plevna a moment too late. On July 18, 1877, General Krudener at Nikopolis received orders to occupy Plevna at once. He seems to have moved promptly, but long before he could arrive Osman's tired but dogged battalions were already in the position.

The Turkish regular of that day must have resembled very closely his fellow of the present. Von Moltke, who knew the Turks well and whose remarkable mind clearly outlined and prophesied the result of several more recent Balkan campaigns, said, "An impetuous attack may be expected from the Turks, but not an obstinate and lasting defence." Historically, the opinion of the great German field-marshal seems very curious. Even in the late war between Greece and Turkey the attacks of the Turkish troops were usually anything but impetuous. They were fearless, but very leisurely. As to the lasting and obstinate defence, one has only to regard the siege of Plevna to understand that Von Moltke was for the moment writing carelessly.

After Plevna, the word went forth that the most valuable weapon of the Turk was his shovel. When Osman arrived, the defences of Plevna consisted of an ordinary block-house, but he at once set his troops at work digging intrenchments and throwing up redoubts, which were located with great skill. Soon the vicinity of the town was one great fortress. Osman coolly was attempting to stem the Russian invasion with a force of these strange Turkish troops, patient, enduring, sweet-tempered, and ignorant, dressed in slovenly overcoats and sheep-skin sandals, living on a diet of black bread and cucumbers.

Receiving the order from the Grand Duke Nicolas, General Krudener at Nikopolis despatched at dawn of the next day six thousand five hundred men with about seven batteries to Plevna. No effective scouting had been done. The Russian General, Schilder-Schuldner, riding comfortably in his carriage in the customary way of Russian commanders of the time, had absolutely no information that a strong Turkish force had occupied the position. His column had been allowed to distribute itself over a distance of seventeen miles. On the morning of the 20th an attack was made with great confidence by the troops which had come up. Two Russian regiments even marched victoriously through the streets of Plevna, throwing down their heavy packs and singing for joy of the easy capture. But suddenly a frightful fusillade began from all sides. The elated regiments melted in the streets. Infuriated by religious ardor, despising the value of a Christian's life, the Turks poured out from their concealed places, and there occurred a great butchery. The Russian Nineteenth Regiment of the line was cut down to a few fragments. Much artillery ammunition was captured. The Russians lost two thousand seven hundred men. The knives of the Circassians and Bashi-Bazouks had been busy in the streets.

After this victory Osman might have whipped Krudener, but the Russian leaders had been suddenly aroused to the importance of taking Plevna, and Krudener was almost immediately re-enforced with three divisions. Within the circle of defence the Turk was using his shovel. Osman gave the garrison no rest. If a man was not shooting, he was digging. The well-known Grivitza Redoubt was greatly strengthened, and some defences on the east side of the town were completed. Osman's situation was desperate, but his duty to his country was vividly defined. If he could hold this strong Turkish force on the flank of the Russians, their advance on Constantinople would hardly be possible. The Russian leaders now thoroughly understood this fact, and they tried to make the army investing Plevna more than a containing force.

The Grand Duke Nicolas had decided to order an assault on the 30th of July. Krudener telegraphed—the grand duke was thirty miles from Plevna—that he hesitated in his views of prospective success. The grand duke replied sharply, ordering that the assault be made. It seems that Krudener went into the field in the full expectation of being beaten.

Now appears in the history of the siege a figure at once sinister and foolish. Subordinate in command to Krudener was Lieutenant-General Prince Schahofskoy, who had an acute sense of his own intelligence, and in most cases dared to act independently of the orders of his chief. But to offset him there suddenly galloped into his camp a brilliant young Russian commander, a man who has set his name upon Plevna, even as the word underlies the towering reputation of Osman Pasha. General Skobeleff had come from the Grand Duke Nicolas with an order directing Prince Schahofskoy to place the young man in command of a certain brigade of Caucasian Cossacks. The prince grew stormy with outraged pride, and practically told Skobeleff to take the Cossacks and go to the devil with them.

The Russians began a heavy bombardment, to which Osman's guns replied with spirit. The key of the position was the Grivitza Redoubt. Krudener himself attacked it with eighteen battalions of infantry and ten batteries. And at the same time Prince Schahofskoy thundered away on his side. The latter at last became furious at Krudener's lack of success, and resolved to take matters into his own hands. In the afternoon he advanced with three brigades in the face of a devastating Turkish fire, took a hill, and forced the Turks to vacate their first line of intrenchments. His men were completely spent with weariness, and it is supposed that he should have waited on the hill for support from Krudener. But he urged on his tired troops and carried a second position. The Turkish batteries now concentrated their fire upon his line, and, really, the Turkish infantry whipped him soundly.

The Russians did not give up the dearly bought gain of ground without desperate fighting. Again and again they furiously charged, but only to meet failure. When night fell, the stealthy-footed irregular of the Turkish forces crept through the darkness to prey upon the route of the Russian retreat. The utter annihilation of Prince Schahofskoy's force was prevented by Skobeleff and the brigade of Cossacks with which the prince had sent him to the devil. Skobeleff's part in this assault was really a matter of clever manœuvring.

Krudener had failed with gallantry and intelligence. Schahofskoy had failed through pigheadedness and self-confidence.

After this attempt to carry Plevna, the important Russian generals occupied themselves in mutual recriminations. Krudener bitterly blamed Schahofskoy for not obeying his orders, and Schahofskoy acidulously begged to know why Krudener had not supported him. At the same time they both claimed that the Grand Duke Nicolas, thirty miles away, should never have given an order for an assault on a position of which he had never had a view.

But even if Russian clothing and arms and trinkets were being sold for a pittance in the bazaars of Plevna, the mosques were jammed with wounded Turks, and such was the suffering that the dead in the streets and in the fields were being gnawed by the pervasive Turkish dog.

A few days later Osman Pasha received the first proper recognition from Constantinople. A small troop of cavalry had wormed its way into Plevna. It was headed by an aide-de-camp of the Sultan. In gorgeous uniform the aide appeared to Osman and presented him with the First Order of the Osmanli, the highest Turkish military decoration. And with this order came a sword, the hilt of which flamed with diamonds. Osman Pasha may have preferred a bushel of cucumbers, but at any rate he knew that the Sultan and Turkey at last understood the value of a good soldier. To the speech of the aide Osman replied with another little speech, and the soldiers in their intrenchments cheered the sultan.

On August 31st the Turkish general made his one offensive move. He threw part of his force against a Russian redoubt and was obliged to retire with a loss of nearly three thousand men. Afterwards he devoted his troops mainly to the business of improving the defences. He wasted no more in attempts to break out of Plevna.

At this late day of the siege, Prince Charles of Roumania was appointed to the chief command of the whole Russo-Roumanian army. But naturally this office was nominal. General Totoff had the real disposition of affairs, but he did not hold it very long. General Levitsky, the assistant chief of the Russian general staff, arrived to advise General Totoff under direct orders from the Grand Duke Nicolas. But this siege was to be very well generalled.

The Grand Duke Nicolas himself came to Plevna. One would think that the grand duke would have ended this kaleidoscopic row of superseding generals. But the Great White Czar himself appeared. Osman Pasha, shut up in Plevna, certainly was honored with a great deal of distinguished interest.

However, Alexander II. did his best to give no orders. He had no illusions concerning his military knowledge. With a spirit profoundly kind and gentle, he simply prayed that no more lives would be lost. It is difficult to think what he had to say to his multitudinous generals, each of whom was the genius of the only true plan for capturing Plevna.

At daylight on the 7th of September the Turks saw that the entire army of the enemy had closed in upon them. Amid fields of ripening grain shone the smart red jackets of the hussars. The Turks saw the Bulgarians in sheepskin caps and with their broad scarlet sashes stuck full of knives and pistols. They saw the queer round oilskin shakoes of the Cossacks and the greatcoats of thick gray blanketing. They saw the uniforms of the Russian infantry, the green tunics striped with red. For five days the smoke lay heavy over Plevna.

The 11th was the fête-day of the emperor, and the general assault on that day was arranged as if it had been part of a fête. The cannonade was to begin at daybreak along the whole line and stop at eight o'clock in the morning. The artillery was to play again from eleven o'clock until one o'clock. Then it was to play again from two-thirty to three.

Directly afterwards the Roumanian allies of the Russians moved in three columns against the Grivitza Redoubt. At first all three were repulsed, but with the stimulus of Russian re-enforcements they rallied, and after a long time of almost hand-to-hand fighting the evening closed with them in possession of what was called the key of the Plevna position. They had lost four thousand men. The victory was fruitless, as anticipating the attack on Grivitza, Osman had caused the building of an inner redoubt. After all their ferocious charging, the Russians were really no nearer to success.

At three o'clock of that afternoon Redoubt Number Ten had been assailed by General Schmidnikoff. The firing had been terrible, but the Russians had charged to the very walls of the redoubt. The Turks not only beat them off, but pursued with great spirit. Two of the scampering Russian battalions were then faced about to beat off the chase. They lay down at a distance of only two hundred yards of the redoubt, and sent the Turks pell-mell back into their fortifications.

At about the same time Skobeleff, wearing a white coat and mounted on a white charger, was leading his men over the "green hills" towards the Krishin Redoubt. There was a dense fog. Skobeleff's troops crossed two ridges and waded a stream. They began the ascent of a steep slope. Suddenly the fog cleared; the sun shone out brilliantly. The closely massed Russian force was exposed at short range to line after line of Turkish intrenchments. They retired once, but rallied splendidly, and before five o'clock Skobeleff found himself in possession of Redoubt Number Eleven and Redoubt Number Twelve.

His battalions were thrust like a wedge into the Turkish lines, but the Turkish commander appreciated the situation more clearly than any Russian save Skobeleff. The latter's men suffered a frightful fire. Re-enforcements were refused. All during the night the faithful troops of the czar fought in darkness and without hope. They even built little ramparts of dead men. But on the morning of September 12th Skobeleff was compelled to give up all he had gained. The retreat over the "green hills" was little more than a running massacre.

After his return, Skobeleff was in a state of excitement and fury. His uniform was covered with blood and mud. His Cross of St. George was twisted around over his shoulder. His face was black with powder. His eyes were blood-shot. He said, "My regiments no longer exist."

The Russian assaults had failed at all points. They had begun this last battle with thirty thousand infantry, twelve thousand cavalry, and four hundred and forty guns, and they lost over eighteen thousand men. The multitude of generals again took counsel. There were fervid animosities, and there might have been open rupture if it were not for the presence of the czar himself, whose gentleness and good-nature prevented many scenes.

It was decided that the Turks must be starved out. The Russians sent for more troops as well as for heavy supplies of clothing, ammunition, and food. The czar sent for General Todleben, who had shown great skill at Sebastopol, and the direction of the siege was put in his hands.

The Turks had been accustomed to re-provision Plevna by the skilful use of devious trails. Todleben took swift steps to put a stop to it, but he did not succeed before a huge convoy had been sent into the town through the adroit management of Chefket Pasha. But the Russian horse soon chased Chefket away and the trails were all closed.

For the most part the September weather was fine, but this plenitude of sun made the Turkish positions about Plevna almost unbearable. Actual thousands of unburied dead lay scattered over the ridges. At one time the Russian head-quarters made a polite request to be allowed to send some men to enter Grivitza and bury their own dead. But this polite request met with polite refusal.

On October 19th the Roumanians, who for weeks had been sapping their way up to the Grivitza Redoubt, made a final and desperate attack on it. They were repulsed.

In order to complete the investment, Todleben found it necessary to dislodge the Turks from four villages near Plevna.

The weeks moved by slowly with a stolid and stubborn Turk besieged by a stubborn and stolid Russian. There was occasional firing from the Russian batteries, to which the Turks did not always take occasion to reply. In Plevna there was nothing to eat but meat, and the Turkish soldiers moved about with the hoods of their dirty brown cloaks pulled over their heads. Outside Plevna there were plenty of furs and good coats, but the diet had become so plain that the sugar-loving Russian soldiers would give gold for a pot of jam.

On the cold, cloudy morning of December 11th, when snow lay thickly on all the country, a sudden great booming of guns was heard, and the news flew swiftly that Osman had come out of Plevna at last and was trying to break through the cordon his foes had spread about him. During the night he had abandoned all his defences, and by daybreak he had taken the greater part of his army across the river Vid. Advancing along the Sophia road, he charged the Russian intrenchments with such energy that the Siberian Regiment stationed at that point was almost annihilated. A desperate fight went on for four hours, with the Russians coming up battalion after battalion. Some time after noon all firing ceased, and later the Turks sent up a white flag. Cheer after cheer swelled over the dreary plain. Osman had surrendered.

The siege had lasted one hundred and forty-two days. The Russians had lost forty thousand men. The Turks had lost thirty thousand men.

The advance on Constantinople had been checked. Skobeleff said, "Osman the Victorious he will remain, in spite of his surrender."

THE STORMING OF
BURKERSDORF HEIGHTS

When, in 1740, Wilhelm Friedrich of Prussia died, the friends whom his heir had gathered about him at his pleasant country-house at Reinsberg were doomed to see a blight fall on their expectations such as had not been known since Poins and Falstaff congratulated themselves on having an old friend for their king.

When the young prince came to the throne as Frederick II., thought these trusting people, Prussia, instead of being a mere barracks overrun with soldiers and ruled by a miser, would become the refuge of poets and artists. Its monarch would be a man of peace, caring for nothing beyond the joys of philosophy, poetry, music, and merry feasts—this, of course, providing for an indefinite extension of the enchanted life he and his companions led at Reinsberg.

They had the best of reasons for this belief: the antagonism between the prince and his father had begun almost as soon as the rapture of having an heir had become an old story to Friedrich Wilhelm. The tiny "Fritz," with a cocked hat and tight little soldier-clothes, drilling and being drilled with a lot of other tiny boys,—and frightfully bored with it all the time,—was a standing grievance to his rough, boorish father. "Awake him at six in the morning and stand by to see that he does not turn over, but immediately gets up.... While his hair is being combed and made into a queue, he is to have his breakfast of tea." This was the beginning of his father's instructions to his tutors when, at seven, he passed out of his governess's hands.

Notwithstanding the fine Spartan rigor of this programme, the boy came up a dainty, delicate little fellow, who turned up his nose at boar-hunting and despised his father's collection of giants, and loved to play the flute and make French verses. Friedrich Wilhelm was anything but a bad monarch; he was moral in a century when nothing of the sort was expected of monarchs; he made the Prussian army the best army in the world; he even had affections; but for a man of these virtues he was the most intolerable parent of whom there is a record.

The brilliant Wilhelmina, Frederick's dearly loved sister, whose young portraits show her as very like her brother, has this characteristic scene in her "Memoirs:" Their sister, Princess Louisa, aged fifteen, had just been betrothed to a margrave, and the king asked her—they were at table—how she would

442

regulate her house-keeping when she was married. Louisa, a favorite, had got into the way of telling her father home-truths, which he took very well, as a rule, from her. On this occasion she told him that she would have a good table well served; "better than yours," said Louisa; "and if I have children, I will not maltreat them like you, nor force them to eat what they have an aversion to." "What do you mean by that?" said the king. "What is there wanting at my table?" "There is this wanting," she replied: "that one cannot have enough, and the little there is consists of coarse potherbs that nobody can eat." The king, who was not used to such candor, boiled with rage. "All his anger," says the Princess Wilhelmina, "fell on my brother and me. He first threw a plate at my brother's head, who ducked out of the way, then let fly another at me." After he had made the air blue with wrath, directed at Frederick, "we had to pass him in going out," and "he aimed a great blow at me with his crutch,—which, if I had not jerked away from it, would have ended me. He chased me for a while in his wheel-chair, but the people drawing it gave me time to escape into the queen's chamber."

One always imagines this charming young princess in the act of dodging some sort of blow from Friedrich Wilhelm, who was nicknamed "Stumpy," privately, by his dutiful son and daughter. The habit of hating his son became an insanity; to kick him and pull his hair, break his flute, and take away his books and his brocaded dressing-gown—that was ordinary usage; it came to the point where he nearly strangled him, and later he condemned him to death for trying to run away to his uncle, George II., in England. When this sentence had been changed to a term of imprisonment, the poor young prince had a much better time of it: his gaolers were kinder than his father.

By the time he emerged from this captivity he had gained much wisdom—the cold wisdom of selfishness and dissimulation. In after years the father and son became profoundly attached to each other, but Frederick was always obliged to humor and cajole his pig-headed sire, to lie more or less, and generally adopt an insincere tone, in order to avert wrath and suspicion—a very hateful necessity to a natural truth-teller, for Frederick was by nature a great lover of facts. Although his training as a politician and a soldier included a thorough education in guile, the tutors of his childhood were simple, honest people, who gave him a good, truthful start in life.

Friedrich Wilhelm, now that his heir was twenty-one years old, thought it high time to put an end to various vague matrimonial projects, and get a wife for him straightway. Frederick having found that obedience was, on the whole, better than captivity, was submissive and silent—to his father; but his letters to his friends and his sister shrieked with protestations against a marriage in which his tastes and feelings were not so much as thought of. Above all things he wished to be allowed to travel and choose for himself, and he had a morbid horror of a dull and awkward woman. It did not much matter, he thought, what else his wife was if she were clever conversationally, with grace and charm and fine manners. Beauty was desirable, but he could get along without it, if only he could feel proud of his consort's wit and breeding. The bride of his father's choosing was the Princess Elizabeth of Brunswick-Bevern—a bashful and gawky young person, with as little distinction as a dairy-maid. But he subdued his rage and married her, and, indeed, seems always to have treated her with kindly deference, although he made no pretence of affection.

Still carrying out his father's wishes, he served in a brief campaign, and afterwards regularly devoted a portion of his time to military and political business. Friedrich Wilhelm was now pleased with his son to the extent of buying for him a delightful residence—Reinsberg—and giving him a tolerable income, and Frederick revelled in his new freedom by building conservatories, laying out pleasure-gardens, playing his flute to his heart's content, writing poor French verses, and solacing himself for the "coarse potherbs" of his childhood by exquisite dinners. They had the best musicians for their concerts at Reinsberg—the crown prince and his friends, with the crown princess and her ladies. It was here, in 1736, that Frederick began—by letter—his famous friendship with Voltaire, that survived so many phases of illusion and disillusion.

It must be said of Frederick's friends—who were mostly French—that they were men of highly trained intelligence, but they were not acute enough to know what sort of king their prince would make.

When his father passed away, Frederick felt as sincere a grief as if there had never been anything but love between them; always afterwards he spoke of him with reverence, and he learned to place a high value on the stern discipline of his early life—which is still to some extent a model for the bringing up of young Hohenzollerns.

It was a handsome young king who came to the throne in 1740. His face was round, his nose a keen aquiline, his mouth small and delicately curved, and all was dominated by those wonderful blue-gray eyes, that, as Mirabeau said, "at the bidding of his heroic soul fascinated you with seduction or with terror." Even in youth the lines of the face showed a sardonic humor. One can well imagine his replying to the optimistic Sulzer, who thought severe punishments a mistake: "Ach! meine lieber Sulzer, you don't know this—race!" In the old-age portraits the face is sharp and hatchet-like, the mouth is shrunken to a mean line, but the great eyes still flash out, commanding and clear.

The reign began with peace and philanthropy: Frederick II. started out by disbanding the giant grenadiers, the absurd monstrosities that his father had begged and bought and kidnapped from everywhere; he started a "knitting-house" for a thousand old women; abolished torture in criminal trials; set up an Academy of Sciences; summoned Voltaire and Maupertius; made Germany open its eyes at the speech, "In this country every man must get to Heaven in his own way;" and proclaimed a practical freedom of the press—all in his first week.

The fury of activity now took possession of Frederick which lasted all his life. He had the Hohenzollern passion for doing everything himself: the three "secretaries of state" were mere clerks, who spared him only the mechanical part of secretarial duties. His system of economy was rigid. While looking over financial matters one day he found that a certain convent absorbed a considerable fund from the forest-dues, which had been bequeathed by dead dukes "for masses to be said on their behalf." He went to the place and asked the monks, "What good does anybody get out of those masses?" "Your majesty, the dukes are to be delivered out of purgatory by them." "Purgatory? And they are not out yet, poor souls, after so many hundred years of praying?" The answer was, "Not yet." "When will they be out, and the thing settled?" There was no answer to this. "Send me a courier whenever they are out!" With this sneer the king left the convent.

Stern business went on all day, and in the evening, music, dancing, theatres, suppers, till all hours; but the king was up again at four in the summer—five in winter. In early youth Frederick had known a period of gross living, from which he suffered so severely that his reaction from it was fiercely austere. After his accession, a young man who had been associated with this "mud-bath," as Carlyle has named it, begged an audience. The king received him, but rebuked him with such withering speech that he straightway went home and killed himself.

Only five months of his reign had passed when the event occurred that put an end to the ideal monarch of Frederick's subjects. Charles VI., Emperor of Germany, was dead. For years he had worked to bind together his scattered and wabbling empire, and by his "Pragmatic Sanction" secure it to his daughter, Maria Theresa, contrary to the rule that only male heirs should succeed, and she was on the day of his death (October 20th) proclaimed empress.

If the young Maria Theresa had been married to the young Prince Frederick of Prussia, as their reigning parents had at one time decided, European history would undoubtedly have been different, though historians may be mistaken in thinking that much trouble would have been saved the world. In view of the fact that both these young people were extravagantly well endowed with the royal gifts of energy and decision, one must be permitted to wonder whether Frederick, as the spouse of the admirable Maria Theresa, would have ever become known as "the Great." But at all events it would have prevented him from rushing in on her domains and seizing Silesia as soon as she was left with no one but her husband—a man of the kindly inert sort—to protect her; and we should have lost the good historical scene of Maria Theresa appearing before her Hungarian Diet, with the crown on her beautiful head, thrilling every heart as she lifted her plump baby, Francis Joseph, and with tears streaming down her face implored its help against the Prussian robber.

We can still hear the thunderous roar of the loyal reply, "We will die for our sovereign, Maria Theresa!"

Nevertheless, by December the Prussian robber was in Silesia with thirty thousand men, engaged in finding out that he was really made to be a warrior. By May he held every fortified place in the province; by June Maria Theresa was forced to cede it to him—since which time it has always been a loyal part of Prussia. "How glorious is my king, the youngest of the kings and the grandest!" chanted Voltaire in a letter to Frederick—who, one is pleased to know, found the praise rather suffocating.

The genius of Frederick was next put to a considerable test in the way of match-making—a delicate art, particularly when practised for the sake of providing the half-barbarous Empire of Russia with mated rulers.

The Czarina Elizabeth—Great Peter's daughter—wished the king to find a German bride for her nephew-heir, who was afterwards Peter III. A true Hohenzollern, Frederick felt himself quite equal to this task—as to any other. From a bevy of young princesses he selected the daughter of the poverty-stricken Prince of Anhalt-Herbst, because of the unmistakable cleverness the girl had shown, though not fifteen. She was handsome as well, and Elizabeth renamed her "Catherine," changed her religion, and the marriage came off in 1745. Frederick had displayed great acumen, but it would puzzle a fiend to contrive a more diabolical union than that of Peter and Catherine!

Meanwhile, Maria Theresa had been preparing to fight for Silesia again. Without waiting for her, Frederick pounced upon Prague and captured it. After her armies in Silesia and Saxony had been put to flight by her adversary, at Hohenfriedberg and Sorr and Hennersdorf and Kesselsdorf, the empress yielded. On Christmas Day, 1745, when the treaty was signed that gave Silesia again to Prussia,—it was known as the Peace of Dresden,—Berlin went wild, and for the first time shouts were heard among the revellers, "Vivat Friedrich *der Grosse!*" The Austrians might call him "that ferocious, false, ambitious King of Prussia," but as a matter of fact he was not more false and ferocious than the other rulers, only infinitely more able. Frederick had made for himself a great name and raised his little kingdom—of only two-and-a-half millions of people— to a noble standing among nations. The eyes of the world were fixed upon the hero to see what he would do next. What he did was to swear that he "would not fight with a cat again," and to build himself a charming country home—his palaces, and even Reinsberg, were too large. In May, 1747, he had his housewarming at little Sans Souci, where for the next forty years most of his time was spent. There were twenty boxes of German flutes in the king's cabinet at Sans Souci, and infinite boxes of Spanish snuff; and there were three arm-chairs for three favorite dogs, with low stools to make an easy step for them. There was another favorite at Sans Souci who was said to lcok like an ape, although he was mostly called the "skinny Apollo." How one would like to have seen the king walking the terraces, with "white shoes and stockings and red breeches, with gown and waistcoat of blue linen flowered and lined with yellow!" while men with powdered wigs and highly colored clothes, and women whose heads bore high towers of hair unpleasantly stuffed and decorated with inconsequent dabs of finery followed him, all talking epigrams and doing attitudes—polite people had to hold themselves in curves in the eighteenth century.

These were good years for Prussia: her law courts were reformed; her commerce flourished, and so did agriculture; potatoes were introduced—they were at first considered poisonous; a huge amount of building was done, and the army was drilled constantly under Frederick's eyes. Each year saw it a better army; its chief must have known that he was preparing for the great struggle of his life, although he took as keen an interest in keeping up the high standard of his new opera-house in Berlin, both as to music and ballet, as he did in the skilfullest manœuvres of his troops.

Maria Theresa had never for a moment given up Silesia in her heart. She was a woman of austere virtues, but these did not stand in the way of schemes which she would have thought too despicable to be used against anyone but the King of Prussia. The Czarina of Russia had been made to hate him by a series of carefully-devised plots,—she looked on him as her arch-enemy,—and within six months after the Peace of Dresden she had signed, with Maria Theresa, a treaty which actually proposed the partitioning of Frederick's kingdom, which was to be divided between Russia, Austria, and Poland, while he was to become a simple Margrave of Brandenburg!

To get the signature of Louis XV. involved harder work still for the virtuous empress—but she did it. It was to ask it of the Pompadour—in various affectionate letters, beginning "My dear cousin," or "Madame, my dearest sister." The Pompadour was also shown some stinging verses of Frederick's with herself as subject, and she (representing France) became the firm ally of Maria Theresa.

Through an Austrian clerk's treachery Frederick became aware of this stupendous conspiracy against him—but not till 1755, when it was well matured. It seemed incredible that he could think of keeping these great countries from gobbling up his little state. He could not have done it, indeed, if it had not been for a certain Englishman. It was an Englishman who saved Frederick and Prussia—the "Great Commoner," Pitt, who, having on hand a French war of his own, raised a Hanoverian army to help himself and Frederick, and granted him a welcome subsidy of six hundred and seventy thousand pounds a year.

His ten years' drilling had given Frederick a fine army of one hundred and thirty thousand men. The infantry were said to excel all others in quickness of manœuvres and skilled shooting, while the cavalry was unsurpassed.

Frederick, without waiting for his foes to declare war and mass their mighty forces, began it by a stealthy, sudden move into Saxony, September, 1756. October 1st, at Lowositz in Bohemia, he defeated von Browne, and, returning, captured the Saxon force of seventeen thousand and took them bodily—all but the officers—into his own army.

England was delighted with this masterly act of her ally. He was known there as "the Protestant hero," which was not quite true to facts; certainly Frederick protested against the old religion, but he was far from being on with the new one. His saying, "Everyone shall go to Heaven in the way he chooses," had been applauded in England, but they were not familiar with his reply when a squabble as to whether one or another set of hymn-books should be used was referred to him: "Bah! let them sing what tomfoolery they like," said the "Protestant hero." Had France and Austria, however, succeeded in obliterating Prussia, it is likely that Protestantism too would have been done for in Germany.

Frederick having himself begun the Seven Years' War, the confederated German states, with Russia, France, and Sweden, formally bound themselves to "reduce the House of Brandenburg to its former state of mediocrity," France— very rich then—paying enormous subsidies all around. England—with Hanover—alone espoused Prussia's cause. During 1757, four hundred and thirty-seven thousand men were put in the field against Frederick. Only his cat-like swiftness saved him from being overwhelmed again and again. In April he made another rush—like an avalanche—on Bohemia, and won another great victory at Prague, but he was terribly beaten by General Daun in June at Kolin. Still he kept up courage, and played the flute and wrote innumerable French verses of the usual poor quality in odd moments. In November, at Rossbach, he met an army of French and Imperialists over twice as large as his own, and by a swift, unexpected movement broke them, so that they were scattered all over the country. Every German felt proud of this French defeat, whether he were Prussian or not. It was the first time the invincible French had ever been beaten by a wholly German army, with a leader of German blood. The brilliant victory of Leuthen followed Rossbach.

But although the world was ringing with Frederick's name, and he was acknowledged to be one of the greatest generals of history, the resources of his powerful enemies were too many for him. At last it seemed that a ruinous cloud of disaster was closing around him and darkening the memory of his glorious successes.

The defeat of Kunersdorf in 1759 would have completely wiped out his army if the over-cautious Austrian General Daun had followed up his victory. "Is there no cursed bullet that can reach me!" the Prussian monarch was heard to murmur in a stupor of despair after the battle. He carried poison about him, after this, to use when affairs became too bad. A severe blow followed Kunersdorf,—George II. died, October, 1760; George III. put an end to Pitt's ministry— and this was the end of England's support.

The winter of 1761-'62 saw Frederick at his lowest ebb. England's money had stopped; his own country, plundered, devastated in every direction, afforded no sufficient revenue. Fully half of the Prussian dominions were occupied by the enemy; men, horses, supplies, and transport could hardly be procured. The Prussian army was reduced to sixty thousand men, and its ranks were made up largely of vagabonds and deserters—the old, splendidly disciplined troops having been practically obliterated.

He played no more on his flute—poor Frederick! At Leipzig an old friend sighed to him, "Ach! how lean your majesty has grown!" "Lean, ja wohl," he replied; "and what wonder, with three women [Pompadour, Maria Theresa, and Czarina Elizabeth] hanging to my throat all this while!"

The Allies felt that it was only a matter of a short time before they should see their great enemy humbled to the position of Elector of Brandenburg. From this abasement Frederick was suddenly saved in January, 1762. Life held another chance for him. The implacable old czarina was dead; her heir, Peter III., was not merely the friend, but the enthusiastic adorer of Frederick of Prussia. Although thirty-four years old and the husband of Catherine (the young lady Frederick had taken such pains to select for him so many years ago), Peter had been kept out of public affairs as if he were a child. Neither he nor Catherine was allowed to leave the palace without permission of the czarina; they were surrounded with spies, and kept in a gaudy and dirty semi-imprisonment—the traditional style for heirs to the Russian throne. Under this system they became masters of deceit. Catherine, in her cleverly unpleasant "Memoirs," tells how they managed to escape and visit people without being found out; how she, when ill and in bed, had a joyous company with her, who huddled behind a screen when prying ladies-in-waiting entered. But the most painful part is the account of Peter, who seems to have had more versatility in hateful ways than any one outside of Bedlam. Crazily vivacious over foolish games, brutal when drunk, and silly when sober, one wonders how for so many years Catherine endured him.

There was a saving grace, though, in him: he worshipped the King of Prussia.

Frederick adroitly rose to the occasion: releasing all his Russian prisoners, he sent them, well clad and provisioned, back to their country. February 23rd the czar responded by a public declaration of peace with Prussia and a renunciation of all conquests made during the war. His general, Czernichef, was ordered to put himself and his twenty thousand men at the disposal of the Prussian hero, and on May 5th a treaty of alliance between Prussia and Russia was announced—to the horror and disgust of France and Austria. They had relied on Czernichef, but Czernichef himself was a sincere admirer of his new commander-in-chief and delighted in the change. The Russian soldiers all shared this feeling: they called Frederick "Son of the lightning."

The French were being held by the Hanoverian army; Sweden had retired from the war; with Russia on his side, Frederick felt that he might hold out against Austria till peace was declared by the powers—peace with no provision made for the partition of his kingdom.

In planning his next campaign—the last of the war—it was evident to Frederick that nothing could be done without recapturing the fortress of Schweidnitz, recently captured by Loudon, the Austrian general. The Austrians held all Silesia, and they must be put out of it, but with Schweidnitz in their hands this was impossible.

Fortunately for Frederick, Daun was appointed commander-in-chief of the Austrians, the general who had been execrated throughout the empire for his failure to follow up Frederick after Kunersdorf. In mid-May Daun took command of the forces in Silesia, and with an army of seventy thousand men made haste to place himself in a strong position among rugged hills to guard Schweidnitz. Schweidnitz, with a garrison of twelve thousand picked men and firm defences, it was impossible to attack while Daun was there. Frederick made repeated efforts to force Daun to give up his hold on the fortress, threatening his left wing, as his right wing seemed impregnably situated; but Daun, although forced to change his position from time to time, kept firmly massed about Schweidnitz. Frederick at last, then, resolved to attempt the impossible, and, his forces now augmented by Czernichef's to eighty-one thousand, determined on storming the Heights of Burkersdorf, where Daun's right wing was firmly intrenched. The last of Frederick's notable battles of the war,—a conflict upon which the destinies of Prussia turned,—it was planned and executed by him with a consummate brightness and cleverness that more than justifies the Hohenzollern worship of their great ancestor.

Burkersdorf Height, near the village of the same name, which was also occupied by Daun, lies parallel to Kunensdorf Heights, where Frederick's army lay. It is a high hill, very steep, and half covered with rugged underbrush on the side next to Frederick's position, and Prince de Ligne and General O'Kelly—serving under Daun—had made it bristle with guns. Artillery was Daun's speciality; his guns were thick wherever the ground was not impractically steep, and palisades—"the pales strong as masts and room only for a musket-barrel between"—protected the soldiery; they were even "furnished with a lath or cross-strap all along for resting the gun-barrel on and taking aim." In fact, Burkersdorf Height was as good as a fortress. East of it was a small valley where strong intrenchments had been made and batteries placed. Farther east, two other heights had to be captured,—they were also well defended,—Ludwigsdorf and Leuthmannsdorf.

By the 17th of July Frederick had all his plans matured, and had made his very first move—that is, he had sent Generals Möllendorf and Wied on a march with their men to put the enemy on a false scent—when he received a call from Czernichef at his head-quarters. It was paralyzing news that Czernichef brought: Peter, the providential friend, had been dethroned by the partisans of his clever wife, Catherine.

After a reign of six months the young czar had completely disgusted his subjects: he had planned ambitious schemes of reform, and at the same time had made despotic enroachments. After delighting the church with important concessions, he proposed virtually to take away all its lands and houses. He overdid everything, like the madman he was. He offended his army by dressing up his guards in Prussian uniforms and teaching them the Prussian drill, while he wore constantly the dress of a Prussian colonel, and sang the praises of our hero until his people were sick of the name of "my friend, the King of Prussia."

Russian morals in the eighteenth century were like snakes in Ireland—there were none. In this respect Catherine was not superior to her husband, but in mental gifts she was an extraordinary young woman. Her tact, her poise, her intelligence, would have made a noble character in a decent atmosphere. Peter had recognized her powers and relied on them, and she had endured him all these years, thinking she would one day rule Russia as his empress. But since his accession he had been completely under the dominion of the Countess Woronzow, a vicious creature, who meant to be Catherine's successor. And Catherine, when Peter threatened her and her son Paul with lifelong imprisonment, had on her side finally begun a plot, which resulted in her appealing to the guards, much as Maria Theresa had appealed to her Diet of Hungary. Everyone was tired of Peter, and no voice was raised against his deposition, whereupon Catherine assumed the sovereignty of Russia, to the great relief and satisfaction of all Russians. The brutal assassination of poor Peter by Catherine's friends—not by her orders—followed in a few days.

It was the intention of Catherine, on beginning her reign, to restore Elizabeth's policy in Russian matters and recommence hostilities against Frederick; but on looking over Peter's papers she found that Frederick had discouraged his wild schemes, and that he had begged him to rely on his wife and respect her counsels, and this produced a revulsion of feeling. She resolved that she would not fight him; nor, on the other hand, would she be his ally; the secret message that had come to Czernichef, and which he communicated to Frederick, was that Catherine reigned, and that he, her general, was ordered to return immediately to St. Petersburg.

One can only guess at Frederick's emotions at this news. Life must have seemed a lurid melodrama, presenting one hideous act after another. "This is not living," he said, "this is being killed a thousand times a day!" On the eve of the attack on Burkersdorf his ally had been taken away from him; his own forces were now weaker than those of Daun, and he did not see his way to a victory.

But the genius of Frederick could not allow him to give in to the destinies. His resourcefulness came to his rescue. He simply begged Czernichef to stay with him for three days. Three days must elapse before his official commands came. Frederick, with all the potency of his personal fascination, implored the Russian during that time to keep the matter secret, and, without one hostile act against the enemy, to *seem* to act with him as though their relations were unchanged. Czernichef consented; it was one of the most devoted acts that was ever done by a man for pure friendship; he well knew, and so did Frederick, that he might lose his head or rot in a dungeon for it, but—his own heroism was great enough to make the sacrifice.

The drama accordingly went on. On the evening of the 20th, with the forces of Möllendorf and Wied, who had puzzled the enemy and returned, with Ziethen and Czernichef,—this last, of course, only for show,—Frederick silently marched into Burkersdorf village and took by storm the old Burkersdorf Castle,—an affair of a few hours,—while Daun's forces fled in all directions from the village. Then, through the night, trenches were dug and batteries built— forty guns well placed. At sunrise the whole Prussian army could be seen to be in motion by their opponents.

At four o'clock Frederick's famous cannonade began, concentrated upon the principal height of Burkersdorf. General O'Kelly's men were too high to be reached by the cannon, but it was Frederick's object to keep a furious, confusing noise going on, to help draw attention from Wied and Möllendorf, who were doing the real fighting of the day. Möllendorf was to storm O'Kelly's height, and Wied the Ludwigsdorf height beyond, but Frederick had arranged a spectacular drama by which the foe was to be deceived as to these intentions. It was not for nothing that Frederick had personally overlooked his theatres and operas all these years. His knowledge of scenic displays and their effect on the minds of an audience stood him in good stead this day.

The Prussian guns continued a deafening roar, hour after hour, with many blank charges, and the bewildered commanders of the allied Austrians watched from their elevation the small man on his white horse giving orders right and left. He wore a three-cornered hat with a white feather, a plain blue uniform with red facings, a yellow waistcoat liberally powdered with Spanish snuff, black velvet breeches, and high soft boots. They were shabby old clothes, but the figure had a majesty that everyone recognized. The difficulty among the officers on the heights was to find out what were the orders Frederick was giving so freely. His generals, who were much smarter in their dress than he, dashed off in all directions, and marched their troops briskly about, keeping the whole line of the enemy on the alert.

Daun, ignorant of the St. Petersburg revolution and its consequences, and seeing the Russian masses drawn up threateningly opposite his left wing, which he commanded, dared not concentrate his whole force on Burkersdorf, but from time to time sent bodies of men to support de Ligne and O'Kelly. As no one could tell what spot to support, no line of action could be agreed upon. The commandant of Schweidnitz, General Guasco, with twelve thousand men, came out of the fortress to attack the Prussian rear, but, fortunately for Frederick, one of his astute superiors sent him back.

Meantime, while this uproar and these puzzling operations were going on, Wied had taken his men out of view of the Austrians by circuitous paths to the gradual eastern ascent of Ludwigsdorf and moved up in three detachments. Battery after battery he dislodged, but when he came in sight of the huge mass of guns and men at the top, it seemed wild foolishness to try to get there. It could never have been done by a straight, headlong rush; they crawled along through thickets and little valleys, creeping spirally higher and higher, dodging the fire from above, till at last a movement through a dense wood brought them to the rear and flank of the foe. Then, with a magnificent charge of bayonets, they sent them flying, and passed on to the easy rout of the troops on Leuthmannsdorf.

On Burkersdorf Height O'Kelly's men were looking for an attack on the steepest side, where they were best fortified, but Möllendorf's troops had gone by a roundabout route to the western slope, where after some searching they found a sheep-track winding up the hillside. Following this, they came to a slope so steep that horses could not draw the guns. And then the men pushed and pulled them along and up, until the Austrians spied them from above, and the cannon-balls came crashing down into them. But under this fire they planted their guns, and did such gallant work with them that they were soon at the top, dashing down the defences. It was a tough struggle: the defences were strong—there were line after line of them—and the Austrians had no idea of yielding. They fought like tigers until the fire from the muskets set the dry branches of their abatis ablaze, and Möllendorf quickly closed in around them and forced them to surrender. Frederick's orchestra still boomed on, and the show of officers on prancing steeds and parading troops kept re-enforcements from coming to assist the men on Burkersdorf.

It was noon when Möllendorf had achieved his task, and Daun ordered the army to fall back. But Frederick kept his cannon going as if with a desperate intention till five, to make matters appear more dangerous than they really were to Daun. He was successful; at nightfall Daun led his entire army away, silently and in order, and he never troubled Frederick again.

He left fourteen guns behind him and over one thousand prisoners, and quite two thousand deserted to Frederick in the next few days.

And Czernichef, who had stood by him so nobly? He was full of warmest admiration for Frederick's curious tactics and their success, and the king must have been eternally grateful to him. He marched for home early next morning—and he was neither beheaded nor imprisoned by Catherine when he got there: one is very glad to know that.

Frederick was now enabled to besiege Schweidnitz; its re-conquest gave him back Silesia and left him to long years of peace at Sans Souci. It is fair to conclude that these were happy years, since his happiness lay in incessant work; it needed the most arduous toil to get his country into shape again, but Prussia deserved it—"To have achieved a Frederick the Second for King over it was Prussia's great merit," says Carlyle.

THE STORMING OF BADAJOS

In studying the campaign in the Peninsula, one must remember first of all that the man who was made Earl of Wellington for the victory at Ciudad Rodrigues was not the great potentiality who, as the Duke of Wellington, influenced England after Waterloo. During the Peninsula campaign Wellington was afflicted at all times by a bitter and suspicious Parliament at home. They had no faith in him, and they strenuously objected to furnishing him with money and supplies. Wellington worked with his hands tied behind him against the eager and confident armies of France. We ourselves can read in our more frank annals how a disgruntled part of Congress was forever wishing to turn Washington out of his position as head of the colonial forces. Parliament doled supplies to Wellington with so niggardly a hand that again and again he was forced to stop operations for the want of provisions and arms. At one time he actually had been told to send home the transports in order to save the expense of keeping them at Lisbon. The warfare in Parliament was not deadly, but it was more acrimonious than the warfare in the Peninsula. Moreover, the assistance to his arms from Portugal was so wavering, uncertain, and dubious that he could place no faith in it. The French marshals, Soult and Marmont, had a force of nearly one hundred thousand men.

Wellington held Lisbon, but if he wished to move in Portugal there always frowned upon him the fortified city of Badajos. But finally there came his chance to take it, if it could be taken in a rush, while Soult and Marmont were widely separated and Badajos was left in a very confident isolation.

Badajos lies in Spain, five miles from the Portuguese frontier. It was the key of a situation. Wellington's chance was to strike at Badajos before the two French marshals could combine and crush him. His task was both in front of him and behind him. He lacked transport; he lacked food for the men; the soldiers were eating cassava root instead of bread; the bullocks were weak and emaciated. All this was the doings of the Parliament at home. But Wellington knew that the moment to strike had come, and he seems to have hesitated very little. Placing no faith in the tongues of the Portuguese, he made his plans with all possible secrecy. The guns for the siege were loaded on board the transports at Lisbon and consigned to a fictitious address. But in the river Sadao they were placed upon smaller vessels, and finally they were again landed and drawn by

453

bullocks to Eloas, a post in the possession of the allies. Having stationed two-thirds of his force under General Graham and General Hill to prevent a most probable interference by Soult and Marmont, Wellington advanced, reaching Eloas on the 11th of March, 1812. He had made the most incredible exertions. The stupidity of the Portuguese had vied with the stupidity of the government at home. Wellington had been carrying the preparation for the campaign upon his own shoulders. If he was to win Badajos, he was to win it with no help save that from gallant and trustworthy subordinates. He was ill with it. Even his strangely steel-like nature had bent beneath the trouble of preparation amid such indifference. But on March 16th Beresford with three divisions crossed the Guadiana on pontoons and flying bridges, drove in the enemy's outposts, and invested Badajos.

At the time of the investment the garrison was composed of five thousand French, Hessians, and Spaniards. Spain had always considered this city a most important barrier against any attack through Portugal. A Moorish castle stood three hundred feet above the level of the plain. Bastions and fortresses enwrapped the town. Even the Cathedral was bomb-proof. The Guadiana was crossed by a magnificent bridge, and on the farther shore the head of this bridge was strongly fortified.

Wellington's troops encamped to the east of the town. It was finally decided first to attack the bastion of Trinidad. The French commander had strengthened all his defences, and by damming a stream had seriously obstructed Wellington's operations. Parts of his force were confronted by an artificial lake two hundred yards in width.

The red coats of the English soldiers were now faded to the yellow brown of fox fur. All the military finery of the beginning of the century was tarnished and torn. But it was an exceedingly hard-bitten army, certain of its leaders, despising the enemy, full of ferocious desire for battle.

Perhaps the bastion of Trinidad was chosen because it was the nearest to the intrenchments of the allies. In those days the frontal attack was possible of success. On the night of the 17th of March the British broke ground within one hundred and sixty yards of Fort Picerina. The sound of the digging was muffled by the roar of a great equinoctial storm. The French were only made wise by the daylight, but in the meantime the allies had completed a trench six hundred yards long and three feet deep, and with a communication four thousand feet in length. The French announced their discovery by a rattle of musketry, but the allies kept on with their digging, while general officers wrapped in their long cloaks paced to and fro directing the work.

The situation did not please the French general at all. He knew that something must be done to counteract the activity of the besiegers. He was in command of a very spirited garrison. On the night of the 19th a sortie was made from the Talavera Gate by both cavalry and infantry. The infantry began to demolish the trench of the allies. The cavalry divided itself into two parts and went through a form of sham fight which in the darkness was deceptive. When challenged by the pickets, they answered in Portuguese, and thus succeeded in galloping a long way behind the trenches, where they cut down a number of men before their identity was discovered and they were beaten back. General Phillipon, the French commander, had offered a reward for every captured intrenching tool. Thus the French infantry of the sortie devoted itself largely to making a collection of picks and spades. Men must have risked themselves with great audacity for this reward, since they left three hundred dead on the field, but succeeded in carrying off a great number of the intrenching tools.

Great rain-storms now began to complicate the work of the besiegers. The trenches became mere ditches half-full of discolored water. This condition was partly improved by throwing in bags of sand. On the French side a curious device had been employed as a means of communication between the gate of the Trinidad bastion and Fort San Roque. The French soldiers had begun to dig, but had grown tired, so they finished by hanging up a brown cloth. This to the besiegers' eyes was precisely like the fresh earth of a parallel, and behind it the French soldiers passed in safety.

Storm followed storm. The Guadiana, swollen past all tradition by these furious downpours, swept away the flying bridges, sinking twelve pontoons. For several days the army of the allies was entirely without food, but they stuck doggedly to their trenches, and when communication was at last restored it was never again broken. The weather cleared, and the army turned grimly with renewed resolution to the business of taking Badajos. This was in the days of the forlorn hope. There was no question of anything but a desperate and deadly frontal attack. The command of the assault of Fort Picerina was given to General Kempt. He had five hundred men, including engineers, sappers, and miners, and fifty men who carried axes. At nine o'clock they marched. The night was very dark. The fort remained silent until the assailants were close. Then a great fire blazed out at them. For a time it was impossible for the men to make any progress. The palisades seemed insurmountable, and the determined soldiers of England were falling on all sides. In the meantime there suddenly sounded the loud, wild notes of the alarm-bells in the besieged city, and the guns of Badajos awakened and gave back thunder for thunder to the batteries of the allies. The confusion was worse than in the mad nights on the heath in "King Lear," but amid the thundering and the death, Kempt's fifty men with axes walked deliberately around Fort Picerina until they found the entrance gate. They beat it down and rushed in. The infantry with their bayonets followed closely. Lieutenant Nixon of the Fifty-second Foot (now the Second Battalion of the Oxfordshire Light Infantry) fell almost on the threshold, but his men ran on. The interior of the fort became the scene of a terrible hand-to-hand fight. All of the English did not come in through the gate. Some of Kempt's men now succeeded in establishing ladders against the rampart, and swarmed over to the help of their comrades. The struggle did not cease until more than half of the little garrison were killed. Then the commandant, Gasper Thiery, surrendered a little remnant of eighty-six men. Others who had not been killed by the British had rushed out and been drowned in the waters of that inundation which had so troubled Wellington and so pleased the French general. Phillipon had estimated that the Picerina would endure for five days, but it had been taken in an hour, albeit one of the bloodiest hours in the annals of a modern army.

Wellington was greatly pleased. He was now able to advance his earthworks close to the eastern part of the town, while his batteries played continually on the front of Fort San Roque and the two northern bastions, Trinidad and Santa Maria.

But at the last of the month Wellington was confronted by his chief fear. News came to him that Marshal Soult was advancing rapidly from Cordova. It was now a simple question of pushing the siege with every ounce of energy contained in his army. Forty-eight guns were made to fire incessantly, and although the French reply was destructive, the English guns were gradually wearing away the three great defences. By the 2nd of April Trinidad was seriously damaged, and one flank of Santa Maria was so far gone that Phillipon set his men at work on an inner defence to cut the last-named bastion off from the city. On the night of the 2nd an attack was made on the dam of the inundation. Two British officers and some sappers succeeded in gagging and binding the sentinel guarding the dam, and having piled barrels of gunpowder against it, they lighted a slow-match and made off. But before the spark could reach the powder the French arrived under the shelter of the comic brown cloth communication. The explosion did not occur, and the inundation still remained to hinder Wellington's progress. On the 6th it was thought that three breaches were practicable for assault, and the resolute English general ordered the attack to be made at once. To Picton, destined to attach his name to the imperishable fame of Waterloo, was given an arduous task. He was to attack on the right and scale the walls of the castle of Badajos, which were from eighteen to twenty-four feet high. On the left General Walker, marching to the south, was to make a false attack on Port Pardaleras, but a real one on San Vincente, a bastion on the extreme west of the town. In the centre the Fourth Division and Wellington's favorite Light Division were to march against the breaches. The Fourth was to move against Trinidad, and the Light Division against Santa Maria. The columns were divided into storming and firing parties. The former were to enter the ditch while the latter fired over them at the enemy. Just before the assault was to be sounded a French deserter brought the intelligence that there was but one communication from the castle to the town, and Wellington decided to send against it an entire division. Brigadier-General Power with his semi-useless Portuguese brigade was directed to attack the head of the bridge and the other works on the right of the Guadiana.

The army had now waited only for the night. When it had come, thick mists from the river increased the darkness. At 10 o'clock Major Wilson, of the Forty-eighth Foot (now the First Battalion of the Northamptonshire regiment), led a party against Fort San Roque so suddenly and so tempestuously that the work capitulated almost immediately. At the castle, General Picton's men had placed their ladders and swarmed up them in the face of showers of heavy stones, logs of wood, and crashing bullets, while at the same time they were under a heavy fire from the left flank. The foremost were bayoneted when they reached the top, and the besieged Frenchmen grasped the ladders and tumbled them over with their load of men. The air was full of wild screams as the English fell towards the stones below. Presently every ladder was thrown back, and for the moment the assailants had to run for shelter against a rain of flying missiles.

In this moment of uncertainty one man, Lieutenant Ridge, rushed out, rallying his company. Seizing one of the abandoned ladders, he planted it where the wall was lower. His ladder was followed by other ladders, and the troops scrambled with revived courage after this new and intrepid leader. The British gained a strong foothold on the ramparts of the castle, and every moment added to their strength as Picton's men came swarming. They drove the French through the castle and out of the gates. They met a heavy re-enforcement of the French, but after a severe engagement they were finally and triumphantly in possession of the castle. Lieutenant Ridge had been killed.

But at about the same time the men of the Fourth Division and of the Light Division had played a great and tragic part in the storming of Badajos. They moved against the great breach in stealthy silence. All was dark and quiet as they reached the glacis. They hurled bags full of hay in the ditch, placed their ladders, and the storming parties of the Light Division, five hundred men in all, hurried to this desperate attack.

But the French general had perfectly understood that the main attacks would be made at his three breaches, and he had made the great breach the most impregnable part of his line. The English troops, certain that they had surprised the enemy, were suddenly exposed by dozens of brilliant lights. Above them they could see the ramparts crowded with the French. These fire-balls made such a vivid picture that the besieged and besiegers could gaze upon one another's faces at distances which amounted to nothing. There was a moment of this brilliance, and then a terrific explosion shattered the air. Hundreds of shells and powder-barrels went off together, and the English already in the ditch were literally blown to pieces. Still their comrades crowded after them with no definite hesitation. The French commander had taken the precaution to fill part of the ditch with water from the inundation, and in it one hundred fusiliers, men of Albuera, were drowned.

The Fourth Division and the Light Division continued the attack upon the breach. Across the top of it was a row of sword-blades fitted into ponderous planks, and these planks, chained together, were let deep into the ground. In front of them the slope was covered with loose planks studded with sharp iron points. The English, stepping on them, rolled howling backward, and the French yelled and fired unceasingly.

It was too late for the English to become aware of the hopelessness of their undertaking. Column after column hurled themselves forward. Young Colonel Macleod, of the Forty-third Foot (now the First Battalion of the Oxfordshire Light Infantry), a mere delicate boy, gathered his men again and again and led them at the breach. A falling soldier behind him plunged a bayonet in his back, but still he kept on till he was shot dead within a yard of the line of sword-blades.

For two hours the besiegers were tirelessly striving to achieve the impossible, while the French taunted them from the ramparts.

"Why do you not come into Badajos?"

Meanwhile, Captain Nicholas of the Engineers, with Lieutenant Shaw and about one hundred men of the Forty-third Foot, actually had passed through the breach of the Santa Maria bastion, but once inside they were met with such a fire that nearly every man dropped dead. Shaw returned almost alone.

Wellington, who had listened to these desperate assaults and watched them as well as he was able from a position on a small knoll, gave orders at midnight for the troops to retire and re-form. Two thousand men had been slain. Dead and mangled bodies were piled in heaps at the entrance to the great breach, and the stench of burning flesh and hair was said to be insupportable.

And still, in the meantime, General Walker's brigade had made a feint against Pardaleras and passed on to the bastion of San Vincente. Here for a time everything went wrong. The fire of the French was frightfully accurate and concentrated. General Walker himself simply dripped blood; he was a mass of wounds. His ladders were all found to be too short. The walls of the fortress were thirty feet in height. However, through some lack of staying power in the French, success at last crowned the attack. One man clambered somehow to the top of a wall and pulled up others, until about half of the Fourth Foot (now the King's Own Royal Lancaster Regiment) were fairly into the town. Walker's men took three bastions. General Picton, severely wounded, had not dared to risk losing the Castle, but now, hearing the tumult of Walker's success, he sent his men forth and thousands went swarming through the town. Phillipon saw that all was lost, and retreated with a few hundred men to San Christoval. He surrendered next morning to Lord Fitzroy Somerset.

The English now occupied the town. With their comrades lying stark, or perhaps in frightful torment, in the fields beyond the walls of Badajos, these soldiers, who had so heroically won this immortal victory, became the most abandoned, drunken wretches and maniacs. Crazed privates stood at the corners of streets and shot everyone in sight. Everywhere were soldiers dressed in the garb of monks, of gentlemen at court, or mayhap wound about with gorgeous ribbons and laces. Jewels and plate, silks and satins, all suffered a wanton destruction. Napier writes of "shameless rapacity, brutal intemperance, savage lust, cruelty and murder, shrieks and piteous lamentations."

He further says that the horrible tumult was never quelled. It subsided through the weariness of the soldiers. One wishes to inquire why the man who was ultimately called the Iron Duke did not try to stop this shocking business. But one remembers that Wellington was a wise man, and he did not try to stop this shocking business because he knew that his soldiers were out of control and that if he tried he would fail.

THE BRIEF CAMPAIGN AGAINST NEW ORLEANS

(December 14, 1814-January 8, 1815.)

The Mississippi broad, rapid, and sinister, ceaselessly flogging its enwearied banks, was the last great legend of the dreaming times when the Old World's information of the arisen continents was roseate but inaccurate. England, at war with the United States, heard stories of golden sands, bejewelled temples, fabulous silks, the splendor of a majestic barbarian civilization, and even if these tales were fantastic they stood well enough as symbols of the spinal importance of the grim Father of Waters.

The English put together a great expedition. It was the most formidable that ever had been directed against the Americans. It assembled in a Jamaican harbor and at Pensacola, then a Spanish port and technically neutral. The troops numbered about fourteen thousand men and included some of the best regiments in the British army, fresh from service in the Peninsula under Wellington. They were certainly not men who had formed a habit of being beaten. Included in the expedition was a full set of civilian officials for the government of New Orleans after its capture.

A hundred and ten miles from the mouth of the Mississippi, New Orleans lay trembling. She had no forts or intrenchments; she would be at the mercy of the powerful British force. The people believed that the city would be sacked and burned. They were not altogether a race full of vigor. The peril of the situation bewildered them; it did not stir them to action.

But the spirit of energy itself arrived in the person of Andrew Jackson. Since the Creek War, the nation had had much confidence in Jackson, and New Orleans welcomed him with a great sigh of relief. The sallow, gnarled, crusty man came ill to his great work; he should have been in bed. But the amount of vim he worked into a rather flabby community in a short time looked like a miracle. The militia of Louisiana were called out; the free negroes were armed and drilled; convicts whose terms had nearly expired were enlisted; and down from Tennessee tramped the type of man that one always pictures as winning the battle—the long, lank woodsman, brown as leather, hard as nails, inseparable from his rifle, in his head the eye of a hawk.

The Lafitte brothers, famous pirates, whose stronghold was not a thousand

459

miles from the city, threw in their lot with the Americans. The British bid for their services, but either the British committed the indiscretion of not bidding enough or the buccaneers were men of sentiment. At any rate they accepted the American pledge of immunity and came with their men to the American side, where they rendered great service. Afterwards the English, their offer of treasure repulsed, somewhat severely reproved us for allowing these men to serve in our ranks.

Martial law was proclaimed, and Jackson kept up an exciting quarrel with the city authorities at the same time that he was working his strange army night and day in the trenches. Captain John Coffee with two thousand men joined from Mobile.

The British war-ships first attempted to cross the sand-bars at the mouth of the river and ascend the stream, but the swift Mississippi came to meet them, and it was as if this monster, immeasurable in power, knew that he must defend himself. The well-handled war-ships could not dodge this simple strength; even the wind refused its help. The river won the first action.

But if the British could not ascend the stream, they could destroy the small American gun-boats on the lakes below the city, and this they did on December 14th with a rather painful thoroughness. The British were then free to land their troops on the shores of these lakes and attempt to approach the city through miles of dismal and sweating swamps. The decisive word seems to have rested with Major-General Keane. Sir George Pakenham, the commander-in-chief, had not yet arrived. One of Wellington's proud veterans was not likely to endure any nonsensical delay over such a business as this campaign against a simple people who had not had the art of war hammered into their heads by a Napoleon. Moreover, the army was impatient. Some of the troops had been with Lord Ross in the taking of Washington, and they predicted something easier than that very easy campaign. Everybody was completely cock-sure.

On the afternoon of December 23rd, Major-General Gabrielle Villeré, one of the gaudy Creole soldiers, came to see Jackson at head-quarters, and announced that about two thousand British had landed on the Villeré plantation, nine miles below the city. Jackson was still feeble, but this news warmed the old passion in him. He pounded the table with his fist. "By the Eternal!" he cried, "they shall not sleep on our soil!" All well-regulated authorities make Jackson use this phrase—"By the Eternal!"—and any reference to him hardly would be intelligible unless one quoted the familiar line. I suppose we should not haggle over the matter; historically one oath is as good as another.

Marching orders were issued to the troops, and the armed schooner Carolina was ordered to drop down the river and open fire upon the British at 7.50 in the evening. In the meantime, Jackson reviewed his troops as they took the road. He was not a good-natured man; indeed, he is one of the most irascible figures in history. But he knew how to speak straight as a stick to the common man. Each corps received some special word of advice and encouragement.

This review was quaint. Some of the Creole officers were very gorgeous, but perhaps they only served to emphasize the wildly unmilitary aspect of the procession generally. But the woodsmen were there with their rifles, and if the British had beaten Napoleon's marshals, the woodsmen had conquered the forests and the mountains, and they too did not understand that they could be whipped.

The first detachment of British troops had come by boat through Lake Borgne and then made a wretched march through the swamps. Both officers and men were in sorry plight. They had been exposed for days to the fury of tropical rains, and for nights to bitter frosts, without gaining even an opportunity to dry their clothes. But December 23rd was a clear day lit by a mildly warm sun. Arriving at Villeré's plantation on the river bank, the troops built huge fires and then raided the country as far as they dared, gathering a great treasure of "fowls and hams and wine." The feast was merry. The veteran soldier of that day had a grand stomach, and he made a deep inroad into Louisiana's store of "fowls and hams and wine."

As they lay comfortably about their fires in the evening some sharp eye detected by the faint light of the moon a moving, shadowy vessel on the river. She was approaching. An officer mounted the levee and hailed her. There was no answer. He hailed again. The silent vessel calmly furled her sails and swung her broadside parallel. Then a voice shouted and a whistling shower of grape-shot tore the air. It was the little Carolina.

The British forces flattened themselves in the shelter of the levee and listened to the grape-shot go ploughing over their heads. But they had not been long in this awkward position when there was a yell and a blare of flame in the darkness. Some of Jackson's troops had come.

Then ensued a strange conflict. The moon, tender lady of the night, hid while around the dying fires two forces of infuriated men shot, stabbed, and cut. One remembers grimly Jackson's sentence—"They shall not sleep on our soil." No; they were kept awake this night at least.

There was no concerted action on either side. An officer gathered a handful of men and by his voice led them through the darkness at the enemy. If such valor and ferocity had been introduced into the insipid campaigns of the North, the introduction would have made overwhelming victory for one people or the other. Dawn displayed the terrors of the fighting in the night. In some cases an American and an English soldier lay dead, each with his bayonet sheathed in the other's body. Bayonets were rare in the American ranks, but many men carried long hunting knives.

As a matter of fact, the two forces had been locked in a blind and desperate embrace. The British reported a loss of forty-six killed, one hundred and sixty-seven wounded, and sixty-four missing. In this engagement the Americans suffered more severely that in any other action of the short campaign.

On the morning of December 24th, Sir George Pakenham arrived with a strong re-enforcement of men and guns. Pakenham was a brother-in-law of Wellington. He had served in the Peninsula and was accounted a fine leader. The American schooners Carolina and Louisiana lay at anchor in the river firing continually upon the British camp. Pakenham caused a battery to be planted which quickly made short work of these vessels.

During the days following the two armies met in several encounters which were fiery but indecisive. One of these meetings is called the Battle of the Bales and Hogsheads.

Jackson employed cotton-bales in strengthening a position, and one night the British advanced and built a redoubt chiefly of hogsheads containing sugar and molasses. The cotton suffered considerably from the British artillery, often igniting and capable of being easily rolled out of place, but the sugar and molasses behaved very badly. The hogsheads were easily penetrated, and they soon began to distribute sugar and molasses over the luckless warriors in the redoubt, so that British soldiers died while mingling their blood with molasses and with sugar sprinkling down upon their wounds.

Although neither side had gained a particular advantage, the British were obliged to retire. They had been the first disciplined troops to engage molasses, and they were glad to emerge from the redoubt, this bedraggled, sticky, and astonished body of men.

On the opposite bank of the river a battery to rake the British encampment had been placed by Commander Patterson. This battery caused Pakenham much annoyance and he engaged it severely with his guns, but at the end of an hour he had to cease firing with a loss of seventy men and his emplacements almost in ruins. The damage to the American works was slight, but they had lost thirty-six in killed and disabled.

Both sides now came to a period of fateful thought. In the beginning the British had spoken of a feeble people who at first would offer a resistance of pretence but soon subside before the victorious colors of the British regiments. Now they knew that they were face to face with determined and skilful fighters who would dauntlessly front any British regiment whose colors had ever hung in glory in a cathedral of old England. The Americans had thought to sweep the British into the Gulf of Mexico. But now they knew that although their foes floundered and blundered, although they displayed that curious stern-lipped stupidity which is the puzzle of many nations, they were still the veterans of the Peninsula, the stout, undismayed troops of Wellington.

Jackson moved his line fifty yards back from his cotton bale position. Here he built a defensive work on the northern brink of an old saw-mill race known as the Rodriguez Canal. The line of defence was a mile in length. It began on the river bank and ended in a swamp where during the battle the Americans stood knee-deep in mud or on floating planks and logs moored to the trees. The main defences of the position were built of earth, logs, and fence-rails in some places twenty feet thick. It barred the way to New Orleans.

The Americans were prepared for the critical engagement some days before Pakenham had completed his arrangements. The Americans spent the interval in making grape-shot out of bar-lead and in mending whatever points in their line needed care and work.

Pakenham's final plan was surprisingly simple and perhaps it was surprisingly bad. He decided to send a heavy force across the river to attack Patterson's annoying battery simultaneously with the deliverance of the main attack against Jackson's position along the line of the Rodriguez Canal. Why Pakenham decided to make the two attacks simultaneously is not quite clear at this day. Patterson's force, divided by the brutally swift river from the main body of the Americans, might have been considered with much reason a detached body of troops, and Pakenham might have eaten them at his leisure while at the same time keeping up a great show in front of Jackson, so that the latter would consider that something serious was imminent at the main position.

However, Pakenham elected to make the two attacks at the same hour, and posterity does not perform a graceful office when it re-generals the battles of the past.

Boats were brought from the fleet, and with immense labor a canal was dug from Lake Borgne to the Mississippi. For use in fording the ditch in front of Jackson, the troops made fascines by binding together sheaves of sugar-cane, and for the breastwork on the far-side of the ditch they made scaling ladders.

On January 7, 1815, Jackson stood on the top of the tallest building within his lines and watched the British at work. At the same time Pakenham was in the top of a pine-tree regarding the American trenches. For the moment, and indefinitely, it was a question of eyesight. Jackson studied much of the force that was to assail him; Pakenham studied the position which he had decided to attack. Pakenham's eyesight may not have been very good.

Colonel Thornton was in command of the troops which were to attack Patterson's battery across the river, and a rocket was to be sent up to tell him when to begin his part of the general onslaught.

Pakenham advanced serenely against the Rodriguez Canal, the breastwork, and the American troops. One wishes to use here a phrase inimical to military phraseology. One wishes to make a distinction between disinterested troops and troops who are interested. The Americans were interested troops. They faced the enemy at the main gate of the United States. Behind them crouched frightened thousands. In reality they were defending a continent.

As the British advanced to the attack they made a gallant martial picture. The motley army of American planters, woodsmen, free negroes, ex-convicts, and pirates watched them in silence. Here tossed the bonnets of a fierce battalion of Highlanders; here marched a bottle-green regiment, the officers wearing furred cloaks and crimson sashes; here was a steady line of blazing red coats. Everywhere rode the general officers in their cocked hats, their short red coats with golden epaulettes and embroideries, their skin-tight white breeches, their high black boots. The ranks were kept locked in the manner of that day. It was like a grand review.

But the grandeur was extremely brief. The force was well within range of the American guns when Pakenham made the terrible discovery that his orders had been neglected: there was neither fascine nor ladder on the field. In a storm of rage and grief the British general turned to the guilty officer and bade him take his men back and fetch them. When, however, the ladders and fascines had been brought into the field, a hot infantry engagement had already begun and the bearers, becoming wildly rattled, scattered them on the ground.

It was now that Sir George Pakenham displayed that quality of his nation which in another place I have called stern-lipped stupidity. It was an absolute certainty that Jackson's position could not be carried without the help of fascines and ladders; it was doubtful if it could be carried in any case.

But Sir George Pakenham ordered a general charge. His troops responded desperately. They flung themselves forward in the face of a storm of bullets aimed usually with deadly precision. Back of their rampart, the Americans, at once furious and cool, shot with the quickness of aim and yet with the finished accuracy of life-long hunters. The British army was being mauled and mangled out of all resemblance to the force that had landed in December.

Sir George Pakenham, proud, heart-broken, frenzied man, rode full tilt at the head of rush after rush. And his men followed him to their death. On the right, a major and a lieutenant succeeded in crossing the ditch. The two officers mounted the breastwork but the major fell immediately. The lieutenant imperiously demanded the swords of the American officers present. But they said: "Look behind you." He looked behind him and saw that the men whom he had supposed were at his back had all vanished as if the earth had yawned for them.

The lieutenant was taken prisoner and so he does not count, but the dead body of the major as it fell and rolled within the American breastwork established the high-water mark of the British advance upon New Orleans.

Sir George Pakenham seemed to be asking for death, and presently it came to him. His body was carried from the field. General Gibbs was mortally wounded. General Keane was seriously wounded. Left without leaders, the British troops began a retreat. This retreat was soon a mad runaway, but General Lambert with a strong reserve stepped between the beaten battalions and their foes. The battle had lasted twenty-five minutes.

Jackson's force, armed and unarmed, was four thousand two hundred and sixty-four. During the whole campaign he lost three hundred and thirty-three. In the final action he lost four killed, thirteen wounded. The British force in action was about eight thousand men. The British lost some nine hundred killed, fourteen hundred wounded, and five hundred prisoners.

Thornton finally succeeded in reaching and capturing the battery on the other side of the river, but he was too late. Some of the British war-ships finally succeeded in crossing the bars, but they were too late. General Lambert, now in command, decided to withdraw, and the expedition sailed away.

Peace had been signed at Ghent on December 24, 1814. The real Battle of New Orleans was fought on January 8, 1815.

THE BATTLE OF SOLFERINO

Italy," said Prince Metternitch, "is merely a geographical expression."

The sneer was justified; the storied peninsula was cut up into little principalities for little princes of the houses of Hapsburg and Bourbon. The millions who spoke a common tongue and cherished common traditions of a glorious past were ruled as cynically as if they were so many cattle. The map of Italy for 1859 is a crazy-quilt of many patches. How has it come about, then, that the map of Italy for 1863 is of one uniform color from the Alps to the "toe of the boot," including Sardinia and Sicily? We must except the Papal States, of course, still separate till 1870, and Venetia, Austrian till 1866, when the "Bride of the Sea" became finally one with the rest of Italy.

This was the last miracle that Europe had looked for. Unity in Italy! "Since the fall of the Roman Empire (if ever before it)," said an Englishman, "there has never been a time when Italy could be called a nation any more than a stack of timber can be called a ship." This was true even in the days of the mediæval magnificence of the city-states, Venice, Genoa, Milan and Florence, Pisa and Rome. But in modern times Italy had become only a field for intriguing dynasties and the wars of jealous nations.

During the latter half of the eighteenth century Italy was strangely tranquil; was she content at last with her slavery? Never that; the people had simply grown apathetic. Their spasmodic insurrections had always ended in a worse bondage than ever: their very religion was used to fasten their chains. Perhaps nothing could have served so well to wake them from this torpor of despair as the iron tread of the first Napoleon. The "Corsican tyrant" proved a beneficent counter-irritant—a wholesome, cleansing force throughout the land. It was good for Italy to be rid, if only for a little while, of Hapsburgs and Bourbons; to have the political divisions of the country reduced to three; to be amazed at the sight of justice administered fairly and taxation made equitable. But the most significant effect of the Napoleonic occupation was this, that the hearts of the Italians were stirred with a new consciousness: they had been shown the possibility of becoming a united race—of owning a nation which should not be a "mere geographical expression."

And although 1815 brought the bad days of the Restoration, and the stupid, corrupt, or cruel princes climbed back again on their little thrones, and the map was made into pretty much the same old crazy-quilt, still it was not the same old Italy: all the diplomats at Vienna could not make things as they had been before. The new spirit of freedom came to life in the north, in the Kingdom of Sardinia, that had made itself the most independent section of the country. In the beginning it was only Savoy, and the Dukes of Savoy, "owing," as the Prince de Ligne said, "to their geographical position, which did not permit them to behave like honest men," had swallowed, first, Piedmont; then, Sardinia; and then as many of the towns of Lombardy as they could. The restoration enriched the kingdom by the gift of Genoa—where, in 1806, Joseph Mazzini was born.

Mazzini, Garibaldi, Cavour—those names will be always thought of as one with the liberation of Italy.

Though frequently in open antagonism, yet the work of each of the three was necessary to the cause, and to each it was a holy cause, for which he was ready to make any sacrifice:

> "Italia! when thy name was but a name,
> When to desire thee was a vain desire,
> When to achieve thee was impossible,
> When to love thee was madness, when to live
> For thee was the extravagance of fools,
> When to die for thee was to fling away
> Life for a shadow—in those darkest days
> Were some who never swerved, who lived, and strove,
> And suffered for thee, and attained their end."

Of these devoted ones Mazzini was the prophet; his idealism undoubtedly made too great demands upon the human beings he worked for, but let us bear in mind that it needed a conception of absolute good to rouse the sluggish Italian mind from its materialism and Machiavellism." Mazzini wore black when a youth as "mourning for his country," and when his university course was at an end he took up the profession of political agitator and joined the Carbonari.

But the greatest service he ever did his cause was the organization of a new society—on a much higher plane that the Carbonari and its like. The movement was called "Young Italy," famous for the spirit it raised from end to end of the peninsula. Among those attracted by Mazzini's exalted utterance was the young Garibaldi, who, taking part in Mazzini's rising of 1834, was condemned to death, and made his escape to South America. In constant service in the wars between the quarrelsome states he gained his masterly skill in guerilla warfare which was afterwards to play so great a part in the liberation of his country. He did not return until it seemed as though the hour of Italy's deliverance was at hand, in 1848, which only proved to be the "quite undress rehearsal" for the great events of 1859.

Garibaldi has been called "not a soldier but a saint." Most great heroes, alas! have outlived their heroism, and their worshippers have outlived their worship, but Garibaldi has never been anything but the unselfish patriot who wanted everything for his country but nothing for himself. He has been described, on his return to Italy from South America, as "beautiful as a statue and riding like a centaur." "He was quite a show," said the sculptor Gibson, "everyone stopping to look at him." "Probably," said another Englishman, "a human face so like a lion, and still retaining the humanity nearest the image of its Maker, was never seen."

The third of the immortal Italian trio, Count Camillo de Cavour, was, like Mazzini and Garibaldi, a subject of the Sardinian kingdom. There was no prouder aristocracy in Europe than that of Piedmont, but Camillo seems to have drawn his social theories from the all-pervading unrest that the great Revolution and Bonaparte had left in the air, rather than the assumed sources of heredity. In his tenth year he entered the military academy at Turin, and at the same time was appointed page to the Prince of Carignan, afterwards Charles Albert, father of Victor Emmanuel. This was esteemed a high honor, but it did not appeal to him in this light. When asked what was the costume of the pages, he replied, in a tone of disgust: "Parbleu! how would you have us dressed, except as lackeys, which we were? It made me blush with shame."

His attitude of contempt for the place occasioned a prompt dismissal. At the academy he was so successful with mathematics that he left it at sixteen, having become sub-lieutenant in the engineers, although twenty years was the earliest age for this grade. He then joined the garrison at Genoa, but the military career had no allurements for him. Taking kindly to liberal ideas, he expressed himself so freely that the authorities transferred him to the little fortress of Bard, till, in 1831, he resigned his commission.

Having by nature a "diabolical activity" that demanded the widest scope for itself, he now took charge of a family estate at Leri, and went in for scientific farming.

"At the first blush," he wrote, "agriculture has little attraction. The habitué of the salon feels a certain repugnance for works which begin by the analysis of dunghills and end in the middle of cattlesheds. However, he will soon discover a growing interest, and that which most repelled him will not be long in having for him a charm which he never so much as expected."

Although he began by not knowing a turnip from a potato, his invincible energy soon made him a capital farmer; his experiments were so daring that "the simple neighbors who came trembling to ask his advice stood aghast; he, always smiling, gay, affable, having for each a clear, concise counsel, an encouragement enveloped in a pleasantry."

Besides agriculture, his interests extended to banks, railway companies, a manufactory for chemical fertilizers, steam mills for grinding corn, and a line of packets on the Lago Maggiore. During this time he visited England, and was to be seen night after night in the Strangers' Gallery of the House of Commons, making himself master of the methods of Parliamentary tactics, that were to be of such value to Italy in later years.

In 1847 Cavour started the *Risorgimento,* a journal whose programme was simply this: "Independence of Italy, union between the princes and peoples, progress in the path of reform, and a league between the Italian states." As for Italian unity, "Let us," Cavour would say, "do one thing at a time; let us get rid of the Austrians, and then—we shall see." After returning from England in 1843 he wrote: "You may well talk to me of hell, for since I left you I live in a kind of intellectual hell, where intelligence and science are reputed infernal by him who has the goodness to govern us."

The king, Charles Albert, had called him the most dangerous man in the kingdom, and he certainly was the most dangerous to the old systems of religious and political bigotry; but his work was educational; gradually he was enlightening the minds of the masses, and preventing a possible reign of terror. In 1848 he wrote: "What is it which has always wrecked the finest and justest of revolutions? The mania for revolutionary means; the men who have attempted to emancipate themselves from ordinary laws. Revolutionary means, producing the directory, the consulate, and the empire; Napoleon, bending all to his caprice, imagining that one can with a like facility conquer at the Bridge of Lodi and wipe out a law of nature. Wait but a little longer, and you will see the last consequence of your revolutionary means—Louis Napoleon on the throne!"

Charles Albert, the king, who, as Prince Carignan, had been one of the Carbonari, and secretly hated Austria, has been accused of treachery and double dealing (he explained that he was "always between the dagger of the Carbonari and the chocolate of the Jesuits"); but the time came when he nobly redeemed his past. In 1845 he assured d'Azeglio that when Sardinia was ready to free herself from Austria, his life, his sons' lives, his arms, his treasure, should all be freely spent in the Italian cause.

In February, 1848, he granted his people a constitution; a parliament was formed, Cavour becoming member for Turin.

In this month the revolution broke out in Paris and penetrated to the heart of Vienna. Metternich was forced to fly his country; the Austrians left Milan; Venice threw off the yoke—all Italy revolted. The Pope, it is said, behaved badly, and left Rome free for Garibaldi to enter, with Mazzini enrolled as a volunteer.

Even the abominable Ferdinand of Sicily and the Grand Duke of Tuscany had been obliged to grant constitutions; all the northern states had hastened to unite themselves to Sardinia by universal plebiscite. At the very beginning, Charles Albert fulfilled his pledge; he placed himself at the head of his army and defied Austria.

But it was too soon: Austria was too strong. On the 23rd of March, 1849, Charles Albert was crushingly defeated by Radetsky at Novara. There, when night fell, he called his generals to him and in their presence abdicated in favor of his son, Victor Emmanuel, who knelt weeping before him. The pathos of despair was in his words: "Since I have not succeeded in finding death," he said, "I must accomplish one last sacrifice for my country."

He left the battle-field and his country without even visiting his home; six months later he was dead. "The magnanimous king," his people called him.

The young Victor Emmanuel began his reign in a kingly fashion; pointing his sword towards the Austrian camp, he exclaimed: "Per Dio! d'Italia sarà." It seemed at the time a mere empty boast—his little country was brought so close to the verge of ruin. The terms of peace imposed an Austrian occupation until the war indemnity of eighty million francs should be paid. Yet Cavour was heard to say that all their sacrifices were not too dear a price for the Italian tricolor in exchange for the flag of Savoy. It was not until July that Rome fell—Rome, where Garibaldi had established a republic and Mazzini was a Triumvir!

At the invitation of the Pope, Louis Napoleon, then president of the French republic, seeing the opportunity for conciliating the religious powers, poured his troops into Rome, and Garibaldi fled, with Anita at his side. The brave wife with her unborn child would not leave her hero, but death took her from him. In a peasant's hut, a few days later, she died, his arms around her. As for Mazzini, the fall of Rome nearly broke his heart. For days he wandered dazed about the

Eternal City, miraculously escaping capture, till his friends got him away.

It was not until April of 1850 that Pius IX. dared to come back to Rome, where a body of French troops long remained, to show how really religious a nation was France. From his accession there had been a Papal party in Italy, who, because of the good manners of the gentle ecclesiastic, had wrought themselves up to believe that Italy could be united under *him*. But as early as 1847 d'Azeglio wrote from Rome: "The magic of Pio Nono will not last; he is an angel, but he is surrounded by demons."

After the events of the 1848 rising, and his appeal (twenty-five pontiffs had made the same appeal before him!) to the foreigner against his own people, the dream of a patriotic pope melted into thin air.

And so Austria came back into Italy, and seemed again complete master there. It would be interesting to be able to analyze the sensibilities of these prince-puppets who were jerked back to their thrones by their master at Vienna. Plenty of Austrian troops came to take care of them. As for the bitter reprisals Italians had to bear, it is almost impossible to read of them. In certain provinces everyone found with a weapon was put to death. A man found with a rusty nail was promptly shot. At Brescia a little hunchback was slowly burnt alive. Women, stripped half-naked, were flogged in the market-place, with Austrian officers looking on. It was after his visit to Naples in the winter of 1850 that Gladstone wrote, "This is the negation of God erected into a system of government."

But Italy had now a new champion. When Victor Emmanuel signed his name to the first census in his reign, he jestingly gave his occupation as "Rè Galantuomo," and this name stuck to him forever after. A brave monarch Victor Emmanuel proved, whose courage and honesty were tried in many fires.

When arranging negotiations with Radetsky after Novara, he was given to understand that the conditions of peace would be much more favorable if he would abandon the constitution granted by Charles Albert.

"Marshal," he said, "sooner than subscribe to such conditions, I would lose a hundred crowns. What my father has sworn I will maintain. If you wish a war to the death, be it so! My house knows the road of exile, but not of dishonor."

The Princes of Piedmont had been always renowned for physical courage and dominating minds. Effeminacy and mendacity are not their foibles. It is hinted by the Countess of Cesaresco, in her "Liberation of Italy," that sainthood was esteemed the privilege strictly of the women of the family, but then sainthood is not absolutely necessary to a monarch. The Piedmont line had always understood the business of kings,—but none so thoroughly as Victor Emmanuel.

He was unpopular at first; the Mazzinists cried, "Better Italy enslaved than handed over to the son of the traitor, Carlo Alberto!" On the wall of his palace at Turin was written: "It is all up with us; we have a German king and queen"—alluding to the Austrian origin of his mother and of his young queen, Marie Adelaide.

These two—wife and mother—were ruled by clerics and made his life melancholy when he began a course of ecclesiastical reform. One person in every two hundred and fourteen in Sardinia was an ecclesiastic, and the church had control of all ecclesiastical jurisdiction and could shelter criminals, among other mediæval privileges. To reform these abuses, the king in 1849 approached the pope with deferential requests, but the pope absolutely refused to make any changes.

However, the work of reform was firmly pushed on, and a law was passed by which the priestly privileges were sensibly cut down, although the king's wife and mother wrung their hands, and the religious press shrieked denunciation. At this time Santa Rosa, the Minister of Commerce and Agriculture, died, and the church refused him the last sacrament, though he was a blameless and devout member of the Roman Church. This hateful act of intolerance reacted on the clergy, as a matter of course, and gave an impetus to church reform.

When, in 1855, Victor Emmanuel was so unfortunate as to lose his wife, his mother, and his brother within a month, and the nation as a whole mourned with him, his clerical friends embittered his affliction by insisting with venomous frankness that it was the judgment of Heaven that he had brought upon himself for his religious persecutions.

Strength was Victor Emmanuel's genius: he was not intellectual in any marked degree, but his ministers could work with him and rely upon him. A union between him and Cavour, the two great men of the kingdom, was inevitable. Up to this time Cavour had no general fame except as a journalist, but the king had the insight to recognize his extraordinary powers, and when Santa Rosa died (unshriven) Cavour in his place became Minister of Agriculture and Commerce. "Look out!" said the king to his prime minister, d'Azeglio, when this had come to pass, "Cavour will soon be taking all your portfolios. He will never rest till he is prime minister himself."

Under the régime of Cavour, railways and telegraph wires lined the kingdom in all directions; he took off foolish tariffs and concluded commercial treaties with England, France, Belgium, and other powers. "Milord Cavour" was a nickname showing the dislike aroused by his English predilections, but through him Piedmont repaired the damage of the war of 1848, and grew steadily in prosperity.

Cavour's brilliant intellectual powers seem to have been so limitless that it is rather a relief to think of him personally as only a dumpy little man with an over-big head. Although a born aristocrat, and living in the manner becoming one, he was capable of quite demonstrative behavior. The occasion for this was a dinner given by d'Azeglio. Cavour, seated at table, joked the premier about his jealousy of Ratazzi; the premier replied angrily; whereupon the greatest of diplomats arose, seized his plate, lifting it as high as he could, and dashed it to the floor, where it broke into fragments. Then he rushed out of the house, crying:

"He is a beast! He is a beast!"

This quarrel, which sounds like an act from a nursery drama, led to a change in the cabinet, with Cavour left out. But a little later on d'Azeglio resigned and Cavour was prime minister.

A marvellous stroke of statesmanship on behalf of his country was Cavour's intervention in the Crimean War in 1855,—three years after Louis Napoleon's coup-d'état. It seemed an act of folly to send fifteen thousand troops from the little Italian state—which had no standing among European powers—to help England and France. The undertaking seemed to Sardinians an act of insanity; Cavour's colleagues were violently against him. But the king stood by him; so the troops were sent and the ministers resigned.

Never was an action more fully justified. At the close of the Crimean War Sardinia had two powerful allies—France and England; and for the first time she was admitted on terms of equality among the "powers." A significant thing had been said, too, in 1855: "What can I do for Italy?" asked the Emperor Napoleon of Cavour. Cavour was not slow to tell him what could be done; he was convinced that he must look for aid to the vanity and ambition of Napoleon III.

No diplomatic pressure of his, however, availed. During the next two years the attitude of Austria became constantly more unendurable, but still Napoleon would make no move.

It proved to be the most unlikely of events that brought about a consummation of the wishes of Cavour.

On the evening of January 14, 1858, a carriage drove through the Paris streets on its way to the opera. With the appearance of its two occupants all the world is familiar; the wonderful Spanish eyes of the lady, the exquisite lines of her figure—who has not seen them pictured? The smallish man with her had been described by the Crown Prince of Prussia as having "strangely immobile features and almost extinguished eyes." His huge mustache had exaggeratedly long waxed ends, and his chin was covered with an "imperial."

The terrible crash of Orsini's bombs, thrown underneath their carriage, failed to carry out the conspirators' purpose. The emperor had a slight wound on the nose and the empress felt a blow on the eye. That was all, except that her silks and laces were spattered with blood from the wounded outside the carriage. They continued their drive and saw the opera to its finish before they were told of the tragedy that had befallen. Eight people had been killed and one hundred and fifty-six wounded by the explosion.

The Empress Eugenie, it is said, showed the greatest composure over the event, but this was not true of her husband. Probably no man of modern times had had so many attempts made on his life as Louis Napoleon, and always, before, he made light of them, but this last one, resulting in such cruel slaughter, completely unnerved him. He now lived in a tremor, dreading the vengeance of still others of the revolutionary ex-friends of his youth, but he dared not relax the despotic grip with which he ruled his land. How could he placate them? He wore a cuirass under his coat; he had wires netted over the chimneys of the Tuileries, so that bombs should not burst on his hearth; a swarm of detectives were around him wherever he went, and always the question asked itself in his mind: What should he do to take off the curse of fear from his life?

Cavour, Victor Emmanuel, the whole of Italy, were filled with rage and disgust at the news of Orsini's attempt. Orsini—an Italian! That must be the end of all their hopes of help from France! But in the summer of 1848 Cavour was summoned to the Emperor at Plombières, and during two days there the agreement was formulated by which France and Italy united against Austria. This was Louis Napoleon's solution of his problem—to help Italy at least sufficiently to annul the hate of every assassin on the peninsula. According to the Prince Regent of Prussia, he chose "la guerre" instead of "le poignard."

No written record was made of the bargain between Napoleon and Cavour; but we know that it gave Savoy and Nice to France, and made one innocent royal victim, the young Princess Clotilde, Victor Emmanuel's daughter, who was there betrothed by proxy to Prince Jerome Napoleon.

It was at Plombières that Napoleon with some naïveté said to Cavour: "Do you know, there are but three *men* in all Europe; one is myself, the second is you, and the third is one whose name I will not mention." Napoleon was not alone in his high estimate of Cavour. In Turin they said: "We have a ministry, a parliament, a constitution; all *that* spells Cavour."

At his reception on New Year's Day, 1859, Napoleon astounded everyone by greeting the Austrian ambassador with these words: "I regret that our relations with your government are not so good as they have been hitherto." This ostentatious expression was equal to publication in a journal. Immediate war was looked for by everyone. Piedmont, France, and Austria openly made bellicose preparations.

Although on the 18th of January, 1859, a formal treaty was made, by which France was bound to support Piedmont if attacked by Austria, Napoleon hesitated and tried to back out of his agreement. It will never be known by what tortuous system of diplomacy Cavour compelled Austria herself to declare war, but it was done, April 27th.

Cavour's intrigues during these days were dazzlingly complicated; he had to deal on one hand with his imperial ally, and on the other with shady revolutionary elements—and to keep his right hand in ignorance of what his left hand did. He summoned Garibaldi to Turin; Garibaldi, in his loose red shirt and sombrero with its plume, with his tumultuous hair and beard, struck dismay to the heart of the servant who opened the door. He refused to admit him, but finally agreed to consult his master. "Let him come in," said Cavour. "It is probably some poor devil who has a petition to make to me." This was the first meeting of the statesman and the warrior. When told of the French alliance, Garibaldi exclaimed: "Mind what you are about! Never forget that the aid of foreign armies must be, in some way or other, dearly paid for!" But his adherence was whole-heartedly given to Victor Emmanuel, and at the end of the short campaign Italy rang with his name.

For months past Austria had been pouring troops into Italy—there seemed no limit to them. Garibaldi, by the end of April, was in command of a band of Cacciatori delli Alpi, a small force, but made up of the iron men of North Italy, worthy of their leader.

On May 2nd Victor Emmanuel took the command of his army; it comprised fifty-six thousand infantry in five divisions, one division of cavalry in sixteen squadrons, with twelve field-guns and two batteries of horse artillery. May 12th the French emperor rode through the streets of Genoa amid loud acclamations; the city was hung with draperies and garlands in his honor. At Alessandria he rode under an arch on which was inscribed, "To the descendant of the Conqueror of Marengo!" In all he had one hundred and twenty-eight thousand men, including ten thousand cavalry.

It was a short campaign, but the weeks were thick with battles, and the battle-fields with the slain.

The first engagement was at Genestrello, May 20th. The Austrians driven out, made a stand at Montebello, where, though twenty thousand strong, they were routed by six thousand Sardinians. The armies of the emperor and king forced the Austrians to cross the Po, and there retire behind the Sesia. On the 30th the allies crossed the Sesia and drove the foe from the fortified positions of Palestro, Venzaglio, and Casalino.

Next came Magenta—a splendid triumph for MacMahon; the Austrian loss was ten thousand men; that of the French between four thousand and five thousand. Meantime, Garibaldi had led his Cacciatori to the Lombard shores of Lake Maggiore, had beaten the Austrians at Varese, entered Como, routed the enemy again at San Fermo, and was now proceeding to Bergamo and Brescia with the purpose of cutting off the enemy's retreat through the Alps of the Trentino.

On the 8th of June Victor Emmanuel and Napoleon III. made their triumphal entry into Milan, from whence every Austrian had fled. Everyone remembers how MacMahon, now Duke of Magenta, caught up to his saddle-bow a child who was in danger of being crushed by the crowd.

The emperor and the king soon moved on from Milan. By the 23rd their head-quarters were fixed at Montechiaro, close to the site of the coming battle of Solferino.

On the day before the battle, the lines of the allies lay near the Austrian lines, from the shore of the Lake of Garda at San Martino to Cavriana on the extreme right. On the evening of the 23rd there was issued a general order regulating the movements of the allied forces: Victor Emmanuel's army was sent to the extreme left, near Lake Garda; Baraguay d'Hilliers was given the centre in front of Solferino, which was the Austrian centre; to his right was MacMahon, next Marshal Niel, and then Canrobert at the extreme right, while the emperor's guard were ordered here and there in the changes of the battle.

The enemy, under Field-Marshal Stadion, held the entire line of battle strongly, with one hundred and forty thousand men.

Solferino has been the scene of many combats; it is a natural fighting-ground, and the Austrians had barricaded themselves at all the strong points of vantage.

At five in the morning of the 24th, Louis Napoleon sat in his shirt-sleeves, after his early coffee, smoking a cigar, when tidings came to him that the fighting had begun. In a few minutes he was driving at full speed to Castiglione, and on the way he said to an aide: "The fate of Italy is perhaps to be decided to-day." It was he indeed who decided it; whatever else is said of him, it was he who struck a great blow for Italy at Solferino.

It was the great day of Napoleon III.; he has never been considered a notable soldier, but throughout this day, in every command issued, he displayed consummate military ability.

The sun glared in the intense blue above with tropical heat, when, at Castiglione, Napoleon climbed the steeple of St. Peter's Church and beheld the expanse of Lake Garda, growing dim towards the Tyrolean Alps. There was the remnant of an ancient castle—a sturdy tower—guarding the village of Solferino, called the "Spy of Italy." Already a deadly fire from its loopholes poured on Baraguay d'Hilliers's men, who faced it bravely, but were falling in terrible numbers.

He could see the Austrian masses swarming along the heights uniting Cavriana with Solferino. The Piedmontese cannon booming from the left told that Victor Emmanuel was fighting hard, but his forces were hidden by hills. It was at once plain to him, from his church steeple, that the object of the Austrians was to divert the attack on Solferino—the key of their position—by outflanking the French right, filling up the gap between the Second and Fourth Corps, and thus cutting the emperor's army in two. Coming down from his height, Napoleon at once sent orders to the cavalry of the Imperial Guard to join MacMahon, to prevent his forces from being divided. Altogether the emperor's plan seems to have been clear and definite; his design was to carry Solferino at any cost, and then, by a flank movement, to beat the enemy out of his positions at Cavriana. Galloping to the top of Monte Fenil, the emperor beheld a thick phalanx of bayonets thrust its way suddenly through the trees of the valley; it was a huge body of Austrians sent to cut off the line of the French. There was not a minute to be lost; he sent orders to General Manêque, of the Guard, to advance at once against the Austrian columns. With magnificent rapidity the order was executed, and the Austrians—a great number—were beaten back far from the line of battle.

The Austrian batteries placed on the Mount of Cypresses and on the Cemetery Hill of Solferino were keeping up a deadly fire on the French.

Baraquay d'Hilliers brought Bazaine's brigade into action against the one, and the First Regiment of zouaves rushed up the other, only to be hurled back by the enemy as they reached the steep slope. A horrible confusion followed these two repulses, the zouaves and General Negrier's division being fatally mixed and fighting with each other like furies. But General Negrier kept his head and collected his troops, scattered all over the hillocks and valleys. Then, with the Sixty-first Regiment of the line and a battalion of the One Hundredth Regiment, he started resolutely to mount the Cemetery Hill. It was a deadly march; the enemy, holding the advantage, disputed every turn and twist of the ascent. Twice Negrier's troops rushed up along the ridge-like path, but the circular wall of the cemetery, bored with thousands of holes, through which rifles sent a scathing hail, was strong as a fortress to resist them. It was sheer murder to take his men up again; Negrier abandoned the attack.

The enemy's cannon-balls from the three defended heights fell thick and fast on Monte Fenil, where Napoleon and his aides breathlessly watched the progress of the drama.

Many of the Cent-Gardes who formed the imperial escort were shot down; the emperor was in the midst of death. The Austrians had been strongly re-enforced and held to tł.e defence of Solferino more obstinately than ever.

But, notwithstanding this, the French were gaining ground; the left flank of the Austrians was at last broken by the artillery of the French reserve, and the whole army felt a thrill of encouragement.

A number of French battalions were now massing themselves about the spur of the Tower Hill of Solferino, but it was impossible to proceed to the attack while solid Austrian masses stood ready to pounce upon their flank.

A few fiery charges scattered the enemy in all directions, and a tempest of shouts rang out when Forey gave the order to storm the Tower Hill. The drum beat, the trumpets sounded. "Vive l'Empereur!" echoed from the encircling hills. "Quick" is too slow a word for French soldiers. The Imperial Guard, chasseurs, and battalions of the line rushed up with such fierce velocity that it was no time at all before the heights of Solferino were covered with Napoleon's men. Nothing could stand against such an electric shock—the Tower Hill was carried, and General Lebœuf turned the artillery on the defeated masses of Austrians choking up the road that led to Cavriana.

The convent and adjoining church, strongly barricaded, yielded after repeated attacks, and then Baraguay d'Hilliers and Negrier made a last attempt